Exile's Vengeance

LEGENDS OF LAIRHEIM

BOOK 4

ALSO BY TORA MOON

LEGENDS OF LAIRHEIM (SCIENCE-FANTASY)

Ancient Enemies (Book 1)
Ancient Allies (Book 2)
The Scourge Incursion (Book 3)
Exile's Vengeance (Book 4)
Redemption - A Novel

THE SENTINEL WITCHES (URBAN FANTASY)

Crossroads to Destiny (Book 1)
Descent Into Darkness (Book 2)
Well of Sorrows (Book 3)

INDIE AUTHOR GUIDES

Business & Accounting for Authors
Business Plans for Authors (forthcoming)

To get an up-to-date listing of all my books or to purchase visit
ToraMoon.com

LEGENDS OF LAIRHEIM

EXILE'S VENGEANCE

BOOK 4

TORA MOON

Lunar Alchemy Publishing

Lunar Alchemy Publishing Company
ToraMoon.com

Cover design: Deranged Doctor Design
Map design: Tora Moon
Map illustrations licensed from Map Effects Fantasy Map Builder

Paperback ISBN: 978-1-946132-10-9
Ebook ISBN: 978-1-946132-09-3

ACKNOWLEDGMENTS

An author may sit alone at the computer, but no book is completed without help. My sister, Angelique, is my greatest supporter, cheerleader, and encourager.

Thank you to all the authors I've had the pleasure of reading their stories and making me want to tell my own. Without story, this world would be a much poorer place.

And especially to my daughter, Sasha, you have made me become a better person by being your parent. I couldn't have asked for a more amazing daughter. You believe in me, even when I struggle with my self-doubts.

Thank you to all my readers. Thank you for spending time with my stories and letting me be a part of your life. I hope you love them as much I loved writing them.

EXTRAS

The world of Lairheim isn't a re-imagining of Earth. It has its own culture, language, and landmasses. I've created several extras and resources to help you enjoy this fantasy world more. You can find these on my website: ***ToraMoon.com/Legends-Extras***.

Extras you may like:

Pronunciation audio - While the appendix includes a cast and glossary, fantasy names and words can be difficult to figure out how to say. I've recorded audios for each name and Posair word.

Maps - There is a map at the beginning of the book to help you orient into the world of Lairheim. A black and white pdf map is available to download for free. Or if you love maps, I've created a beautiful, hand-drawn, color map you can purchase.

Merchandise - I've created some fun merchandise centered around the books and the world of Lairheim. Check them out in my shop!

MAP OF LAIRHEIM

Prologue

The first time he'd heard the woman had been in a dream. The dark velvet voice held him in thrall, promising him the pain he craved. None of his pack-mates understood his need to experience and inflict pain, or the pleasure he derived from it. He'd learned after the first few incidents as an adolescent boy to hide his yearnings, as his alphas believed them to be the aberrant behavior of a rogue. And the Posairs killed rogues. So he hid his pleasures, finding ways to impose pain and suffering on animals and on himself.

Then came the glorious day while fighting one of the new control-janacks when her voice called to him again. He followed the lure of her darkness, like the scent of sweet perfume, deep into the nearby swamp. But before he sank fully into her depths, the bore, Eidstrun, rudely attacked him. Eidstrun had chased him, like an errant child, driving him out of the swamp. He growled at the memory and fisted his hand—being careful not to drive his long claws into his palm—vowing someday he'd exact his vengeance on Eidstrun.

The bitch Rizelya turned him over to a White Priestess, who rummaged through his mind with her filthy Talent, installing a block to the dark woman's voice. Chedans later, he finally broke it, and, using the distractions of the continuous Malvers' monster attacks, he escaped into a large swamp. Her voice immediately caressed him and drew him deeper.

He eventually learned her name. Malviana. He whispered it and licked his lips, savoring the taste. She hadn't reneged on her promise. He fell into a pool filled with delicious, potent magic. And when sweet, luscious pain enveloped him, he'd opened himself fully to the ecstasy it brought. Time had no meaning in that place of pleasure-pain.

Four lunadars later, he'd awakened as the first bite of winter snows covered the swamp to discover he was no longer a Posair. Malviana changed him into something more.

He now yearned for more than just pain as pleasure. He craved blood and death. Following Malviana's call, he left the swamp in Strunlair Territory and made his way south, killing and maiming wherever he went. Sometimes, he hunted with the Malvers' monster. Now, with his mistress's power steadily growing, they were no longer confined to their nests. He took victims to sacrifice to Malviana and her god—and to feed upon.

Finally, he crossed the Barrens and entered the great southern swamp. He felt her pull even stronger. Soon, he would join her.

Soon, he'd be with his love.

Chapter 1

Wisah - 25 de Ahdar, 1076

Sunlight filtered through the library windows, set high in the walls. With a huge sigh, Wisah closed the book she'd been reading. Sheekeek glanced up from the books littering the table in front of them.

What's wrong? He placed a talon on the corner of his book, marking his place.

Wisah winced, hoping he wasn't poking a hole in the aged manuscript. "Nothing... everything. It's been two lunadars since we returned to the Sanctuary, and all we've done is read these old, moldy books and scrolls. I thought when Rizelya found the ancient book, and we rushed here with it, there was some urgency."

It was my impression as well. Sheekeek shook his head feathers, resettling them. *Perhaps the Goddess needed to keep it out of the Scourge's hands.*

Wisah rolled her eyes and shrugged. "But why? Their translators, the Volkern, couldn't read Posarian. Plus, what little I glimpsed from the cover, I doubt we could read it. It was that old."

Even so, they would have destroyed it if they'd found it.

"True." She shuddered. She'd seen some truly awful things the alien invaders inflicted on her people. In some ways, she was very glad to be in the Sanctuary and away from the war front. She pushed her book aside. She couldn't read any more about long dead people. The Supreme gave Wisah and Sheekeek authorization to read several histories about the Great War. While some were enlightening, most were boring.

Fiddling with a pen, she studied Sheekeek. They hadn't talked about what had occurred when they discovered the book. Had he experienced anything extraordinary, like she did?

"Do you ever think about what happened that day?"

Sheekeek sighed, put a marker in his book, and sat back on his haunches. *I do. It's strange the monstrous sandstorm revealed the temple, and as soon as Rizelya recovered the book, the temple disintegrated.*

"The Goddess wanted it found." Wisah hesitated. She hadn't told anyone what had befallen her. But the Goddess had also called Sheekeek to her service. He'd understand. She leaned forward. "It was the first time the Goddess clearly spoke to me."

Sheekeek pulled back slightly and cocked his head to the side. *I didn't know that. I'd received other messages from her. What did she say, if you don't mind me asking?*

Wisah closed her eyes, letting the incident flow to the top of her consciousness. Slowly, quietly, she recounted the experience to Sheekeek.

> *Wisah, my child,* a voice whispered to her.
>
> She sat up straight and looked all around her, but no one was near her.
>
> *I have need of you, child,* the voice said. It wasn't mind-speech, but something else. A loving presence filled her, and she finally realized who was speaking to her—the Goddess! *The time has come to reveal what was once hidden. You will help heal my people and bring an ending to those who pervert my gifts and my world. Go find Rizelya. She has recovered what you need. Take it to the Supreme. Go quickly now, before it is lost again.*

Wisah opened her eyes and leaned back in her chair. "I walked through the camp in a daze to the edge of the Barrens, where I met Rizelya and Glork. I came to my senses when Rizelya handed me the book." She gazed down at her hands, remembering the sharp jolt of energy that pulsed from the ancient tome when her fingers touched it. "You found us moments afterward."

The Goddess had spoken to me, Sheekeek said, *telling me to find you and take you to the Supreme. Has she shared with you what is so special about the book?*

Wisah shook her head. "I didn't have time to tell Jaehaas goodbye, or let him know I was leaving."

I'm sure Rizelya told him. He'd understand you left because you'd been called by the Goddess.

"But for what?" Wisah threw her hands in the air. "To read books about ancient history or political plots? I should be at the war front, helping my friends. What do you think is happening in the war with the invaders?"

Fighting. Sheekeek shrugged and rubbed his beak on his furry shoulder. *I'm unaware of The Supreme receiving a messenger from Histrun, so they must still be fighting.*

"I can't help feeling guilty for being here, safe, while they're fighting for their lives—and our freedom."

Sheekeek pushed the book Wisah had been reading back toward her. *Right now, all we can do is follow the Supreme's orders and read these books and scrolls, until she tells us otherwise.*

Wisah sighed, knowing he was right, and pulled the dry history closer to her. Even as she tried to concentrate, her mind kept wondering what was so important about the ancient tome Rizelya had found.

Later that night, Wisah sat on her bed, her knees tucked under her chin, unable to sleep and fighting off her loneliness. She glanced over at the empty bed across the room, the covers a bit wrinkled where Chariel had hastily pulled them up. On the shelf over the bed, she'd knocked over a small carved sabertiger in her rush to leave. Wisah sighed, wishing her friend was here in the Sanctuary with her, rather than far south, fighting the invaders.

She wiped the tears from her face and blew her nose, admitting to herself who she really missed: Jaehaas. As a White Priestess, she hadn't ever expected to fall in love, and especially not with a centaur. But sometime during the journey to find the Posairs' long-lost allies, the Gryphons, she and Jaehaas had become close. They couldn't have a normal relationship because of the choice he'd made many years ago to shift into half man, half horse. Once made, the change was irreversible. Jaehaas could never shift back into his natural form and make love to her, but she didn't care. She loved him anyway.

Her thoughts returned—as they always did these days—to the powerful book. Rizelya had miraculously found it in an ancient temple, uncovered by a sandstorm in the middle of the Barrens. As far as Wisah knew, the Supreme hadn't opened it yet. She wondered why the Supreme was waiting. It had seemed important at the time for her and Sheekeek to bring the book quickly to the Sanctuary. She, Sheekeek, and the other Gryphons escorting her had nearly killed themselves to reach the Sanctuary as fast as possible. She hadn't slept well since then. The ancient tome called to her, begging her to open it. She didn't know why something so old, so powerful, wanted her, a lowly White Priestess.

She scrubbed the tears off her face and stood to straighten Chariel's figurine. As she reached for it, power thundered through her, dropping her to her knees.

At last, the Supreme had opened the book!

Throwing on a cloak and shoes, Wisah ran from her room, through the dormitory, and out the door. The nip in the night air made her glad she'd grabbed a cloak. Although it was Ahdar, spring came later to the mountains. Kelar, the largest moon, was nearly full, providing her with enough light to make her way across the cloister grounds and to the temple. She slipped through a side door into a dimly lit corridor. Few people would be wandering the temple's halls so late at night, and those would be the occasional Red Guard patrolling the temple.

Wisah dashed through the temple, skidding to a stop at the doors to the Supreme's quarters, panting and out of breath from her run. The two Red Guards, veils covering their faces and dressed head to toe in red, crossed their helbraughts in front of the door, blocking Wisah from entering.

"The Supreme gave orders not to be disturbed," the taller of the two said.

"But I have to see her," Wisah implored. "It's important."

The shorter one narrowed her eyes, and leaned on her helbraught. "Is anyone dying, or is there an attack on the gates?"

Wisah shook her head.

"Then your business with the Supreme can wait until morning. She's doing important work and doesn't want any interruptions."

"I know. I have to be in there to help her."

"She gave no such orders." The taller guard sighed. "Go back to bed, Wisah. We can't let you in."

Supreme, Wisah called softly in mind-speech, *I need to talk to you. I need to see the book.*

Wisah waited for an answer. When she didn't receive one, she spun on her heel, intending to return to her room, but the powerful presence of the Goddess stopped her. *No, stay. The Supreme needs you.* Wisah's eyebrows rose at this direct communication and obeyed the order.

The energy of the book seeped through the door and caressed her skin like a lover. She rubbed her arms and paced the hallway to relieve the sensation. Finally, it ceased, and Wisah guessed the Supreme had finished reading the book. She attempted to contact the Supreme again, using mind-speech. But when she still didn't receive an answer, she assumed the Supreme had placed a shield over the door to block any such types of communication.

A few octars into her vigil, the Red Guards changed, and she tried wheedling her way past the new ones. But they were just as obnoxiously efficient as the first two and wouldn't let her in. Throughout the long night, Wisah paced the hallway in front of the Supreme's door, or sat slumped against the wall waiting for the Supreme to open the door.

A blast rocked the island, knocking Malviana from her feet to land in a crumpled heap on the damp cave floor. Above her, a giant stalactite cracked, and with a loud snap, it broke off and dropped toward her. She rolled quickly to avoid being impaled by it, only to have another, and then another, break off as the island continued to rock and buck. Unsteadily, she regained her feet, holding onto her laboratory table. A blast of energy ripped through her, and she collapsed forward, gasping for breath. Her heart thundered in her ears, and she reached out with her senses.

Whatever caused the blast had torn through the barrier that kept her and her people locked on the miserable island of their exile. "Thank you, Mordaga!" she cheered, tears wetting her cheeks, even as the earth continued to shake.

With the recent increase in her power, Malviana had almost pulled it down already, and this earth shake finished the job for her. After the invaders had arrived and used her pets inside their corrals, the Malvers had fed well for the first time since their exile, and their powers steadily strengthened. She scowled. A few chedans ago, the invaders suddenly stopped using the corrals. No matter. She'd gained enough power to create new mounts for her people, anticipating when they could leave the hated island. Malviana grinned.

The day had finally arrived!

She reached out with her senses, pushing them farther than they'd gone since her incarceration. Fear—an unfamiliar emotion—coursed through her. A wall of water bore down on the island, taller than the highest peak.

"Magdelyn! Borgedier!" she yelled.

Her two most trusted lieutenants rushed to her side. They were the closest she had to friends. Friends made a person weak and could be used as leverage against one.

"Gather everyone," she ordered. "We have to leave. Now!"

"What's happening?" Magdelyn asked. "I thought we had more time, Your Grace."

"Our time is out. The earth shake caused a tidal wave, and it's coming straight for us."

Magdelyn's eyes widened, and her already pale gray skin grew paler. She straightened her shoulders and gave a curt nod. "We'll be ready to leave in—"

"Half an octar. Less would be better. Have my mount prepared for me. I have one last thing to do."

"Yes, my queen. It will be done." Magdelyn curtsied and hurried from the cave.

"Borgedier, stay. I need your strength." Malviana hated needing to rely on another. But even with the increase of death essence through her pets, she wasn't as strong as she had once been—and what she vowed she'd return to. She slid into the nearest chair.

He dropped to one knee in front of her and thumped a fist to his chest. "I am yours. Take what you need, my queen." He bowed his head and raised his wand. It already pulsed as he released his power into it.

She placed a hand on his shoulder, closed her eyes, and accessed her magic. Malviana pushed it outward, far across the ocean and deep into the White Mountains. She followed the thread of magic that held the magical barrier back to its source—the Supreme. She didn't have to go far. The Supreme's mind was speeding toward where the barrier should be. Malviana wrapped her power around the Supreme's mind, trapping it, then squeezed.

The Supreme collapsed.

Malviana came out of her trance with a cackle of glee. Her opponent was dead!

Still laughing, she ran to the cave serving as the stables for their mounts, with Borgedier following a few steps behind her. She worried for a moment she'd pulled too much from him. But to kill the Supreme would be worth it, even if it killed him.

Magdelyn held her mount steady as Malviana leaped onto the saddle behind its reptilian shoulders, taking the whip Magdelyn handed to her. It hissed at her, and she laughed again.

"Is everyone here?"

"Yes, my lady," Magdelyn said.

"Let us ride to freedom!" Malviana slapped the banthu with the whip, and it sprang up, spreading its wide wings to sail out of the cave mouth and into the sky. Malviana glanced back as it gained altitude. The wave overtook the peak behind the cave.

"Hurry!" she yelled, willing her people to get out.

The last person, Borgedier, escaped the cave and furiously whipped his beast to fly faster. The water crashed over the cave system, the edge catching Borgedier's beast's tail, making it spin out of control. Malviana flung out her wand, extending her magic, and caught them before they plunged into the water. The banthu regained its equilibrium and flapped its wings, flying higher with each down stroke.

Malviana guided her beast to the barrier, then beyond.

Home! The word sang in her heart.

She was going home at last.

Malviana blinked at the bright sun—the first she'd seen since her exile. A blinding headache bloomed behind her eyes, and she pulled her hood over her head, which helped alleviate her headache. Below her, the blue ocean sparkled. It was so full of life, so full of potential power! She drank in the life essences of the small fish and sea creatures, their bodies floating to the surface in her wake. The increase of power filled her until she buzzed with it. She sensed her people were also feeding from the ocean's bounty. It didn't provide the depth of power, or the nourishment, a sacrifice to Mordaga did, but it was much, much more than they'd partaken of in ages. The deaths caused by her pets had kept them alive, but it hadn't delivered any satiation.

Soon, she and her people would feed properly.

Rizelya - 25 de Ahdar, 1076

The bomb the invaders left as they fled from the planet's atmosphere detonated. The land under Rizelya's feet rolled, and she hastily reached out a hand to steady her heart-sister, Kaieli. She held her breath, waiting to discover if their Faeorn allies had spoken the truth. After several milcrons, nothing more happened. Her world was safe from the invaders. Laughing with joy, she pulled Kaieli into a hug, careful of the delicate egg Kaieli clutched to her chest.

Tre'nok, the last Volkern to enter the ship, stopped on the ramp and turned around. "The bomb. See, your planet survives." He tilted his head and smiled. "But quite a few fish did not. Take care, Kaieli." He disappeared into the ship, the door sliding shut behind him. A blast of steam jetted from the engines.

Everyone stepped away quickly. The interstellar ship rose above the ground, then zoomed diagonally across the sky. Rizelya watched it vanish over the horizon. The Scourge's former slaves, the Volkerns and Faeorns, were heading home.

A rush of homesickness swamped Rizelya. She wanted to go home, too. She hadn't seen Strunland Keep for nearly a year.

Rizelya glanced at Blazel standing by her side. His long, dark-auburn hair, still twisted into locs, hung nearly to his waist. He grinned at her. The scar running down his cheekbone and chin made him appear ruggedly handsome to her. She knew it continued down his neck and chest and left arm. He'd received it, and the four scars on his back, from a sabertiger as a young man. At six foot, he stood nearly a foot taller than her measly five foot-something. She smiled and squeezed his hand. She wanted to show Blazel the places she loved in her home territory and explore the old ruins near the keep with him.

At least they had a home to return to, unlike the Vhelopsi refugees. Their leader, Hairan Aziru, stood rigid as he watched the scout ship punch into the sky. The sunlight gleamed on his golden-toned skin and hair, quite unlike anything found on a Posair. He and his people—nearly four hundred of them—were now stranded for the rest of their lives on Lairheim. Rizelya doubted she could start over in a strange world like they were doing. But no matter what happened in the future, they were better off here than remaining as Scourge slaves, waiting for the day when they became food.

Rizelya followed Blazel's gaze to their friend, Chariel, a Gray who was gifted—or cursed—with receiving prophetic visions from the Goddess. Chariel had unusual charcoal-gray hair and eyes. Right now, a silver film didn't cover her eyes as it did when she received a vision, but they were bleak. What could she be unhappy about? They had just won the war against the Scourge. When Blazel looked back at Rizelya, he wore a grim expression.

"What's wrong?" She didn't think they had mind-spoken.

He shrugged and opened his mouth to speak, but her best friend from childhood, Aistrun, lightly punched him on the arm.

"Hey, Blazel," Aistrun said, a grin lighting up his gold eyes. The sun glinted off his red-gold hair. "Get a move on it. Let's go fishing."

Fresh fish sounds good, Graak said, dropping his beak. *I'm tired of dried meat.* The Gryphon shook out his sandy-brown head feathers, which turned to a creamy-white flecked with light brown and black feathers on his chest. Dark brown fur covered his feline body. His head was nearly even with Blazel's.

Their Gryphon friends, Glork and Broogk, bobbed their heads in agreement.

"Me too," Blazel agreed. "I'd like to do something besides fight for a little while."

Rizelya nodded enthusiastically in agreement. The war with the Scourge had lasted nearly six lunadars. She was so tired of fighting and of watching friends die.

She brushed her hand over Glork's creamy-tan and brown fur. "How is your wing? It's only been six days since your injury. Are you well enough to fly with me on your back?"

He nodded, and the breeze shifted his light brown and white feathers. He lifted his left wing. *The hole from the invader's projectile is healed. See?*

She examined it closely. New feathers formed next to the metacarpal bone where an invader had shot him. Satisfied, she threw her leg over his back, buckled on the harness, and laid forward. A few milcrons later, Blazel and Aistrun finished buckling their harnesses on Graak and Broogk. Several other fighter-Gryphon teams joined them.

As the Gryphons leaped into the air, Rizelya sensed the pulse of magic helping the huge Gryphons fly. They flew east over the plains, where below them horses raced the Gryphon's shadows. Rizelya laughed with joy. Blazel and Aistrun joined her.

Soon, the ocean came into sight. Instead of a clear expanse of blue and the expected bounty of fish, strange creatures flew on the horizon. As they drew closer, Glork trembled from nose to tail. Rizelya could just make out people riding the creatures.

"What's wrong? What are they?" Fear filled Blazel's voice.

A big problem, Graak replied. *They are beasts we thought long extinct. They were the Malvers' mounts during the Great War.*

"Does this mean those are Malvers riding them?" Aistrun asked.

I can't see them clearly, Glork responded, his head feathers standing on end. *And I should be able to. I don't like this at all.*

How could that many Malvers survive all this time? Graak shook violently from head to toe. If Blazel hadn't securely buckled his harness, he would have fallen off.

"We know at least one of them survived," Rizelya said, her voice trembling. "The woman who keeps haunting my dreams." Terror gripped her as she remembered the evil delight the woman took in the death caused by the Malvers' monsters.

Blazel narrowed his eyes as he watched the creature's trajectory. "If they continue in the same direction they are now, their flight path will take them to the black castle Graak and I found in the southern swamp. That thing was pure evil. We need to return quickly and warn Histrun and Moraak."

The fish were forgotten as the Gryphons circled to go back to camp.

Glork suddenly slowed, beating his wings furiously to hover in place. *Wait!* he cried. *There's something else out in the ocean.*

Rizelya gaped, and her heart thundered. A monstrous fast-moving wave barreled toward the shore.

"Oh, Sweet Mother! A tidal wave!" Aistrun yelled.

"We didn't escape unscathed from that damnable bomb, after all," Blazel swore.

Morru, Graak ordered, *you and Leistral warn the keeps along the coast. As soon as we're close enough, I'll have Kaaik and Baekeek help you. Go! Go! Fly fast!*

The smaller, faster, falcon-type Gryphon sped away.

Glork put on more speed as they dashed back to camp. Histrun, Keshanal, and Moraak needed to know about the new threat from the Malvers people, and they had to save the people near the coast from the tidal wave.

Blazel - 25 de Ahdar, 1076

Blazel lamented the loss of a quiet day of fishing and relaxing. Over the past lunadars since meeting Rizelya, he hadn't experienced many of those. When they approached the camp, it seethed with activity. As soon as they'd been within range, Graak had mind-spoken with his leader, Prince Moraak, who obviously had passed on the message to the Supreme Alphas, Histrun and Keshanal.

People rushed to harness a flight of Gryphons, while two dozen of the huge, black Thunder Wings leaped into the air. Blazel nodded to himself in approval. They were a large enough company they could evacuate many people from the keeps in range of the tidal wave. As soon as they cleared the sky, thirty fighter-Gryphon teams—some carrying women dressed in the bright-green clothes of healers—took off, speeding toward the coast.

Graak landed next to the command tent, and Blazel jumped off, having already unbuckled his harness. He and the others hurried inside.

"Where do you want us, sir?" Blazel asked Histrun as soon as they entered the tent.

Histrun bent over a table, studying the map covering it. The old man's red hair, dulled with age, had become paler and thinner during the trial of the Scourge War. Worry lines now creased his face, and his grass-green eyes were puffy from exhaustion. He slowly stood, and Blazel noticed his shoulders and back were more stooped. He worried about the man who had been his mentor, teacher, and friend. Histrun had taught Blazel how to shift into his warrior form and how to be an honorable Posair male, even if, until recently, he'd never been in a pack.

"I knew I shouldn't have sent you three," Histrun growled. "You always seem to find trouble."

"Hey," Aistrun objected, "trouble finds us."

Rizelya put her hands on her hips and glared at Histrun. "We didn't do anything to cause the tidal wave. The blame for it is squarely on the Scourge's bomb."

"Did Graak tell you about the Malvers returning?" Blazel asked.

Histrun rubbed his eyes. "Yes. As if we didn't have enough to deal with. They will have to wait until we get our people to safety."

We should take a large force to the castle in the swamp and wipe them out, Moraak said, his tail swishing in agitation. It crashed into a small table, flinging the taevo pot and mugs on it into the air. Moraak flattened his golden head feathers tightly to his head, and his tawny-gold fur stood on end. At seven feet tall, he towered over the Posairs in the tent. *We must kill them before they can kill us!* Moraak banged his talon onto the map table, causing the markers on it to jump and several to tip over.

Naila, Rizelya's sister and the Posairs' battle commander, reached over and righted the overturned markers. "Do you know how?" she croaked in her rough, gravelly voice. A long time ago, a janack had strangled her, and the injury had ruined her voice. She switched to mind-speech. *I don't. Our ancestors tried to kill them—* she flung a hand toward the Barrens *—and that is the result. Instead of killing the Malvers, they devastated the land.*

We should at least send a force to determine what we're up against, Moraak said. *Graak could not see the creatures well enough to tell how many there were.*

Some sort of spell distorted the air around them, Graak said. *None of us could see them properly.*

"I concur. We need to know." Histrun held up a hand to forestall Moraak. "But it should be a small scouting party. We don't know what we're up against, except that it's evil."

"Graak and I could lead them," Blazel offered. Inwardly, he shuddered at the thought of returning to the castle. The malignant magic of the place had twisted the vegetation until they barely resembled the trees or plants they'd once been. Twisted, monstrous beasts had overrun it, making it their homes.

Graak flinched, and his rear paw twitched. One of those beasts had been intelligent enough to use a magic rope to try to ensnare Graak as they had flown over the castle. It had left a scar on his paw where the fur wouldn't grow. Blazel glanced down at his right palm, where the backlash of the magic in his helstrablade had collided with the malignant magic of the rope. It burned the pattern of his helstrablade hilt into his palm. Bethlyn had healed the wound, but couldn't do anything about the scar.

Histrun shook his head. "No, that won't be necessary right now. I need you two for something else. Graak, do you have any idea when we can expect the wave to make landfall?"

Graak gazed at the tent ceiling while he thought, scratching the side of his beak with a talon. *Based on the wavelength and the speed, I estimate we only have two or three octars.*

Histrun swore. "We don't have much time to evacuate five keeps."

Rizelya lifted a hand. "What about me? What do you want my battalion to do?"

"Most are gone already," Naila said with a smile. She tossed her thick braid of bright-red hair back over her shoulder and pointed to the map. *They are in Posanvenlynde, Posanvendean, and Posanvenir, evacuating those keeps. I want you and your squad-pack here, at Posanvende Keep. It should be far enough inland to escape any damage, and it's a large enough keep to hold everyone. We'll use it as the evacuation center. We've informed the keep alphas, Camerposan and Dalnevah, to expect an influx of evacuees. Help them make sure their people are safe, especially since so many people will attract the damned Malvers' monsters. Your new techniques should be useful there. I've already sent Maheli on ahead. Maybe together you can figure out how to create a shield like the Scourge used.*

Rizelya tucked a lock of her dark auburn hair, which had escaped from her braid during the Gryphon ride, behind her ear. "We'll do what we can. We don't have their technology. But we'll eventually think of something that will work."

"Come on, Little Red," Aistrun said with a sigh, looking down at the much shorter Rizelya. "We have work to do. Too bad about those fish." He sighed deeply again and made a sad face.

Rizelya laughed at him, then turned to leave, but Keshanal stopped her. "Take Kaieli with you, Rizelya. A change of scenery and something else to occupy her mind might do her some good."

Blazel nodded in agreement. Rolstrun had been a casualty of the final battle with the Scourge. He had been Blazel's first Posair friend after he returned from his sojourn into the swamps, and he still mourned his friend. Kaieli and Rolstrun had become lovers during their enslavement by the invaders, and she'd taken his death hard. Blazel glanced at Rizelya and didn't want to imagine the grief he'd feel if something were to happen to her.

As Rizelya and Aistrun left the tent, the Vhelopsi leaders, Hairan Aziru and Sangasu Musa, entered.

"We heard the news about the catastrophe," Hairan said. "Is there anything we can do to help?"

Histrun shook his head.

"This is our world too, now." Hairan jammed his fists on his hips. His lips lifted in a snarl, revealing his fangs. "Please, let us help."

Histrun considered the map again, his chin resting on his fist. After several moments, he nodded and pointed to a keep near a river. "I'll send your people to Posanvelden. They need to move away from the Borleano River. When the wave hits, it will travel quickly upriver. There's a group heading that direction, and they'll drop you off."

I've let them know to expect you, Naila said. At Hairan's blank look, she swore, then said to Histrun, "Translate, please." The Vhelopsi didn't have the magic or aptitude to communicate via mind-speech. They could only hear the Gryphons, who had the ability to make themselves understood by everyone.

Histrun translated, adding, "Hurry, they're waiting for you."

Hairan and his entourage bowed and rushed from the tent.

Blazel raised an eyebrow at Naila. "What do you want Graak and me to do?"

Naila stepped to a chest, unlocked it, and pulled out an old scroll. She carefully laid it on the table over the map, setting stones on the corners to hold it down. It appeared blank except for some faded print along the edge. Blazel leaned closer to see it more clearly. He'd learned to read the ancient script at the Sanctuary. He read the words in a low voice and blinked in surprise when he awakened the magic in the scroll. A map in bright colors appeared, showing the eastern coastline and the southern subcontinent. Dots glowed where villages and cities once stood. But the dark island far from the eastern coast caught his attention. It would take Graak several octars of flight to reach it.

Histrun pointed to the large island, not touching the map. "This is where I want you and Graak to go. Our ancestors exiled the Malvers there after the Great War."

Blazel sucked in a breath, and chills ran down his spine. Graak squawked, his head feathers lifting.

Histrun ignored their reactions. "We need to determine if all the Malvers returned to the mainland or if some remained on the island. I don't want to fight a two-front war with them. Take a small force with you in case you find trouble."

"I'd like Rizelya and Aistrun to go with me."

"I know, son." Histrun slumped onto a stool. "But I don't want her anywhere near that Malvers woman. If she can affect Rizelya from the island, and behind a magical barrier, I'm terrified of what she'd do to Rizelya when she's close."

Blazel skimmed a hand over his hair, where a gray streak ran through it.

"Ah, sir." He swallowed and hung his head. "Um, I've had dreams about her too."

Histrun scowled at him. "Why haven't you said anything, boy?"

"They weren't as bad as Rizelya's, and I never saw anything more than she did. I don't know if it would be safe for me to go to their home or not."

Histrun scrubbed a hand through his hair, mussing it up. He looked at Naila for a long moment, then at Moraak. They seemed to be having a private discussion in mind-speak. Finally, Histrun huffed. "You're the only one we have available right now. Everyone else is helping with the evacuations. Visit

Saffren and have her help you with a mind block like she did with Rizelya."

She should go with you, Moraak added. *I've felt her mind-blocks, and they are strong. She can protect your group from a mind-attack if needed. Take Kaaik. He is also good with mind-blocks. I've called him back, and he should be here by the time you're ready to leave.*

Blazel saluted, and Graak dipped his head. They both studied the map again.

Blazel groaned. "Come on, Graak. We have a long flight ahead of us, and we need to gather supplies and our people. I don't want to stay there overnight."

Me either! Graak said with feeling, shaking his head feathers. *We will fly fast.*

Apprehension filled Blazel as they hurried to find their teammates. What if the Malvers woman hadn't left the island? Could he and Saffren fight her off? As he thought about it, he decided to check if Chariel remained in camp, and if so, he'd take her with him, too.

Chapter 2

Rizelya - 25 de Ahdar, 1076

Rizelya raced to the healers' sleeping tent in search of Kaieli. As Rizelya slipped through the tent flap, she allowed her eyes to adjust to the dimness within. She found Kaieli curled around a carved egg on her cot, weeping softly. Her dark brown hair curtained her face. Their Volkern ally, Tre'nok, had given her the egg. One image on it was of Rolstrun, and it was the only likeness of him Kaieli had. Rizelya sat on the edge of the cot and placed a hand on Kaieli's shoulder.

"Dear Heart," she said. "I know you're hurting. But there's an emergency, and we need you."

Kaieli brushed at the tears on her face and turned to Rizelya. Grief clouded her gray eyes. "What emergency? What could possibly be wrong now?"

"The Faeorn didn't account for the bomb to cause a huge tidal wave when it exploded. One is barreling toward the coast and could wipe out the entire eastern seaboard. Several Posanlair Keeps are in danger."

Kaieli sat up, still hugging the precious egg. "What does Histrun and Naila want us to do?"

"We're helping the alphas at Posanvende Keep prepare for the people evacuated from the smaller, minor keeps. Naila wants you to go because there might be serious injuries."

Rizelya studied Kaieli as she carefully wrapped the egg in a blanket, then placed it in a nest of clothes in her chest. It wrenched her guts to watch her former lover so heartbroken, and uncharitably, she hoped she'd never have to experience such pain herself by losing Blazel.

While she waited, Rizelya considered the net-shield she and her team had created to stop the invader's aerial projectiles. During her captivity, Kaieli had developed a way to weave all the Talents together to create something akin to Black Talent. Before, Rizelya had been too busy fighting to explore its possibilities, but now she wondered if there could be another use for it.

"Posanvenir is in the direct path of the tidal wave," Rizelya said, tapping her chin with her fingertips. "The wave will destroy it if it hits it. Do you think with your Black Weave we can create a shield to protect it?"

Kaieli straightened, her eyebrows furrowed. "I don't know. We never tried anything like that. But Chariel mentioned your team created a net-shield. It may be possible to combine the two."

"That was my thought. We should at least try. If we evacuated all the people and livestock first, then if we can't do it, the only loss will be the buildings."

"We need one person from each of the seven Talents, plus a male to anchor the energy." Kaieli's eyes filled with moisture. "Rolstrun did that for us."

"Most of my pack has already left," Rizelya hurriedly said, not wanting Kaieli to break down again. "We'll have to make do with whoever we can find. Let's grab Chariel and Loshera. Their Gray and White Talents will be the hardest to find elsewhere. I have Red and you have Brown, so we'll only need someone with Blue, Green, and Yellow, and those are now common in the fighting-packs." She grinned. It had been her innovation which allowed women with Talents other than Red to join the fighting-packs. "Aistrun is coming with us, so he can be the anchor."

"I can be the anchor for what?" Aistrun said, sticking his head into the tent. "Are you two ready yet?"

Kaieli nodded, and they rushed from the tent.

"We're going to try to stop the wave from destroying Posanvenir Keep," Rizelya explained as they ran.

"Then why are we headed to the temple?"

"We need a White Priestess, and Chariel's been spending a lot of time there."

"I know," Aistrun huffed. He and Chariel had become lovers during their quest to find the Gryphons. She'd spent three lunadars in the invader's slave camp cleansing the crater rocks of nucla. After returning, they'd been too busy fighting the invaders for anyone to spend much time alone. "Whenever we haven't been fighting, she's been in the temple, trying to cleanse herself of the slave camp's evil."

They reached the white tent serving as the temple for the war host. Rizelya tore back the tent flap. "Are Loshera and Chariel here?"

A woman passing from her middle to elderly years bowed to the altar before standing. As a White Priestess, her snow-white hair indicated her White Talent, not age. Serenity shone from her light-yellow eyes. "I'm here," Loshera said. "Chariel is in the back. What do you need, Rizelya?"

"We're going to try to save Posanvenir Keep from the tidal wave caused by the invader's bomb," Rizelya said. "We need the Black power to do so."

"Ah, I see."

Chariel entered the main chamber of the tent, pushing back her damp charcoal-gray hair. In the candlelit tent, her charcoal-gray eyes appeared black. She wore trousers and a tunic rather than her priestess robes. "I'm ready."

"Are you reading minds now, Chariel?" Rizelya smiled.

She shook her head. "I heard the commotion and figured you'd be coming for me soon. Let's go."

They raced through the camp to the grassy outskirts. Besides Glork and Broogk, three other Gryphons awaited them.

You may ride me, honored healer. A hawk-type Gryphon with rust-red fur and medium brown feathers crouched in front of Kaieli. *It is my pleasure to work with you.*

"Thank you—" Kaieli blushed.

Keeru, he supplied.

Glork introduced the two nearly identical Gryphons as nest mates, Morlek and Torlek. They had light tan head and chest feathers, and dark tan wings and fur. Loshera awkwardly climbed into the harness on Morlek's back, while Chariel, with more grace, mounted Torlek.

On their way to Posanvenir Keep, the Gryphons flew a short distance over the sea. Rizelya gasped at the incoming wave. It now rose twenty or more feet, stretched over ten measures, and was traveling faster than when they'd first seen it. Instead of the two octars they'd predicted, it would hit land within the octar. The Gryphons flew faster, and Glork mind-spoke with Moraak, updating him with the new time frame.

They circled Posanvenir Keep before landing, and the lack of people indicated the residents had left. Herders drove flocks of sheep and herds of multa deeper inland. The wild billocks herd had already moved on its own. As they landed near the gate, several teenage Browns chased a flock of fowl inside the courtyard, trying to capture them and stuff them in crates.

A Gryphon with bluish-gray feathers and fur darkening to black along his back and the top of his head flew over the teenagers. His face and chest were white, and the black streak over his eyes looked like a mask. A young woman with sunny-yellow hair rode on his back. Rizelya recognized the pair: Korrik and Eiden.

"You have ten milcrons to catch those birds," Eiden shouted. "Whatever you haven't caught by then will either find their own way to higher ground or drown."

Eiden! Rizelya called. *I'm glad you're here. Ask Korrik to land, please. We need your help.*

Eiden and Korrik turned away from the teenagers and landed next to where Rizelya waited. "What do you need us to do, Rizelya?"

"We're going to try to save this keep. We need a strong Blue and Green to complete our team. Do you know any who are still here?"

"I think Grazeen and Noriana are here," Eiden said.

Yes, they are, Korrik said. *I've asked them to join us. They were getting ready to leave with the last carts.*

Rizelya glanced at the keep's now-empty courtyard. "Is everyone out?"

I don't sense anyone, Glork said. *Brogkek and Leistrun are making a final sweep to check for any stragglers.*

A short, slender woman with dark forest-green hair ran around a corner. Grazeen stopped in front of Rizelya and held her ribs as she panted for breath. "I got here as fast as I could," she gasped.

A moment later, an older woman with cornflower-blue hair and pale green eyes jogged to the group. "What do you need, Kaieli, Rizelya?" Noriana asked.

"We're going to try something new with the Black Weave," Rizelya said.

Noriana's forehead creased. "The what?"

"The Black Weave. You know the thing you do with Kaieli that creates Black Talent?" Rizelya shrugged. "It needed a name."

"Oh," Kaieli brushed back a dark brown curl. "That's a good name."

Rizelya quickly explained her idea of creating a magical wall to stop the wave before it hit the keep.

"But won't it just divert the wave to the other keeps along the coast, making it worse for them?" Aistrun asked.

"No," Noriana said. "If we can break the wave, it will dissipate. Kaieli can use my water magic to control the subsequent waves."

We don't have much time for whatever you're going to do, Broogk said, pointing a talon to the ocean.

The water was being sucked out to sea, exposing the sand and the harbor's rocky floor. A few measures beyond the harbor rose a wave fifty-feet high.

Rizelya gaped, then shoved her fear aside. "Kaieli, what do we need to do to merge our Talents?"

"We found we need to touch for me to weave the magics together."

I'd prefer if you were above the ground on our backs, Glork muttered, his tail thumping a quick staccato. *You'll be safer if it doesn't work.*

Korrik gazed at Eiden, ruffling his head feathers. *It would be difficult to snatch you to safety while fighting that massive wave. We can't fly through it.*

We can't. Broogk glanced back at the wave, his dark brown fur standing on end.

"How about if we sit on your backs while holding hands?" Rizelya suggested. "We'd be touching, and if you need to get us away quickly, you can."

Glork bobbed his head in assent. *That is acceptable. But first, let's move higher on the cliff.*

"As soon as you touch the person on either side of you," Kaieli instructed, "open up your magic, and I'll weave them together."

They all remounted, with Grazeen climbing behind Aistrun, and Noriana behind Rizelya. Glork and Broogk, as the largest Gryphons, could easily handle the double weight. A thunderous rumble echoed from the ocean as the wave approached them. The Gryphons leaped to the cliff which overlooked the harbor. As soon as they landed and formed a circle, the Posairs joined hands.

Kaieli's grip on Rizelya's hand tightened painfully. Noriana wrapped her arms around Rizelya's waist and nearly squeezed the air from her. Chariel grabbed Kaieli's hand, adding her Gray Talent and completing the circle. As soon as she did, Rizelya sensed Kaieli latch onto each person's magic and weave them into a single stream of energy. The strands of magic merged together as she built one thick black band of power.

Kaieli gasped, and the power flickered a moment before Kaieli regained her composure. Rizelya surmised this was more power than Kaieli was used to having at her disposal. Everyone in this group possessed strong Talents. When Kaieli added Aistrun's magic, the black braid pulsed in the rhythm of a heartbeat. Suddenly, the Gryphon's power and magic surrounded the rope and Kaieli wove it in with the rest.

Rizelya instantly knew what had to be done, but she wasn't directing the magic. All of them were! Not only did her magic weave into an intricate rope with the others, but her mind also melded with theirs into something extraordinarily complex. They became part of the whole, connected not only to each other, but also to the whole of creation.

They reached out and touched the wave, which now seemed insignificant to them in this state. It smashed into their might, not only in this small section of shore, but up and down the entire coastline. They absorbed its energy, taking it in as their own, adding it to the power they held. Wave after wave crashed against them, each one growing smaller and smaller, until at last, the ocean spent its fury.

Intoxicated with the power, they knew they could do anything, control everything. With this came the deep knowing they could only use this gift for good, to help their people or to vanquish the evil seeped into the land. If they ever used this gift for greed, the consequences would be dire. Their souls would be lost forever in the nothingness, and they'd never be accepted back into the womb of the Goddess.

Blazel - 25 de Ahdar, 1076

Blazel and Graak walked to the tent Blazel and Rizelya shared with their squad-pack, hoping to find Saffren. Before they reached it, the beautiful woman strolled toward them. She'd pulled her sapphire-blue hair into a thick braid that hung past her waist, and she wore red leathers. Maestrun and Nelstrun strode on either side of her. Maestrun, at over six feet, towered over both Saffren and Nelstrun. He wore his long rust hair in a complicated braid, with the sides shorter, and two braids kept his long beard tamed. In contrast, Nelstrun wore his fern green hair short and was clean shaven. The two men were never far from Saffren. They served as her bodyguards while fighting, and from living in the close quarters of the tent, Blazel knew the threesome were lovers.

"Naila wants me to go with you," Saffren said, her silky voice as beautiful as the rest of her. "But she didn't tell me where we're going or why you need me."

"We're scouting the island the Malvers came from." Blazel turned toward the tent serving as the camp's temple.

Saffren drew in a sharp breath. "Surely, we're not going to someplace so evil. Remember, I've helped Rizelya block her mind. I know how evil and depraved the Malvers woman is."

"Because you've blocked Rizelya's mind, you can help me block mine. The woman has also interfered with my dreams."

"Oh, Blazel, why didn't you say anything earlier? Wisah and I could have helped you." Saffren gently cupped Blazel's face with her hands. "I'll help you all I can."

He felt a delicate touch on his mind and suddenly smelled a fresh, sweet breeze. It reminded him of the first breezes of spring blowing off the snow above the Sanctuary and over the blooming cherry trees. He loved that scent and time of year. He inhaled deeply and coughed as the grit of the war camp replaced the scent.

"There." Saffren lowered her hands. "It's begun. We can continue as we fly."

Blazel pulled out the thong tying his long locks behind his neck, scrubbing a hand through his matted locs before retying them. He hadn't expected her to delve into his mind so soon. What had she seen?

"I want to check if Chariel is available to go with us, too. Between the two of you, we should be protected."

"Who else is going?"

"Besides us, your two bodyguards, and Kaaik and Delestrun. Moraak mentioned Kaaik had good mental shields. We want a small party. We're simply looking and getting an idea of what we're up against, not engaging in any fighting. The rest of our pack is helping evacuate the Posanlair keeps in danger from the tidal wave."

"What about Ambrelya?" Maestrun asked. "Her sniper abilities would come in handy if we run into trouble."

Blazel raised an eyebrow as he considered it. "That's a good idea, if she's available."

I shall ask Naila if she is, Graak said. *She's in charge of assignments.*

Blazel waited while Graak mind-spoke with Naila.

Ambrelya is here and will meet us at the temple. Naila approves of our team.

They arrived at the tent, and Blazel stepped inside. He breathed in the familiar temple scents of kehani and frankincense, and a White Priestess approached him.

"Is Chariel here?" he asked.

"No, Blazel. You just missed her. She left with Rizelya and Kaieli."

Blazel bit back a curse. He'd hoped to take Chariel with him to reconnoiter the island. He'd have to trust Saffren and Kaaik could protect them if the Malvers woman was still there. Blazel bowed to the priestess and quickly exited the tent.

Outside, Ambrelya ran to the waiting group, tucking her chin-length vibrant red-brown hair into a tight-fitting leather cap. Peeking over her back was a pulser. The Posairs had converted the invader's weapon to use either helstrim projectiles or focus the shooter's Talent. Two full bandoliers of cartridges crisscrossed her chest. She saluted him, thumping her right fist on her left side above her heart. "I'm ready, sir."

While Blazel had been in the temple, Graak had called several Gryphons to help them convey the entire group. Everyone was already in their harnesses. Ambrelya nodded to the Gryphon with striped reddish brown and tan head feathers waiting for her. Maeaak's brighter tan feathers between his pale yellow eyes formed sharp eyebrows. A knob of bright yellow sat above his sharply hooked beak. "Maeaak, good to fly with you again."

The Gryphon preened and settled his dark brown and rust wings over his striped rust and tan fur. *This should be exciting.*

Ambrelya laughed as she climbed onto his back and buckled her harness with practiced ease. The two had flown together multiple times during the Scourge War.

Blazel slid into Graak's harness and buckled in. As he adjusted his goggles over his eyes, he blessed Maellyn for inventing the devices. He hadn't had a bug stuck in his eye since he'd started wearing them. He patted Graak on the shoulder, letting him know he was ready.

Graak crouched and leaped off the ground. With great sweeping flaps of his huge wings and a pulse of magic, the Gryphon rose high into the air. Blazel loved flying with Graak and watching the landscape below them shift and change. Pink, white, and purple flowers dotted the bright green grass, waving in the breeze at the edge of the plains. As they flew east, the plains gave way to scrub lands filled with sagebrush and blooming lavender, and plants with tall thin stalks covered in orange flowers. Short, stocky junipers sprinkled with white blossoms provided the only shade.

They soon reached the rocky coast, where great redwood trees clung to the sides of the cliffs. Blazel remembered when he'd traveled to the southern peninsula the first time. He'd used a small boat and hugged the rocky shore to pass undetected into the Barrens. No one traveled much more than a measure from the shore due to the fearsome sea creatures haunting the ocean. From his reading in the Sanctuary library, Blazel had discovered the Posairs had been mighty seafarers before the Great War and the sea monsters created during it. Now ships, no matter their size, weren't safe from becoming dinner.

The tidal wave grew higher and wider the closer it came to shore. Blazel swore. It would destroy Posanvenir Keep, located on a narrow peninsula. The invaders had decimated enough keeps, and his people didn't need to lose another one. He was torn between continuing east and asking Graak to head north along the coast to help with the evacuations.

Our mission is too important to abandon, Graak said, sensing Blazel's thoughts. *Besides, Glork informed me he and Rizelya are at Posanvenir Keep. Rizelya has a crazy idea to save it.*

Blazel snorted. Rizelya's crazy, innovative ideas had helped them many times during the war. She came by the tendency naturally. He remembered when he was a lonely boy at the Sanctuary, listening to Histrun talk about how clever his mate and Rizelya's mother, Zehala, had been.

They flew farther out over the ocean, leaving behind the coast and the encroaching tidal wave. Graak and the other Gryphons dove and swooped to catch the thermals. Saffren continued to work with Blazel until he clumsily formed a mental block by himself.

Two octars into their flight, a behemoth shape four times Graak's fourteen-foot length and nearly as wide as his thirty-foot wingspan rose to the water's surface. It kept pace with them for quite some time. It had small, lidless black eyes, and a dark-gray body streaked with bright-orange jagged stripes. When it dove, dread washed over Blazel.

He watched the ocean while urging Graak to fly higher. Suddenly, the sea creature launched at them. Three rows of large, sharp, triangular teeth filled its wide-open mouth. Graak flapped harder to gain more altitude as the creature honed in on him. Blazel swore, unable to believe it leaped so high from the water until he sensed a throb of magic.

"Higher, Graak, higher!" he yelled.

I'm trying, Graak squawked. He wrapped Blazel in a protective layer of magic before flaring.

Even with Graak's shielding, sweat broke out on Blazel's face from the intense heat. He heard several loud pops, and projectiles streaked past him, burying into the creature's nose. Green ichor gushed from its wounds, and it crashed back into the water.

"That was close." Blazel wiped the sweat from his forehead. He turned to Ambrelya. "I'm really glad now I added you to our team."

Graak put on a burst of speed and climbed higher. When they were so high the ocean became a smudge of blue, Graak leveled out. He bent his head, peering at his chest, and rubbed it with a talon.

It plucked me! I have a bald spot, Graak shrieked.

Blazel leaned over as far as possible and laughed. Sure enough, a bare spot marred Graak's creamy-white chest.

It isn't funny, Graak harrumphed.

Blazel stopped laughing. "No, it isn't. It could have caught more than just your feathers. I'd be down his gullet with you, my friend."

The other Gryphons joined them at the higher altitude, and they continued flying toward the island. After three octars, Graak descended.

He peered intently at the ocean, dropping lower. *It should be right here.*

Nothing but waves broke the ocean's surface.

"There!" Ambrelya pointed. A rocky point poked from the water.

Graak flew as low as he dared after the incident with the sea creature and circled the rock.

Blazel shivered. "I think that's it. I can feel the remnants of malignant magic coming from it. We won't have to worry about any Malvers attacking us from here. We'll only have to deal with however many escaped. I couldn't tell. Graak, could you?"

No, they wrapped some sort of obscuring magic around themselves.

"Oh, Sweet Goddess," Nelstrun said, gazing out into the ocean. His golden honey eyes widened as he pointed. "Would you look at that!"

Graak turned in the direction Nelstrun pointed. Five plumes of molten lava shot hundreds of feet into the air, and a haze of sulfuric dust hung over the ocean between them. The water hissed where the lava struck it, quickly cooling the lava.

"The bomb did more than cause a tidal wave," Saffren noted. "Those are volcanoes. We might be witnessing the birth of a new island."

It would be a good thing, Kaaik said, *since the Malvers' island is gone. There isn't anywhere to exile them to now.*

Blazel's heart sank at the realization. "We can't let the Malvers win. I doubt they have returned in peace."

No, they will want vengeance for being exiled. Graak turned away from the smoking volcanoes and flew back to the mainland. *Hopefully, we'll have some time to regroup before we must fight another war. I remember our histories. We barely defeated the Malvers before, and then it was only through Shandir's great magic. We don't have anyone like that anymore.*

Blazel hoped they could use the technique Kaieli had developed to cleanse the malignant magic from the crater's rocks against their ancient enemy. If not, they'd be defenseless.

Rizelya - 25 de Ahdar, 1076

The black power released them, and Rizelya was once again alone in her mind. She slumped over Glork's shoulder, who sprawled flat on his stomach. Noriana's weight on her back pressed down on her. Rizelya slowly turned her head from side to side. The other Gryphons also lay flat on the ground. The pounding in her head receded, and she realized it was the sound of the waves on the jetty. They were higher than normal, but not much.

Noriana groaned and pushed off Rizelya, then crawled off Glork's back. Rizelya forced herself to move so she could unbuckle herself and slid off Glork. She sat slumped on the wet ground against his shoulder, wrung out and exhilarated, but mostly in shock at what had happened. The others soon crawled off their Gryphon's backs and slouched against them. The waves' spray soaked them, but they were too exhausted to move.

"Well," Kaieli said after a while, "that's never happened before."

"If it had," Chariel added, repositioning herself so she sat up straighter, "we could have cleared the nucla in the pillar."

"I've never experienced anything like it before." Awe filled Noriana's voice.

"None of us have." Aistrun moaned and rubbed his face. "Hey, I certainly haven't. I'm not sure I like it."

Rizelya rubbed her temples. "I think... I think it happened after the Gryphons joined us. They were never part of your weave before, Kaieli."

I'm surprised. Glork shifted to crouch on his paws. *I have never heard of our magic melding with yours.*

I didn't think it was possible, Morlek said.

It is not only possible, but astonishing! Torlek rolled off his stomach to sit on his back haunches. *I would like to do it again.*

"Me too," Kaieli said with a smile. "But just not too soon. I'm still drained."

Rizelya nodded in agreement. "As soon as you're able to fly, Glork, we need to report back to Histrun and Moraak and tell them what we accomplished." Rizelya grimaced as she remembered they hadn't gone to Posanvende Keep where they were supposed to, instead veering off to Posanvenir Keep. She had taken this task on herself and would be in deep trouble. While trying to gain the energy to remount Glork, she reflected on the incredible experience. Had they really saved the entire coastline from the deadly wave?

She sat up quickly. "Glork, we need to check the other keeps."

What? he asked sleepily, then shook his head, yawning. *Why do we need to check them? They're safe.*

"Are you sure? I need to find out if it really happened, or if I was dreaming."

"Well, if you were dreaming, Rizelya," Kaieli said, stretching, "then so was I."

"Me too," added Chariel, sitting up and peering over Morlek's back. She reached over and roused Aistrun.

Aistrun groaned. "Argh, what a nightmare." He paused when he realized everyone was staring at him. "What?"

"That was the most amazing thing I've ever experienced," Chariel said, "and you're calling it a nightmare?"

He drew his eyebrows together and rubbed his eyes. "Yes, it was for me. I don't want to do it ever again. Having so much power was too much for me. I still have a blazing headache."

Kaieli stood and walked to where he lay with his head on Broogk's shoulder. "Here, let me help you."

"How does everyone else feel?" Rizelya asked as Kaieli worked on healing Aistrun's headache.

Grazeen stood and swung her arms in a circle. "Other than being tired, I feel great. And I would definitely be part of that again."

"Same here," Noriana said with a shy smile.

Me too! Keeru shifted to sit on his haunches.

Loshera pushed her snowy-white hair back from her face. "I feel blessed to have been part of the melding of our spirits into one. I think we touched the well where all our magic springs from. Even the Gryphon's magic comes from the same wellspring." She paused, gazing at the sky, and a sunbeam lit her face. Loshera sighed deeply as the sunbeam seemed to soak into her skin. "The Goddess has given us this gift to heal her land of the malignant magic infecting it. It is our responsibility to teach others how to merge into the Black Weave."

"More teaching," Rizelya groaned, leaning forward to put her elbows on her raised knees. "I thought I was done with teaching."

"You have a gift for it," Grazeen said. "Look at all you've done. I wouldn't be here now, or part of this wonderful event, if you hadn't taught me I have value in a fighting-pack." She looked pointedly at Aistrun. "This is simply another way to fight and keep our people safe."

"Not everyone can fight in the same way," Chariel said. "This isn't Aistrun's way. I'm thankful he was here to share the first Black Weave with me, even if he chooses never to do so again." She squeezed his hand, and he gave her a weak smile.

I agree with Aistrun, Broogk said, *It was astounding, but I don't want to repeat it.*

Let's do it again, Morlek said, dropping his beak in a grin. Torlek and Keeru nodded in agreement, their head feathers bobbing enthusiastically.

"What about you, Eiden and Korrik?" Rizelya asked.

Eiden stood and walked several feet away. Korrik ambled to join her, and she draped an arm over his shoulder. Together, they stared for several milcrons at the harbor, where waves only slightly higher than normal rolled into the shore.

She turned back to the group. "Korrik and I will fight the evil in our land. It has gone on for too long and has brought stagnation to our people—both of our peoples. We believe this technique will work against the Malvers' evil as much as it will the malignant magic pools."

Rizelya turned to the only one in their group who hadn't expressed his opinion yet. "Glork?" She heard the entreaty in her voice. Over the course of the war with the Scourge, she'd come to rely on him. She counted him as one of her good friends, as much as Aistrun or Kaieli. She didn't want to do this without him—or Blazel, for that matter.

Glork bobbed his head once. *I'm in.*

Rizelya stood and briskly rubbed her hands together. "Great!" Her stomach rumbled, and she realized she hadn't eaten anything since breakfast. When she'd left the camp, she hadn't thought to grab any supplies. She placed her hand over her stomach as it grumbled again. "I'm starved. We'll have to wait to try it again later."

Yes, I need to eat before using so much energy again. Glork stood and shook his fur. *Let's go check on the other keeps on our way to Posanvende Keep. They will be worried about us.*

The group mounted and flew first in the direction the Posanvenir people had fled, then checked on the other keeps along the coast. They discovered them all safe and sound, with only a higher tide than usual. Finally, late in the evening, Rizelya's group landed in Posanvende Keep's courtyard, the place they should have originally gone. Her legs trembled when she slid off Glork's back, and her stomach hurt from being so empty. She studied her people, and they all looked as exhausted and famished as she did. She nearly wept when Keep Alpha Dalnevah offered them food.

While they ate, Rizelya let Aistrun tell the keep alphas what they had accomplished to save the keeps in their territory from the deadly tidal wave. The storyteller in him made it sound heroic, and none of his distaste for the process came through. It wouldn't surprise her if the story passed from keep to keep like wildfire.

As Rizelya listened to Aistrun, joy filled her. For the first time in her life, she'd been able to help her people without fighting or killing anything to do so. She considered the Black Weave's power and its potential. If they could eradicate the malignant magic which formed the Malvers' monsters, their entire culture would change. What would it be like if she didn't have to fight all the time? She wasn't sure, but she'd like to find out.

Chapter 3

Malviana - 25 de Ahdar, 1076

Malviana led the procession southwest away from the lost island and back to the place which had transformed her into the person she was now—Mordar's Castle. Initially, she hated the castle and Mordar as he tortured her mind and body until one day the naive girl she'd been disappeared. She'd experienced true power for the first time in her life. The little magics she'd done with her Black Talent were nothing compared to what she could do with the power Mordar and his god, Mordaga, gave her.

Over time, she'd grown to love Mordar and the castle, becoming his queen. Together, they began their conquest of the land for their god, killing those who opposed them or turning them into slaves. Life had been glorious! Until that wretched Shandir discovered a way to stop them.

Malviana's mouth tightened in a bitter line. Shandir had killed her beloved Mordar. Even after a thousand years, Malviana's heart ached, and she yearned for his touch. No man satisfied her like he did. Malviana exacted her revenge on Shandir by twisting her last, great spell. Instead of negating the Malvers' powers, the spell destroyed every living organism in a one hundred measure radius of the blast zone and created an immense crater. Nothing lived there now.

The twisted spell's backlash had robbed Malviana of her power long enough for the hated Supreme to bind her. By the time Malviana recovered, the Posairs had exiled her and her people to that vile island with nothing on it to sustain them. They almost died from starvation. But Mordaga upheld his promise of immortality, and they'd discovered a way to survive.

To the west, the black sand of the Barrens glimmered in the late afternoon sun. Jumbles of petrified wood littered the ground where a vast forest once stood. Malviana smirked at the desolation of Malvernlair Province. Shandir's twisted spell had been in its center. Her former clan, the Malverans, had sought to overthrow her and Mordar's rule. She considered their destruction justice.

After another few octars of flying, the black sand gave way to the muted greens of a vast swampland. Life filled the area, and Malviana sensed an underlying, delectable magic affecting everything. Mordaga's residual power distorted the animals here. She inhaled deeply.

She beckoned Borgedier and Magdelyn to come forward to ride alongside her. "Ah! Home!" she said. "Do you remember it?"

"The memories of it have kept me sane these interminable years, my queen," Borgedier said. He, too, inhaled deeply. "Can you sense all that luscious power waiting for us to harvest?"

"Yes, I can. I have long waited to regain the power I lost to Shandir. It is now within my grasp."

Below them, the vegetation changed, becoming a twisted, sinister parody of life. The trees turned from dark green to black. The trails of water darkened, and vines with orange and black flowers draped between tree limbs. She glimpsed a rabbit, now warped into a carnivorous beast.

At last, as night gained dominance over the day, they arrived at the black castle. As she caught sight of her beloved castle, she gasped, clutching her heart and tears springing to her eyes. The turrets were crumbling, and sludge filled the moat. Even though vines clogged the courtyard, someone had cleared the encroaching vegetation from the main altar. The obsidian block absorbed the light, and rust-colored blood stains from past sacrifices dripped down its sides. Twisted beasts milled around its foundations and gave them baleful glares.

Anger replaced her dismay. "How dare they defile my altar!" Malviana guided her banthu to fly over the courtyard and touched her necklace. Drawing on the stored power in it, she directed it through her wand. A blast of power and jagged bolts of light struck the ground, burning a twisted beast to a crisp. She absorbed its death essence, wringing the last, pitiful drop of power from it.

The sound of leathery wings drew her attention back to her approaching people. Only the higher ranks of nobility retained any semblance of their former strength. She needed everyone to quickly regain their full power. Clearing the castle of unwanted tenants would begin restoring the lower ranks. Besides, it was beneath her dignity to kill rabbits.

"Borgedier, have the lower ranks clear this infestation from the castle," Malviana ordered.

Her two trusted vassals saluted, and orders rang out. Before they began, a ten-foot-tall creature exited the castle. Sharp antlers spread above his head. His face was Posarian, except for his glowing orange eyes. Long brown fur covered his muscular body, but there was no mistaking his maleness. His lower portion was a multa's hindquarters which ended with wide, cloven, platter-like hooves. He held a coiled black rope, reeking of power in his clawed hand. He looked up at Malviana and grinned, showing sharp fangs.

"My queen!" he hailed her. "A moment, and I'll have a space cleared for you to land."

She dipped her head in acknowledgment, pleased to have one of her twisted Posairs, Korand, already at the castle.

He bellowed. The smaller warped creatures scurried into the tangled vines. A large canid stalked from the opposite side of the altar. The sharp spikes all along the length of its tail whistled as they whipped through the air, hitting a carnivorous rabbit. The spines impaled the rabbit, and the floxidor dragged its squealing prey toward it. Two rows of triangular teeth bit down, shearing the rabbit in half.

"Hai!" Korand yelled, as he snapped the rope out like a whip. It wrapped around the floxidor's straight horns. Another twist of his wrist, and Korand secured the canid's long muzzle with the rope. With a jerk, he tightened the rope, pulling the creature's jaws closed. The spiked-tail lashed toward him. He sidestepped, then stomped on it with his hoof. Spikes shattered, and the floxidor wailed, thrashing to escape. Power pulsed through the rope, and the floxidor stilled.

"A present for you, milady," Korand said with a bow.

Malviana's senses told her it wasn't dead, just stunned. She directed her banthu to land next to Korand. Borgedier landed immediately after her, quickly dismounted, and hurried to her side. He limped, and pain pinched his mouth, but otherwise he seemed hale. He hadn't suffered much from her use of his energy.

She took his proffered hand and threw a leg over the saddle, grimacing at the ache in her thighs, no longer accustomed to such long flights. Her knees threatened to buckle, and Borgedier's strong grip kept her from falling. Korand awkwardly knelt on one knee—still holding the rope—and bowed his head. His huge antlers nearly touched the ground. She walked around him, studying the way the magic had transformed him from a Posair male to this stunning creature. He quivered, and she inhaled, tasting his anticipation and eagerness.

The rest of her people landed, quickly mobilizing to clear the small pests from the area, while she turned her attention to the captured floxidor. It would do.

"Put it on the altar," she ordered.

"Yes, Your Majesty." Korand stood, stooped over, and easily picked up the creature. He carried it to the black obsidian altar, where he tied it, using the rings driven deep into the stone for that purpose.

Ten of the higher-ranking nobles, along with Borgedier and Magdelyn, gathered around the altar. Magdelyn placed the sacred matte black bowl under a slot on the altar. The same bowl Malviana had collected the death essence from her pets, using the device she'd constructed. She sighed. She'd never have to use it again.

Malviana removed her jewelry, placing it and her wand in the bowl. Throwing her cloak back from her shoulders, she stood at the head of the altar, raised her arms to the sky, and tilted her head back.

"Great Mordaga! Hear us, your faithful servants, as we once again come before you and give offerings of blood to you. Drink deeply of this offering, and grant us immortality and power!"

The malevolent power gathered around her, and a dark presence hovered over her, breathing its sulfuric breath upon her neck. She shivered in delight. Her god had come to her. A cold hand gripped her throat, and exquisite pain exploded through her, filling her body and mind. As the ecstasy carried her higher, she plunged her long, stiletto claws into the creature's chest, puncturing its heart. Hot blood pumped over her hand and poured into the bowl. A black mist of power swirled from the bowl, then thrust sharp fingers into her. She absorbed the death essence of the creature, but it wasn't enough. She pulled her hand from its carcass.

Examining the faces around the circle, she knew her trusted advisers had also fed. But like her, it hadn't been enough to fill the emptiness.

She turned to Korand. "Are there more large creatures?"

"Yes, my liege."

She flicked her eyes at Borgedier. He nodded and stepped away from the altar.

"Jorvelden," Borgedier called. "Gather ten men and go with Korand. Bring us more of these creatures, so we may feed."

The men saluted and followed Korand from the courtyard. Malviana glanced at the bowl. The blood was gone, and the gemstones set in her jewelry glowed with dark power. Her lips quirked up. It was a start.

Blazel - 25 de Ahdar, 1076

Night had fallen by the time Blazel and his team returned to the war host camp. The exhausted Gryphons landed as close to the command tent as possible. Even though he hadn't done anything other than hang on, Blazel was so tired that his fingers fumbled at the buckles of his harness. He sent Kaaik, Delestrun, Ambrelya, and the others to find their dinner and beds, while he, Graak, and Saffren trudged to the command tent to report to Histrun and Moraak.

He almost stepped on the paw of the huge, black Thunder Wing guarding the tent. Blazel mumbled an apology to the Gryphon, who had blended with the shadows. Lanterns hanging on the ridgepoles brightened the makeshift headquarters, and he jerked to a stop. Histrun's face scrunched in anger as he stared into the cup in his hands. Keshanal sat back in her seat, shaking her head. She'd pulled her faded copper hair into a bun. The wrinkles lining her dark brown eyes crinkled as she chuckled softly.

Histrun glared at her. "It isn't funny," he mumbled.

Naila slumped on a stool, holding a mug. She appeared dazed. Moraak's tail was curled around his golden body as he sat on his haunches, the tip of it thumping the ground.

Fear trembled along Blazel's spine. "What happened? Weren't the keeps evacuated in time? How many people did we lose?"

"Thanks to Rizelya and Kaieli, none." Keshanal grinned.

"She disobeyed orders," Histrun grumbled. "No matter what they did, they didn't go where they were supposed to. Too many people look up to her for her to go off with some harebrained idea." He slammed his cup on the table and Blazel heard it crack. "It could have killed her and the rest."

Not true. Moraak lifted a talon. *My Gryphons were ready to carry them to safety.*

"Except she pulled them into her spell," Histrun huffed. "If it hadn't worked, we'd have lost them all."

Blazel remembered Graak mentioning Rizelya had gone to Posanvenir instead of Posanvende Keep. "What did she do?"

Keshanal smiled and shifted into a more comfortable position in her chair. "The brilliant girl figured out how to stop the tidal wave and save the entire eastern coast. She and Kaieli formed what they're calling a Black Weave. It's similar to what Kaieli's been doing to cleanse the nucla, but much, much more. They haven't even skimmed the surface of what the power can do."

She stopped the tidal wave? Graak's head feathers stood on end. *We saw how monstrous it was. It would take incredible power to stop it.*

"Well, she did," Naila croaked. *She and the others stood in front of the wave and commanded it.*

"Where is she? Is she all right?" Blazel searched the tent for her.

"She's fine," Keshanal assured him. "They're just exhausted and are staying the night at Posanvende Keep. They'll return tomorrow."

"And then she can explain to us what in the Crones' fires she did!" Histrun growled.

Blazel crossed his arms and grimaced. "Our news seems anticlimactic after this."

Histrun sat up straighter. "What did you see, boy?"

"Nothing. The island is gone."

Any Malvers who stayed on it would have drowned, Graak added, satisfaction in his voice.

"We must assume the woman in Rizelya's visions is on the mainland," Saffren spoke up. "I've seen her in Rizelya's mind when I've helped her create the mind-blocks. That woman is evil incarnate. She revels in blood and death. From what I gather, she created the Malvers' monsters. They are her pets."

Naila sucked in a breath, and Keshanal pursed her lips.

"So we only need to deal with the Malvers who made it off the island and to the mainland." Histrun stroked his beard thoughtfully. "It would be good to know how many there are. It can't be very many. We must outnumber them."

It doesn't matter how many there are. Moraak's tail thumped harder. *Any Malvers are too many. In the Great War, a single one could decimate an entire village. We can only hope they no longer possess the power to create their beasts and followers. If they do, they can make an army, and in a few lunadars, we'll be the ones outnumbered.*

Memory stirred in Blazel, along with it a foreboding. "Graak, do you remember the twisted creature we encountered in the swamp?"

Graak's hind paw twitched. *Of course I do. Do you think it could be one of the Malvers' creatures?*

"It certainly was intelligent, and I haven't encountered anything like it before."

If they are already creating creatures, we're in trouble. Moraak's fur bristled. He stood up suddenly, knocking over a small table. *I must inform my father about this news.*

"Wait!" Histrun held up a hand. "Shouldn't we send a scouting party to the swamp first?"

No, it doesn't matter how many Malvers are there, Moraak replied. *Their queen, Malviana, has returned. She is the one who has plagued Rizelya's dreams. If she is on the mainland, trouble is here now. He needs to know. The one-hundred and eighty Gryphons who survived the war with the Scourge are not enough to keep the Malvers from our home.* Moraak strode from the tent, and with a crack of thunder, he and his bodyguards soared away.

"I believe finding out more about our enemy is a good idea," Keshanal said. "Graak, Blazel, you know where the black castle is. You'll lead the reconnaissance team. Graak, when will you be rested enough to leave?"

I can be ready in the morning, Graak said, although his ears and tail drooped with fatigue.

How about late morning? Naila scratched the side of her face. Histrun and Keshanal nodded in agreement, and Naila continued. *Most of the evacuation teams should return by then. Saffren, go with them. Your mind-block would be useful. Take Chariel and Kaaik too. But Rizelya stays here.*

"Yes, ma'am." Saffren's eyes were wide.

"Go get some sleep," Histrun ordered.

As soon as they exited the tent, Saffren swore. "I really don't want to go. I've felt Malviana's malice. And I want to find out what Rizelya and Kaieli did. It sounds much more interesting, and fun, than going to that dark place."

"I agree with you." Blazel put an arm around Saffren's shoulders. She was shivering, and the spring night wasn't that cold.

As Blazel laid in his cot, missing Rizelya's warmth, he worried about what they would find in the castle. The malignant magic saturating the swamps had twisted its denizens bad enough. How much worse would it be with the queen of evil in residence?

Wisah - 25 de Ahdar, 1076

The first gray light of predawn crept through the high windows of the hallway. Wisah sensed a shift in the energy. It felt uneasy and dangerous. She stood and turned slowly in a circle, trying to determine where it originated. She finally stopped when she faced the southeast and frowned. If the danger came from the invaders, or if Rizelya and her pack were in trouble, it would come from due south.

Wisah opened her mind and lightly touched the veil separating the physical world from the psychic plane. Usually, she just sensed its presence, so it surprised her when she clearly saw it. The veil shimmered a pale silvery-gray with fine filaments attached to it. She looked at the one fastened to her heart. She smiled with joy. Each filament was a soul in the astral or physic plane. The cords kept their bodies anchored in the physical world so they wouldn't cross the veil into death before their time.

The veil vibrated. She heard a dissonance in the sound. Something was wrong! She searched the veil and found a dark filament reeking of rotting malignancy. Gagging, she firmed her resolve and followed it. Within moments, she heard an evil, malicious cackle reverberate along the thread she held. A moment later, a scream of pain resounded on both planes. Wisah dropped the thread, quickly returning to her body.

"The Supreme!" she cried, running for the door. "She's in trouble. Let me in!" She gathered her magic to her, determined to use force if she must. She'd learned a few offensive tricks while she was part of Rizelya's squad fighting the invaders. The guards took one look at her face and opened the door for her.

The fire had died down to embers, making the room dark. A small puddle of light from a reading lamp on the desk showed the Supreme slumped in her chair. Her limbs convulsed, and she moaned in pain.

"Get a healer in here quickly," Wisah yelled at the guards as she ran to the Supreme's side. "She's having a heart attack!"

She gently laid the Supreme on the floor, kneeling by her side. Wisah searched the Supreme's pockets for the tin of heart medication she always carried. Fumbling it open and dropping several of the small pills, Wisah finally picked one up in her shaky hands and placed it under the Supreme's tongue.

"I'm here, Supreme," Wisah crooned softly, holding the old woman's hand. "You're not alone."

"Malvers... Malvers..." the Supreme muttered.

Terror slammed into Wisah. Because of Rizelya, she knew who the Malvers were. Their ancient enemies were locked behind a magical barrier and exiled on an island in the eastern ocean. Wisah's eyebrows rose. The malevolence and danger had come from that direction.

The Supreme's hand fell limp, and her breathing stilled. "Where is the healer?" Wisah yelled.

"She's coming!" a guard said from the doorway.

The Supreme was slipping away. The healer wouldn't reach them in time. She couldn't die. They didn't have a replacement. They couldn't be without a Supreme to lead them. Frantic, Wisah reached for the Supreme's soul. Horror filled her as the filament connecting the Supreme's soul to her body started to fray and an opening formed in the veil.

No, Wisah cried, *you can't go.*

The Supreme turned from her plunge toward the opening. In the astral plane, she appeared as a young woman, not much older than Wisah. Her white eyes shone with power. *I don't want to go, Wisah, but my body is failing, and the Goddess is calling me home.*

No, Wisah shook her head. *She sent me here to save you. You have to fight, Supreme. We still need you!*

You are right. I have too much to do, and there is too much danger to our people. The Supreme visibly pulled her power closer to her. Her eyes shone brighter, and her astral body became more defined. She struggled to move away from the veil. *Wisah, you have to help me. The pull is too strong.* She held out a hand.

Wisah grabbed it and tugged. Another strand of the Supreme's filament snapped and came out of the weaving. Wisah became aware of the healer working on the Supreme's body. Wisah let go of the Supreme's hand and concentrated on repairing the filament connecting the Supreme's soul to her body. A presence touched her shoulder, and additional power flowed into her. Using it, she gathered astral dust, formed it into a long, thin strand, and wove it into the Supreme's rope.

The Supreme moved away from the veil and gripped Wisah's hand. *Whatever you did to save me worked. I haven't felt this good in ages. Thank you.*

"She's coming around," the healer said, relief in her voice. "She'll be okay."

Wisah blinked her eyes and found herself crumpled on the floor next to the Supreme, holding her hand.

The healer, Jordelyna, sat back on her heels. "You gave us a scare, Your Grace. But you're back." She gently patted the Supreme's shoulder, then looked at the guards surrounding them. "Help me get her to her bed."

Jordelyna maneuvered a board underneath the Supreme, and six Red Guards lifted it up carefully and carried the Supreme to her bedroom adjoining her office. Jordelyna followed close behind them.

Left alone, Wisah slowly stood, groaning at her aching body. She gripped the edge of the desk for support and glanced down. The ancient book lay open. The old script swam before Wisah's eyes, calling her to read it. She resolutely averted her eyes. What if it caused the malignant energy she'd sensed that had attacked the Supreme?

Her gaze fell on two small portraits. One depicted a beautiful young woman with black hair and yellow eyes, her cheeks glowing with health and a mischievous smile curving her lips. The other showed a mature, thin woman, with charcoal-gray hair, pale gray skin, and black eyes lacking the whites. The planes of the face and the shape of the eyes suggested the portraits were of the same person. *Who is this woman? Is she the Malvers woman plaguing Rizelya?*

Wisah picked up the portrait and sensed the same malicious, malevolent energy as she had in the astral plane. She shuddered.

A Red Guard entered the office from the Supreme's bedroom. She cocked her head and studied Wisah for a long moment. "The Supreme wants you to stay with her. I don't know how you knew she was in trouble, or what you did to save her, but thank you." She bowed her head, touching her right hand to her forehead in a gesture of deep gratitude and respect.

Wisah shrugged, unsure herself what exactly had happened. She followed the guard into the Supreme's room and sank into the empty chair next to the bed. The other guards filed from the room.

Jordelyna paused at the doorway. "She's sleeping now. But I'll be outside if you need me. I'll have someone bring in some food for you. You look drained."

Wisah sighed and shook her head. "I am. Don't send for anything, I'm too tired to eat. Thank you for saving her."

Jordelyna gave a small snort. "I didn't do much. It was you." She ran a hand through her emerald-green hair, and the light caught on the white strands in it. "She was gone, and there wasn't much I could do. Then I sensed you doing something on the astral plane, but I don't have enough White Talent to enter there, and suddenly the Supreme returned." She smiled at Wisah and gave her the same gesture of respect the guard had given her.

Wisah stared at the Supreme, watching the slow rise and fall of her chest. She wasn't sure what she had done, except the Goddess's presence had guided her actions. Why was the Goddess suddenly interested in her? She was a lowly White Priestess, nothing special. Wisah inwardly shrugged as she settled more comfortably in the chair. She'd ask the Supreme about it when she recovered.

Chapter 4

Malviana - 26 de Ahdar, 1076

Malviana squinted in the late morning light, still unused to sunshine. She stepped back from the head of the obsidian altar in the central courtyard, now stained red from the blood of many twisted creatures. Blood from the last victim still trickled from the body, along the channels carved into the altar, and dripped into the black crystal bowl sitting on a small platform. Her and her children's implements of power and symbols of rank gleamed in the bottom of the bowl. A satisfied smile crossed Malviana's lips as the gemstones in the jewelry sluggishly slurped up the last of the blood. At last, all the gemstones in her jewelry and wand pulsed with power and couldn't absorb any more.

Dark power thrummed through her body, and she felt strong and alive for the first time since her exile. She stretched her neck from side to side. Vertebrae popped, and she sighed at the relief of tension. She'd stood at the altar throughout all of last night and all day. Malviana glanced to the west. The sun hung low on the horizon. No wonder exhaustion pulled on her.

Malviana surveyed her children and the high-ranking nobles—her court—surrounding the altar. The long octars had been worth it. Their starved gauntness had fleshed out, and power radiated from them. Their gemstones had also drunk deeply of the death essence and could now be used to work the Malvers' magic.

Magdelyn lifted the bowl from its pedestal, carried it to Malviana and dropped to her knees, holding the bowl as an offering. Her arms trembled with the weight of it. No one but Malviana was permitted to touch her jewelry. Another's energy would contaminate it and dilute the available power.

Malviana first removed her jet earrings and threaded them through her ears. Next, she put on her rings, a different gemstone for each finger. Lifting her necklace from the bowl, she admired the gleaming diamond, sapphire, emerald, ruby, axinite, apatite, and hematite jewels set in black gold before clasping it around her neck. Let the Supreme and her White Priestesses wear a single paltry diamond. Malviana drew in a breath as the jewels touched her skin, and the sharp taste of power bit her tongue.

Lastly, she extracted her wand, smiling as she gripped the Gryphon talon handle. Affixed to it was a six-sided obsidian, the length of her forearm. Embedded into one side were the same seven crystals, with the light-colored ones at the bottom and the darkest, the hematite, near the tip. The wand allowed her to focus and direct incredible power, much more than possible using her own magical reserves.

Suitably adorned, she gave a regal nod to the others. "You may retrieve your jewels of power."

Her eldest son, Prince Mordeven, as heir to her throne, stepped up first. She admired the sharp planes of his face and his thin, sensuous lips. A pain of longing filled her. He looked so much like his father. He brushed his long black hair from his face and reached into the bowl. After removing his hematite and black diamond earring, he fit it through the hole in his ear. Then he withdrew his rings, sliding them onto his fingers, three on his left hand and four on his right. Each ring symbolized a level of power and rank achieved. As was right, only Malviana wore more rings than he. Smirking at his sister, Morvana, he reached for his onyx wand and purposely picked up one of her rings as he did so.

"Oh, is this yours?" he asked innocently, holding it out for her.

"Damn you, Mordeven." She scowled at him, her pearl gray eyes snapping, and grabbed it from him. "You know it is. Now it's ruined until the next sacrifice." She slipped it on her left pinkie, anyway. None of them could squander what power they had right now. She fished out her other five rings and put them on her long, slender fingers. The tightly braided ropes of her taupe gray hair swung free as she tilted her head to thread her iridescent black moonstones earrings on. She held her black tourmaline wand with its four gemstones protectively against her chest. Silver charms hung from the black gold handle.

Morvana stepped back, smoothing a hand down her leather-clad thigh. "Your turn, Malvidor."

Malviana's youngest child gave his sister a crisp bow, his light gray eyes hooded. He rarely showed what he was thinking through his eyes. He smoothed his dark hair back which, unlike most of the noble men, he wore cut close to his head. Without fanfare, he retrieved his five rings, black sapphire earring, and sardonyx wand.

Then, one by one, in order of rank, the nobles reached into the bowl and retrieved their wands and jewelry. Most wore three or four rings and perhaps an earring. As a mark of rank, none of their wands held more than five gemstones.

Malviana turned her attention to the small altar on the east side of the courtyard where the lower ranked Malvers, led by Duchess Valdorian, had sacrificed the smaller animals. Malviana gave a crisp nod to see the lower ranks were also recovering their lost power. As a low-ranking lord withdrew his wooden wand with a single clear crystal on it, Malviana glanced down at her own ornate, bejeweled one. Rank had its privileges.

Wisah - 26 de Ahdar, 1076

Wisah awoke to the sound of the Supreme calling out in her sleep. She pulled her chair closer to the bed and held the old woman's hand, murmuring reassurances. The Supreme's restlessness eased, and she drifted deeper into sleep. Still holding the Supreme's hand, Wisah dropped her head onto the edge of the bed.

She couldn't imagine life without the Supreme's guidance and influence. She had a gruff exterior, but Wisah always found her to be loving and compassionate. When Wisah recently rejected tradition and fallen in love, while the Supreme disapproved, she hadn't stopped Wisah from leaving the Sanctuary to fight the invaders. She had seen more death than she had ever wanted to. Wisah shuddered at the memory of her and the other White Priestesses escorting thousands upon thousands of souls through the veil. She recalled the Supreme's muttered words, Malvers, and hoped it didn't mean they had escaped their exile.

Jordelyna interrupted her thoughts as she walked through the door. "I can sit with her," she whispered, "while you go eat and freshen up."

Wisah glanced at her rumpled nightgown and ran a hand through her tangled hair. A bath and fresh clothes sounded good. Instead, Wisah shook her head, fearful the Supreme would slip away while she was gone. "Could you have someone bring me clothes and food? I want to stay here until I know she's out of danger."

Jordelyna lightly placed her hand on the Supreme's chest and closed her eyes while she scanned the Supreme with her healing talent. "Her heart is beating strong." The healer smiled. "Stronger than it has in years. I don't think she's leaving us anytime soon."

"It isn't her heart I'm worried about." Wisah stroked the old woman's hand. "She nearly crossed the veil."

"Ah, I see. I'll send someone up with food and clothes for you."

Throughout the day, Wisah sat vigil over the Supreme. Every so often, she paced to the door separating the bedroom and office and stared at the open book and the pictures beside it. When she found herself standing over the ancient tome the second time, with no memory of entering the office, she hurried back into the bedroom. As she passed the bookshelf, she grabbed a random book, slamming the door behind her. Leaning against it, she breathed hard, like she'd just run across the cloister grounds.

Wisah took several long, deep breaths until her breathing returned to normal. She looked at the book she'd randomly selected and giggled. *Hymns of Praise* should work to dispel the tingle of power crawling over her skin. She settled into the chair and started reading the poetry.

Some of the poems begged to be read aloud, so she quietly recited them, especially those the author had written for and about her lover.

"What in the world are you reading, Wisah?" the Supreme grumbled.

Wisah's face flushed, and she guiltily held up the book showing the title to the Supreme.

She chuckled. "Ah, you've found the naughty bits."

"How are you feeling? Do I need to call Jordelyna in?"

"I'm fine, child." The Supreme struggled to sit up, and Wisah hurried to put pillows behind her, then tucked the blankets more securely around her. The Supreme leaned back and studied her.

Uncomfortable with standing over the Supreme, Wisah sat back down.

"How long have you been able to manipulate the astral plane and the veil?" the Supreme finally asked.

"Not long. Just to help you." Wisah twisted her fingers together, unsure if she was in trouble.

"Who taught you?"

"No one, Your Grace." Wisah paused, her gaze sliding to the ceiling as she thought about it. "If anyone did, it was the Goddess. I felt Her presence. Until then, I didn't know doing something like that was possible."

"It shouldn't be possible." The Supreme plucked at the bed covers. "Why were you here?"

Wisah glanced at the door, then bowed her head. "The book, Your Grace..."

"It calls to you, doesn't it?"

Wisah nodded.

"I should have known," the Supreme whispered. She scrutinized Wisah for a long time. "The Goddess truly does work miracles. I'm quite grateful you were here and dragged me back."

"You were willing."

"Yes. There is much you must learn. First, our ancient enemies have escaped their exile. Malviana attacked me as she broke free."

"I sensed something wrong in the astral plane, just before you cried out. Was it her?"

The Supreme nodded. "I'm too old to fight her. But you are young and strong. It will be up to you to keep her from subjugating our people. Bring me the book and the pictures on my desk."

"You should eat first and let Jordelyna examine you." Wisah wasn't sure she wanted to touch the ancient text.

"Fine. Call Jordelyna."

Wisah stood and headed for the door.

Her hand was on the knob when the Supreme said quietly, "Wisah, the book isn't evil. It didn't hurt me. Malviana did."

Her face grew hot as she flushed with embarrassment. She'd forgotten the Supreme could read people. She snatched the door open, poked her head out, and told the Red Guard the Supreme was awake. A few moments later, Jordelyna came in and examined their leader, scanning her thoroughly.

Jordelyna stepped back from the bed, shaking her head. "You're better than I've seen you in lunadars, maybe even years, Your Grace. Even so, I want you to stay in bed and rest for the next few days. I want to make sure you're fully recovered."

The Supreme grumbled, but eventually agreed to the healer's demand.

While the Supreme ate under Jordelyna's eagle-eyed watch, Wisah cleaned up and put on fresh clothes. When she returned, she moved around the room, lighting candles and lanterns.

"Go fetch me the book, dear," the Supreme said.

Wisah glanced at the door, her gut churning. "But aren't you tired?"

The Supreme shook her head, pursing her lips. "I've slept long enough. We don't have enough time for your training as it is. There is nothing to fear, Wisah. Go get it for me."

Wisah ducked her head at the admonishment. She slowly approached the closed door to the Supreme's office. Taking a deep breath, she opened it and rushed into the room. The book sat open on the desk, the miniature paintings next to it. As she reached for the tome, a jolt of power sizzled from it to her hand. She jerked her hand back, shaking it, as the book slammed shut on its own. Bracing herself for another shock, Wisah grabbed the book and pictures, ran into the bedroom, and dropped the items on the bed beside the Supreme.

The Supreme chuckled.

"It bites." Wisah frowned at her and crossed her arms over her chest.

"It's only the protection spell on the book. Come, sit by me." The Supreme patted the bed.

Wisah felt like a child again as she climbed onto the Supreme's bed. She'd sat like this many timeswhile the Supreme read to her and Chariel.

"First, you must learn the sigils and the spell for opening the book. Here, let me show you." The Supreme lifted her hand and drew a glowing symbol in the air with her finger. It hung between them. "Now you try."

The Supreme gently guided Wisah as she performed the magic. In the back of Wisah's mind, she knew the spells and sigils were of the highest magnitude and sacredness. She wondered why the Supreme was teaching them to her, a lowly priestess.

She finally managed to do the magic correctly. The sigil she'd drawn in the air sank into the book, and with a click, it fell open. The script swam before Wisah's eyes.

"I can't read it," she sighed. "It's all blurry."

"That's also part of the protection spell, so those not initiated can't read it. You need another spell."

She taught Wisah the spell, and suddenly the words flowed into place. But even then, Wisah couldn't read the ancient language until she reached the last few pages. She skimmed over them.

"What's so special about this?" she asked, disappointed. "It seems to be a journal."

"Not any journal." The Supreme pulled the book back onto her lap. "This is a special journal, written before and at the time of the Great War." She thumbed through the pages until she found the entry she wanted and then tapped the two pictures. "These are both Malviana, before and after Mordar turned her to his cause and the corruption of death magic." The Supreme read aloud the passages about the torture Malviana had endured at Mordar's hands.

Wisah listened to the tale, aghast. It was a testament to Malviana's strong will that she had survived such evil. What could she have accomplished if she'd focused her determination on good instead of evil?

The Supreme wanted Wisah to defeat Malviana? Wisah mentally shook her head, doubting she possessed the capabilities and strength.

Malviana - 26 de Ahdar, 1076

Malviana examined her people more closely, and it appalled her how few of her people had survived the war and their exile. She tapped a long nail against her cheek as she considered what needed to be done. The sacrifices had cleared many of the creatures infesting the castle.

A banthu belched fire at a twisted creature that came too close to it. Using its tail, it tossed the charred beast into the air, tilted its triangular head back, and closed its jaws around the morsel. With morbid fascination, Malviana watched the bulge travel down the banthu's long, sinewy neck while two other banthues fought over a twisted canid. One of the mounts forked tail crashed into the side of the castle, and several stones tumbled to the ground. Malviana huffed in irritation. Her castle was literally falling apart. The banthues needed food and a stable, and her people required shelter. She heaved a sigh at the delay in building her army.

Malviana strode to the steps and climbed them, turning to face her people. "We have escaped our exile, praise Mordaga."

"Praise Mordaga!" Her people cheered, raising a fist to the air, then thumping their chest.

"We have fed, and our powers are returning, but we have much to do before we can exact our revenge on the Posairs. Prince Mordeven, you're with me."

He looked down, both literally and figuratively, at his sister and gave her a smug smile as he stepped forward.

He lost his smile when Malviana continued. "Princess Morvana, Prince Malvidor, Duke Borgedier, Duchess Valdorian, you're also with me. The rest of you, help Duchess Magdelyn make this place habitable again enough so we can at least sleep. The banthues need stables. Korand, Baron Jorvelden, capture the remaining creatures for additional sacrifices."

"As my queen wills," her people chorused, snapping their heels together and dipping their heads. In a short time, only her children and the duke and duchess remained in the courtyard with her. Malviana grimaced at the grime covering the steps. She'd prefer to sit on her throne, but doubted she could reach it until Magdelyn cleared a path to it. Instead, Malviana gingerly sat down on a grungy stair. The women sat on a lower one, while the men stood.

"We are sorely understaffed. I had not realized until today how many people we've lost over the centuries of our exile. From the quick count I did, only 225 of us returned to our home, and of those, most are the mid and lower ranks. And we are still weak."

"Even so, we are a match for any Posair." Mordeven jutted out his chin with indignation.

"We do not want to test that, my son," Malviana said, giving him a stern look. "It will take time to turn more Posairs to my side. There are always those whose hearts yearn for the power Mordaga can give them. But we'll have to wait to start that project. We first need to secure our new home from unwanted visitors."

"Do you think the Posairs will send a scout party?" Borgedier rested his hand on his wand, where he'd secured it in a sheath at his hip.

Malviana nodded. "I do, and soon. I have no intention of allowing them to learn anything about us until we're ready to seek vengeance and resume our quest to conquer the land.

"Borgedier, Malvidor, your job is to create a distortion fog around the castle grounds' perimeter." She needn't use their titles now that people weren't around to impress with their rank. "I don't want any pesky Posairs or Gryphons able to see what we're doing. Valdorian, Morvana, I'm tasking you to create a spell of disorientation. I want any who enter the fog to become confused, and the only direction they can find is back to the place they started—unless you capture them." She grinned at the thought of once again torturing and sacrificing her enemies to her god. Her court bowed or curtsied to her and hurried off to accomplish their assignments.

"And what do you want me to do, Mother?" Mordeven asked.

"You and I will create a barrier much like what kept us on that miserable island."

His eyes widened. "But won't it trap us in here?"

She sighed inwardly. Morvana truly was more intelligent than her eldest. But Mordar had proclaimed Mordeven his heir, and Malviana wasn't ready to go against his wishes, even though he'd been dead for a millennium. He had been a high priest to Mordaga, and as such, death wasn't always permanent. If she pleased Mordaga sufficiently, he would bring Mordar back. Unfortunately, the backlash of twisting Shandir's spell had caught her, and she'd been exiled before she could make the appropriate sacrifices. But she would soon remedy the situation.

"We'll be able to leave, but they won't be able to get in," she explained. "And we're going to add some nasty surprises for them."

An evil grin crossed his face, and he rubbed his hands together. "Oh, I like that. This will be so fun."

"Yes, it will be, my son. Let's get to work."

She stood and walked outside the fortress until she climbed a small hill and could see the entire complex. Picturing what she wanted to do clearly in her mind, she drew upon her newly filled reservoirs of power, raised her wand, and released her magic. Slowly, a magical barrier surrounded the castle, then expanded to cover ten measures of land. Darkness had settled while she worked.

Finished, she examined Mordeven's spells and the surprises he'd created for any unwanted visitors. She tipped her head back and laughed. In this, he was truly his father's son. She added a few flourishes to his diabolical creations.

Malviana studied the spells her children had wrought, pleased with the results. Morvana had a deft and subtle hand. Her disorientation spell compelled the person to travel in circles as if they were in a maze. The deeper into it they went, the more the magic affected their mind, making them unbalanced and ready to be added to Malviana's army.

"Cunning girl," Malviana praised her daughter. Morvana preened, smirking at her older brother.

"Malvidor, your distortion fog expands each time someone not of our ilk tries to penetrate it. Good job." Her youngest pulled his shoulders back and stood up straighter.

"And Mordeven, it was pure genius to add the bansholos to the barrier." Her eldest crossed his arms over his chest and sneered at his siblings.

"Let's go see what Magdelyn has done with our home." Malviana yawned. "I'm ready for bed."

"That was so much fun," Mordeven crowed, a bounce in his stride as they walked toward the castle. "What more can we do?"

"Much, much more, my dear," Malviana smiled at his exuberance. "But we must rest. We've expended a lot of energy. It's been a long two days since leaving the island." Malviana looked forward to sleeping in a dry castle without the constant and annoying drip of water.

Blazel - 26 de Ahdar, 1076

Blazel sat on the edge of his cot with his head in his hands and groaned. He hadn't slept much during the night, and whenever he did, nightmares plagued him. They hadn't been visions of Malviana, simply old-fashioned bad dreams. He dreaded returning to the black castle. It radiated evil and reeked of malignant magic, worse than any other place he'd been, even inside the crater.

During breakfast, the evacuation teams trickled in. Everyone excitedly talked about the tidal wave breaking on the invisible wall, and the tremendous power they'd sensed. Anticipation thrummed through him as he waited to see Rizelya and hear from her firsthand what had happened. He wished he'd been there instead of Aistrun to support the magic and experience it. It had to have been exciting. And now Histrun was sending him off in the opposite direction again. Would he ever be able to discover what it was like to wield so much magic?

Blazel sat in the mess tent, sipping taevo and dawdling, hoping Rizelya and her team would return before he and his left for the southern swamp. He raised his head at the commotion overhead. "Rizelya's back!" the sentry shouted.

Blazel hurried from the mess tent, arriving at the command tent at the same time as Glork landed. Even though she could do it herself, Blazel helped Rizelya unbuckle her harness. As soon as she dismounted, he wrapped her in his arms and kissed her deeply. He didn't care who saw them. He'd missed her.

With his arm around her shoulders, they walked to the command tent. "I hear you tilted our world and the way things are done again. You just couldn't let nature alone, could you?"

"That wasn't nature," she huffed. "It was the damned invaders, and I couldn't let them kill more innocent people. I had to at least try to stop it."

"I know you did, and that's why I love you. Although I wish I could have been there with you."

"Hey, I wish you'd been there, too," Aistrun said, thumping him on his shoulder blades. "Then I wouldn't have had to be part of it."

Blazel stopped in his tracks, whirling to face Aistrun. "You didn't like it?" His eyebrows nearly brushed his hairline.

"No. Way too much power and responsibility for me." Aistrun made a show of shivering. "You two can deal with the burden. I'm still trying to get out of leading the squad-pack you foisted on me."

Chariel, walking beside him with her hand linked through his arm, leaned into him. "One day, you'll be able to. But not anytime soon."

He gave her a quizzical look. "Is that a prophecy?"

She laughed. "No. Simply an educated guess. The Malvers are back. It's doubtful they've repented and given up their perversion. We'll have to fight them."

The group silently processed this information as they walked the rest of the way to the command tent. Blazel lifted the tent flap, and they entered in a more somber mood. Blazel noted Torlek and Kaieli were already inside.

Histrun glared at Rizelya with his arms crossed over his chest. "Well, girl, it seems I can't punish you for your disobedience. You're too much of a hero." He stood and pulled her into a tight hug. "What were you thinking? You could have been killed. I watch you fight, because we don't have a choice, but that... that was—"

"Brilliant," Keshanal interrupted. "Aistrun, were you part of it?"

He nodded, his face flushing scarlet. "Yes, ma'am."

"Good," she clapped in delight and resettled in her chair. "Then you can tell us about it. If we let Rizelya tell it, we'll only get the bare bones. But you have a rare gift for storytelling."

Knowing it would take Aistrun more than a few milcrons, Blazel and the others pulled camp stools into a circle around Aistrun and facing Histrun, Keshanal, and Naila. Blazel frowned at Moraak's absence, wondering what was so important that he would miss the evacuation reports. Listening to the story, he again wished he'd been part of the historic—and heroic—event.

"Do you think you can replicate it?" Histrun asked.

Rizelya and Kaieli exchanged a glance. "We think so," Rizelya said. "We need to experiment to find out what works best."

"Such as which people work well together," Kaieli said, a look of grief quickly crossing her face. She swallowed hard and continued. "And if it makes a difference how strong the various Talents are. I suspect it does. Eiden is a much stronger Yellow than Jaelena. That aspect of the Weave was correspondingly more powerful."

"This is intriguing," Keshanal said. "But it will have to wait. We need Chariel and Saffren to accompany Blazel on a mission. They are the strongest Gray and Blue Talents in the camp, if not in all of Lairheim. They should be part of the first team."

"First team?" Rizelya's eyebrows creased.

"There will, of course, be more than one team." Keshanal smiled. "I have faith this is a gift from the Goddess we can use to cleanse Lairheim of the filthy magic infecting it. And Lairheim is a big place. One team can't do it all."

Torlek, Chariel, Naila said, *when would you be ready to leave?*

Where are we going? Torlek asked, his head feathers lifting with interest.

"Nowhere good," Blazel told him. "The black castle in the southern peninsula swamp."

Oh. Torlek's feathers flattened. *If we're not trying to fly there in one day, I can leave at any time. I rested well last night. The Posanvende sands were warm.* He sighed and gave a trill of pleasure.

"I need to pack a travel bag," Chariel said.

Histrun nodded. "Plan to leave within the octar. May you fly with the blessings of the Goddess."

As Blazel and the others filed out, he inwardly cursed Histrun. The time allotted wouldn't give him long enough to spend some private time with Rizelya. He glanced over at Aistrun, who wore an equally unhappy expression for much the same reason.

"Would you like to come with us?" Blazel asked his friend. "We could use another warrior. Even without the threat of the Malvers, the southern swamp is dangerous."

Aistrun's face lit up. "Yes, I would. I didn't get to go with you and Graak last time."

Blazel rubbed the scar on the palm of his hand. If they were lucky, the Malvers would drive off the creature who had given him the scar. But then again, the creature had felt as evil as the castle, and the Malvers may have welcomed it with open arms.

"This won't be a sightseeing or pleasurable trip," Blazel warned Aistrun.

"I know." He shrugged, raised Chariel's hand entwined with his and kissed it. "But I'll be with my lady love. And I won't be dragged into Rizelya's experiments."

Rizelya laughed. "I can wait until you get back." She laughed again at Aistrun's groan. "I can't experiment without my best people—Blazel, Chariel, Saffren, and Graak. Too bad you don't want to play with us."

"On second thought," Blazel said, "ask Leistral and Leistrun to join us. More warriors would be good to take with us." The burn on his palm itched. "Oh, let's add Ambrelya. Her sharpshooting skills could be useful, especially if we run into that creature Graak and I encountered."

Aistrun saluted. "Maestrun and Nelstrun will want to come to protect Saffren."

"That's fine."

As they reached their shared tent, he and the other selected pack members raced in, tossing things into their packs. Besides his few belongings, Blazel gathered the herbs he needed to create the ward boundary to keep the swamp's twisted beasts from intruding into their campsites. He put the packet on the top, where it would be easily accessible as soon as they landed. The others were still packing, so he pulled Rizelya outside behind the tent and kissed her, savoring her warmth.

"Hey, we're ready to leave," Aistrun called a few milcrons later.

"All of us except Leistrun," Leistral said loudly. "He can't make up his mind which blue shirt to pack."

"The turquoise one, of course," Leistrun replied.

"They're all Strunland turquoise!"

Blazel imagined Leistral throwing her hands in the hair. Chuckling at the sibling's banter, he reluctantly broke away from Rizelya. Holding his hand, she walked with him to the field where Graak, Broogk, and the other Gryphons waited.

"I wish I was going with you," Rizelya said as she watched him buckle his harness. She gave him a rueful smile. "But I know why I can't. I don't want to be anywhere near Malviana."

"Neither do I. I'll see you in a few days."

She stood on her tiptoes to kiss him again. "Hurry back."

When she stepped back, Blazel glanced at his waiting team, and his face grew warm, embarrassed at the public display of affection. "Okay, Graak. Let's go."

Graak bunched his legs beneath him and jumped into the air. His huge wings quickly carried them high over the war camp before flying over the Barrens. The desolate place held only black sand-glass, petrified wood, and Malvers' monsters. Their flight path took them over Shandir's Crater and the remnants of the invader's compound. The monolithic pillar inside the deep crater, now reduced to a knobby hill, still oozed malignant magic. Blazel wondered if the Black Weave would be strong enough to clear the nucla in the pillar. Although he trusted the Faeorn had disabled the Scourge's navigation system, he'd feel better if the stuff that had attracted the alien species to his world no longer existed.

Malviana - 26 de Ahdar, 1076

Malviana's delight over the fiendish traps she and her children set around the castle grounds faded when she returned to her castle. Although Magdelyn and her people had accomplished much in the octars while Malviana cast her spell, they hadn't fully restored it to its previous glory.

Along the eastern wall—far enough from the castle she wouldn't smell their stink—they'd reconstructed the stables, and housed the banthues in them for the night. During the day, her underlings would release them to feed in the surrounding swamp.

Lights shone in the western wing, showing the crumbling stones had been repaired or replaced, and the creeping vines removed. The area around the outside altar was now cleared of plant and animal debris, as well as the remains of the sacrifices.

Malviana smiled. The grimy steps she'd sat on earlier were now cleaned, and the red veins in the black marble glowed in Kelar's moonlight. Malviana strode up them to the thick, black ironwood door.

Magdelyn met her in the dark foyer. "My lady, we've made your bedchamber habitable. We require additional resources to restore it to its former grandeur, and it will take time to finish the rest of the castle. However, we at least have beds to sleep in tonight. I've drawn a bath for you and set out fresh clothes."

Pleasure thrilled through Malviana at the thought of sleeping in a real bed with mattresses rather than on hard, cold stone. She smiled at Magdelyn. "You've accomplished quite a bit in such a short time. I'm ready to wash the stink of the island from me."

"Yes, Your Grace." Magdelyn curtsied, then led the way through the corridors and up a flight of stairs.

Memories of the first time Mordar led her through these corridors assailed Malviana. She'd been so young and dazzled by the luxury on display. She grimaced at the empty niches and the crumbling statues. They reminded her of how long she'd been gone. Malviana nodded absently to the two men standing guard at her door.

"Wait a moment, Magdelyn," she ordered, then entered her chambers alone. In the antechamber, a small fire burned in the fireplace. A settee and two wing-backed chairs flanked it. She scowled at the threadbare fabric and the faded, holey curtains pulled over the large window which dominated the south wall. Malviana lifted an eyebrow in surprise at how well the two desks sitting in front of the window had stood against the ages. Fond memories floated to the surface of her and Mordar working at their desks with their quills scratching across the paper as the only sound in the room.

She glanced up at the portrait over the fireplace. The preservation spell on it made the colors as bright now as the day they'd been painted a millennium ago. Malviana crossed the room and reached out her hand. Her fingertips hovered over the painting as she traced Mordar's long, straight nose, his thin lips pulled into a cruel smile, and his black eyes. *Mordar, I miss you. Even after all these years, I long for your touch. Soon, my love. We'll be together again.*

The portrait portrayed him standing behind her chair, one hand on her shoulder and the other on Mordeven's, who stood on one side of her. Morvana, her hair in curls, leaned against her on the other side, while a baby Malvidor sat on Malviana's lap. In the portrait, her hair was still black, but her yellow eyes had changed to the pure black they were now. Those had been the days before she'd lost the ability to procreate, before any of the Malvers had. She thanked Mordaga her mate had given her three children before she couldn't bear any more.

She turned away from the portrait before the moisture gathering in her eyes could spill and called Magdelyn to her. They strode into the bathing chamber attached to her bedroom. Fragrant steam rose from the large oblong tub, and Malviana fought back the memories of making love to Mordar in it. She stripped off her clothes, and Magdelyn honored Malviana with her personal attention to scrub her skin clean until it shone pearly gray.

As Malviana soaked in the hot water, she wrinkled her nose in distaste. The sulfur stench still lingered on her from the hated cave she'd lived in for so long. It would take time for it to fade.

Dressed in a clean nightgown, she finally entered her bedchamber. A wardrobe stood on the right-hand wall with a vanity next to it. The stool for it had long since crumbled to dust. Her large canopy bed sat under a stained-glass window. The drapes for it were gone, but Magdelyn had created a mattress and fresh linens. Malviana wondered momentarily at the magical cost the luxury had taken from someone, then brushed the concern aside. Her comfort was worth it.

In the corner next to the bed, a pleasure device waited for her to strap a lover into it. She sighed, again wishing for Mordar, then thought of the muscular Korand, and her nether regions tingled as she imagined the pleasure he could provide her.

While the animal sacrifices improved her magical reserves, it wasn't enough. Malviana took off her jewels, except her rings, and placed her wand within easy reach on the bedside table before climbing into bed. She pulled up the covers, shivering in the cool night air. She didn't like the smoke from a fire in her sleeping chamber, except in the dead of winter when she'd freeze without one.

As she drifted to sleep, she worried about how to gain the power she and her people needed to fully restore her castle and build her army. Her thoughts wandered to her pets, the janacks and brechas, and her eyes flicked open. A ready power supply—the magic pools—was at her disposal. They hadn't existed when she'd lived on the mainland. The pools fueled and created her pets. She could siphon the power from them for herself and her people. And even better, they were located all over Lairheim. Malviana smirked as she closed her eyes again. She drifted to sleep, imagining a myriad of ways she could use the magic pools against the Posairs.

Blazel - 27 de Ahdar, 1076

A green smudge appeared on the horizon, growing larger over the next few octars until they reached the edge of the swamp. It covered the entire southern subcontinent, although it had been fertile land before the Malvers had started using their perverted death magic. The sunset lit the sky with oranges and reds, and he directed Graak to a clearing large enough for the fifteen Gryphons.

As soon as Blazel's feet touched the ground, his body ached from the long ride. He groaned, stretched, and then pulled the herb pouch from his pack. He paced around the clearing, strewing the herbs and chanting a spell. As he completed the circle, he sensed the ward engage.

"We're safe inside this circle," he told his group. "You won't be safe outside of it. Don't disturb it, and while inside, don't kill anything. The twisted beasts can't cross it."

We can fly out to go hunting, Graak added. *Just be careful of your wings and tail. I want two Gryphons to stay with our friends at all times. There are some tasty creatures, like the jallopitar—* he clicked his beak *—and some not so tasty, like the dracur. The anguletes aren't too bad, but not my favorite.*

Broogk, Oslerru, Torlek, and Baekeek remain here and take the first watch. The rest of us will go find our dinner, and you can take turns when one of us returns.

The Gryphons took off singly or in pairs until Graak was the last of the hunting party to leave.

"Graak," Blazel called, "can you bring back a couple of swamp rats for our dinner?"

He looked disdainfully down his beak at Blazel. *And I suppose you want me to roast them for you too?*

"Well... if you're offering..."

I'm not! Graak ruffled his head feathers and, grumbling, launched into the air.

Blazel shrugged and helped his pack set up camp. Dirt flew as Oslerru enthusiastically dug a fire pit. The stripe of tufted taevo brown feathers between his forehead and over the top of his head jiggled. A band of the same brown swept from his yellow eyes across his cheeks on his otherwise ivory face. His tufted feathers and sharply hooked beak gave him an intense visage.

"Easy, there, my friend," Maestrun called, laughter in his voice for his partner. He lugged twice the load of firewood the smaller Leistrun did. "We don't need quite that large of a pit."

Oops! I got carried away. Oslerru dipped his head and resettled his taevo brown wings across his back. Almost delicately, he pawed dirt back into the hole, lifting his white tail high over his head for balance. Clods of dirt speckled his ivory fur.

"It's okay." Maestrun dropped his load and strode to the Gryphon, easily stroking Oslerru's feathers. At over six feet, Maestrun's head was level with the Gryphon's. The two matched each other in size. Oslerru was slightly larger than Graak.

"Really? That's all you could find?" Leistral stood with her hands on her hips, frowning at Leistrun's pile of wood. "Baby brother, I thought you were a big, strong man now." She playfully tousled Leistrun's strawberry blond hair and pulled him into a hug. Scowling, he pulled away from her. Laughing, she carefully laid wood in the pit and lit the fire. Soon, a pot of taevo bubbled over it.

Heads up! Graak called, flying into the clearing and dropping two charred lumps to the ground, then flew away again.

From the long, skinny tails, Blazel recognized the meat as swamp rats. The creatures were ugly, but they were one of the few edible, and somewhat tasty, swamp animals. He had only been kidding Graak and hadn't really expected him to hunt for them. He and Aistrun carried the meat to the fire. When they cut into it, they found Graak's flames had burned the hide while roasting the meat inside.

After eating, they sat around the campfire, and a twisted rabbit hopped by and sniffed at the herbs, sneezing and rubbing its nose with a paw.

"Oh, how cute," Saffren cooed. The firelight momentarily glinted on its long, sharp claws before it hopped away. Saffren blinked and snapped her open mouth shut. "I take that back."

A few milcrons later, a large squirrel with a bottle-brush tail curling over its back appeared. But unlike a normal squirrel, a rack of sharp horns extended over its head, and fangs peeked from its upper jaw. Its red glowing eyes unnerved Blazel as it sat watching them for a long moment before wandering off. Throughout the evening, other perverted beasts entered the bounds of the firelight. However, Blazel's magical barrier kept them from doing more than sniffing curiously at their campsite.

As the group flew deeper into the swamp the next afternoon, the vegetation changed below them, and, like the animals they'd encountered, it twisted into unnatural shapes and forms. Blazel's heart raced. They'd reached the area surrounding the black castle. Suddenly, a black fog rose like a wall in front of them. Blazel squirmed at the evil emanating from it.

"No, Graak!" Chariel shouted. "Don't go into it!"

Graak squawked and darted straight up—and up. There seemed to be no end to the fog. *This isn't natural,* he hissed. As he turned to fly back down, his wingtip hit the fog, and he screeched in agony.

The feathers touched by the fog were shriveled, like something had sucked the life from them. As Graak flapped his wings, the individual barbs dropped off, leaving only blackened and deformed rachis. By the time he landed, the affected feathers had fallen out. Graak held his wing out, still moaning with pain.

Chariel and Saffren ran to him and examined his wing. Chariel's mouth tightened, and her eyes narrowed.

"It's very like nucla poisoning," she said. "We can't heal it here, and we don't have enough people to form a Black Weave. I think Saffren and I can halt it from spreading further. Hold still, Graak. The pain will go away in a moment."

She quickly explained to Saffren what to do, and they joined their magic. A blue-gray light enveloped Graak's wing, and sank into it.

He blinked, carefully folding his wing over his back. *Thank you! That is better.*

"Will you be able to fly?" Blazel didn't want to leave his friend here. Wounded, he wouldn't last more than a few octars.

Graak nodded. *A few missing feathers won't stop me.*

"We did some exploring," Aistrun said, scowling at the fog. "We discovered if you enter the fog from the ground, you can only take a few steps before you find yourself back where you started." He shuddered. "There are scary things in it, too."

"None of us can sense any farther than a few inches," Saffren added. "And what's in there is pure evil."

Blazel crossed his arms over his chest and studied the fog. "This wasn't here the last time. I think it's safe to assume the Malvers are inside and are settling into the castle. However, we still need to know what's happening here. Baekeek, you and your scouts stay here and watch the area. Let us know if there's any change or movement. There's no need for the rest of us to linger."

While the scouts were smaller than the hawk-type Gryphons like Graak or Broogk, they were still large enough to take on any of the swamp's twisted beasts. Except maybe the one Blazel and Graak had encountered at the castle. The half-dozen scouts should be safe.

Blazel and the rest flew back to the war host. They hadn't learned anything other than the castle and swamp were even more dangerous. Could the Black Weave penetrate it? If it could, he was sure it would ignite the war with the Malvers.

His people needed to regroup and recover before they fought another one so close on the heels of the Scourge War. Hopefully, the Malvers weren't ready to engage yet, either.

Chapter 5

Rizelya - 28 de Ahdar, 1076

A warning cry of "Malvers' monsters!" broke the quiet as Rizelya exited the mess tent. She changed directions and sprinted to the southwest portion of the camp where it bordered both the Barrens and the plains. She skidded to a stop. Rizelya gulped as she counted five control-janacks, seventeen regular janacks, and over fifty brechas barreling toward them. The fighting-pack guarding the perimeter couldn't handle such a large mob. They hadn't seen nests like this since the invaders used the monster corrals.

Shaydan, Maheli, she yelled, using mind-speech. *I need your packs, now!* She started to call for Leistral, then recalled she'd accompanied Blazel. Rizelya wasn't sure who was in camp and who wasn't. As Histrun's battle commander, her sister would know. *Naila, we have an enormous problem. Get as many fighting-packs here as possible.*

She ran toward the monsters, feeding fire magic into her helbraught as she closed the distance. She glanced up at the sound of wings overhead. Twenty Gryphons dropped to the ground, letting off their passengers. She spotted Maheli, Calistrun, and Alestrun, along with several others from Maheli's fighting-pack. The Gryphons rose back into the air, winging toward the oncoming horde. Other fighters streamed from the camp, the men already in their warrior forms. Rizelya wished Blazel and Aistrun were here to fight at her side.

Eidstrun shifted and strode across the field to stand next to her. His warrior form—a perfect meld of human and wolf— was impressive at almost ten feet tall. Eidstrun's already wide shoulders were even wider, and his claws were nearly eight inches long. His massive jaws gaped open at her in a grin.

Laynar and the other gathered Reds split up and raced forward to form a wide semi-circle encompassing the approaching monsters. Rizelya nodded to Eiden, who ran by her side. Together, they would take on the control-janack.

Now! Rizelya ordered, and the Reds touched their glowing helbraught blades to the ground. A wall of fire blazed up, blocking the monsters from reaching the camp.

Calistrun and Alestrun howled and raced to meet the leading brechas, ducking and dodging the spines the brechas released from their backs. Calistrun punched a brecha's side, his claws tearing a huge hole in it. As he pulled his hand back, it dripped with ichor and venom. The brecha turned, snapping at him with its three rows of sharp teeth. Alestrun slashed with his claws, severing its head. Rizelya ran past them as other warriors tore into the loping brechas. Above them, the Gryphons dove and flared, coordinating their attacks with their partners on the ground.

Rizelya, Eiden, and Eidstrun weaved around the fighting, angling toward a control-janack. A brecha blocking their way burst into flame, quickly becoming ash.

Thanks, Korrik! Eiden called.

Rizelya glanced up at Korrik and Glork keeping pace with them. They finally reached the control-janack, and Rizelya panicked momentarily, expecting the debilitating humming that she alone could hear. This time, though, it was blessedly quiet.

She dropped the tip of her helbraught to the ground and concentrated on building the fire-shield. Normally, she'd have several other Reds to help her cast and hold it, except she'd outrun all the others. Glork added his flames to hers, and the fire-shield burst into being, creating a dome around the control-janack, while leaving an opening in the top for the Gryphons.

The control-janack roared and flung one of its ten tentacles at her. She slashed at it with her helbraught, slicing off a huge chunk, then moved away from the fire-shield. The heat stalks on top of its head waved, tracking her movement. Unlike the regular janacks, this one had a long, thick appendage, with round circles all around it, protruding above the heat stalks. It pointed directly at her, and Rizelya sucked in a breath, quickly tightening her mental shields, preparing for an attack by the Malvers woman. She let her breath out in a whoosh when it never came.

A thirteen-foot long tentacle reached for Eiden while another one slammed toward Eidstrun. He jumped out of the way, and Eiden shot an ice spear from her helbraught. The spear pinned the tentacle to the ground. While Rizelya chopped it off, the air chilled as Eiden cast a cold-air shield to keep the control-janack from sensing them. Rizelya and Eidstrun attacked another tentacle.

Glork and Korrik flared, their bolts of flame striking the control-janack's head and body, leaving smoking holes where they hit. Screeching, Korrik dove. The janack flung a tentacle at him, knocking him to the side. As Korrik fought to regain height, Glork dropped and snatched the protrusion with his talons while flaring. The protrusion burst into flame.

Rizelya leaped onto a tentacle and raced to the janack's head. Orange and red flames danced along her helbraught blade. She buried it in the janack's head, feeding even more magic into the blade. Snatching it out, she jumped off, yelling, "It's blowing!"

She rolled as she landed, then gained her feet and dashed to the edge of the fire-shield. Tucking into a ball, she formed a personal shield around herself just as the control-janack exploded and flaming bits rained on her.

When the debris stopped pelting her shield, she rose from her crouch and searched for Eiden and Eidstrun. She found them only a few feet from her. Eidstrun shook his fur, dislodging a few globules of monster guts. Eiden calmly stood and dusted ash off her shoulders.

"Glork, how are the others doing?" Rizelya asked.

It's almost over. You can lower your fire-shield. There aren't any monsters near you.

Rizelya gratefully released the magic, drained from holding it by herself. She leaned on her helbraught for support as she surveyed the battlefield. Shaydan and Dukaaik brought down the last control-janack. None of the regular janacks remained, and only a few brechas were left on the field. One turned into lava, and Rizelya spotted Maellyn standing over it. A few feet away, Raeleen thrust her helbraught into the last brecha, and brownish-gray streaks spread out from it, covering the brecha a mottled brown and gray. As she pulled out her weapon, the brecha crumbled into pebbles.

Anyone hurt? Rizelya asked.

One by one the fighting-pack alphas answered her. There were a few injuries, but thankfully, none were serious, nor were there any deaths.

Rizelya and the other Reds walked the battlefield, burning the monster detritus. The Gryphons joined them, making the work go faster, but even so, they didn't finish until the sun sat low on the horizon. When Glork landed beside Rizelya, she puffed out a breath, relieved she didn't have to walk back to camp.

"We need to tell Histrun and Naila about this," Rizelya said as Glork rose into the air.

My thoughts as well.

In a few moments, they reached the command tent. It seemed strange not to see a humongous Thunder Wing lying in front of it.

"Where's Moraak? It isn't like him to be absent."

He's returned to Alkaak, Glork said, his head feathers drooping. *He doubted King Zorlaak would believe any messenger except for himself about the return of the Malvers. We need more Gryphons for the coming war. We lost too many in the last one.*

They entered the tent and nearly bumped into a pacing Naila, her hands clasped behind her back and a scowl on her face.

"Tell me," Naila ordered.

Rizelya and Glork made their report, detailing the battle. "It's like they were working together." Rizelya observed. "I've never seen five nests mature at the same time, in the same place."

"Our numbers are attracting them," Histrun said, running a finger around the edge of his mug.

"But we've been here lunadars, and with more people," Rizelya protested. "And there hasn't been an attack like this before."

The Malvers are back. Glork's feathers ruffled as he shivered. *These are their pets. It stands to reason they would increase the attacks to thin our numbers.*

"It makes sense." Histrun stroked his chin while resting his ankle on the opposite knee. "If they could direct them from that remote island, they can certainly control them from a few hundred measures away."

Expand the patrols, Naila suggested, gesturing outward. *And send warnings to the nearby keeps. It's a good thing the border keeps are still empty.*

Histrun dismissed Rizelya and Glork, and they went their separate ways to find dinner. As she walked to the mess tent, Rizelya wondered what would happen to the border keeps and their people. During the Scourge War, they'd evacuated the borders keeps the invaders hadn't captured, to prevent more people from the Scourge's slave pens. No one had returned to their homes, and now they would have to stay away even longer.

A wave of homesickness washed over her. She hadn't been home to Strunland Keep in nearly a year. Rizelya wanted to go home and sleep in her own bed rather than a cot. She cursed the Malvers. Why couldn't they have stayed exiled?

Malviana - 28 de Ahdar, 1076

Malviana slept deeply, exhausted from her toils. A disturbance in the barrier jerked her to awareness. Someone, a Posair or Gryphon, was trying to penetrate the fog surrounding her castle. She pulled on a robe, grabbed her wand from the bedside table, and ran into the antechamber.

She stood in front of the large black mirror, taller and wider than she, affixed to the wall opposite the window. Her eyes narrowed at the peeled and cracking gilt on the frame, afraid the mirror had also suffered the deprivations of time. She stepped closer and examined the mirror, smiling when she discovered it was undamaged. It had taken many lives, and Mordar's and her combined power, to create the magic in the mirror. And right now, she didn't have the power or strength to replicate the feat.

Malviana directed her wand at the mirror and recited the incantation to activate it. "Show me!" she ordered. Mist formed on the surface, and as it cleared, she saw a small group of Posairs riding Gryphons gathered at the border of her barrier. A Gryphon held out its sandy brown wing and keened in pain. She grinned. When it tried to enter the fog, a bansholo had taken a bite out of it. Malviana needed to make a sacrifice to Mordaga, thanking him for giving her the strength to erect the barrier in time to protect them from their enemies. His strength was truly magnificent.

Pleased the spells were working, she climbed back into bed and snuggled into the covers, drifting back to sleep.

The sounds of banthues keening to be let out to feed drew Malviana from her sleep. She stretched, luxuriating in the feel of a soft mattress under her and silky sheets covering her. Pale light filtered through the curtains. She considered going back to sleep—it had been so long since she'd had such luxury—but then remembered her thoughts before going to sleep.

Giddy with excitement, she danced into her bedchamber, threw open the wardrobe, and grinned. Magdelyn had filled it with new clothes. Malviana selected a long black velvet gown and slid it over her head. She stepped to the glass mirror beside the wardrobe to admire herself, frowning at how loose the dress hung on her. Malviana preferred more tight-fitting clothes that hugged her curves. She'd lost weight during her incarceration, but she'd soon fill out. One of Mordaga's gifts was staying young forever. She clasped her necklace of power around her neck, and the lowermost jewel, the diamond, nestled between her breasts. The low-cut bodice was designed to show off both the necklace and her bosom. Men, she'd found, were easy to lead and distract by showing a little skin. The back of her gown plunged past her waist, and the long, slender sleeves ended in a point over her hand.

Before calling in her council, she wanted to test her theory. She moved into the sitting room and stood in front of her black mirror and activated it. Searching, she found a pool of dark, luscious magic within the boundaries of her castle and called on the power. It came quickly to her, like a dutiful child eager to please. She channeled the magic through the mirror, gasping with pleasure as the magic filled her body, then her jewels and wand. It was nearly as powerful as the death magic from sacrifices. "Oh, Mordaga, this will do. This will do nicely."

She reached for the bellpull and tugged it. One of the low-ranking ladies tapped on her door before entering. Bowing low, she waited for Malviana's command.

"Tell my council I wish to see them. And bring me bloodwine." As the woman turned to leave, Malviana stopped her. "How long have I slept?"

"A full day and night, my lady."

No wonder I feel so refreshed and energized. Unable to sit with so much power filling her, Malviana paced the room while she waited for her retainers.

Magdelyn arrived first, brushing dust from her skirts and a smudge of dirt from her cheek. She'd pulled her black hair into a neat, tight bun. A serving girl followed her in and quietly placed a decanter filled with dark bloodwine and a tray of goblets on a side table, bowing as she exited.

"We've accomplished much, Malviana," Magdelyn said, "to clean the castle and put it to rights." She stopped in front of the settee, her eyebrows furrowing at the threadbare cushions, and pointed her wand at them. Light swirled from its end, wrapped around the cushions, and when it dissipated, dark blue velvet covered them. Magdelyn turned to the other seating in the room and performed a similar spell.

"I didn't have an opportunity to fix these before you retired, and you were sleeping so deeply, I didn't want to disturb you."

"No matter," Malviana waved the apology away. "It's done now." She studied Magdelyn's wand, noting the gemstones still gleamed even with the magic she'd just completed. "You're feeding well?"

Magdelyn grinned. "I am. As is everyone. This swamp is filled with life we can drain."

"I look forward to when we can sup on more than animal death."

"And when will that be, Mother?" Mordeven swept into the room and sat in a winged-back chair. His face had filled out while she'd slept, and his black hair shone with renewed vitality.

"Soon, my son."

Morvana and Malvidor entered next, discussing the status of the banthues. Morvana, as usual, wore a pair of black trousers and a red corset. She plopped into an armchair, throwing her leg over an arm. Malvidor chose to sit on the settee beside Malviana. Borgedier and Valdorian hurried in. Magdelyn filled each of their glasses with bloodwine then found a seat.

"Now that we have rested, we'll begin drawing Posairs to us. We need an army to fight our enemies. They have grown and prospered while we languished in exile." Her lips tightened with anger at the injustice of it. She waved at the mirror. "We'll be able to see what our enemies are doing with this."

Borgedier's eyes lit up. "I remember Mordar using this mirror."

Malviana ignored the pain of loss Mordar's name still brought to her. She reactivated the mirror and searched for the nearest Posairs. On the boundary between the plains and the Barrens, an enormous force camped. Her eyebrows rose with surprise. "They can't have gathered to fight us so quickly, could they?"

"I don't know how they could," Borgedier said. "Even using those damned Gryphons, they couldn't have moved so many people south in just a few days."

"Is this where they fought those hateful invaders?" Morvana asked. "I remember you telling us they camped close to the Barrens."

"Yes. That's correct, daughter." Malviana adjusted the spell, requesting to see the invaders. The mirror only showed an abandoned compound at the crater's edge.

Mordeven leaned forward in his seat, staring. "That isn't possible! How in Mordar's name could the Posairs and Gryphons win a war against such a formidable force?"

"More importantly," Valdorian said, "do they now have weapons that would work on us?"

Malviana shook her head at the absurdity. "How could they? Mordaga's magic is much stronger than the paltry magic of their goddess. He will protect us."

She returned the mirror's view onto the war camp. At first, her enemies' numbers and proximity unnerved her, but then she smiled slowly. After fighting a war, many Posairs would be ripe for her manipulations.

Two nearby pools gave her an idea, and she formed a larger mass of her pets than she'd ever accomplished before. She was pleased when she didn't have to take them through a larval stage. Without the Supreme's barrier blocking her magic, and with the new influx of power, she could do many things she hadn't been able to do for a long time. She directed the swarm of monsters to attack the Posair army.

"Oh, that's marvelous, Mother!" Malvidor said, clapping with delight. "Sending so many monsters against them will surely cull their numbers."

"Yes, it serves that purpose, plus it will keep them busy for a while. We're not ready to fight them—and won't be for several lunadars. We need to build our army first. To that end, watch carefully for those with the necessary temperament to become a Malvers."

"There," Magdelyn pointed at two men at the edge of the fighting.

The corner of Malviana's lip lifted as she wove a summoning spell and flung it at the men, luring them into the Barrens. Her pets distracted the other Posairs from noticing the men flee.

Before leaving her pets to their fate, she gathered more magic, chanted the spell, and called a wind to blow her spell over the fighting.

"Soon," she explained to her retainers, "my spell will infect those Posairs with a kernel of cruelty or greed in their souls, and their transformation will begin. They'll make their way across the Barrens and to the castle, where we can mold them into our army."

"And those not worthy of our army," Mordeven said, rubbing his hands together, "will become our food."

Pleased with her work—and the power available from the magic pools—she taught her children and retainers how to access the pooled magic. Although refueling this way was quicker, it wasn't as satisfying as sacrificing a victim to Mordaga. It wouldn't be long before they were strong enough to sacrifice something much better than the swamp animals.

Wisah - 28 de Ahdar, 1076

Wisah sat at the Supreme's bedside, learning to read the ancient language the book had been written in. It worried Wisah how weak the Supreme remained from Malviana's attack on her.

"I shouldn't be learning this," Wisah protested, and not for the first time. "I'm not your heir."

Even as she said it, she wondered why the new Supreme hadn't been born yet. Throughout history, before the old Supreme reached her elderly years, a new Supreme was born and trained to take over the spiritual reins of their people. But no one had delivered a white-eyed, white-haired child to the Sanctuary during the Supreme's long life. After this latest attack, Wisah worried their people wouldn't have a leader. The Supreme's heart was weak and faltering. If Wisah hadn't been near the Supreme's quarters, drawn there by the book she struggled to understand, the Supreme would be dead. Wisah still questioned why the book called to her.

The Supreme patted Wisah's hand. "It isn't blasphemy if I'm the one to teach you, child. My heir is coming. Have faith. The Goddess has shown me her face. Until then, I will teach you. The Malvers are a problem now, not in some distant future. Back to work." She tapped the text they were reading—not the ancient, magical book—but a primer. "Read this to me."

Wisah bent her head over the book and puzzled out the words, reading them slowly out loud. Every once in a while, her eyes flicked to the ancient tome lying, not so placidly, on the table across the room. It still called to her.

"Pay attention, Wisah," the Supreme admonished. She glanced at the ancient book and sighed. "You can't read that one until you can understand this one. In addition, there are powerful spells in it you aren't ready to work yet. Have patience."

"Tell that to the book," Wisah huffed, glaring at it. "I can't sleep. It calls to me in my dreams, begging me to open it."

"Ah. Bring it to me."

Wisah crossed the room and rubbed her palms on her skirt, staring at the tome. She closed her eyes, picturing the sigil for protection the Supreme had taught her, and drew it over the book. Hesitantly, she picked it up, expecting a jolt of energy to sting her. She sighed when nothing happened. She carried it over to the Supreme and lowered it onto the bed. Before she let go of it, a shock tingled through her hands.

"Dammit!" She dropped the book and rubbed her hands. At the Supreme's raised eyebrow, she growled, "It bites me! Every time I touch it, it shocks me with energy."

"Just love bites, child." The Supreme chuckled. "It likes you. I wondered why you were using the protection sigil. It isn't going to hurt you."

"Well, its love bites hurt."

The Supreme smiled, then drew several sigils over the book and murmured a spell. "There, that should help you. Do you sense it calling to you now?"

Wisah canted her head to the side, listening. When she didn't hear anything, she closed her eyes. After a few moments, she opened them and grinned at the Supreme. "Nope, nothing!"

"This is only a temporary fix. You need to study hard so you can read this book." The Supreme threw her blankets off. "Here, help me. I have a safe place to put this until you're ready."

"But Jordelyna doesn't want you out of bed."

The old woman waved her hand dismissively. "Oh, posh. I'm fine. Walking a few steps over there—" she indicated the east wall "—won't hurt me."

Wisah helped the Supreme onto her feet, and with slow shuffling steps, the Supreme crossed the room. She touched a stone, and a hidden alcove appeared, revealing a panel with ancient symbols carved into its surface. Lifting her heavy necklace over her head, the Supreme turned it around, so the diamond faced the wall, then pressed her token of office into the corresponding eight-pointed star. The diamond flared with bright white light, and she turned the key in a set sequence. The panel unlocked. Behind it lay a deep shelf. She placed the book next to a gold and silver coffer.

Wisah glimpsed several other objects inside before the Supreme swung the door shut and relocked the panel. The stone slid back into place, hiding it once more. Wisah gulped, sure she shouldn't know about it. These were secrets known only to the Supremes or their heirs. She wasn't the heir. She couldn't be. The Supreme must be confused from the recent attack—and her age.

She helped the old woman back into bed, then sat by her side, working through the primer.

The next morning, Wisah joined the Supreme for breakfast in her quarters consisting of scrambled eggs, toast slathered with mookti berry jam, and taevo.

"I'm moving you from the cloister to the room next to mine," the Supreme said in between bites of her toast.

Wisah choked on the taevo she'd just sipped. Only the highest-ranking priestesses lived in the temple with the Supreme.

"You can't be running back and forth for your training," the Supreme continued and nodded toward the ancient book sitting on her desk. "You have much to learn. We've only started. Besides, I need a personal assistant, and I've chosen you."

"It's a great honor, Your Grace. I will do my best."

The Supreme pushed her plate away. Wisah frowned at how little the old woman had eaten. If she were to recover fully, she needed to eat more. She made a mental note to talk to the house matron about having the kitchen send up the Supreme's favorite foods. A knock sounded, and Wisah shoveled the last of her eggs into her mouth and gulped her taevo. Wiping her mouth off, she crossed to the door and opened it for Jordelyna.

The Supreme's nose wrinkled. "I suppose you're going to poke and prod me?" she grumbled. "I feel fine."

Jordelyna smiled widely as she swept into the room. "You're sounding more like your old self this morning, Supreme. I know the crankier you get with me, the better you feel. Now, let's see just how well you're doing." Jordelyna helped the Supreme to her feet and ushered her into her bedroom, closing the door behind them.

Wisah returned to her room in the cloister to pack her few belongings and clothes. The temple provided her with all she needed, but she possessed a few precious, personal things. She opened her wardrobe and removed her priestess gowns, folding them neatly in a stack on her bed. Wisah paused when her hands fell on the special gown she'd worn at Alkaak, the Gryphon city. She'd spoken on the Supreme's behalf to convince King Zorlaak to allow his people to help the Posairs in their fight against the Scourge. Without the Gryphons, the Posairs would never have defeated the alien invaders.

Next came the fur cloak she'd worn to cross the cold mountains. She lifted the soft fur to her cheek and inhaled. The faint scent of smoke filled her nostrils, and memories of sitting in front of the fire with Rizelya, Blazel, Chariel, Aistrun, and especially Jaehaas traipsed through her mind. She'd fallen in love with Jaehaas during their journey. Still holding the fur, tears leaked from her eyes. As the Supreme's new assistant, it didn't seem like the Supreme would release her any time soon to return to her friends—or her love. Wiping away her tears, she finished packing.

A little while later, two young women, who served the White Priestesses, arrived to help her carry her things across the grounds to the temple. As Wisah headed out the door, Chariel's carved sabertiger caught her attention. She picked it up, tucking it into her pocket. It would remind her of her friend in the coming days. She wished she had a keepsake from Jaehaas to hold when she missed him.

As soon as she settled her belongings into her new quarters, the Supreme called Wisah to her side, and Wisah's training began in earnest. Besides learning to read the ancient language, her lessons included spells and incantations Wisah knew were far beyond her current level within the hierarchy of priestesses. By the time the Supreme released her for dinner, Wisah was wrung out. After eating, Wisah dragged herself to her room. She saw the pile of history books sitting on her desk and groaned. She still had a lot of reading to do before she went to bed.

Much later, she lay in her strange new bed, unable to sleep. Too much new information jumbled her mind. She wondered how much worse it would be when the Supreme recovered enough to return to her duties. Wisah covered her face with her hands and huffed out a breath. She'd rather be back on the front lines fighting the Scourge than deal with all the politics that were the Supreme's responsibilities.

Chapter 6

Rizelya - 30 de Ahdar, 1076

After her fifth battle in two days, Rizelya slumped on a bench in the mess tent. She stared at the mug of taevo in front of her, debating if she had the energy to lift it to her lips. Swarms of Malvers' monsters attacked the camp from every quarter. As soon as they defeated one horde, another one cropped up. With the Gryphon's help, the fighting-packs were able to contain the monsters—but just barely. It reminded her of the time wave after wave of monster attacks had hit her original squad-pack on their way to Strunlair Keep from Strunven Keep. It had seemed the Malvers woman didn't want her team to reach the Clan Keep—and it was when Keandran had disappeared. Rizelya sat up straight, bumping her shoulder into Dehali, who sat next to her.

"Huh?" Dehali rubbed her face. "What's up, Rizelya? You look like you've seen a ghost."

Rizelya shook her head. "No, but I thought of one. Do you remember Keandran?"

"How could I forget that caitiff and what he did to those poor horses?"

"I just realized when he disappeared, the monsters were harassing us much like they are right now."

"You don't think there's a connection, do you?" Dehali's eyebrows furrowed.

"I don't know, maybe?" She shrugged. "I'm going to talk to Histrun and Naila."

Rizelya strode quickly to the command tent. Twilight cast long shadows across the camp. At least with the coming night, the fighters would receive a reprieve from the monsters, and so far, narhili beasts hadn't bothered them. When she entered, Histrun, Keshanal, and Naila were sitting at a small table to one side, eating.

"Sorry to bother you," Rizelya said. "But have any people disappeared?"

Keshanal narrowed her eyes, set down her fork, and leaned back in her chair. "Why do you ask?"

From Keshanal's reaction, Rizelya assumed there had been. "When Keandran vanished, we were being ambushed like this. I thought maybe the monsters were providing a distraction now Malviana has returned. Could she be luring people away to their deaths like she did Keandran?"

"It's possible." Histrun picked up his goblet, stared into it for a long moment before taking a big gulp. When he looked up, the past haunted his eyes. "Keep an eye on your people and look for any strange black spots."

"Mendehan," Naila croaked and put a hand over the scar on her throat. *Could the infection be returning?*

Histrun lifted a shoulder. "It's possible. We'll have to pass word to the battalion alphas to watch their people, especially those who've developed a taste for war and cruelty."

"So, have there been people who've gone missing?" Rizelya pressed. She wasn't sure what infection they were talking about.

Keshanal nodded and held up two fingers. "They were under guard for questioning about their cruelty. If found guilty, we would have killed them as rogues. Somehow, two brechas made it inside the camp and to the tent where we were detaining them. While the guards fought the brechas, the prisoners escaped. We thought—hoped—it was only a coincidence." She gave a harsh laugh. "Thank you for the information, Rizelya."

Dismissed, Rizelya turned to leave, when several Gryphons landed outside.

"Now what?" Naila said, gazing at the tent roof.

Blazel, Graak, Aistrun, and Chariel strode into the tent. Rizelya covered her mouth with both hands at the sight of them. Graak's right wing was missing numerous long primary feathers. A bloody rag was wrapped around Aistrun's right thigh, and Chariel had one around her left forearm. Rizelya wanted to rush into Blazel's arms, but now wasn't the time.

"What happened?" Keshanal leaned forward. "We didn't expect you for a few more days."

"We almost didn't make it back," Blazel said, wiping at the blood dripping from a gash on his cheek.

"The Malvers?" Histrun's goblet dangled between his fingers, forgotten.

Blazel shook his head. "No, just normal, twisted swamp beasts."

There was nothing normal about those beasts, Graak argued, his tail thumping the ground. *They didn't behave like they did the last time we were in the swamp.*

Rizelya frowned in confusion. Keshanal, Naila, and Histrun also wore confused expressions.

"Hey, you need to tell the story in the proper order for them to understand," Aistrun huffed. He stepped forward, limping, and Histrun motioned for them to take a seat while they reported.

"The first night," Aistrun recited, "Blazel cast his ward boundary, and all was well." He told them about the twisted creatures and their flight to the Black Castle. But rather than the clear view of it they expected, a fog surrounded it. "We couldn't see through the fog or penetrate it—every time we tried, we'd end up in the same spot—"

Or we'd get injured, Graak held out his wing. *There is something evil living inside it.*

Aistrun grimaced in sympathy with Graak. "We left Baekeek and the scouts to watch the area in case the Malvers left, and we headed back. As soon as we landed for the night—"

"And before I could cast a ward boundary," Blazel added.

"—the twisted beasts came at us," Aistrun continued. "There were things I have no name for, strange combinations of animals. A monstrous tall beast with huge antlers and a body and face that resembled a man led them."

The beast Blazel and I encountered previously at the castle, Graak interjected.

Aistrun scowled at him. "Hey, who is telling this story? Let me tell it."

Graak ducked his head, his feathers plastered flat.

"Anyway, we fought our way free and flew into the Barrens, where we stayed the night in the northern fortress."

"I don't know if the scouts we left behind are still alive." Blazel's shoulders drooped.

"The beast-man was once a Posair," Saffren said quietly, rubbing her forehead. "I glimpsed into his mind before he shut me out. He likes what he's become. He is a creature of pure evil and a willing servant of Malviana."

"I sensed the same thing," Chariel added. "The other creatures are simply a product of being around the malignant magic pools for generations until they are now a new species. But the man-beast had been a rogue before he heard Malviana's call. His soul is as twisted as his mind and body. He is no longer a Posair."

Histrun dropped his head into his hands. When he lifted it, his eyes were bleak. "She's begun calling others to her. Thank you for your report. Go see a healer, then find food and sleep. We'll take care of this."

Blazel helped Aistrun to his feet, who then leaned against Chariel as he limped out. Rizelya reached out and clasped Blazel's hand, squeezing his fingers.

"Oh, Rizelya and Blazel," Keshanal's voice stopped them at the tent doorway. They turned back around, and Keshanal continued, "We're giving command of your battalion to Alpha Maheli—temporarily. We want you to concentrate on forming the Black Weave teams. After this news, it's your top priority. We have to stop Malviana from using our people against us."

"Yes, ma'am, sir." Rizelya bowed to them and left the tent with Blazel.

Elation should have surged through her at finally being relieved from the responsibility of leading so many people, but instead, sadness and disappointment washed through her. She'd come to love the people in her battalion. Maheli would take good care of them. She'd been the guard-pack alpha at the northern fortress when the Scourge had attacked it. Without Maheli's leadership, more of their people would have died in the slave camps. After spending so many years of avoiding being even a squad-pack alpha, the past year had taught Rizelya she was a good leader, and she liked being in charge.

"It's only temporary," Blazel reminded her, seeming to read her mind.

A bitter smile pressed his lips together in disappointment. Blazel's position as a battle commander gave him a sense of purpose and belonging he'd never experienced before. Until this past year, he'd been a lone wolf, never part of a pack.

She bumped her hip into his. "We're still pack. And wait until you experience the Black Weave! We'll be closer than ever."

He smiled at her as he pulled her into an embrace. "I can think of many ways I'd like to be closer with you."

"So can I." She grinned and kissed him.

The others had already gone into the healers' tent. She and Blazel hurried to the mess tent and gulped down food. While their pack-mates were still eating dinner, they returned to their empty tent and made love, falling asleep in each other's arms.

Blazel - 31 de Ahdar, 1076

The next morning, Blazel and Rizelya sat in the mess tent eating breakfast with their core team. As the group laughed at one of Aistrun's stories, Blazel scanned those sitting with them and scowled. "Does anyone know where Jaehaas is? I haven't seen him since the hectic day of the bomb blast and the resulting tidal wave."

"He went to help evacuate Posanvendean Keep," Rizelya said and crunched on her toast. "Histrun doesn't expect those teams to return for another few days."

Blazel nodded. After Wisah returned to the Sanctuary and the war with the Scourge ended, Jaehaas had been moping, missing Wisah horribly. At least she was still alive and Jaehaas would see her again. Unlike Kaieli. As though his thoughts had conjured her, Kaieli entered the mess tent. His heart ached at her red, puffy eyes and the dark circles under them. He glanced at Rizelya as she laughed at Aistrun's silly joke. If she died, he'd be in worse shape than Kaieli was. He didn't think he'd be able to function.

Rizelya followed his gaze. "She's not dealing well with Rolstrun's death. I'm worried about her. Our new mission will help. She won't be so alone." She raised her arm and waved her hand. "Hey, Kaieli, over here."

Kaieli looked over and nodded. Carrying her porridge bowl and mug, she wended her way around the tables and sat down next to them.

"You're going to see a lot of us shortly," Rizelya beamed.

Kaieli lifted an eyebrow. "Why? Not that I mind, but I don't anticipate you spending much time in the infirmary, Rizelya."

Rizelya crinkled her nose. "No, and you're not either. You're going to be spending time with us."

Blazel took pity on Kaieli's confusion. "Histrun and Keshanal have ordered us—and you—to make the Black Weave our top priority. We need to discover the best way to form it, and who makes the most effective and powerful team members. And while we're at it, determine if we can use it to clean the malignant magic pools."

"Oh, that makes perfect sense." Kaieli's eyes brightened as she surveyed those at the table. "We have enough people here to start, although I wish everyone on my original team were here. Jaelena sent word that she's staying at the Sanctuary with her children. She's had enough of war and terror. I don't blame her. I'd like to run away too." She turned her head away for a moment, then heaved a huge sigh, and slapped her hands on her thighs as she looked back at them. "There's no time for such self-indulgence. Everyone who was with us the other day, Rizelya, has strong Talents, except Noriana. We could try swapping Saffren in her place. And we'll need someone to replace Aistrun."

"That would be me," Blazel said, lifting a finger. "And I was trained to use my Red Talent, so it might be easier with me as the anchor."

"You were?" Kaieli asked.

"By the Supreme herself. She told me I'd need it someday. I guess that day has arrived." He quirked an eyebrow. "When I was twelve, Histrun spent the winter at the Sanctuary, recovering from Zehala's death. I was the only boy in the Sanctuary, and I desperately wanted to leave the Sanctuary with Histrun when he returned home in the spring. But the Supreme forbade it." Blazel gave a lop-sided grin. "I was so furious with her. But as I consider my life, if I'd left the Sanctuary with him, I would never have traveled to the Deep Mountains and met Graak. The Gryphons wouldn't have become our allies against the invaders—and now against the Malvers." He gazed at Rizelya, and she squeezed his hand. "Nor would I be the man I am today. I've never forgiven her for her decision. Until now."

Chariel touched his shoulder and smiled softly. "You should write her a letter later, expressing your gratitude. She'll appreciate it."

Blazel nodded. And they continued to eat quietly for a few moments.

Kaieli idly made patterns with her finger in a puddle of taevo that had spilled on the table. "Noriana will be heartbroken if she can't participate," she said, "so will Faliciden. She's been part of this since the beginning. We stumbled on the Weave when we were trying to save Posanreande Keep from a plague. Faliciden and Loshera both helped me."

"There will be more than one team," Blazel said. "Keshanal is already making plans for more."

"Yeah, and sending me—us—here and yon, teaching." Rizelya's forehead creased.

"Keshanal can plan all she wants," Kaieli said, "but the Weave requires someone from every Talent. As far as I'm aware, Chariel is the only Gray Talent we have. And there aren't that many White Talents here."

"True." Blazel's mouth pursed, and he gazed at the ceiling for a moment. "I'll tell the Supreme Alphas of our limitation. Histrun or Keshanal can send a message to the Sanctuary and ask the Supreme to assign us some strong Gray and White

Priestesses who would be willing to help. Although, even there, strong Grays are rare." He leaned back and reached behind Rizelya to tap Chariel on her shoulder. "How many Grays are in the Sanctuary, Chariel?"

"I assume you're talking about priestesses to create Black Weave teams with?"

"Yes."

She settled her chin on her fist and gazed into the distance. "Ten total."

"That's it?" Rizelya asked incredulously.

Chariel nodded, her eyes sad. "The Malvers targeted Grays almost as much as Blacks until the Talent is nearly extinct. There are plenty of Whites to choose from who would be willing to do this. And some of those have a decent level of Gray as a secondary Talent." She smirked at Blazel. "Your mother, Blenora, is one of them. Do you think she'll come?"

Blazel thought his eyes would pop out. "My mother! You can't be serious." He couldn't imagine his sweet, gentle mother leaving the Sanctuary and entering a war zone. Besides, she'd never leave his grandmother.

Chariel laughed. "Oh, I'm serious. Blenora has spunk and determination. She talked the Supreme into letting her keep you beyond the time when most other little boys were turned over to their father's clans. If she can do that, she can face whatever we have to do."

Blazel crossed his arms over his chest and huffed. "I don't like it."

Rizelya patted his leg. "Sorry, dear. You don't have any say in the matter. I like your mother, and she'd be a great addition."

Blazel stared at her, stunned at the outrageous idea.

Rizelya studied the women of her squad-pack, drumming her fingers on the table. "I think we should see if Noriana and Faliciden can work with Raeleen as their Brown Talent, Gehan for Yellow, and Dehali as their Red. Maheli can't participate since she's been promoted to my position as the Strunland battalion alpha. From what I know of Noriana and Faliciden, I believe they'll get along well with that group. While we wait for the Supreme to send us women with Gray Talent, we'll interview the White Priestesses who are here. They've already shown they have the mettle needed to be part of the war host."

"We'll also need to find suitable men to anchor the working." Kaieli squeezed her eyes shut for a moment, then took a deep breath. "When we stopped the wave, the Gryphons with us joined our weaving. But I don't know how many are required for the Black Weave to work."

"Graak and Glork are eager to join us," Blazel said. He slapped the table and stood up. "Enough talk. Let's gather the people we've agreed on for the first team and start experimenting. My testing tent is available, and it's out of the way."

While Rizelya and Kaieli talked to the other women, Blazel contacted Graak, and then informed Histrun of the lack of Grays. He prayed his mother wouldn't hear about the project. He didn't want her in danger.

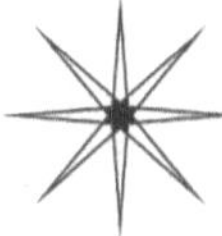

Blazel - 31 de Ahdar, 1076

By the time Blazel and the others arrived at the tent he'd used to brew his poison, Graak and Glork were waiting for them. Also, with them were the Gryphons who had flown with the members of their selected team.

Kaieli explained to the newcomers what to do. Those chosen for the first team formed a circle, clasped hands, and extended their magic. Since Kaieli had the most experience with the technique, she directed the melding of magic.

When she drew on Blazel's well of magic, he sucked in a breath at the rainbow braid of light shining in each of the Talent's colors. As Kaieli added his magic, the braid pulsed in the rhythm of his heartbeat, and the individual strands merged into one thick rope of Black Talent. His consciousness floated in a beautiful ocean. He sensed each elemental power—air, water, earth, and his own fire—in a way he'd never imagined. Although their energies were merged, he could pick out each woman's beam of light and sense her soul. Such amazingly exquisite women!

Then he heard—felt?—Kaieli say, "Now," and a different energy merged with theirs. She added first Graak, then Glork and Korrik's magic and essence, weaving it in with the others. Blazel's consciousness expanded further, and he saw the veil separating the physical and astral worlds. A heartbeat later, they passed through it, and he-they—there was no separation anymore—became pure energy. Anything they could conceive, they could accomplish in this state.

It was both glorious and frightening.

He sensed a mass of nasty magic squirming in the nearby swap. The wrongness of it perverted the natural order the Goddess decreed for this world. The malevolent energy irritated him, making him want to set it to rights. He-they stretched out their hand and began the process of returning it to wholeness. The magic wiggled, attempting to escape them, but they were too strong, too powerful for it. He spoke a sacred word, and power blasted the malignant magic. If he had physical eyes, the intense bright light would have blinded him. When it waned, none of the baneful magic remained, and the ground started to dry. In a few chedans, it would return to fertile land, growing tall plains grass.

Suddenly, the energy spit him out.

Blazel shook his head, blinking his eyes to clear them, and found himself sprawled on the ground, Rizelya's hand a few inches from his. A headache thundered behind his eyes.

"Oh, sweet Mother!" Rizelya cried. "Someone tell me they noted where the swamp was located."

I can find it, Graak croaked. *But not for a while. I can't fly just yet.*

"Did the Black Weave knock you on your butts last time?" Saffren ground out, gingerly sitting up.

"It did." Eiden groaned. She eased up to lean against Korrik's side. "Although not as bad."

"We must find a way to protect ourselves better." Saffren brushed her hair from her face. "We can't turn into mush like this and fight the Malvers."

"Hey, it's a good thing you have me," Aistrun spoke up.

Blazel turned his head, all he had the energy to move. Aistrun and Broogk stood over them.

"Us," Leistral added, slinging her arm over Morru's shoulder.

Beside her, Eidstrun lounged against Sterkek's side. Brogkek's tail curled around Leistrun's feet. Maestrun and Nelstrun shadowed Saffren, as always, but were now joined by the Gryphons, Oslerru and Daerik.

"Now you know why I don't want to be part of the Black Weave, Blazel," Aistrun said. "I don't like being incapacitated. So what did you do?"

Rizelya scratched her head. "We think we cleared the malignant magic from a nearby swamp."

Broogk, go check it out, will you? Graak asked. He sent a mental image of the spot.

"I'm coming with you." Aistrun swung a leg over Broogk's back. Leistral and Morru also took off.

Finally, Blazel maneuvered into a sitting position, and Eidstrun handed him a canteen of cool water. He drank and passed it on to Rizelya. After a few milcrons, his headache eased. He had mostly recovered by the time Broogk and Morru returned.

"What did you find?" Kaieli asked, leaning against Keeru for support.

I couldn't smell or detect any malignant magic in the swamp, Broogk said. *A rotting stench lingers, but it is dissipating.*

"We saw a herd of twisted rabbits," Leistral said, her eyes glistening with unshed tears. "They were dying. As awful as they were, they were just animals."

Blazel frowned. The energy he'd experienced wouldn't kill innocents, and no matter how they looked, most of the twisted swamp creatures weren't evil. Sure, normal rabbits weren't carnivores, but eating meat didn't make them evil.

"They aren't dead," Chariel and Loshera said together.

Chariel ran a hand through her hair. "If you go back in a few octars, you'll find they've reverted into their natural form and are all right."

"For the larger creatures," Loshera added, "it will take a few days, perhaps a few chedans, for them to finish the transformation."

Blazel was glad they hadn't killed all the swamp creatures. "Do you think the Black Weave will work on any people the Malvers twist, like that man-beast?"

Loshera shrugged, her eyes sad. "He willingly chose the path of evil. I doubt it."

"It worked!" Rizelya said, thrusting her fist into the air. "We can finally rid our world of the Malvers' monsters!"

Blazel hadn't considered that as a possibility. What would their world be like if they weren't fighting the Malvers' monsters for survival? He recalled the books he'd read in the Sanctuary's library written before the Great War. Once, his people had achieved amazing things. What could they accomplish now?

A short time later, he and the others tromped through the camp to inform the Supreme Alphas what they'd done. The task ahead of them daunted Blazel. Their team cleared one swamp out of thousands. It had taken him three years to visit the majority of them. They'd need many, many more teams before they eliminated the Malvers' monsters from their world.

Wisah - 34 de Ahdar, 1076

A chedan after the Supreme's heart attack, Jordelyna finally allowed the Supreme to return to work, and Wisah's duties as her personal assistant increased. While the housekeeping staff removed the remains of breakfast, Wisah moved around the Supreme's office, lighting braziers and stoking the fire. Sweat dripped from her upper lip as the room heated to a stifling level. But the Supreme wrapped a thick, wool shawl around her shoulders as she settled into her desk chair.

"You can sit there." The Supreme pointed to a small desk behind hers, holding stacks of paper, pens, and a full jar of ink. "Take notes of what transpires and be ready to discuss it with me later."

Wisah sat down, wiggling to find a comfortable position on the hard chair, sighing in frustration at the impossibility. She removed the top sheet of paper, placing it before her, and sharpened a quill before dunking it in the ink. "I'm ready," she informed the Supreme.

The Supreme pounded her cane on the floor, the sound making Wisah wince. When the Red Guard on duty stuck her head through the door, the Supreme said, "Send in the first petitioner."

Throughout the morning, Wisah took notes of the various meetings. After a light lunch, the Supreme grilled Wisah on her interpretation of the meetings and events. During the afternoon, the Supreme drilled her on the new spells.

Wisah hoped she'd receive a reprieve after dinner, but the Supreme called her into her bedroom, where she reclined on the bed. The Supreme tapped the book beside her, and Wisah groaned inwardly. Resigned, she picked up the primer and struggled to learn the ancient language.

A few days later, the Supreme didn't have any morning appointments, and Wisah sat on a chair before her, reading out loud.

"You're doing very well, Wisah," the Supreme said, leaning back in her chair and sipping her taevo. "You'll soon be able to read the ancient spell book."

Wisah lowered the primer and peered toward the Supreme's bedchamber. Since being placed in the safe, the book hadn't called to her. Until last night. She'd dreamed of opening it and reading about Malviana and Shandir. The dream had morphed, like dreams do, and she had suddenly been watching Shandir casting her last great magic.

"Did Malviana twist Shandir's spell?" Wisah asked, still looking at the bedchamber.

"Why do you ask? Where did you get that idea?"

Wisah took a deep breath and turned back to face the Supreme. "I dreamed about it last night. I don't know why the book wants me to read it so badly."

"Because someone needs to know what happened, so we can correct the great wrong that was committed long ago." The Supreme put down her mug and steepled her hands in front of her chin. "I'm too old to leave the Sanctuary. The Goddess has called you to face Malviana. Otherwise, the book wouldn't draw you to it. It is old, even older than the Great War, and contains powerful spells. If Malviana gets her hands on it, she could corrupt the spells and do even greater damage to our world. It's why the book is so well protected. The section that's important for our purposes right now pertains to Shandir's next-to-last spell."

"Wait, I thought her last spell created the crater."

"No," the Supreme said quietly as she shook her head. "Her last spell was to hide the book where Malviana couldn't find it. It was one of the greatest spells ever cast."

Wisah raised her eyebrow.

"Her spell placed the book, and the temple housing it, into a pocket out of time and not part of this world anymore. The book would reveal itself only when the one who could right the wrongs done was ready. And that, I believe, is you."

Wisah's heart thundered in her chest, and her mouth went dry. "But I'm not anything special. I'm just a White Priestess. Rizelya found the book."

"To give it to you. Although she must have a role to play." The Supreme lifted a shoulder.

"You said there was a section that's important to us. What is it about?"

"The book details Shandir's spell that ended the Great War. Her intent was to cleanse all the death magic from the land and render its users powerless. Somehow, Malviana found out about the spell and contrived to twist it. The combined magics resulted in killing every living organism in a one-hundred-measure radius of the blast zone. Malignant magic flooded the area and fused with the molecular structure of the rocks—the only thing left in the Barrens."

"The nucla the invaders wanted," Wisah nodded. During her time with Rizelya at the battlefront, she'd seen the rocks and felt the evil magic locked inside of them. "Before I returned here, Kaieli and her team had discovered how to cleanse the malignant magic from the rocks."

"I don't fully understand what they do." The Supreme gazed toward her bedroom—and the safe with the ancient tome. "But the book speculates Black Talent can undo the spell, since two people with Black Talent created it."

Wisah sat up. "I didn't know Shandir had Black Talent. All I've ever heard of her says she was a White Priestess."

"Back in those days, Blacks were common, most of them served as priestesses. Shandir was one. The Malvers systematically killed everyone with Black and Gray Talent they could find, trying to eradicate the Talents from our bloodlines. They accomplished their goal with Black. Shandir was the only remaining person with Black Talent by the end of the war. They almost succeeded with the Grays, too. It's why Gray Talent is so rare today.

"When you are ready, you'll be able to read the book, and, I believe, work the magic to defeat Malviana. But until then, you must study and practice."

The Supreme suddenly pushed her chair back and stood, grabbing her cane. "Come, child. I have something to show you."

The Supreme led Wisah through the corridors linking the temple with the library. Sunlight fell through the high windows of the library, filling the cavernous room with warmth without touching the fragile books and scrolls. Long lines of shelves marched the length of the room with books stacked in neat order and scrolls in their cubbyholes. Wisah and the Supreme ambled past the well-kept stacks to the far back corner of the library. Dust covered everything. A patina of cobwebs laced the shelves, and only the skittering of mice disturbed the silence.

They finally stopped at a door hidden in the gloom. Dirt encrusted the frame, and age rusted the bar across it; however, a new, shiny lock had been placed on it.

A corner of the Supreme's mouth quirked up as she pulled a key from her pocket. "Blazel broke the last lock. The door sticks, so you'll have to open it for me." She unlocked the door, and Wisah gripped the handle and tugged it open.

A dark hole lay behind it. Wisah crossed to a nearby reading table, grabbed the lantern on it, and went back to the door. Holding the light before her, she peered into the darkness, barely able to discern the steps leading down.

"Are we going down there?" Wisah asked.

"What I want to show you has been hidden a long time. I'd forgotten this place existed until Blazel stumbled on it. He set off the alarms placed on the door, and I had to come save him from his folly." She smiled. "It's a good thing he did. We need what's down there now. Lead the way, child. There are torches below."

The light from Wisah's lantern revealed only two sets of footprints had recently disturbed the thick layer of dust: Blazel's and the Supreme's. The air smelled musty with age. Wisah slowly descended, holding the lantern high while grasping the iron railing. The Supreme's shuffling steps and their breathing were the only sounds.

Down and down they traversed until finally the stairs ended. The light from her lantern formed a small circle around them, unable to penetrate the oppressive dark. Using the lantern, she lit an old torch in a wall sconce. The additional light revealed more torches affixed to the wall. As she lit them, the light revealed an enormous room filled with ancient relics.

Wisah stood in the center of the room, turning in a slow circle as magic tingled against her skin. Dozens of staffs leaned against the wall, but one laid on the ground where it had fallen. She picked it up to return it to its place. Magic thrummed from her hand to the staff and a fireball burst from it, slamming into the wall and leaving a black spot.

"Oops," she gulped. She carefully placed the staff with the others.

Crystal globes filled with various shades of light glowed on a worktable. A shelf stacked with books and scrolls drew her attention, and as she passed by the crystal globes, her fingers brushed against one pulsing with indigo-blue light. At her touch, blue light crisscrossed the ball's surface, gathering into a swirl of snapping energy, until it released with a crack like lightning. It hit the wall with a muffled boom, and the light fizzled out. She jerked her hand back. With her arms crossed in front of her so she wouldn't touch anything else, she walked to the bookshelf and perused the titles. They were books from before and during the Great War.

She turned around to find the Supreme sitting on a bench by a worktable, her hand resting on her cane. Wisah couldn't quite interpret the look on the old woman's face.

"What is this place?" she asked. "What are all of these things?"

"This is where we hide what we once were," the Supreme said sadly. "And what we once could do. These are weapons used in the Great War. We will fight the same Malvers and their creatures that our ancestors created these weapons to fight a millennium ago." She gestured at the room. "I suspect most of these artifacts no longer function after such a long time of disuse, and others need Black Talent to activate them. But there may be some viable ones we can use with our current levels of magic. Our magic has changed over the years. It's grown more specialized—and I hope more powerful."

Wisah wandered around the room, carefully examining the objects, many of which were entirely unfamiliar to her. "We should have Maendy and her daughter, Maellyn, come study these weapons," she said, continuing to explore the room. "They are both innovative. I think they can create new ones based on the old models. Maendy is a helstramiester."

The Supreme leaned on her cane, considering, then nodded. "Helstrim wasn't around during the Great War. It's something we've developed since then to battle the Malvers' monsters. We haven't completely stagnated in our fight for survival. But we aren't nearly as advanced as our ancestors were. I'll send for them immediately."

"Sheekeek is still here. He and I could go fetch them." She missed traveling across Lairheim with her Gryphon friend, meeting new people, and having adventures.

"No, you'll stay here while he goes." The Supreme gave a short bark of laughter. "I hadn't realized how valuable and convenient it is to have the Gryphons around. They make sending messages and people to where they're needed much easier. Would they remain in contact with us after we defeat the Malvers?"

Wisah tapped her chin for a moment, thinking about the Gryphons she'd met. "I think some of them would like to stay. Graak and Glork have formed tight bonds of friendship with Blazel and Rizelya. Sheekeek and I are good friends, too. It will be more a matter of convincing King Zorlaak to allow them to stay than if they want to."

The Supreme smiled. "I'll have to practice my best diplomacy to ensure he agrees." She glanced around at the artifacts. "Your job will be to study these weapons and catalog them. This is in addition to your other studies. Once Maendy and Maellyn arrive, they will assist you. We must have weapons and spells to help us defeat the Malvers once and for all. Our ancestors' compassion has led us to fighting another war with the Malvers. This time, I'm determined we'll end it for good."

Wisah groaned. Hundreds of relics and artifacts filled every corner of the huge room. When Sheekeek returned, she'd enlist his help and his sharp intellect to make sense of the sundry articles.

The Supreme stood and limped to the bookcase, studying the titles. Wisah joined her. The Supreme pulled out several books and handed them to Wisah. "Start with these."

She read the titles. *Shandir's Great Magic, The Malvers' Rise to Power: A Treatise on Corruption, Effective Fighting Techniques and Spells,* and *Making and Using Magical Weapons.* She thought the last two would be highly useful.

Wisah extinguished the torches and relit the lantern. Then she and the Supreme climbed the stairs back to the library, which was now dark. The sun had set some time ago. She hadn't realized how long they'd been in the secret room. Wisah's belly fluttered when the Supreme locked the door and handed Wisah the key.

Chapter 7

Malviana - 37 de Ahdar, 1076

Malviana yawned and stretched, then threw off the warm quilts she slept under. Still yawning, she drew back the thick, dark red brocade curtains hanging around her bed, and shivered in the cold draft they'd kept out. Flinging on a warm, cozy robe, she slid from her bed, grateful for the luxurious rugs softening the stone floors. Padding to the necessary room, her gaze fell on the black velvet drapes hanging over her windows and the plush upholstery covering the furniture. "Thank you, Mordaga!" she prayed with ardent gratitude.

When she'd lived in the castle, Malviana had taken such luxuries for granted. But after the years of nothing but damp stone and cave walls, she delighted in the return of comfort every time she walked through her suite. One of her greatest joys was not hearing the steady drip of water. She'd thought she'd go mad listening to it and watching the slow growth of the stalagmites and stalactites. *If I never see a cave again, it will be too soon! I much prefer sleeping on a soft mattress than the hard stone bench that served as my bed for so long.*

After dressing, Malviana pulled her hair into a loose braid, noticing it had grown thicker in the twelve days since leaving the island. Her dresses now didn't hang as loosely as they had when she'd first escaped. She left her suite to check the status of her domain.

After accessing the power within the magic pools, the castle's reconstruction progressed quickly. Malviana strolled down the corridor. Thick carpets muffled her footsteps, paintings covered on the walls, and priceless artifacts—from the time before her birth—decorated accent tables. Warmth filled her chest, and after ensuring she was alone, she whirled in a circle. After the years of asperity, Malviana appreciated, more than ever, the power of Mordaga's death magic. With it, the Malvers could transform one substance into another. From death, came life and power.

The west wing was the first one Magdelyn's team had restored to a clean and habitable state, free of vermin. The wing housed the top-tier of the nobility—her children and the dukes and duchesses, and they deserved to live in luxury. As Malviana passed the door to Magdelyn's suite, a smile tugged her lips as she recalled Magdelyn chasing a pack of swamp rats from her bedroom. She'd run out with her skirts pulled above her knees, flinging magic at the scurrying rodents. Their death had fueled the magic to transform a scrap of rotting fabric into a bolt of lush velvet.

The heels of Malviana's shoes clicked on the steps as she descended. She paused at the foyer and considered inspecting the southern wing, which housed the mid-tier nobility—the counts and barons. She vaguely recalled from her limited time as a countess that the furnishings weren't quite as luxurious as those in the west wing. Malviana wrinkled her nose at the thought of dipping her toes back into less opulent surroundings. She'd never entered the northern wing where the lords and ladies, the lowest ranking nobility—and the most numerous—had their quarters. She continued down the stairs, trusting Magdelyn to take care of those wings and deal with any complaints.

The fresh air beckoned her, and Malviana nodded at the guards at the door to open it for her. She stepped outside, tilting her head back and breathing deeply. Mordeven's fog filtered the harsh sun enough so that she didn't have to squint or be blinded by a pounding headache. A pleased smile lifted her lips at the clean courtyard, and the main obsidian altar shone in the pale light. The tangy, coppery smell of blood lingered from the sacrifices she'd made last night to Mordaga—and every night since returning to the castle. Malviana raised her hand, admiring her gleaming rings pulsing with power. It waited, like an eager puppy, for her to use it.

She wandered around the courtyard, making her way toward the east wing and the stables. Malviana winced at the cacophony created by the banthu's shrieks and cries as they demanded to be let loose and hunt. She paused in her walk, studying the wing. It would provide housing for her new army. They would need it restored when Malviana's infection took root and brought the Posairs in the process of being transformed into Malvers to her.

Magdelyn stepped from the building, pushing back a wisp of hair that had escaped the tight bun holding it in place. She saw Malviana and dipped a quick curtsy.

"I'm pleased with your progress," Malviana said, gesturing at the castle grounds. "You and your team have done well."

"Thank you, your Grace. When do you think we'll need to fully restore the barracks? I've inspected them, and they need some work."

Malviana snorted. "As much as I wished otherwise, it will take time for infected Posairs to reach the transformation stage to voluntarily leave and seek me out." She tapped her chin as she thought. "Before I had access to the magic pools, it took several lunadars to warp someone into another creature. But with so much power at my disposal, I'm hopeful it will only take a few chedans. Mordaga, may it be sooner!"

"May it be so," Magdelyn said, touching her fingertips to her forehead as she bowed her head. "We could receive new Malvers, or even Maldiers, within the next chedan. I'll have my team start working on it today."

Not all the Posairs caught in Malviana's net would transform into Malvers. The majority would become Maldiers—those transmogrified like Korand—and those would make up her infantry. She rubbed her hands together, anticipating discovering what glorious forms her magic twisted the Maldiers into. Delighted with the prospect, she returned to her suite. Now, if they could capture one of those pesky Gryphon's spying on her, she could really create a magnificent creature.

Later in the afternoon, a messenger arrived at Malviana's suite, breathless from running through the large castle.

"Your Grace," the messenger said, kneeling before her. "A twisted Posair is at the gates. Shall we let the Maldier in?" The lady looked up and breathed out. Lust filled her eyes. "He is glorious."

Malviana inwardly shouted in triumph. Although, even with the boost to her power, her magic couldn't create a fully formed Maldier so soon. This one had to be one she'd worked on from behind the barrier.

"Yes, show him to the throne room, but wait outside until we are ready to receive him. Have Korand escort him. Also, tell my children and Duke Borgedier, Duchess Magdelyn, and Duchess Valdorian, to join me there."

The woman bowed her head, then backed out from the room before turning and scurrying to do Malviana's bidding.

Malviana changed into a gown made from several layers of sheer fabric. As she moved, it revealed glimpses of her skin. Small diamonds and rubies sparkled on the field of black. Her maid brushed Malviana's long charcoal-gray hair into an elaborate updo, weaving diamonds and rubies into the mass. Malviana opened a coffer, removed her crown from its satin cushion, and admired its beauty. Diamonds, emeralds, rubies, blue and black star sapphires, and marcasite adorned it. She placed it on her head, picked up her wand, and swept from her bedchamber.

Duke Borgedier waited in her sitting room. He was resplendent in a black velvet jacket and black tight-fitting trousers tucked into shiny black boots. "My lady, may I escort you?" He held out his arm for her.

She dipped her head and placed her hand on top of his. They strolled from her suite and through the corridors. A few moments later, Duchess Valdorian curtsied, then stepped in line behind them. She wore a simple velvet gown in dark blue-gray. Malvidor grinned as he slipped into the procession, his outfit a near duplicate of Borgedier's. Malviana lifted her eyebrow at Morvana's curve-hugging indigo bustier and trousers with a long brocade coat in jet and gold. Morvana grinned back at her unapologetically. Her daughter liked to flaunt protocol and stereotypes.

Mordeven stepped from his room, tugging the lace at his sleeves into place. Black lace spilled from his throat and blood-red leather pants were tucked into tall black boots that clung to his calves. "Mother," he said with a bow. "Who do you think it is?"

"I managed to lure four into the swamps while we were still imprisoned. Korand is already here. We'll soon find out which of the other seeds took root."

She picked up her pace, and in a few moments, the entourage swept into her throne room. Those nobles, not otherwise engaged, stood in small groups in their finery and bowed as she entered. She strode to her throne, a piece of carved obsidian. Twisted beasts from the past cavorted on its surface. A thick black velvet cushion softened the hard seat. Her children took their places on their much smaller seats, while the duke and duchess stood on either side of the dais, their wands held ready.

Magdelyn slipped in—a smear of dust on her cheek—to stand at the foot of the dais. Her work on reclaiming the east wing had started none too soon. Valdorian mimed rubbing her cheek to Magdelyn, who quickly scrubbed the dirt away.

Queen Malviana nodded to the guards to open the doors. Korand had to turn slightly sideways to maneuver his wide antlers through the doorway. At his side strode a creature who had once been a Posair.

His pale, watery-blue eyes gleamed from a wolf-like face with elongated jaws, sharp teeth, and pointed ears. A set of twisty ram horns, starting from behind his ears, curved around his face. Blond fur covered his seven-foot humanesque frame and did nothing to hide his manly assets. The lady had been correct. He was splendid. The muscles in his torso rippled as he moved. His legs were those of a wolf, with short claws, and a tail swayed behind him. With a quick glance, he took in the assembled Malvers, and just as quickly, dismissed them. He fastened his eyes onto Malviana's and grinned with lust as his phallus engorged.

Her groin throbbed in response. As she considered putting her pleasure device into service with him strapped into it, a slow grin crossed her face, and her left hand brushed her breast. He gave her an answering leer.

He stalked down the aisle toward her, his gait surprisingly graceful. She flicked her eyes to Korand, who glared at the newcomer with his clawed hand flexing at his side. While Korand was taller than the new creature, he wasn't nearly as well-endowed. Korand thrust out his arm to stop the Maldier from climbing the dais steps.

He turned and snarled, pulling back his lips to show impressively sharp teeth, his own clawed hands flexing, ready to fight.

"Bow to the Queen, knave," Korand growled as he shoved the man, who rocked forward but didn't move.

He snarled again at Korand before turning to Malviana and bowing deeply. "My queen, I am yoursss." His wolf-jaws slurred and mangled the words, but even so, she understood him clearly.

She flicked her hand, and he stood straight. She shifted in her seat, recrossing her legs, knowing her movements flashed a peek of her thigh. Malviana smirked as he licked his lips, wondering what his long tongue and sharp teeth could do, and resisted squirming.

"Tell us who you once were, and how you came to our castle," she ordered, resting her forearms on her throne's arm rest and thrusting out her chest.

"I am Keandran, vassal to Queen Malviana."

Malviana remembered him. He'd been with the hated Rizelya, who, for some reason, could spy on Malviana through her visions. She'd learned to turn those around and show Rizelya what she wanted her to see and had drunk deeply of Rizelya's resulting terror. Her mouth twitched. She sensed Keandran had the rare gift of equating pain with pleasure. Not only did he enjoy inflicting pain, but he also relished receiving it. Tingles shot from her groin, and she hid her shivers of desire, deciding then she would take him to her bed. She'd deprived herself of carnal pleasures for too long.

"Last spring," he continued, "I heard your voice calling to me. I followed your sweet perfume of darkness into a swamp in Strunlair Territory, where I became what I am now, something more than Posair. I awoke with the bite of winter and traveled south, hunting and killing Posairs on my way. Until I finally arrived here." He awkwardly bent to kneel on one knee. "How may I serve, my queen?"

"I shall find many ways for you to serve me," Malviana purred. Then grimaced at the mud and muck caked onto his fur. "But first, Magdelyn, show him where to bathe and give him quarters. Bring him to me after the evening sacrifices."

Magdelyn lifted an eyebrow and smirked. "As you will, my queen." She bowed and beckoned Keandran. "Come with me." She led the way from the throne room, her hips swaying seductively. Keandran following closely behind with his wolf nose twitching.

Malviana sensed Magdelyn's lust—and many other women's—for Keandran. Magdelyn would have some fun first and prime him for Malviana later. They had played this game frequently in the past. She grinned. It was good to resume such pastimes.

Rizelya - 38 de Ahdar, 1076

Rizelya sat with the others on the Black Weave in Blazel's old poison-making tent on the edge of camp where the team practiced every day to perfect the technique. She scowled when shouts and a blaring horn broke their concentration.

Graak cocked his head, listening to the Gryphon conversation Rizelya couldn't hear. *It's another Malvers' monster swarm.*

"Let's try using the Black Weave to destroy them." Excitement thrilled through Rizelya. "If we can fight from a distance, it will keep us safe during a battle when we can't hide out in a tent. Then we won't have to have babysitters."

"Hey," Aistrun protested from where he lounged by the tent doorway. "Leistral, Eidstrun, Leistrun, and I aren't babysitters. We're your bodyguards."

"Same here," Maestrun grunted. He and Nelstrun sat cross-legged on the floor near Saffren, playing two-handed keshe. Their Gryphon partners, Oslerru and Daerik, stretched out along the side of the tent, dozing.

During the Black Weave team's experiments over the past chedan, they'd discovered they needed at least two Gryphons contributing their magic. However, the team's Gryphon partners participated, except Boreek, Grazeen's partner.

"Even so," Rizelya said, "it would be nice not to have to rely on you while we're out of it."

Grazeen nodded enthusiastically as she stroked Boreek's dark umber chest fur, and the Gryphon chirped with pleasure.

"Not that we don't appreciate you." Chariel gazed lovingly at Aistrun.

"It just makes us vulnerable," Blazel finished, a small shudder running through his body.

"Let's try it." Saffren pushed her sapphire-blue hair back from her beautiful face. "It will be nice to kill the monsters without the threat of monster acid splashing on us."

The Posairs joined hands while their Gryphon partners curled up behind them. Kaieli initiated the Weave, and Rizelya noticed each time they did, it was easier than before. Their consciousness zoomed to the fighting, which flared like a bonfire in their augmented sight. In this state, Rizelya could see strings of malignant magic formed the janacks and brechas. She grimaced. Nothing about them was natural. A brecha collapsed under a warrior's claws. The strings unwound and burrowed into the ground.

I can see where it's going, Grazeen said, disgust filled her voice. *It's flowing back to the pool it came from. They don't really die. The rancorous magic they're formed from just recycles over and over into more monsters.*

No wonder we can't get rid of them, Rizelya said. *Our power can eradicate the malignant magic in the pools, so we should be able to actually destroy these monsters.*

Kaieli concentrated and pushed their magic toward the monsters, but it seemed like it hit a barrier. Through their connection, Rizelya sensed that Kaieli, as a healer, was having trouble killing the monsters, even though they weren't truly alive. Rizelya figuratively stepped forward and took control of the Weave. She'd been fighting—and she believed, killing—these things for most of her life. She didn't have a problem directing their power to destroy the monster's unnaturalness.

Their power flowed over the battle, wrapping the monsters in a gray mist. Rizelya accessed more of Chariel's Gray Talent and Loshera's White, directing it into a bright light which burst through the mist, dissolving the malignant strings inside the monsters. Grazeen added her element of earth and formed a layer over the ground, absorbing any trace particles of the cancerous magic. Together, they gathered the residual magic into a ball. Another blast of their magic burned it into nothingness. Not even ash remained.

Rizelya broke the contact, and her consciousness rushed back to her body. This aspect of the Weave was also getting easier with practice. She no longer returned to awareness sprawled on the ground. After a few deep breaths, she'd regained her equilibrium.

"Sweet Mother, did we do it?" Rizelya jumped to her feet, excitement tingling through her. "Let's go check the battlefield, to be sure. I still don't trust what we see in our joined state."

"I'm with you," Blazel said.

Shortly, the entire group headed to the battle scene. When they arrived, the fighting-packs stood in the middle of the battlefield, muttering together in confused shock. Rizelya and the Black Weave team jogged to Maheli.

"Did you do this?" Maheli gestured to the empty field.

Rizelya nodded. "We did it! We destroyed the magic in the monsters. Those particular beasts will never bother us again."

Maheli crossed her arms over her chest. "What are you talking about? We kill the monsters all the time."

"Ah, but we just discovered we've only been killing their outer shells. They are evil incarnate. They aren't hatched like we believed, rather, they're formed out of the malignant magic. We can now destroy the magic that creates them."

Grazeen walked onto the battlefield and knelt to examine the ground. She dug her fingers deep into the earth, then turned to them, a smile brightening her face. "There's no residual malice. It's gone! Boreek, will you take me up? I'd like to track where this nest came from. I'm interested in if what we did affected the mother pool."

Of course, we're partners. Boreek dropped his beak in a grin as he crouched for her to climb onto his back.

"I want to see too," Rizelya said. "This discovery is too important to leave out the Supreme Alphas. If we leave Histrun out, he'll be angry with us." Rizelya shuddered. She didn't want him to yell at her—again.

Graak's head feathers lifted. *Good idea. I'll ask them to join us along with Gryphons to carry them.*

During the war, the Supreme Alphas hadn't formed a working relationship with any particular Gryphon. In a few milcrons, Histrun, Keshanal, and Naila joined the Black Weave team. They followed Grazeen and Boreek across the plains to a small swamp a few measures from the camp. On its outskirts, numerous twisted rabbits, squirrels, and birds lay scattered on the ground. The Gryphons hovered over the area.

Keshanal gasped. "They're all dead! Is this what your magic does?"

"Wait a moment," Rizelya told her.

With a twitch, a rabbit lurched to its feet and rubbed its nose. Its paws no longer sported long, sharp claws, and its teeth were again those of an herbivore. Within half an octar, all the animals had hopped, run, or flown off.

"That's amazing," Histrun said. "But what about the malignant magic in the swamp? Is it gone?"

Blazel shrugged. "Let's find out."

The Gryphons landed, and Blazel led the group deeper into the swamp on foot. Rizelya followed reluctantly, expecting to sink into the marshy ground. Instead, they walked on quickly drying mud. In a clearing, they found the remnants of a Malvers' monster nest. Rizelya blinked. The pool of thick greenish-black, putrid liquid was visibly shrinking. It grew smaller until it was only a few feet wide.

"How come it isn't going away?" Rizelya scowled at the pool when it didn't dwindle any more.

Chariel stared at the pool thoughtfully. "We need to drain malignant magic from this pool, otherwise it will spawn more monsters."

"We only destroyed the monsters originating from here, not the magic itself," Loshera reflected.

Blazel studied the dank water, stroking his chin. "If we attack the monsters, it weakens but doesn't destroy the rancorous magic unless we annihilate all the monsters spawned from it. But if we eliminate the malignant pools, no more monsters can form. I like the second option better."

"Yes!" Histrun pumped a fist into the air, grinning. "All my life I've dreamed about ridding our world of the Malvers' monsters, and now it's a possibility." He laid a hand on Rizelya's shoulder. "I wish your mother was here to see this. It's what we were trying to accomplish with our Zehis method. She would be so proud of you. Like I am."

Rizelya stared at him. She knew him more as a mentor than a father and wasn't sure what to say or do at this rare praise and show of affection. She finally settled on giving him a hug, grinning when his face turned a bright red with embarrassment.

"While we're here," Kaieli said, "let's clean this pool."

Rizelya nodded her agreement. The team dropped to the ground and sat in a circle. Blazel's shoulders rubbed Rizelya's on one side, with Kaieli on her other side. Glork settled his bulk at her back and rested his chin on her head. In a few breaths, they formed the Weave. When Rizelya tried directing the magic toward the pool, nothing happened. Kaieli took control of the Weave, gathered Loshera's White Talent, and sent it to the pool. With her expanded consciousness, Rizelya realized a healer had to direct the Weave to heal the malignant magic. They had just learned something new. One of the Talents must also be a healer.

After Kaieli broke the connection, Rizelya and the others gazed at the dark ground where the malignant pool had been. In half an octar, the spot was bare earth, and the itchy feeling of evil Rizelya had been trying to ignore was gone.

"Sweet Mother!" Histrun said, lifting his eyes to the sky. Then he smiled happily at Rizelya and the team. "You did it! Our Vhelopsi friends need a home, but I've hesitated to give them a keep because they can't protect themselves from the Malvers' monsters well enough. If you clear the swamps around, say, Posanreande Keep, we can settle them there. There are too few people remaining from there to repopulate it."

"As a former resident," Loshera said, "I wouldn't mind the Vhelopsi living there. They helped us against the invaders. Most of the people I've talked to don't want to return to the keep."

"They have told us the same thing," Keshanal said. "We wouldn't give it to the Vhelopsi without the consent of the former residents. Most wish to resettle far from the Barrens. The war decimated several other keeps along the border, which we plan on making garrisons. The guard-packs would have a much easier time guarding against the potential Malvers' invasion if they didn't also have to fight Malvers' monsters."

Rizelya bowed to the Supreme Alphas. "We'll travel to Posanreande Keep tomorrow and start cleaning the area."

On the short flight back to camp, Rizelya fretted. Dehali, Gehan, and Raeleen would eventually be part of another Black Weave team when the Gray and White Priestesses arrived from the Sanctuary. But until then, Rizelya would be leaving half her pack behind as she fulfilled this new role. She liked fighting and loved the adrenaline rush of physically pitting herself against an opponent. However, this new aspect allowed her to fight and serve her people differently. But it would eventually put her out of a job. What would she do when her fighting abilities weren't needed anymore?

Blazel - 39 de Ahdar, 1076

As they flew to Posanreande Keep, Blazel ground his teeth against the bile in the back of his throat. The winter storms hadn't completely obliterated the trail of death. The forced march of the captured people into the Barrens had left behind a trail of bodies. They'd known then the aliens who had landed on their planet weren't friendly. He glanced over at Kaieli flying on Keeru. A mask of terror contorted her face, and tears streaked her face. She'd been on that march and had survived lunadars of slavery at the invaders' hands.

Sunshine-yellow and creamy-white flowers dotted the ground between the gray sagebrush. The spring landscape appeared inviting. As they drew closer to the keep, a stunted tree here and there poked the sky. They became more frequent and taller as the keep came into sight.

Shoots of grass grew in the pasturelands, although the bleached bones dotting the green expanse ruined the beauty. Blazel recalled his shock when he'd seen the slaughtered animals. The invaders had killed all the livestock, including the horses. The crops in the fields had rotted with no one to tend them, and weeds grew profusely. In the vegetable plots, a few volunteer plants sprouted where the untended vegetables from the prior season had gone to seed. Life was reasserting itself. The stone fences surrounding the pastures and fields still stood, keeping the land from being poisoned by passing Malvers' monsters.

Black spots marred the white sheadash stone walls of the buildings where the invaders had blasted them with their weapons. Several windows were shattered, and a few walls had crumbled from the impact of large projectiles, one of which was still lodged in the side of a pack-house. The winter storms had washed the blood from cobblestones. Earlier, while preparing the Keep for the Faeorn, a team of Posairs had rehung the gates and cleaned the keep-house and dining hall. The Faeorn had stayed at the keep, repairing the scout ship they used to escape and return home.

Graak, Glork, and Broogk landed in the courtyard—all the Gryphons who could fit in the small space. Blazel, Rizelya, and Aistrun quickly dismounted, pulling their bags off and moving out of the way. The Gryphons huddled into the side streets radiating from the courtyard.

Blazel tossed his pack over his back, and with an arm around Rizelya's waist, they walked to the keep-house. After setting their bags inside the door, they waited on the porch for the others to disembark. Aistrun waited in the courtyard for Chariel to land.

Chariel, Kaieli, and Loshera were the next to dismount. Aistrun escorted the ladies to the keep-house. He looked up and grinned.

"Hail, the keep alphas!" He saluted Blazel and Rizelya. "May we enter the keep and seek sanctuary from the dark?"

Blazel and Rizelya glanced at each other, then noticed they were standing in the traditional place where keep alphas welcomed guests. They burst into laughter.

Rizelya sobered. "Welcome to Posanreande Keep. Come in and rest your tired bones."

Laughing, Aistrun and Chariel climbed the stairs. Kaieli and Loshera followed slowly, each wearing a haunted look on her face. They had lived here when the Scourge attacked it.

"Kederposan and Kothera were good keep alphas." Loshera stroked the porch railing. "They would be proud to see you two standing in their stead."

Rizelya tipped her head in acknowledgment of the praise. "It will be a long time before we're keep alphas. Maybe someday. But I'd rather lead my home keep of Strunland."

Next, Eiden, Saffren, and Grazeen climbed the stairs to the keep-house. Leistral, Nelstrun, and Leistrun hopped off their Gryphon partners, who quickly vacated the courtyard. Gryphons peered from the packed side streets, and Blazel wondered where the two huge Gryphons, Oslerru and Sterkek, would stand.

Sterkek, as a sea-eagle type Gryphon, out sized Graak by several feet, both in length and height, although he wasn't as large as a Thunder Wing. Even landing, they would fill the small courtyard. Oslerru's feet barely touched the ground when Maestrun jumped off, and the Gryphon leaped back into the air. Blazel moved aside to let the big man onto the crowded porch.

In a flurry of white and black feathers and fur, Sterkek dropped into the courtyard. He tucked his black wings tight against his feline body and curled his white tail around his paws. The tuft of short black feathers sitting between his eyes and above his prominent hooked beak gave the big Gryphon a perpetual, angry mien. Although it belied the Gryphon's easy-going attitude. He gave an unhappy chirp. *Hurry, Eidstrun, I can barely breathe in this tiny space.*

Eidstrun rolled his eyes, even as he slid off Sterkek's side and hurried to stand in front of the Gryphon. At over six feet, Eidstrun's head was a bit shorter than Sterkek's shoulder. He reached up and stroked Sterkek's chest. "You're fine, big boy. There is plenty of space for you to take off again."

The Gryphon shivered as he gently touched his prominent yellow hooked beak to Eidstrun's cheek. Eidstrun stepped onto the lowest stair of the porch, and with a burst of magic, the enormous Gryphon launched into the sky.

Even though the team was the only occupants in the keep, their bodyguards would watch over them while they worked on draining the territory's malignant magic pools. The team still fell into an insensate state while in the Weave.

"Let's settle our things," Blazel said. "We need to find a place where we can include the Gryphons."

Rizelya surveyed the keep, then narrowed her eyes, studying the Gryphons. Her gaze paused on Sterkek and Oslerru, circling overhead. "I don't recall seeing any bodies inside of the practice arena. Even for a keep this small, it should hold the team. However, our guards may have to remain outside."

The pasture will hold us, Sterkek said. *When we cleared this keep for the Volkern's to work on their ship, we removed the animal bones.* He and Oslerru snapped their wings back into a dive, then backwinged to gracefully land in the pasture.

Rizelya rubbed her arms as she shuddered. "The bodies may be gone, but I feel like there are ghosts here."

After she said it, Blazel realized he'd been feeling a bit antsy, as if he was being watched. He touched the loc on the side of his face where gray swirled in it. Once in a while, his minuscule amount of Gray Talent allowed him to sense ghosts.

Chariel closed her eyes. "One or two souls are still lingering, lost. I'll guide them across the veil this evening. Twilight is the best time for these things. The veil thins and makes it easier for souls to cross it."

"I'll help," Loshera said, straightening out her skirts. "These were my people. They know me and will listen to me."

Chariel nodded her thanks. The group went inside, found rooms, and stored their belongings before tromping over to the largest building in the keep: the practice arena. The Posairs gathered in the center.

Graak, we're here. Blazel sent a mental image of the space.

In a moment, Graak appeared over his head. The Gryphons could pass through matter, but they needed to know what was on either side. The Gryphons, who were part of their team, followed him through and settled on the sands. Blazel sensed the bodyguard Gryphons spreading out around the building. Aistrun strode down the aisle between the stands and leaned on the railing. Broogk filled the aisle with his bulk.

Ugh, Glork complained. *These sands are cold.* A nimbus of flame extended from him to the sands.

Graak, Keeru, Torlek, Morlek, Florrik, and Boreek joined him, and within a few milcrons, the sand was toasty warm.

Grazeen shook out a blanket. "I didn't want to sit on the sand."

Blazel grabbed a corner and helped her spread it out. "I'm glad you thought of this. It will be much more comfortable, and sand won't get all over me."

The team sat on the blanket while the Gryphons settled on the sand behind them. Before they'd left, Blazel and Rizelya had obtained a map of the surrounding area from Kothera. Seven swamps needed malignant magic drained from them. Blazel hadn't spent any time in this territory during his sojourn studying the swamps. He removed the map from his inner jacket pocket and spread it out in the center of the blanket.

"Let's do this one first," he suggested, pointing to the nearest swamp.

"Looks as good as any of the others." Saffren held out her hands.

Everyone nodded in agreement as they clasped hands, and Kaieli initiated the melding. Blazel didn't think he'd ever get over his amazement and the rush of merging his magic with the others.

They sent their combined consciousness to the swamp they'd chosen. The inky greenish-black pool was bigger than the first one they'd drained, and Blazel briefly feared they wouldn't be able to do the job. Then the calm, deep presence of the Goddess, which always accompanied their workings, brushed his cheek like a fleeting kiss. Confidence replaced his fear. They could empty pools much larger than this one. Their magic encompassed the pool and slowly sucked the infected magic from it, leaving fresh water behind. This dry land needed the ponds and springs.

When Kaieli released the connection, Blazel sagged against Graak's chest.

"Finally!" Aistrun exclaimed. "I was beginning to worry. You've been out of it for nearly two octars."

Chariel rubbed her face. "To us, it only seemed like a few milcrons."

"Then it's a good thing you have bodyguards."

"I'm famished," Grazeen said. Her stomach grumbled loudly, and she stood up. "I'm going to fix dinner."

"I'm so glad you're part of our group, Grazeen," Aistrun said with feeling. "None of us can cook. If Rizelya offers to help, don't let her!"

Rizelya glared at him. "I'm not that bad."

"Um, yes you are," Blazel argued. She punched him lightly on the arm.

Graak stood, shaking the sand from his fur. *We'll go hunting. There should be some game in the nearby plains.*

The Gryphons zipped through the walls to go hunting. Blazel paused outside the arena, stretching while he enjoyed the glorious sunset of dark red and purple clouds. Shadows crept over the cobblestones. Chariel and Loshera excused themselves, hurrying to the temple. Blazel slung an arm over Rizelya's shoulders as they walked with the rest toward the keep-house.

As they passed the stables, Blazel sighed with longing. "I miss Lighzel, and even Tejen." Recently, he'd only ridden his horse for a short ride. "It's great riding the Gryphons and getting to places quickly, but..."

"It isn't the same thing as riding a horse," Rizelya finished for him.

"Exactly."

He and Rizelya followed the rest into the keep-house and downstairs to the bathing room. Saffren purified the water, while Rizelya and Leistral heated the huge tubs and the water tanks. After bathing, they walked to the mess hall, following the delicious smells wafting from the kitchen. Grazeen hummed happily as she stirred a pot. She stood on a stool with her evergreen hair pulled back in a ponytail. It reminded Blazel of the first time he'd met her. Everyone helped carry dishes to the table and sat to eat.

"The ghosts are gone," Chariel said, as she and Loshera joined them. "They didn't understand what had happened to them or why their people were missing."

It took three more days for the team to clear the other six malignant magic pools. When they overflew the area, Blazel could see a change in the land already. The plants looked healthier, and several of the pools were reverting to their natural state as small lakes and ponds. In a few lunadars, this would be a completely different place. The Gryphon's shadows startled a ducorn herd, drinking in the new pond. They bounded away from the Gryphons, but Blazel was confident they'd be back once the Gryphons departed. He hadn't realized how much the healthy animals avoided the swamps.

The Vhelopsi should like this place now, Graak observed. *There'll be good hunting and fishing.*

"And fertile pasturelands and fields," Blazel added. "The Vhelopsi deserve a home of their own after helping us defeat the invaders. I hope Histrun can convince them we still have a war to win before our world is safe."

Their fighting skills will be beneficial against the Malvers. While we currently outnumber them, they have superior magic.

Blazel shivered. The Posairs barely defeated the Malvers in the Great War and only an act of tremendous magic had saved them then. What would it take this time?

Chapter 8

Wisah - 40 de Ahdar, 1076

Wisah sat at her desk in the small reception office outside the Supreme's office, busy scribbling notes from the Supreme's latest meeting. Wisah wondered again if she was being trained to take the Supreme's place. But why? She didn't have the necessary qualifications, but she wouldn't question the Goddess's living representative. Wisah recalled fighting to bring the Supreme back from across the veil and bent her head to her task. She'd learn all she could. Wisah knew, better than most, how fragile the Supreme's hold on life really was.

A runner burst through the door. "A Gryphon approaches!" Her eyes gleaming with excitement.

"I'll tell the Supreme." Wisah dropped her quill, disregarding the smear of ink marring her paper. Her heart hammered in her chest. Maybe it was news about her friends. Wisah's new duties and studies kept her so busy that she didn't have time to miss her friends. Every night, she tumbled into bed, exhausted, and immediately, fell asleep. Thankfully, the book left her alone, and dreams of the past didn't disturb her sleep. She hurried into the Supreme's office.

A few milcrons later, Wisah and the Red Guard helped the Supreme shuffle the short distance to the audience chamber. As they passed a window, Wisah glimpsed a Gryphon land in the inner courtyard, and her shoulders drooped when she saw his beige and brown fur and feathers. It wasn't Glork, which meant his rider wasn't Rizelya.

The Supreme took her place on her crystal throne, indicating for Wisah to remain on the dais next to the throne. Wisah squirmed at this outward show of prestige. The Supreme then motioned to the Red Guards to allow the messengers into the audience chamber.

Wisah recognized Kaaik and Delestrun as they strode toward the dais. She longed to ask them about her friends, especially Jaehaas, but protocol demanded she wait until after they'd delivered their message. Delestrun made the gesture of obeisance, while Kaaik simply bowed his head.

The Supreme bade them rise. "You have news for me?"

"Yes, Your Grace," Delestrun said. "The bomb the invaders left behind created a tidal wave, threatening to destroy the eastern coast." He told them about the tidal wave and the astonishing magic Rizelya, Kaieli, and the others had worked to save the coastal keeps. "This isn't the only thing they can do with their new Black Weave." He rocked back on his heels, his hands clasped behind his back, and grinned.

Oh, don't make them wait, Kaaik said, as he gave a happy trill. *They can destroy the malignant magic pools!*

The Supreme leaned forward in her seat, her drumming fingers stilled. "This is good news. I, and my predecessors, have tried over the years to accomplish that feat. Now the Malvers are back, it is even more imperative to destroy those pools."

"You knew the Malvers had returned?" Delestrun's eyebrows rose. "But then, you're the Supreme. You know everything. I was waiting to tell you that last. You know, deliver the good news first and all."

"Tell us how this Black Weave is done," the Supreme said. Wisah noted she didn't disabuse him of the notion she was all-knowing.

We don't know. Neither of us has participated in it, yet. Kaaik lifted his shoulder feathers in a shrug.

"Gryphons are part of this magic?"

He dipped his head. *Yes, it makes the difference. At least, it's what I'm told. Graak says it's like connecting to the void and listening to the Goddess's will. Melding their magic creates a form of Black Talent. If they had more people, they can clear the malignant magic faster.*

"It's why we're here, Your Grace," Delestrun added. "The technique requires someone from each Talent, plus a male, to be part of the melding—"

"And there aren't enough Grays and Whites," the Supreme observed.

Delestrun shook his head. "No, Your Grace, there aren't. The only full Gray is Chariel. Histrun is requesting you send us more priestesses with Gray and White Talent. The stronger they are, the better."

Chariel was the strongest Gray in the Sanctuary. But Wisah could think of three or four who came a close second.

The Supreme resumed tapping her fingers on the arm of her throne, her rings chiming against the crystal. "I have a few I can send. Let me talk to them. I'll advise you of my decision."

Delestrun and Kaaik bowed and retreated from the chamber.

"Wisah, help me back to my office."

As soon as the Supreme sat at her desk, she pulled a sheet of paper to her, scratched out a list, and handed it to Wisah.

She studied the dozen names. As she read the last one, she looked up sharply. "Blenora? Are you sure?"

"I am. Her secondary Talent is Gray, and quite strong. Since her mother died, she's been begging me to send her to serve at a temple. Bring those women to me."

"Um... I'm a strong White. Shouldn't I be on the list?"

The Supreme put her pen down and leaned back in her chair. "No. You have other work to do, which is just as important—more so. You shall stay here."

Wisah bowed her head to hide her disappointment. "Yes, ma'am."

"Go fetch them for me, will you?"

Wisah nodded, and returned to her small office, brushing away the tears. The ruined document on her desk stared accusingly at her. Working the Black Weave sounded exciting, more so than taking notes for the Supreme. A lump formed in her throat. Seeing Delestrun had reminded her how much she missed her friends—and Jaehaas.

Deciding to take a detour, Wisah hurried from the temple, hoping to catch Delestrun and Kaaik before they left the temple's grounds for the guest quarters. The pair strolled toward the gates. She smiled at Kaaik's swaying gait, his wings held slightly away from his body as he walked. Delestrun strode at his side, and a young girl led the way.

"Delestrun! Kaaik!" she hailed them. "Wait." She lifted her skirts and ran to them when they stopped.

"Wisah! I thought that was you lurking beside the Supreme's throne." Delestrun threw his arms around her and pulled her into a hug. "Are you coming back with us? We brought plenty of Gryphons."

We were hopeful the Supreme would grant Histrun's request, Kaaik said.

She sadly shook her head. "No, I can't leave. How is everyone?"

"They are doing well. But we lost so many during the last battle."

Tears pricked Wisah's eyes. "I know. I've read the reports." She'd studied every one with dread, hoping not to see the names of her loved ones listed. "I have to get back to work right now. But I'll come visit you after dinner."

Delestrun hugged her again. Then he and Kaaik followed the young girl to the guest quarters. She sighed, wishing she could join them. With a pang of longing, she remembered the fun she'd had staying with Rizelya, Blazel, and Jaehaas the last time they were here. She hadn't played the throwing stick game, jelehan, since leaving the war to bring the ancient book to the Supreme.

She turned on her heel and headed to the cloisters to collect the women on the Supreme's list.

After the Supreme detailed the mission, each one of the dozen women chosen agreed to go. The group consisted of six of each Talent, including Blenora and Ardela—the strongest Gray next to Chariel. Ardela—like Chariel—hadn't ever left the Sanctuary since her arrival as a baby. Wisah returned to the cloister with Ardela and helped her pack while sharing stories about Chariel's first experience with the outside world.

Before going to bed, Wisah wrote a long letter to Jaehaas, explaining why she left. Her continued absence wasn't because she didn't care or want to be with him. She remained in the Sanctuary at the Supreme's will—and the Goddess's call.

The next morning, she accompanied the departing priestesses to the practice area where the Gryphons Kaaik had brought with him waited. She helped the women strap into the unfamiliar harnesses, then approached Delestrun.

She pressed the letter into his hands. "Can you give this to Jaehaas for me?"

He tucked it into the inner pocket of his jacket. "I will."

On impulse, Wisah wrapped her arms around Delestrun and kissed him. "Give that to him as well."

Blushing, Delestrun hopped onto Kaaik's back.

Farewell, Priestess Wisah, Kaaik said, dipping his head. *I'm sure we'll see you again soon. Trouble is brewing.*

"Yes, it is," Wisah agreed. She stepped to the far side, wishing she could convince Sheekeek to go against the Supreme's wishes and take her back to the front lines.

As Wisah curled up on her lonely bed, she longed for Jaehaas's loving, soothing presence. She didn't want to be the next Supreme. She wanted to serve in a temple in Strunlair or Haaslair Province, where she and Jaehaas could be together. Wisah prayed for a white-eyed, white-haired baby girl to be brought to the temple—and soon.

Malviana - 40 de Ahdar, 1076

Malviana stretched, wincing as muscles she hadn't used for a long time protested. She glanced at the sex device and smiled at the blood coating it and the wall. She'd been correct. Keandran loved her games and gave her as much pleasure—and pain—as he'd received. And he had incredible stamina. They'd played for two days.

She sat up, and the whip lashes across her abdomen broke open, oozing blood. She dipped a finger in it and licked it, savoring the residual pain and pleasure. Such delicious foreplay! Between it and the sacrifices, Malviana felt quite satiated.

After bathing and dressing, she called her children in, and they gathered around her black mirror. "It's time—"

"Ooh," Malvidor said, eying the mirror and bouncing on his toes, "are we going to learn how to use it?"

"Don't interrupt," Malviana scolded him.

He ducked his head and mumbled an apology.

"Yes, it's time you learned how. We have much work to do to build our army."

Morvana tapped a finger on her chin as she contemplated the mirror. "I've been thinking—"

"Dangerous," Mordeven snipped.

Morvana glared at him. She flicked her fingers at him, and he yelped as a tiny bolt of lightning struck him. "As I was saying, we can use the larger swamp creatures as our initial army. There certainly are enough of them, and the magic pool under the swamp means we can create even more. We could transform the little dracurs into more banthues."

Malviana beamed at her daughter. "Very good, Morvana. I had the same thoughts. Other creatures live outside this swamp we can use, too. In our absence, our magic worked to pervert the animals of Lairheim." She rubbed her hands together in anticipation. She loved this aspect of her magic, even though it reminded her of the hateful Posair magic.

"To use the mirror, first concentrate on what you want to see. Once it's in focus, draw this sigil—" she demonstrated with her wand the correct pattern of movements "—and say this spell to activate it."

As she chanted the spell, a silver fog formed over the mirror, and when it cleared, the Posair army encampment appeared. An old man, slightly stooped, his red hair dulled with age, standing in front of a white tent, came into view. His grass-green eyes shone with sharp intelligence, and his broad shoulders still held strength. She'd asked to be shown the Posair leader. A woman with faded copper hair stepped from the tent. Malviana cringed at the wrinkles lining the woman's face. Gratitude filled her. Mordaga's gift of immortality kept her young and wrinkle-free.

"Why are there two leaders?" Mordeven asked.

"The Posairs have a penchant for balance, and their leaders are usually a male and female pair," Malviana explained.

"Why would anyone have sex with someone that wrinkled and ugly?" Malvidor's face crinkled in disgust.

Malviana felt the same way. "They may or may not be lovers. They don't use sex for power like we do." A younger woman pushed open the tent door. Her bright red hair streaked with gold was pulled into a thick braid. An ugly scar encircled her neck. "Interesting. It seems they have three leaders. Make note of these people. They need to be taken out of the picture."

Morvana stared at the mirror with her eyes narrowed. "Can we hear what they're saying?"

Malviana shook her head. "It can only show us what we desire. We can't attack through the mirror, either. If you try it, your spell will backfire and strike you. And if it's a powerful enough spell, it could shatter the mirror." She shook her finger and glared at each of her children. "Do not break my mirror. We don't have the lives to spare to make a new one."

She waved her wand. The image of the hated Posairs dissolved in a silver fog—too bad she couldn't do the same to people—and the mirror's surface returned to a matte black. She considered which creature she'd observed through her pets to use first, and her eyes lit up. The insectoid creature would be an excellent addition to her army.

She activated the mirror once again, and a five-foot long insect appeared. Orange spots dotted its lime-green body. It had a long, thin face, six eyes, and four antennae. It stalked a ducorn, and suddenly, its long, supple middle antennae whipped out, lassoing the ducorn and wrapping around its throat. The creature reared back, tightening the loop, and the ducorn slumped, either unconscious or dead, Malviana couldn't tell which. The skeaeter's sharp mandibles clicked as it bent and chomped the ducorn's head off. Perfect! They were as deadly as she'd suspected.

"We can, however, attract and affect creatures of a similar nature through the mirror, like so." Malviana sent her power to the skeaeter. It lifted its head from its feeding, its eyes whirling as it sought her. She spoke another spell, and a black mist enveloped the creature. When she made a jerking motion with her wand, the creature collapsed.

"What happened? Is it dead?" Mordeven asked. "What use is killing it when we can't use its death?"

"Patience, my son," Malviana said through gritted teeth. She wove a different sigil with her wand. The scene changed to the castle's outer courtyard, where two women were working on removing the tangled vines from the wall. The mist formed behind them, and the creature stepped out. It wobbled on its legs, but when it saw the women, it immediately skittered toward them, waving its middle antennae. One woman sensed the danger and whirled around. Her shriek penetrated the closed window. The other woman calmly turned and raised her wand. Sparks danced on its tip.

"No!" Malviana yelled. "I need it!" She threw a shield between the woman and the creature just as the woman released her spell. Malviana's shield absorbed the magic, and she shifted the composition of the shield to cage the creature. It hit the cage and reared, its mandibles clicking in anger. The women recognized Malviana's magic and quickly retreated from the courtyard.

"The skeaeter is nearly perfect," she purred. "But we can make it better, more deadly to the Posairs. Mordeven, what changes will you make to it?"

Mordeven nibbled on his bottom lip as he studied the creature as it scuttled around the confines of its cage. Finally, he raised his wand, drawing a sigil, then pointed the wand at the image of the skeaeter while chanting to release the spell. The giant insect shuddered as the spell slammed into it. Within moments, it grew larger, filling the small cage. Its carapace darkened until it was completely black. The mandibles extended like tusks from its jaw, even sharper than before. Its six eyes whirled and changed to blood red.

Mordeven stepped back, lowering his wand, and smirked. "Its favored food is now Posairs. It will seek them out above all other prey. Its jaws are strong enough to sever a person's head. And they will follow our orders."

Pride filled her. "Nicely done, Mordeven. Now, make me two hundred more, using that one as your template. Will they come when you call them?"

Mordeven nodded. "They will."

"Then place them in the swamp outside the castle walls. We don't want them feeding on our people. We have too few as it is."

She moved to sit on a comfortable chair to watch him while he worked. Normal food no longer nourished her body as it had before she became a Malvers. Now, as a higher ranking Malvers, she only fed on the death essence of the sacrifices to Mordaga. But she still liked the taste of wine and blood. She rang a bell, and the lady serving as her maid crept in, quickly leaving after Malviana gave her order. A few milcrons later, the servant brought in a decanter of dark bloodwine and poured Malviana a large goblet. She sipped it while Mordeven worked.

Almost two octars later, the required two hundred creatures milled in the northeastern swamp. Mordeven panted from his efforts and flopped into a chair next to her. He poured himself a goblet of wine. "Beat that, Morvana," he crowed.

She stepped up to the mirror. "We need more banthues to combat the Gryphons. We don't want to risk losing our mounts before we're ready to leave the castle." She drew a pattern with her wand and released her spell. A dracur, a distant relative of the much larger banthu, appeared with a squawk in the outer courtyard. Before it could escape, a dark rope snaked around its rear leg and pulled it to the ground. In a few milcrons, it had transformed into a large banthu. Morvana turned, grinning at her mother. "How many do you need? A hundred, three hundred?"

"A hundred will do for now. We need enough for our initial attack."

"No fair," Malvidor complained. "I saw you practicing that spell earlier."

Morvana flung her hair over her shoulder and smirked at her younger brother. "I anticipated Mother's needs. You had the same opportunity as I did, and access to the same magic pools. I can't help it if you're lazy."

She returned her attention to the mirror. In less than an octar, a hundred new banthues milled in the paddock, snapping at each other. "Your turn, little brother." She sauntered to the wine decanter, poured herself a glass, and sat primly on the settee.

Malvidor pursed his lips and crinkled his nose, then huffed out a breath. Ignoring his siblings, he addressed his mother. "Why not use those canids, the floxidor? If they fought in packs instead of individually, they'd be even deadlier than they are now. Of course, we require them to come to our call and do our bidding."

Malviana lifted her goblet in a toast. Leave it to her youngest to take the easy, but smart, way. "That will do nicely. Five packs of thirty should be a good start. Proceed."

He turned to the mirror and released his spell.

Malviana winced at his shrill whistle. About fifteen milcrons later, she heard yips and yowls outside. The mirror cleared and showed canid after canid running toward the castle, their long, spiked tails held out behind them. They converged on the castle, passed through a small door in the eastern wall, and loped directly to the empty kennels. The kennel gates shut behind them. The floxidor snarled and snapped at each other for several milcrons until they finally settled down. Three of the larger ones circled a smaller one, who lifted its lips, snarling. Two of the males attacked each other.

"Oops!" Malvidor grinned. "I forgot she was in heat." After a quick battle, the largest male approached the female. He batted aside the third male and continued to stalk the female. She led him on a chase around the kennel, but he finally caught her and, sinking his teeth in her ruff, mounted her.

"There are several females in heat or ready to go into heat," Malvidor explained. "We'll have pups with the new qualities in a few chedans. We won't have to expend so much energy making more. The floxidor will mature quickly, ready to fight for us in less than a lunadar. The litters will also be larger than normal, ten to twelve pups in each one."

Malviana shook her head slightly while smiling. Sometimes, her youngest was the smartest of her children. They now had a naturally perpetuating creature to fight for them. All the others required their magic to reproduce.

"Shall we see what our new creatures can do?" she asked.

The three youngsters nodded eagerly.

"Release them. Send them to the Posair encampment."

Her children released the floxidor and skeaeter first. The canids ran ahead of the insects, snapping as they passed. They quickly traversed the swamp and headed into the Barrens.

"Do you need the mirror to track your creatures?" Malviana asked, bored with watching the animals.

"No, Mother," Malvidor answered quickly.

Mordeven screwed up his face in concentration, finally shaking his head. "No, I can track them without it."

"Good. Morvana, release your banthues so they will arrive at the encampment at the same time as the other creatures. Now leave me. Return when they approach the camp."

Once alone, Malviana considered where to strike next. There must be those luscious, dark magic pools all over Lairheim. She suspected they sprang up wherever atrocities had been committed during the Great War, and both sides had perpetuated plenty of those. She activated the mirror, and a map appeared.

Malviana scowled at the lack of pools north of Strunhelos and in the White Mountains. She and her people had never penetrated those mountains. The Posairs' Goddess had protected the inner sanctum of her priestesses. The farthest north the Malvers had attacked had been Strunhelos Keep. No matter. She'd break through the pass this time and crush the Sanctuary and its White Priestesses under her boot heel. Then she'd have a sacrifice worthy for Mordaga to return her beloved Mordar to her.

Her gaze traveled the map down to the southern peninsula. Her eyes widened as she took in the vast pool sitting under the crater. *No wonder it was so easy to create my pets there.* If ever there had been an atrocity, the spell she and Shandir had loosed on the Marvenden Forest was one of the worst. If she could harness the power in the crater pool long distance, she'd possess enough magic to blast through Strunhelos Pass and level it to the ground. But, alas, the mirror was affixed to the castle and couldn't be moved. Perhaps she could create a smaller one, but she'd need a large supply of slaves even with the power available from the crater pool. A pang of loneliness stabbed her, and she reached out to caress the mirror's frame. She and Mordar had spent lunadars together making this one.

Shaking off her melancholy, Malviana drew upon the magic in the crater pool, gasping at its strength. She set her spell of corruption and loosed it on every malignant magic pool in Lairheim. Malviana focused on Strunhelos Keep and smiled in satisfaction as a black mist rose from the nearby swamps. A breeze blew the contagion away from the swamp and into the keep and its surrounding fields, settling on the plants and stone. It would infect anyone who touched it, and had a seed of greed, cruelty, hatred, or anger, and begin transforming them into a Malvers. She regretted it was the only way for the Malvers to procreate any longer.

The power from the crater pool was so great, it wouldn't take long for the transformations to begin or to complete. Within the next lunadar or two, her new subjects would arrive.

Blazel - 43 de Ahdar, 1076

The Black Weave team flew back to the base camp, exhilarated and exhausted from their work on Posanreande Keep. The keep only needed the Vhelopsi, livestock, and seed for it to be reopened. Happiness filled Blazel. He'd helped his people and world without fighting. Last night, Rizelya had confided in him that she was worried about the future and what she'd do if they didn't have to fight for their people's survival. But the future excited Blazel as he dreamed about what they could accomplish. This work was just the beginning.

Pops of pulser fire and bursts of magic lit up the sky ahead of them.

It's coming from the camp. Graak's long-distance vision was better than Blazel's. *They're under attack.* Graak's huge wings swept faster, and he angled their flight toward the conflagration.

As they approached, Blazel swung his pulser around in front of him. He, like many other fighters, had adapted their fighting style to use the converted Scourge weapons in addition to their traditional ones. For the men, the pulsers allowed them to fight Gryphon-back. His brows knitted together at the creatures the fighting-packs battled. Besides the normal janacks and brechas, a pack of canids with straight horns sticking from their heads swarmed three warriors. A floxidor swung its long tail like a whip and struck the back of a warrior's legs with the sharp spikes along its length. The warrior howled, blood dripping from the wounds. Blazel had seen the canids in the southern swamp, but never outside of it, or in such large packs.

Another warrior with pale-yellow hair shot a blast of freezing air from his pulser at the floxidor, instantly freezing it as it raised its tail to strike again. The wounded warrior punched the frozen beast, shattering it into pieces.

The Vhelopsi Prince, Hairan, led a group of Vhelopsi fighters. Blazel had become friends with the prince along with several other Vhelopsi during the Scourge War.

"Hairan has a new weapon," he observed to Graak. Hairan used a curved knife similar to the women's helbraught blade, but much longer. With a sweep of the blade, Hairan sheared the spines off of a floxidor's tail, while Ninsun bashed his pulser into the canid's muzzle.

He often talked about wanting to recover his family's sword, Graak said. *That must be what it is.*

A flaming arrow struck the side of a floxidor as it leaped at Hairan's uncle, Agabus. Agabus jumped out of the way and saluted Jaehaas as he fired another arrow into the floxidor pack.

From their vantage point, Blazel glimpsed a long, thin black creature skittering through the tall grass toward the fighters. It reminded Blazel of the skeaeter he and Graak had fought in the Gryphons' territory. Although those had been lime green with orange spots. He hadn't run across the insectoids anywhere else on Lairheim. It raised onto its rear four legs, standing taller than the Vhelopsi. Its large, sharp mandibles, extending from its jaw like tusks—much larger than Blazel remembered— clacked in eager anticipation.

"Hairan!" Blazel yelled at the Vhelopsi. "Watch out!" He wished the Vhelopsi could hear mind-speech, but they didn't have any magic.

The long supple antennae on the middle of its head whipped out to lasso Hairan around the neck. He managed to insert his sword between his throat and the antennae, the sharp blade easily slicing through it. Hairan dropped to the ground on all fours, gasping for breath. Agabus fired his pulser. Red light streamed from it to the skeaeter, and it exploded in a blazing fire.

Graak and Blazel were now in range, and he rapidly shot the four remaining skeaeters, slithering toward the Vhelopsi and Haaslair fighters. Graak flared, burning the beasts Blazel missed.

The Vhelopsi looked up and saluted to them, then turned back to the fight.

Good to have you back, Jaehaas, Blazel said, pleased to see his friend.

I'm not so sure it be a good thing. You seem to have attracted new critters to fight while I was gone.

It wasn't me. It's those damned Malvers. Blazel shot a skeaeter before it could throw its antennae at his friend. Jaehaas reared and stomped it with his hooves.

Overhead, a Thunder Wing shrieked.

Tuueek is in trouble! Graak flapped furiously, taking them higher. *We have to help him. Great warrior, he's fighting a banthu!* His wing beats faltered. *I'd hoped those things were extinct.*

Blazel gaped at the flying reptile locked in combat with Tuueek. Sterkek and Eidstrun dove toward the battle. The creature was slightly larger than Sterkek, but still smaller than Tuueek. It snapped its long, forked tail at Sterkek, slamming into his side. Sterkek tumbled end over end several revolutions before righting himself. The banthu struck Tuueek again, slicing gashes along his flank. Graak zipped in, flaring. The banthu opened its great jaws and belched a ball of sulfurous-smelling gas. Graak dove so hard and fast, Blazel's forehead slammed into Graak's neck. An explosion shattered the air, and Blazel looked behind them.

"Sweet Mother! Graak, put out your flame!" The exploding gas continued to follow the trail of Graak's flare. Another few inches and Graak's tail would be on fire.

It's out! Graak cried, fear in his voice.

A sheet of water suddenly drenched them, extinguishing the fire and exploding gas. Saffren and Florrik above flew them, and a bolt of frozen water streamed from her helbraught. The ice spear pierced one of the banthu's wide, leathery wings before burying into its body. She flung more bolts at the creature, ice spreading from where they hit. The banthu's wings grew heavy with ice, and it was having trouble keeping aloft. Tuueek screeched and dove at the banthu, striking with his sharp talons, while Sterkek hit it from the other side. Eidstrun shot at the banthu, but it ignored the projectile buried in its shoulder. Graak swooped, striking the creature's long neck. The creature opened its mouth, and Blazel fired his pulser, the projectile slamming into the back of the banthu's throat.

"Fly!" Blazel yelled. "Get out of here, now!"

Graak, Florrik, Sterkek, and Tuueek zoomed away.

The beast coughed as if to belch its gas—or spit out Blazel's projectile. Instead, the fire magic in the projectile reacted with the gas, blowing the beast's head off. The body spiraled downward.

Ware! Graak called. *Move!*

The fighters on the ground looked up at Graak's warning, saw the danger, and raced out of the way. Several of the floxidor weren't fast enough, and the banthu's body smashed them when it crashed.

In the brief lull, Blazel searched the sky, trying to find Rizelya. He spotted her and Eiden fighting another banthu. It belched its gas, only to shake its head as the gas sped back at it, followed by a bolt of Rizelya's fire magic. The gas ignited in the banthu's maw. Small explosions blossomed all along its neck. Blazel's eyes widened, and he swore.

"Graak, move! When that hits the banthu's belly, it's going to be a huge eruption."

Graak squawked and put on a burst of speed. Blazel glanced over his shoulder. "Faster! It's exploding!"

I'm flying as fast as I can! He tumbled as the shock wave hit him.

Blazel tensed, but a sphere of hardened air contained the debris. He waved his thanks at Eiden.

Tuueek joined another Thunder Wing in attacking the remaining banthu, tearing chunks of flesh from it. Long gashes covered its neck and back from their talons. It broke away from them and flew toward the Barrens, out-distancing the larger Gryphons.

Below them, only a few individual battles were still being fought. Six floxidors raced into the Barrens, and three skeaeters skittered after them, their coloring blending with the black sand-glass. A warrior killed the last brecha. The fighters still standing helped injured comrades to their feet, or called for healers to attend to those who were too badly wounded to move. The Reds walked the battlefield burning the creature's corpses, not wanting them to attract scavengers so close to their camp. Boreek dropped Grazeen dropped off, and she worked on the banthu corpse, using her snelks to rapidly rot and consume the beast.

Blazel and Graak hovered over the cleanup, keeping watch to ensure the escaped creatures didn't return. Glork and Rizelya joined them.

"I wonder," Blazel said, unbuckling some of the straps to sit straighter, "if we'd had time for us to join, if the Weave could kill the creatures."

Rizelya shrugged. "I doubt it. They seemed different from the Malvers' monsters to me. These creatures were more like the twisted beasts found in the swamp, and the Weave only changes them back to their natural form. It didn't kill them."

I only sensed residual malignant magic on them, Graak said. *It was nothing like how the janacks or brechas reek of it.*

"If we have a chance," Rizelya said, "the next time we encounter these creatures, we can try using the Weave against them."

Blazel nodded in agreement. "Right now, though, we should report in with Histrun."

"He'll want to know about our success." Rizelya gave him a tired smile.

As they flew toward the command tent, Blazel gasped. Several tents were overturned, their contents scattered. He clenched his teeth when he glimpsed two bodies lying amid the wreckage of one. Histrun walked through the ruins, surveying the damage. As they landed, he turned to face them. The scar on his cheek stood out on his stark face.

"I hope you have good news," Histrun said to them. "I could use it. This is the third attack by those damned creatures since you left."

"Yes, we have good news." Blazel turned his head away from the tent and its gruesome contents. Floxidor had killed the two people, whom he didn't know.

"We successfully cleaned all the swamps in Posanreande Keep's territory," Rizelya said, a grin crossing her face as she rocked back and forth on her heels. "You won't believe how much the land has changed. It's no longer a desolate place."

The Vhelopsi should have an easier time settling there now, Graak added. *The natural game herds are returning to the area.*

White Priestesses had arrived and were wrapping the bodies in white shrouds. A team waited to carry them to the temple tent. Histrun ambled to the command tent, his head bowed, and his hands clasped behind his back.

"We can't stay here," he said at last. "This isn't defensible against those creatures, or whatever army the Malvers sends. We're moving deeper into the plains to Haaslornde Keep. It, and Dehanranle Keep on the other side of the river, should be large enough to hold our numbers."

After seeing the aftermath of the attack, Blazel understood the wisdom of the plan.

"When are we moving?"

"Bethlyn and Faelyn are preparing the infirmary to leave now. The rest will depart in the morning." Histrun put a hand on Blazel's shoulder. "Boy, I want you and the Black Weave team to cleanup Haaslornas and Dehanrandevir Keeps. Both of them are currently abandoned, and they lost most of their original people in the slave camp. We're going to use them as garrisons, but I can't have the guards fighting Malvers' monsters at the same time." He ran a hand through his hair. "Perhaps cleaning the swamps will keep the other creatures away, too."

"We can only hope, sir," Blazel said.

"Which keep do you want us to clean first?" Rizelya asked. Blazel reached out and rubbed a smear of soot from her cheek.

"Haaslornas Keep. It's the nearest." They arrived at the command tent and entered it. Histrun walked to the map and studied it for a moment. "Kothera and Metherposan will accompany you as the new keep alphas. Their packs will follow you on horseback."

Blazel leaned on the table, scrutinizing the map. "The area has a few more swamps than Posanreande. It should take us four—" he glanced at Rizelya, who held up five fingers "—five days to clear the area."

"That will do." Histrun tapped the map, indicating a spot in Dehanlair Province a few measures from the Barrens border. "Once you're done, go directly to Dehanrandevir Keep. By the time you reach it, Norvela and Aradehan should already be there with their people. Go with the Goddess's blessings."

Another long trip. Glork sighed as they left the tent. His head feathers drooped. *At least I'll get to see more of Lairheim.* He brightened, his head feathers lifting.

Graak yawned. *Until morning, Blazel, Rizelya. I'm going to get some food and sleep. As should you.* He dipped his head to them, then he and Glork strolled toward the Gryphon section.

"He has a good idea." Rizelya linked her arm around Blazel's. "Let's go tell the others, then eat. I'm famished."

Blazel's stomach growled, and he realized he hadn't eaten since breakfast. They'd skipped their midday meal to reach the camp before dark. Together, they went to find their team. He hoped the garrisons would provide protection from the new Malvers' creatures.

Rizelya - 43 de Ahdar, 1076

Rizelya strolled to the mess tent, arm in arm with Blazel. The new creatures they'd fought disturbed her. "If the Malvers can manipulate such creatures," she mused out loud, "what can they do with Posairs or Gryphons?" Keandran's strange behavior before he'd disappeared crossed her mind. She was sure now Malviana had influenced him. *How do we protect our people?*

"We continue to do what we've been doing," Blazel said, giving her a quick squeeze. "We fight and clean the malignant magic pools."

She hadn't spoken the last aloud. He must have sensed it through their connection, which scared her more than the Malvers. It meant they were becoming bond-mates. Rizelya tucked her thoughts securely behind a mind-shield. She wasn't sure she wanted that deep of a commitment, at least not now, while their lives were so unsettled and endangered. Either one of them could die during the next battle. Becoming heart-sisters—one step below bond-mates—with Kaieli hadn't bothered her. As a healer, Kaieli's life was rarely in danger.

"Oh, I saw Jaehaas with the Vhelopsi during the battle," Blazel said.

"How is he?"

"He went with the Haaslair contingent to help with the tidal wave and seems to have made friends with the Vhelopsi. I think it's a good thing. With Wisah still in the Sanctuary, and us flitting everywhere on the Gryphons, he's been feeling a bit out of place. You know how he hates to ride in the Gryphon nets."

Rizelya wrinkled her nose. As a centaur, the only way for Jaehaas to travel with the Gryphons was to be carried by them. After finding the Gryphons, a sabertiger had severely injured Jaehaas, and unable to run, the Gryphons conveyed him in a sling. He'd complained for days about how much the ropes chaffed his belly, besides it being undignified and embarrassing.

"I wouldn't want to travel that way either," Rizelya agreed.

Blazel pushed open the mess tent flap for Rizelya. Inside, a familiar blue-gray striped chestnut rump stood in line at the buffet tables. Blazel pushed forward and clapped Jaehaas on the shoulder, startling the centaur into rearing slightly.

"Ho, Blazel! Rizelya!" Jaehaas cried, clasping Blazel's wrist and pulling Rizelya into a hug.

"When did you get back?" Rizelya asked.

"A few days ago. I just missed you when you traipsed off to Posanreande Keep." Jaehaas scooped up a large portion of mashed tubers, then he gazed at the dessert table. He put half the tubers back. "I need to leave room. There be mookti berry pie!"

Blazel laughed, knowing how much Jaehaas loved the berries. They filled plates with food and joined their teammates. The others warmly greeted Jaehaas, and soon they were laughing, exchanging stories of the evacuation.

"Histrun is sending the Black Weave team to Haaslornas Keep in the morning," Rizelya informed them as she pushed her empty plate aside. "He wants to make it a garrison. And he's moving the camp."

Saffren shivered. "After fighting those new creatures, I can understand why. I didn't think anything could be worse than the janacks and brechas, but those banthues are awful." She made a face.

"I don't think those will be the worst we'll fight," Blazel said.

"No, they won't." Chariel's eyes were bleak, but not the silver orbs they turned into when she had a prophecy vision. "We'll soon see more twisted Posairs, like the creature you and Graak encountered at the black castle."

"I'll protect you." Aistrun winked at Chariel and kissed her cheek.

Rizelya looked down the table. "Loshera, you'll be traveling with old friends. Kothera and Metherposan are the new keep alphas of Haaslornas Keep."

"They are good people," Loshera said and sipped from her mug. "Metherposan showed great courage during our captivity."

Rizelya mentally pictured the map in her head and the distance to Haaslornas Keep. She'd become used to riding trussed up on Glork's back, but she missed the freedom of riding horseback. "Why don't we ride with them rather than fly? It's only a few octars from here."

"Won't Histrun be angry?" Grazeen asked.

Rizelya snorted. "He'll have too many other things to worry about moving the camp. Besides, I want to take my things with me, and Glork doesn't like being a pack multa. He's okay with toting me around, but my belongings—" she shrugged "—not so much."

"It's the same with Graak." Blazel smiled, twirling his empty fork. "I doubt two octars will make much of a difference. It will give the Gryphons a couple extra octars of rest. They've flown a lot the last few days."

Eiden laughed. "Korrik says they would gladly take the extra octars of sleep. He grumbled he didn't like being a multa either."

"Our multa, Kressy, is here," Leistral piped up. "We can take her. She's a sweet thing."

"Why don't you ride with us, Jaehaas?" Blazel said.

Jaehaas finished chewing, then shook his head. "Thanks for the offer, Blazel. But I be needed here more. Hairan and the Vhelopsi could use help in settling into Posanreande Keep. The Posanlair Clan Alphas were so impressed with the Vhelopsi, they be sending a herd of horses and multas to them." Jaehaas finished off the last of his pie, licking his lips. "Besides, once you get to Haaslornas Keep, you'll be flitting off again on the winged beasties."

Blazel gave him a wry smile. "You're right, of course. I miss your company."

Early the next morning, Rizelya said farewells to half her pack. Maellyn, Raeleen, Dehali, and Gehan were going with the main army, while Jaehaas was traveling with the Vhelopsi. The other person who'd become part of her pack, Laynar, had moved on. She'd done so well as a platoon alpha, Histrun had promoted her to a company alpha. A moment of grief pressed on Rizelya, remembering Laynal, Laynar's young sister, who'd so joyously joined their squad, only to be killed during the war.

Behind Rizelya tromped the Black Weave's support team, Aistrun, Leistral, Leistrun, Eidstrun, and Saffren's lovers, Maestrun and Nelstrun. She grinned. She still had a fairly large pack accompanying them on this mission.

Rizelya's mare, Kymaya, greeted her with a happy whinny, laying her head on top of Rizelya's shoulder and dribbling horse drool.

"I'm happy to see you, too, my old friend." Rizelya rubbed the horse's nose. She'd had Kymaya since she was fourteen, and in a way, the horse was a last link to her mother. Her mother's mare, Kylara, and Histrun's stallion, Telen, were Kymaya's dam and sire. She quickly put on Kymaya's tack and swung into the saddle as the others mounted their horses.

Rizelya's squad-pack seemed to be more fluid than most, gaining and losing members as Histrun and Naila sent her and Blazel on errands. She chuckled. With the addition of the people on the Black Weave team, including the Gryphons, her squad-pack would soon be a platoon. Once the fighting began in earnest with the Malvers, she was sure Histrun would give her battalion back to her. And to think, just a year ago, she hadn't wanted to be an alpha at all.

Her pack joined Kothera and Metherposan's people, and they left the main army, heading northwest. The farther they rode from the Barrens, the thicker and healthier the grass grew. The landscape changed into tall plains grass, sweeping vistas, and rolling hills. New buds sprouted on the few trees they passed, and pollen dusted the air.

Rizelya stretched in her saddle, breathing deeply the heady scent from the small white and lavender flowers dotting the green fields, and delighting in the spring day. Flying on Gryphon-back, she couldn't enjoy the countryside like she could from horseback. She expected the territory to be overrun by Malvers' monsters, since the keep was empty, and kept a constant watch for marauding monsters. It startled her when the outlying stone fences of the keep came into view, and nothing had attacked them.

The fields lay fallow and the pastures empty, with signs that the invaders had killed all the livestock here, as well. Since this keep would become a garrison, and the first line of defense against the Malvers, Rizelya doubted the new inhabitants would replant the fields or replace the livestock.

She twisted in her saddle, surveying the people in Kothera's group. All of them carried a pulser across their backs and bandoleers of projectiles crisscrossed their chests or were strapped to their waists. None were field hands or herders. A few support staff for the kitchens and stables traveled with them, and even they carried weapons.

The group stopped in front of the gate, which hung lopsidedly on its hinges. Dark stains covered the cobblestones inside the gates. Teams of Reds and a White Priestess had come through a long time ago to burn the bodies, but they hadn't cleaned away the evidence of bloodshed and death.

Kothera sat still on her horse, surveying the gates. Multiple emotions crossed the older woman's face: rage, terror, sadness. Kothera closed her brown eyes for a moment. When she opened them, strong-willed determination shone from them.

"All right," she ordered, "let's put this place to order, pronto! We were lucky we didn't have to fight any monsters or creatures along the way. I don't think our luck will hold. I want these gates secured. Derenposan, take a team and ride the wall's perimeter to ensure there aren't any breeches. Anyola, you and the other young ones, start cleaning. Begin with the keep-house. We'll all sleep there tonight."

The new keep residents streamed through the gates and set to work.

Rizelya considered what they'd needed to do at Posanreande Keep to make it habitable. "Saffren will check the well," she offered to Kothera, "and purify it if necessary. Leistral and I will heat the baths. This evening, Chariel and Loshera will escort any ghosts haunting the keep through the veil."

Kothera's face paled. "I hadn't thought of ghosts, but if what happened here was anything like at Posanreande Keep, there will probably be a few."

"There were only two at Posanreande Keep," Chariel said gently.

As they rode into the courtyard, the damage from the invasion became more apparent. The temple doors swung open on the breeze, and a huge hole gaped in the dome covering the outer sanctuary. Deep gouges marred the keep-house porch and railing, part of which was missing, as were the doors. A pack-house roof had collapsed, and another had two walls missing.

Grazeen and another woman with Green Talent hurried into the dining hall. Grazeen came out a moment later, a smile on her face. "The kitchen is intact. We'll have a hot dinner tonight." She turned back inside, followed by several men and women with green or brown hair.

Rizelya gladly left the men in her pack to work on clearing the bleached horses and multa bones littered the paddock's grounds. They needed to remove the bones so they could let out the horses to graze in the morning. While they worked, the Gryphons arrived and helped.

By the time Rizelya fell into bed next to Blazel, her body ached with exhausted. The keep still needed a lot of work to make it habitable again, but at least people slept in beds and had clean water to drink and bathe in. The gates and holes in the outer walls had been repaired, and Chariel and Loshera had led the half dozen ghosts through the veil.

Rizelya - 45 de Ahdar, 1076

Rizelya and her team crossed to the practice arena, where the Gryphons had roosted for the night. They sat in a circle on the sands, and Kaieli initiated the connection for the Black Weave. It startled Rizelya when it snapped into place. One breath she was alone in her mind, and the next, she was part of a greater consciousness.

Octars later, when Rizelya came out of the trance, she was still sitting in the same position as she'd started rather than sprawled on the ground.

"Well, this is new," she commented, looking around the circle to see the others were similarly seated.

Kaieli stretched. "A very welcome change. I'm not as tired either, and we drained three swamps."

Graak arched his back. *We're getting stronger. Perhaps one day, we won't go so deep and need bodyguards.*

"Ah, I don't mind Graak," Aistrun drawled from where he lounged on a bench. "It's easy work."

Well, I don't like my safety dependent on someone else.

Leistral leaned against the low wall separating the practice sands from the observation stands. "We should make sure you can come out of your trance quickly, if needed."

"That's a good idea, Leistral." Blazel stood and worked out the kinks in his body. "We'll try it in the next session. Right now, I'm starved."

Eidstrun strode into the arena, balancing a tray filled with meatrolls. Behind him trailed Anyola with a tray of steaming mugs. She gave large handleless mugs to the Gryphons, who had developed a love for taevo. Their people didn't have anything similar.

Rizelya sipped on her taevo, letting it slide down her parched throat. After being in such a connected state with the others, it seemed a bit strange to be alone in her body and mind.

An octar later, she was again in the Weave, floating in the joy it brought. They hadn't started draining the malignant pool that set her teeth on edge—did she have teeth?—when she heard her name being called.

"Rizelya, come back. We need you here, now."

The voice came from far away. *Who is it? What is wrong?*

It's Aistrun. We must end the connection, the Kaieli part of their consciousness said.

A moment later, Rizelya returned to her body, but her mind reeled, making her feel queasy. Holding a hand to her stomach, she recalled Aistrun was going to try calling them out of the trance.

"It worked," Blazel said, looking a bit green. "But not fun. I think I'm going to be sick."

"Take a few deep breaths," Chariel said. "It's just disorientation from coming back to your body too quickly. It will pass."

Chariel looked fine, chipper even. Rizelya groaned and dropped her head between her knees, taking deep breaths. A few milcrons later, the dizziness and queasiness stopped. Someone tapped a cool container on her arm. When she glanced up, Leistral handed her a canteen of water.

"Let's hope we don't have to be pulled out of the melding until we're ready." As Rizelya sipped more water, she felt better.

Glork stood, fluffed his feathers and shook his fur, then resettled on the sand. *I suspect it is like everything else. Practice will make it easier.*

The team practiced being pulled from the connection interspersed with draining the malignant magic pools. As Glork predicted, each time became easier than the last. Disorientation still hit Rizelya when she was jerked from their melding, but at least nausea no longer plagued her.

On the fifth day, Rizelya, Glork, Blazel, and Graak flew over Haaslornas Keep's lands. Not one swamp remained. They landed at several known nest sites to discover dry ground and no sign whatsoever of the nests. As with Posanreande Keep, the land changed, becoming healthier than ever before.

They met with the keep alphas in the practice arena since the Gryphons were too large to fit in their office. Kothera waited on a bench at the bottom of the stands, while Metherposan lounged with his butt pressed against the railing, and his arms crossed over his chest. Blazel joined him at the railing, leaning his elbows on it and facing the stands.

"Your new lands are clear of malignant magic." Rizelya sank onto the bench next to Kothera. Even though going in and out of the Black Weave trance was easier, the cleansing still exhausted her. "You won't have to worry about any Malvers' monsters attacking you."

"That's good news," Kothera said, running her hand through her pale red hair. "We've fought some of those new creatures—the floxidor and skeaeters—while you worked. But, thank the Mother, none of the banthues have shown up."

I doubt you'll see banthues if there aren't any Gryphons here, Graak said, rubbing a talon on his beak. *The Malvers created them to counteract us.*

Metherposan huffed out a breath. "That's a relief."

But be watchful. Graak's tail thumped on the sand, flinging small puffs of dust in the air. *The Malvers can twist many creatures, even Posairs.*

Metherposan stood up straighter, frowning. "A man went missing yesterday, before you drained the last swamp. A few days before that, I caught him beating up Anyola."

Rizelya leaned forward, resting her elbows on her knees. "Did you notice anything unusual about him? Did he have any black spots?"

Metherposan scratched his jaw. "Aye. When I hauled him off her, I noticed he had a black splotch on his neck. We confined him to his quarters, but he escaped."

Rizelya's stomach turned at the news. "I'd check everyone to make sure they don't have any black spots. Histrun seems to have experience with this disease. I suspect it's caused by the Malvers."

Nothing good comes from them. Glork shivered.

"Now we've drained the malignant magic pools," Blazel added, "you might not have any more cases. But it'd be good to check."

Graak dropped his paw that was scratching at the underside of his wing and fluffed his fur. *I'll send Daerik and Nelstrun to Histrun, and let him know. Saffren can get by with only one of her lovers for a few days.* He winked. *They'll return with any suggestions or instructions on what to do if you find more.*

"Thank you." Kothera inclined her head.

Rizelya held out her hand, and Blazel helped pull her to her feet. She stifled a groan. "Our work here is finished. We'll be leaving at first light. It was a pleasure to help you."

As Rizelya settled into bed next to Blazel, news of the infection spreading here bothered her. Perhaps they should hurry to Dehanrandevir Keep on the Gryphons rather than ride the horses. Except, she wouldn't abandon Kymaya to strangers or in a dangerous place like the garrison. And she didn't know if draining the magic pools would help stop or prevent the infection from spreading.

Chapter 9

Wisah - 50 de Ahdar, 1076

Wisah sat in her office, just outside the Supreme's, studying the book on making magical weapons. She didn't understand a quarter of it. She put the book down and rubbed her temples to ease the headache blooming behind her eyes. A young girl ran into her office.

"Priestess Wisah," the girl panted. "Gryphon Sheekeek is back, along with several other Gryphons."

Although the priestesses could use mind-speech, they usually didn't. The Posairs developed the ability to aid them while fighting the monsters. Instead, the Sanctuary community relied on the young girls living there to run messages.

"Thank you, Lorenda. Wait a moment, and I'll find out where you can tell the gatekeepers to send our new guests." Wisah walked to the Supreme's office door and poked her head inside. "Sheekeek and Maendy have arrived. Where would you like to meet with them?"

The Supreme put her fingers to her lips as she considered it. "Do you think Sheekeek can fit in here?"

"He should be able to. He's smaller than the other Gryphons."

"Then here will be good."

Wisah kept the concern from her face as she returned to the outer office and told Lorenda. She smiled as the girl sped off on her errand, fondly remembering the days when she ran errands for the higher level priestesses. Wisah summoned a housekeeper and placed an order for refreshments.

While straightening the papers scattered on her desk, Wisah glimpsed the Supreme, leaning her head back on her chair. Even after four chedans, the Supreme hadn't fully recovered from the psychic attack and the resulting heart attack, although she tried to act like it. Wisah had caught her napping in her chair more and more frequently, and she fretted that a new Supreme hadn't been born yet. This one was old and frail and could pass on at any time. Why hadn't the Goddess sent her replacement? As she was learning from being the Supreme's assistant, the duties and obligations of the Supreme were enormous and would take a long time to learn. Time the Posairs didn't have.

Hearing the distinct click of Gryphon talons on the marble floors, Wisah shook off her worry and plastered a smile on her face. A few moments later, Lorenda showed the new arrivals into her office, and with a quick bow, she hurried on to her next errand.

"Welcome to the Sanctuary." Wisah inclined her head, touching her heart before hugging Maendy and Maellyn. Her smile turned into a grin, and she stroked Sheekeek's soft feathers. "Welcome back, my friend. Thank you for bringing them here."

He trilled and leaned into her hand. *It was my pleasure, Wisah. I've wanted to visit the great helstrim forges. Maendy generously gave me a tour.*

"Do you know why the Supreme summoned us?" Maendy asked, her red eyes flaked with gold held a worried look. A colorful band held back her dark, chocolate-brown hair. She had broad shoulders, and her arms were muscled from years of work at the forge. At just under six-feet tall, she towered over Wisah.

Maellyn had the same hair and eyes flecked with gold as her mother. Although she was a few inches shorter and wasn't as broad-shouldered. She'd been in Rizelya's first squad-pack, which included other Talents besides Red. She carried a helbraught and used it to kill the monsters and invaders with lava. Her greatest accomplishment, though, was creating glass in the goggles propped on her head. They protected people's eyes when they rode on the Gryphons. Wisah smiled as she remembered the story Maellyn had told her of getting a bug stuck in her eye, which prompted her to make the eye protection.

"I do, but I'll let the Supreme tell you. Maellyn, you can leave your helbraught in here." Wisah led them through her office to the Supreme's, picking up the book she'd been reading as she passed her desk.

"Supreme, may I introduce you to Helstramiester Maendy and her daughter, Maellyn. You already know Sheekeek."

They entered the room, and Maendy and Maellyn made the gesture of obeisance: hands clasped together, fingertips resting on their bowed forehead. Sheekeek simply dipped his head.

"Blessings. Come in. Sit." The Supreme waved to the chairs in front of her desk. As they settled into seats, with Sheekeek sitting on a large cushion placed on the floor, a housekeeper entered with the refreshments, handed them out, and then left.

After allowing her visitors a few moments to relax and drink some of their taevo, the Supreme set aside her cup. She leaned forward with her elbows on her desk. "The Malvers have escaped their exile. They have one driving purpose: to seek vengeance on those who imprisoned them. They will kill or subjugate any who stand in their way or try stopping their evil. We can't let that happen.

"During the Great War, we possessed magical weapons effective against the Malvers and their perverted magic. But many are no longer useful, either due to age or because they need Black Talent to function. We need you to create new weapons, based on the old, we can use to fight the Malvers and their creatures."

Wisah handed the book on making magical weapons to Maendy. "This may help you. I don't understand it, but maybe it will make sense to you."

Maendy took the book and flipped through the pages, then placed it on her lap. "We have a similar one in the helstramiester library. It's required reading for our final exams to become a helstramiester. We should be able to get some of the ancient weapons working." She rubbed her hands together. "I'm excited to start. I've heard about them my whole life, but I haven't ever seen them. Our hall didn't have any of the old weapons."

"They were all stored here after the war," the Supreme said, "to protect them against misuse. And then, I'm unhappy to admit, my predecessors forgot them because we had little need for such weapons. When the Malvers' monsters appeared, the men gained the ability to shapeshift, and so we still didn't need them. Wisah will show you the cache. I'd prefer the ancient weapons stay here at the Sanctuary for safekeeping and that you work here."

"But there isn't a forge here," Maendy objected.

"You'd be surprised what you can find in the Sanctuary." A rare smile lifted the corners of the Supreme's mouth. "Why don't you examine the weapons and the room where they're kept first before making any assumptions? Wisah will show it to you in the morning. Sheekeek, you're welcome to join them if you desire."

Sheekeek dipped his head. *I very much do, Your Grace. Our people didn't hide our history away like yours. We have stories of the weapons of old. I'm interested to see them.*

If the Supreme took offense at Sheekeek's subtle rebuke, she didn't show it.

Maellyn shifted in her seat and raised a finger. "What's my role?"

"You are here because of your inventiveness." The Supreme pointed to the goggles on Maellyn's head. "You are gifted in creating new things. The weapons of the past may not work as we wish. Your task is to make new ones to work with our current Talents and abilities."

Maellyn blushed.

"I had a cottage prepared in the village for you. I imagine you'd be more comfortable there than the guest quarters, since you'll be here for some time. You've had a long journey, and I'm sure you could use some rest. Afterward, Wisah will take you to the weapons cache. Report back to me when you have results."

Wisah stood up, signaling the end of the audience. The others stood and bowed before leaving the Supreme's presence. Wisah led the party through the temple, outside, and around the grounds to the small village of temple staff, where she showed the two women their new cottage.

She joined them for dinner. "Last I saw you, Maellyn, you were at the war front. How did you end up here?"

"We're living in a different world." Maellyn scratched her head and appeared bemused. "The Gryphons relayed a message to Histrun that the Supreme required my services. Jorreek volunteered to fly me to Strunlair Keep, where we picked up Mother. He flew me here, too. The Gryphons are great companions. I almost envy the Black Weave teams and their Gryphon partners. I'd like to partner with Jorreek."

Wisah grinned. "It's amazing how the Gryphons have integrated into our lives. Sheekeek is now one of my best friends. I couldn't imagine life without the Gryphons in it." She leaned her elbows on the table and rested her chin on her fist. "Now, tell me about what happened after I left the war front."

Maellyn must have sensed her need to hear about Jaehaas and told several stories about him. When Wisah went to bed, she missed him more than ever. She wished he could join her at the Sanctuary. He'd love learning about the old weapons and discovering new ones.

Wisah - 51 de Ahdar, 1076

Wisah led Maendy and Maellyn across the temple grounds to the library. Spring roses, freesia, and sweet peas perfumed the early morning air, and red tulips and yellow daffodils brightened the walkways. Wisah took a deep breath, happy to be outside and for the winter snows to be gone. She wished Jaehaas were here. He'd enjoy the beauty spring brought to the Sanctuary. She waved at Sheekeek, where he waited for them at the library entrance.

Maellyn stopped to stare at the massive building. "This whole thing is a library and filled with books and scrolls?"

"It is." Wisah nodded and headed toward the doors.

Maendy's forehead creased. "The weapons cache is in the library?"

"Not in it, but under it. Far fewer people visit the library than the temple." Wisah continued up the stairs and into the building while she considered the incongruity. "Or perhaps our ancestors built the library on top of the workshop to hide it."

"Wow!" Maellyn turned in a circle, taking in the rows and stacks of books and scrolls. "All this available knowledge. I may never leave. Strunell Keep only has about a hundred books, and I've read them all. Several times. And I've been on the Scourge War frontlines for lunadars with Rizelya. We didn't have much time for reading there."

Wisah smiled. She hadn't realized how much she missed the library until after she'd traveled all across Lairheim with Rizelya with nothing to read. "You'll find plenty to read here and in the weapons cache. It includes a library of books the previous Supremes didn't want our people to have access to."

Maellyn shook her head. "How sad."

"You won't think so after you've read some of them!" Wisah shivered, remembering her horror when she'd read *The Malvers Rise to Power: A Treatise on Corruption*. "Some are rightfully hidden and should be kept that way."

Sheekeek tilted his head and studied her. He lifted a talon and gently tipped her head, so the sunlight filtering through the high windows shone on her face. *Interesting.*

"What?"

Your eyes are changing color. They used to be a pale blue.

Maellyn stepped closer to peer into Wisah's eyes. "He's right. They're darker than I remember them."

Wisah closed her eyes to hide them from their scrutiny. *It can't mean what I think it does. It's just the lighting in the library.* She took a deep breath, trying to center herself.

"Come on, the lab is this way." Wisah wound through the stacks toward the back.

How is your training with the Supreme going? Sheekeek asked as they walked.

"Busy." Wisah sighed, tucking a strand of hair behind her ears. "Between it and becoming her assistant, I haven't had any time to myself. And now you're here, I'll have help in cataloging the weapons cache."

They reached the back corner where the shadows hid the door. Wisah pointed to the several lanterns sitting on a nearby table. "Grab one of those to take with you. The stairs are dark."

She lit a lantern, then unlocked the door and muscled it open. "I need to remember to bring some oil next time to oil the hinges. I keep forgetting." She shrugged.

"Here, let me help." Maendy reached up and placed her hand on the top hinge. Golden-brown light flared from her palm to surround the metal. She squatted and did the same for the bottom hinge. "Now try it."

Wisah tugged on the handle, and the door nearly banged her nose as it flew open. "Be careful going down the stairs. They're steep. We need to shut the door behind us so no one unauthorized comes down."

"I can fix that too," Maendy said, her eyes gleaming. "Are only the four of us and the Supreme authorized?"

"For now, until you decide if you need help."

Maendy plucked a strand of her hair, then held out her open hand. "Wisah, Maellyn, give me a strand of your hair. Sheekeek, give me a feather and some fur." She cupped the items in her hands and murmured a spell over them. She placed her hands flat on the door, continuing to chant. A dark brown light beamed from her hands to cover the door. After a moment, it faded and Maendy removed her hands. The hairs, fur, and feather were gone. "Now only those authorized may open the door, or even see it. I'll need a hair sample from the Supreme to add her to the authorization spell."

Wisah narrowed her eyes and studied the door. It appeared the same to her. She mentally shrugged as she picked up the lantern and motioned for Maendy to go down first. Maellyn followed her mother, and Sheekeek went next. His claws and talons clicked on the stone steps as he descended. Wisah stepped onto the stairs, shutting the door behind her. With the lanterns, and Sheekeek's natural glow, she didn't have any trouble seeing the stairs. Soon, she stood at the bottom.

As she walked around the room, lighting torches, the others gasped in awe as the light revealed the room's contents.

"This is a treasure trove!" Maendy's eyes shone with delight. "It's even better than I imagined it." She wandered to the various tables and piles of weapons. "Ooh, these are interesting." Maendy sat at the table with the crackling lightning globes, pulled a pad of paper and a pencil from her jacket and started writing notes.

"We've lost her now for a while," Maellyn said with a smile. "What else is in here?"

She wandered around the room, exploring, poking into corners, and perusing the titles on the bookshelves. Wisah and Sheekeek tagged along behind for a while until they became absorbed in their own exploration of the ancient artifacts.

Wisah pulled out a scroll with an interesting title and sank to the floor, reading. The tale about a White Priestess—not Shandir—fighting in the Great War engrossed her. She dropped the scroll when Maellyn called out, "Wisah, Sheekeek, you need to see this!"

Maellyn stared at a spot on the wall that didn't seem to have anything on it. Her forehead crinkled, and she nibbled on a fingernail.

"What is it?" Wisah asked. She couldn't figure out what had Maellyn so fascinated.

"I think there's another room behind this one," Maellyn finally said.

Ooh, a secret room! Sheekeek gushed as he and Wisah joined Maellyn. *How exciting.*

Wisah examined the wall with both eyes and fingers. She discovered symbols faintly etched into the stone that tugged at her memory.

Do you think there are more weapons and books in it?

Maellyn shrugged. "Only one way to find out. Although I work better with metal than I do stone. Here goes." She rubbed her hands together, and sandy-brown light spun between her palms. Before she placed her hands on the wall, Wisah stopped her.

"Wait! I think I can open it without destroying the wall."

She'd finally recognized the symbols as the same as those in the spell books she was studying with the Supreme. Wisah doubted just touching the symbols in order or even randomly would open the door. The key was to use the correct pattern. She closed her eyes, picturing the pattern the Supreme used to unlock her safe. Wisah's eyes flew open, and she leaned closer to the wall. There! In the center of the symbols was a depression carved into the stone. She removed her necklace of office from her neck and pressed the pendant into the notch. It clicked into place. The symbols glowed a pale silver, and Wisah turned it in the same sequence as for the Supreme's safe. A bright light crisscrossed the area, forming an eight-pointed star before the stone grated, revealing a door slowly sliding to the side.

She jumped aside as stale, pungent air whooshed from the room. She recovered her necklace and put it back on. After the air cleared, she, Maellyn, and Sheekeek peered inside.

"Mother!" Maellyn called. "You need to come look at this."

Maendy looked up and blinked at them. "What's so important?"

"Come see." Maellyn motioned with her hand. "You'll want to see this."

Maendy reluctantly put down her pencil and the globe she'd been examining and joined them at the new doorway. "Oh my!"

Inside was an enormous laboratory. A preservation spell had kept its contents in immaculate condition. Glass bottles and apparatuses filled several tables. On one table sat a partially assembled staff. Another table held a globe with several pieces around it. It appeared similar to the one Maendy had been studying. A cabinet on the wall revealed multiple tools. Some were miniature, and some Wisah had no idea what they'd been used for. Near the far wall, a circular forge squatted with a huge bellows hanging above it and a stone trough lay on the floor. A channel for water crawled along the ceiling, running down the wall and to the trough. On the anvil sat a hammer along with a cube of metal.

To Wisah, it looked like the previous workers had left the workshop in a hurry, intending to return, but never did. What could have pulled them away?

Maendy and Maellyn explored the laboratory and workshop, emitting excited "oohs" and "ahs" as they discovered new things.

Maendy turned to Wisah, her face glowing with happiness. "This is fabulous! We'll definitely be able to create weapons— and other amazing tools—with this equipment. Where to start first?"

"How about getting dinner?" Maellyn suggested. "I'm starving. We can start working in the morning when we're fresh. Why don't you study the book Wisah gave you? It should give you a starting point."

Now Maellyn had mentioned food, Wisah's own stomach grumbled. They'd been down here all day.

Rizelya - 51 de Ahdar, 1076

Rizelya and her pack exited Haaslornas Keep while the sunrise painted the sky with soft pinks and oranges. The Gryphons flew high above them. Green shoots poked through the ground in the fallow fields. Two women with brown hair, pulsers strapped to their backs, herded the few multas Kothera and Metherposan had brought with them to a pasture. Rizelya's group clattered southwest along the crushed sheadash stone road and away from the keep's fenced grounds. A few startled rabbits hopped into the brush as they passed. A flock of starlings wheeled overhead.

An octar from the keep, they crossed the remnants of the first swamp they'd drained. The marshy ground in the middle of the savanna was the only evidence it had existed. The budding leaves on the widely spaced oak trees gleamed with health and vitality. In the distance, Rizelya heard the *tap-tap-tap* of a woodpecker.

They stopped at a former swamp, now a lake, for their midday meal. The roots of the tall cypress trees sank deep into the water, and the tree's branches provided shade in the warming sun.

"This is remarkable!" Grazeen squatted next to the water and sifted through the dirt. "The grub and insect life are a hybrid of what you'd find in a savanna and in a swamp. Our magic must have changed them so they could live in this new environment." She lifted a handful of dark earth to her nose and sniffed. "The earth is regenerating. This will be fertile ground, capable of supporting grazing livestock and herds of billocks and ducorns by next summer. I don't see any trace of damage from monster slime, and I haven't noticed any since we left the keep." She stood, dusting her hands together to rid them of the residual dirt.

Saffren dipped her hand in the water, closing her eyes. "The water is a mix of swamp and freshwater. As the winter rains fill the lake, it will become fresher, and those fish needing the swamp's murkiness will die."

"Unless they, too, have been changed," Loshera said, hope in her voice.

Saffren gracefully stood and shook the water off her hands. "It's a possibility. I can't tell for sure unless someone wants to try their hand at fishing."

Did you say you needed a fish? Oslerru asked, hope filling his voice. As an osprey-type Gryphon, he loved to fish, and the Barrens hadn't offered much opportunity for him to indulge. Not waiting for an answer, he soared into the blue sky.

Rizelya swallowed the bite of trail bar she'd just taken and shook her head. "We don't have time. We need to reach the safe-house before dark."

"Do we need to stay at safe-houses anymore?" Blazel tossed a pebble into the still water. "If the Malvers' monsters can't form without the malignant magic pools, then we should be safe."

"There are other dangers besides the monsters, like narhili beasts." Rizelya's left calf cramped in sudden phantom pain as she remembered being poisoned during a narhili attack. "I doubt the lack of malignant magic will affect them. No, we stay at safe-houses." She popped the last of the trail bar into her mouth.

Oslerru dove, his long sharp talons held in front of him, and his eyes glued to the water. He struck without making a splash, then rose. A fat fish wiggled in his talons.

Saffren, do you want to examine this before I eat it?

"Yes, I would, thank you." She strode over to him and held the proffered fish for a short time before handing it back to him. She smiled. "It has been altered. The Goddess truly guides our magic."

Oslerru gripped the fish in his talons as he tore chunks off it. Meanwhile, Graak and Glork dove into the middle of the lake, swimming under the water. A few moments later, Glork's head cleared the surface, a fat fish wiggling in his beak. He swam to the nearby bank and climbed out, water streaming from his fur and feathers to eat his catch. Graak joined him a moment later, while the other Gryphons took turns diving into the lake. Soon, Gryphons lazing in the sun sprinkled the lake shore.

When everyone finished eating, they remounted their horses.

We will catch up to you, Glork said sleepily, his head resting on his front talons. *The sun feels so good.*

"Nap safely," Rizelya said, and kicked Kymaya into a trot.

During the ride to the safe-house, Rizelya noted how healthy the landscape had become.

"I wonder how Lairheim will look in a few years when there aren't any swamps," she commented to Chariel.

Chariel's eyebrows furrowed. "What do you mean?"

"Look how healthy everything is now. I think the malignant magic pools draw their substance from the land around them."

"And like parasites, they infect the host."

"That's an interesting thought." Rizelya considered it while they rode to the safe-house.

The next day, as they traveled farther south, the oak trees grew less frequent and the grass shorter, and clumps of sagebrush covered in purple blooms dotted the landscape. They needed to travel nearly to the Barrens to reach a place to ford the Storengher River. Late in the afternoon, black sand-glass glittered on the horizon, and Rizelya loosened her helbraught in its holder on her saddle. The group's chatter quieted, and the Gryphons drifted lower until they flew only a few feet above their heads.

An octar later, when they reached the shores of the river without incident, Rizelya let out a relieved, "We made it!" She reigned in Kymaya. "Let's camp on this side tonight. Once we cross the river, we'll be in Dehanlair Province, and we haven't drained any malignant pools there yet."

The others agreed and dismounted.

Blazel waved at the Gryphons. *Graak,* he called. *We're camping here tonight.*

The Gryphons tilted their wings and soon landed. Graak staring at the river. *It's shallow here, only a few feet deep. Do you think there are any fish in it?*

A silvery tail shone in the fading light, and a fish plopped into the water as it jumped in search of insects.

"That answers your question," Blazel laughed. "We could use a few fresh fish ourselves."

Graak lowered his head feathers and glared at Blazel. *I'm not your errand fledgling.*

Glork dropped his beak in a Gryphon smile. *I don't mind. I'll fetch you a fish.* He waded out into the river, his tail lifted high, as he stared intently into the depths. A few moments later, he snapped his head under the water, and when he raised it, he had a large fish gripped in his beak. With a flick of his head, he tossed it at Blazel's feet.

Let the real fishers take care of it, Glork. A creamy white Gryphon with a stripe of short brown feathers on top of his head and a matching stripe across his cheeks and necks streaked to the river. His talons flashed, and Oslerru rose with a fat fish gripped in his talons. He flapped his dark brown and tan wings to fly over and dropped the fish at his partner's feet. Maestrun grimaced as he picked up the slimy fish, then thunked it on the head.

"Do you want the entrails?" he asked as he slid open the fish's belly.

Please! Oslerru snatched the offering as Maestrun tossed it to him, gulping it down with obvious relish.

By the time Rizelya and the other women had gathered wood and started a fire, Glork and Oslerru had caught them five good-sized fish. Grazeen wandered the riverbank and found watercress, onions, and carrots, which she stuffed into the fish, putting them over the fire to cook.

The group sat around the campfire, sipping taevo and listening to the chirping of the crickets and the low-pitched buzz of the cicadas. Aistrun wrapped his arm around Chariel, and Rizelya rested her head against Blazel's shoulder. Saffren sat cuddled with Maestrun, while Eiden leaned against Leistrun, who was twirling the end of her yellow braid in his fingers. Loshera sat tucked between Morlek's front talons, his head resting gently on the top of hers. Grazeen squatted in front of the fire, feeding twigs into it. Kaieli sat with her legs tucked up and her arms wrapped around them, her cheek resting on her knees. Eidstrun and Leistral sat next to each other, their fingers entwined. Their Gryphon partners stood like sentinels as they guarded the perimeter.

"It was nice not having to deal with Malvers' monsters today," Rizelya said, breaking the silence. "We should drain the closest magic pool in the morning before we cross the river and enter Dehanlair Province."

Kaieli stretched and yawned. "That's a good idea. At each safe-house we stay the night in, we should cleanse the nearby pools. If we do that, we'll have a good portion of them cleared by the time we reach the keep. I'm beat." She crawled into her bedroll and curled up in it with her back to the fire and the others.

Rizelya gazed at her, wishing she could do something to help her heart-sister heal her grief.

"It's been a long day for all of us," Blazel said. "I'll take the first watch, Aistrun you do the second, and Eidstrun you'll have the last one." Aistrun and Eidstrun nodded in acknowledgment. While everyone settled into their bedrolls, Blazel pulled his flute from his pack.

I'll sit watch with you, Blazel, Graak said, crouching behind Blazel.

Rizelya fell asleep to the soothing sound of Blazel's flute.

The next morning, after a cold breakfast of trail bars, the Black Weave team gathered in a circle. Rizelya's consciousness instantly blended with the others, and the malignant magic pool drew them like a beacon. Their melded energies had just about finished when Rizelya heard Aistrun's voice urgently calling to her. Unwilling to leave the job unfinished, the group quickly purified the last of the rancorous magic.

Rizelya blinked her eyes open, swearing as she grabbed her helbraught from where it lay next to her and jumped to her feet. On the other side of the fire-shield Leistral had formed around the insensate team, Aistrun and the other men, in their warrior forms, battled a large pack of floxidor. The fire-shield shook from a fireball spewed by a banthu. Boreek, who wasn't part of the melding, screeched as he attacked the larger creature. Above them, Morru, Brogkek, Sterkek, and Oslerru fought with several banthues.

Jezhan, Aistrun's red sorrel gelding, kicked his hind leg, catching a canid in the side. Kymaya, Rizelya's mare, reared and dropped down, stomping on a floxidor sprawled on the ground.

Rizelya added her strength to the fire-shield. Kaieli, Chariel, and Loshera huddled on the ground, still groggy from the melding. Blazel shook his head clear and picked up his pulser. Eiden, Saffren, and Grazeen were on their feet, their helbraughts glowing with their magic.

Torlek and I will protect the priestesses and healer, Keeru said. He and Torlek stood next to the women and stretched their wings over them, then flared, creating their own type of fire-shield. Loshera's Gryphon partner, Morlek, hovered above the shield. He'd protect them from the air.

Rizelya nodded to Leistral, and they released their hold on the shield. As soon as it was down, the remaining Gryphons leaped into the air, and Blazel shot his weapon into the floxidor pack, taking down a large canid. Six floxidors broke from the pack and rushed toward them. Saffren and Eiden threw ice spears from their helbraughts, while Rizelya and Leistral attacked the beasts with fire.

Rizelya swung her blade at a floxidor, but it blocked the strike with its horns. It twisted its head, and she would have lost her helbraught if she hadn't been gripping it so tightly. As it was, it pulled her off balance, and she stumbled to the side. Before it could drive its horns through her, Grazeen drove her helbraught into its side with a guttural yell. Grimacing, she pulled it out and turned to block the slavering jaws of another beast. Rizelya lifted her helbraught high and brought the blade down, severing the canid's head.

She sensed something behind her and whirled in time to slice through the skeaeter's antennae reaching for her. On the back swing, her blade bit deep into its neck. Another of the creatures had wrapped its rope-like antennae around Leistral's neck. It rose onto its four rear legs, jerking the noose tight. A bolt of yellow light struck its belly. The poison from the projectile quickly spread and turned the creature's insides into a glutinous substance. Leistral hung limply, still captured by the dying insect. Rizelya raced to her and cut off the antennae. *The damned things have a temporary paralyzing toxin.*

Ware! Glork yelled.

Rizelya's eyes widened as a flaming chunk of banthu descended on them. She huddled over Leistral, forming a shield around them. The debris struck the shield and burned to ash. As she stood, Eiden killed the last skeaeter.

Kaieli hurried to Leistral, who was still having trouble breathing. She put her hands on Leistral's chest and bronze light pulsed from them. Leistral took a deep, stuttering breath, and the color returned to her pale face.

"Anyone else hurt?" Kaieli glanced around.

People shook their heads.

"Where did they come from?" Chariel stared at a floxidor corpse.

"We're only about a dozen measures from the Barrens." Rizelya toed a skeaeter with her boot. It twitched, and she blasted it with fire.

Eiden leaned on her helbraught, gazing south. "Do you think the Malvers know what we're doing with the magic pools and are trying to stop us?"

Rizelya shrugged. "It's a possibility." Since Malviana had broken free of her prison, she hadn't bothered Rizelya's dreams. In a way, it worried her more than the new creatures did. The dreams could clue them into what Malviana was doing.

Loshera bent and examined a floxidor corpse, then motioned for Chariel and Kaieli to join her. They spoke quietly for a moment. Kaieli unsheathed her helstrablade, sliced open the creature's belly, and pulled out its organs. While they studied them, Rizelya worked her way around the battlefield, burning the corpses. Leistral, finally recovered, joined her.

"Rizelya, leave a skeaeter body for us, will you?" Chariel asked, glancing up.

She nodded and continued her work. By the time she finished, the priestesses had completed their examinations and had her burn the bodies they'd been studying. Blood and gore covered Kaieli up to her elbows. She stood holding her arms out to the side, her nose wrinkled.

"Well," Aistrun said, tapping his foot, "what did mucking around the insides tell you?"

"These aren't normal creatures," Kaieli said. "Oh, they started out that way at least the skeaeter did. The canid is a swamp creature, twisted by loathsome magic. I'm going to wash this off." She strode to the riverbank.

"Magic has altered them," Loshera said, hunching her shoulders. "The Malvers had their hand in changing these creatures. But although malignant magic wrought the changes, the creatures aren't dependent on the foul magic. I'm afraid we'll see more as the Malvers regain their powers."

Rizelya scowled. Fighting the Malvers' monsters made life hard enough, but now they'd have to contend with these new beasts. She'd hoped cleaning the rancorous magic from the swamps would put an end to living in constant danger. With a heavy heart, she gathered her things, scattered by the fight, and mounted Kymaya.

They forded the river and rode quickly through the landscape. This side of the river hadn't had a chance to heal yet. The plants were wilted, and the few animals they encountered seemed scrawnier.

While in the security of the safe-house, the Black Weave team cleaned the pools in the surrounding area of the vile magic. When Rizelya came out of the trance, she frowned at the scraping and snorting noises around the outside fences.

"Narhili started nosing around," Aistrun said, "shortly after you began your work. I don't think the Malvers like you messing with their power sources."

"They'll like it less when we purge the biggest one," Kaieli said, crossing her arms.

Rizelya's forehead creased. "Which one?"

"Shandir's Crater. Once we're strong enough, we have to clear it."

Rizelya shuddered. If the magic pools fueled the Malvers' magic for creating the new horrendous beasts, how much worse would the creatures be if the Malvers accessed the crater's massive one?

Chapter 10

Blazel - 54 de Ahdar, 1076

As the sunset struck the clouds a brilliant red, Blazel and his pack rode through Dehanrandevir Keep's gates. After the first attack, the new creatures hadn't bothered them again, and they made good time. Even so, Norvela and Aradehan had arrived before them. Blazel surveyed the keep as they rode through the courtyard. Norvela's people had cleaned it already and repairs were underway. His team wouldn't need to help make it habitable. He smiled at the keep alphas waiting for them on the keep-house porch. He'd missed the traditional greeting when they arrived at Posanreande and Haaslornas Keeps.

"Welcome, Blazel, Rizelya." Norvela waved at them, the beads at the ends of the tiny braids in her orange-red hair clicking together. "How was your journey?"

"Uneventful," Rizelya answered, "except for right before we crossed the river. A pack of those new creatures attacked us."

"Was anyone hurt?"

Rizelya shook her head, then indicated Kaieli slightly behind her. "Nothing Kaieli couldn't heal. It's a nice perk about traveling with a healer."

"We've had trouble with them, too," Aradehan said, brushing his strawberry-blond hair from his yellow-green eyes. His thick beard was a darker red. "We sent patrols to the nest sites southeast of here, but they reported there aren't any swamps or nests there. Is that your doing?"

"It is." Blazel threw his leg over Lighzel's rump and stepped off her saddle. He stretched, then turned and helped Loshera from her horse. He knew the priestess was quite capable, but he'd grown up in the Sanctuary and showing respect and courtesy to the White Priestesses was ingrained in him.

"We're draining the malignant magic pools as we travel." Blazel climbed the porch steps and gripped Aradehan's wrist in greeting. "We won't have to stay as long as we planned."

Several younger fighters jogged to them to take their horses to the stable, while Blazel's group dismounted and wearily climbed the keep-house stairs. Cleansing the pools with the Black Weave took a lot out of them, and combined with the days of travel, they were all exhausted. Both Loshera's and Kaieli's faces were drawn and pale. They still hadn't completely recovered from the lunadars as Scourge captives. As they entered the keep-house, Blazel hoped they wouldn't be fighting any pitched battles with the Malvers anytime soon. He and the other fighters could use some rest after the war with the Scourge. He snorted to himself at his wishful thinking.

Norvela led them to the entertainment room, where the large table easily accommodated them all. Blazel's eyes lit up at the bowls piled high with mookti. He loved the sweet purple berries. Steaming mugs of taevo accompanied the snack.

Norvela rolled her mug between her palms. "Will draining the swamps also stop the attacks by the new creatures?"

Chariel shook her head, wiping the berry juice from her chin. "No. We necropsied both a floxidor and a skeaeter. While foul magic had altered them, it didn't create them like it does the Malvers' monsters. Even killing their makers may not eradicate them."

"We'll deal with them as we can," Aradehan said, stroking his beard. "They're easier to fight than the janacks and brechas, and they don't damage the land with their slime. The damned banthues are a pain in the ass. They fly over the walls."

"They don't like ice, though." Norvela chuckled. "Several of our fighters use the pulsers to shoot ice spears. The ice mixes with the banthues' sulphuric gas, and they explode. As much as I hate the invaders, I love we now have weapons to use on these new menaces."

"Now, if they would work on the Malvers," Rizelya said with a sigh, "it would give us a definite advantage. From what the Supreme said, the Malvers are nearly immortal. We'll be fighting the same people our ancestors did. I don't know if it also means we can't kill them."

"We should be able to." Blazel gazed at the ceiling as he tried to recall what he'd read in the ancient books he'd found in the Sanctuary's library as a young man. "Our ancestors killed them in the Great War."

"But they used Black Talent." Chariel leaned back in her seat. "The only Black Talent we have is us—" she pointed to the Black Weave Team "—and we're not actually Blacks."

"I believe we're something more." Loshera placed her hand over her priestess medallion. "Something better. The Goddess brought us together and taught us how to form the Black Weave for a reason. It isn't any coincidence we found this technique now, just when the Malvers return to Lairheim."

"You think the Weave can kill them?" Eiden asked, leaning forward.

Loshera nodded. "I do."

The talk turned to other things until dinnertime. After dinner, Aistrun entertained the garrison with stories, including some featuring the people in the garrison and their heroic fights with the invaders. It had only been by the grace of the Goddess, and their allies, the Gryphons and Vhelopsi, that the Posairs had defeated the Scourge and remained free. A rush of anger flushed Blazel's face as he thought about the Malvers and their desire to subjugate his people. The Posairs had already stopped an enemy from forcing them into slavery. They would stop this one, too.

Over the next two days, the Black Weave team emptied the surrounding malignant magic pools. Packs of the new creatures attacked the keep by day while at night, narhili beasts left their tracks in the fields. Before they could drain the last pool, a nest of Malvers' monsters erupted from it, fully formed without going through the larval stage. Eidstrun, as a skilled tracker, accompanied the platoon Aradehan sent after the monsters, while Sterkek and Boreek flew above them, bored with watching the team sitting in silence.

"We should try draining the pool these monsters came from," Rizelya said as the platoon clattered from the garrison. "It would allow us to discover what effect it has on the monsters. Can they survive without the malignant magic that created them?"

Blazel shrugged. "I like your idea. None of the pools we've cleared recently spawned monsters. This will be a good experiment."

"We're still learning what we can do," Chariel said, fiddling with the tiny braids at the side of her face. "While it feels like anything is possible while we're in the Weave, we need to discover our limitations. Better now than in the middle of a battle with the Malvers."

"Good point," Grazeen said. "I agree. Let's get started before the platoon catches up to the monsters."

The team entered the practice arena, where the Gryphons waited for them. Warmth oozed from the sands, and Blazel shook out a blanket for him, Rizelya, and Kaieli, while Aistrun spread one for the other ladies.

We haven't tried drawing off the magic from a pool while the monsters are being killed and flowing back to it, Graak reminded them, as they settled into place. *We don't know what effect it will have on us.*

"Yeah," Saffren shuddered. "It could knock us on our butts like the first few times we melded."

"Or make us sick, like it did when we're jerked out of it." Blazel rubbed his stomach and scrunched his nose.

Everyone settled into their favorite positions, and Kaieli held out her hands. Blazel joined his hands with her and Rizelya, closing his eyes and taking several deep breaths. A few moments later, he became one with the blended consciousness of the Black Weave. As their minds flew to the pulsing, corrupt energy signifying a large pool of malignant magic, he sensed smaller dots of the same corruption below them. Fire magic flared nearby, and a dot snuffed out. The fighting-pack had found some of the Malvers' monsters and were engaged in battle with them.

The larger mass of evil tugged at them, drawing their consciousness to it like a magnet. Kaieli wrapped their Black Talent around the sickening magic, squeezing it from the land and eliminating it. Malevolent energy streamed into the pool, and Blazel surmised the fighters had killed a monster. More and more energy streaked to the pool, where it was absorbed, before the Black Weave wrung it out. Eventually, no more streams returned to the pool, and they finally neutralized the last of the malignant magic. The entity that was their melded consciousness rose from the pool, extending its awareness outward. One pinprick of evil remained. They zoomed after it, unwilling to allow the aberration to continue to exist.

The pinprick resolved into a brecha hurtling toward the Barrens. They formed an energy net, blocking the brecha's headlong retreat. It fought, lashing out with its spines, but the entity didn't have a physical body. From their perspective, the brecha appeared to be nothing more than magic given form. They pulled on the string of evil energy, unwinding it from the brecha.

Kaieli released the melding, and Blazel blinked as he came back into awareness. The shadows in the arena told him they'd been in the trance for quite some time. He lay sprawled on the ground, his cheek pressed into the blanket. He sputtered and sat up, grateful they'd started sitting on a blanket. Otherwise, he'd have a mouthful of sand. The others were also pushing themselves up.

"Hey, are you all okay?" Aistrun asked, helping Chariel to sit up. "You've been out of it for nearly three octars."

Blazel nodded, but immediately regretted it. Pain flared behind his eyes. Leistral handed him a cup of cool water. After drinking it, his headache eased.

"We're good," Rizelya croaked and took another drink of water. "That wasn't fun."

No, it was not, Glork agreed. His head drooped, and only the tip of his tail flicked. *Draining the pool while parts of it kept returning isn't efficient and takes longer.*

"It will be much easier, and better," Loshera observed, rubbing her temples, "if we drain a pool when there aren't any monsters out of it."

Agreed, Graak said. *But we may not always have that luxury.*

Blazel concurred. As he stood, his legs felt wobbly and weak. "I'm glad we don't have to do any more work today. I feel as drained as the swamp we cleaned."

"Me, too," Rizelya agreed as she held out her hand for him to help her up.

A short time later, the platoon rode through the gates. Eidstrun joined their group as they relaxed in the entertainment room. His pale blond hair was still damp from his bath. He eased his tall frame into a chair and gratefully accepted the cup of taevo Maestrun offered him.

"So, Eidstrun, what was it like on your end?" Aistrun asked after telling him about their experiment.

Eidstrun wrinkled his nose. "Odd. The monsters weakened during the fight, but they didn't simply die or disappear. I assume it occurred at the same time you were cleansing the swamp. It seemed as if their energy escaped from them, like water draining from a water skin, which made them easy to kill. The lone remaining brecha tore off, heading south toward the Barrens. Sterkek, Boreek, and I chased it. Damn, the bugger moved fast. We'd almost caught up to it when it suddenly stopped."

He shuddered and stared into his mug. He took a long drink before continuing. "Strands of ugly, dark energy bristled from it, and it looked like it was unraveling. It was the weirdest sight I've ever seen. I hope I don't see it again."

Rizelya reached over and poured more taevo into her mug. "You just might. It aligns pretty much with what I saw happening." She yawned. "I don't know about the rest of you, but as soon as dinner is over, I'm going to bed. That last session wore me out."

"I'll be right behind you," Blazel said.

Later, after eating, Blazel and Rizelya tiredly climbed the stairs to their room. As she flopped on the only bed in the room, he shut the door, leaning against it, watching her with hooded eyes as she stretched. Norvela had given them a single room, and he planned on taking advantage of being alone with her.

Rizelya looked over at him. "What?"

"I'm thinking of how best to ravish you. We have this lovely room all to ourselves."

"Ooh. We do." She languorously raised her arms over her head and arched her back. The thin top she wore under her red leather jacket stretched taut over her breasts.

He felt his manhood harden in response. All tiredness left him as he sauntered across the room, divesting his jacket and shirt as he went. He knelt on the bed, straddled over her, and bent his head to kiss her. One hand found the soft globe of her breast. She moaned as he massaged it and deepened their kiss. A very long time later, they laid together under the sheet, exhausted but satisfied. As he drifted to sleep, he thought about the years he'd spent as a lone wolf. He hadn't ever imagined he'd love anyone as deeply as he did Rizelya. He blessed the events that had brought them together.

Malviana - 58 de Ahdar, 1076

Malviana walked through the halls of her castle, pleased to see it returned to its former glory. She paused by a large window, pushing aside the thick velvet curtains to gaze into the eastern courtyard. Nearly two hundred twisted Posairs, now known as Maldiers, practiced their new magic. They'd arrived in a steady stream over the past two and a half chedans. Their individual hatred and cruelty fueled their transformation, making each one unique. She expected more to arrive in the coming chedans. Malviana held hope some would make the full transition to Malvers.

Keandran and Korand, her first Maldiers, were by far the most magnificent of the new species. To her delight, several women also answered her song, and if Keandran and Korand weren't careful, their leadership would be in jeopardy. The women were meaner and more ferocious than any of the men.

She propped open the window and stood by it transfixed, watching black whips snake out in unison to strike straw targets, representing Posairs in their warrior form. The whips wrapped around their victim's necks or extremities, holding them, while the wielder injured or incapacitated them with the greatest amount of pain possible.

A Maldier woman, her olive-green scales shimmering in the pale light, jerked her magical rope. The wings attached to her back rippled, and her forked tongue slithered from between her long fangs as she tugged. She spat a spell, severing the straw head from its neck. The woman caught the head in her taloned hand as it flew to her, her jaws elongating until her open maw engulfed the head. Too bad it had only been straw.

"Damn it, Cloresh," Keandran yelled, stomping over to her. "Stop eating the targets."

"Jusst practissing," Cloresh hissed, her long tongue licking her scaled lips. "Tasstess good. But not as good as Posair flesh. When will we have live victimss?"

Good question, Malviana thought. They'd have to raid the border along the Barrens soon to capture slaves for her new army to practice on. Straw targets didn't struggle or beg for their lives. Nor did they bleed and die.

Keandran looked toward the castle, and his gaze unerringly found hers. Their blood exchanges connected them enough so she could send simple thoughts and emotions to him—but nothing like the mind-speech she discovered the Posairs had developed. They hadn't possessed the ability a thousand years ago when she and Mordar had ravished the land.

"Soon, Cloresh. Soon." Keandran pulled his lips back from his wolf teeth. "I, too, hunger for their blood and screams." He returned his attention to the troops and barked an order.

The troop rolled their whips into circles and hung them on belt loops while servants set up clay targets. The Maldiers brought their hands, paws, or whatever passed as hands in front of them, several inches apart. Dark magic crackled in the space between their hands, and when they threw it, lightning balls sizzled and zoomed toward the targets. Sparks of electricity struck some of the targets, and had they been alive, they would've danced and writhed with excruciating pain, allowing the Maldier to strike a killing blow. Malviana noted the snake woman, Cloresh, had a deadly aim.

After everyone had a turn with the targets, Korand carried in a cage filled with the bothersome swamp rats. The large rodents burrowed into everything and resisted the Malvers' efforts to change them. Even worse, they provided little death magic. Korand had finally found a use for the vermin.

He put the cage on the ground, opened it, then ran back to the wall. As the rats scurried out, lightning bolts whizzed through the courtyard, a few catching a rat in its grip while most others rolled along the ground, striking unwary Maldiers. Cloresh's lightning bolt gripped a rat in its light, and she stalked to it. She picked it up, and, ignoring the electricity still skittering on its skin, popped it into her mouth, swallowing it whole. She frowned at the wriggling tail poking out and shoved it in, too. Then, with a grin, she looked around the courtyard, aimed at, struck, and ate three more rats.

Malviana smiled in appreciation. *Cloresh is one to watch. Too bad I don't like sex with women.* She turned away from the window and continued to the outer courtyard, her long skirts swishing around her feet. The vassals guarding the door opened it for her, and she strode into the sunlight, muted by the distortion fog. The Malvers had spent too many years on the cursed island where the mists blocked the sunlight. They couldn't handle direct sunlight anymore. Besides hurting their eyes, it caused blinding headaches and burned holes in their skin. Before they could directly attack the Posairs, she needed to find a spell to allow them to leave the confines of her castle. They couldn't always skulk in the dark or under heavy, hooded capes.

Duke Borgedier met her at the bottom of the stairs. "We have him ready for you, my queen." He offered his arm to her. She placed her hand on his elbow, and he escorted her to the central courtyard.

A small brown, white-spotted, owl-type Gryphon lay trussed up near the altar. Its bright yellow eyes glared at Baron Jorvelden. The Gryphon flared, trying to burn through the rope, but the magical ropes held it tight, and it screeched in pain and frustration. Malviana didn't believe the rumors that the creatures were intelligent. She certainly hadn't heard them talk.

She strolled around it, examining the perfect blending from bird to feline. "Where is its rider?"

"There wasn't one," Jorvelden said, lifting a shoulder. He murmured another spell, and the Gryphon was suddenly silent, even though its beak opened. "We haven't seen any Gryphons or Posairs, except the flock of small owl-types hanging around our border. They've yet to see our new recruits enter the castle."

"Good. They won't know how large our army is before we want them to."

"Oh, mother," Morvana said, sauntering into the courtyard, "it's beautiful. Are you going to sacrifice it?"

"Of course, as soon as the others arrive. This lovely sacrifice is only for us. The lower ranks can feed on lesser sacrifices."

Malviana studied the animal while she waited for her other children, as well as the dukes and duchesses of her council. She stroked its gray and white fur and sighed, luxuriating in its softness. She'd have to be careful so she wouldn't ruin its pelt. It would make a glorious coat, and perhaps she could find a use for the feathers, too.

"We're all here, Your Grace," Magdelyn said softly.

Malviana nodded and ambled to the Gryphons' head. It followed her every move with its enormous eyes. She raised her arms and prayed to Mordaga. Smiling at the animal, she plunged her long, sharp claws into the side of its neck. It threw back its head and shuddered. She'd been careful not to nick an artery.

"Release its voice," Malviana commanded. "Mordaga revels in the sacrifice's screams."

Jorvelden nodded, and a moment later, a warbled screech echoed from the castle walls.

Malviana contemplated the altar as she decided on how best to wring the most death magic from the animal. She touched the stones on her necklace and pointed her wand at it, chanting a spell. A thin, red light blazed from the end of her wand, cutting into the Gryphon like a sharp knife. With a fine touch, she skinned the fur pelt from it, bright-red blood spraying her face.

"I want a coat made from the pelt," Malviana ordered. Borgedier hurried forward, picked up the bloody skin, and carried it to the castle steps, where a lower ranking Malvers took it from him.

Over the next four octars, Malviana remembered her lessons at Mordar's side. She inflicted as much pain on the dumb animal as possible, glorying in the magnificent death magic flowing into her. By the time she plunged her hands into its heart, releasing it into oblivion, she glowed with power, and her gemstones couldn't hold another speck.

She stood back, panting, as the others placed their jewels in the offering bowl. "If there's this much magic in a small Gryphon, imagine how much more there is in a large one."

"Shall I obtain one for you, Mother?" Mordeven asked, his eyes bright from the infusion of power.

She walked to him, trailing a bloody finger down his cheek. He inhaled deeply, his nostrils flaring. "No, my darling, not yet. We must put this power to a better purpose. We currently can't turn enough Posairs to make a difference. There are too many of them. They spawned like rabbits during our incarceration. What we need to do is produce more creatures to fight our battles for us, to whittle our enemy down—"

"And capture slaves for our use," he said dreamily.

"That too." She turned to leave, then considered the Gryphon's carcass. "Give that to the Maldiers. They will enjoy the meat."

"Yes, Your Grace," Magdelyn said with a bow. "I'll see to it."

"As soon as it's taken care of, join us in the laboratory, Magdelyn. The rest of you, follow me."

Malviana led the others back into the castle and down the stairs to the laboratory. When they emerged three days later, nearly a thousand new banthues, giant baethors, floxidors, and skeaeters wandered the swamp surrounding the castle.

Rizelya - 58 de Ahdar, 1076

Early in the morning, Rizelya and her team gathered in the stables to saddle their horses. She recalled the many mornings she'd done the same thing while traveling across Strunlair Province in search of the cause for the new control-janack. At the time, they'd had to use barding for their horses to announce their clan affiliation, but during the Scourge War, Histrun and Keshanal had discouraged the tradition. Too many packs now included people from multiple clans. But so far, none were as unique as her squad-pack.

Her pack included Blazel, who had once been a lone wolf and not part of any pack, and Chariel, the Gray Seer. Chariel had never left the Sanctuary's territory until a prophecy—and Rizelya—had dragged her out to find the Gryphons. Chariel's laughter rang out, and Aistrun bent down and kissed her passionately. Rizelya smiled at their display of affection. She doubted Chariel would ever return to the confines of the Sanctuary's cloister and relinquish her relationship with Aistrun.

Rizelya looked up at the sound of wings as the Gryphons took flight to scout ahead for them. They didn't belong to any Posair clan. Her fighting-pack only lacked a member from their new allies, the Vhelopsi. She snorted to herself as she stepped into the stirrup to mount Kymaya. It was probably only a matter of time until one or more of the Vhelopsi attached themselves to her pack. She seemed to attract the strange and unusual. Likely because she loved it and invited them in.

She surveyed the courtyard, noting her team stood next to their horses, ready to leave. She and Blazel offered a quick farewell to Keep Alphas Norvela and Aradehan, then led the Black Weave team from Dehanrandevir Keep. They took the road north, their horses' hooves clattering on the sheadash stone. Rizelya breathed in the fresh air scented with last night's rain—one of her favorite scents. She tilted her head back, and a grin crossed her face at the sky clear of clouds. Along the side of the road, Rizelya glimpsed a narhili paw print in the mud.

"Where are the narhili beasts coming from?" she wondered aloud. "They live in the swamps, and we've cleared them in this area."

Blazel leaned over in his saddle to peer at the prints. "If they're still alive, it means they aren't pure malevolent magic, like the janacks and brechas. They're either searching for new homes, or the Malvers could have mutated them."

"Ugh, just what we need," Rizelya moaned. "They're bad enough as nocturnal beasts. I don't want to have to worry about them in daylight." She reached down and rubbed her calf where a narhili had bitten her. She'd almost lost her leg to the poison. The thought of being attacked by the beasts made her jittery, and she kept scanning the grass for dark shapes slinking through it.

"We made it!" she whooped when they arrived at the safe-house without an attack. During the night, they heard scratches at the gates and digging along the walls. The next morning, when Blazel and Aistrun investigated, they found claw marks on the gate and paw prints on the ground.

"I've never seen narhili beasts do this." Aistrun frowned at the gate. "This isn't normal behavior."

"We haven't cleaned the swamps around here," Rizelya said, half-heartedly. "They came from those. Nothing abnormal about that." Even she didn't believe her own words.

Before they left the safety of the safe-house, they drained the nearby swamps. In one, a nest of monsters had been ready to leave, and as they'd cleared the malignant magic, the life force of the monsters winked out.

"I could become accustomed to killing them like this," Rizelya commented when their minds returned to their bodies.

"So could I," Kaieli said, rubbing the back of her neck. "No one gets hurt or injured."

They left the safe-house, confident they wouldn't run into any Malvers' monsters. Birds flew over them in the bright, clear sky, and chipmunks and squirrels dashed off the road at their approach. Around mid-afternoon, they crossed the boundary between Dehanran Territory and Dehanrolos. Purple sagebrush and vivid pink and red wild-rose bushes interspersed the birch trees, their silvery leaves nearly fully budded. A blue jay swooped over them. Wide swathes where nothing grew showed where janacks had rolled through in the recent past, their slime killing the plant life.

They were a measure away from reaching the safe-house for the night when Kymaya pranced to the opposite side of the road. Glowing red eyes peered from the foliage, and a dark brown narhili leaped at them. Its protruding jaws, filled with fangs, snapped at Kymaya's legs. She kicked out, catching the lead narhili in the side. It yelped as it rolled, then righted on its six limbs. Rizelya pulled her helbraught from its holder, flowing her fire magic into it. Other beasts exploded from the bushes, snarling. She sensed the men jump from their horses and shift into their warrior forms. Their thick fur would protect them from the narhili's poisonous claws.

The first beast charged Kymaya. Rizelya swung her blade, catching the narhili's hind legs as it zipped under her horse. She grabbed the pommel of her saddle as Kymaya crow-hopped away from the beast. A shot rang out, and the narhili tumbled, a hole in its side. Rizelya glanced over her shoulder as Chariel chambered another projectile. The men's horses' reins filled Loshera and Kaieli's hands.

Glork dove through the trees with his talons outstretched. He screeched as he dug them into a narhili's back. Flapping his wings hard, he gradually rose from the ground with his burden. The beast snarled and lunged, trying to sink its teeth into Glork's belly. He raked it with his rear claws, shredding its throat and chest. As soon as he'd climbed above the trees, Glork flared, burning the corpse to ash.

A pained yip made Rizelya whirl around. A narhili gripped Leistrun's leg in its jaws. Eiden buried an ice spear into it, but even in death, its jaws clung to Leistrun's leg. Rizelya urged Kymaya toward him and lopped off the narhili's head with her helbraught. Leistrun reached down and pulled the jaws apart. Blood poured from the multiple puncture wounds. He turned as if to resume fighting.

"Leistrun!" Rizelya yelled. "Get your butt onto a horse. Moving will make it worse." He snarled at her, caught up in the fight. She accessed her alpha power and infused it in her voice as she commanded, "Now!"

He jumped, startled by her rare use of her alpha power, and hopped to his horse. A beast stalked him from behind. Eiden tossed another ice spear from her helbraught, jamming it into the narhili's eye.

Kymaya sidled to the right, alerting Rizelya. She jerked her foot out of the stirrup and swung her blade down in time to kill another beast before it could bite her. She turned Kymaya in a circle, surveying the battle, but none of the dozen narhili remained alive.

Leistrun had shifted back to his natural form. Sweat bathed his pale face.

"Eidstrun, help me lay him down," Kaieli cried.

The big man loped over, still in his warrior form, and easily lifted Leistrun from the saddle. Leistrun screamed in pain. Thankfully, he quickly passed out. "Sorrrry," Eidstrun said. He glanced around and found a place that wasn't covered in blood or gore and gently laid his friend down.

Eiden ran to Leistrun, tears streaming down her face. She cradled his head in her lap. "Don't you dare die on me, Leistrun. We still have too much to do together. Remember, we're supposed to visit Alkaak. I can't go without you."

Leistral strode over, a mask of calm plastered on her face. She squatted next to Leistrun. "Dying from narhili poison, little brother, is unacceptable." Her mask faltered and anguish tightened her lips. "Fight it, damn you!" She stood, swiping tears from her eyes, and stalked to the decapitated narhili. She blasted the corpse with her fire magic, burning it to ash.

Kaieli's ashen face was a mask of professional calm as she rushed over and used a scarf to tie a tourniquet around Leistrun's thigh. "He isn't going to die," she assured Eiden. She turned to his calf, bronze healing light streaming from her hands. After a long time, it faded, and she sat back on her heels. "I've stopped the progress of the poison for now, long enough for us to reach the safe-house. How far is it?"

"Only a measure or so," Rizelya said. "We were so close to safety."

"The faster we reach the safe-house to finish the healing, the better."

Brogkek landed, keening in distress, and folded his dark brown and beige wings across his back. *I'll take him. We will be there in a matter of moments.*

Kaieli, you will ride with me, where you should be, anyway, Keeru said from above. His disapproval of her riding a horse, instead of her Gryphon partner, was evident in his voice. The space where they'd fought wasn't large enough for the two Gryphons to land at the same time.

Kaieli grimaced, rolling her eyes at her Gryphon's admonishment. Eidstrun lifted Leistrun onto Brogkek's back. Eiden climbed on, holding Leistrun close, and leaned forward, gripping Brogkek's shoulder fur tightly. As soon as Brogkek vacated the spot, Keeru landed, and Kaieli vaulted onto his back.

"We'll be there shortly," Rizelya told her. "Just take care of Leistrun."

"He isn't going to die," Kaieli said through gritted teeth. "I won't let him die."

Chariel came to stand next to Rizelya and watched Keeru and Kaieli rise above the trees. "That isn't a healthy attitude. We all must return to the Mother's Womb when our time comes. And we don't determine when that is. As a healer, Kaieli should know this."

"She does. She's still grieving Rolstrun's death and doesn't want anyone else to lose a beloved." Rizelya surveyed her pack but didn't see any wounds. "Is everybody else okay? Anybody scratched? Even a scratch is bad."

Her people examined each other and their horses, then shook their heads.

"We're good," Blazel said, standing from peering at Lighzel's belly.

"If malevolent magic tainted these beasts," Chariel observed, "we don't want it to infect any scavengers. We don't know how the Malvers are changing the animals. We should burn the carcasses."

"You're right. Leistral, help me burn these."

"Gladly!" Leistral scowled at the beasts, tromping around the small glade, burning the bodies with more glee than she normally would.

Rizelya sighed as she burned the beasts on the other side of the road. She didn't have a sibling, but she glanced over at Aistrun. They'd been close friends since childhood, and were as close as most siblings in their society. If something happened to him, she'd be as upset as Leistral was over Leistrun's serious injury.

In less than a quarter octar, they'd cleaned the area. Rizelya hauled herself into Kymaya's saddle and kicked her into a gallop, anxious to reach safety and check on Leistrun.

A few milcrons later, they clattered into the safe-house compound, and after settling her horse into the stable, Rizelya strode to the house with Blazel at her side. The rest followed closely. The sharp, pungent scent of healing herbs made her eyes water. Kaieli pressed a poultice on the wound, which still oozed ugly black pus.

Rizelya crossed the floor and stood behind Kaieli, placing her hand on her shoulder. "How is he?"

"Not good. I've done all I can for him."

Loshera approached the cot and laid a hand on Leistrun's forehead. "He's still with us. Why don't we try healing him with the Black Weave? Surely, if we can heal people of the nucla poisoning in the awful conditions of the slave pens, we can heal him of this poison."

Hope lit Kaieli's eyes.

"But the Gryphons can't join us in here," Saffren protested. "It's way too small for them."

"We didn't have any Gryphons with us in the slave camp," Kaieli said. "To cleanse the poison from him, we shouldn't need them. Hurry! Gather 'round. We don't have much time."

The Black Team circled Leistrun's cot, holding hands. This time when they merged, Rizelya didn't sense the melding of their consciousnesses even when Kaieli deftly wove their Talents together. With her enhanced senses, Rizelya could see the pernicious poison seeping into tissues around the wound and spreading. Kaieli first pulled on Grazeen's Green Talent, and instead of snelks, magical leeches formed, sucking the poison from the tissues. They swelled, dropping off when they couldn't hold any more poison. Kaieli tugged on Rizelya's fire magic, using it to burn the poison-filled leeches. Saffren's water magic washed the wound and tissue clean. Kaieli used her own earth magic to knit the damaged tissues and muscles together. Finally, she released the Black Weave.

The world around Rizelya reeled, and she stumbled back to keep her balance. She sank to the floor and put her head between her knees. Soon, the dizziness and queasiness receded. "Next time, we do that sitting down," she said, holding her stomach.

She heard retching and gritted her teeth so as not to join whoever it was losing the battle with the nausea.

"Agreed," Chariel said.

"Did it work?" Eiden asked, crawling to kneel beside the cot.

Kaieli closed her eyes for a moment. She smiled as she opened them. "There isn't a trace of poison in his body. We did it!"

Worry filled Eiden's eyes as she gazed at Leistrun. "Then why isn't he awake?"

"He needs sleep to finish healing and to recover. He'll be all right, I promise."

Grazeen pushed to her feet. "After that, I'm famished. I'll fix us something to eat." She stumbled and Maestrun caught her elbow. He put his arm around her, letting her lean on him, and walked with her to the stove. Soon, the aroma of beans and pan bread replaced the odor of healing herbs.

The next morning, Leistrun awoke, sore and hungry. Eiden covered his face with kisses. He had a limp which Kaieli assured him would disappear in a few days.

After they cleared the surrounding malignant magic pools, they rode through the safe-house gates. Everyone kept sharp eyes on the undergrowth bordering the road. But no one saw any sign of narhili or any other Malvers' creatures. Rizelya pushed them into a fast pace, only slowing to rest the horses. Twilight was lengthening the shadows when they crossed under the gates to Dehanranle Keep. A large bridge arched across the river, joining Dehanranle to Haaslornde Keep on the other side of the river.

The war host had arrived before them, and people filled both keeps to capacity. A tent village covered Haaslornde's fields, and the Gryphons camped along the riverbank on both sides of the river.

Rizelya found Naila in the keep-house. "Where do you want my pack?" she asked, swaying with exhaustion.

"Dormitory room," Naila said, pointing up. *We reserved a large one for you upstairs. The rest of your squad-pack is already settled in. Were you successful?*

"We were. Although, along the way, narhili attacked us. It wasn't even dark yet!"

Naila's eyebrows furrowed, and she swore. *With the other twisted beasts, we don't need those too. I'll alert the sentries. Was anyone hurt?*

"Leistrun. But he's okay." She paused and rubbed her face. "We found another use for the Black Weave. We used it to save him."

When you've rested, you'll have to tell me about it. It sounds fascinating. One day, after we defeat the Malvers, I'd love to experience the Weave. She patted Rizelya's shoulder, then shooed her from the office.

As Rizelya lay in bed with Blazel, she missed the private quarters they had shared in Dehanrandevir Keep. He was a much more enthusiastic lover when they were alone. She grimaced at the sounds of Saffren, Maestrun, and Nelstrun's enthusiastic reunion. Nelstrun had only been gone a few days. Behind the thick sheadash stone walls of the keep-house, Rizelya slept curled up in Blazel's arms, secure they were safe from attack by any of the Malvers' creatures.

Chapter 11

Blazel - 61 de Ahdar, 1076

Blazel was pouring his second mug of taevo when a young boy ran up to him and Rizelya with a message to meet with Histrun and Keshanal.

Blazel stood, wiping his mouth with a napkin. "I imagine they'll want us to start draining the magic pools around here. The practice arena is probably in use as housing. Aistrun, will you find us a place where we can work and is comfortable for the Gryphons?"

Aistrun touched his fingers to his forehead. "Sure. Broogk can help me."

Blazel and Rizelya jogged to the keep-house and climbed the stairs to the keep alpha's office, where they found Histrun and Keshanal. A large square table, with the map of Lairheim spread out on it, took up the side wall. Two large desks sat side by side under the window, open to let in the spring air. The muted noise of people practicing with their pulsers disrupted the idyllic setting.

Histrun put aside a document he was reading and leaned back in his chair. "How did it go? Any progress?"

"Go ahead and sit." Keshanal gestured to the chairs in front of Histrun's desk. She scooted her chair closer to Histrun.

Blazel glanced around the room, a frown furrowing his brow.

"Where's Naila," Rizelya asked, before he could. "She's usually in these briefings."

"More people arrived from Keistanlair Province this morning," Keshanal said. "She's overseeing settling them in."

"Our mission went well," Rizelya said as she sank into a chair. "We've drained the malignant magic pools in both the areas surrounding Haaslornas and Dehanrandevir, as well as the portion of Dehanrolos we traveled through."

Blazel crossed his ankle over his knee. "We didn't have any problems with Malvers' monsters, especially after we cleared an area. But we did with the other creatures." He told them about their findings and the narhili attacks.

"We could make more headway with another Black Weave team or three," Rizelya said. "Have the priestesses arrived from the Sanctuary yet?"

"I expect them this afternoon," Histrun said, glancing out the window. "The Gryphons have taken it easy on them, and they've made several stops along the way. None of them had ridden a horse more than a few measures from the Sanctuary, and riding Gryphon-back is even more strenuous."

"How have things been here, sir?" Blazel asked.

Histrun's forehead crinkled as he scowled. "Not good. In addition to people disappearing, there's an infection sweeping through the army. It's similar to the one I saw years ago at Dehanlair Keep." Histrun swallowed hard and looked away.

Blazel recalled Dehanlair Keep was where Histrun's bond-mate, and Rizelya's mother, had been killed.

Histrun cleared his throat and continued. "The Clan Alpha at the time, Mendehan, wandered into a swamp and contracted a parasite-type infection. But we don't believe any of these people have gone into the swamps. We don't know how they're getting sick."

Keshanal grimaced. "We've had to lock them up for everyone's protection because they become violent. We had to execute a man for murder. The victim said something he didn't like, and he plunged his helstrablade into the man's heart.

People just don't do that. In all my years, I've only seen a few murders committed by rogues, and we'd already exiled them from the clan. Those infected are fine one day, and cruel and violent the next."

Blazel frowned, drumming his fingers on his knee. "I spent three years living in the swamps, and I ran into a few rogues, even though I tried to avoid them. But sometimes they'd find me and attack without provocation. I had to kill them to survive. I don't know if this strange illness infected them, or if they were simply hideous people."

"Did they have black splotches or gray skin?" Histrun asked.

Blazel shook his head. "Not that I recall."

"Then they weren't infected."

Keshanal rubbed her forehead. "We don't want to kill them as rouges, but we may have to. None of the healers or priestesses here can do anything for them. Kaieli is a gifted healer, and Chariel and Loshera are extremely strong in their respective Talents. Perhaps your Black Weave team will have better success."

Rizelya lifted a shoulder. "We can try. Where are they?"

"I'll show you." Histrun pushed his chair back and stood. He selected a key from a cabinet on the wall.

"I've asked Kaieli, Chariel, and Loshera to join us," Rizelya said as they headed outside.

The healer and priestesses joined them in the foyer, and Histrun led them to a storage shed at the back of the keep, guarded by two men. The guards stepped aside, and Histrun unlocked the shiny new lock. A foul stench wafted from the room when the door opened. Inside, four men and a woman slumped on the floor. Even in the poor light, Blazel could see the paleness of their skin. A black patch covered the woman's left cheek and another one spread across her right forearm. She glared at them, hate filling her eyes. Something seemed wrong with her fingers. Blazel squinted at them, blinking when he realized they were longer than normal.

As soon as the woman saw the two priestesses, she went into a rage. "Filthy bitches! Scum!" She continued to yell obscenities as she rushed toward them, her hands raised as if to claw them.

Loshera stepped back, her face pale with shock. "Nelieh?"

Chariel gripped the woman's wrists, struggling to keep from being clawed. She stared into the woman's eyes for a long moment while Nelieh screamed curses at her. She finally shook her head.

"Rizelya, if you would form a shield in front of me, I'd appreciate it."

Chariel's calm voice surprised Blazel. The woman continued to struggle in Chariel's grip.

Rizelya did so, and Chariel dropped the woman's hands and scurried to the door. The woman banged her fists on the shield, ignoring the sparks flying around her. She didn't quit until Chariel and Loshera stepped out of sight.

Histrun slammed the door shut, leaning against it as fists pounded on it. "What was that about?"

Chariel's eyes were bleak. "I don't think there's anything we can do for them, at least not for Nelieh. She's too far gone. The parasite attaches itself to its host's soul and eats away the person's humanity and goodness. I doubt even the Black Weave can cure them."

"I can't believe that was Nelieh," Loshera said, shaking her head, her eyes glassy with shock.

"We have to try." Kaieli turned imploring eyes to Rizelya and Blazel. "I know her. She was a squad-pack alpha at Posanreande Keep. We can't leave them hurting." She rubbed her arms. "They are filled with so much rage, I can barely tolerate standing here."

Blazel put a comforting arm around her. "We don't have to remain near them. We drain the swamps from a distance, so we should be able to do this, too."

Histrun relocked the door and turned to the guards. "I don't want anyone entering here."

They saluted him and returned to their positions on either side of the door.

Blazel and the others walked toward the courtyard. He replayed Kaieli's words in his head. Many people still harbored pent up anger over the horrors inflicted during the Scourge War. He hoped eliminating the malevolent magic would stop the contagion. They stopped at the keep-house, where Aistrun lounged on the steps, waiting for them.

"Let me know if you can do anything for them or not," Histrun said. He turned toward the shed. A haunted look crossed his face before he strode into the keep-house. If Blazel's team couldn't cure those people, Histrun would be the one responsible for putting them down as rogues.

"Did you find a place for us?" Blazel asked.

Aistrun nodded and stood. "Broogk and I found an excellent spot. The others are there now." He frowned and put an arm around Chariel's shoulders. "Hey, what happened? You look like you've seen a ghost, Chariel."

"A living ghost." She shuddered. "I thought the Scourge were evil. But that woman was worse. She craved hurting people more than food or even sex. She wanted to tear people's hearts out and eat them while they were still beating!"

A chill blasted Blazel. He couldn't imagine such a hunger.

Aistrun led them to the small wooded area behind the paddocks. They wound through the trees to a large clearing. The Gryphons, who were part of the Weave, lounged in the dappled sun. Their Posair partners resting either between their forepaws or against their sides. The team's guardian Gryphons crouched around the perimeter as sentinels. As Blazel and the women entered the clearing, Leistrun kissed Eiden's cheek and hobbled to stand next to Brogkek. Leistral, Eidstrun, Maestrun, and Nelstrun joined their Gryphon partners to surround the Black team.

Chariel filled the others in on what they were going to try first, then they clasped hands. Blazel's mind merged with the group's greater consciousness. It sped toward the shed and the dark spots of evil inside it. Blazel sensed a shield-like barrier around each infected person, and no matter what they tried, they couldn't penetrate it. Dejected, their minds returned to their individual bodies.

Tears streamed down Kaieli's face. "We can't do anything for them. I thought our power would be great enough, but it isn't."

"In a way," Loshera said, folding her hands in her lap, her eyes bleak, "it's good to know we aren't all-powerful, and we have limits. But I had hoped we could help my former friend."

Blazel agreed. Too much power could make them hubristic, which would lead to misusing their power and becoming like the Malvers. They merged again and drained the malignant magic pool a few measures from the keep.

Blazel rubbed his face, clearing the last of the trance from his skin. He stretched, tilting his head back. Overhead flew a flight of Gryphons with women dressed in white robes riding on their backs.

"The priestesses from the Sanctuary have arrived," he announced, pointing upward.

Rizelya climbed to her feet and brushed the dirt from her behind. "Let's go greet them! With this new infection, we could use help in cleansing as many of the malevolent magic pools as possible. I believe the pools are causing it, or at least spreading it."

They trooped from the wooded area and crossed the paddock to the courtyard. People were helping the priestesses off the Gryphons.

Blazel squinted at them, then shook his head. "No, no, no, it can't be her," he groaned.

"Who?" Rizelya gazed at the white-and gray-haired women.

"My mother. She's here! What could have persuaded my mother to leave the Sanctuary?" Blazel growled. His face suddenly heated. He pulled his hand from Rizelya's and wiped his clammy palms on his trousers. "She'd only leave it if Grandmother Shanle crossed the veil. I should have been there for her."

"No. You were where you needed to be," Rizelya assured him. "Our people—I—needed you more. When we left the Sanctuary last summer, she was ill and failing. Crossing the veil to the Mother's arms was a blessing."

"I know. But it doesn't stop the pain of losing her."

Rizelya patted his arm. "Just think about how much time you'll get to spend with your mother."

He gave her a small smile. Since leaving the Sanctuary at eighteen, he hadn't returned for more than a few days at a time. "True. Once we train her team, Histrun will send them north, away from danger and the war."

The priestesses turned to face them at their approach. Blenora's gray eyes crinkled with joy.

"Blazel!" she cried and rushed into his arms.

He gathered her in a tight hug, making her giggle when he swung her in a circle. Setting her down, he kissed the top of her head and stepped back.

"I'm glad to see you, Mother," Blazel said. "But... why did you come?"

"The Goddess called. I answered. She had already called your grandmother to her arms, which released me to come here. It is my duty to fight evil and, son, Malviana and her people are evil incarnate. After Rizelya informed the Supreme of her visions of the Malvers, the Supreme opened the forbidden section of the library. I've read the histories of the Great War. When the Supreme told us there was a way to stop the Malvers' evil, I knew I had to do whatever I could."

"Well, I'm glad you and the other priestesses are here," Rizelya said, greeting Blenora with a hug. "We can't cleanse all the swamps in Lairheim by ourselves. Could you please introduce us?"

Blenora did, and then Rizelya introduced the others on the Black Weave team, including their support pack.

"Oh!" Blenora clasped her hands in front of her chest. "The Gryphons are part of the team? Will I be partnered with one? I really like flying with them, and they make the most enjoyable conversation companions."

Blazel laughed at his mother's enthusiasm. "Yes, Mother, the Gryphons are an integral part of our team. And yes, a Gryphon will probably decide to pair with you, although not all the Gryphons choose to join in the blending. Boreek, who flies with Grazeen, doesn't. But he's still a valuable part of the team."

"Ooh, it sounds so lovely," Blenora said. "I can't wait to learn this new technique. But first, we need to pay our respects to Histrun and Keshanal. And I would love a bath to clean off the travel grime." She looked wistfully down at her clothes.

The corner of Blazel's mouth quirked up. "Both can be arranged."

"Good!" Blenora said.

They walked to the keep-house where Histrun and Keshanal waited on the porch.

"Blenora!" Histrun's voice boomed, his face alight with pleasure. Blenora climbed the stairs, and he pulled her into a bear hug. "What are you doing here, my friend?"

"You sent word to the Supreme you needed priestesses, so here I am."

"It's so good to see you again. We'll have to play a game of keshe after you're settled in. This time, I'll win."

"Ha! Only if you cheat."

Histrun held a hand over his heart. "I'm wounded. I never cheat."

Blenora raised an eyebrow.

"I've played keshe with you, Histrun," Keshanal said. "She's right, you know."

Blazel laughed and clapped a hand on Histrun's shoulder. "Admit it, old man. You cheat whenever you can get away with it." He noticed a longing look cross Rizelya's face and remembered she'd never been close to her father. He caught Rizelya's hand and winked at her. "Rizelya plays a mean game of keshe."

"You're all on!" Histrun glared fiercely at them, but a smile played at the corners of his mouth. He turned to the other priestesses and warmly welcomed them to the keep.

A runner raced up the steps.

"Excuse us," Keshanal said, "we have other work to take care of." She entered the keep-house, with the messenger at her side.

"After dinner—" Histrun pointed to Blenora, Blazel, and Rizelya "—be prepared to lose." He hurried after Keshanal.

"Now, can we have that bath?" Blenora gazed wistfully at the Temple.

"Sure," Rizelya said. "I'll show you to the bathing room."

"No need. We know where it is. All the temples are laid out the same way." She gave Blazel another hug, then strode toward the temple with the other priestesses accompanying her.

"It's good to see her," he confided to Rizelya as they climbed the keep-house stairs to their dorm room. "But I really don't like her here where it's so dangerous."

"As long as the Malvers are alive, we're all in danger. Besides, we need all the help we can get. She'll be fine."

"I hope so."

They hadn't had a direct fight with the Malvers yet, only their twisted creatures, and those were bad enough. Blazel shuddered at the thought of fighting their ancient enemies.

Wisah - 62 de Ahdar, 1076

Wisah rubbed her gritty eyes as she trudged to the Supreme's apartment. The damned book hadn't let her sleep for the past several nights. Perhaps working in the old weapons laboratory had sparked the book's renewed interest in her. After octars of tossing and turning, she'd finally given up and worked on learning the language of the book.

The Supreme was eating her breakfast when Wisah entered her rooms.

"You look awful," the Supreme commented. "Didn't you sleep?"

"No," Wisah growled, glaring at the alcove containing the safe. "That damned book has called to me every night for the past chedan. I finished reading the primer you gave me."

The Supreme bit into her toast smeared with fresh mookti berry jam. "Have you eaten?"

Wisah shook her head. "I'm not hungry."

"Sit." The Supreme gestured to the empty chair at her breakfast table. "Show me the sigils you've learned."

Wisah sat and carefully drew the symbols one by one in the air in front of her. Each one glowed for a moment before dissolving. The Supreme eyed them critically as she continued to eat.

"Nicely done," the Supreme said. "You drew them all correctly. Now, demonstrate the sigils for opening the book. But just draw them, and don't activate the spell."

Wisah did so. As she drew the last one, the symbols melded together to form a new sigil she hadn't seen before. It hung in the air for nearly a milcron before fading.

"I see you're ready." The Supreme took off her necklace of office and handed it to Wisah. "Go on, you know the combination. Bring me the book from the safe. But touch nothing else."

When Wisah opened the safe, whispers intruded in her mind, begging her for release. She shivered, then used a sigil spell to wrap a thin coating of magic around the book. She tentatively touched the book, expecting a sharp zing, and sighed when nothing happened. When she removed the book, several strange artifacts sat behind it. Her fingers itched to pick up the one glowing with purple light. Instead, she jerked her hand away and slammed the safe door closed. Wisah placed the book on the table in front of the Supreme.

While she'd fetched the tome, a housekeeper had cleared away the dishes, leaving behind a fresh pot of taevo and two cups. Automatically, Wisah poured taevo for the two of them, and sank into her chair.

"It didn't bite me," she said.

"It knows it's time." The Supreme pushed the book toward Wisah with a fingertip. "Before you open the tome, cast a spell of protection around the room. We don't want anyone walking in here unaware of the book's power."

Wisah drew a complex sigil in front of the door. The symbol blazed a dark gold and spread to cover the door in a web of light. She repeated the spell at each window. Another symbol linked the webs together, covering the room in a network of golden light.

Wisah returned to the table and sat back down, staring at the book. Although she knew it hadn't been the cause for the Supreme's collapse, it still scared her. So much power radiated off it. She didn't feel worthy and questioned again why the ancient tome had latched onto her. A tendril of power seeped from it and reached for her. She leaned back, not allowing the power to touch her.

"Go on, open it," the Supreme urged.

Wisah gulped, pushing her fear to the side. Holding her hands over the book, she slowly drew the sigils. The tendril of power wrapped around her wrist as she did so, then slid up her arm. When she drew the last symbol, they merged and zoomed into the book. Even though there wasn't a physical lock, Wisah heard a click, and the book fell open.

More tendrils blossomed, wrapping around her, until azure light covered her entire body. The power forced her head back, and her mouth to open. It plunged down her throat, making her gag. Her body buzzed painfully. She gasped for breath. Her heart thundered in her ears. As she passed out, a loud *bong* sounded in her mind.

When she came to, Wisah was sprawled in her chair. Sigils of power covered her exposed skin like azure-blue tattoos. "What... what just happened to me?"

Tears shone in the Supreme's eyes, and she smiled happily. "An initiation. A gift."

"What kind?"

"When the time is right, you'll know the full extent of your initiation. Until then, relax, breathe. Pay attention. You may do things you haven't been able to do before."

Since the Supreme wasn't worried about what the power had done to her, Wisah did as she was told and took several long, deep breaths. Her body still buzzed uncomfortably. After another few breaths, the energy faded into the background. Although if she paid attention, she could feel it. The sigil tattoos faded until she couldn't see them, but she sensed them lurking under the surface of her skin.

The Supreme tapped the book, bringing Wisah's attention back to it. "Now, read to me. What does the book want you to know?"

Wisah leaned forward, peering at the script. It swam before her eyes, so she mumbled another spell. The words flowed into place, and she read aloud. The entry talked about how Shandir had lured Mordar into a trap and used a special weapon and spell to kill him. Shandir had lost the weapon when Mordar's dark god, Mordaga, stole his body away.

She finished reading the entry, then looked up at the Supreme. "How is this going to help us now? We don't have the weapon, and the book doesn't include the spell Shandir used."

"Have faith, child. Malviana will be hard to kill, harder than any of the other Malvers, as she is Mordaga's priestess, and he'll protect her. But we now know something exists that will kill her. If it killed Mordar, it will her too. Take the book. It's now yours and will guide you in your calling to rid our world of Mordaga and all his evil followers."

"But why have I been called? I'm nothing special."

"Oh, dear sweet child, but you are." The Supreme reached across the small table and stroked Wisah's jaw. "You have courage, compassion, and heart. You have the inner strength to do what is necessary, even if it's difficult." The Supreme glanced at the chronometer on the shelf. "Now be off with you. I have several other appointments today."

"Don't you need me to attend you?"

"Not today. Go help Maendy and Maellyn with the weapons. How are you doing with the inventory?"

Wisah's lips thinned into a frown. "Slowly. The cache contains so many things we struggle to determine what they are. Are you sure you don't need me?"

"My meetings are all in my office, so I should be fine. But thank you for your concern. If I need you, I'll send for you. Enjoy your day."

Wisah stood, and with a gesture and sigil, released the protection web. It dissolved much quicker than it normally did. She glanced down at her left forearm. On the underside, a glowing tattoo of the same sigil slowly faded. She'd never heard of anyone with this kind of power or Talent. When she picked up the book, power caressed her fingers. She raised her eyebrows. *At least it's better than a painful shock!*

Back in her room, Wisah looked around for a safe place to put the book. A fresco on the wall above her bed glowed. She crossed the room and drew the sigil for opening over the fresco. It popped open, revealing a cabinet in the stone wall the exact size for the book. She put the book in and closed the door, which disappeared, returning to plain stone. *Huh. My own safe.*

She changed from her priestess robes into a sturdy pair of trousers and a tunic and laced on a pair of boots. After braiding her long, creamy-white hair, she tied a scarf over it. She'd been ignoring the dust covering the weapons room and laboratory since finding it two chedans ago, concentrating instead on taking inventory. But she couldn't stand the mess any longer. On the way to the lab, she stopped by the housekeeper unit and grabbed a pail, rags, and a broom.

When she reached the door leading to the basement, she gawked at Maendy's spell on the door to keep unauthorized people out. She hadn't been able to see it yesterday. The spell reacted to her signature energy, and the door swung open. She frowned at the cleaning supplies and the lantern. She couldn't carry it all herself.

"Here, let me help you," Maellyn said, striding into view and carrying a small basket.

Wisah sniffed appreciatively as the scent of mookti berry pies drifted to her nose. Her stomach grumbled, reminding her she hadn't eaten breakfast.

"I thought you'd be in the weapons cache already."

"My mother has been down there since sunrise. I spent the time lazing in bed, reading." She held up the book on making magical weapons. "Quite fascinating really."

"You understood it? I tried reading it, but the information was over my head."

"It would be for most people unless they've had training in the helstramiester hall—" Maellyn smiled and touched her chest "—which I've had."

You have a handful there, Wisah, Sheekeek said, gliding between the book stacks. He squinted. *Something is different about you. What happened?*

Wisah wasn't sure what had happened or if she should share. She shrugged her shoulders. "Nothing. Let's get to work."

If you walk behind me, I can flare enough for you to see the stairs, Sheekeek offered. *We're going up and down so often, we should add modern lighting to them.*

"Good idea." As Wisah considered the problem, the spell for the light globes in the temple corridors, and to adjust their light when people were present, popped into her head. She had the feeling she could cast the spell even though she didn't have any Red Talent. Putting it out of her mind, she followed Sheekeek and Maellyn down the stairs.

Maendy had already lit the torches, and a haze of smoke drifted along the top of the ceiling. They could use light globes down here as well. While Maendy and Maellyn tinkered with the various old weapons, Wisah and Sheekeek cleaned the dust and debris. Then they continued the monumental task of inventorying the multitude types of weapons: staffs, crystal balls, shields, and long knives. They found a cabinet filled with myriad miscellaneous spelled articles they weren't sure what their ancestors had used them for. They finally stopped working when the dinner bell gonged above them.

As they walked past a bookshelf, a sigil marking a drawer glowed, and Wisah's hand itched. She tried opening the drawer, but it was stuck fast. She stepped back, drew the sigil for unlocking, and heard a click. The drawer glided open at her touch. Inside, she found an old scroll, the edges crumpled to dust. Wisah carefully lifted it out, unrolled it, and gasped. It was written in the same language as the ancient tome. She deciphered a few lines of the text.

"Oh, Sweet Mother!" She'd just read about this spell from the ancient book that morning. Fate—or coincidence—was leading her to what she needed.

What is it, Wisah? Sheekeek craned his head over her shoulder to peer at the scroll.

"Something terrible and incredible. This scroll details the weapon and spell Shandir used to kill Mordar. If it could kill him, it's likely to kill Malviana. The Supreme thinks I'm supposed to fight her." The scroll trembled in her shaking hand. It had been one thing for the Supreme to tell her, but quite another for the very thing she needed to fall into her lap.

Maendy gingerly took the scroll, and after looking at it, passed it back to Wisah. "I can't read this."

"It's in the ancient language I'm studying. I'll translate the spell and instructions for you, but it will take a while since I'm still learning it." Wisah meticulously re-rolled the scroll.

"As soon as you do, I'll put aside my other work to make this weapon," Maendy said. "We can't go against the Goddess's decree."

Wisah didn't think it would be easy. Her initial perusal of the spell made her think it was long and complicated—and Black Talent was needed to wield it. *Rizelya's Black Weave team? Is that why they've come together now?* Her eyebrows rose at the thought, and it gave her some comfort. She wasn't really the chosen one.

Rizelya - 62 de Ahdar, 1076

Chariel guided the priestesses from the Sanctuary across the keep to the practice arena where Rizelya, Blazel and the Black Weave team awaited. Blenora and Ardela entered with a bounce to their step, appearing eager for their training to begin. The others crept in, holding each other's hands, and their eyes were wide with fear. Rizelya wondered briefly why they'd agreed to come if they were so frightened. She glanced at Chariel, remembering how terrified she'd been when they left the Sanctuary to search for the Gryphons. But she'd pushed through her dread and accompanied Rizelya's squad-pack into danger and adventure. These women were in the same position—called by the Goddess and completely out of their comfort zone, but willing to deal with their fear to serve their people.

Rizelya studied the women, noting their dark gray or pure white hair, indicating strong Gray or White Talents. Ardela, with her dark silver-gray hair, was nearly as strong a Gray as Chariel. The Supreme had sent her strongest and best priestesses, but she'd only sent six of each Talent. Rizelya's chest tightened, and she blinked back the tears pricking her eyes. She'd hoped for more. *How can we clear the hundreds of malignant magic pools infecting Lairheim with so few people?*

It was a wonder the Malvers' monsters hadn't wiped out the Posairs long ago. After Histrun showed her the map detailing the swamps filling Lairheim, including Blazel's additions, Rizelya now understood how precarious the Posairs' survival was. The enormous quantity astounded her.

One of Chariel's prophecies had sent Blazel to explore the swamps, and he'd finally emerged from them three years later. Over the lunadars, he'd recounted some of his experiences, and it was a miracle he still lived. The Mother had truly watched over him. Rizelya glanced at him. He had so many scars, and not all of them were visible. She squeezed his hand, grateful he stood beside her now.

"Shall we get started?" Blazel asked.

She followed his gaze to the stands filled with people. A full wing of fifty Gryphons waited on the sands. They'd need at least that many to partner with each member of six new teams, plus however many bodyguards each team ended up with. Her team had almost as many guards as people!

The crowd outnumbered the poor priestesses, all anticipating becoming part of a Black Weave team. New compassion for the priestess's situation washed over Rizelya.

Rizelya stepped forward and raised her voice so everyone in the arena could hear her. "As you've noticed, we have quite a few people here, but only enough women with White and Gray Talents for six teams. The Black Weave requires a person from each Talent, plus a male, and at least one Gryphon. It's also stronger if there is a healer in the mix, and if everyone has the same level of Talent. Beyond that, the connection created by the Weave goes deep into your heart and soul, so the people in the Weave must be compatible."

She clasped her hands behind her back and looked at the people gathered, making eye contact with as many as possible. Rizelya smiled at the women from her squad-pack she'd already tagged as potential Black Weave members. "Some of you will be chosen to continue, but most of you won't. We're creating the strongest teams we can find. The fate of our world rests on the work the Black Weave teams do." She paused. All the volunteers had fought in the Scourge War and against the Malvers' monsters. "The Weave can destroy the Malvers' monsters for good. Never again will we have to fight janacks and brechas for our survival!"

She waited for the thunderous cheers and stomping feet to subside.

Blazel stepped forward. "Group one!" he bellowed. "You're up."

Fifty people and ten Gryphons marched onto the sands. The priestesses huddled together, visibly shaking. Rizelya's face flushed. Perhaps she should have introduced the priestesses to a smaller group. But she didn't know how much time it would take to form the teams—or how much time the Malvers would give them. So far, other than forays by twisted beasts, the Malvers hadn't attacked them yet.

"I need a volunteer from each Talent to step forward, please," Rizelya said, changing her plans.

The priestesses pushed Blenora and Ardela to the front of their group. Blenora raised her chin, threw back her shoulders, and took a big step forward. After a moment, Ardela joined her.

It pleased Rizelya when Noriana stepped forward from the group of volunteers. The Blue had been part of Kaieli's original team, clearing the nucla at the Scourge slave camp. After Saffren took her place on the new team, Rizelya worried Noriana would be angry or disappointed, and wouldn't want to join a new one. Rizelya raised an eyebrow as Ambrelya joined the waiting group. The Red was a crack-shot with the pulser weapons, and Rizelya hadn't thought she'd give it up. Then she noticed how Ambrelya gazed at Raeleen, and understood. Dehali, Gehan, and Raeleen held back, giving others an opportunity to go first.

"Form a circle and join hands, thumbs to the left," Rizelya instructed. She waited for the group to do as instructed. "This first exercise is just to get used to connecting your energy. One at a time, concentrate on sending your energy through your hand to the person on your right. As soon as you feel it, send it to the next person until it goes all the way around the circle. Reds, remember to keep your fire low so you don't burn your companions. We've done this exercise before in training."

Ambrelya nodded in understanding. "I can go first," she said.

A moment later, Blenora, standing on her right, squeaked, dropping her hand and shaking it. "It's warm! Is this what fire energy feels like?" She gazed at Ambrelya, who nodded with a shy smile. Blenora held her hand out again.

Fifteen milcrons later, Ambrelya finally indicated the energy had returned to her. Rizelya inwardly groaned. At this rate, it would take chedans to find the correct people for the Weave teams. Groups formed with the other priestesses to do the energy exercise. Kaieli, Loshera, Chariel, and Saffren wandered around the practice area, lending a hand in teaching. When one group finished, another swapped their place.

Three octars later, Rizelya halted the session. Everyone who wanted a chance to join a team had participated in a connection exercise. As expected, many people bowed out, thinning the ranks to a more manageable level. While the candidates exited the arena, the priestesses slumped on the stands, leaning against each other, exhausted from flowing so much energy. Leistral and Eidstrun hurried in, handing out mugs of taevo to the priestesses and the Black Weave team.

"Did you connect with anyone?" Rizelya asked. She'd hoped at least one team would have formed during the session.

Blenora pushed a damp strand of hair from her forehead. "A few, but we didn't experience anything like you described. I liked Noriana and Ambrelya."

"Faliciden had nice energy," Ardela added, staring into her mug. "Since she was part of Kaieli's original group, she knew what we needed to do."

"We'd have better success if everyone wasn't so deferential to us," Blenora huffed. "No one wanted to offend us or show disrespect. Except your other pack members. I don't think Gehan defers to anyone."

"You're right, she doesn't." Rizelya chuckled, remembering the Yellow standing up against her Keep Alpha, Saehala, and demanding to be allowed to fight.

Ardela grimaced and hunched her shoulders. "It was even worse for me. Your pack members are used to Chariel, so they talked to me. But no one else would. I felt like they were avoiding me."

Kaieli leaned against the railing, twirling her mug between her hands. "We've been taught our whole lives to treat priestesses with reverence. It's difficult to change that attitude, especially since normal Posairs don't interact with White Priestesses much outside of the temple. I think it also helped that everyone on our team was friends, or lovers—" she grinned at Rizelya, then glanced at Blazel "—before we attempted the Black Weave. It made it easier for me to weave their energy together."

Blenora rested her elbows on her knees. "But how are we going to convince our potential teammates we're just people, so we can become friends?"

"I don't know." Rizelya shrugged, then rubbed her faced. "Let me think about it." She hadn't considered how her close friendships with her Black Weave team affected their ability to combine their magic. How could she change the training exercises to encourage friendships rather than just working together? Her people's ability to move past simply surviving into thriving depended on the success of the Black Weave teams.

Malviana - 63 de Ahdar, 1076

Malviana sat at her desk, reading one of Mordar's journals, intrigued by the details of his attempts to corrupt a hated Gryphon, even though he hadn't been successful. As she contemplated how she could modify and expand on his ideas, shouts and cheers rang through the castle from the inner courtyard.

She frowned at the open window, and with a flick of her wand, flung it closed and returned to her study. A few milcrons later, the sound grew louder, and she slammed her hands on the desk. "What in Mordaga's seven hells is going on!" Striding to the window, she opened it and leaned out.

In the center of the courtyard, Keandran and Korand faced each other, their lips pulled back in snarls, blood dripping from their clawed hands. With his impressive rack of horns, Korand towered over Keandran, making him seem the stronger fighter. But his height hadn't stopped him from receiving several deep gashes across his chest. He shook his head, flinging droplets of blood from the furrow over his left eye.

It spattered Keandran, who howled with laughter as he licked the blood off his face with his long tongue. In a lightning fast move, Keandran dove under Korand's guard and slashed. Blood welled on Korand's thigh and from a fresh wound on his chest.

"Admit it, Korand," Keandran lisped. "I am the better fighter." He stood tall, preening—not a speck of blood marred his fur—and reached down to stroke his impressive manhood to hardness. "And the better man. It's why I'm the Maldier's captain and why Malviana prefers me in her bed."

Korand roared, dropped his head, and rushed Keandran, intent on skewering him with his horns. Keandran howled and leaped out of the way, kicking Korand as he passed. Korand yowled in pain, and Malviana smiled. Keandran's clawed feet had gouged a sizable wound in Korand's hindquarters. Korand reached for his whip.

"Uh-uh-uh," Keandran made a negating motion with his hand. "No magic."

"I'll teach you, you mangy cur!" Korand's hand flicked out, and his whip sliced Keandran's chest.

A stunned look crossed Keandran's face for a moment before he dove at his opponent. They grappled, rolling across the courtyard, their watchers moving quickly out of the way.

Malviana enjoyed the play of muscles on the two men and licked her lips at the scent of testosterone wafting off them. Keandran hadn't boasted. He was the better fighter—and better endowed. Watching them, Malviana's lust grew. Finally, Keandran knocked his opponent to the ground and straddled him, his hands wrapped around Korand's throat. Beads of blood welled under his claws.

"Enough!" Malviana shouted. She didn't want to lose Korand. He had his uses.

Keandran glanced up, his eyes finding hers. He straightened, rubbing his bloody chest. A leer crossed his face as he slowly licked the blood from his hands, his gaze never leaving her.

Malviana's core tightened, and wetness dampened her crotch. "Keandran, come see me and explain the meaning of this," she called down, trying to keep the lust from her voice.

Keandran grinned triumphantly at Korand and strode toward the door leading into the castle.

Korand slowly rose to his feet, shame filling his face as he gazed up at her.

"You disappoint me, Korand," Malviana said. "I expect much better from my people. A Posair could have bested you. Train harder." She turned her attention to the Maldiers crowding the courtyard's perimeter. "The Posairs aren't sitting around playing. They are training. Now, all of you, back to work!"

The Maldiers saluted her and resumed their training exercises.

The soft shutting of her door alerted her to Keandran's presence. Before she could turn around, he was behind her, his hard manhood pressed against her. She quickly moved her skirt aside, and he rammed into her. The fierce sex only increased her desire. They continued satisfying each other throughout the rest of the day and night. At some point, they made it to her bed, and she fell into an exhausted sleep.

The next morning, Borgedier entered her office and slumped into the chair across from her.

"You look like you don't have good news," Malviana said, studying his face.

"No, your grace, I don't." Borgedier handed her his report.

She inspected it, a scowl creasing her forehead.

"Even with the new Maldiers," he continued, "and the expected new Malvers, the Posairs significantly outnumber our people."

She waved a hand. "Everyone who returned from exile is nearly immortal. They should count three or four times more than a single Posair."

"I accounted for that, and we're still outnumbered. We need something else to even the odds."

The yip of a puppy floated through her open window. Malviana pushed away from her desk and strolled to look out. A dozen floxidor puppies played in the courtyard. One jumped and caught the end of Cloresh's whip in its teeth and pulled. They played tug-of-war for a few milcrons.

Malviana turned back to face Borgedier, smiling. "What we need are more deadly creatures to fight for us. Send for my children. We have work to do."

When they arrived, Malviana activated the mirror and sat back in her chair, studying the twisted animals in the great southern swamp.

"I find it intriguing that the dark magic transformed all the herbivores into carnivores," she said, her fingers tapping a rhythm on the arm of her chair. "But I see little use for the twisted rabbits and squirrels."

"The Maldiers love to hunt them." Mordeven smoothed a hand over his goatee. "It's sad, really. They aren't true Malvers or Posairs or even animals. They need to feed on the flesh and blood of the animals they kill, as well as absorb the death essence."

Malviana turned her attention away from the mirror. "Do they only eat animals?"

He laughed. "Oh no. Several have confided they killed and ate Posairs as they traveled south. Keandran boasted he killed four Posairs, only to have Korand smugly inform him that he'd killed a dozen. It's quite interesting to witness the rivalry between those two."

Malviana smiled and shifted in her seat. The wounds on her inner thighs broke open and burned, bringing with them memories of last night's sex games with Keandran. She glanced at the welts on her wrists from her night with Korand. The mere mention of how much fun she'd had with the other one prompted them to invent new ways to combine pleasure with pain. Although nothing they did compared to her beloved Mordar. Malviana had denied herself the pleasures of the flesh while in exile, mourning his loss. But now that she'd regained her power and strength, it would be sacrilegious not to enjoy the magnificent body Mordaga had given her.

The mirror showed a large flying serpent, an angulete, coiled around a tree. A floxidor passed under it unaware of the danger. The snake spread its wings wide. It struck quickly, burying its fangs into the floxidor's neck. The angulete wrapped its coils around its catch and squeezed. Malviana imagined she could hear the crunching as the beast's bones were crushed. The serpent's jaws unhinged and engulfed its victim head first.

"That creature is promising. Malvidor, see what you can do with them."

"Yes, Mother," her youngest said. "Do you want them twisted further, or leave them as they are only more pliable to our commands?"

"Your choice." She bade the mirror to show her more. The large jallopitar reptiles would also serve her purposes, but she wanted something more terrifying. Deeper in the swamp, they watched a carnivorous vine attack a swamp rat.

"Morvana, you have a gift with plants and poisons. I'm intrigued by those carnivorous plants. We won't remain here much longer, but perhaps we can use those elsewhere against the Posairs."

Morvana folded her right leg onto the chair and draped her arm over her knee. "I already have specimens of those in my laboratory. It's resisting combining with animals, but it might work as an additional defense." She shot a smug grin at Mordeven, pleased she'd anticipated Malviana's request.

Mordeven stuck his nose in the air and pretended he didn't notice her.

Malviana ignored their antics as she instructed the mirror to sweep outward beyond the swamp. The scene flowed over the glittering black sands of the Barrens and to the crater. Her hands clutched the arms of her chair, her knuckles turning white as memories of the fight with Shandir assailed her. Movement at the crater rim caught her attention. "Stop!" she commanded. "Show me this."

A huge abandoned compound came into focus. Bits of cloth stuck on a wire mesh fence fluttered in the breeze. Unusual buildings, most with gaping holes in their walls and roofs, cluttered the space. "The Scourge compound," she breathed.

"What's that?" Malvidor pointed to movement at the edge of the mirror.

It obeyed his wish, and the image in the mirror shifted. A herd of pale gray-green lizard-like beasts, standing nearly erect on their powerful hind legs, milled around several of the pens, rooting for food. Sharp horns curved over their heads, and Malviana spotted dark stains on several of them that appeared like blood.

Excitement rose in her. "Those creatures are magnificent. I'm sure we can make them useful."

Malviana cast the spell to pull creatures to her castle through the mirror's magic. She scowled at the mirror when nothing happened. She sensed her magic touching the creatures, but it couldn't grab them. After the third attempt, she gave up, slumping onto the sofa. "The creatures are either too alien, or they aren't corrupted enough. My mirror magic doesn't affect them. It's like trying to bring an untainted ducorn here. There isn't enough malevolence for my magic to latch onto." Malviana crossed her arms, pouting. "Damn, I wanted to use those creatures!"

"I'll send a team to fetch them for you, Mother," Mordeven offered. "I'm sure our magic can affect them. They are alive after all, but they just may be too alien for the mirror to recognize. If we combined a Gryphon with the lizards, it could be a formidable creature."

Malviana sat up straighter and raised her eyebrows at her son. The idea was outlandish enough that it might work. He usually didn't have such good ideas. She considered Mordar's experiments on the Gryphons. Perhaps she could succeed where he failed. He hadn't had access to the vast amounts of power the magic lake under the crater gave her. Delight filled her at the thought of doing something Mordar couldn't. She rubbed her hands together, looking forward to twisting a Gryphon, a creature Shandir had had a hand in creating so long ago.

Chapter 12

Malviana - 3 de Neydar, 1076

A force of fifty Maldiers and ten Malvers, under Korand's command, ventured from the castle toward the abandoned compound. Mordeven had returned yesterday with several captured alien lizards, and Malviana's initial test showed her magic could affect and twist them. Now, they needed the other half of this new experiment—a Gryphon. Mordeven noted one had followed his team as soon as they'd left the castle's protective barrier.

Malviana sat on her banthu as it hovered behind the distortion spell surrounding the castle and its lands. Mordeven, Malvidor, Borgedier, and Jorvelden rode to the side of her.

On the ground, Korand waited, his whip held ready. "Now!" he shouted.

Keandran and four other Maldiers crossed the invisible barrier and stomped through the swamp, heading north toward the Barrens, with a pack of floxidor pacing at their side. A few milcrons later, a Gryphon broke from the cover of the trees, following them.

Korand flicked his whip. It snapped, capturing the Gryphon's back leg. It squawked in pain and terror, frantically beating its wings, trying to escape. Mordeven urged his banthu forward. A black stream of magic flowed from his wand, snaking around the Gryphon's beak and cutting off its shrill cries. Borgedier waved his wand, and a net dropped onto the Gryphon. It continued to struggle, entangling its wings in the net even more. It flared, flames blossoming to encompass its body, nearly burning away Borgedier's magic. Jorvelden and Malvidor rushed closer, throwing more nets of magic over the Gryphon.

"Don't kill it," Malviana ordered. "I want it alive."

With a swish, Korand wrapped his whip around the Gryphon's other leg. The muscles in Korand's back bulged as he tugged, dragging the Gryphon lower. Cloresh snapped her whip, catching the Gryphon's front talons. With both her and Keandran pulling, and Jorvelden and Malvidor's banthues forcing it down from above, they finally grounded the Gryphon.

Malviana guided her banthu to land next to the heaving Gryphon. The gray and white feathers and wide eyes reminded her of an owl.

"You're a pretty one," she crooned at it. It glared at her. She chuckled. "Your defiance won't last long once I start my experiments. Take him to my laboratory. Mordeven, adjust the barrier spell to ensure none of the remaining Gryphon spies can leave the area. I want them here, in case I need them. And we don't want the Posairs to know what we're doing."

She buried the doubt her experiments would succeed. Her vengeance depended on it. She followed her men carrying the trussed-up beast back to the castle and into her laboratory. As Malviana walked down the steeps stairs, she glared at the trickle of water seeping down the walls. It reminded her too much of the island cave and the constant *drip, drip* of stagnant water. When she and Mordar had ruled here before her exile, there hadn't been any annoying water, but then the swamp hadn't existed at the time, either. Crossing her arms over her chest, she watched the men wrangle the struggling Gryphon into a cage.

The beast crouched, the tip of its tail slashing angrily. It turned as best as it could in the cramped quarters to keep her in sight as she walked around the cage. She approached the cage and threw up an arm to protect her eyes as the creature flared.

"None of that!" she roared, tapping the cage with her wand. The Gryphon trilled in distress as her magic swamped it, drowning its flames. She consulted the spell book, drew the proscribed pattern with her wand, and sent the spell to the cage. The bars glowed a deep maroon. It took several milcrons for the glow to fade.

The beast glared at her and appeared to study the bars. It breathed deeply and tried to flare again. The Gryphon threw its head back, warbling in agony.

"Tut, tut," Malviana said, wriggling her finger at it. "Behave. Anytime you try to flare, excruciating agony will result. Now, let's discover what we can do with you. The best place to start is to replicate what Mordar did. Then I can see for myself what worked and what didn't." She turned away from the cage and flipped through Mordar's notes. "Ah, let's start with this, shall we?"

She turned back to the cage, frowning at the Gryphon. It lay curled in a ball, its head tucked beneath its hindquarters, visibly shaking. "Come here," she cajoled, using the sweetest tone she could manage. One ear flicked toward her, but otherwise, the Gryphon didn't move. "That was only the beginning. It will only get worse."

She waved her wand at the creature and cackled with glee as it writhed with renewed anguish. From Mordar's observations, it would take time, days perhaps chedans, to see any results, even with the additional power at her disposal from the magic lake in the crater. "This will be so much fun," she murmured to herself as she set to work to corrupt the hated Gryphon.

Rizelya - 3 de Neydar, 1076

Rizelya trudged to the alpha office to apprise Histrun and Keshanal of the Black Weave team's progress. She wished she had better news to give them. She still hadn't found a way to convince the candidates that the White and Gray Priestesses were simply people they could become friends with.

"How is your progress with forming the Black Weave teams coming?" Histrun asked as soon as Rizelya entered the office. He folded his hands on top of the desk, piercing Rizelya with his glare.

She sighed as she sat on the hard chair in front of the desk. "Not as well as I'd like. I just can't figure out how to get them to form a pack."

Keshanal leaned forward. "What's the problem? Perhaps we can help. Between us—" she indicated herself and Histrun with her thumb "—we've had plenty of experience in getting people to work together."

Rizelya huffed out another breath, not wanting to seem incompetent, but she needed their insight. "Most of the applicants leave the priestesses alone and won't talk to them outside of the exercises. They're so ingrained with having a deep reverence for them they can't seem to see them as people, or potential friends. The Gryphons don't have the problem. Even though they respect the priestesses, friendships between Gryphons and the priestesses are blossoming. But if the candidates can't relax and see the priestesses as women, I'm afraid they'll never find the closeness necessary for the Black Weave." She'd slouched deeper into her seat as she lamented.

"What exercises are you doing?" Keshanal asked.

"Mostly connecting their energy."

"Ah. While that's good for what I gather you do in the Weave, you need to focus more on developing teamwork. Once they work together as a team, their energies will naturally connect. After our meeting, I'll help you devise some exercises you can do with them."

Rizelya sat up straighter. "Oh, thank you!"

"We need you to get these teams formed as quickly as possible," Histrun growled. "The swamps around here need to be cleared as soon as possible. The twisted beast and the Malvers' monsters have attacked us nearly every day. We can't keep fighting both types of creatures."

Keshanal laid a placating hand on Histrun's arm. "Nelieh escaped a few days after you attempted to cure her, killing the guards on her way out. More people have fallen to the black-splotch infection. Once infected, neither the healers nor White Priestesses can't do anything for them. In some ways, it's fortunate most of those who become victims tend to disappear quickly."

"Where are they going? Do you know?" Rizelya asked. So far, no one she knew had fallen to the terrible affliction.

"South," Histrun grumbled, "to the Barrens and beyond. The Gryphons can't track them past the crater. We presume they are going to the black castle." He slammed his fist onto the desk, making Rizelya jump. "Damn her to the Crone's fires! Malviana is building her army from my people. That's the only reason I can think of why they'd all be heading to the southern swamp. We need you to quickly clear the malignant magic from around here and hope it stops this infection plaguing my people."

"I'm doing my best, sir."

"I know. But it's damned frustrating!"

Over the next few days, Keshanal helped Rizelya to develop more teamwork exercises, which whittled the candidate pool even further. Much to Rizelya's disappointment, Ambrelya bowed out, saying she'd rather be a bodyguard to a team than be in one.

A chedan into finding the right teams, Rizelya ran the candidates through a maze exercise. Keshanal assured her the relay race would build trust while the participants had fun. Rizelya crossed her fingers. This was her last ditch effort in forming the teams.

Blenora guided her blindfolded partner Raeleen around a series of obstacles. "Move your ass to the left," Blenora yelled as she excitedly waved her arms and motioning as if Raeleen could see her. "No, no, the other left. Come on, Raeleen, hurry! The other team is winning." She threw her hands up in the air. "For the love of the Mother, not that way!"

Faliciden, who was on the same team and cheering her teammates on, stopped and gaped at Blenora. Several women gasped, while others stared. Blenora looked around in the sudden quiet, put her hand over her mouth, then burst into laughter.

Noriana, also a teammate, grinned at Blenora, then shouted, "Come on, Raeleen! Turn to your left. The other team is flabbergasted. Now is our chance."

Rizelya inwardly whooped. She'd have to tell Keshanal the maze idea worked.

Afterward, everyone forgot the Grays and Whites were priestesses, treating them in the same fun, irreverent manner as they did everyone else.

Two days later, Rizelya and her team gathered together after dinner to discuss the training results.

Kaieli put her taevo mug down and leaned back in her chair. "We're close to having our teams. The only candidates remaining have similar levels of Talent. After the Blenora incident," she chuckled, "friendships are forming between people and they're naturally forming groups."

Rizelya rested her chin on her fist. "The priestesses understand what we're doing much quicker than the others."

"It's because we do something similar," Chariel said, "when we connect with the veil separating the physical world from the psychic plane." She scrubbed her hands over her face. "I don't understand why we haven't tried to blend our Talents before now."

"We haven't needed this type of power before this." Loshera shrugged. "During the last war with the Malvers, our Talents were different. For one, the men used theirs the same way the women do now, and for another, many people had Black Talent. The Black Weave creates a similar power."

Kaieli, sipping on her taevo, tilted her head in acknowledgment. "We need to test the effectiveness of the teams before adding the Gryphon's influence into the weaving. Once they're added, it deepens the bonding too much to make many shifts to the teams. We were lucky we'd all worked closely together when we switched out Noriana with Saffren and Blazel for Aistrun."

"What do you suggest?" Blazel asked.

"What we did in the slave pens." Kaieli paused, ducking her head and wiping the tears from her eyes. Her beloved, Rolstrun, had anchored their team, and she still grieved his death.

Rizelya reached over and rubbed Kaieli's back, comforting her heart-sister and letting her know she wasn't alone.

Kaieli took a deep breath and straightened her shoulders. "Cleansing the nucla from the crater rocks would test their ability to work together, and build the skills needed for draining the swamps, since they are similar."

Loshera and Chariel shivered. They'd helped cleanse tons of nucla while Scourge captives. Without their efforts, the Posairs would be in danger of the Scourge returning to conquer Lairheim.

Aistrun, standing behind Chariel, placed a hand on Chariel's shoulder and kissed the top of her head. His eyebrows crinkled together at Kaieli's intense gaze. "What do you want me to do, Kaieli? Nothing good, I wager."

"Would you and Broogk go to the crater and retrieve some rocks for us?"

"I was afraid that's what you wanted," he grimaced. "Those things make my skin crawl. Do you absolutely need them?"

Kaieli nodded.

Aistrun huffed. "Fine. We'll leave in the morning."

Malviana - 7 de Neydar, 1076

As Malviana dressed, preparing to go to her laboratory for another long session with the Gryphon, a messenger hurried into her room.

"Your Majesty!" the messenger said, breathless with excitement. "A newly changed Malvers has arrived."

"Show them to the throne room."

Malviana's hands shook as she threaded her earrings into her ear. *So soon! And a Malvers not a Maldier. This one must be filled with hate or anger to have transformed already.* She hadn't expected her new followers for another few chedans. Malviana's children joined her as she walked toward her throne room. She sat on her throne, fingers drumming the arm. Would it be a man or a woman?

The throne doors opened, and a woman strode through them, a belligerent scowl on her face. A few spots of brown skin showed through the black splotches covering her, which would soon fade to gray. Bands of dark gray streaked her formerly red hair, and her yellow eyes shone in the dark background where the whites used to be. The woman ran her elongated fingers through her hair. Shortly, her fingers would become claws. This one was well into her transformation from Posair to Malvers.

The woman's head swiveled from side to side as she surveyed the people crowding the throne room. Her footsteps faltered when she caught sight of Keandran and Korand, but she took a deep breath and continued her journey to the dais. She stopped a few feet from the bottom stair, straightened her back, and looked up at Malviana.

"Are you she? Are you Malviana?"

Malviana inclined her head. "I am."

The woman dropped to her knee. "I'm here to serve you."

"Welcome, child, welcome." Malviana's heart raced. "You are the first in the new generation of Malvers. What is your name?"

The woman licked her lips. "Nelieh, Your Grace."

"Magdelyn, show her to her quarters and help her through her final stages of transformation. Inform me when it is complete." Malviana smiled down at her new subject. She wanted to jump up and down with joy. Instead, she said calmly, "Nelieh, go with Magdelyn. She'll feed you."

Nelieh raised her head, and her eyes glowed red. "Good. I'm so hungry, but food doesn't satisfy me anymore."

"I know, child. Magdelyn will give you something that will." Malviana recalled the cage of swamp rats. She'd found another use for the vermin—feeding her new subjects. Too bad they didn't have any Posairs to feed her. Their bodies provided the best sustenance for transitioning Malvers. Her new Malvers wouldn't need any flesh to sustain her once she completed her transformation—only blood and death essence. Although, the meager amount from the rats wouldn't satisfy a newly transformed Malvers for long.

Excitement coursed through Malviana as the woman left the throne room. "Borgedier, post a squad on banthues at the edge of the Barrens."

"What should they look for, your grace?"

"Nelieh is just the first of the influx of new Malvers to journey here. I want them here as quickly as possible to begin their training. Have the squad pick up any new Malvers they find entering the Barrens and carry them to the castle."

He bowed. "It will be done, my queen. Do you have an estimate of how many we should expect?"

She shook her head. "Not yet. I hadn't expected such early results of my spell. Once you make the arrangements, join me in my suite. I should have some numbers by then."

He bowed again and left the throne room.

Instead of going down to her laboratory for another day of failure, Malviana returned to her suite and stood in front of the black mirror. "Show me," she demanded. "Show me my new followers."

A mist gathered on the mirror, covering its surface. When it cleared, pinpricks of light overlaid a map of Lairheim. She whooped at the hundreds of dots. As expected, the largest cluster centered where the Posair army hunkered.

Borgedier's sharp knock on the door interrupted her counting. When he saw the mirror, he thrust a hand in the air. "Yes! I like seeing so many, and especially from the Posair army."

"I estimate it will provide us with six to seven hundred new Malvers. And look," she gestured at the mirror, "there are another three or four hundred scattered all over Lairheim. They will travel south to join us."

"Those will take chedans, perhaps lunadars, to arrive here. What happens if we've left and are marching north?" He dropped into a parade-ready stance, his feet spread wide and his hands behind his back.

"It doesn't matter. No matter where I am, they will find me."

"I'll talk to Valdorian. She's in charge of training the new Malvers, to discuss accelerating their training using death magic as soon as they arrive."

"Also meet with Keandran and Korand." Malviana poured herself a cup of bloodwine and sat in her favorite chair. "Unfortunately, not all of those infected will make the transition to Malvers, and instead, will twist into Maldiers. They should prepare to add new members to their ranks and get them up to speed quickly. I want our new people ready as soon as possible to march against the Posairs. I've spent too many years waiting for a chance to exact my vengeance. The Posairs, especially the Supreme, will pay for locking us on that wretched island."

"As we all have," Borgedier said. He gave her a quick salute. "I'll go make the arrangements."

Rizelya - 10 de Neydar, 1076

The final candidates for the Black Weave teams lounged in the keep-house's entertainment room, relaxing after a grueling day of training. All they needed now was the nucla to test them. Rizelya hoped this final exercise would bond the groups into teams.

As if on cue, Aistrun strode in, carrying a bag slung over his shoulder. When he dumped the lumps of nucla on the table, Blenora put her hand to her chest and gasped for air. Ardela threw her hand over her mouth, and the color drained from her face.

"What... is... that?" Blenora finally spat out. "It's awful, whatever it is."

"It's nucla," Kaieli explained. "The Scourge prized the substance, and it's what brought them to our planet. We learned to merge and form the Black Weave to cleanse the malignant magic fused into the rock."

Ardela gagged, then rushed from the room.

"I'll go make sure she's okay," Faliciden said, then followed Ardela to the necessary room.

Rizelya watched Blenora, uncertain if she'd be sick too.

But Blenora took several long, deep breaths before straightening her back. "Crone's Fires, I don't know how you did it," she said to Kaieli and the others who had worked cleansing the nucla in the slave camp. "I admire you for being able to handle so much malevolence for lunadars."

Noriana shrugged. "We didn't have a choice."

After Ardela and Faliciden returned, Kaieli explained how they cleansed the nucla, using the Weave. "It isn't a full weave without the Gryphons. Your consciousness won't merge, but you'll still combine your Talents. The Gryphon's magic is what shifts it into a power akin to Black Talent."

Rizelya studied the groups for a moment. "Blenora," she said, "I want you, Ardela, Faliciden, and Noriana, to join with Raeleen, Dehali, Gehan, and Delestrun. You seem to work well together, and you're all strong in your respective Talents." They'd gravitated into a group over the course of the training, often working together.

They nodded and moved to sit on the floor in a circle.

"Faliciden, you have experience doing this," Kaieli added. "You take the lead. Besides, when doing this type of working, having the healer lead the merge seems to work the best. Noriana, help her as you've also done this."

The group joined hands and closed their eyes. Within a few moments, they'd merged, and Rizelya could sense the power emanating from them, even before they began clearing the nucla. She folded her arms and nodded crisply to herself. They were nearly as powerful together as Rizelya's team.

"That was satisfying," Ardela said, tapping the now inert rock.

"Just wait until you clear a swamp," Loshera said, grinning.

After the first team's success, the other candidates sorted into groups, chatting excitedly. They pushed furniture aside to sit in circles on the floor. Rizelya walked around the room, checking on them as they wove their energies together.

"Yahoo!" she whooped as the last team emerged from their trance after successfully purging the nucla. "We have our six teams! We just need to add the Gryphons."

"It shouldn't be difficult," Blenora said. "Most of us have formed friendships with a Gryphon. Blueek and I are quite good friends now, and have discussed partnering."

"So have Nealaak and I," Ardela added.

"Let's move into the practice arena, where the Gryphons can join us," Blazel suggested. "It's up to them who they choose to partner with, and they need to experience the Weave to decide if they want to be part of it."

"Yeah, like Boreek," Grazeen piped up. "He loves working with me, but dislikes the blending of his consciousness with others."

The new teams swarmed from the entertainment room. Some of the younger members ran to the practice arena, calling to their Gryphon friends to join them. By the time Rizelya's pack arrived, the groups had arranged themselves in circles. Every single person had a Gryphon sitting behind them. Just like with the Posairs, who came from every clan, the Gryphons came from nearly every flight which had joined the Posairs to fight the invaders.

Rizelya raised her eyebrows. This part of forming the teams was going to be easier than the rest. "For the weave to transition into a Black Weave, at least two Gryphons need to participate in it. Any Gryphon who wishes not to be part of the Weave can still be partnered with their chosen Posair."

"After all," Blazel said, winking at Graak, "the teams will be flitting across Lairheim to stop the Malvers' malignant magic. Having a Gryphon partner will make this much easier."

It's one reason I wish to be part of a Weave team, Chekraa said. Even sitting, the dark brown and white Gryphon towered over Dehali. White feathers covered his face and neck, but a dark taevo brown crest of feather stood in a ridge over the top of his head. He crouched deeper and lowered his bright orange beak, tipped with blue-gray, gently on top of Dehali's head.

Geraaik resettled his cinnamon brown wings over his back. Only the light brown wingtips showed where his wings ended and his fur started. *Gehan assures me we'll have an adventure, and our work will stop the hated Malvers. This is a worthy endeavor.* As he spoke, the three long feathers on his crest bounced and his yellow-orange eyes blazed with intensity.

Since Rizelya didn't know what the Gryphons did when they joined the Weave, she turned the instruction over to Graak. Instead of speaking with his people in mind-speech, he explained the procedure in the Gryphon language. She still couldn't understand much more than a few words of the screeches, clicks, and clacks.

They know what to do and are ready to begin, Graak said after a few milcrons, bobbing his head to Rizelya.

Rizelya rubbed her hands together, excitement building within her. "Okay, healers, initiate the blending with your group. Gryphons, join in as you will."

A few moments later, the faces of the Posairs relaxed, and a few sighed as they blended with their teammates. Rizelya could tell when the Gryphons entered the weave because everyone stiffened and their postures straightened. Then the Posairs grinned. Rizelya silently cheered, not wanting to break their connection. They'd achieved the Black Weave! She reached out and gripped Blazel's hand. His fingers interlaced with hers. Kaieli leaned against her side, and Rizelya wrapped her arm around her shoulder. Joy filled her with the two people she loved the most in the world at her side, witnessing this miracle.

A quarter of an octar later, the new teams slumped to the ground as the Weave released them. Leistral, Eidstrun, and Maestrun entered the arena, carrying trays loaded with mugs of taevo and light snacks. They balanced them on the railing while Kaieli added a reviving spell to the natural stimulant of the taevo.

"I'm glad someone thought about how drained we were after our first few blendings," Rizelya said.

"It wasn't us," Leistral said. "Loshera made the arrangements."

Blenora moaned as she sat up, rubbing her eyes, then gripping her head.

Blazel snatched a mug of taevo from a tray and hurried to his mother. "This will help the headache." He handed her the mug.

"Oh, Sweet Goddess!" Blenora gripped the mug tightly in her hands. "That was incredible. I sensed the Goddess like I've never done before. This truly is Her gift."

I also sensed Her, Blueek said, curling his tail around Blenora. The black tuft on its tip caressing her. *Thank you for allowing me to be part of it.* He rubbed a talon along his beak and the black feathers outlining his red eyes, and clicked in distress.

"Here, drink this." Blenora handed him her mug.

Within a few milcrons, everyone had revived from their profound experience and was sipping on mugs of taevo. Only a few Gryphons chose not to re-experience the blending of their consciousnesses.

"Oh," Blenora waved her hand, "we should give each team a name. We can't just be called team one, team two, etc."

Rizelya cocked an eyebrow. "That's a good idea. What do you suggest?"

"How about animal names? Our team could be the foxes, because we're so cute... and cunning."

Laughter filled the arena.

"I like it," Blazel said. "We could be the sabertigers, because we're so fierce."

The sabertigers are our enemies, Graak protested.

"But, you have to admit they are ferocious fighters and never give up." Blazel fingered the scar on his face he'd received from a sabertiger attack.

Fine, Graak harrumphed.

Soon, the other teams had given themselves names: Lynx, Bear, Wolf, Badger, and Ducorn.

"Now comes the difficult work," Rizelya commented, "of ridding Lairheim of the malignant magic tainting it and freeing us from the Malvers' monsters."

The new Black Weave teams cheered. A sense of calm eased the tightness in Rizelya's chest as she surveyed them, confident they could accomplish such a momentous task. Hopefully, the Malvers would hold off attacking them until they did.

Chapter 13

Wisah - 12 de Neydar, 1076

Wisah's days flowed into a routine. During the morning, she learned politics and diplomacy while attending the Supreme's meetings, and in the evenings, the Supreme taught her advanced spells from the ancient tome. In the afternoons, while the Supreme dozed in her chair, Wisah worked with Maendy, Maellyn, and Sheekeek in the library basement.

They were making progress in developing new weapons based on the ancient relics. To Wisah's relief, they still couldn't make the weapon in the scroll she had uncovered. Although she didn't fully comprehend the spell, its potential terrified her. But since reading Shandir's entries in the ancient tome, Wisah knew Malviana—and her god, Mordaga—must be stopped.

After learning about the horrors of the Great War from the hidden texts, Maellyn focused their efforts on making globes which anyone could activate, regardless of their magical Talent. The Malvers wouldn't spare anyone, therefore, everyone needed some type of weapon to defend themselves—and to fight the Malvers. Although the Posairs currently outnumbered the Malvers, it wouldn't remain the case.

As Wisah worked on her portion of the spell for the globes, she shuddered at the memory of reading the text detailing how Malvers were created. Even before the Great War, the Malvers had lost the power of procreation. Had Malviana already released her spell? Were Posairs suffering through the transformation? Wisah's thoughts flew to the twisted beast Blazel and Graak had described, and her heart ached. At least one Posair had become a Maldier. Because of the Scourge War, more would succumb to Malviana's evil.

"These should work," Maendy said, gazing at the prototypes laying on the workbench.

The globes looked beautiful in a rainbow of colors. Each color denoted a different type of spell contained within the globe. Having fought on the front lines, Maellyn had insisted they color code the globes so it'd be easy for fighters to grab the one they needed. In a fight, they wouldn't have time to sort through them.

Maendy brushed an errant strand of hair back from her face, then rubbed her hands together. "The next phase is the most fun. While I enjoy creating new devices, I love testing them. It's always a challenge to figure out why my creations aren't working as intended and then to fix them. We need people who don't have much Talent to test the globes so we can determine what adjustments we need to make."

"The Sanctuary's support staff includes all levels of Talent," Wisah said. "We even have a few warriors as guards, which will show us if our fighters can use these. I'll make the arrangements for test subjects."

"Maellyn and I will set up the tests. The practice arena in the guest area would be perfect. It's designed to contain errant magic."

Although I have magic, Sheekeek added, *it would be interesting to discover if Gryphons can also use our devices. We need every advantage we can develop if we're to win against the Malvers.*

The next day, several support staff, along with four men serving as guards for the Sanctuary, gathered in the practice arena. A table sat to the side of the sands with the various prototypes. The rainbow of colors glowed in the sunlight shining through the windows.

The men looked at each other, confusion written on their faces. A large man with pale yellow hair and brown eyes stepped forward, running his hat brim through his hands. "Um... Priestess Wisah... why are we here? We don't have any magic. We can't use those things."

"Ah, Celedon, but you do have magic," Wisah said, smiling at him. "You shapeshift, do you not?"

He nodded, his manner still skeptical. "I do."

"Well, it takes magic to shapeshift." She picked up a red globe and handed it to him. It fit easily in the palm of his hand. "Hold it out in front of you, focus on a target—" she pointed to the painted boards across the arena "—and say, 'Oyt.' The nonsense word activates the globe." She'd added it to the spells after remembering what Jaehaas said to activate his fire arrows. Wisah sighed as loneliness assailed her. She hadn't seen him in over three lunadars.

Gingerly, Celedon held out the globe. "Oyt, you said?"

As soon as the word left his mouth, lights danced across the globe. Startled, he pointed it at the target as a red beam of light shot from the globe. It struck the target, which burst into flames.

"How do I turn it off?" he exclaimed. The beam blinked out.

"You just did. 'Off' works to shut them down."

"It worked beautifully!" Maendy crowed, hugging Maellyn. "And he doesn't have a speck of Red Talent."

She'd studied the invader's weapons extensively and modified their light technology to work with the Posair magic. Maendy had created the pulsers the fighters now used, which used both magic and projectiles. However, she'd crafted the globes to absorb the elemental energies in the environment so they'd never run out of power.

Maendy excitedly handed an orange globe to a woman with pale blue hair and green eyes. "Go ahead, you try it."

"But... I can't hurt anyone," the woman protested.

Maellyn rolled her eyes. "The target isn't going to complain. Go on. Activate it."

The woman held the globe out as far as her arm would reach, turning her head away before whispering, "Oyt." At the loud crackling sound, she whirled her head around. Lightning flickered over the surface of the globe before a bolt sizzled into the target.

"Off! Off!" the woman shouted. The globe still crackled with electricity as she thrust it into Maendy's hands and ran from the arena.

Wisah watched her disappear. "I doubt she's ever used so much power before."

"I know how she feels, ma'am," Celedon said. He rubbed his jaw, gazing at the globes. "I never dreamed I could do anything like that. Can I try again?"

Maendy grinned as she handed him a purple globe.

This time, Celedon confidently held the orb away from his body and commanded, "Oyt." Steam whooshed from the globe and struck the target. He scowled at it. "What good will water do?"

"Have you ever lifted a lid from a boiling pot?" Maendy asked him. When he nodded, she said. "This steam is quite a bit hotter and will instantly burn anyone it hits."

"Oh!" He looked at the globe in his hand and the dripping target. He hefted the globe, tossing it lightly in the air and catching it again. "You know, if these were smaller and lighter, you could fit a whole arsenal in your pockets."

"That's brilliant!" Maendy's eyes glowed, and she kissed him on the cheek.

After testing the various globes, they dismissed the test subjects. The globes formed a bright rainbow of color.

Sheekeek walked to the table and picked up a mustard-colored globe. *We now know these work for Posairs with little magic, but do they work for me?* He held the globe in his talons and activated it.

A cyclone of air spun from it, growing larger as it barreled toward the target. Wisah threw up a hand to shield her eyes from the sand swirling into a gathering tornado. It struck the target, sucking it into the central funnel, then contracted on itself. It crushed the target with a loud popping sound.

Impressive, Sheekeek eyed the globe. *It's exhilarating to focus magic through an object. The cyclone would be effective against a large force if it could grow bigger.*

"It will," Maendy assured him, taking it from him and placing it on the table. "I've set the spell to limit its destructive capabilities while we're inside. It wouldn't do for us to be killed during our testing."

Sheekeek resettled his wings on his back. *Do you think our allies, the Vhelopsi, will be able to use these? They don't have any magic. Our kind can speak with them, but it takes great effort.*

Maendy shrugged. "Unfortunately, there aren't any Vhelopsi here we can include in our tests. I have to assume if one as un-Talented as that Blue could make them work, a Vhelopsi could as well. I believe I can adjust the spell to make it more responsive."

Maellyn packed the globes back in a padded box. "But we don't want our enemies, the Malvers, to be able to pick them off the battlefield and turn them against us." A shudder went through her. "It happened frequently during the war. But if we hadn't been able to use the Scourge's weapons against them, they might have won."

"We need to know more about them than we do now," Maendy wrinkled her nose. "For one, they use magic, but can they access the same type we do?"

Wisah leaned against the table. "They can't. At least they couldn't before their exile. Their magic is based on death and misery, while the foundation of ours is life and growth."

Sheekeek rubbed his chest feathers. *And how do you know that, Wisah?*

"It's something I read recently." She hadn't told anyone about the spell book, and she didn't think it was a good idea now. "The Supreme has me reading all sorts of esoteric stuff."

The globes repacked, Maendy and Maellyn hoisted the box between them and carried it back to the workshop, with Wisah and Sheekeek trailing behind them. As they climbed the stairs to the library, Maellyn tripped, the box slipping from her fingers. Without thinking, Wisah sketched a sigil in the air. The box halted in midair before it crashed, then rose until it was level. Wisah drew another sigil.

"You can let go, Maendy," Wisah said. "I have it."

Eyes wide, Maendy carefully and slowly opened her hands and pulled them away from the box. It floated. With a flick of Wisah's fingers, it trundled ahead of them on a cushion of air.

"How... what are you doing?" Maendy asked.

Sheekeek touched her shoulder with his beak. *And why are you glowing? Does it have anything to do with the change in your eyes? They are now almost black.*

Wisah pushed up her left sleeve. A tattoo of the sigil she was using to float the box glowed with azure light. She sighed. If she used the magic she'd received from the spell book, she shouldn't complain when someone noticed it. "I think it does. For some reason, the Goddess has gifted me with new powers."

Maendy's eyes sparkled. "How many other sigils tattoos do you have?"

Wisah shrugged. "I don't know. They cover my entire body. And before you ask, no, I didn't put them there. They simply appeared one day." She internally winced. Opening a book was simple, except this book wasn't an ordinary one.

Wisah concentrated on maneuvering the box down the stairs. The light globes she'd installed last chedan brightened as the group stepped down the stairs. Once she settled the box safely on a table, she turned to face her friends.

"As far as I can tell, they only show when I access the power of the sigil." She pushed back her sleeve again. Only a faint outline of the symbol remained on her arm, and within moments, it completely faded.

"Fascinating. I've never seen or heard of anything like it." Maendy held Wisah's arm as she examined it. She dragged Wisah to a table with a lantern on it, and using a magnifying glass, she peered at Wisah's arm. "They are there, just under the skin. We'd have to experiment to discover which ones you have."

"I think I have all of them."

Maendy whistled. "There are hundreds of sigils. Are you sure?"

Magic thrummed under Wisah's skin. "Pretty certain."

What about the symbol for darkness? Sheekeek lifted his hind leg to scratch his ear.

Wisah drew the sigil in the air in front of her. Magic flared over her back right hip, and then every light in the workshop was extinguished, plunging them into darkness. Sheekeek squawked and Maellyn gasped. Maendy's fingers squeezed Wisah's arm. She sketched the symbol for light and sensed a tracery of power on her left pectoral muscle. She glanced down at the sigil glowing in the spot she felt the magic. The lights flickered on again, including the torches they hadn't lit when they entered the room.

Sheekeek blinked in the sudden light. *That was amazing, but also a bit frightening.* His fur stood on end and a feather floated to the ground. *Well... a lot frightening.*

Wisah rubbed her arms, slight jolts of energy shocked her fingertips. She shook her hands to rid them of the sensation. "It scares me too. I'm not sure what's happening to me."

Maendy studied her for a long moment. Wisah squirmed under her intense gaze. She felt like a strange, alien bug being examined under a magnifying glass.

"Something that has bothered me finally makes sense now." Maendy turned away and glided to the worktable she used as a desk. She rummaged through the piles of paper and pulled one out. She opened the cabinet and removed the scroll Wisah had found two chedans ago. Maendy unrolled it and placed a sheet of paper next to it. Wisah wandered over and recognized her translation of the scroll.

"See these. I couldn't figure out why the spell included them." Maendy tapped a symbol on the scroll, then another one, then a third. "We don't use sigil magic."

"The Supreme does," Wisah said absently, staring at the scroll, finally noticing the sigils buried within the text's fancy script. She squinted at them, visualizing them combined into one in her mind, and gasped, covering her mouth with her hand. "It can't be," she breathed.

"What?" Maendy looked up at her sharply. "What's wrong, Wisah? You've turned pale."

Wisah swallowed hard. Now she understood what terrible spell Shandir had used to kill Mordar. She slumped into the nearest chair, burying her face in her hands and shaking her head. How could the Goddess ask her to do something so horrible?

She heard the clicking of Sheekeek's claws on the stone floor as he approached the desk. *Maendy, what did you show her?*

"Just these sigils." Confused, Maendy pointed at the scroll. "I don't recognize them, but the spell needs them to work."

As Maendy touched the parchment, the dry crinkle sounded like death peals to Wisah. A few moments later, Sheekeek warbled in distress.

Oh, my poor friend. He laid a comforting talon on her shoulder. *The Goddess only asks the strongest of us to do such a terrible deed.*

"What? What does it do?" Maendy asked, her voice high in alarm.

Wisah lowered her hands. "It's the darkest spell imaginable, a spell of unmaking. The spell doesn't just kill someone. It unmakes them as if they had never existed, destroying even their soul, so there's no hope of rebirth. Using it was the only way to stop Mordar. And now it's the only way to stop Malviana."

Wisah glanced at her hands. The faint outlines of two of the three necessary sigils glowed faintly on the backs of her hands. She didn't doubt the third one was somewhere on her body.

Her hands trembled. Only one person in the world was capable of performing the spell: her. What would it do to her to cast something so ghastly?

Blazel - 13 de Neydar, 1076

Blazel surveyed the keshe board, looking for a good move so he could take the most pieces from his fellow players while losing him the fewest. Eight players made the game more exciting. They had played several times since his mother had arrived. It reminded him of the nights he and Chariel had played with Histrun and Blenora whenever Histrun visited the Sanctuary. After the first time Histrun came to the Sanctuary grieving Zehala's death, he'd returned two or three times a year. Although Blazel didn't want his mother in danger, he enjoyed spending time with her.

As Blazel's hand hovered over one of his pieces, he glanced at Histrun. The gleam in Histrun's eye made him change his mind, and he moved a different piece.

"Drat you, boy," Histrun harrumphed. "I wanted you to make the other move!" Even as Histrun growled, he quickly took his turn.

"Ha! Wrong move, Histrun," Chariel chuckled. She made a complicated move, clearing seven of Histrun's pieces, three of Keshanal's, two of Aistrun's, and the last three of Naila's.

"I'm out," Naila groaned, leaning back in her chair. She stood and stretched. "Let me know who wins. I'm headed to bed."

"So early?" Histrun asked.

"It's past midnight."

"It's that late already?" Keshanal looked at the chronometer on the wall. "My old bones are tired and ready for bed. Aistrun will take my last pieces with his move. I'll go upstairs with you, Naila."

Naila waited for Keshanal to lever herself out of her chair and then offered her arm to the older woman. Keshanal leaned heavily on Naila as they walked out of the entertainment room. Blazel hadn't realized how much the last few lunadars had aged Keshanal. He turned back to look at Histrun with fresh eyes, noticing the deep worry lines etched on the old man's face. *Will they survive leading another war?*

The banter quieted as the remaining players concentrated on the game. As each player reduced the number of pieces on the board, it became harder to make good plays. Histrun made his next move.

"Hey," Aistrun protested, "you can't move that way, Histrun. That's cheating!"

"Nice try," Blenora laughed. "He caught you. Now you have to forfeit a piece of his choosing."

Blazel laughed with the others as Histrun growled. His forfeit and Chariel's next move left Histrun with only two pieces, which Rizelya took on her turn.

"See, Histrun," Blenora said with a smile. "You can't win, even when you cheat. Especially when you cheat."

A few moves later, Chariel won. The rest headed to bed while Blazel and Rizelya stayed to put away the game.

"This is nice," Rizelya said, stacking the pieces in their container. "I've never spent so much time with Histrun before. Until a few days ago, I hadn't ever played keshe with him."

"Really?"

"I was raised in the crèche and rarely saw him, except in training. I've played lots of jelehan with him, but only because it teaches hand-eye coordination. He's always been more of a mentor to me than a father."

"He's been both to me. I'm sorry you didn't experience the same with him."

Rizelya shrugged and, putting the last piece in its place, handed the box to him to put in the cabinet. "I didn't miss what I didn't have. Children born to those in the fighting-packs rarely have any type of relationship with their parents." A sad look crossed her face. "Although I vaguely remember my mother visiting the crèche, singing to me and reading me stories. Treasure the time you have with Blenora and the relationship you have with her. It's unique in our world."

As Blazel tucked the box on the shelf, he considered the closeness he shared with both Blenora and Histrun. Now, he was grateful his mother had fought to keep him in the Sanctuary and raise him rather than send him to his birth father's clan. When he'd turned twelve, Histrun had become his father figure.

He turned around, leaning against the cabinet. "Weren't you lonely? Did anyone show you love and affection?"

"No, I wasn't lonely. I had Aistrun and the other children in the crèche to play with. The caregivers gave us plenty of love, so I grew up fine."

"I can't imagine what it was like for you. My experience was so different. Well, you're getting to know Histrun as a father now. And you're well-loved. I love you." He pulled her into an embrace and kissed her gently.

She returned it and deepened the kiss. Her hands caressed his back and slid down to grip his buttocks. His wandering hands slid over the softness of her breasts, and his manhood hardened. Upstairs, over two dozen people shared their room. Here, they were alone. He needed to feel her skin against his. He quickly divested her of her clothes, and his soon followed hers to float to the floor.

Still kissing her, he picked Rizelya up and carried her to the fur rug in front of the fireplace. Blazel admired how the coals cast a soft light over her flushed skin. He sank into her soft, warm depths. As they moved together toward climaxing, her magic reached for him, and in answer, his magic rose from his deep core. With a jolt, their magic merged. It curled around him, through him, and through her until there was no beginning, no end, no separation between them. It carried him higher and higher, into an ecstasy he'd never experienced before.

Later, as she cradled her head on his shoulder, he marveled at the magic still infusing his skin. "Have you ever experienced your magic doing that before?" he asked quietly, not sure if he really wanted to know the answer.

She turned to face him and lightly traced the scar over his eyebrow and down his cheek. "Never. It was amazing! The blending we do in the Black Weave must have attuned our magic and our energies. I wonder if it will happen every time we make love?"

He kissed her fingertips. "I wouldn't be averse to it!" He slid his fingers along the curve of her side. "Bond with me."

"I think we just did." She smiled and kissed him.

"No. Be my bond-mate. Agree to spend the rest of your life with me." He held his breath, waiting for her answer. Once they bonded, there would be no going back. The ceremony was more than an exchange of bond-mate torques. It joined their souls.

"Yes," she whispered. "For as long as we have left, whether it is only a few days or thousands of days, I want to spend them with you."

Overjoyed, he pulled her closer to him and made love to her again.

Blazel and Rizelya awoke before anyone else in the keep-house. He bounced down the stairs to the bathing room. His steps were as light as his heart, and he couldn't stop grinning. Rizelya had agreed to be his bond-mate! He'd never be alone again. Blazel tilted his head back on the rim of the big redwood tub with his arm around her shoulders. He gazed into the depths of her dark brown eyes, amazed at the beautiful soul who loved him shining in them.

"When do you want to do the ceremony?" he asked. "My mother would be overjoyed to officiate."

"I wish Wisah could be here for it." Rizelya trailed her hands in the water. "I'd love for her to also officiate. But I doubt the Supreme is going to release her just for our bonding. We can't have the ceremony without bond-torques, and those will take time to make." She made a face and splashed the water. "Damn! Maellyn isn't here to make them for us. The Supreme called her to the Sanctuary for some secret work. I want Maellyn to make yours for me."

"Histrun is constantly sending messengers to the Sanctuary. Maybe we can slip a message to Maellyn and ask her. I, too, would prefer someone I know well to make the tokens of our bonding. After all, I'll be wearing it the rest of my life, so I want it to last."

"But what if I die before you, years before you?"

He fingered his throat as if the bond-torque already laid against his skin. "I'll be like Histrun. Even though it's been nearly twenty years since Zehala's death, he still wears her bond-torque."

He kissed her. Before they could do much more, people entered the bathing room.

Aistrun poked his head into the area which held the soaking tubs. "Hey, so this is where you two are! Histrun wants to see you after breakfast."

A few milcrons later, Aistrun, Chariel, Kaieli, and the rest of their team climbed into the big tub, their skin rosy from their scrubbing. Blazel averted his eyes, still not quite comfortable bathing with others.

Chariel peered at Blazel and Rizelya and raised an eyebrow. "Something is different about you two. What's happened? You're both positively glowing."

"We're going to become bond-mates," Blazel blurted. He was too happy about it to keep it quiet.

"Congratulations!" Leistral said, looking shyly at Eidstrun. He smiled at her and put his arm around her, pulling her close.

"That isn't just it," Chariel said, after the others congratulated them. "Your energy is different."

Rizelya squeezed his hand and grinned. "Our magic merged when we made love last night."

Heat flushed over Blazel, and he wanted to duck under the water. He was extremely glad his mother still bathed with the priestesses.

Chariel smiled. "Ah, that's it. I've never heard of it happening before, but then, no one has ever blended like we do with the Black Weave."

"Do you think it will happen to us?" Aistrun waggled his eyebrows at Chariel.

She laughed. "Possibly."

Embarrassed by the intimate talk, Blazel changed the subject. "My stomach's growling. I'm starved."

"It's all that lovemaking," Aistrun teased.

"Why yes, it is," Rizelya said, grinning at Blazel. "I'm hungry, too."

Blazel blushed and quickly climbed out of the tub.

He and Rizelya held hands while they walked to the dining hall, and Blazel grinned at the open display of affection. It didn't happen often. "When should we talk to Histrun about our bond-mating ceremony to arrange a time?"

"He isn't the one to set it. We are. But we can't determine when to have the ceremony until after we've cleared the swamps around the two keeps. Come on, I'm starved." Rizelya hurried to step into the line for food.

Blazel knew she was right. But he didn't want to wait. He wanted to be bonded to her as soon as possible.

Malviana - 17 de Neydar, 1076

Malvidor rushed into Malviana's laboratory. "Mother! Come look," he squealed, bouncing on his toes.

She put down her knife and turned away from the bloody Gryphon. "What is it, my son?"

"You have to see the new creature I've transformed for you. I think you'll love it." He pulled on her hand, urging her off her stool.

Laughing, she allowed him to drag her from the room and up the stairs and hallway. She needed a break from her efforts to twist the Gryphon. None of her attempts had worked any more than they had for Mordar. It would be nice to witness something that had succeeded.

A loud roaring broke the quiet. Intrigued, Malviana hurried to the balcony overlooking the rear courtyard. Below her, thirty monsters turned as one to gaze up at her and Malvidor. They reminded Malviana of the jallopitar inhabiting the swamps, but these were much, much larger. The beast's elongated snouts were those of a jallopitar, except they had a short, curving horn on the end of it. A frill of sharp horns haloed their heads.

"I used the jallopitar to make those." Malvidor waved his hand at his creations milling in the courtyard. "They have a good sense of smell and are tenacious trackers. I call them jallopsitor. Do you like them?"

"If they kill Posairs, I love them."

"I programmed them to kill Posairs over all else, and we can control them through the magic pools. Shall I let them loose?"

Malviana took his face between her hands and kissed his forehead. "Yes, my sweet, clever son. Let's see what damage they cause."

His eyes sparkled, and he grinned. Lifting his wand, he set a spell over the beasts. "Seek our enemies and destroy," he commanded. Malvidor used a tendril of magic to open the back gate. The largest beast turned a red eye on him and roared, then charged out, followed by the rest of its herd. Trees quaked and fell as the jallopsitors barreled through the swamp. Soon, only trembling leaves and crushed vegetation showed their path.

Malviana watched them until they were out of sight. With a sigh, she returned to her laboratory. Perhaps this time, she'd find the right combination of spells to transform the damned Gryphon.

Blazel - 18 de Neydar, 1076

Blazel and Rizelya slid into the chairs in front of the alpha's desk. On their way in, they'd passed Keshanal hurrying down the stairs to take care of some personnel disagreement.

Histrun grimaced at the tall stack of papers in front of him before moving them aside. "Are the other Black Weave teams ready to go it alone?"

"Yes, sir," Blazel said, slouching in his seat, with his arms dangling over the armrests. "After the last nine grueling days, clearing the rancorous pools near both Haaslornde and Dehanranle Keeps and the surrounding areas, they've had plenty of experience."

"Good work on training them and clearing the malignant magic pools." Histrun relaxed back in his chair, his hands threaded behind his head.

Rizelya perked up at Histrun's praise.

"Thank you, sir," Blazel said, rubbing his tired eyes.

"We've seen a huge difference," Histrun continued. "We haven't fought a janack or brecha in days, although the twisted creatures are becoming a bothersome nuisance."

Naila grimaced while fiddling with a pen. *The damn things creep up on us at any time, from any direction. We moved all the troops behind the stone walls of the pastures and fields to protect them.*

"The Black Weave doesn't seem to affect them," Rizelya said, crossing her ankles in front of her. "We've tried."

"I know you have, girl. I'm not upset at you." Histrun dropped his hands and leaned forward. "We're seeing more—and different—creatures. Just this afternoon, Blazel's antlered beast led a raid on the keep. We had an up-close encounter with him banging on the keep's gate. He appeared like some twisted

version of a Posair, and there were several others with him."
Histrun shuddered. "Great Mother! Is that what the infection is
turning our people into?"

Blazel shrugged, even though the question seemed
rhetorical.

Naila grinned at them. *Thankfully, since you cleared the
swamps, we haven't had any more people fall to the black-
splotch infection.*

"That's a relief to hear," Rizelya said.

"But before then, a hundred people have disappeared. That's
too many to lose to our enemies. Damned Malvers woman!"
Histrun slapped the desk with the palm of his hand. He took
a few deep breaths. "We drove the twisted Posairs off, and our
scouts followed them. The damned things are slithering from
the swamp beyond the Barrens."

Blazel fisted his hands. "Have you had any word from
Baekeek and the other scouts we left there? They should have
notified us when these creatures left the swamp."

Histrun shook his head. "No, nothing from them. I fear the
worst. Moraak would be able to tell me if his people were alive,
but he's still in Alkaak."

"Perhaps Graak can contact them. He's leading the
Gryphons while Moraak's away. Well, he was until we snagged
him as part of the Black Weave." Blazel chuckled.

Please ask him, or whoever replaced him, Naila said.
*We're worried about what mischief the Malvers are doing
inside their compound.*

"Mischief?" Rizelya snorted. "That's too mild of a word. We
know what they're doing. Creating new monsters to plague us."

"Damn Malvers!" Histrun swore, then stood and paced to
the window, gazing out of it for a moment.

While waiting for Histrun, Blazel contacted Graak and
asked about the status of the scouts. He slumped further in
his seat. "Sir, the news isn't good. None of the Gryphons can
contact the scouts. They aren't sure if the barrier around the
castle is causing the problem, or if something has happened to
them. They want permission to check."

Histrun turned away from the window and leaned against it
with his arms crossed over his chest. "We need more intelligence
about the Malvers. But we now know it's too dangerous to have

people watching the castle. Until we obtain more information, I don't want to risk any more Gryphons. I fear the worst has happened to them." He gazed at Naila for a moment, and his eyes slightly glazed as he silently communicated with her.

"Not a good choice, but necessary," Naila ground out in her gravelly voice.

Histrun sighed. "We're reopening the crater fortresses. They're a safer place to watch, and possibly stop, the creatures slithering out of the swamp before they leave the Barrens."

Blazel leaned forward, his elbows on his knees. "Is that wise, sir? Anyone stationed there will be in danger from the nucla poisoning."

"It's why your team, the Sabertigers, by the way I like the use of animal names for your teams, and the Fox team are going there. There's too much malignant magic in the Barrens for a single team to purge."

Blazel's heart plummeted. His mother was part of the Fox team.

"I'm disbursing the other teams throughout Lairheim." Histrun paced the small office, then stopped at the table with the map on it. He gestured for them to join him.

"The Lynx team is to go directly to Strunlair Province. We need it cleared before the army reaches it. Once they finish, they're to travel to Ronanlair Province. I'm sending the Bear team north ahead of the army, through the Haaslair plains." Histrun indicated the route on the map. "They will clear the swamps as they go, creating a path for us in case we must retreat. I want a corridor of safety between here and Strunlair Province. It means Haaslair and Strunlair Provinces will take the brunt of the fighting. But I'm intimately familiar with Strunlair Province and can fight the Malvers better there. Of course, the best option will be to stop them here.

"Once the Bear team reaches Strunlair Province, they're to head west into Dehanlair. The Wolf team will go through Posanlair, then into Andranlair. I'm assigning the Badger team to Keistanlair Province and the Ducorn team to Ledonlair."

Blazel whistled. "If our Black Weave teams accomplish this, we'll clear the entire Lairheim continent north of the Barrens of malignant magic!"

"That's the goal," Naila rasped.

Histrun turned back to the map and studied it. After a few milcrons, he sighed and faced Blazel and Rizelya. "I'd considered having them meet us in Strunhelos after they finish clearing the malignant magic pools in their assigned areas, but I'm unsure how long it will take them. I don't want them coming to Strunhelos in the middle of the siege and risk Malviana capturing them. If they finish, they're to stay at the respective Clan Keeps. Do they know how to create your net-shield?"

Rizelya nodded. "They do."

"Good. They can protect the Clan Keeps from the Malvers if needed." Histrun leaned against the table and crossed his arms over his chest.

"What exactly do you want us to do at the crater, sir?" Rizelya asked, a furrow creasing her forehead.

"Why, empty the malignant lake in it, of course."

Rizelya sputtered. "But... but, sir. Kaieli tells me it's huge. I doubt it's possible."

"Do whatever you can. Malignant magic forms the swamps, and you can drain them, so it stands to reason you could do the same with the crater."

"I suspect they aren't exactly the same." Blazel scowled as he crossed his ankle over his knee. He'd seen the crater and felt its power during the Scourge War.

Histrun curled his lip. "If the Malvers used the magic in the swamps to create their foul monsters, what could they do with the immense power in the crater? I don't want to even think about it. Although we're seeing some examples in the creatures attacking us."

Blazel shuddered. The twisted floxidor, skeaeters, and banthues were bad enough—almost worse than the janacks and brechas. However, the new beasts were easier to kill.

Chapter 14

Blazel - 20 de Neydar, 1076

The sabertiger and fox Black Weave teams and their guards flew toward the Barrens. A larger force followed on horseback along with a half-flight of Gryphons flying with them to staff the fortresses.

Below them, the landscape changed from fertile plains grass to sagebrush and cedar trees, and then to the scrublands bordering the Barrens. Blazel reflected on how much had transpired in the year since he'd left the southern swamp as a lone wolf. He glanced over his right shoulder, grinning when Rizelya waved and threw him a kiss. On the other side of him, Aistrun and Broogk seemed to be deep into a conversation. Knowing Aistrun, he was telling Broogk some wild story. Behind them, his best friend Chariel lay across Torlek's back, her eyes glued to the terrain speeding past them.

Kaieli on Keeru and Loshera on Morlek both wore pained expressions the closer they flew to the Barrens. They had both spent lunadars in the Scourge slave camp, but if they hadn't, they wouldn't know about the Black Weave. Kaieli had first developed the technique to fight a plague, which he now suspected was another Malvers infection. She'd further evolved the Weave in the slave camp, healing the men from nucla poisoning. The Posairs wouldn't be able to cleanse their land of the evil magic contaminating it if the Scourge hadn't captured Kaieli. Sometimes, the Goddess worked in mysterious ways.

Before darkness fell, Graak landed next to the Storengher River in a small copse of trees. While the Posairs set up camp, Graak, Glork, and Broogk graciously tossed several big, fat fish onto the shore. Grazeen found wild onions and carrots along the riverbank, and Eiden discovered watercress in a pool. Soon, the scent of roasting fish made Blazel's mouth water.

As they relaxed around the campfire after eating, Blazel rubbed at the prickling sensation on the back of his neck. He peered beyond the fire, but nothing appeared in the dark to explain his uneasiness. "We need to set watch rotations tonight, with at least three people for each shift. A woman with fighting experience, a warrior, and a Gryphon." He gazed around the fire, and everyone nodded in agreement. "Rizelya, Graak, and I will take the first watch. Eiden, Leistrun, and Korrik, if you'll take the second?"

We shall, Korrik answered.

"Dehali, Aistrun, and Broogk, will you take the last one?"

"Sure thing," Aistrun said with a yawn.

A few milcrons later, the party crawled into their bedrolls. Soon, soft snores filled the campsite. Rizelya sat next to Blazel, leaning against his shoulder. She shivered as the flames died down. He put another log on the fire, then pulled her closer, rubbing her arm. Graak's eyes reflected yellow in the light as he blinked slowly. The three talked quietly, needing to stay awake. Blazel couldn't shake the feeling they were being watched, but nothing approached their fire. Every so often, he stood and stalked the perimeter of their camp, staring into the dark.

Blazel's anxiety strung his nerves so taut, he felt he'd break. Finally, his watch ended, and he awoke Leistrun and Eiden for their shift. He crawled into his bedroll, and Rizelya curled up next to him. Unable to sleep, Blazel gazed at the stars. How many nights had he watched them alone? Rizelya murmured in her sleep and cuddled closer to him for warmth. He put his arm around her and kissed the top of her head.

Kaaik's shrill cry woke him. *We're under attack!*

Large shapes loomed in the dark. Blazel kicked out of his bedroll, grabbed his pulser, and jerked to his feet. Rizelya stood beside him, her helbraught blade glowing. Its light revealed more shadows slinking toward the camp. Soon, more helbraughts glowed brightly as the women fed their magic into them. The men snarled as they shifted into their warrior form.

A dark shape leaped at Blazel, and he threw the pulser up, blocking the huge jaws from sinking into his throat. He gagged on the fetid breath. Someone kicked the fire, causing a shower of sparks. In the flickering light, a red reptilian eye blinked at him. A short, curved horn rose from the end of the elongated snout, and serrated teeth filled its open jaws. A frill of sharp horns extended from its neck.

Rizelya ducked under his upraised arm and thrust her helbraught into the creature's underbelly. The heated blade slid into the scaly hide. Fire danced from the blade as she gutted the beast, and it flopped down.

"Duck!" Blazel yelled, firing as she dropped. The projectile slammed into the back of another creature's throat.

Rizelya stood back-to-back with him. Another beast rushed him, its smaller front clawed legs grasping for him. The creature warbled and emitted a pulse of magic. Blazel dodged to the side, the hairs on his arm raising as the energy slid past him. He fired his pulser, swearing as he missed, and the projectile bounced off its frill of horns. Before he could fire again, a beast hit him from the side, throwing him into the air. He rolled as he hit the ground and came up to a knee, still clutching his pulser. He adjusted the settings, chambered another round, and fired. A red light zipped from his weapon, burying deep into the side of the creature that had hit him. The red glow grew larger as the fire ate at the beast's innards. He shot two more rounds into it before it toppled over.

Blazel ignored the warmth trickling from his calf. Rizelya fought with a beast, the staff end of her helbraught keeping its snapping jaws from her. A Gryphon flared, and in the light Blazel saw dozens more of the creatures rushing toward them. He glanced around. The beasts had surrounded them, and were pushing them into a smaller and smaller circle.

Graak! Blazel called. *We have to get out of here, or we'll be overrun.* They'd lose their supplies, but they could return for them later.

Coming!

Blazel fired into the open mouth of another creature as it reached for him. Wing beats cracked above him, and Graak landed beside him. Blazel flung himself onto Graak's back, squeezing his legs to stay on as Graak leaped into the air. Blazel shot into the melee below him, providing cover as the other Gryphons landed and quickly took off again with their riders. He searched for Blenora and Ardela. Panic flooded him. The two priestesses didn't have any fighting abilities or training. What was he thinking, bringing them into such a dangerous situation without giving them any weapons?

Graak, where are Blenora and Ardela? I don't see them.

They're safe. We carried them away as soon as the attack began.

Blazel sagged against Graak's back, wrapping his arms around the Gryphon's neck, holding tight as Graak continued to fly higher, leaving the creatures behind. *Did everyone get out?*

Maestrun was killed. Leistrun is badly injured, and so is Brogkek. Several others, both Gryphon and Posair, suffer from minor injuries. It's a good thing we have Kaieli and Faliciden with us.

A few milcrons later, Graak angled to land. *Brogkek can't fly any longer without treatment,* he said before Blazel could protest. *Leistrun also needs healing quickly. We should be far enough away from those creatures. Kaieli wants to treat our injured before we reach the Barrens.*

When Graak landed, Blazel slid off him. Feet thudded the ground as the others dismounted. The Gryphons flared, providing them with light. Kaieli and Faliciden rushed to Leistrun and Brogkek. Blazel limped toward them, and the fire in his calf grew with each step.

Rizelya approached him and frowned at the blood dribbling down his leg. "That looks bad."

Blueek and Nealaak, carrying Blenora and Ardela, arrived. Blenora jumped off and ran to Blazel. "Sweet Mother!" she cried, her hand flying to her mouth and her eyes wide. "You're hurt!"

He shrugged. He'd had worse. "It isn't that bad."

"No, no, you need help now," Blenora insisted.

"I can wait until Kaieli heals Leistrun and Brogkek."

Blenora's eyes widened when she noticed Kaieli kneeling over Leistrun. "Oh, Mother save us! He's horribly injured. Kaieli can't heal you just yet. But we must stop your bleeding until she can." She put her arm on his.

Blazel gritted his teeth. He wasn't used to having someone fuss over him. He glanced over at Rizelya for help.

She rolled her eyes at him, took off her belt, and made a tourniquet. "That will hold until Kaieli treats you."

With Blenora on one side of him and Rizelya on the other, Blazel hobbled over to where Leistrun lay on the ground. He gagged when he saw Leistrun's bloody stump. His left arm ended at his elbow. Kaieli worked feverishly to staunch the blood flow. Eiden knelt by him, tears streaming down her checks as she brushed his hair from his face and murmured to him.

Blazel shuddered. With that type of injury, Leistrun would never shapeshift into his wolf form again. They'd learned from the Scourge war the loss of limbs didn't necessarily mean the men couldn't shift to their warrior form. It depended on the man's determination. And with the new pulsers, they could still fight.

His sister, Leistral, bent over the top of his head. She abruptly stood, whirled around, and kicked the dirt, swearing at him for being slow and at the Goddess for allowing him to be injured. "Damn those Malvers! Why do they have to create such awful creatures?" Leistral railed. Eidstrun strode to her and wrapped her in his arms, and she dropped her head into his chest. Her sides heaving as she cried.

Faliciden worked on healing the deep gash in Brogkek's side. As the golden-green light streamed from her hands and bathed the wound, it started to knit together.

Saffren sobbed in Nelstrun's arms, while tears streaked down Nelstrun's face. Oslerru bowed over them. Blazel winced at his high-pitched keening. The rest of the group gathered near her. Worry and pain etched on their faces. Blazel took quick stock of his pack and let out a relieved breath. Everyone else's injuries were minor.

"Does anyone know what happened?" he asked.

Saffren lifted her head. "It's all my fault. I woke up and had to pee. Maestrun wouldn't let me leave by myself. Suddenly, one of those creatures appeared out of the dark and snapped Maestrun's neck. He didn't have time to fire his pulser. More beasts attacked, and Leistrun and Brogkek rushed to save me. Several creatures swarmed them. I couldn't help them. I hadn't thought to carry my helbraught with me." She buried face into Nelstrun's shoulder, sobs shaking her slender frame.

"It isn't your fault, Saffren," Blazel said, patting her shoulder.

"What were those creatures?" Rizelya's eyebrows furrowed. "I haven't seen anything like them before."

I think we have new Malvers' monsters to contend with, Graak said. His head feathers drooped.

Rizelya cursed. "Great, it's all we need."

"Hey, we were just getting rid of the janacks and brechas," Aistrun growled.

The others murmured agreement.

The prickling sensation crawled on Blazel's skin. He held up a hand for silence and breathed deeply. The same fetid stench he'd smelled on the creatures filled his nostrils. "Kaieli, you about done there? Brogkek, can you fly?"

"What's wrong?" Rizelya's head swiveled as she looked all around. "Are we in danger?"

The creatures are coming! Glork squawked from behind them. *Hurry, they'll be here in milcrons.*

I can fly. Pain laced Brogkek's voice. *But I can't carry Leistrun.*

I'll take him, Korrik said. He stood protectively over Eiden and Leistrun.

"Are we running from them?" Leistral incredulous stare burned into Blazel. "We can't let them get away with this!"

"There's more of them than us," Blazel said. "We barely escaped our last encounter with them."

Rizelya placed her hand over Leistral's, gently lowering her helbraught. "We need to move Leistrun to safety. We either stand and fight those creatures, and allow Leistrun to die, or we flee to save him."

Leistral grimaced and looked at where her brother laid on the grass. Faliciden had joined Kaieli, and together, they worked feverishly. Kaieli grimaced as a bright bronze light flashed from her hands.

"There," Kaieli said, sitting back on her heels. "We've stopped his bleeding. He'll hold on until we reach somewhere safer."

"The fortress is the only place close by with walls," Blazel said. His skin crawled, and the stench grew stronger. "Come on, we have to go!"

Aistrun and Nelstrun lifted Leistrun's limp body onto Kaaik's back. Eiden climbed on behind him, wrapping her arms around him.

"Wait!" Nelstrun cried. "Maestrun's body. We can't leave it for the monsters."

I've already done what I could. Oslerru dipped his head and rubbed his black beak against Nelstrun's cheek. *By the time I reached the fight, a big brute in the herd was eating Maestrun. I burned his remains.* He stretched his neck, warbling a distressed cry, then snapped his sharp beak. *And the beast.*

"No more time!" Blazel yelled as he helped Blenora into her Gryphon's harness. He sprinted to Graak and scrambled onto his back. As soon as their partners settled onto them, the Gryphons leaped into the air.

The new monsters burst through the brush as Brogkek lumbered into the sky. The lead creature raised on its toes, its broad tail supporting its weight, and snapped its jaws. Brogkek jerked his tail up before the monster could nip it. Blazel looked back over his shoulder. The creatures snuffled the bloody ground where Leistrun had lain. Red glowing eyes turned to watch their escape. Unbelievably, the beasts ran after them.

"Go, Graak, Go!" Blazel yelled. He clung onto Graak's neck, digging his fingers into the fur. Blazel winced as the wind stung his eyes. None of them, except Blenora and Ardela, had harnesses—or goggles. They had a long flight across the Barrens to reach the northern fortress. Blazel prayed no one would fall during the journey.

Rizelya - 21 de Neydar, 1076

Rizelya hung onto Glork, her head pressed into his neck, and her eyes squeezed closed. They'd fled without retrieving their goggles, harness, or other belongings. Her arms ached from holding him tightly, afraid she'd fall the thousands of feet to her death. The nightmare of the attack replayed over and over. She'd spent her life battling the Malvers' monsters, the symbiotic pair of janacks and brechas, and had thought they were the worst thing she would ever fight. Just when she thought they'd found a way to eradicate the miserable beasts from her world, new monsters popped up to take their place. But nothing tied the new creatures to the malignant magic pools. *Goddess help us!*

The air became drier, and grit tickled the back of her throat. She opened her eyes, squinting against the glare of the afternoon sun glittering off the black sand-glass below them. Dark, glossy boulders of petrified wood thrust into the sky. On the horizon, the steep slope of Shandir's Crater rose like a black snake. Glork descended, and she tightened her grip. The white sheadash stone walls of the fortress shone like a beacon of light in the black sea of sand.

Glork landed in the courtyard, panting, his wings drooping at his sides. They hadn't stopped during the long flight since fleeing in the middle of the night, afraid the damnable new monsters would catch them. Dust rose in the Barrens from the running beasts as they followed Rizelya's pack. Rizelya forced her cramped fingers to open and slid off, leaning against Glork's side as pins and needles raced up and down her legs and feet. *We made it!* They never would have if they hadn't had the Gryphons. How would the troops cross the Barrens with those new creatures dogging them?

The only time she'd been inside one of the guard fortresses was searching for survivors after the Scourge landed. She hadn't paid much attention to it then, and looked around her with interest. Other than the location, it seemed like any other keep she'd visited. Then she noticed there wasn't a temple sitting prominently next to the keep-house. She was stretching her legs when her gaze landed on the sturdy gate.

The open gate.

"Blazel! Aistrun!" she yelled, running. "The gate!"

Blazel cursed, and he raced behind her. They reached the gate and started shoving it closed. One side banged into place, and they rushed to the other side. They'd nearly pushed it closed when a long snout poked through. Claws gripped the edge of the gate and pulled. With renewed effort, Rizelya shoved the heavy door. Eidstrun, Delestrun, and Nelstrun added their strength.

A spear of ice zoomed past her ear to embed in the monster's nose. Its high-pitched screech rang in her ears. Saffren tossed another ice spear. A blast of freezing air hit the monster, pushing it back. Rizelya stepped away, letting the bigger and stronger men close the gate. Fury filled Eiden's face, and her helbraught glowed bright yellow. Energy streamed from it, slamming into the beast like a brick wall. The snout crumpled, crushed. The gate banged shut, and the bar locking it clanged into place.

Loud scratching noises came from the other side. Rizelya ran up the battlement stairs, with Blazel, Aistrun, Eiden, and the others following closely on her heels. She leaned over the balustrade. Below them, the monsters dug into the ironwood, their claws striking sparks as they hit the helstrim strips. Suddenly, as one, they pulled back and turned their heads to look at the Posairs staring down at them. Hatred and malevolence glowed in their eyes, along with an intelligence that the janacks or brechas had never exhibited, not even the control-janack. They milled around the door, then several broke from the group to stalk the wall. Ambrelya and Leistral trailed them on the battlement walk, their pulsers trained on the beasts.

Rizelya turned to study the courtyard. "Are there any other entrances?"

Aistrun shrugged. "I haven't been here before."

"No," Blazel said, still watching the monsters below.

"How would you know?" Aistrun looked at Blazel askance.

"I've been here. This is where I met Rolstrun and Maheli."

"Oh, that's right. I remember you telling us the story. Damn, would you look at that!"

Rizelya whirled back around. The largest monster backed up and ran at the gate with its horned head down. "I hope the gate holds."

The beast hit the gate with a resounding thud. The wall trembled, but the gate held. A smaller monster bunched up its legs and jumped toward them. Reflexively, Rizelya jerked her head back, even though she doubted the beast could jump twenty-five feet. She whistled when it missed by just a few feet.

"What are those creatures?"

Blazel leaned over the wall, studying the beasts milling below them. "At first glance, their long snouts, tusks, and greenish-brown scales appear similar to a jallopitar. But those are much smaller and don't have a frill of horns surrounding their heads or the barbed tails. And they slither through the swamps, not run semi-upright like these creatures."

Those front claws appear good for ripping apart their prey, Graak added.

Ambrelya joined them, finished with her saunter around the fortress. "Can we see if our pulsers will kill them?"

Rizelya nodded, raising her pulser to her shoulder and focusing her magic to it. She shot a gout of fire at the monsters. She preferred using her helbraught, but the pulser had a greater firing distance. Ambrelya's pulser popped beside her. The sound grew into a drone as the others also opened fire. Three beasts fell to their onslaught before the others moved out of range.

"Stop!" Rizelya ordered. "We're wasting ammunition. Leistral, Dehali, help me burn those carcasses. I don't want to smell rotting corpses."

The three Reds focused their fire magic, and two of the bodies burst into flames. Rizelya swore at the third, which had fallen too far for them to reach.

Let me do it, Oslerru said. He flew over the wall, hovering twenty feet over the carcass as he flared.

The largest monster raced toward him.

"Oslerru, get out of there!" Rizelya yelled.

Oslerru looked over his shoulder and flapped wildly to gain altitude as the beast leaped. He pulled his tail up as the monster snapped at it. Oslerru squawked as tufts of dark brown fur floated in the air. He flared, catching the beast's nose. It rubbed it on the ground, putting out the fire.

Blazel whistled. "Damn, they can jump high. I wouldn't suspect it possible for an animal so large."

Chariel shook her head, her eyes wide. "It must be the magic in them."

Oslerru landed in the courtyard, flipping his tail to examine it, and keened softly. Rizelya couldn't see any blood. Oslerru's dignity had suffered more than anything else.

Weariness tugged on Rizelya from the long night. While the monsters stayed out of their weapon's range, she couldn't harm them. She needed sleep. She turned away from the wall, rubbing her gritty eyes. "Eidstrun, Leistral, keep watch. Inform me if there's any change, especially if they leave." They saluted and took positions against the wall, their eyes and pulsers trained on the beasts below them.

Rizelya trudged down the steps, Blazel at her side. She remembered they'd used this fortress as a way station for the men escaping from the crater. "Blazel, do you know if there are any supplies here?"

"I think so, at least travel bars. I came here to recruit the Vhelopsi to ally with us against the Scourge. At the time, the well was clear, so we should have water."

"Good. After last night, we all need some food and rest."

"The travel bars won't feed the Gryphons," Aistrun said.

Blazel grunted. "True. But they can leave to go hunting. After they rest, those not part of the Black Weave teams should fly back and retrieve our supplies. And we need to warn the troops." The scar on his face and neck stood out against his pale skin, and dark circles had formed under his eyes. "We can kill the new monsters. Because they stink of malignant magic, perhaps the Weave will affect them the same way it does the janacks and brechas."

Rizelya shrugged. They'd wouldn't know until they experimented. Before she sought her bed, she checked on Leistrun in the infirmary. She smiled at Eiden sleeping on a cot pushed next to his, with her hand resting on his uninjured arm.

"How is he?" Rizelya quietly asked.

Kaieli looked up from applying a poultice to his arm. "He'll live, unless infection sets in. In this environment, that's a possibility. There's also the risk the nucla will poison him."

"Cleansing the nucla from the fortress will keep that from happening." Rizelya leaned against a cot, struggling not to sink into it. She was so tired. She and Kaieli hadn't been alone for quite some time. "How are you doing?"

"As well as anyone else."

"You know what I mean."

Kaieli turned away from Leistrun with a sigh. "The hole from Rolstrun's loss is still there, but I'm coping. Having something to do keeps me occupied. But I still miss him."

"I know you do, dear-heart. I still love you, you know."

Kaieli gave her a sad smile. "It helps." She turned back to Leistrun.

Rizelya left to find a bed and flopped into it next to the already sleeping Blazel. She studied his face for a long moment, adoring his rugged handsomeness. The scar running from his right cheekbone, over his chin, and across his neck and chest only made him more handsome in her eyes. She kissed him lightly, not wanting to wake him, thanking the Goddess she had sent him into her life and praying to the Mother to keep him safe. Rizelya didn't want to go through the type of grief Kaieli suffered.

Wisah - 22 de Neydar, 1076

The clatter of hooves in the outer courtyard broke Wisah's concentration as she tried to master the spell the Supreme was teaching her. She took the opportunity to rub her tired eyes. Her days were so busy between her work with the Supreme in the mornings, her time spent in the laboratory, and her studies, she felt perpetually exhausted. She longed to return to the simply life traveling with Rizelya, Blazel, Jaehaas and the others. Even fighting the Scourge hadn't been as tiring as her days had become.

A few milcrons later, a young messenger burst into the Supreme's office. "Supreme! There's a contingent from Ronanlair Keep. Clan Alphas Mujeen and Hadronan need your help." Lorenda's eyes grew round, and she lowered her voice. "There has been a rape."

The book Wisah held clattered to the desk. Rape was a serious charge and rarely occurred. The Supreme judged—and punished—a few crimes rather than the province Clan Alphas. The short list included rape.

"Send them to the audience chamber," the Supreme told the girl. As soon as Lorenda sped through the door, the Supreme turned to Wisah. "Bring me my judgment robe and my amulet of office, then walk with me."

Wisah ambled through the corridor with the Supreme leaning heavily on her arm, as heavily as the dread sitting on her heart. Each footstep they took toward the audience chamber reverberated in her mind like a death knell. If the Supreme found the man guilty, the Clan Alpha would execute him immediately. Once Wisah helped the Supreme into her throne, the Red Guards opened the doors. Wisah's heart thudded in her chest as several more Red Guards slipped into the room and hurried to stand guard around the dais. The red veils covering their faces hid their emotions, but their tight grips on their helbraughts worried Wisah. Chills iced her veins. More was happening than a simply rape charge.

Wisah's nose crinkled, and she gagged at the noxious stench wafting from the man being dragged between two burly men. He snarled curses while pulling against their grip, but with his hands tied behind his back, he couldn't do much. A black splotch on his neck peeked from his collar. Clan Alpha Hadronan stalked behind them, resting his hand on his helstrablade.

A slender young woman, about twenty years old, limped at the side of Clan Alpha Mujeen. Wisah gasped as the woman brushed aside her cornflower hair, revealing dark bruises covering one cheek and both her sage eyes. Her delicate beauty shone through the bruises. Men beating women rarely occurred in their society. The woman hunched her shoulders and hugged herself as she threw nervous glances in the direction of the prisoner.

The group stopped the requisite ten steps in front of the dais. Everyone dropped to their knees, giving the Supreme the gesture of obeisance—except the man. He refused to kneel or bow his head, instead glared at the Supreme. A sensation of biting insects crawled over Wisah's skin as his eyes met hers. She suppressed a shudder. Even fighting against the Scourge, she hadn't experienced such malice.

After the Supreme bade them to rise, Clan Alpha Hadronan stepped forward. "Gedronan has always had a problem with wanting more than his fair share, and feeling like he deserved more because of his warrior status. In the past, this showed up as belligerence toward non-fighters, and we caught him taking items from crafters without giving them a fair exchange." Hadronan glowered at the man.

"But recently, his outrages escalated, becoming more vocal and saying blasphemous things about the Goddess and the priestesses. He ranted about how they were a parasite on our society, not contributing anything valuable, and should be exiled, if not killed."

The Supreme's tapping fingers stilled, and she gripped the armrest of her throne. Wisah gulped. She'd read similar sentiments expressed by the Malvers when they began their campaign to overthrow the Supremes' rule and take control of Lairheim.

"Elaehara here—" Hadronan gestured to the young woman "—brews an excellent mookti berry and honey mead. Gedronan entered her shop and demanded she give him some. Like all crafters, Elaehara gave him a flask of the mead, showing her respect for his work as a fighter. But Gedronan wanted a full barrel, but didn't want to exchange any work or other token for it. When she refused to give it to him, he leaped over the counter and beat her."

Tears filled Elaehara's eyes, and she shook. Alpha Mujeen wrapped an arm around her. "But that wasn't all he did," she ground out. "Gedronan raped her."

"He nearly killed me, Your Grace," Elaehara stammered. "If Alpha Mujeen hadn't heard my mental cry for help and sent men to my shop, I'd be dead." She pulled down the collar of her tunic, revealing a bruise in the shape of a hand print circling her neck.

Wisah narrowed her eyes, whispering the spell for revealing the hidden. Her left shoulder blade tingled. Oily, slimy energy shrouded Gedronan. Tentacles of magic—reminding Wisah of a janack's—oozed from him, seeking to ensnare his guards, but slid off them. Neither man held any malicious feelings for it to latch onto. Wisah had little doubt he had committed the terrible act.

The Supreme gestured him forward. "Gedronan, come and allow me to see into your mind to determine the truth."

"I'm not letting a foul creature like you in my mind!" Gedronan yelled, jerking from his guard's grasp. He kicked at them and fought against his bonds. "Let me shift, you bitch," he screamed at Mujeen.

Although Wisah couldn't sense it, Mujeen must be using her alpha power to suppress Gedronan's ability to shift into his warrior form.

Six red guards rushed forward, and, within moments, subdued Gedronan. They dragged him to the dais. One thrust his head toward the Supreme, who grasped it between her hands.

"Wisah, I need your help," she whispered urgently.

"What do you want me to do?"

"Put your hands over mine."

After she did, the Supreme taught her the spell only the Supremes knew for reading a person's mind. Wisah gagged as her mind entered Gedronan's, and she witnessed the awful things he'd committed. His rape of Elaehara wasn't his only crime. Once the black splotch appeared, he lost all the inhibitions previously stopping him from acting on his desires. The Supreme ended their connection.

"Kill the cur!" The Supreme ordered. "He is guilty. There is no remorse within him."

"As you will," Hadronan said. His guards, along with the red guard, dragged the now insensate criminal from the audience chamber.

As Wisah helped the Supreme back to their quarters, she couldn't help wondering why she'd been taught the spell. She wasn't the new Supreme. How could she be? Never before had a Supreme not been born with white eyes and sent to the Sanctuary to be trained from birth. But ever since Malviana had attacked the Supreme, and she'd almost died, she'd treated Wisah as her heir. The Supreme seemed desperate to have an heir ready in case she died before the true Supreme was born.

"Malviana," the Supreme swore and slapped her palms on her desk. "She has loosed her contagion on Lairheim."

"The black splotch on Gedronan's neck and chest is a symptom of it, isn't it?"

The Supreme nodded. "If we examined him, he'd have more covering his body. It's the first sign of a Posair transforming into a Malvers or transmogrifying into a Maldiers."

Wisah's hand flew to cover her open mouth as her stomach plummeted. "She's building her army. We need to inform Histrun and Keshanal to prepare for another war."

"I suspect they already know, dear." The Supreme patted Wisah's hand. "The disease attaches to hate, greed, and anger. After fighting the Scourge, Histrun's army will be ripe for her contagion to find fertile ground. But for it to infect someone as far north as Ronanlair Province, Malviana must be more powerful than before. I'm afraid this is the first sign of trouble, and we'll receive more cases to judge." Tears gleamed in the Supreme's eyes as she covered her face with her hands. "I don't know how to stop it or help my people," she murmured.

Wisah doubted the Supreme meant for her to hear the last bit. Perhaps the ancient tome held the answer, or another of the books in the hidden library. She'd search in hopes she could help the Supreme.

Rizelya - 22 de Neydar, 1076

Rizelya sleepily rolled out of bed. The monsters had rammed the gate during what little had remained of the day and throughout the night. The dull booms, the shaking walls, and the crack of pulsers being fired left Rizelya's nerves rattled and had disturbed her sleep so she didn't feel rested. She cocked her head, listening as she pulled on her boots. "Oh, thank Goddess! They've stopped attacking the gate."

She and Blazel went down to the dining hall. She sniffed and breathed in the welcome scent of taevo.

"How did it go last night?" she asked Aistrun as she poured a cup of taevo.

He yawned and plucked the mug from her hands, ignoring her frown. "Nelstrun, Eidstrun, and I took turns firing shots at the monsters while on our watch. Their damned horny frill protects them too much. We only managed to kill two more of the beasts. The herd is still roaming in front of the gates and patrolling the walls."

"Are you rested enough to retrieve our abandoned supplies?" Blazel asked Aistrun, as he handed Rizelya a replacement cup of taevo.

"Yes," Aistrun nodded. "I took the first shift. Who do you want to go with me and Broogk?"

"Good," Blazel said with a curt nod. "Take Boreek, Leistral, and Morru with you. Leistral and Morru can warn the ground troops about these new monsters, unless we're too late and the monsters have attacked them already."

"Also take Ambrelya and Maeaak with you," Rizelya added. "Ambrelya can help if you run into any other creatures. Oh, and Eidstrun and Sterkek. You'll need their strength to carry all the gear we left behind."

Aistrun finished his taevo, then collected his team.

As they flew off, Rizelya and the Black Weave teams gathered in the courtyard, the only space large enough for their Gryphon partners to join them. Rizelya rolled her shoulders to release the tension in her neck. She hadn't tried purging such vast amounts of nucla before. She glanced at the women who had as part of Kaieli's group while Scourge captives. Wariness pinched Noriana and Faliciden's faces, while dread filled Loshera's and Chariel's eyes.

Chariel shook her arms and hands. "Okay, let's do this... again."

"It should be easier this time," Kaieli observed, then glanced fondly over her shoulder at Keeru. "We have the Gryphons to help us. Since this is new to many in both teams, let's start with the sabertiger team. Fox team, watch how we're clearing the nucla from the black sand and rocks within the fortress. It's a bit different from the small rocks we used for testing or draining the pools."

As soon as Kaieli initiated the Weave, Rizelya saw the wriggling nasty worms she associated with the malignant magic crawling all over the fortress. When they came out of the trance, Rizelya took a deep breath, then smiled. The air didn't stink! She hadn't realized how much the malignant magic had pervaded the fortress, or how quickly she'd become accustomed to it. Certainly, this should help Leistrun's wound to heal.

Faliciden initiated the Weave for the fox team. Rizelya sat back, sipping on a mug of taevo and leaning against Glork's shoulder and resting. The rancorous magic was so compacted in this area it took more effort for them to purge it. An octar later, the fox team came out of their trance.

Blenora beamed. "We did it! We cleansed the nucla surrounding the fortress. I'm really happy I volunteered. We're doing good work for our planet."

Rizelya grinned at her and her enthusiasm. "We have quite a bit to do before it's all cleared. I'm not sure if it's possible to clear it all before the Malvers start attacking."

"They already have." Blazel motioned toward the gate, where a dull boom resounded.

Rizelya grimaced. The monsters had resumed ramming the gate while they worked.

"We can only do what we can," Blenora said. "The Goddess only asks us to do our best."

Rizelya resettled into a comfortable position. "Then let's see what we can accomplish."

She held out her hands to the side. Blazel grasped her right hand and Kaieli her left. Chariel held Blazel's other hand. Loshera grinned and grasped Saffren's hand. Eiden glared at the gate, then completed the circle, holding Grazeen's and Kaieli's hands. The Gryphons settled behind their partners. Rizelya closed her eyes and breathed deeply as Kaieli formed the Black Weave. Rizelya's heart expanded as her consciousness blended with her teammates and beloved friends.

This time, their joined consciousness spread from the fortress. Malignant magic writhed within the etheric shapes of the monsters, but unlike the janacks and brechas, these creatures weren't fully magic. The team tugged on the magic, easing it from the creatures. Roars of rage pulled Rizelya out of her trance.

"What in the Crone's fires is that?" she yelled, holding her hands over her ears.

Nelstrun leaned over the railing at the top of the wall. "Whatever you've done made the beasts go crazy."

Rizelya jumped to her feet, grabbed her weapons, and ran up the stairs, the others on her heels. Below them, the monsters tore into each other. The intelligence that had guided them was gone. Nelstrun, Baederposan, and Kami shot into the melee below them. The largest monster clamped his jaws around a darker one's shoulder, behind the protective horn frills. Blood poured from the wound. It tossed the smaller animal, flinging it on its back. Using the short horn on its snout, it gored the downed beast. It had its back to them, and Rizelya sighted her pulser on it and fired at the same time as Blazel. Their projectiles slammed into it. Blazel's had been a fire projectile, and flames bloomed under its hide, and it threw its head back, keening. Blazel fired again. His shot hammered into the base of the creature's skull, and it toppled over. The rest of the beasts lay dead on the black sand, or fled across the Barrens and toward the southern swamp.

Rizelya pumped her fist in the air, cheering along with the others. After making sure the animals weren't returning, she, Dehali, and the Gryphons left the fortress and burned the carcasses.

The next afternoon, Aistrun and his team returned with their belongings and supplies.

"Leistral and Morru flew back to warn the troops," Aistrun said as he slumped on the keep-house steps. "We saw more of those beasts. Damn, I thought we were ridding our world of monsters."

"We are, Wolf." Rizelya patted his shoulder. "We are. But the greatest monster isn't any of the beasts, it's their masters, the Malvers. Once we destroy them, our world will be safe."

"I wish they'd stop playing these games with the monsters and twisted animals and just come at us and fight."

Blazel leaned his elbows on the railing. "They will. But not until they have regained their strength. From what I remember reading about the Great War, the Malvers prefer to loose their creatures on us to deplete our numbers before they engage. We're at a distinct disadvantage this time. The only Black Talent we have is our new Black Weave teams, and we don't exactly provide any offensive tactics."

Rizelya's eyebrows rose. "I think we do. We take away the Malvers' base of power, the malignant magic pools, and they'll have to fight us on our terms."

Not true, Graak said, fluffing out his head feathers. *They will still have their death magic. It's what gives them power and makes them different from Posairs. The pools only formed after the Great War.*

Glork rested his head on the rail beside her, and Rizelya absently petted his soft feathers. He chirped with pleasure. *But draining the pools does deny them access to additional power. We must continue.*

Rizelya agreed with him. They hadn't tackled draining the huge pool within the crater yet. But luckily, they wouldn't have to leave the fortress to do so. The crater rim was only five measures from the fortress.

"Well, on that note," she said, pushing away from the railing. "Let's get back to work."

Malviana - 23 de Neydar, 1076

Several days after releasing his new creatures, Malvidor stormed into Malviana's laboratory, in such a rage sparks flickered from his body. "I can't believe it!" he shouted. "They stole the magic from my jallopsitor."

"What?" Malviana frowned, trying to make sense of what he was saying as she pulled her attention from her notes. She and Mordeven were still having trouble finding the right spell to transform the Gryphon and lizard into something new and ferocious.

"My magic controlling my jallopsitor is gone," he repeated, spitting out the words.

Malviana's heart thundered in her chest. "How could that happen?"

"I have no idea." He paced the room, tugging at his hair. "One milcron I sensed them in the back of my head, harrying the fortress, and the next they disappeared. Whoosh!" He moved his hands to the side of his face and flicked his fingers, opening his hands wide.

Malviana jolted from her desk, knocking over her chair, and marched upstairs, her sons running to catch up to her.

"Show me!" she ordered her mirror.

The jallopsitor fought each other in front of a fortress. Men and women lifted strange stick-like weapons to their shoulders. Projectiles spit out, hitting Malvidor's beasts and killing them. A man with long, tangled hair shot at the largest beast. It toppled over. The rest of the creatures fled into the Barrens.

She waved her wand, and the mirror focused on the new weapons. They looked vaguely familiar, but she couldn't place where she'd seen them. "Could those be the cause? They certainly are effective in killing our creatures."

"Maybe." Mordeven shrugged. "Mother, check his other beasts, will you?"

Malviana made the adjustments to the mirror's spell, and the perspective of the scene swept outward, away from the fortress and deeper into the Barrens. A herd of Malvidor's creatures approached a Posair contingent crossing the black sand-glass. Rather than the wild beasts shown at the fortress, these ran as a coordinated herd.

Mordeven's eyebrow raised, and he shook his head. "Whatever shattered your control appears like it only affected your jallopsitor around the fortress. Did you even access the others before you interrupted us?"

"Huh?" Malvidor scrutinized the image, then closed his eyes. After a moment, they flew open. "Ah, thank Mordaga! The rest of them are fine." He turned on his heel and left, muttering about making his spell stronger.

Malviana returned the mirror's view to the fortress and stared at the scene, trying to place where she'd seen the weapons before. An auburn-haired woman pumped her fist in the hair. "Her!" Fire zipped from Malviana's fingertips, and a nearby vase exploded. "What in Mordaga's name is she doing there?"

Mordeven shrugged. "I don't know who she is or why she's upsetting you so much."

"It's that damned woman who intruded into my mind those last few lunadars we were exiled."

"Ah."

Malviana paced, cursing under her breath and casting venomous glances at her hated nemesis—Rizelya. She'd discovered her name from her new Malvers. She wished she could hurl her curses at the woman through her mirror. Alas, all she could do was watch her.

"I have the feeling," she said when she finally calmed down, "whatever caused the loss of Malvidor's magic wasn't the weapons but that awful woman. She's becoming as much of a nuisance as Shandir." Malviana spit at the thought and mention of her ancient foe. Her eyes hardened, and she shook her fist at the mirror. "By Mordaga's will, when we meet on the battlefield, Rizelya will be one of the first to fall!"

Even more determined to make the new Gryphon-lizard combination work, Malviana stalked back to her laboratory. Mordeven followed her, and she ignored his smirk. She turned her attention onto the Gryphon, still bound to the metal table.

Much later, she stepped away from the Gryphon. "Damn it to Mordaga's seven hells!" she swore.

"What's wrong?" Blood smeared Mordeven's face and apron.

She tossed the knife she'd been wielding, and it clattered on the metal table. "It's dead. Can't you sense it?"

Mordeven stared at the Gryphon, then he too swore.

She untied her apron, putting the soiled one in the bin with the others, before trudging upstairs. Furious with her continued failures, Malviana grabbed the first servant who crossed her path. "Tell Jorvelden and Korand to join me in my suite. And have someone remove the Gryphon's carcass from my laboratory. Give whatever is left of it to the Maldiers." At least some good would come from the beast.

Malviana glowered at the sticky blood covering her hands. *My spells should have worked!* She finished washing her hands and face when Jorvelden and Korand entered her suite.

"I need another Gryphon," she said, patting her face dry with a towel. "The first one had the audacity to die on me today."

"We'll capture another for you, my queen," Jorvelden said, thumping a fist on his chest.

"On second thought, how many Gryphons are spying on us?" Malviana poured a glass of bloodwine.

Korand scratched the side of his face. "I believe there are five more."

"Bring me all of them. Their damned magic is resisting my spells. And I don't want them to escape before I can figure out how to make it work."

While she waited for her people to capture the Gryphons, she called Keandran to her. She needed to release the tension and frustration bottled inside of her. Keandran was almost as adept as her beloved Mordar at inflicting the right combination of pain and pleasure for her to forget her worries.

Two days later, Jorvelden entered Malviana's suite. She lay naked on her bed, languorous from her most recent session with Keandran. With hooded eyes, she swiped at the blood and semen pooling on her stomach. She slowly and sensuously licked it off her fingers, watching Jorvelden. A pleased smile crossed her lips as he squirmed and adjusted the fit of his trousers.

"My lady," he stammered and cleared his throat. "We've completed our task, and the Gryphons await you in your laboratory."

"Thank Mordaga!" Malviana scrambled from her bed, quickly washed, and put on clean clothes. She raced down the stairs. Four animals glared at her from their cages. They all had the same owl-like heads. Her nose wrinkled at their small size. She'd fought much larger ones during the war.

"Is this all of them?" she asked Jorvelden.

"Yes, my queen."

"I'll have to make do with what I have and hope it's enough."

Chapter 15

Wisah - 45 de Neydar, 1076

Wisah splashed water on her face and glanced in the mirror, then took a double-take, leaning closer to peer into her eyes. Their normal pale blue had darkened to an azure a few shades darker than her tattoos. Gray strands streaked her creamy white hair. She lifted a strand, and after examining it, decided it wasn't as dark a charcoal-gray as Chariel's. Wisah leaned her hands on the sink. "What are you becoming?" she asked her reflection. "Who are you?"

The question played on her mind as she performed her duties for the Supreme. Throughout the morning, Wisah opened her mouth to ask the Supreme if she was, indeed, training Wisah to become the next Supreme. The Supreme would raise her eyebrow in question, as if she knew what Wisah wanted to ask. However, Wisah shut it without asking. The last time, disappointment filled the Supreme's eyes. But if Wisah didn't ask, she could continue pretending she didn't know the answer.

By the time the Supreme released her for the afternoon, Wisah felt drained. A quick lunch revived her, and she hurried to the hidden laboratory. Yesterday, she found a book on making artifacts for healing battle wounds and wanted to try creating them. During their quest to find the Gryphons, a pride of sabertigers had attacked them. In the fight, a sabertiger had inflicted awful wounds on Jaehaas's rump. His flanks still showed the scars from where they'd cauterized the wounds to stop the bleeding. During the Scourge War, many fighters lost limbs, simply because the healers couldn't do anything fast enough to save them. The devices described by the book would keep them from having to resort to such drastic measures.

Wisah wanted to use her newfound gifts and powers to help people, not for killing. But Maendy insisted they concentrate on creating weapons. Killing went completely against Wisah's upbringing and training as a priestess for the Goddess, who revered life.

In the laboratory, Wisah sat at her workbench and opened the book on healing artifacts. She jotted down a list of materials, then wandered over to the cabinets. Over the chedans, Maellyn had organized them, making it easier to locate the parts they needed for the various devices. As Wisah selected the supplies, Maendy approached her with a scowl on her face.

"What are you working on?"

"A healing device. I showed it to you yesterday."

Maendy shook her head, the furrows in her forehead deepening. "No, no, we need you working on *the* weapon."

Wisah gritted her teeth, swallowing hard. She didn't want to create the Unmaking device. Even though she knew, better than anyone else, how imperative stopping Malviana was, Wisah hated she'd have to kill to accomplish the task. No, not kill, completely annihilate Malviana.

"But we need healing devices as well as weapons," she huffed, jutting out her jaw. She thrust her fists on her hips. "You weren't on the battlefront during the Scourge War. We lost too many people simply because the healers couldn't reach them in time, or fighters lost limbs. This device could save lives!"

"It won't help anyone to heal them if we can't stop Malviana and her Malvers. In fact, it would be better if we didn't." Maendy softened her voice. "If we have time, we'll work on those, too."

Wisah stomped back to her workbench and pushed aside the book and her list. She jerked the pieces of the Unmaking device toward her. She struggled to lay the correct spells on them. The longer she worked on it, the more guilt and anger assailed her, choking her. *How can I continue to make devices that destroy life?* She abruptly pushed the components away from her and ran to the stairs.

"Wisah, what's wrong?" Maellyn called after her.

"I need some air." She sped up the stairs, through the library, and outside. She stood panting on the grass between the library and the temple, leaning over with her hands on her knees. The sun warmed her back. The weather had grown warmer over the past chedan. In a few days, it would be the first day of Sandar and the beginning of summer. She straightened, tilting her head back and closing her eyes, letting the sun caress her face. The soft breeze carried the scent of roses, lilacs, and fresh-cut grass. She breathed in the life-affirming scents.

Brushing back her hair, she wandered through the garden. Its beauty soothed her tattered soul. The gardens had always been her favorite place since the day Histrun had brought her to the Sanctuary when she was five-years-old. She hadn't chosen to be a priestess. It had been a happy accident of birth, and one she rarely regretted. Once, maybe, when as a child she watched the flames dance on Rizelya's hand, she'd envied Rizelya her fire Talent. But the first time she'd sensed the veil and the world beyond it, she'd never looked back, never questioned the rightness of her White Talent. Even when she fell in love with Jaehaas, she hadn't wanted to stop being a White Priestess.

Wisah frequently dealt with death as she ushered souls across the veil into the Mother's arms. But she hadn't killed anyone, not even while helping Rizelya during the Scourge War.

She held up her hands, and the sun highlighted the two sigils of the unmaking spell a darker shade under her skin. Her heart tightened. She doubted she *could* cast the spell. Wisah now knew from her studies and lessons that the Malvers hadn't begun as a separate species or people. They were once Posairs—her people, those she'd vowed to serve when she'd passed from apprentice to full priestess years ago. The death and blood magic they used was evil and wrong. But did it make them evil and deserving of such a horrendous fate? Malviana had been a victim of Mordar's evil. The things Malviana had suffered—and survived—under Mordar's hands would break anyone. Was Malviana responsible for what she did now?

Her footsteps echoed on marble floors, and Wisah glanced around. Her wanderings and musing had taken her into the temple sanctuary. She stopped in front of the mural of the Goddess in Her fierce warrior aspect. The helbraught in Her hands glowed with fire and dripped with blood. The painting showed Her red cape flung over one shoulder, and wearing dented and scratched battle gear. Wisah's gaze was drawn to the Goddess's eyes. Instead of triumph and gloating over the victory of Her enemies, Her eyes held compassion and sadness.

"I thought I'd find you here," the Supreme's voice broke into Wisah's reverie.

Wisah turned. The Supreme stood behind her, leaning heavily on her cane. Since her near-death experience, she hadn't ventured farther than the audience chamber. A sheen of sweat shone on the Supreme's upper lip, and her shoulders trembled. The white veil over her hair, symbolizing the veil between the physical and spiritual worlds, floated around her as if it had a life of its own.

The Supreme reached out her hand, the gemstones in her rings catching the sunlight. She laid it to rest gently on Wisah's cheek. "I sensed your disturbance, sweet child. Why do you fret so?"

Wisah covered the old woman's hand with her own and dropped to her knees. "I don't want to be the new Supreme. I want the freedom to love Jaehaas. All these new weapons we're making are to destroy life. But how can I do that as Supreme? Why is this happening to me?" She lowered her head, weeping and letting all her fears flow with the cascade of tears. Finally, she ran out of words and tears.

At some point during her tirade, they had sat on the bench under the mural. The Supreme pulled a handkerchief from her pocket and wiped Wisah's tears away. "My dear child, it is good you are so upset over what you've been called to do. I'd be worried if you weren't. These fears and worries show you haven't succumbed to the power at your disposal and that the Goddess has chosen well."

"After everything Mordar put Malviana through," Wisah said, sniffing, "is she still responsible for her actions? Won't I be committing as heinous of crimes if I use the unmaking spell?"

"To answer your question, yes, Malviana is responsible for her actions. She may have started out as a victim, but she chose to follow Mordar and his god, Mordaga, a long time ago. Before we exiled the Malvers, we offered them a chance to return to the Goddess, and they refused. Your compassion isn't misplaced. Look back at the Goddess in the mural and her eyes."

Wisah turned around and gazed at the beautiful painting.

"She, too, is filled with compassion," the Supreme said, "but it doesn't keep Her from doing what needs to be done, even if it is difficult and unpleasant. If we leave Malviana and her people unchecked, they will kill and enslave our people, using them as sacrifices to their god. You have the choice to allow evil free rein or to stop it." The Supreme lifted Wisah's left hand, and the sigil tattoo lit up briefly. "The Goddess has given you the means to destroy the evil. It is in your hands whether or not you use it."

The Supreme patted Wisah's cheek and tottered toward the door leading to the inner sections of the temple. Healer Jordelyna waited just inside the door. Wisah nodded to Jordelyna as the Supreme took her proffered arm, happy the Supreme hadn't been foolish enough to make the long walk alone.

Wisah lit a votive candle and placed in on the altar under the Goddess as Warrior mural. She knelt and prayed she'd be strong enough to do the right thing when the time came—whatever that was.

Malviana - 47 de Neydar, 1076

Malviana slumped dejectedly on a stool, nearly in tears. Only one Gryphon remained caged, the rest having succumbed to her experiments. It lay curled in a ball with his beak tucked under the tattered remains of its wing, quietly keening. The once magnificent creature now looked ragged, with patches of fur missing on his side and tufts of feathers pulled from his head.

"I can't understand why my spells aren't working." Malviana leaned her arms on the table, dropping her forehead onto them. "They should have."

"Perhaps you need more power," Mordeven suggested. Dark circles smudged his red-rimmed eyes. His usually immaculate hair stuck out from his head, from pulling at it in frustration.

Malviana rubbed at her gritty eyes, and ran a hand over her hair, grimacing as her needle-sharp nails snagged in the snarls. Neither of them had slept much in the last chedan. She needed a weapon to bring down the Posairs, and a transmogrified Gryphon would strike terror into their hearts. It took a few milcrons for his words to sink into her exhausted mind.

She sat up straighter. "Yes! That must be the answer, and I shall have more power. Come, we need to clean up. We can't appeal to Mordaga in this state."

Malviana marched upstairs with Mordeven on her heels. After washing, she selected a servant and sacrificed her to Mordaga, allowing only herself and Mordeven to absorb the servant's death essence. The next morning, filled with power, determination, and hope, Malviana returned to her laboratory to resume her work on metamorphosing the Gryphon and lizard.

Later in the afternoon, Malviana glared at the Gryphon, then turned to study her notes. It emitted shrill whistles as it struggled to breathe. Her head jerked up in the sudden quiet.

"You will not defy me!" she yelled. Frustrated and angry, she grabbed Mordeven's hand and drew more power from the crater pool than she'd done before, channeling more power than ever.

Dark, evil, luscious magic filled her. Power burned under her skin, and tiny flames lit her body. Her long hair floated away from her. The space between her thighs throbbed. Pointing her wand at the mangled and bloody Gryphon, she drew the runes of power and spoke the words of the spell.

Power rolled off her to surround the Gryphon, then it expanded to encompass the equally bloody lizard, and pulled them together. She held the image of what she wanted in her mind even as her arm shook and a red haze of blood filled her vision. A great weight pressed on her chest, forcing the air from her lungs. Her heart pounded loud in her ears. With a cry, she pushed the magic into the spell. A thunderclap cracked through her laboratory. Power streaked like lightning, bouncing off every surface and into the two creatures. Pain sizzled along her nerve endings, and she crumpled to the floor as darkness descended on her.

Malviana awoke sprawled on the ground with a splitting headache and the taste of blood in her mouth. Rubbing her temples, she sat up and glanced around her laboratory. Mordeven lay curled in a fetal position, and the slight rise and fall of his chest assured her he still lived. Glass shards covered the floor and workbench. Fluids from broken beakers dripped, reminding her of the hated cave.

The Gryphon cage stood empty. She hung her head. After all of that effort, her spell hadn't worked. Tears pricked her eyes. She brushed the hated sign of weakness away.

A squawk sounded in the lizard's cage.

Malviana's head flew up, and she pushed herself to her feet. Staggering, she made her way through the mess. She stared at the creature, blinking wide eyes at her, then burst into laughter. "Yes!" she threw her fist into the air. "It worked!"

Now that she had one, she could make many, many more.

Malviana - 50 de Neydar, 1076

Malviana awoke to the crackle of death magic. She stared at the ceiling and stretched, grimacing as her body protested the movement. Exhaustion still pulled at her from the effort expended from transmogrifying the Gryphon and lizard. She'd have to decide what to call the new creature.

Tendrils of death magic snaked into her bedroom and caressed her like a lover before sinking into her skin. Malvina sat up in bed, now fully awake and aware. "Wait, that only happens when a lot of magic is being used, more than my few Malvers would account for."

She tossed on a robe and rushed to the practice hall and stood at the doorway, stunned. While she'd been locked in her laboratory for the past three chedans, hundreds of newly turned Malvers had arrived. Humming, she returned to her bedroom and dressed.

Malviana paused in the courtyard, leaning against the wall in the shadows to watch her new people practicing their magic. Women outnumbered the men. Her eyebrows furrowed at the men struggling to maneuver their new wands and focus their magic through them. In the past, it hadn't caused men a problem. It seemed as if they hadn't ever used magic before. *But why? Everyone has some degree of magic they use.* Malviana paced, attempting to make sense of the problem. Some of the women also struggled to direct magic through their wands, while a majority picked it up much quicker. Red streaked the hair of those who easily wielded their wands and magic.

Nelieh, her first new Malvers, used her wand almost as easily as the older Malvers. Her patterns weren't always correct, but somehow, she made it work. Curious, Malviana sauntered to Nelieh.

"This doesn't seem foreign to you, unlike others." Malviana adjusted Nelieh's wand into the correct pattern. "Why isn't it?"

"Using patterns is unfamiliar." Nelieh bit her bottom lip as she concentrated. "But directing my magic through the wand isn't much different from feeding my magic through my helbraught." She waved her wand correctly, and runes flared before her, then zipped to the swamp rat in front of her. It squealed as bloody sores appeared, quickly spreading to cover its body. It convulsed, and a mist of death energy rose from it and zoomed into Nelieh. She gasped, throwing her head back. "Yes!"

Malviana smiled, remembering the first few times the death magic had filled her with ecstasy. "Helbraughts?" she asked when the pleasure released Nelieh.

"The weapons the Reds use to fight the monsters. The helstrim in them focuses our magic. When the janacks and brechas showed up centuries ago, we needed something to fight them with, so we developed the helbraughts." Nelieh's shoulders slumped, and she toed a rock with her toe. "I wasn't able to retrieve mine when I left. It was an extension of me for twenty years. These are great for directing magic—" she held up her wand "—but they aren't weapons like the helbraughts."

Malviana's eyebrows crunched together. She pointed to the dead rat. "Didn't you just kill it with your wand? How is it not a weapon?"

"Helbraughts have a sharp blade on the end, useful for killing Malvers' monsters, or Scourge bastards. Until recently, only women with fire magic could use them. It's a good thing we had more fighters when the Scourge arrived."

Malviana's jaw clenched as she remembered the foul creatures that had killed one of her people while still on the island, and she'd lacked the power to stop it. She admired the weak Posairs had not only stood up to the Scourge, but had thrown them off the planet. Her teeth ground, infuriated the Posairs could do something she couldn't. A small part of her mind feared her enemies had grown too strong while her people had languished. She squashed the thought like a loathsome bug.

"What changed?"

"Rizelya discovered the other Talents could use helbraughts and be just as effective against the control-janack as the Reds."

"Her!" Malviana's lip lifted in a snarl. Somehow, the girl had peered into her mind through her pet. She still wasn't quite sure how she did it. When Malviana finally realized she was being spied on and she'd backtracked the connection to destroy the intruder, but she couldn't reach the spy's mind. By the time it flared into existence again, Malviana had decided to use the link to terrorize the girl. She growled in remembered frustration. It hadn't worked the way she expected. The damned girl had fought back, putting blocks on her mind Malviana couldn't breach.

"Yes, her," Nelieh wrinkled her nose. "Even though I'm glad we had the manpower to fight the invaders, I still think it's wrong for Blues—Blues, of all people—to fight. Reds and their fire magic are much better suited to fighting."

"So are those who were fighters the ones picking up how to use the wands faster?"

Nelieh nodded. She pointed to several women with red streaks in their gray hair, showing they were still transitioning into a Malvers. "Anyone with red in their hair were Reds who battled against the janacks and brechas, like me, and also fought in the Scourge War. A few with other Talents wielded helbraughts—" she sneered "—but most of them were support staff for the war host, cooking, doing the laundry, that sort of thing."

It made sense her magic was first affecting those who'd just been in a war. It actually surprised her that more Posairs weren't succumbing to her spell, which fed on anger, fear, and greed—all emotions war fostered.

"What about the men? They are struggling even worse than the support women."

"They don't use magic like we do. When the Malvers' monsters arrived, the men's magic changed, allowing them to shapeshift into warriors."

"Ah!" Malviana had seen creatures which appeared to be a mix of human and wolf through her pet's eyes. But she'd assumed they were similar to her Maldiers, and once transmogrified, they remained in that form. "It explains why fewer men have transformed into Malvers. I suspect most will turn into Maldiers. Keep practicing, Nelieh, and you'll become a formidable Malvers." She patted the woman on the shoulder.

Nelieh ducked her head, and a rosy tinge blossomed on her gray cheeks. "Thank you, Your Grace."

Malviana strolled to the eastern courtyard where the Maldiers lived, practiced, and made their sacrifices to Mordaga. She estimated six hundred Maldiers now filled the enclosure with more in the barracks and performing chores. When she'd descended into her laboratory, only two hundred had arrived. Her eyes widened at the multitude of configurations of Posair and animals they'd transmogrified into. She threw back her head, flung her arms wide, and laughed. Mordaga's magic was truly magnificent!

Her laughter drew the Maldiers' attention, and they turned as one toward her. Their eyes glowed with feral hunger. Keandran cracked his whip and roared, "Bow to your queen, you curs."

The host bowed in whatever way their new forms allowed. Malviana stood straighter and lifted her chin. A satisfied smile curved her lips. "As you were."

While the Maldiers returned to their training, Korand and Keandran loped to her.

Korand dipped his huge antlers in a bow. "My lady, we have missed you." He straightened, and grinning, flung out an arm toward the troops. "Are you pleased with the army we are creating for you?"

"I am." She gazed between the two Maldiers, her lips pursed, as she decided which one to put in command. She considered their many squabbles and remembered Keandran rarely lost. "Korand, I'm putting you in charge of training the new ones, and once they are proficient in using the death magic, they will be added to the army—"

Korand puffed out his chest and smirked at Keandran.

"Which Keandran will lead."

Keandran tilted his head back and howled with glee. "Once again, Korand, I am the better man."

Malviana rolled her eyes at their rivalry. As she returned to her study, warmth blossomed in her chest. Soon, her army would be strong enough for her to march north and exact her revenge on those who had taken her beloved Mordar from her.

Chapter 16

Malviana - 3 de Sandar, 1076

Malviana blew at the stray strand of hair falling into her eyes, unwilling to break her concentration to brush it away. This last part of the spell to transmogrify the Gryphons required all of her focus. With her mind, she reached for the lake of power inside the crater, drawing vast quantities to her. She directed it at a small dish of blood and tissue in the middle of the empty cage. After creating the first grifflyn, she hadn't needed another full Gryphon and Scourge lizard, only bits of them—and their blood. Pulling on Mordeven's strength, she formed a pattern with her wand and shouted the final phrase of the spell. Her wand spat out strands of jet-black filaments. They wrapped around the contents in the dish, writhing and pulsing. With each throb, they grew larger, forming a cocoon of magic where the new creature would develop.

"No! Don't let it go, Mordeven," she cried, sensing Mordeven's hold on the spell slipping. If he lost it now, they'd have wasted the past four octars of effort. And they only possessed this final bit of raw material. This was the last grifflyn they could make until they obtained another Gryphon—hopefully a female this time. Since both donors were male, all the new species were also male and couldn't procreate.

The spell steadied, and the glistening black threads gave a final throb. As the cocoon dried, it lightened to an ash gray, then the mound shuddered and broke apart as a new grifflyn shattered it. The creature squawked as its horned, reptilian head banged on the top of the cage. Before it belched a flame, a servant tossed a chunk of bloody meat at it, which it snatched out of the air. It turned hungry eyes on the servant, who had another gob ready for it. The creature followed the trail of meat from the cage to the outer northern bailey where would join its fellows. The servant tripped, and the grifflyn snaked out its long, sinewy neck and plucked up the hapless man, gulping him down.

Malviana slumped onto a stool in the castle wall's shade. After working nearly non-stop for the past two chedans, she and Mordeven had created a flight of three hundred twisted Gryphons. To test their effectiveness, she'd released thirty of the beasts to harass the eastern fortress. She planned to go north via that route and needed the fortress under her control. The early results had encouraged her during the last push to finish her task.

"Creating those last ten grifflyns was brutal." She gazed at her hands, grimacing at the dullness of the jewels in her rings and on her wand. The spell required enormous amounts of energy, and even with the influx of power from the crater pool, she couldn't do it by herself. She hated having to rely on Mordeven's help.

"I'm so exhausted," Mordeven grumbled. He slumped on his stool, leaning his elbows on the table. His head rested on his fists. "I'm not sure I can climb the stairs to my suite. I'm going to sleep for days."

"Help me up, and then we can both sleep."

Finally, after several more milcrons, Mordeven levered himself to his feet and held out his hand for Malviana. She stood up shakily, steadying herself with a hand on Mordeven's shoulder. Leaning heavily on him, Malviana wearily trudged up the stairs to her suite from the outside work area they'd built in the bailey. For some reason, the magic from the crater pool hadn't flowed to her as easily or as quickly in the past few days. Her thoughts swirled in a whirlpool as she considered the possible causes of the magic to be so sluggish. She chided herself for becoming so reliant on it. The power from sacrificing to her god was more satisfying, but it also required more effort.

As she poured herself a cup of bloodwine, the big, black mirror gleaming in the candlelight caught her attention. She paused in front of it and thought of the map of magic pools. Could something be wrong with them? She activated the mirror, and her knees buckled. She crumpled to the floor, gazing at the pinpricks of light.

"So many gone! How can that be?" Malviana gripped the back of a chair and pulled herself to her feet. The vast lake in the crater had shrunk significantly. "No wonder the magic felt sluggish. I doubt I used so much, though. But Malvidor and Morvana have also been accessing it for their creatures." She scrutinized the map again and let out a relieved breath. None of the magic pools in the great southern swamp had disappeared. They still had them to draw upon.

Her eyes narrowed as she considered the smaller disappearing pools. Although she no longer needed her pets, the janacks and brechas, to collect death essence for her to survive, they played an important part in her vengeance. She'd abandoned the device when she'd fled the island and hadn't thought much about them since returning home. Unlike the beasts she and her children were currently creating, which were transmutations of real animals, her pets were constructs of magic. They served only one purpose: to feed her and her people during their exile. Without the magic pools, they couldn't exist. Malviana cursed. She'd planned on using them to continue harassing—and killing—the Posairs where she wasn't actively attacking.

The stench of blood and consumed magic gagged her, and she couldn't tolerate it any longer. While she'd contemplated the mirror, her maid had filled her tub with hot water. Shedding her filthy clothes, Malviana slipped into the water. As the heat and steam relaxed her tired body, the problem of the disappearing magic pools beyond the crater swirled through her mind.

Except for setting her spell to create the new Malvers, neither she nor her people had drawn from those pools. It didn't make any sense. She sank deeper into the warm water, leaning her head against the back of the tub, and closing her eyes, letting her mind wander as she relaxed.

She suddenly sat up, sloshing water onto the floor. "No! It can't be. The only way to cleanse the perverted magic from the ground is with Black Talent. We destroyed all those with that Talent and their families so it wouldn't return. How are the Posairs doing it?" She stepped out of the tub, put on a nightgown, and climbed into bed. The puzzle perplexed her. Even though her mind churned with worry, her exhaustion pulled her into sleep.

After a night of nightmares, worrying about the restoration of Black Talent, Malviana awoke in a foul mood. The Malvers were susceptible to Black Talent. If it had returned, they were in trouble.

The servant brushing her hair hit a tangle, pulling Malviana's hair. She lashed out, striking the careless woman. The servant cowered, and red, oozing blisters popped up on her skin where Malviana's hand had struck her. "Be more careful," Malviana admonished. "Continue."

With shaking hands, the woman resumed brushing Malviana's hair until it glistened. Malviana sighed, pleased to have servants again. Those transformed Posairs who didn't possess enough power to become full Malvers, nor change to Maldiers, became servants. The woman helped Malviana into her black gown, fastening the ties on the sides. "Go fetch Lady Nelieh and bring her to me," Malviana ordered. The servant dipped a quick curtsy and scurried out.

Malviana paced her suite's sitting room, her skirts swishing at her feet, pondering the Black Talent problem. Shortly, a knock sounded on the door and Nelieh stepped in. Since coming to the castle, her hair had darkened to a charcoal-gray, and her skin had lost the black splotches, turning the same pale gray as the other Malvers. Pale yellow streaked her black eyes where they hadn't completely changed. If Nelieh kept progressing at her current rate, she'd soon raise to the rank of Baroness.

Nelieh bowed deeply. "How may I serve, my queen?"

"Are there any Posairs with Black Talent?"

Nelieh stood at attention, her hands clasped behind her back. Her lips puckered. "None I know of, my lady. Although, just before I left, I heard rumors Rizelya and her pack-mates had discovered something they were very excited about. It was related to how Kaieli cured the men in the slave camp of the nucla poisoning."

Malviana's forehead creased, and she tilted her head to the side. "What is that, and how did she cure it?"

"Nucla is what the Scourge called the malignant magic fused in the rocks," Nelieh explained. "It infected the men who mined it, and Kaieli and some other women discovered a way to heal it. But I don't know how they did it. They never invited me to participate." Nelieh's dark eyes glinted, and bitterness filled her voice.

Malviana's heart raced. She hadn't known about the encapsulated magic or what it could do. She settled into her favorite chair. "Tell me everything you know and can remember. Even the smallest detail will be valuable."

She grilled Nelieh on how the Scourge had used the nucla. She crowed with delight when she discovered embedding the nucla under a man's skin made it impossible for him to shapeshift. The men in their warrior form were formidable, and she feared they could defeat her new creatures. Malviana loved the idea of grinding the rocks and making a poison to use against the Posairs.

Malviana whirled her goblet in her hands while she considered Nelieh's information. She could use this substance against her foes. She sent a servant to fetch Jorvelden to her.

"This nucla," she said after he arrived, "will give us an edge we need over the shapeshifters. They are formidable fighters, and we need every advantage. Baron Jorvelden, take Lady Nelieh and a dozen others to the crater and procure some of those lovely nucla rocks. She can show you which ones."

"Your will, my queen," Jorvelden bowed. The two Malvers left to do her bidding.

Malviana sipped her bloodwine and stared at the portrait of her family as she pondered the new information. She had a sudden preposterous thought. Could the Posairs merge their Talents to form Black? Malviana shook her head at her silliness. *Disparate Talents can't be combined. But what if the Posairs had found a way to do the impossible?*

Anxiety ate at her insides. She adjusted her crown, smoothed her skirts, and swept from her suite, her bodyguards falling in behind her, and stalked down to the dungeons. Her spell had infected a few people who didn't have enough evil within them to complete the transformation, and they remained Posairs. Slipping a thick leather apron on over her gown, she interrogated several of them, but they didn't possess the information she needed. By the time she completed her questioning, the Posairs were good for only one thing. She sacrificed them to Mordaga, relishing in the power flowing into her and filling her gemstones with their death essence. The power from animals was well and good, but it didn't compare to the amount and quality that came from Posairs.

The corpses of her sacrifices were divided between her still transitioning Malvers and the Maldiers. Malviana wanted her army strong. And the flesh would speed the Malvers' transition.

Malviana - 5 de Sandar, 1076

Malviana sat in her favorite chair and arranged her skirts around her while she waited for her children to arrive to report their progress on their projects. Her gaze fell on the mirror. She flicked her wand at it, activating it. "Show me Rizelya," she commanded.

The mirror misted over, then cleared, showing a bright, blue sky. Malviana blinked and held a hand up to block the light. Even after all this time off the island, she still couldn't tolerate the sunlight. She murmured another spell, and the light dimmed enough so she could look at the mirror without squinting. Rizelya came into view, walking the battlements of a fortress located near the crater. Malviana frowned. Why would Rizelya be there and not with the rest of the Posair army? Suspicion crept up Malviana's spine.

"Damn you to Mordaga's hells!" Malviana swore, glaring at the mirror.

"Who?" Mordeven asked, entering her suite and coming to sit on one arm of her chair. He glanced at the mirror. "Oh, her."

"Yes. Her." Malviana's lip curled. "Didn't you notice how sluggish the magic had become?"

His brows furrowed as he gave a small nod. "I thought it was because we were so exhausted."

"It wasn't that. Somehow, the magic pools are being drained! I can't shake the feeling she—" Malviana jabbed a finger at the mirror "—is behind the loss."

Her fingertips crackled with suppressed anger. Malviana whirled away from the precious mirror lest she damage it. Lightning sizzled, and a vase across the room shattered. She took a deep breath and shook out her hands, then turned back to the mirror and cleared the hated image from it.

She returned her attention back to Mordeven. The wide lapel of his short jacket set off his broad shoulders. Skin-tight trousers hugged his legs. He brushed his shoulder-length dark hair away from his face. Her heart hitched. She flicked a glance at the portrait over the fireplace. He looked so like his father.

The door opened, and Malviana shoved her grief back into its box. "Ah, Malvidor, Morvana, good timing. Come, tell me about your projects. How close are they to being done?"

"I've completed everything you've assigned me," Malvidor said, pulling a straight-backed chair closer to hers. He twirled it around and straddled it, leaning his arms across the back of it. "The jallopsitor are reproducing quickly, as are the floxidors and skeaeters. They're flourishing in the swamp. They each now number over five thousand."

Morvana chose a soft chair, flinging her leg over the arm. Malviana sighed. She just couldn't convince her daughter to wear gowns, except for formal occasions.

"I created over a thousand banthues," Morvana said, "enough for every Malvers, our servants, plus any Malvers marching toward us. Also, I found colonies of our baethor hiding in the far northern mountains, although I'm unsure how they bypassed the Sanctuary to reach so far north." She shrugged. "I called them home and increased their size so they can now compete with the larger Gryphons. Unfortunately, the carnivorous plants were a failure and aren't useful unless we're stationary for some time. Are we going to march soon? I'm ready. My power is fully restored." In response, the gemstones in her ears and on her wand glowed.

"As is mine," Mordeven said. His wand pulsed brighter than Morvana's.

Malviana laughed at the show of power and allowed her gemstones to gleam. Their light eclipsed Mordeven's stones. It never hurt to remind her children of her power and strength.

"Malvidor, you've overseen the training while Mordeven and I worked on the grifflyns. How goes it with our new recruits?"

He sat up straighter and grinned. "Very nicely. Korand is finishing up with the last batch. We haven't had any arrive for a few days, though."

"Not to worry. They'll find us wherever we are."

He threw his leg over his chair, standing, and paced. "The Maldiers are itching to fight. How much longer are we going to hide here?"

Malviana pursed her lips. "We're not hiding. We're preparing."

She stared at the mirror, tapping her long nails on the chair arm. With Rizelya's separation from the rest of the army, now was her chance to destroy the pest. Malviana nodded sharply, more to herself than to her children.

"Yes. It is time to march. Give your people the order. We leave tonight."

As her children scurried from the room, excitement thrilled through her. Finally, the blood of her enemies would pour over her hands, and their death essence would fuel her magic.

Blazel - 6 de Sandar, 1076

The early summer sunshine beat on Blazel's back as he flew with Graak and the others across the crater. It had taken them two chedans to clear the northern fortress and had spent another two at the western one. He rolled the kinks out of his neck. Some days, Blazel would scream with frustration. It seemed like they were trying to empty a lake one cupful at a time. Other days, he could sense a perceptible drop in the magic.

He smiled, remembering Rizelya's joy when she'd discovered a green sprout growing through the cracks in the western fortress's courtyard. Nothing had grown in the Barrens for over a thousand years. This proved their work was healing the land. Before they'd left the fortress, more grass grew in the courtyard—and beyond, pushing through the black sand-glass.

Thankfully, their time at the southern fortress had passed without incident. A few packs of floxidor and skeaeters attempted to slither past the fortress, but the troops had stopped them. Blazel and the Black Weave teams now flew toward the eastern fortress. They'd saved it for last because too many of their members had nightmares of being Scourge slaves. The Scourge compound squatted only a few measures from the fortress.

The central pillar of pure nucla rock rose before them. Before the Scourge had come for the mineral—and to conquer their world—the pillar had stood well above the crater rim. The Posairs and other slaves had hacked off so much from it that it was now a short, squat spire only a few hundred feet high. After working so long with the Black Weave, Blazel easily sensed malignant magic, and the pillar crawled with the stuff.

He squinted, pushing his senses to the lake of malignant magic underneath it. He whooped. *We're making progress,* he told his companions. By now, they could all communicate in mind-speech, even the White Priestesses, and they didn't have to shout at each other while riding the Gryphons. *Look at the lake with your senses!*

The others did and released their own yells of excitement.

It's about half its original size, Rizelya said. *I estimate we need at least two more lunadars to completely cleanse the area.*

I doubt we have that much time, Graak grumbled, *before the Malvers leave the swamp to engage us directly.*

Sooner than we expect. Blazel whispered, shivering.

Graak turned his head over his shoulder to peer at Blazel. *What aren't you telling us?*

Glork increased his pace to fly wingtip-to-wingtip with Graak, and Rizelya frowned at Blazel. *You had more than a nightmare last night, didn't you? What did you see?*

Blazel fingered his loc with the gray stripe. He'd noticed over the past few days it had darkened and grown thicker, and his hair had more gray streaks in it—and so did Rizelya's. Her eyes were a darker brown than he remembered, too. The others were also showing signs of changes happening within them.

Last night, I dreamed about Malviana. Blazel shuddered. *I haven't had any dreams about her since the Malvers escaped their confinement.*

Neither have I, Rizelya assured him. *But after my experiences with her, I keep my mind-block up all the time.*

Blazel hunched his shoulders in chagrin. *I haven't practiced it after Saffren taught me when we checked on the Malvers' island. The dream was so vivid, as if I was watching the scene as it happened. Hundreds of twisted creatures, like the one at the black castle, all powerful and filled with hatred, marched through the southern swamp. Above them flew a thousand banthues, each one with a Malvers sitting on its back. Malviana in the lead, held a dark wand, sparkling with glowing jewels. It radiated repulsive power.*

We didn't see that many when they escaped, Glork commented. *Even cloaked, I doubt there were more than a few hundred.*

Where are they coming from? Blenora asked.

Rizelya's eyes widened, and she covered her mouth with her hand. *The infection! It's creating Malvers and hybrids like the twisted creature you saw, Blazel.*

What else did you witness? Chariel asked. *This wasn't a dream, but a vision sent by the Goddess.*

Blazel took a deep breath, delving deeper into his memory, trying to recall more. *Behind them flew thousands of banthues, over sized baethors, and another kind of creature I haven't seen before.* He swallowed the bile rising in his throat as dread swamped him. He wrestled his fear back down, then continued. *Thousands of floxidor, skeaeters, and the new monsters trailed the twisted men. In my dream, I couldn't see them all.*

*Sweet Mother, protect us!** Blenora prayed.

*How can we even hope to fight so many creatures?** Kaieli slumped deeper into her saddle harness. *So many will die.**

*We survived the Scourge invasion and won,** Rizelya said, confidence radiated through her mind-voice. *And our ancestors fought these same monsters in the Great War. We can win this one, too.**

Memories of fighting the Scourge assailed Blazel. His people had survived and beat those impossible odds. They could do so again against the Malvers and their foul followers.

Below them, the broken remnants of the invaders' energy dome came into sight, and they flew over the ruins of the Scourge compound. Many of the buildings still stood and, unbelievably, a herd of ten sheezet, the Scourge's large lizards mounts, rooted around their pens. Blazel assumed they'd killed all the beasts. He wondered how they survived in this desolate place.

Graak turned and swept away from the compound. Following the curve of the crater rim, he flew northeast. The white sheadash keep rose from the black depths of the Barrens. Blazel squinted at the bright flashes from the noon sun sparkling on the mica within the stone. Glossy mahogany and striped dark gray shapes jutted from the ocean of black sand-glass like deserted islands. The jumble of petrified wood stretched across the sands, reminding him this had once been a large forest. He prayed they wouldn't need to unleash such terrible magic to win the fight against the Malvers this time. One such desolate place in their world was more than enough.

His heart and mood lightened when he recalled the greening in and around the western fortress. Hopefully, this area would one day thrive with life. That is, if the Malvers didn't destroy it again with their filthy death magic.

A shout arose from the fighters in the fortress as they circled above it. When Blazel glanced down, he gulped at the pulsers trained on them.

"Can't they tell you're a Gryphon? Graak, why don't you flare?" he suggested. "Let them know it's us and not banthues."

Graak's magic gathered and heat washed over Blazel. The crack of a pulser firing startled him. Graak flared again, and this time, his flame formed a shield around them.

"What in the Crone's fires is going on?"

They're afraid of us! Graak's tone held disbelief. *Our people have never harmed a Posair.*

"Isn't Candriel the alpha there? Talk to her. Tell her it's us."

A few moments later, the fighters on the battlements lowered their weapons.

She said flying creatures that look like Gryphons have attacked them. I don't understand this, Blazel. My race was created during the Great War to protect your people. We can't hurt a Posair. Graak's head feathers drooped.

"We'll find out what's been happening," Blazel assured his friend.

Graak spiraled down and landed in the courtyard, with Glork right behind him. Before Blazel had finished unbuckling his harness, Rizelya jumped off Glork and stomped toward the woman standing at the bottom of the keep-house steps. Pale yellow striped the woman's scarlet hair.

"What in the Crone's fires, Candriel?" Rizelya demanded, her hands on her hips as she glared at the much taller woman. "Why did you shoot at us?"

"Sorry, Rizelya." Candriel rubbed her forehead. "Gryphons have attacked us recently."

"Are you sure they were Gryphons? I can't believe our allies would turn on us. Glork says they can't. As in, it's impossible for them to harm a Posair."

"They look like Gryphons." Candriel's eyes narrowed at Graak and Glork. "You'll find out for yourself soon enough. They've hit us every day we've been here. Come on, I'll get you and your people settled in. Although I'm not sure where we can house the Gryphons."

We will be fine in the rear courtyard, Graak said.

She nodded to him, then limped into the keep-house. Her leg still wasn't fully healed from the injury she'd sustained during a fight with the Scourge. She showed them a large dormitory with enough beds for both Black Weave teams and their bodyguards. Blazel and Rizelya chose a bed near a window and were putting their belongings in a chest when an alarm blared. He dropped his shirt, grabbed his pulser, and bolted down the stairs.

As he and Rizelya ran out the door, Candriel pointed up. "Now, you'll see what we've been fighting."

Blazel craned his neck. Large, dark shapes soared above them. He thought he saw a flash of red as one flew over him. He narrowed his eyes, trying to focus better.

That is no Gryphon, Graak said, coming to stand next to Blazel. Puffs of dust rose as his tail thumped the ground hard as he glared at the flying creatures.

Blazel wrapped the harness around Graak's middle, having a harder time than usual from trying to avoid Graak's thrashing tail. He jumped on. "Let's go find out what these things are."

With pleasure, Graak growled. He leaped into the air, along with Glork, Broogk, Morru, Kaaik, and Sterkek. Their partners rode snugged into their harnesses. Others from the Black Weave teams shot into the air a few moments later.

I can understand Candriel's confusion, Blazel said in mind-speech to his packs, as they closed on the creatures.

Me, too, Eidstrun added. *From below, their shape would appear like a Gryphon.*

The wide wings and feline-like bodies were similar to a Gryphon. But these creature's heads were reptilian on long, sinewy necks, instead of the familiar birdlike Gryphon front half. Sharp horns curved over and behind the creature's heads, similar to the invader's sheezet. A red stripe ran along the underside of their gray bodies, starting below their jaw and ending at the tip of their tail. The same red edged their gray and white wings.

A beast opened its mouth, and a gout of flames streamed from its maw. Graak veered to the side, barely avoiding the flames.

Abomination! Graak cried and chased the creature. Suddenly, it careened. An ice spear protruding from its side.

Blazel saluted to Saffren vend Florrik. After Maestrun's death, Blazel had expected the Blue to withdraw, but instead she focused her grief on any Malvers created monster they encountered. Overhead, Oslerru screeched, and attacked the largest creature. Saffren grimaced, urging Florrik to catch up to their pack-mate. Nelstrun on Daerik sped past Graak on their way to help Oslerru.

Graak dove at another beast, flaming, and Blazel grabbed the harness straps. Graak squawked as his fire washed over it without any effect. While Graak sputtered and swore, the beast twisted in a sinewy move and closed in on Graak. Blazel pulled his pulser forward, chambered a round, and fired. The creature jerked when his projectile struck it. Another pulser fired, as Maeaak and Ambrelya flew over the beast. Blazel and Ambrelya fired again and again, hitting it each time.

"Damn beast won't die!" he swore. "Ambrelya, aim at its head."

Blazel took a deep breath and carefully aimed at its head. Body shots weren't stopping it. His pulser slid from his grip, making his shot go wide, when the creature slammed into Graak. Its jaws snapped at Graak's neck, and its clawed feet tried to shred Graak's belly. Maeaak zipped over the tumbling fight. The creature screeched, and a red trail streaked from Ambrelya's pulser. Her projectile zoomed into the creature's open mouth and embedded into its brain. It finally spiraled toward the ground in death. Blazel saluted Ambrelya, grateful she'd decided to join the fox Black Weave team as one of their bodyguards. Her marksmanship had saved him and Graak.

Rizelya and Glork battled a much larger beast below them. Graak dove with his talons outstretched. He screeched as he dug them into the creature's back. It snaked its long neck around, spewing fire. Graak flared. Blazel ducked behind the shield, laying his cheek against Graak's shoulder. Intense heat washed over him, and he dropped his pulser before the metal burned him. Graak's sharp beak bit into the creature, gouging out a chunk. It violently spasmed, and Blazel glanced over Graak's side. Rizelya jerked her helbraught, glowing a deep orange, from its belly.

"Graak, let go!" she yelled. "It's going to blow."

Graak bit another hunk from the beast before unhooking his talons, flapping hard to gain altitude while Glork soared to the side. A few moments later, the animal exploded. Blazel searched the skies, but couldn't see any more of the flying creatures.

They're gone, Graak spat. *The cowards fled. Too bad there aren't more of us here to chase them down and annihilate* *the abominations.** He spiraled to fly back to the fortress. Their fight had taken them far into the Barrens.

"It looked like someone mashed together a Gryphon and a lizard-mount."

I thought the same. But where would they get a Gryphon?

Blazel considered the coloring of the creature's wings and how it was the same as the owl-type scouts. "Baekeek and the other scouts," Blazel said in horror. Guilt followed closely. He'd been the one to suggest they stay to watch the black castle.

We don't know that for sure.

"You nor the other Gryphons could contact them. Now we know why." Blazel slumped against Graak's neck.

If that's what happened to them, I am to blame, Graak said softly. **I ordered them to stay behind.**

They flew back to the fortress in silence, both lost in their own guilt.

Chapter 17

Blazel - 9 de Sandar, 1076

Since the Black Weave team's arrival at the eastern fortress, attacks by the new flying Gryphon-sheezet hybrid—now called grifflyns—kept interrupting their work. The teams hadn't cleansed much nucla from the surrounding area. Instead of just a flock of grifflyns, this latest attack also included a dozen banthues and a handful of giant baethor.

"Fly over the fortress, will you, Graak?" Blazel asked as the last of the creatures fled. "I want to study it. The banthues and baethors appearance reminded me about my dream, vision, of the Malvers army."

You believe this heralds their approach? Graak tilted and slowed his flight, gazing down at the fortress.

Ants crawled over Blazel's skin. The hundred fighters wouldn't stand a chance against the swarm he saw in his dream. "We can't defend this. It would be suicide to stay."

Agreed. Graak flew higher, arrowing toward the crater. It blocked their view of the Barrens beyond it. Before they reached it, far on the horizon, dust filled the air, making the sky appear black. Blazel's mind bucked with terror.

Graak warbled in distress. *That isn't dust! It's the Malvers army.*

He turned so fast Blazel's head smashed into his shoulder. Graak sped back to the fortress.

"Rizelya! Candriel!" Blazel yelled as they landed. He scrambled from Graak's back and raced into the keep-house.

Rizelya caught up to him on the stairs. "What's wrong? Where did you go after the fight?"

He groped for her hand. "The banthues are the leading edge of Malviana's army. The Malvers are coming."

"How do you know?"

"Graak and I just flew toward the crater. The army is so large, it blackens the sky."

Rizelya gasped. "Your vision! It's happening." She quickened her pace, running up the stairs and down the corridor. Blazel lengthened his stride to keep up with her. They burst into Candriel's office without knocking.

"We have to leave," Rizelya said in a rush.

Candriel glanced up, a protest on her lips. It died when she looked at Rizelya's face. "Why? When?"

"Now!" Blazel slapped the desk and leaned forward on his hands. "Tonight. We don't have much time. Those banthues were scouts for the Malvers' army. Graak and I saw them."

"We should leave under the cover of darkness," Rizelya said, "and get as far across the Barrens as possible."

"We can't defend this fortress," Blazel added, "against the hoard barreling toward us."

Candriel's eyes widened. "That many?"

Rizelya nodded.

"Sweet Mother!" Candriel sprinted from the room.

A moment later, the alarm bell pealed, the strident sound making Blazel's heart beat faster. Organized pandemonium broke out as people rushed to pack and load the supply carts. They couldn't cross the Barrens without food or water. Blazel regretted the two dozen Gryphons, who were part of the Black Weave teams, couldn't evacuate everyone in the fortress. However, they could provide cover for the ground troops. His thoughts flew to the White Priestesses on the teams. He still hadn't taken the time to train them to fight.

Graak! Morlek! he called as he jogged to where the Gryphons roosted.

Morlek blinked at him, shaking his fur as if he'd just woken from a nap. *What's going on?*

"We're leaving here. Tonight." Blazel caught Graak's eye. He knew the urgency. "Morlek, I'd like you to lead Blueek and Nealaak in taking the White Priestesses ahead of us to safety. Ambrelya and Maeaak will accompany you as additional protection. Leave as soon as it's dark and fly as fast as you can. Even if they argue with you, which my mother is likely to do, take them to safety. They still can't fight. Graak, the rest of our team needs to provide cover for the ground troops if everyone is to survive the coming army."

Morlek dipped his head and put a talon gently on Blazel's shoulder. *We shall fly the priestesses to safety. Loshera is just as likely to be upset we're going ahead. But I agree with you, it's best to remove them from the fight to come. What about Chariel?*

Blazel paused. While the other priestesses didn't know how to fight, Chariel did. "Take her and Torlek. They can help you protect the others if needed." Blazel grimaced. Chariel was going to skin him, but she'd be safe.

Relieved, Blazel returned to the keep-house to quickly pack his few belongings. He hoped they left in time.

Rizelya - 9 de Sandar, 1076

Under the cover of darkness, the fighters at the eastern fortress slipped out the gates and into the Barrens. Rizelya felt like a coward as they ran ahead of the Malvers' army. She rubbed her eyes as exhaustion swept over her. The Black Weave teams had spent the last few octars draining as much of the malignant magic from the area as possible to deny the enemy any additional power. Morlek's team, carrying the White Priestesses—and a loudly protesting Chariel—had sped away with the garrison's people. They could replace all the Talents for the Black Weave teams, except the priestess's Talents of White and Gray.

The Gryphons, as the rearguard, left the fortress well past midnight, cutting it close when a wave of banthues appeared on the horizon. Graak, as the Gryphon's leader, had to force Oslerru to leave and not fight the banthues. Ever since Maestrun's death, Oslerru had fallen into an almost suicidal funk, flinging himself into the most dangerous fights with the grifflyns and banthues. When they returned to the main army, she hoped he'd find another partner or rejoin the Gryphon flights. His attitude was putting them all in danger.

Leistrun and Brogkek were the opposite, refusing to fight unless absolutely necessary. Leistrun's amputated arm had healed, and Blenora was working on healing his traumatized mind, but he still refused to shift into his warrior form. Ambrelya had devised a sling to hold his pulser, so he could use it. Once he started practicing with it, his demeanor had perked up. Not being able to shapeshift herself, Rizelya couldn't understand everything Leistrun was going through. She tried not to pity him. But sometimes, the line between pity and compassion was very thin.

Laying against Glork's shoulder, Rizelya squinted her eyes at the morning light sparkling on the black sand-glass below them. She lifted her head at the rush of wings, then pushed as upright as the harness allowed.

You're back. Rizelya's tired mind caught up to the inane observation. She slapped her cheeks to revive herself. *What did you see?*

Aistrun and Broogk had risked flying toward the army to scout for them.

It's like in Blazel's vision, Aistrun reported. *Thousands of beasts march or fly across the Barrens. Some, we've already encountered, but there are new ones, too.*

Hundreds of the twisted conglomeration of beasts and Posairs marched with them, Broogk added. *And even worse, at least a thousand Malvers ride banthues.*

The news chilled Rizelya. Her thoughts strayed to Nelieh and the black splotches covering her face and arms as she screamed profanities at Chariel and Loshera. There couldn't have been so many in the army infected by the illness, could there?

If so, how many former friends and family would they face across the battlefield?

Between beasts and Malvers, Blazel said, his mind-voice sounding tired, *the two armies seem to be roughly equal, with the Posairs slightly ahead. We can draw a few thousand more from the northern keeps.*

Graak's wing beats faltered a moment, and he righted himself. If Rizelya was exhausted, the Gryphons were worse. They'd not only worked as part of the Black Weave team, but had flown all night.

As it stands now, Graak said, *the Gryphons are sorely outnumbered. If Moraak convinces his father, King Zorlaak, to send more to fight against our ancient foes, we'll be fine.*

I can't believe he won't, Glork added. *He knows the danger the Malvers pose.*

The Gryphons took turns soaring into the higher altitude to catch thermals to briefly rest. Late in the afternoon, Glork circled over a jumble of large petrified logs leaning against each other, providing the fleeing fighters shelter to rest out of the blazing sun. Rizelya frowned at Morlek and Torlek, waiting for them. They should have been much farther ahead. As Glork landed, Rizelya blinked at the tracks of hooves and cart wheels leading to the rest stop, her tired mind screaming at her. Finally, she understood what she was seeing.

"Blazel, we need to do something about our tracks," she pointed at the ground.

He swore. "All our enemy needs to do is follow the broken sand-glass to know where we are."

"We could use the Black Weave to make a wind storm to hide them," Eiden suggested. "I could guide us. It would be nice to use our powers for something different."

Rizelya considered it for a moment, then shrugged. "We might as well try. If it doesn't work, we'll be no worse off than we are now."

The team found a quiet spot, and Rizelya's consciousness joined with the others as Eiden and Korrik initiated the blending. They flew over their trail, the wind from their ethereal wings sweeping away the tracks of their passing. Suddenly, they brushed against an evil presence. One Rizelya recognized. She quickly pulled them away at the same time as Chariel, Ardela, and Saffren threw up strong mental shields. Graak added in the magic of the Gryphon's invisibility spell. Rizelya snapped back into her own body just as the presence sent questing fingers toward them. She held her breath, eyes wide open, praying Malviana wouldn't find them.

"Do you think she sensed us?" Kaieli whispered.

"She did." Loshera wiped the sweat off her forehead. She nodded to Graak. "But thanks to Graak's quick thinking, I believe we've hidden our psychic tracks, as well as our physical ones."

"We need to hide what we can do for as long as possible," Chariel said. "Our lives and those of our people depend on it."

Rizelya glanced over at her, but Chariel's eyes were clear of the silver film that covered them when she spoke prophecy.

Chariel saw her and shook her head. "No, it wasn't a prophecy, but a warning from the Goddess just the same. Although I keep receiving glimpses of Wisah and Malviana battling in the snow."

"Then it won't be anywhere near here." Blazel stretched his legs out in front of him with a grimace. "It doesn't snow this far south."

"It feels more like we're in the mountains," Chariel added. She scrunched her face in thought. "It isn't the Sanctuary, but close. Strunhelos, maybe?" She shrugged.

Rizelya groaned. "That means not only will we be fighting all summer, but we'll also have to travel north."

"This is good news," Saffren said, leaning her head back to rest on Florrik's side and closing her eyes. Nelstrun, rarely far from her side, sat next to her. Daerik rested his head over Florrik's back, while Oslerru curled in the sand alone. "Our people will resist the Malvers at least through the summer and autumn. I have complete faith the Goddess will provide a way for us—and Wisah—to prevail against this evil. She has before. But right now, I'm too tired to stay awake any longer."

Exhaustion pulled at Rizelya. Her eyes felt heavy, and her extremities leaden. A snap of fabric roused her. Blazel spread out their bedroll and patted it in invitation. It would be more comfortable than sleeping on the hard rocks. She crawled over to him, curled up against his side, and was asleep in moments.

A gentle nudge woke her. She sat up, resisting the urge to rub her gritty eyes.

"Here, this will help." Blazel handed her a damp cloth.

She wiped Barrens dust, filled with fine particles of glass, from her face. Traveling by Gryphon eliminated being coated in the stuff. She traded him the cloth for a water canteen. She drank deeply, easing her raw throat.

"The fighters have left already. We're following behind, both as rear guard and to cover their tracks." Blazel looked over to where Eiden, Dehali, and Grazeen conferred with their Gryphon partners. "Eiden thinks she can erase the passage with Dehali and Grazeen's help."

"How can Grazeen help?"

"Haven't you noticed she now has yellow streaks in her hair?"

Rizelya shook her head, then squinted at Grazeen. In the dying sunlight, she glimpsed golden threads amid Grazeen's dark forest-green hair. She turned back to Blazel and lightly picked up the dark gray loc, which had been light gray when she'd met him. "She isn't the only one picking up new Talents."

He laughed. "You haven't looked closely in the mirror lately, have you? Your eyes are so brown now, they're nearly black, and there is quite a bit of gray in your hair."

"Really?" She touched it softly. She wasn't one to spend much time in front of a mirror and hadn't noticed anything different. She studied the others in the Black Weave teams, marking slight changes in all of them. Her eyebrows raised at the shocking dark purple strands streaking Saffren's hair. Water and fire Talents never mixed! What did it all mean? Rizelya mentally shrugged. Time would tell.

"Where's Aistrun?" she asked as she dug in her pouch for a travel bar.

"He and the priestesses are accompanying the fighters." Blazel helped her to her feet, then rolled up the bedroll.

She chewed on her travel bar while buckling the harness onto Glork. In a few milcrons, the Gryphons launched in the darkening evening. Before the light completely gave way, Rizelya saw an eddy of wind wiping away the fighter's trail. When they landed to rest during the heat of the afternoon, Rizelya couldn't spot a single hoof print. Somehow, Eiden, Dehali, and Grazeen had found the trail in the dark.

Wisah - 11 de Sandar, 1076

Wisah entered the weapons laboratory and groaned at the two new devices sitting by themselves on Maendy's worktable. She scowled at the large pyramid-shaped device made from helstrim, and what appeared like a headband.

The pyramid was large enough she'd have to hold it with both hands. Maendy had deeply etched one of the three sigils of the unmaking spell into each pyramid face. She'd inlaid one sigil with gold, another with silver, and bronze covered the third. A double-terminated clear quartz point jutted from the pyramid's apex.

Dread filled Wisah as she approached the table. Maendy had started assembling the unmaking device over a chedan ago.

"I finished the device on the scroll," Maendy needlessly announced. She pointed to the pyramid-shaped object. "This is the projector and will focus the spell on whatever—whoever—you wish to unmake. And this is the activator." She held out the helstrim headband, decorated with sigils and crystals. A large crystal dominated the center.

Wisah stared at the articles, loath to touch them, fearful she'd accidentally arm the weapon.

"You have to wear the headband in order for the device to work," Maendy explained. She placed two fingers on the center of Wisah's forehead. "This is where the third symbol of the spell is tattooed. I attuned the crystal in the headband to the crystal in the pyramid. When you're ready to use the weapon, chant the spell while holding the device in both hands. Place your palms over the corresponding symbols tattooed on the back of your hands. Point it at what you want to destroy. The magic will flow from you through the crystal in the headband and to the crystal in the device and..." She made an explosion sound as she pulled her hands away from each other.

Wisah gingerly touched the pyramid with a fingertip, and warmth crept into it. The symbols on her hands blazed with azure light, then deepened to an indigo so dark it seemed black. She didn't have a mirror, but she guessed the sigil on her forehead also shone, especially from Maendy and Sheekeek's wide-eyed expressions. Power coursed through her, and the words of the spell whispered seductively in her mind, begging to be used. She jerked her hand away, lest she succumb to their seduction, and turned it on her friends. She'd wrongfully assumed she'd have to practice with the device in order to use it.

Maendy slipped the pyramid-shaped device in a leather pouch with protective sigils and spells thickly laid on it. As she pulled the ties closed, the whispering in Wisah's mind hushed, and she sighed in relief.

"You should keep the pieces separate," Maendy said, holding out the headband, "until you're ready to use it. I doubt anyone else can use them, but we don't want Malviana to get this."

"No, we don't. It would be very bad for her to have this device and spell."

"Wear the headband," Maellyn suggested. "It's decorative enough that it looks like it's simply holding your hair back from your face."

"Then even if this—" Maendy hefted the pouch "—gets stolen, it won't work. Both pieces are required for the device to function."

Maellyn held the headband out to Wisah. She warily touched it with her fingertips. When nothing happened, she took it from Maellyn. Her forehead throbbed in time to her heartbeat, and the central crystal pulsed in concert. Taking a deep breath, Wisah jammed the headband on. Power flooded her as the crystal came into contact with the sigil, making her throw back her head in a scream. She wasn't sure if it was pain or pleasure. She felt as if she could do anything, create anything, she desired. As the power began to subside to a manageable level, Wisah remembered the last symbol was for creation. In order to unmake something, you had to understand its essence.

Sheekeek trilled a nervous laugh. *When you said you had all the sigils, you weren't joking.*

Wisah lifted a quizzical eyebrow at him.

He pointed a talon at her. *When you put the headband on, your body lit up with sigils.* He leaned down to peer more closely at her. *I don't think there's a speck of skin not covered with a symbol.*

"You'd have to do that again nude," Maendy added, "for us to be sure. But from what we could see, it certainly looked like it."

Wisah held her arms out in front of her. The sigils tattooed on them still glowed with azure light. Was there anything she couldn't do? The saliva in her mouth suddenly dried, and she wished she had a glass of water. A tiny pulse of power throbbed in her forehead. Her eyes widened when, a moment later, a glass of water appeared on the table. She pointed at it, her mouth moving, but no sound came out.

"What?" Maellyn asked, then glanced at the table and gasped. "Where did that come from?"

"I think... I think I created it," Wisah whispered. "I wanted a glass of water, and it appeared." With shaking hands, she picked up the glass, water sloshing over the sides. She gulped it down.

Maendy took the empty glass from her and examined it. "It looks like an ordinary glass, like those in the kitchens. I wonder what else you can do. Imagine a rose."

"A rose? Why?" Wisah wrinkled her nose. "Ouch!" A pale pink and white rose rested in her hands. A drop of blood welled on her palm where a thorn had pricked her.

Ooh... amazing! Sheekeek took the rose. *Look here at the stem, it's been freshly cut. So I'm not sure if you're creating things or teleporting them.* He handed the blossom to Maendy, who scrutinized it.

"Were you thinking of a single rose or a rosebush?" Maendy asked.

"A rose. Exactly like that one."

"Hmm... it started after you put on the headband," Maendy observed. "Can you still do it when you're not wearing it?"

Wisah shrugged, glad she had someone with Maendy's logical mind to guide her through discovering how this new aspect of her power worked. She removed the headband, fluffing her hair. Her head felt oddly strange without the headband's weight, even though she'd only worn it for a few milcrons.

Maendy took it from her and put it on the table. "Now, think of a different rose."

Wisah held her hands out, palms up, as she visualized a yellow rose. After several moments, with nothing materializing, she laughed, relieved. "Thankfully, it's only when I wear the headband. Do you have another pouch for it?"

Maendy picked up a blue velvet bag from the table and held it out. "You can use this. But I suggest you wear the headband all the time. You need to learn to control your power. You don't want to manifest something awful just by thinking about it when you're frightened."

Sheekeek tapped the headband with his talon, making it chime softly. *I agree with Maendy. We'll be going into war soon, and Malviana will have created some frightening creatures. It would be horrible for you to drop them into the middle of our people because you'd thought about them.*

Wisah put the headband in the bag and tied it to her waist. "I want to do some more reading before I experiment further. For one, am I'm creating objects from thin air or teleporting them from elsewhere? It makes a huge difference which one I'm doing. Where is the scroll?"

Maendy rubbed her chin and leaned against the table. "It's in the cabinet over my desk, but I don't recall the spell saying anything about this aspect of it."

"Perhaps I didn't translate that part. I missed the sigils, after all." Wisah walked to the desk and found the scroll. Leaving the pyramid device in the workshop, she returned to her room. Something about the spell niggled at the back of her mind. She wanted to compare the scroll with the spell book.

Octars later, several old tomes and scrolls from the Supreme's private library lay spread out in a jumble on Wisah's bed. She held a scroll so ancient the ink was barely legible. As she read, her hands began to tremble, and she carefully laid the scroll down so her shaking wouldn't damage the fragile parchment. The mysterious sigil tattoos had appeared over the ages on several Supremes when the world was in dire need. But they'd all had one or two sigils, not the thousands Wisah now wore.

Except one.

Sigil tattoos also covered the first Supreme chosen by the Goddess. Wisah dropped her head into her hands and sobbed. This destroyed her last hope for a semi-normal life with Jaehaas. She wanted to blame the damned spell book for the sigils, but she couldn't. It had only been the delivery mechanism for the Goddess's will. Not even a shred of doubt remained within Wisah. When the current Supreme died, Wisah would take her place. The why was irrelevant. The Goddess had made her choice, and it was irrevocably Wisah.

She locked herself in her room, trying to accept her new calling and the changes it would bring. Sadness, guilt, surprise, confusion, amazement, and even anger traipsed through her, as Wisah processed the fact she was not only the next Supreme, but a new type as well.

Rizelya - 12 de Sandar, 1076

The unmistakable stench of Malvers' monsters pulled Rizelya from her sleep. She leaped to her feet, feeding fire magic into her helbraught, and kicking the bedroll aside. The men, except for Leistrun, had already shifted into their warrior forms. Leistrun awkwardly fit his pulser into the sling. He grimaced with a mixture of determination and distaste. The nimbus of fire always surrounding the Gryphons grew brighter. Eiden leaped on Korrik's back, and together, they rose into the air, her helbraught glowing a golden-yellow. Boreek launched a moment later with Grazeen.

"Where are they coming from?" Rizelya swiveled her head from side to side, trying to find the monsters. Candriel's people had already left the campsite. Rizelya hoped this wasn't a large nest. She doubted they had enough people to kill the monsters. But they couldn't let them chase after the fighters.

"There," Blazel growled, and pointed a claw southwest.

She nodded as Dehali, Kami, Ambrelya, Raeleen, and Leistral moved into position to form a fire-ring. She raised an eyebrow as Saffren stepped into place. Her helbraught glowed red, tinged with purple. Rizelya still didn't understand how Saffren could wield both fire and water Talents.

Rizelya put the thought aside as the first brecha ran into view, its spines quivering as it sought a target. She hadn't fought a janack or brecha in many chedans. Five brechas ran unerringly at their small group. A single janack trundled after the brechas, its heat stalks waving. She tilted her head, listening intently, but didn't hear the telltale hum of a control-janack. When nothing else appeared out of the gloom, she signaled, *Now!*

The fire-ring sizzled, forming a circle around the fight. With a swoop of wings, Korrik dove and Eiden unleashed an ice spear into a brecha looming behind her twin, Eidstrun. A brecha ran toward Saffren, releasing its spines. Before they could hit her, a wall of flame flared in front of her. Korrik screeched as he drove his talons into the back of the brecha, lifting it several feet in the air, then dropping it.

Blazel and Eidstrun tore into the janack as Leistrun fired projectiles at it. The janack was a large enough target that he could shoot it and not hit his pack-mates. Delestrun teamed up with Baederposan in taking out a brecha. Ambrelya broke from the fire-ring to help Korhaas with his brecha. Aistrun worked with Nelstrun, fighting the fifth brecha.

Something seemed off to Rizelya. Without thinking, she reached out with her senses as if she were in the Black Weave. A dozen pinpricks of baneful energy surrounded them and were closing in. She concentrated and sucked in a breath. Jallopsitor!

It's a trap! she yelled, assessing the fight. The janack wobbled, missing four of its ten tentacles. Nelstrun dug his claws into the side of the last remaining brecha. *They're just decoys. We have to get out of here.*

Glork dropped down beside her. Abandoning her bedroll, she grabbed her pack dend his harness. She hurriedly snugged it on him and flung herself onto his back. The others were throwing harnesses on their Gryphon partners, their rucksacks strapped on.

"Blazel!" she screamed. "Leave it! It'll collapse in a few milcrons. We have to go now!"

He turned from the janack to face her, a snarl on his lips. She gasped at how feral he looked. He shook his head, then shifted as he raced to Graak. He was still buckling his harness when one of the nasty creatures loomed out of the dark, snapping at Graak. With a screech and a burst of flame, Graak leaped into the air. The jallopsitor let out a high-pitched warble as it ducked its burning snout to the ground and rubbed it with its stubby forelegs.

"Go! Go!" Rizelya urged Glork. The jallopsitor ran after them. "Don't follow the fighters. We'd just lead these creatures to them."

Agreed. The fighters don't have enough of a head start to outrace these monsters. Glork passed the message to the other Gryphons.

Glork tipped his wings to veer in the opposite direction the fighters had taken. Several octars later, they finally lost the jallopsitors. They searched for Candriel's people, but the dark made one jumble of rocks appear like the next. With no discernible landmarks, they spent two more octars searching for the protecting jumble of petrified boulders where the fighters camped. Glork wobbled with exhaustion. As he landed, Rizelya noticed the scuffed-up sands. There'd been a fight here recently.

After sliding off Glork, she searched for Candriel. Blazel caught up to her in a few strides. She found Candriel with a bloody bandage wrapped around her right biceps. "What happened?"

"A pack of floxidor waited for us when we arrived." Disgust laced Candriel's voice. "How in the Crone's fires did they know this is where we'd stop?"

Rizelya started to shrug, then stopped. "This is where the guard-packs always stay on their way to the eastern fortress, isn't it?"

"Yes..."

"The Malvers now include Posairs subverted by Malviana's disease. They know our regular routines and routes."

Candriel's mouth dropped open. "You can't be serious!"

"Anyone with black splotches has been infected and, I suspect, will become a Malvers."

Candriel covered her face with her hands and groaned. "I've seen several people with those splotches in my command. Do you think they're spies?"

"Most likely. We need to take a different route..." Rizelya hesitated. What if she'd made an erroneous assumption about the connection of the illness and the increase in the Malvers population? She gritted her teeth and paced, wishing she knew for sure. If it was how new Malvers were made, the most practical thing would be to kill the infected. She'd killed plenty of monsters in her lifetime—including the monstrous invaders—but she'd never killed another Posair before. If she were wrong, she'd commit murder. Her stomach knotted, and sweat broke out on her face. She couldn't do it.

"We have to leave the infected people behind. Tie them up, but loose enough they can escape after we're long gone."

"That's a bad idea," Blazel said, crossing his arms over his chest. "We'd be leaving an enemy at our backs."

"Can you callously kill them? Because I can't."

The muscles in Blazel's jaw tightened. After a moment, he let out his breath in a whoosh. "No. No, I can't. There'll be enough killing and atrocities in this war. I don't want to be the first to commit such an act."

Candriel hunkered down and gestured to them to join her. Once Rizelya and Blazel crouched next to her, Candriel pulled a map from her pack and laid it out on the ground between them. She pointed out the route they'd been following. "This is the most direct way to Haaslornde Keep, with a stop at Haaslornas tonight. If we go this way instead—" her finger trailed a different course "—we'll bypass the garrison, but it will add an extra day to our travel."

"Haaslornas is in the direct path of the advancing army," Rizelya noted. "We have to warn them. Kothera and Metherposan don't have enough people in the garrison to stop the coming horde. Histrun will need them with the rest of our army rather than having them stay in a suicide position."

"True," Blazel agreed. He studied the map for a moment. "Why don't we head this alternate way, but turn here, back toward Haaslornas Keep. It will only be a half-day's delay, but would still throw off our spies."

When darkness fell, and they continued on their journey, they left behind three men and two women blindfolded, tied, and gagged.

The force pushed through the heat and exhaustion, arriving at the garrison late in the afternoon.

"So it's begun," Kothera said, pacing her office. "Why didn't you stay and fight, Candriel? You were there specifically to hold off the Malvers' advance."

"We ran to fight another day. This was no advance party. My hundred fighters weren't a match for their thousands."

"But how can they have such a big army?" Metherposan eyebrows furrowed in confusion. "I didn't think there were that many Malvers still alive."

Rizelya reached up to rub her face and stopped. Barrens dust coated her skin. She slumped in her chair. "They have twisted creatures fighting for them. Some we believe were once Posairs. You've fought the floxidor, skeaeters, and banthues. Those are nothing compared to their newest creations. And they have thousands of them. You need to leave here, too. You can't stop them, and Histrun will need you more to fight in the battles to come rather than wasting your lives to hold this pile of stones."

Reluctantly, Kothera and Metherposan agreed. While they prepared their people to evacuate the next morning, Rizelya and her team washed off the Barrens dust and went to bed for some much-needed sleep.

Rizelya's teams waited to leave the garrison, again serving as the rearguard. As Glork circled the keep before flying after the fleeing fighters, Rizelya saw a dark smudge on the horizon. They were only a day or so ahead of the Malvers' army.

"Leistral, you and Morru fly directly to Haaslornde as quickly as you can," Rizelya ordered. "Warn Histrun trouble is following us."

She watched the two speed away. The Posairs had just defeated the much larger Scourge army. She had to have faith they could defeat this one, too. But these enemies had something the Scourge hadn't.

Death magic.

Chapter 18

Wisah - 16 de Sandar, 1076

Wisah awoke and stretched. After three days sitting alone in her room, she'd finally accepted her new calling, and she'd slept well last night for the first time in chedans. She rolled over, her gaze landing on a book on her bedside table. *Huh? Where did that come from? It wasn't there when I fell asleep.* She sat up, piling pillows behind her back, and picked up the book. Wisah gasped as she thumbed through it. "Oh, Sweet Mother! This is the first Supreme's journal!" Priestesses had lovingly copied it many times over the centuries to preserve its contents.

Wisah reverently held the book as she read, pausing when she read the first Supreme's name. She'd never heard it before— no one had. Once the woman had ascended to the Sanctuary's Throne and became the living representative of the Goddess, she'd lost her name. Someday, at her own ascension, Wisah would become known only as the Supreme. Wisah trailed her fingers over the name as she whispered it. "Wyshera." She marveled at how similar their names were.

She wondered what the current Supreme's name had been. The Supreme had hinted her safe contained a logbook of the

Supreme's lineage, which contained the only record of the past Supreme's names. Wisah could open the safe and look at it, but it felt like an invasion of privacy. She would wait to read it when she added her own name to it—hopefully many years in the future.

Wisah's heart lightened. The First Supreme, Wyshera, had gone through the same emotions she was experiencing when she'd been called to serve as the representative of the Goddess. Wyshera's trial by fire had set the path the Posairs now lived. Her calling had brought the Posairs from living in caves to building the first temple, cultivating the first fields, and writing the first books. Everything the Posairs believed in and the practices they followed could be traced back to the teachings of Wyshera—and yet no one knew. It had been thousands of years ago, and they still followed the same precepts. In Wisah's opinion, it just proved the eternal nature of the Goddess.

Wisah held out her arms and gazed at the sigils covering them. *If Wyshera's ascension changed the world, and she had these, how will my trial change it?*

The thought frightened her—and brought a thrill of excitement.

Later in the afternoon, Wisah emerged from her room, needing to share with the Supreme about her internal reflections.

The Supreme cupped her face in her hands and smiled at her with understanding. "I will show you and guide you all I can, daughter of my heart. But for reasons known only to the Goddess, your path to ascension is different from any others, including the First Supreme's. Certainly unlike my own. I trained from birth to lead our people. You will have but a few short lunadars."

"Don't say that, Supreme!" Wisah flung herself into the Supreme's frail arms. "You'll be around for a long time to come."

"We both know that isn't true." The Supreme patted Wisah's back. "I'm living on borrowed time. Time you gave me. Now, dry your tears and walk with me."

Curious, Wisah scrubbed the moisture from her face, then held her arm out for the Supreme to hold on to. They strolled to the audience chamber. When Wisah headed for her usual place in an unobtrusive spot behind the crystal throne, the

Supreme motioned for her to stand by her side. Wisah fidgeted when the Supreme called to the red-veiled guards to allow the supplicants to enter.

The enormous black ironwood doors swung open, and Maendy and Maellyn, dressed in finery, stepped through. With great ceremony, they strode through the chamber, stopping the customary ten feet from the dais. Maendy carried something long wrapped in a cloth. She carefully laid the object on the floor before joining Maellyn in making their obeisance to the Supreme. It felt odd to Wisah to also receive the gesture of respect and honor. The Supreme bade the two smiths to rise.

"Supreme, we have completed our task, as per your instructions." Maendy balanced the object on her open palms while Maellyn unwrapped it, revealing a beautifully carved staff. "Wisah, please accept this gift."

"Go ahead, child," the Supreme urged her, "take the staff." Excitement filled the Supreme's voice, and she leaned forward in her seat, her eyes shining brightly.

Maendy hurried up the steps and knelt, offering the staff to Wisah. As she reached her hand toward it, power surged through her. Energy crackled between her fingertips and the staff, and the sigils visible on her arms glowed. She suspected they all did.

A thin helstrim wire spiraled the length of the golden wood, polished to a high sheen. A beautiful piece of clear crystal topped the staff. As Wisah wrapped her hand around the wood, light blazed from the crystal and traveled through the wire, and sigils flared into existence on the wood.

Maendy's eyes grew wide at the display. "I didn't carve those," she whispered. She cleared her throat. "The wood is kehani, capable of holding a vast amount of power."

"The wood is from the sacred tree in the inner courtyard," the Supreme added. "It will help you focus and direct your sigil magic, or so the Goddess informs me."

Tears sprang to Wisah's eyes, and she swallowed the lump in her throat. She had worried how she was going to control her newfound Talent, especially with the headband that activated the unmaking device. She hugged Maendy and Maellyn. Later, in private, she'd thank the Supreme. The Supreme didn't like public displays of emotion—or affection.

"We've done all we can here," Maendy continued when Wisah stepped back onto the dais. "Alone, we can't create enough globe weapons for the army. There's a school of helstramiester apprentices and journeymen at Strunlair Keep. With their help, perhaps we can even make some new projectiles for the pulsers based on what we learned when we adapted the weapons from the Scourge."

"Some good, then, came from the invaders," the Supreme said, leaning back in her throne. "Do you have all you need?"

Maellyn held up the book on making magical devices. "Yes, Your Grace. Sheekeek asked the Gryphons assigned to Strunlair to give us a ride. They arrived this morning."

"Wisah," Maendy bowed, "until we see you on the war front. Supreme, call us again if you require our services. We are always willing to serve the Goddess."

The Supreme inclined her head and motioned them forward to receive her blessing. Once done, they left the audience chamber. Wisah vacillated between wanting to rush behind them to give them a proper farewell and staying to examine her new staff.

The Supreme smiled at her. "Go on. It will take them a few milcrons before they'll be ready to leave. The staff and I can wait."

Wisah bowed and quickly bent to brush a kiss on the Supreme's cheek. With a swirl of her skirts, she was exiting the audience chamber before the Supreme had finished sputtering her surprise. Wisah hurried to her room and placed the staff gently in the corner, then raced down the stairs. She arrived in the outer courtyard before Maendy and Maellyn climbed onto their Gryphon's backs. As she hugged her friends goodbye, she vowed she wouldn't become so entrenched in the persona of the Supreme that she'd forget to be a person and have friendships. One relationship, in particular, she refused to relinquish. Jaehaas.

Malviana - 16 de Sandar, 1076

Malviana pulled the hood of her cloak lower over her eyes against the bright sunlight. Below her, the Barren's black sands gave way to scrub grass. *Thank Mordaga the unbearable heat of the Barrens is behind us!* After the centuries of living on the dank island, she'd forgotten what summer heat felt like. As sweat dribbled down her back and between her breasts, she regretted regaining the experience.

Twenty measures later, a stone edifice surrounded by high stone walls rose out of the grass like a sentinel. Walled pastures and fields—barren now, but showing signs they'd once been fertile—radiated from the main structure like spokes on a wheel. She steered her banthu to fly over it, out of arrow range. It resolved into a decent-sized compound, much smaller than her Black Castle, but large enough to hold several thousand people. The architecture reminded her of the garrisons and fortresses built during the war.

She directed power into her wand, ready to strike the first blow to her enemies before they knew what hit them. Malviana scowled, bitting her bottom lip at the lack of movement below her. She withdrew a dark crystal from the pouch around her waist, sure this was the place the jallopsitor had tracked her quarry.

Borgedier dropped below her, and Jorvelden and a squad of fighters, including Nelieh, followed his lead. The banthues screeched as gusts of fire erupted from their jaws. The attack didn't elicit any movement in the citadel. Her pulse sped up, and her heart pounded. *No, not again!* Her people landed in the courtyard without incident. A few milcrons later, a flash from Borgedier's wand signaled she could safely land. Fury rushed through her.

"No!" Malviana shouted. This place was empty, just like the fortress in the Barrens. Furious, she released a bolt of magic. It slammed into the abomination of a temple, and her magic crackled over it. When it dissipated, black scorch marks and fine cracks danced over the surface. She gathered more power and blasted the building, the magic singeing the hair on her arms as it escaped through her wand. The stones shattered, raining debris on the courtyard. Borgedier jumped back as a chunk nearly smashed into him. He shot her a dismayed look, which she ignored. Malviana had waited more than ten centuries to avenge her love. How could they simply run from her?

Even after venting her fury, most of the compound remained habitable enough to house the Malvers in her army. She was pacing in her commandeered quarters, still seething, when Keandran slipped into her room late in the night. She'd chosen this particular room because of the large bed she'd found in it. Malviana eyed Keandran as he stalked toward her, the muscles under his fur rippling with strength. *Pity I had to leave my pleasure device at the castle.* The swing of his whip tied at his waist caught her attention, and she grinned. It would work to bring the sweet pleasure of pain to the surface. She reached out her hand for it, but quickly drew it back. As angry as she currently was, she might kill him during their foreplay, which she couldn't afford to do. She needed him to lead the Maldiers.

"I did not know you were so powerful, my love," Keandran said, nuzzling her neck. "You destroyed the Temple. Nothing the Posairs can do can match your power. We're sure to win."

"That is, if they stop running." She moved away from him, poured a cup of bloodwine for them both, then curled up on the settee by the fireplace, patting the empty place next to her. Instead, he sat at her feet and laid his head on her lap. He groaned with pleasure as she ran her long, needle-like nails through the fur covering his face. "When will the cowards stand and fight? I expected more from them, especially after watching Rizelya for all those lunadars."

Keandran jerked away, and her nails left a bloody furrow in his cheek. "Her! May she suffer agony in Mordaga's seven hells!"

"I take it you don't like the bitch?"

"She tried to keep me from hearing your call. She had the damned White Priestesses block your song from my mind."

Malviana vaguely recalled the incident. She'd managed to infect several Posairs from behind the barrier and hadn't kept track of them all. She didn't want to know the potential

Maldiers. Why should she when she'd never meet them while still exiled?

Keandran pushed to his feet, stomped to the window, and threw it open. He leaned on it for a moment, then whirled around. "Her pet, Aistrun, nearly killed me, and she stood by and watched him. I hate her almost as much as Histrun. I begged to go to Strunland Keep specifically to train with him, and he foisted me into Rizelya's squad-pack." He rushed back to her, sliding onto his knees before her. "Please, My Queen, let me be the one to kill them both."

She laid a hand on his head as if in benediction. "Perhaps I'll allow you to kill this Histrun. But Rizelya is *mine* to destroy." She tangled her fingers in his fur and guided his sharp teeth to her throat. He nipped her, drawing blood. By the time they finished with their sex, she'd satiated her craving for violence.

The next morning, Malviana stood on the battlement walls, contemplating the wide expanse of the Storengher River. Her objective, Strunhelos Keep and the pass to the Sanctuary, lay far to the north on the eastern side of the river. The shortest route was straight north, following the river. If her entire army continued together, she left the whole western half and a wide swath of the east available to outflank her. That wouldn't do at all. Besides being a horrible tactical strategy, she needed slaves and sacrificial victims.

"Mordeven! Malvidor!" she called. "Meet me in the keep office."

Malviana stalked back to the room where she'd discovered a recent map of Lairheim conveniently hanging on the wall. She grinned at the Posairs' lack of foresight in not taking it with them, leaving her with valuable information. She'd have someone search the office for smaller maps to give to her sons. When she left this miserable stone heap, Malviana would take this one with her.

Within moments, her sons rushed into the office. They gazed curiously at the map.

"Yes, Mother?" Malvidor bowed.

"I have an important job for you. Malvidor, I'm giving you command of the Malvesh Division. Go east across the Storengher river, and to the Kreistan Sea, to this passage here." She pointed to the narrow opening of the sea. "Fly across the sea, then march northeast toward the Tregano River. Destroy any keeps you encounter and capture the occupants as slaves. Once you pass the plains, turn east toward Strunhelos." She pointed out the route she wanted him to take.

Malvidor's eyes gleamed, and he threw his shoulders back as he pounded his fist to his chest. "As you will!" He shot a gloating glance at Mordeven for being given a division.

"Mordeven, you'll lead the Mordesh Division west and across the Borleano River, then north until you reach northern Strunville Province. There's a place to cross the Borleano again, before you're locked in the mountains. Then push northwest toward Strunhelos, also destroying keeps and capturing slaves."

Mordeven saluted her, then sneered at his brother. He'd received command of a larger division.

"No matter what—" Malviana shook a finger at them "—you're both to meet me at Strunhelos no later than the first of Rokdar. The entire army must attack the pass before the winter snows close it.

"Morvana and I will lead the remaining army straight up the middle of the continent on the east side of the Storengher and to Strunhelos. I expect our divisions to take the brunt of the fighting."

Although the routes she'd assigned her sons left a swath of Ledonlair Province unmolested, it couldn't be helped. She needed a bigger army to cover the entire breadth of Lairheim. The map showed mountains covered most of Ledonlair.

Several octars later, with an unexpected pang of worry, Malviana watched her sons fly to the south, leading their portion of her army. *They will be victorious*, she assured herself, *and meet me at the appointed time.*

As soon as her son's divisions cleared out from the keep, Malviana led her army north. The sparkle of the late afternoon sun on the water made her head ache and her eyes water. Vast plains stretched on either side of the river. Patches of grass, turning summer golden-brown, clustered amid the dark green of spring's growth. Animals with two twisty horns bounded away from the banthue's shadows. She breathed in deeply, savoring the luscious life available to fuel her magic.

Blazel - 17 de Sandar, 1076

Blazel and the Black Weave teams kept pace with the retreating fighters as they raced from Haaslornas Keep ahead of the Malvers army. They'd fought a few skirmishes in the past two days with advance packs of floxidor and skeaeters. Blazel flexed his arm, grimacing as the movement pulled at the wound he'd received from a floxidor's claws.

The Supreme Alpha's pennant flying high over Haaslornde Keep came into view. Tents covered the outlying fields and pastures. Across the river, at Dehanranle Keep, a few crops still remained.

"I don't see any livestock," he commented to Graak. "Did they slaughter them all to feed the war host?"

No, they're out on the plains. Graak's long-range vision was much greater than Blazel's. He tilted his wing to give Blazel a better view of the undulating grass.

As they flew closer, the black, brown, white, and green spots scattered across the plains resolved into the missing livestock herds.

"I'm happy to see our efforts to drain the surrounding swamps were successful, and long lasting."

As am I.

A group of people industriously working on the outermost pasture fence drew Blazel's attention. Without asking, Graak dipped a bit lower. The workers added blocks of stone to the already high fence. Fifteen feet from the fence, a team dug a trench and filled it with thick, black pitch that would burn hot for a long time when lit. Another team installed a line of tall, sharpened spikes twenty feet in front of the trench. And beyond those, a team of Blues and Reds placed the mental bomb spells they'd developed in the Scourge War. Those efforts would protect the outer perimeter of the Keep.

While they waited for the arriving fighters to clear from the courtyard so they could land, Graak and the other Gryphons circled the keep. It gave Blazel a birds-eye view of the two keeps. Men balanced vats of black pitch on top of the keep's wall with pots filled with Blazel's poison interspersed between them. Fighters could easily push them over the edge, dropping their contents on those below. Youngsters carried baskets of ammunition, both arrows and projectiles, up the stairs and placed them every few feet along the battlements, within easy reach of the fighters.

Blazel assessed the fortifications. "Histrun received our message and is preparing the keeps for a siege."

I see no good in this, Graak growled. *It is too open. They can come at us from three sides. Moraak must not be back yet. He'd advise against hiding behind walls and risk being trapped. Our histories tell many horror stories of sieges.*

"A few stories survived in ours, too. I remember one winter when Histrun stayed at the Sanctuary, and he told me the story of the Strunhelos siege. We used keshe pieces to reenact the battle." Blazel smiled at the memory. "The keep never fell to the enemy, which stopped them from advancing on the Sanctuary. Histrun viewed the strategy lessons as invaluable."

Finally, the courtyard cleared enough for the Gryphons to land inside. Graak hit the ground and immediately snapped his wings over his back and stepped to the side to allow room for Glork. Graak purred in pleasure when Blazel slid his harness off and dipped his beak to groom his sweat-soaked fur.

I hope the sands in the practice arena are warm, Graak said. *I could use a good grooming.*

"Later, after the meetings, I'll come help you," Blazel promised. Over the last year together, Graak had grown to enjoy Blazel brushing out his fur. Blazel reached for Rizelya's hand. "But first we need to find Histrun and Keshanal and give them our report."

"They'll skin us if we don't," Rizelya agreed. They headed toward the keep-house porch. She paused and looked over her shoulder. "Aren't you coming, Graak?"

Graak furiously rubbed his beak on his fur. *Yes, coming. Damned fleas! We never have trouble with them in the mountains.* After a last scratch, he resettled his wings and climbed the stairs. The wide door built for centaurs allowed him to easily pass through.

They found Histrun and Keshanal in a front office. The map of Lairheim, with colored markers placed on it, covered the large table. Histrun and Hairan bent over the map.

Blazel greeted Hairan warmly. During the Scourge War, he'd worked closely with Hairan and admired his courage in leading his people to fight the Scourge.

Histrun straightened, putting his hands on his lower back and groaning. "I'm getting too old for this. Leistral warned me we have trouble coming. How much?"

Blazel and Rizelya filled him in on what they'd seen of the Malvers army.

"I estimate we have a day, maybe two, before they arrive," Blazel said.

Histrun whistled. "I didn't think so many Malvers had been exiled."

Blazel's nose wrinkled as he frowned. "There are now more than those who escaped their island."

"Where did they come from?" Histrun leaned against the table, crossing his arms over his chest.

"The strange illness." Rizelya shrugged. "It's what I sensed while in the Black Weave."

"Could be," Histrun agreed. "We've had enough people disappear after exhibiting symptoms of the disease to account for the additional numbers of Malvers. They're predominately those who survived the Scourge slave camp." He looked over at Hairan. "Have any of the Vhelopsi fallen ill? Could it have something to do with the Scourge?"

Hairan shook his head. "I've never heard of the illness you describe, except here. All my people are healthy." He beamed. "In fact, many of our women are pregnant, including my wife, Zebba."

"Congratulations!" Blazel said, clapping Hairan on his back.

Histrun paced in front of the table. "Rizelya, your report dashes any hopes I had of easily defeating the Malvers. We still don't understand how their magic differs from ours, other than the source is different—and apparently they can convince Posairs to change their allegiance." He pounded his fist on the table, causing the markers to jump. "Damn those Supremes for hiding our enemy from us! I can't prepare for the upcoming battles because I don't know what the Malvers can throw at us besides twisted beasts."

"We have magic they aren't familiar with too, sir," Rizelya reminded him. She gestured at Blazel. "They've never seen our men in their warrior form, except what Malviana glimpsed through her control-janacks."

"Our women use their Talents differently now than they did a thousand years ago," Keshanal added, folding her hands over her stomach. Her serenity contrasted with Histrun's agitation. "We focus our Talents through the helstrim in our helbraughts. We invented those after the Great War. They don't have all the advantages."

Our magic has grown and evolved, too, Graak said. He chirped in distress as he scratched at his fur again with his beak. *We're also much larger than our ancestors, especially the Thunder Wings.*

Blazel ran a hand through his tangled hair, scratching his itchy scalp. "And don't forget the new pulsers or the Black Weave technique. We haven't explored everything we're capable of doing within the weave yet."

Sir? Graak clicked his beak and resettled his wings. *Why are you preparing for a siege and risking being trapped? Only the river offers some protection. Wouldn't it be better to draw the Malvers north, where there are natural fortifications, like at Strunhelos?*

"It's precisely because we don't know what the Malvers are capable of. I'd rather have a stout sheadash stone wall between me and a blast of unknown magic than thin air. Besides—" Histrun grinned and stroked his beard "—most of those tents are empty. I've sent two-thirds of our army north to Haasneven Keep. It's larger and more defensible than this one. Once we determine what we're up against, we'll pull back. This keep is perfect because of the river docks. While the Malvers watch the front gates, we'll slip out the rear entrance and travel upriver." Histrun scratched his head and huffed out a breath. "Graak, have you received any word from Moraak? With as many flying beasts as the Malvers are fielding, we could use more Gryphons."

Graak shook his head, his feathers drooping. *No. I had hoped he'd be here when we returned. I can't imagine what the delay is, unless something happened to the king, and his son Daelaak took control of the Gryphons while Moraak was gone.*

"We can only pray nothing has happened King Zorlaak. We could lose without the Gryphon's air support." Histrun rubbed his face in his hands.

"Ancient enemies coming to light. No allies, the enemy wins and all die," Rizelya murmured softly. "That's what Chariel's prophecy said, the one which sent us on a quest to find the Gryphons in the first place."

"But wasn't it referring to the Scourge?" Keshanal asked.

Rizelya shook her head. "I don't think so. They weren't an 'ancient enemy.' We need the Gryphons in this war as much as we did against the Scourge."

They sat around the table while discussing battle plans and exploring possible contingencies. Rizelya, Blazel, and Graak shared their experiences fighting the new twisted creatures. The shadows on the wall lengthened as the sun lowered, and Blazel's stomach growled loudly, interrupting the discussion.

He put a hand over it, embarrassed. "We've only eaten travel bars the last few days, and we didn't stop for a midday meal today."

Histrun slumped back in his chair. "My apologies. I sometimes forget the young need to eat more often. The older I get, the less food appeals to me. I didn't realize it was dinnertime. Go clean up and eat dinner." He waved to the door.

At the foyer, Graak took his leave of them, and Blazel and Rizelya headed down the stairs for a much-needed bath.

Refreshed from the quick wash, Blazel and Rizelya entered the dining hall, where they stepped into line and filled their plates. Blazel caught sight of their friends and pack-mates sitting at a tall table, eating and talking with a familiar centaur.

"Jaehaas!" Blazel cried with delight. After putting his plate on the table, he hugged Jaehaas, thumping him on the back. "It's good to see you, my friend. I saw Hairan earlier. When did you arrive?"

Jaehaas brushed a strand of chestnut-brown hair from his slate-blue eyes. "This afternoon, shortly before you did. Aistrun be filling me in on what you two be doing."

Blazel bit into a billocks rib smothered in tangy sauce, savoring the flavor, happy to eat something more substantial than trail bars.

"How are the Vhelopsi?" Rizelya asked, twirling her taevo mug.

"They be settling in. I can't believe the changes in Posanreande territory with the lack of Malvers' monsters. The Vhelopsi renamed the keep Vhelkansti: the first of Vhel." Jaehaas pushed his plate aside and stared at the table for a long moment. "Have you heard from Wisah?"

Rizelya sipped her taevo, then shook her head. "No, but I'd expect her to be recalled soon now the Malvers are attacking."

"I hope so. I miss her." Jaehaas pressed a hand against his chest.

"Hey, Jaehaas," Aistrun said, winking at Rizelya, "did I ever tell you about when Rizelya set Wisah's hair on fire?"

Jaehaas's eyes widened. "You didn't!"

Rizelya's face flushed. "I was only five and just learning how to use my Talent."

By the time Aistrun finished telling the story, the friends were all laughing, and Jaehaas appeared less lonely. Blazel glanced over at Rizelya, glad circumstances hadn't separated them. With a start, he realized he'd met her nearly a year ago and hadn't spent many days away from her since then. His hand strayed to his throat, wishing a bond-mate torque laid against his skin. He agreed with Jaehaas that Wisah couldn't return fast enough. Rizelya would no longer have an excuse to delay their bond-mate ceremony. The friends sat around the table, drinking taevo and talking, until the kitchen staff booted them out to clean the dining hall.

Blazel - 18 de Sandar, 1076

The two Black Weave teams gathered in the practice arena. The spelled building would protect others in case they lost control of their magic. In this safe place, they didn't need protection, so Aistrun and the other bodyguards had joined in the siege preparations.

Rizelya idly doodled in the sand with her fingertips, while waiting for everyone to settle into a circle with their Gryphon partners behind them. She cleared her throat. "We'll be engaged in battle with the Malvers soon, and we should experiment with different ways we can use the Black Weave technique."

"What do you suggest, Rizelya?" Kaieli's voice held wariness.

"I propose our first experiments should be for defense. As we develop more, we can expand to offensive measures."

Loshera folded her arms across her chest. "I'm unsure we should use our gift to cause harm. We don't know what that path would lead us to do. Would we become power hungry, like the Malvers?"

It would never happen with us here, Graak protested. *We'd keep you from going over the brink.*

Grazeen snorted. "Loshera, you forget we've destroyed Malvers' monsters with the Weave. Aren't we causing harm to them?"

"It doesn't count," Loshera huffed. "They are pure evil."

"And so are their masters, the Malvers."

Rizelya held up a hand to stop the argument between the two. "Let's not get ahead of ourselves. I trust all of us here—" she glanced around the circle "—to do the right thing. Unlike the Malvers, we have the Goddess guiding us through her priestesses. Loshera, do you doubt your connection to the Goddess as her priestess?"

"No." Loshera blushed and bowed her head while shaking it.

"Our teams include White and Gray priestesses for a reason," Rizelya continued, "beyond simply adding their Talents. They'll keep us on a path of righteousness to use our gift for the good of our people."

"And sometimes," Chariel added, placing a hand on Loshera's knee, "it means fighting for what is right. Malviana wants to hurt and enslave our people, as much or more, than the Scourge did. The Goddess has given us this gift to protect our people and keep us free."

Blazel leaned his elbows on his knees and rested his chin on his fists. "Loshera, I read ancient books while in the Sanctuary about the Great War. We must stop Malviana and her people. You can't imagine the atrocities she and Mordar committed. I agree with Chariel. The Goddess blessed us with this gift to stop them."

Across the circle, Blazel's mother raised an eyebrow at him. "I'd wondered what occupied you so much in the library. War stories. I should have known." She shook her head. Then turned her attention to Loshera. "The Supreme, our leader and the living avatar of the Goddess, sanctioned our coming here. She knew our goal, and I believe, what we could become. The Supreme has directed us to protect her people in any way possible. Even if it means we must take the life of another to save the many."

Ardela, the Gray who traveled from the Sanctuary with Blenora, nodded in agreement. "The Goddess has called us—" she indicated the circle of Posairs and Gryphons "—to be a front line defense for her people. We are strong enough to resist any temptation to use our new gifts for evil. I feel the Goddess's presence in the Black Weave guiding us. Don't you?"

Blazel nodded enthusiastically with the others. He'd certainly noticed the loving presence every time they blended their consciousnesses.

A joyful smile crossed Loshera's face. "I do. She's always there with us. I guess you're all correct."

"As Rizelya suggested," Ardela continued, "let's focus first on defensive measures. When the time is right, I'm sure the Goddess will show us any offensive tactics we need. Rizelya, what do you propose we start with?"

Rizelya shifted, leaning deeper into Graak's chest. "We need to shield people from whatever evil magic the Malvers hurl our way. I believe we can adapt the net-shield we developed to protect our people from the Scourge projectiles to defend us against the Malvers' magic."

"Good idea," Blazel said. "But if we're going to be part of the coming war, we need to evaluate how we initiate the Weave. Our current practice of holding hands or touching severely limits what we can do, especially during a battle. And it puts us in danger. When you worked the spell against the Scourge, you didn't hold hands."

"No, we didn't," Saffren said, folding her hands in her lap, "but what we did then was different. We simply joined our magic, not merged our consciousnesses, like we do in the Weave."

"But do we still need to be touching to merge?" Blazel glanced around the circle. "I can sense every one of you in the back of my mind all the time now."

Loshera lifted an eyebrow. "Hmm... so can I. I hadn't thought about it, but I've been able to for a while. I knew you were in danger after you sent us ahead of you. By the way, Blazel, I'm not too pleased with that. Chariel and I are part of this team. You shouldn't shunt us aside just because we're priestesses."

He shifted uncomfortably under her glare. "I only thought of your protection. You can't fight—"

"You're forgetting I trained with Histrun," Chariel interrupted, her eyes narrowed at him. "I can fight. Don't treat us like children, Blazel."

"I trained every week with the other women in the keep," Loshera added, "even though I wasn't required to do so. Besides being good physical exercise, I thought I might need it someday. That day has arrived."

Rizelya laid a hand on his thigh. "You should have talked to me, love, before you sent them off. I could have told you it wasn't necessary. Every noncombatant—even the priestesses serving in the temple—is taught basic fighting techniques. They can defend themselves, the children, and the keep if Malvers' monsters slip past the fighters and attack it."

"Oh!" He hadn't known. Life was different in the Sanctuary than in the keeps. "But the priestesses in the Sanctuary aren't taught to fight. Mother, do you know how?"

Blenora and Ardela both shook their head. "But," Blenora said, holding up a finger, "while we don't have any fighting experience, we also learned the fighting forms as exercise."

Blazel's mouth dropped open at this revelation. "I didn't know that!"

"You were always in the library or off doing something else during our practice sessions." Blenora chuckled as heat flushed Blazel's face.

"Back to the subject at hand," Kaieli said. "When we were testing ways of cleansing the nucla, we found we had to be in physical contact for it to work."

But you didn't have us with you then, Kaieli, Keeru said, his tail curled around her.

She stroked his fur. "True. It could make a difference. Let's try first with the sabertiger team. If it works, the fox team can attempt it. We should test combining the two teams. We might need the added strength when we face Malviana."

"That's a good plan," Blazel said. And the others indicated their agreement.

"I usually start the blending," Kaieli said. "Since this is a fighting technique, Rizelya, why don't you initiate it?"

"Sure." Rizelya closed her eyes. She started to reach out her hands, then dropped them onto her lap and clasped them together. Blazel closed his eyes and concentrated on connecting with the others. Suddenly, his consciousness melded with them. A few moments later, he sensed the net-shield hovering a few inches under the practice arena's ceiling. Blazel opened his eyes and gasped at the beautiful rainbow filaments of magic woven together in a tight net. He'd never seen magic with his physical eyes before and stared at it in fascination. Annoyance flared when Rizelya deactivated the melding. He didn't want the wonder to cease.

Dehali, Raeleen, and Gehan had all participated in creating the net-shield, and the fox team also easily formed it.

When they attempted to join the two teams, at first, the blended consciousnesses fought the connection. Then Blenora and Loshera took charge of the blending. Love poured into Blazel, and the two consciousnesses became one. He gaped in astonishment at the beauty, love, and kindness shining in his mother's soul, and he appreciated anew the relationship they were developing.

Rizelya - 18 de Sandar, 1076

The Black Weave teams quickly became proficient with the net-shield, and moved into experimenting with various defensive, and even a few offensive spells, to use against the Malvers. Knowing the enemy approached, they pushed through the afternoon, attempting as many spells as possible.

Bells pealed a warning cadence, interrupting their practice session.

"What's happening?" Rizelya scowled at the ceiling, reeling from being unceremoniously pulled from the Weave.

The Malvers have arrived. Glork surged to his feet, displacing Rizelya. He mantled his wings and warbled a distressed cry.

Rizelya threw her hands over her ears at the cacophony of sixteen Gryphons screeching. When she pushed to her feet, spots swam before her eyes. Blazel put a steadying hand behind her back, and she gave him an appreciative smile. They raced from the practice arena with the teams on their heels—and what seemed like the keep's entire population—to the balustrade. In the waning light, Rizelya peeked over the wall. Her stomach knotted with anxiety at the enormous force assembled on the plains beyond the keep.

In the center, the Malvers had erected a huge black pavilion. The breeze caught the pennant raised above it: a black banthu flying on a blood-red background. A tall, charcoal-haired woman exited the tent, and Rizelya's breath caught in her throat. She clasped Blazel's hand in a crushing grip.

"Malviana!" Rizelya whispered. The woman's head jerked up as if she'd heard her name called. Malevolence radiated from her in waves.

Their enemy was real, and she was here.

Rizelya strengthened her mental shield, worried the dreams—nightmares—about Malviana would begin again, now with her so close. She didn't want to be privy to that woman's evil mind. Rizelya continued to stare down at the gathered army, even after Malviana reentered her tent.

The campfires in a large section of the Malvers camp revealed monstrous creatures. Somehow, all sorts of beasts were mashed with a Posair. She suspected the strange illness created Malvers, but where did these creatures come from? Had they once been Posairs?

One stood out from the rest and appeared to be the alpha. The malignant magic had turned and twisted his warrior form into something grotesque rather than beautiful, like the true warrior form. For some reason, he seemed familiar, but she'd never seen such a creature before. With a shiver that had nothing to do with the summer breeze, she turned away from the wall and climbed down the stairs. Morning would come all too early, and they'd find out what the Malvers—and their creations—could do.

When Rizelya and Blazel made love, the magic they'd experienced before rose to tingle along her flesh as she climaxed. Their skin glowed with power, and streamers of magic filled the room, slowly dissipating as her and Blazel's breath returned to normal. He held her in his arms, his fingers leaving a tracery of light on her skin. She loved whatever was happening with their magic. Rizelya didn't need a bond-mating ceremony. A magic, much greater than any a White Priestess could bestow, joined them together. She wasn't sure why Blazel felt the need for a public ceremony.

Malviana - 18 de Sandar, 1076

The setting sun glinted on the white stone of a walled community. Another town sat on the other side of the river. A delicate, arching bridge connected the two villages. A flotilla of boats anchored at the docks. Hope rose in Malviana's chest.

Finally, her enemy lay before her.

Her army stopped when the Keep came into sight and set up camp. Relieved to be in the dim light of her tent, Malviana relaxed against the soft cushions of her couch. Weariness seeped into her limbs from the long octars riding a banthu. She let the sounds of her people moving around wash over her as she dozed. A half-octar later, she pushed off the couch and strode out of the tent for some fresh air. Now wasn't the time to become lazy. Her enemy was within striking distance!

Malviana surveyed the stone walls, smirking at the heads of people peeking over the edge. *Good, they're afraid of me.* She needed more information before she could finalize her plans. She sent a runner for Nelieh, then returned to the comfort of her cushions to wait.

"What is this place called?" she asked after the woman dropped to her knees and bowed at Malviana's feet.

"Haaslornde Keep, Your Grace." Nelieh rose gracefully to stand tall. "And the one across the river is Dehanranle Keep."

Malviana searched her memory, but the names were familiar to her only because of the map she'd discovered. Other than her Black Castle, the cities of her youth were long gone, replaced by these fortified communities the Posairs called keeps.

"Which one is the leader... the Supreme Alpha likely to be in?"

"The Supreme Alpha flag flies over Haaslornde, my lady."

"Tell me everything you know about these keeps and the Supreme Alpha."

Nelieh's information aligned with what Keandran, Korand, and Cloresh had told her earlier. By the time she dismissed Nelieh, it was late.

Malviana leaned back against her cushions and closed her eyes, touching her necklace to draw a bit of extra power to her. Although she hadn't connected with Rizelya's mind since leaving the island, she reached for it anyway. She sensed the girl was close, but couldn't penetrate her mind. With a start, Malviana's eyes flew open. In the past, she'd been hooked to the damned device. She hated using the device to collect the death magic through her pets. Eating the pearls it created reminded her of her adversity and near starvation. She'd abandoned the device on the island when she'd escaped, never wanting to use it again. And now, it lay buried at the bottom of the ocean.

Swearing, she picked up her goblet and threw it. Liquid dribbled down the tent's dark fabric. Still fuming, she stood and paced, sparks flying unnoticed from her fingertips and burning small holes in the rugs covering the dirt floor. The portable black mirror sitting on the table by her cushions caught her attention. It couldn't show her as much, or over as much distance, as the large one in her quarters at the Black Castle, but it had its purposes. She concentrated on the woman she sought and whispered the activation spell.

The mirror misted over, then cleared, showing a darkened room with lovers deep in the sex act. She recognized the man's long, matted hair as the other mind she occasionally touched. Malviana directed the mirror to give her a closer look at him. His back bore puckered furrows from a sabertiger attack, and well-defined muscles flexed as he rode the woman. He arched up and flung his head back as he climaxed. She wrinkled her nose at the scar running from his cheekbone to chin, marring his once handsome face. Strength, both physical and magical, radiated from the couple.

Grief, like she hadn't experienced in a long time, punched her in the gut. She gasped in pain, dropping the mirror as she clutched at her chest. She and Mordar had once enjoyed the same power and strength. How dare anyone have that when she couldn't! Her scream of jealous rage shattered the glass in every light globe in her tent, throwing it into darkness. She crouched in the dark, her arms wrapped around her knees, hot tears streaming down her face, as she rocked back and forth.

Mordaga's promise of returning Mordar to her with the sacrifice of the Supreme intruded on her grief. She angrily brushed away her tears, and clenching her fists, she resolved the bitch would die, and her own love would live again.

Chapter 19

Rizelya - 19 de Sandar, 1076

The loud clanging of the alarm bell woke Rizelya from a sound sleep. Darkness still shadowed her room, and she groped for her clothes where she'd tossed them last night. She hopped to the window as she slipped on her pants. Flashes of bright light came from the keep's outer wall.

"Can you see what it is?" Blazel mumbled, as he tugged his shirt over his head.

"No, not clearly. Apparently, the Malvers aren't waiting for daylight to begin their attack."

She dropped down on the bed and pulled on her boots, quickly lacing them tight. She grabbed her helbraught and pulser while Blazel strapped his pulser over his shoulder. They raced from the keep-house and up the nearest steps leading to the wall rampart.

Archers and sharpshooters hastened to their positions, checking their stockpiles of ammunition. Below, in the practice field, riders buckled harnesses on Gryphons. Rizelya and Blazel joined Histrun and Naila, where they gazed over the battlements. A flash of light in the vicinity of the first set of defenses flared.

Howls and screams of terror erupted as the emotion bombs exploded. Rizelya could just make out the outlines of twisted creatures falling to their knees in anguish.

"They tripped the outer wards," Histrun said with an evil grin.

The seven-foot tall warrior-Posair monstrosity uncurled a whip from his belt, indiscriminately striking the wailing creatures with it, yelling, "Get up, you cowards!"

Rizelya's forehead crinkled. The voice sounded familiar, but she couldn't place it. Histrun sobered when the creatures, under the lash of the twisted wolf-man, slowly pushed to their feet—or what passed as feet. They paced in front of the line of bombs, but no amount of cajoling by their leader would force them to pass it again.

"The bombs have stopped those beasts," Histrun said, "but we can't assume they'll stop all the creatures. Who knows what the Malvers will throw at us first? Be prepared for anything."

"They'll definitely use their flying beasts," Blazel observed, "believing we're vulnerable from an overhead attack."

Rizelya glanced at the practice field. The last of the riders were climbing onto their Gryphons and fastening their harnesses. "But we won't be. Once the Gryphons are aloft, we'll cast a net-shield. It should protect those on the ground from falling debris and magic strikes from above."

"Good," Naila croaked, then switched to mind-speech. *Be prepared to modify the spell for the Malvers' unknown magic. It could pass through where the Scourge's projectiles couldn't.*

"We've already discussed it. We're ready... I think." She and Blazel headed toward the tall corner tower of the wall.

"Where are you going?" Histrun called after them. "Why aren't you joining your team?"

Blazel turned around, and walking backward, said, "We've found a new way to work together. Rizelya and I need to be where we can see the battle to know where we can best utilize our Black Talent."

A breeze washed over Rizelya, and Graak and Glork landed on the tower battlements with Sterkek right behind them. The huge Gryphon loomed over the rest, and the growing light of dawn outlined their silhouettes. Even as Glork hopped gracefully down to the walkway, Graak stretched his wings wide and let out a challenging shriek. Scowling—that hadn't been part of the plan—Rizelya quickened her pace and rushed to the tower. She needed to be in physical contact with Glork to initiate the blending and cast the net-shield over the keep.

The dark shadow of a grifflyn flew over the no-man's-land where the Posairs had laid their ground defenses and sped toward Graak. Rizelya sped up, her feet flying up the curving stairs inside the tower, chanting the spell as she ran. She flung the door open and leaped at Glork, her outstretched fingers snatching at his fur even as her mind sought out her teammates. The grifflyn belched a gout of fire at them.

Rizelya stared as it zoomed toward her and shouted the last words of the net-shield spell just as she sensed the Black Weave settle into place. She threw up an arm to protect her face from the fire. When she didn't feel any searing heat cascading over her, she cautiously lowered her arm and gaped at the dome of brilliant light protecting the keep. The grifflyn's flame hit it and bounced off, much like their magic had done with the Scourge's energy dome. Behind the shield, Graak crowed with delight and taunted the grifflyn.

"Graak!" Blazel yelled, his hand on the Gryphon's flank. "What are you doing, my friend? You'll get yourself killed—or us."

Getting its attention. Quickly Blazel, shoot it.

Blazel made a frustrated sound. "Rizelya, can you maintain the net-shield if I let go of this idiot to shoot?"

"I think so." Rizelya let her senses flow into the shield. She considered how the Scourge had anchored their energy field, and did something similar to her shield, affixing it to the keep's walls.

But before Blazel shouldered his pulser, Eidstrun slid to a stop in front of them.

"Don't worry, I've got this." Eidstrun knelt, chambered a projectile, and shot at the grifflyn.

Yellow light smashed into the beast's chest. A blossom of dark fluid spread from the wound. The beast keened in pain, sounding very much like a Gryphon in distress. Gritting her teeth against the sound, Rizelya lifted her own pulser and fired a helstrim projectile into the creature's throat. The back of its head exploded, and it tumbled backwards to the ground.

Amazement filled her when she realized she'd let go of her physical contact with the net-shield, and it remained in place.

"What are you doing here?" Blazel asked Eidstrun.

"My job. Protecting you. You focus on the Black Weave magic, and Sterkek and I will keep you safe."

Graak hopped off the tower battlement. *None of those abominations should be allowed to live,* he hissed.

A shock wave blasted the keep. By now, the sun had risen high enough to light the battle. Three Malvers stood beyond the field of spikes, pointing their wands at the keep. Magic flashed from their wands, and a moment later, the walls trembled. Rizelya ducked from the shards of stone flying in all directions.

Arrows whizzed through the air from further down the wall. One slammed into the chest of the tallest Malvers and exited his back. He scowled at the shaft protruding from his chest and put a hand on it. The shaft disintegrated, and the arrowhead plunked to the ground. On a Posair, it would have been a fatal shot.

The Malvers grinned, pointing his wand at the arrows embedded in the ground. Two dozen arrows rose, twisting around to face the keep. With a flourish of his wand, they catapulted in a beeline toward the archers. Rizelya held her breath. Because the arrows were Posarian, she didn't know if they'd penetrate the net-shield. They'd designed it to stop foreign materials and magic. She let out a whoosh of relief when the arrows shattered against the invisible barrier. The Malvers shouted in anger. He and his companions waved their wands, and what appeared to be a thousand arrows filled the sky like black hornets.

Eiden! she called, *more hardened air. Gehan, help her. Grazeen, add your rotting spell. Raeleen, lava!* While she sensed their magic flowing into the shield, Rizelya quickly added her fire element to it as the arrows arched past the tallest tower. They hit the dome and ignited, immediately fizzling to ash.

Overhead, Gryphons and their riders fought banthues with Malvers on their backs, grifflyns, and the over sized baethor. A pack of floxidor wove through the spiked fence but a flaming arrow whooshed down, lighting the trenches of pitch, and stopping them. Rizelya coughed, gagging on the noxious odor that a breeze blew toward the keep. Immediately, Eiden and Gehan created a wind funnel, gathering the fumes and carrying them over the Malvers army.

As the day wore on, the Gryphons and sharpshooters kept the banthues, grifflyns, and baethor away from the keep. Rizelya and the Black Weave teams continued to maintain the net-shield for several octars even after the Malvers halted their air strikes for the night. The fire from the pitch trenches still blazed, sending eerie shadows over the no-man's land. So far, their ground forces hadn't breached the searing flames.

Histrun and Naila joined Rizelya on the wall. Malviana, and what appeared to be her captains, stalked the keep's perimeter.

"Let them search," Histrun growled. "They won't find a weak spot in our defenses."

Histrun had studied siege tactics well. He'd ensured even the docks and river gate were protected from easy entry. Finally, after midnight and no new attacks from the Malvers, Histrun sent the exhausted Black Weave teams to their beds.

Rizelya - 20 de Sandar, 1076

Rizelya and Blazel again stood in the tallest tower as the sun rose over the horizon. Below, in the courtyard, both the sabertiger and fox Black Weave teams waited with their bodyguards surrounding them. Aistrun had vacillated between protecting Rizelya and Blazel or Chariel. Rizelya smirked when he'd decided Chariel needed him more. Instead, Ambrelya joined Eidstrun on the battlement wall. Her sharpshooting skills would be more useful up here. Maeaak and Sterkek settled on towers on either side of them, tucking their wings along their backs and staring out over the battlefield. They looked like sentinels carved into the stone, until one noticed the nimbus of flames outlining them.

Rizelya checked the net-shield. Her eyebrows lifted in surprise. "It's still up! I didn't expect it to hold while we slept."

"Yes, the anchoring worked," Blazel whooped. "Too bad we couldn't do this before. It would protect the keeps from the janacks and brechas."

"We still don't know how much the net-shield will block."

Eidstrun jerked his chin toward the Malvers army. "We're about to find out. They're coming."

A frisson of fear washed over Rizelya as Malviana swept from her tent, her black cloak billowing behind her, and the hood pulled low over her face. She stalked through her camp, stopping at the edge of the emotion bombs. The woman raised her obsidian wand and waved it in a complicated pattern, dark light streaming from the jewels on it. A thick fog formed over the buried bombs and seeped into the ground. Suddenly, the small disks containing the spells popped from the ground, and with a sweep of Malviana's arm, sped toward the keep.

Through their connection, Saffren and Chariel saw the danger and threw a layer of mental blocks into the shield. The disks slammed into the wall and dome. The shield defused those that hit it.

Rizelya cheered, thinking they'd dodged the peril, but a few milcrons later, black fog seeped through tiny cracks in the stone walls. Blazel turned to say something to her, and Rizelya screamed as the skin sloughed off his face. His eyes burned with dark green fire, and instead of words coming from his mouth, he spewed huge black spiders. She frantically waved her arms in front of her. The spiders slammed into her, clinging like sticky syrup and biting deep into her flesh, making it burn. She shrieked, horrified, when the spiders burrowed into her flesh. She slumped against the wall, still screaming, unable to move as the spiders ate her alive.

A cool breeze washed over her, and the spiders disappeared. Her mind cleared. With dread, she lifted her arm to see how much damage the spiders had caused, only to find it whole, and the red leather of her jacket undamaged. Blazel leaned against the wall, trembling with remembered terror, but otherwise healthy.

Eidstrun slumped on the ground, shaking. Sterkek huddled next to him, butting his head against his friend's hand. *You're *okay. It isn't real,** Sterkek crooned over and over again. Finally, Eidstrun lifted a shaky hand to stroke Sterkek's black fur.

As she levered herself to her feet, Rizelya glanced down at the courtyard. Pockets of fighting between friends and pack-mates were breaking up with the people shaking their heads and muttering in confusion. If everyone experienced the terror and illusions she had, the army would be immobilized, making them easy targets for the Malvers' beasts and creatures. Rizelya sent a prayer of thanks to the Mother the full blast hadn't hit them.

"What stopped the attack?" she muttered.

Her stomach heaved from the spell's aftereffects, and she leaned over the balustrade, spewing the contents of her stomach. Rinsing out her mouth, she turned back to the courtyard. In the center, Chariel, Loshera, Kaieli, Faliciden, Blenora, Ardela, and Saffren stood in a tight circle, arms around each other, murmuring a spell. Another cool breeze washed over Rizelya's hot face, and her nausea evaporated.

Still trembling, she joined Blazel, leaning against his side. "That was awful. We can't let it affect us again."

He pointed a shaking hand at the wall, where wisps of black fog continued to seep through it. "The priestesses and healers are only clearing the effects. The spell is still working. We have to stop it."

Rizelya nodded her head. "Glork, you okay? I need you."

I'm here. Glork lay curled in a tight ball. He slowly unwound and glared at Sterkek and Maeaak. **Why aren't you suffering from the spell?**

Sterkek shrugged. **We're not part of the Weave. Our natural immunity to Malvers' magic protected us.**

Something we need to keep in mind. Glork ungracefully stumbled to Rizelya and then flopped back down at her feet.

Placing one hand on Glork's flank and holding Blazel's hand, Rizelya re-initiated the melding. Working carefully, she extended the shield to the other side of the keep's walls and, for good measure, a few feet beyond them. She anchored the shield deep into the earth. A few milcrons later, the priestess and healers cleared the poison from the air. Rizelya took a deep breath, then another, regaining her equilibrium.

A flock of banthues and grifflyns arrowed toward the keep. Gryphons and their riders met them before they could reach it, and fire blossomed in the sky as they fought. Malvers stood just beyond the still-burning pitch, their wands trailing dark light as they cast their spells. Magic slammed into the net-shield, making Rizelya's teeth ache from the aftershocks. The Malvers sent wave after wave of magic, trying to weaken the Posairs' shield. But it held.

Rizelya - 21 de Sandar, 1076

Several octars later, Rizelya leaned against the tower wall, resting and sipping on the taevo Leistral had brought with her when she'd relieved Eidstrun. Blazel slumped next to her, staring at his cup held between his bent knees. Graak and Glork crouched in the tower's shade.

Even though anchoring the shield in the earth made it easier to hold, the constant bombardment was wearing her and the team out. She wasn't sure how much longer they could hold it. She almost wished she was physically fighting. At least then, the adrenaline would keep her from feeling the exhaustion. As she pushed away from the wall, she caught movement out of the corner of her eye. Several dark shadows flew over the burning pitch and dropped something behind the outermost fence. The stooped and heavily burdened figures ran toward the Keep's wall.

Sound the alarm! Rizelya called. *We have incoming.* She pulled on the magic from her teammates and strengthened the net-shield.

Archers and sharpshooters fired at the approaching fighters, but after their projectiles bounced harmlessly off them, they stopped wasting ammunition. Teams rushed to the prepared vats of pitch and pots of poison. The first of the figures, a twisted amalgamation of a Posair, billocks, and boar, stopped several feet from the wall. He threw down his burden while another pair, a blend of Posair and fox, raced forward and began to assemble something.

"It's a siege engine," Histrun said. "If you can't hit the people because of their shields, target the materials. We don't want them to finish building it."

Archers dipped their arrows into the vats of pitch before letting them fly. Rizelya heard soft murmurs of "oyt," and the arrows burst into flame, burning hotter with the addition of the pitch. Soon, the Malvers leaped away from their burning project. The Posairs stopped cheering when grappling hooks plunked along the wall. The siege engine had just been a diversion!

Rizelya frowned. Somehow, the hooks had passed through the net-shield. She and Blazel hurried to the nearest one. He picked up the jar of poison and upended it over the monstrosity climbing the rope. The creature sputtered and wiped its face, its red eyes glaring up at them.

"The poison doesn't work on them!" Blazel yelled.

Rizelya used her helbraught's blade to hack off the rope attached to the grappling hook. As the creature fell, its arms wind-milling, she sent a blast of fire magic through her helbraught, hitting it in the chest. She gaped when her fire didn't kill it. Leistral ran to their side, and she and Blazel shot helstrim projectiles into it. Finally, after being struck multiple times and crashing to the ground, the creature stopped moving.

Blazel glared at the creature. "Damn, these things are hard to kill."

"Evil usually is," Rizelya said. "How did the grappling hooks pass through our shield?" She worked one free and examined it. It didn't look unusual. She studied the hook with her magical senses. Nothing. She slapped her forehead. "It's an ordinary, normal hook. It didn't trigger the shield's protections because it's Posarian made, not something foreign."

"The Malvers must have picked it up at Haaslornas Keep," Blazel said. "We left in a hurry. They could have found all sorts of tools. We were more concerned with getting people out than with what we were leaving behind."

"They now have weapons they can use against us." Rizelya then mind-spoke with Histrun and Naila, informing them of the latest observations.

Leistral whirled around to stand between Rizelya and Blazel and the monstrosity stalking toward them. She held her helbraught in front of her and added her fire magic to it. Other Malvers fighters had also climbed over the wall.

Two men, in their warrior form, rushed to the angulete and Posair mash up and attacked it, turning its attention away from Rizelya. She struggled with the urge to join in the fight. Blazel growled, and she flung out an arm to stop him from surging forward. "No, we can't, as much as we want to. Our skills are better used with the Black Weave team." She leaned to the side to peer past Leistral to watch the battle, wanting to evaluate how the twisted creatures fought.

The warriors harried the creature. He leaped straight up to escape a warrior's claws. His flapping wings carried him higher, but they didn't support his weight for sustained flight, and he dropped back down, swinging his long claws at them. One man ducked, ramming his shoulder into the twisted Posair. The creature snarled and stepped back, snapping a whip from his side. He lashed the warrior several times, cutting through the warrior's thick fur. His wounds seeped yellow pus, and the warrior's movements grew sluggish and disjointed.

The creature flung out an arm and caught the injured warrior by the throat, its claws puncturing the man's skin. The twisted Posair ducked his head, lapping up the blood with a long tongue. Leistral screamed, feeding fire into her helbraught, but before she unleashed it, the creature jumped over the wall, taking the injured man with it. He opened his wings and glided over the trenches and stakes.

Bile rose in Rizelya's throat when the creature sank his fangs into the warrior's neck. It tore out a chunk of flesh, and ate it, even as the man struggled weakly. Other twisted creatures converged on it and tore into the Posair. Rizelya turned away and vomited in the corner.

Later, a Malvers woman climbed over the wall and laid devastation on the keep. Arrows and projectiles passed through her harmlessly as she blasted the Posairs with magic, killing twenty-five, all dying in horrendous ways. And with each death, the Malvers seemed to grow more powerful.

Rizelya screamed in terror as the Malvers stalked toward the Black Weave team in the center of the main courtyard. Even though he knew it was useless, Leistrun pounded her with projectiles from his pulser. Eiden dashed from behind him to throw an ice spear at the woman. It shattered against her shield. Saffren nudged Nelstrun aside and tossed boiling water at the Malvers, while a pool of lava formed at her feet. Grazeen cast her rotting spell. But she only laughed and absorbed the magic. Other twisted creatures attacked, and their bodyguards fought with them, defending the team and leaving Aistrun and Kami to fight the Malvers.

Horror clogged Rizelya's throat. The two of them wouldn't stand a chance against the powerful Malvers woman. As Rizelya dashed down the steps, she gathered her magic to her, including that available through the Black Weave, and fed it into her helbraught. With a yell, she attacked the Malvers. The woman spun, and with a sneer, pulled a long blade from her robes, easily blocking Rizelya's strike. Power thrummed through the wooden staff of Rizelya's helbraught, making her hands tingle. Gritting her teeth, she gripped her helbraught tighter and thrust it. The Malvers parried her strike, and countered, driving Rizelya back.

While they fought, Rizelya scowled at the woman's fighting technique. She moved like a Posair. Rizelya gaped when she landed a fatal blow and the wounds closed before her eyes. Finally, Rizelya swept her leg out, wrapping her foot behind the woman's knee, knocking her off her feet. As she fell, Rizelya hefted her blade high over head, and swung down with all her might, decapitating her foe. A surprised expression crossed the Malvers' face before her eyes went blank.

Later, when the fighting stopped for the night, Histrun examined the body. Sadness pinched his face. "This was a woman with the strange illness who escaped. This confirms the purpose of the disease and what happens to the infected people."

Rizelya hated she'd been right about the illness. She stared at the woman's corpse before she touched her helbraught to it, burning it. *What had caused her to fall to the illness?* Rizelya thought of her friends and loved ones and prayed none of them would succumb to the hateful sickness.

As they climbed the stairs to the keep-house, Histrun surveyed the battered walls. "We can't hold them back here," he said. "Give the order to retreat up the river. We'll go to Haasneven Keep, where it's more secure." He turned to Rizelya. "Do you think your team can use the Weave to create an illusion that our ships are still here? Hopefully, the Malvers will continue focusing on the keep while we evacuate on the boats."

"We can try, sir," Rizelya said. She wasn't sure what their limits were—if they had any.

It might be possible to extend our invisibility Talent with the Weave, Graak suggested. *If we can, we could hide the ships. If it works, it would keep the retreating army safe until we're far from the Malvers' reach.*

"Do it," Histrun ordered. "We leave at midnight."

Rizelya hurried to the dorm room, quickly packing her meager belongings. As they packed, she and the teams discussed ideas on how to accomplish the requested spell. They finally decided they'd have to be spread across several ships to cover them all. When Rizelya climbed on the boat assigned to her, she turned and gazed longingly at Blazel and Graak boarding a different one.

Blazel - 21 de Sandar, 1076

In the boat's stern, Yellows coaxed a stiff breeze to drive the fleet up the Storengher River. Blazel huddled on the ship's deck as it silently pushed away from the dock. It seemed strange not to have Rizelya at his side. Graak curled around him, with his tail tucked protectively under him after scurrying deckhands had stepped on it twice. Blazel wished he was flying on Graak rather than stuck on a boat. But if they wanted their attempt to extend the Gryphon's invisibility to succeed, the Black Weave teams needed to be scattered throughout the fleet. Eidstrun hunkered next to Blazel, and Aistrun rode with Rizelya. Happily, Ambrelya accompanied Blazel's mother, Blenora, while Leistral, Korhaas, and the other bodyguards were distributed in the boats with their teammates.

Overhead, the Gryphons in the army flew on silent wings. Blazel couldn't even see an outline of them. Between their natural coloring and their invisibility spell, they blended in with the night sky.

Blazel sensed Kaieli's mind first, quickly followed by Rizelya's familiar patterns, then one by one, the others in the two Weave teams connected with him. A moment later, his consciousness floated over the ships on the river. Eiden led them in forming the illusionary boats.

"Did it work?" Blazel whispered to Eidstrun. From his augmented perspective, a phantom fleet appeared tied to the docks.

Clothing rustled as Eidstrun stood. "Aye. It looks pretty damn real. It should fool the Malvers."

Chariel took the lead of the blending, and her gentle touch coaxed the Gryphon's invisibility spell into their weaving. Gasps sounded around Blazel as the ships in the river disappeared. Astounded they'd succeeded, Blazel's hold on the complicated spell slipped. He dropped his head to his knees, closed his eyes, and breathed in Graak's musky, cinnamon scent. It helped him focus on his connection with his teammates and the spell, and ignore the activity around him.

As the octars passed, the soft sounds of people resettling, a suppressed cough, or the quiet creaking of the sails seeped into Blazel's consciousness. Finally, when the light of dawn caressed the sky, the Black Weave spit the members from it. Blazel slumped against Graak, heaving heavy breaths as if he'd been running.

It's a good thing we didn't try that while flying, Graak mumbled. His feathers drooped with exhaustion. *I couldn't have maintained it and flown at the same time.*

"How far have we traveled?"

"Much farther than Histrun expected. Here, you'll need this." Eidstrun handed Blazel a canteen of water and a travel bar. "You were in the Weave so long, we started worrying. If you hadn't come out of it when you did, Aistrun was going to pull you out."

Blazel gulped the water. Eidstrun set a bowl of water and a dish of chopped meat in front of Graak. Graak warbled his thanks, quickly tossing the meat down his throat. Blazel had assumed the thoughtful care the big man showed the team was because of Leistral. But now, with her on another ship and nowhere around, Eidstrun gave Blazel the same attention.

"Thanks," Blazel said, his thirst finally slacked. "You're a good man, Eidstrun. I'm glad you're part of our pack."

Eidstrun's pale face flamed bright red, and he ducked his head. "To answer your first question," he said, "we should reach Haasneven Keep in three days, if we continue at this pace."

"Graak, can the Gryphons keep up?"

Easily. Graak settled his head on his forelegs and closed his eyes. A few milcrons later, he snored softly.

Before he joined him, Blazel reached for Rizelya's mind. A sleepy mutter greeted him, but the faint contact comforted him, and he drifted to sleep with a smile.

Blazel - 22 de Sandar, 1076

A blast of heat jolted Blazel awake. He winced at Eidstrun's pulser popping near his ear. The other fighters on his ship pointed their weapons toward the fight overhead, and the crack of pulsers firing both magic and projectiles filled the air. Black smoke, and the stink of the banthue's sulfurous gases, cast a pall on the sunset. Bright flashes of fire lit the sky from the fierce battle between a phalanx of Gryphons and dozens of banthues, grifflyns, and baethors.

Blazel placed a hand on Graak's shoulder, intending to jump onto his back and join the overhead fight. Instead, the Black Weave, led by Rizelya, swept him into it. She wove the net-shield over the fleet. He sensed Eiden and Dehali add hardened air underneath the layer of water Saffren and Noriana spun into the net. He'd learned he didn't have to be completely absorbed by the Weave for it to work. Blazel pulled out enough of his mind from the Weave to remain coherent.

As the shield fell into place, malignant magic lanced toward the Posairs aboard Blazel's ship. Without thinking, he followed the magic to its source: a Malvers sitting on a banthu high above the skirmish. Blazel recognized the man, even though he now had gray skin and hair. Gelposan had survived the Scourge's slave camp.

A burst of anger warmed Blazel's face. *We risked our lives to free him, and this is how we're repaid? How dare he?*

Sparks flickered on the ends of Blazel's fingers, and he imagined closing his claws around Gelposan's throat, pumping venom and fire into the traitor. In Blazel's mind's-eye, the man's eyes bulged, his face turned blue, then purple, and bloody foam frothed from his mouth as his limbs convulsed. A terrible scream pierced the battle noises as the man tumbled from his banthu. Pain contorted his face, and his throat bled from multiple punctures. He splashed into the river, waves covering him.

"Is he dead?" Blazel whispered to Graak, whose height allowed him to see better over the railing.

I think so. His head isn't bobbing to the surface.

Blazel's stomach churned. He hadn't just imagined the attack! He'd killed Gelposan with his thoughts. But how? At Haaslornas, when a Malvers woman had climbed over the wall, warriors had injected their venom into her as they fought, and it hadn't killed her. *Was it because I was in the Black Weave? Can I do it again?*

Through their connection, Blazel sensed Graak's fury at the perversion the grifflyns represented. A particular grifflyn caught his attention. It arrogantly harassed a much larger Thunder Wing, like a crow teasing a hawk. Blazel imagined gripping the creature with his warrior's claws below its jaw and injecting it with his venom. He allowed Graak's anger to flow through him and into the beast.

Oh, I like this!

Graak added to the image of him ripping the grifflyn's belly open with his talons, tearing out the abomination's heart, and biting through its jugular with his beak. A warm, coppery-salty taste filled Blazel's mouth. He spit, surprised when green-tinted blood spattered the deck.

That was satisfying, Graak said, a smug tone to his voice.

It appears we can affect the physical world with our thoughts while in the Black Weave. Blazel shivered from head to toe at the implications. *Does it have limits? Could we create as well as destroy?* He hoped so. *We'll have to watch our thoughts carefully.*

But not before we destroy more of those abominable creatures. That one there is ideal. Graak pointed with his talon to another grifflyn, who concentrated its fire on the net-shield above Rizelya's ship.

Fear and anger cascaded through Blazel. He again imagined his warrior's claws digging into the grifflyn's throat while Graak tore open its belly. Milcrons passed, and he poured more venom and fire into the creature. Finally, the grifflyn gurgled, dropped from the sky, and splashed into the river. Waves crashed into the ship, and the captain cursed as she fought to keep it upright.

Flashes of lightning flickered over head. *Is a Malvers attacking the net-shield?*

No, it's Rizelya and Chariel, Graak replied. *They added an electrical charge to the net.*

Whenever a banthu flew within a few feet of the net-shield, bolts of electricity struck the creatures, leaving huge burning patches on their hides. A sustained strike hit two banthues, each carrying a rider. The electricity sizzled from the banthues to the Malvers. They twitched violently in their saddles, and their hair frizzed in a halo around their heads.

Blazel held his breath. *Would the lightning kill the Malvers?* He let it out with a curse of dismay when the Malvers jerked on their reins and pulled the banthues away from the ships. Even though the strike hadn't hurt or killed the Malvers, their banthues weren't as impervious. The burning patches continued to grow, and their wing sweeps became uncoordinated and awkward. The two Malvers managed to guide their banthues to the shore and leap from them before the creatures crashed onto the plains, exploding into balls of fire. Another Malvers blew a rhythm on a horn, and the surviving banthues and grifflyns retreated from the fleet.

The people on the ships cheered. Blazel stumbled back into Graak when Rizelya released him from the Black Weave. Spots danced in front of his eyes, and his stomach whirled.

"That was spectacular!" Eidstrun shouted, thumping Blazel on the shoulder. "Did you kill Gelposan?"

Bile rose to Blazel's throat, and he weakly nodded. He sank onto the deck, putting his head between his knees, breathing deeply until the nausea passed. When he finally lifted his head, he grimaced at the sight of Graak. His head hung over the side of the ship, and his feathers and fur drooped.

Ooh, my head hurts. Graak keened with pain.

"Mine, too. I wish Kaieli was on our boat," Blazel said aloud. He rubbed his eyes and temples, trying to ease his horrendous headache. "Killing while in the Black Weave isn't without its cost."

But we did kill a Malvers and two of those abhorrent creatures. Graak lifted his head to rest it on the railing. *The cost of a headache and queasy stomach is worth ridding the world of their evil.*

"Yes, it is. We now know of two ways to kill the Malvers." Blazel considered reaching out to Kaieli and asking her for help. But his head hurt too much to mind-speak.

"Would you ask Kaieli to come heal us?" he asked Eidstrun.

"I already did. Keeru is bringing her over."

Blazel dropped his head back onto his knees and closed his eyes, groaning at every lurch and roll of the ship. He didn't have to wait long before the angry staccato of boots stamping toward him made him raise his head. He winced at the fury in Kaieli's eyes. Keeru balanced on the railing a few feet away, muttering angrily at Graak in their language.

Kaieli stopped in front of him with her hands on her hips, and her toe tapping in irritation. "What in the Crone's fires did you do? I sensed you pulling energy from the Weave, but I couldn't tell what you were doing. When Rizelya released the Black Weave, both you and Graak collapsed in terrible pain."

Blazel grinned. "Did you see that Malvers die? It was me and Graak!"

A look of horror crossed Kaieli's face. "You killed while in the Black Weave?"

Graak enthusiastically bobbed his head. *And we destroyed two of those detestable creatures!*

"Then you deserve to be hurting." She whirled around to stalk away from him.

"But Kaieli, my head is killing me. Can't you ease it?"

She stopped and turned back to him. "No. You profaned the Goddess's gift! She gave us this gift to protect life, not take it away."

Blazel's forehead crinkled. "We talked about this when we started developing offensive spells. You agreed with it, then. So what's different now?"

Kaieli's shoulders sagged, and tears filled her eyes. "I know we have to fight them. But I recognized the Malvers. Gelposan was my patient. I treated him for nucla poisoning several times while in the slave camp. I thought I could do it, and when it's some nameless, evil Malvers, it isn't as difficult. But seeing someone I know die because of what we do goes against every instinct I have as a healer."

Blazel took the two steps separating them and wrapped Kaieli in his arms. She didn't have anyone else to comfort her. Even as her tears wet his shirt, she eased the pain in his head. He'd been furious at the former Posairs' betrayal, but hadn't personally known him. What was she feeling to have a previous patient trying to kill her?

His jaw clenched. He'd thought Malviana, and her kind, evil, but to turn their own people into enemies full of hate was pure diabolism. Before this war ended, how many friends, lovers, and siblings would have to destroy their loved ones?

Chapter 20

Blazel - 24 de Sandar, 1076

Blazel stepped off the boat onto Haasneven's dock and into the chaos of people from multiple ships disembarking at the same time. Earlier, Graak had flown off to join the other Gryphons, billeted in the paddocks and wooded areas of the Keep. Blazel froze as people streamed past him. He'd never been in this type of Keep before. As a lone wolf, the Posairs hadn't welcomed him into their towns and cities. Lately, he'd had Rizelya at his side to guide him through the intricacies of entering a Keep.

Someone bumped his shoulder, and he whirled with a snarl.

Eidstrun backed up a step with his hands in the air. "It's just me. What's the plan?"

"I... I don't know. I don't know where to go."

"The rest of our pack probably headed to the Keep House to find out which barracks we're assigned to stay in."

"Oh, that makes sense." Blazel glanced around him. Everyone moved toward the gates at the end of the dock. He adjusted his rucksack more comfortably, took a deep breath, and stepped into the crowd.

Blazel and Eidstrun hadn't gone far when they ran into a knot of Vhelopsi standing on the dock in front of the ship they'd disembarked from. They appeared as confused—or more so—than Blazel. At least he had Eidstrun at his side to guide him. They didn't have anyone. Hairan waved at him, and a relieved look crossing his face. Both Blazel and Eidstrun had worked with the Vhelopsi during the Scourge War.

Hairan and his uncle, Agabus, approached them. Hairan gripped their wrists in greeting. "Can you tell us where we should go?" he asked. "Nobody told us."

"We're trying to find out the same thing," Blazel said. "You can come with us."

Clopping hooves echoed from behind them. Jaehaas carefully maneuvered down the gangplank and hurried to them.

"You disembarked before I could find you," Jaehaas said. He slung his pack over one shoulder and his bow and quiver peeked over the other one. He looked better than Blazel had seen him since Wisah had left for the Sanctuary. Jaehaas wore a sleeveless dark brown leather vest tied with turquoise thongs, and he'd recently shaved his beard.

"Blazel! It be good to see you." Jaehaas clasped Blazel's wrist in greeting. A huge grin on his face. "But why you be with the Vhelopsi?"

He pointed to himself and then to Hairan. "We're unsure where to go. And there's so many people!" Even after spending time with the war host, being around crowds still bothered him. In the war camp, they'd been spread out, not jumbled together like this.

"Ah." Jaehaas squeezed his shoulder in understanding. He'd helped Blazel the first time he'd had an anxiety attack being in a crowded safe house. "I be just the person you need. Come with me, and I'll show you where you be billeted."

"Thank the gods!" Hairan said with feeling. "Many people at Posanvelden reacted to our presence with fear, and they were close to the war front. Here, where they don't know who we are, I'm unsure what our reception will be like going into the keep alone. But with you and the war hero, Blazel, we shouldn't experience any problems."

Blazel jerked back, his mouth gaping open. "War hero? Me? I'm just an ordinary Posair."

"No, you be much more." Jaehaas lifted a loc of Blazel's now almost black hair. "You and the rest of the Black Weave teams be turning into something new."

"He's right," Eidstrun said. "You and Rizelya are legendary, especially after creating the net-shield protecting Haaslornde."

Blazel frowned, cocking an eyebrow in disbelief. "It wasn't just us. The sabertiger Black Weave team, actually both teams, made it."

Eidstrun chuckled. "But you were the most visible. You tend to only mingle with our pack. I talk with others, and everyone is in awe of what you're doing."

"Even we Vhelopsi, who don't understand your magic," Agabus added, "know who you are, and how important you are in this new war. And to us, you're our hero. You helped us escape slavery and now we have a chance to raise our children in freedom."

Blazel ducked his head as his cheeks flamed. He wasn't sure he liked being considered a hero when he was only doing what was necessary to save his people. The crowds on the dock had thinned while they talked, allowing him to breathe easier.

"Let's find our rooms." He strode off, wanting to end this uncomfortable conversation.

Jaehaas, Eidstrun, and Hairan quickly caught up to him. The Vhelopsi troops fell in line behind them as they tromped down the docks toward the keep. As they entered, the crowd grew, and people jostled them as they tried to pass. A few stopped and stared at the strangers. Hairan put a hand up his golden hair in a self-conscious move.

A small boy chasing a group of older youngsters bumped into Hairan's legs, and he steadied the boy, smiling at him. The boy gasped and his eyes widened. Hairan's smile fell.

"Oh, I'm so sorry to frighten you." Hairan covered his mouth with his hand.

The boy grinned and pointed to Hairan's mouth. "You have fangs! I have them too, see?" The boy shifted into a wolf pup and pulled his lips back, showing off his tiny fangs. He changed back. "But how come you have fangs when you not be in your wolf or warrior form? I want fangs all the time, too."

"I don't have a warrior form, so I have these instead."

Now the boy appeared truly horrified. "Be you... how can you... what be you?" the boy stuttered.

Jaehaas put a comforting hand on the boy's shoulder. "He not be a Posair, boy, nor be he a rogue. He be our new friends, a Vhelopsi."

"A Vhelopsi?" The boy tripped over the unfamiliar word. He looked Hairan over from head to foot, then peered around him to stare at Ninsun and the other Vhelopsi. "You be beautiful! Do you have any little boys I can play with?"

Hairan smiled again. "No, not yet. But I hope to have one like you soon."

Blazel grinned as the boy trailed along with them as they walked to the courtyard, asking non-stop questions. A brown-haired, harried looking young woman swept the boy up. "Julhaas, what be you doing, bothering these fighters? You should not be out of the crèche."

"But Nanna, Borhaas and the others left, and I wanted to see all the fighters, too."

"I be sorry if he bothered you," Nanna said.

"He not be a problem," Jaehaas assured her. "I remember being so inquisitive when I be a youngster."

The woman tugged the boy's hand, leading him toward the center of the keep and the crèche. The boy chattered to her non-stop about his new friends.

"Someday," Hairan sighed, "Vhelkansti's courtyard will hold laughing children. Perhaps both Vhelopsi and Posair. It's wonderful that your children are as curious and fun-loving as ours—when they're not slaves."

Blazel smiled at the thought of the two species of children playing together. He and his Black Weave team weren't the only ones changing Posair society. But first, they had to win the war against the Malvers, otherwise, none of them would be free to discover how the Vhelopsi and Posair would integrate their societies.

"Why are there still little ones here?" Hairan asked. "The Malvers army isn't far behind us. Shouldn't they be evacuated already?"

Blazel gaped, stunned. He hadn't considered it when he'd seen the children. "I'm sure Histrun has a plan for their evacuation, as well as the other non-combatants in Haasneven."

Jaehaas led them through the crowded plaza, pausing at the Keep House.

"Thanks, Jaehaas," Blazel said. "We'll catch up later. Stay safe, my friend. Hairan, I'm sure we'll meet again." He and Eidstrun jogged into the building.

Rizelya sat on the steps leading upstairs. "You're here!" She leaped to her feet and hugged Blazel. "What took you so long?"

"We ran into Jaehaas and the Vhelopsi." Blazel didn't want to admit he'd been frightened and lost.

"They made a new friend," Eidstrun chuckled, then recounted the incident with the child. "Why are the children still here?"

Rizelya grimaced. "I had the same question. Histrun told me he was sending them upriver on the boats we brought. They should leave this evening. Blazel, our teams will create another phantom fleet tonight, in case Malviana has spies in our midst." She slipped her arm around Blazel's waist. "Come on, you two, and I'll show you where we're staying and you can drop off your bags. Then we'll join the others in the practice arena."

Blazel sighed. He'd hoped to rest before being put to work. But the Malvers army wasn't far behind them. They needed to set up protections as quickly as possible.

Malviana - 27 de Sandar, 1076

Malviana frowned at the fortified community. Why did these new Posairs hide behind walls? Their ancestors had fought her face-to-face. She hadn't discovered her quarry had escaped from the last keep until the next morning and she'd had to scurry to catch up to them. And when she finally did, they'd snugged behind thick walls again.

She stood at the edge of her camp, the hood of her cloak shielding her from the harsh daylight, observing the battle. Morvana casually leaned against Gordelven as she tossed her tightly woven tiny braids over her shoulder. Gordelven brushed back an errant braid from her neck and nuzzled it.

"Now isn't the time," Malviana growled. It irritated her the younger Malvers had adapted to the sunlight. Only the older Malvers, like herself, still had to wear a hooded cloak to block the sunlight, or risk a raging headache.

A banthu belched flames at the Posairs standing on the wall. Malviana swore when the flames halted several feet above them. "Damn those Posairs! They've erected that strange shield again."

"It shouldn't matter," Morvana scoffed. "Surely, Mother, your magic can penetrate it. You did once before."

Malviana ignored her daughter's sarcasm, and mentally searched her repertoire of spells and selected a particularly nasty one to fling at her enemies. A wicked smile played at the corners of her mouth as she contemplated the terror and pain the Posairs would soon experience. This time though, it wouldn't be illusions striking her enemy, like at the last keep. Malviana channeled the stored power in her necklace through her wand and released the spell. She cocked her head to the side, listening with gleeful anticipation. A few milcrons later, the awaited screams came from her troops, not from behind the walls. Beside her, Morvana wailed, curling into a ball and gibbering in terror. Gordelven clutched his head between his hands and hunkered on the ground, tears freely flowing down his cheeks.

The smell of sulfur drifted down, and she glanced up. The grifflyns continued to fight the Gryphons, but the banthues veered away with their riders gripping their heads and their faces pulled in a rictus of terror. A Malvers lost hold and slid from his saddle, tumbling to his death. Every Malvers and Maldier around her wailed and moaned as the spell ate into their brains, filling them with nightmarish images from Mordaga's seventh hell.

"Damn them all to Mordaga's seven hells!" Malviana fumed. Her spell hadn't permeated the shield, but somehow, the shield reflected it back on her troops. Only her power kept it from affecting her. Malviana furiously worked to reverse her spell.

The huge gate swung open, and Posairs on horseback poured through. The fighters would annihilate her troops! Panic choked her. She couldn't stop unweaving her spell or it would kill her people. Those on the outer edge of her camp remained unaffected, but they were too far away to stop the oncoming Posairs. On the edge of her awareness, she detected a herd of jallopsitor. Elation swept over her as she sent them to intercept the Posairs. The massive beasts would engage the enemy long enough for her to unravel her spell—she hoped.

A few milcrons later, Morvana moaned, her face pale and tear-streaked. "What happened, Mother?"

"The damned Posairs turned my spell back on us," Malviana grumbled. "Something they shouldn't be able to do. Only a powerful Black Talent can stop me. Help me undo this, before the Posairs push through the jallopsitor." Already, several of the beasts lay unmoving in the tall grass.

Morvana unsteadily climbed to her feet, then drew on the power in her jewels. Malviana quickly explained what to do, and together, they feverishly worked to undo the effects of her spell. In ever-widening circles, Malviana's troop revived, but not before the Posairs cut down those nearest the keep's wall. Finally, the unaffected Malvers troops reached the skirmish line, and the Posairs retreated back into the keep.

Malviana scowled at the keep, wiping away the sweat dripping into her eyes. "I swear, by Mordaga, I'll crush these Posairs hiding behind their walls!" Afterward, she would push north toward her goal and finally be reunited with her beloved.

Wisah - 31 de Sandar, 1076

Wisah brushed an errant lock of hair away from her face, gripped her staff, and focused on the spell she was learning. Her headband pulsed once, then a sigil on her right inner elbow glowed. Red light surrounded a melon on the table in front of her. It floated into the air, and with a sweep of her staff, the melon flew across the room to strike a straw dummy. Fire engulfed the target. With another thought, Wisah smothered the flame.

Very good, Sheekeek said. *That was better. The fire covered more of the target.*

"Thank you for helping me." Wisah took off the headband and rubbed her forehead. She'd only wheedled a few melons from the kitchens, and she'd just used the last of them. "Your invaluable guidance has helped me learn to control my new powers."

Sheekeek preened.

"I'm so tired, though," Wisah moaned, leaning on her staff. "Between studying the secret spells only known by the Supreme, learning how to manage the Sanctuary, and practicing my sigil magic, I barely have time to sleep." They exited the large room next to the laboratory and entered the main section of the hidden library.

Wisah collapsed on a comfy chair she'd transported down to the lab. The wooden benches didn't allow for relaxation after a hard workout. She propped her feet on the matching ottoman and balanced her staff on her lap. "Sheekeek, I'm worried I don't have much time left to learn everything I need to."

Why do you say that? He looked up from the scroll he'd picked up.

"I feel a sense of urgency, like chaos will break loose at any moment. I wish we knew what was happening with the Malvers."

Sheekeek lifted a shoulder. *We'll find out when the time is right. Until then, we study all we can.* He returned to his scroll.

Sighing, Wisah stood, put her headband back on, and carrying her staff, she ambled to the testing lab while considering which spell to practice next. All morning she'd worked on offensive spells. "Sheekeek," she called, "can you come help me?"

Sure. What do you need? His silver feathers and fur glowed in the lanterns she'd replaced the torches with.

"Your fireballs. I need to practice defending myself and others, too. And whatever else you can toss at me. Don't hold back. Malviana won't."

Sheekeek dropped his beak into a grin. *I rarely use my magic like this. It's so fun.* Without warning, he flared, shooting a fireball at her.

Wisah blocked it with her staff, uttering the word to activate a shield spell. She'd learned she could use only a word or two of the spells rather than saying the entire thing. In a fighting situation, she'd only have a few moments to react. Sheekeek tossed another spell, and another. She spun and whirled, casting counter spells, and light shimmered in an afterglow of energy from her staff. Sheekeek continued lobbing fireballs and other spells at her until sweat dripped down her face and soaked the back of her shirt. Her skin glowed with azure light from the myriad sigils she'd used.

She missed a fireball, and the heat singed her hair.

Enough for the day, Sheekeek said. His sides heaved. *We're both tired. You're doing better.*

"Our next step is learning how to fight together."

Sheekeek drew back, his eyes widening and lifting his wings. *No, I can't do that! I'm a mystic. I don't fight.*

Wisah shrugged. "And I'm going to be the new Supreme. Times are different for us, my friend. We're setting new traditions. I sense I'll need you in the coming battles with Malviana. You're more than my ride. You're my partner."

I can't argue with your reasoning. What do you propose? Sheekeek resettled his wings along his back, and using his beak, smoothed his feathers into his fur where they met at his shoulder.

"We kept a few of the magic orbs. Celedon and the other guards can use them to spar with us. It will also be good practice for them, in case Malviana breaches the pass at Strunhelos and attacks the Sanctuary. We know it's her ultimate goal."

The next day when they went to the practice arena, Wisah discovered the protections Maendy had placed on it when they tested the orbs were still holding. Celedon and another guard joined her and Sheekeek.

A few days later, a contingent of Red Guards approached Wisah, wanting to practice with her. Shrugging, and not thinking anything of it, Wisah welcomed them. Before the women joined the Red Guard, they had fought the Malvers' monsters.

As they continued to practice, the Red Guards split into two teams. One team would join Wisah and Sheekeek, while the other one became their opponents. Wisah appreciated learning to fight in a group. She'd been on the front lines during the Scourge war and knew how important it was to fight as a unit, not solo. Solo fighters lost their lives. Two Red Guards, Jaena and Dejah, most often attached themselves as Wisah's bodyguards during their practice skirmishes.

As the days passed in a frenzy of activity, Wisah's unease grew. Soon, she'd leave the safe confines of the Sanctuary and meet her adversary in battle.

Rizelya - 36 de Sandar, 1076

Between creating and holding the net-shield and running from wall to wall to assist the fighters against the more powerful Malvers, Rizelya drooped with exhaustion. They'd fought multiple battles with the Malvers over the past ten days since Malviana and her army arrived at Haasneven Keep.

Histrun had sent several platoons to fight skirmishes on the ground with the twisted Posairs. The information gained would allow him to design battle strategies for when the Posairs pushed north toward Strunhelos. The beasts were brutal fighters, although quite often, they'd fall into a blood frenzy and stop fighting to feed on a Posair held in their clutches. While sickening, it made them easier to kill.

Rizelya slid to the ground, leaning against the battlement wall, and rested her head on her bent knees, taking advantage of the lull in the fighting. Her stomach growled and thirst pulled at her. Before finishing her breakfast, she'd raced to stop a banthu and grifflyn attack on the south wall, and hadn't grabbed a canteen on her way. *I'll rest a few more milcrons, then drag myself down to the dining hall.*

She jerked awake at the cold sensation on her shoulder.

"Here," Leistral said, holding out a water canteen.

Rizelya gratefully took it and swigged several gulps of icy water. Since the fighting began, either Leistral or Eidstrun, often both, attached themselves to Rizelya and Blazel. Besides protecting them while deep in a Black Weave spell, the two friends also ensured Rizelya and Blazel had food and drink.

Below, Blenora, Adara, Loshera, and Chariel hurried toward the Temple. Whenever they had a break from the fighting, the priestesses of the Black Weave teams used the time to commune with the Goddess. As Chariel had told Rizelya, even though they knew the violence they participated in was necessary, it still pulled on their hearts and souls. Knowing this, those used to fighting shielded the priestesses as much as possible when they needed to work an offensive spell against the Malvers.

Aistrun and Baederposan strolled behind the priestesses, and when they went inside, the men stood at the door, guarding it. Neither man wanted to leave their lover unprotected. One never knew when the Malvers would attack or attempt to infiltrate the keep. Apparently Chariel's example of tossing aside tradition and developing a close relationship with Aistrun had influenced the other White Priestesses. Over the chedans, Noriana and Baederposan had become lovers.

Leistral plopped beside Rizelya and gave her a meat roll, warm from the ovens. Rizelya bit into it, savoring the melted cheese mixed with ground billocks. Leistral nibbled on her own meat roll. Several feet away, Eidstrun and Blazel sat, eating their lunch.

"Do you know how much longer Histrun is going to hold here?" Leistral asked.

"No." Rizelya shook her head. "He wants to learn as much as he can about our enemy while we have stout walls to protect us. I doubt we'll stay here more than four or five chedans. We have to wait for the fleet to return from taking the evacuees out of the danger zone."

"If there's such a place." Leistral sighed deeply and gazed toward the northeast. "Do you miss home? Our quick jaunt around Strunlair Province, that was only supposed to be a lunadar, has morphed into being gone for over a year. Sometimes, I miss the simple days of riding to a monster's nest, killing the beasts, and going home."

"So do I." Rizelya took another bite of her meat roll, washing it down with some water. "At least we have friends with us." She pointed toward the courtyard where members of the Black Weave teams played an impromptu game of kickball.

Eiden's laughter rang as she kicked a ball a child had left behind, keeping it from Leistrun. He was learning to compensate for his missing arm, and moved well. Eiden punted it to Saffren, who moved it across the makeshift playing field. Rizelya grinned when Nelstrun took it from her—in an illegal move by tickling her—and kicked it to Delestrun. After a jallopsitor killed their partner, Maestrun, the two had become glum and sullen. This display of good-natured teasing assured Rizelya they were healing.

Saffren responded by using her Talent to snatch the ball from Delestrun and lift it over Nelstrun's head to score a goal. Rizelya's eyebrows rose. She'd detected air magic mixed with Saffren's water Talent.

"Hey, no fair!" Delestrun objected, his arms akimbo.

Leistral squinted, then turned to study Rizelya. "You're all developing cross Talents. I doubt it will be long before you can work all the Talents by yourself and not need to meld in the Black Weave."

Rizelya blinked. Her mind stuttering at the idea. Outside of the Weave, she hadn't tried to do much with her Talent, especially after Blazel had killed Gelposan with only his thoughts. The power available to them, and the potential to abuse it, terrified her.

Activity on the north battlement caught her attention. Hairan anxiously gesticulated, pointing at something. Bren squinted, shook her head, and appeared to argue with him. Hairan threw his hands in the air. Suddenly, he jumped to the top of the wall and leaned over it, while Ninsun held his feet. He fired his pulser.

"Holy Mother!" Bren's shout rang across the keep. *Rizelya! Blazel!* she shouted in mind-speech. *We need help over here. We're being attacked by a hoard of angulete. At least that's what Hairan is telling me.* Surprise and confusion filled her voice.

Rizelya leaped to her feet.

"What's going on?" Leistral snatched her helbraught as she stood.

"Trouble. Glork, we're needed."

Coming Glork dropped from the tower above her and hovered near the walkway so she could slide onto his back. A moment later, Morru picked up Leistral. Graak and Blazel were already zooming across the courtyard, with Sterkek and Eidstrun on their tails.

Even as they flew the short distance, the Vhelopsi continued to fire. Rizelya squinted, but she couldn't see anything until Hairan's strike killed an angulete. She gaped at the huge flying snake that was sliding off a pasture fence.

"Those aren't the normal size," Blazel commented. "I've never seen any so large!"

Graak whistled. *Just one of those will feed a Thunder Wing. While not my favorite, they'll supplement our rations.* Every time the Gryphons left the Keep to hunt for fresh meat, they risked being attacked by banthues and grifflyns.

"Watch out!" Ninsun called. He fired at an angulete, poised to strike Bren.

Bren's face drained of color as she stared at the angulete draped over the edge of the wall. With obvious loathing, she pulled the snake onto the walkway. "I didn't see it. The damned spell on it makes it invisible. How can you?"

"We don't have magic, so it doesn't work on us?" Hairan shrugged.

The snake's thick coils twitched and writhed.

It isn't dead. Glork dove, and Hairan and Ninsun leaped aside as Glork snatched the snake behind its head with his talons. A quick twist, and the angulete fell limp.

"You'll pay for thisss!"

Rizelya and the others whirled at the angry shout. A Posair woman twisted with an angulete landed on an outer fence. A grimace crossed her olive-green scaled skin. She stretched her leathery wings wide out as she balanced on top of the stone, and she held a black whip coiled in her talons. She thrust a fist into the air, shouting a command. A flock of banthues and baethor rose from the plains, flying toward those on the north wall.

Graak screeched. A flight of Gryphons, including several Thunder Wings, launched into the sky in response.

A Malvers man flew to the twisted Posair and reached a hand down to pull her onto his banthu. Eidstrun fired. The Maldiers nearly lost her grip when red blossomed on her clavicle. Hairan, his Vhelopsi, and the Posairs manning the wall shot pulsers and arrows at the banthues. The Gryphons reached the battle and clashed with the Malvers' aerial forces.

Rizelya and Blazel leaped off their Gryphons and rushed to stand at the battlement edge, while Graak and Glork landed next to them. A moment later, Leistral and Eidstrun jumped down and flanked them. Rizelya began raising the net-shield, but paused when the hair on her arms and the back of her neck stood on end.

Blazel looked at her in confusion. "Why aren't you initiating the net-shield?"

"Something new is happening. I don't think it's what we need."

Two banthues hovered over the outer most pasture fence wall. So far, the sturdy sheadash stone had protected the keep from the new Malvers' monsters as much as it had the janacks and brechas. Behind the fence waited a large, squat, lizard-like creature with thick bony plates covering its head. Spiky scales covered its body and protruded from its sides. Its gold, dark brown, and reddish scales shimmered in the afternoon sun, making the scales along its back look like it had a thousand eyes watching them.

The two Malvers pointed their jeweled wands at the fence, shooting foul magic at the stone. The creature dropped its head and rammed into it.

Rizelya gasped as the stone splintered. More rock flew as it rammed the fence again. Its third hit created a hole large enough for it to amble through. The creature barreled across the field, where the Malvers men targeted the next pasture fence with their magic. Three more creatures eased through the gap and raced to join their companion.

"They shouldn't be able to break those walls," Bren said, fear filling her voice. "Sheadash stone is impervious to malignant magic."

"Not their magic, apparently," Hairan pointed out as the creatures breached another fence, trampling the vegetables under their huge feet.

Only two more fences stood between the lizards and the Keep. "Whatever those Malvers are doing is softening the stone. We can't let them attack the Keep's walls." She reached for Blazel's hand while placing the other one on Glork's flank. In the back of her mind, she sensed the rest of her Black Weave team. The fox team had already established and held the net-shield over the Keep. At her direction, they moved it further out.

Rizelya studied the two Malvers. *Blazel, we need to stop them. What did you do to kill Gelposan?*

No! We can't use the Black Weave like that, Kaieli protested.

It's a profanity of the Goddess's gift, Loshera added.

I hate the idea, too, Rizelya said. *But we have to stop them, otherwise everyone here is in danger if they breach the Keep.*

It's necessary, Blazel said, in a tone of finality. *I'll take the lead, and the responsibility. We'll try the reflection spell first. But they may now have a counter-spell. If it doesn't work, we'll have to hit them directly.* Blazel gripped Rizelya's hand tighter, then spoke to her in a private mind-link. *Help me shield the priestesses and Kaieli. Before, I imagined what I wanted to do, and it happened.*

Rizelya's mind rocked with the simplicity of it.

Blazel gathered control of the weaving and placed the reflection spell between the stone fence and the Malvers' stream of magic. The Malvers' magic sped back toward them. The jewels in the lead man's wand sparked and absorbed the attack. He grimaced in pain, then scowled at Blazel and Rizelya. He made a complicated pattern with his wand and flung his spell at them.

Holy Mother! Rizelya swore. If the death spell hit them, they'd be dead. And most likely, their teammates, too.

Without thinking too much about what she was doing, she wove Raeleen's lava in with her fire, and Saffren's ice into a deadly weapon. She threaded in a bit of Kaieli's earth magic. She imagined the combined magic wrapping around the Malvers' heart, the ice stopping it, while the lava boiled his blood. He didn't even shriek as he toppled off his banthu. She watched in fascination as the jewels in his wand cast a rainbow of light as it spiraled to the ground.

The other Malvers jerked on his banthu's reins, twisting it around. "Retreat!" he ordered as he sped back to their encampment. Immediately, the air battle stopped, and the remaining riders followed him.

The giant, horny lizards shook their heads, like they were shaking off a bad dream. The lead lizard dropped his snout, rooted in the crushed vegetables at his feet, and started munching. Meanwhile, the others wandered through the holes to graze on the alfalfa fields.

Bren studied the lizards, her forehead crinkling. "Those look like overgrown cardrolon horned lizards. But the ones I've ever seen are this big." She held up her hands about three hands-width apart. The creatures below them were about seven feet long and six feet tall. "They're usually very gentle. It's so sad to see them changed so dramatically from what the Goddess designed them to be."

"Do you think we can make them work for us?" Hairan asked. "To have such a fearsome creature on our side might make a difference later."

"I don't know about making them work for us," Blazel said slowly, studying the creatures. "But we should capture them. It would deny the Malvers a valuable tool."

"Maybe a Brown, who specializes in animals, can tame them," Rizelya speculated. "I'll ask Naila to assign someone to try. She'll know who is here and capable." She turned toward the place the Malvers lay crumpled. "We have an opportunity to study the Malvers' magic. One we haven't had before. Glork, would you take me down to retrieve that man's wand?"

Of course, Glork dipped his head, hopped off the tower, and crouched for her to climb onto his back.

"We're coming, too," Blazel said, as he mounted Graak's back.

They flew to the field, landing next to the Malvers.

"Should we burn him?" Rizelya asked, staring down at him. The darker tint to his gray skin indicated he was one of the newly turned Malvers. All the exiled Malvers' skin was a much lighter gray. Luckily, neither of them knew the man.

Yes, Graak said, his wings tucked tight to his side. He glanced at the hole in the fence, which no longer protected the field. *His body will attract scavengers, and we don't know what it will do to ordinary animals. Step back.*

As soon as Rizelya and Blazel moved away, Graak flared. His fire quickly immolated the body. Rizelya sensed Grazeen's snelk magic, and in a moment, not even ash remained of the Malvers.

"Let's find his wand," Rizelya said.

The Gryphons joined her and Blazel in searching for it. Finally, a glint in the tall grass caught Rizelya's eye. She bent over and picked up the wand. Heat seared her, and slimy magic wrapped around her hand. She swore, dropping the wand and flinging the magic from her. "The damned thing burned me!"

Blazel dug into the pocket of his jacket and pulled out a cloth. "Here, wrap it in this."

Rizelya held up her uninjured hand. "No, you do it. I'm not touching it again." She held out her palm.

Blazel took her hand in his, and after examining it, showed her his scarred palm. "It's the same magic. Their magic doesn't like us."

"That's an understatement." Rizelya grimaced as the pain in her hand grew. "I need to see Bethlyn about this burn."

"Histrun and Keshanal need to examine this." Blazel carefully wrapped the wand in the cloth. He started to put it in his jacket.

That isn't a good idea, Glork said. *It could still burn you.*

Blazel wrinkled his nose and held it away from him as he climbed onto Graak's back. As they flew toward the keep-house, Rizelya wondered if this find could help them in their fight with the Malvers. If anyone could determine if they could turn it to their use, it would be Maendy.

Malviana - 38 de Sandar, 1076

Malviana sent wave after wave of Maldiers and twisted beasts at the keep. Two days ago, the cardrolon lizards had nearly reached the keep's walls. Malviana swore. They'd lost control of the beasts during the battle.

She glared at the keep. She hated these sieges. Somehow, whoever was casting the damn shield had strengthened it from when they'd first encountered it at Haaslornde Keep. The shield not only covered the outer fields and pastures, it stopped even the Malvers from penetrating it to infiltrate the keep.

A scout raced up to her, sweat shining on his face. "My queen," he said in a rush, "a group of Posairs is escaping the keep!"

Malviana's heart leaped with joy. Finally, she'd be able to face these cowards outside of the walls. She ran to her banthu, with Borgedier and Jorvelden at her side. The banthues' wide wings soon had them aloft and flying after the throng of thirty Posairs on horseback.

"They won't get far," Borgedier said. "I've directed a band of skeaeters to block them on the ground, and a flock of grifflyns to attack them from the air."

The grifflyns overtook the banthues and raced ahead. Faint pops came from the keep, but Malviana ignored them. They'd flown too far for the Posairs' weapons to reach them. She gaped at the two men who were half horse, half man. But unlike her Maldiers, they were a perfect meld, not some twisted monstrosity. One was a chestnut with dark blue-gray stripes. The feathers on his legs and his tail were the same blue-gray. His chestnut hair flowed behind him as he galloped, holding a bow in his hand.

"Capture that centaur," she ordered Borgedier, pointing at the one who'd caught her interest. "I want to study it. How did he manage to become one, and so beautiful?"

"As you will, my queen."

The leading grifflyn released a gout of flames, and fire engulfed the lead horse and rider. Malviana grinned as his screams filled the air. The centaur shot an arrow, and flames lit the arrowhead right before it thunked into the side of the grifflyn.

"I really must have one of those of my own," she crowed, impressed by the centaur. A speculative gleam entered her eyes when the centaur reared, revealing he was a stallion. She stared at him, and he glanced up. His beard did nothing to hide his beauty. "You're mine!" she shouted.

He glowered at her as he shot an arrow at her. Laughing, she knocked it away with a casual wave of her wand.

The men in the group lifted strange weapons to their shoulders. With a bang, projectiles streamed from the weapons, striking the grifflyn. It turned and shrieked at them. A woman carefully aimed and fired her weapon. This time, red light, instead of a metal projectile, streaked toward the grifflyn. The beast snapped its jaws shut, but not fast enough. The light zipped into its maw. Blooms of fire erupted along the entire length of the grifflyn's neck, even as the other grifflyns attacked.

Suddenly concerned, Malviana pulled her banthu back and flung up a shield just as the grifflyn exploded. She expected the burning debris to fall on the escapees. Instead, they landed on a dome of fire and hardened air. The other grifflyn's flames slammed into the shield and bounced off it. They had to veer to avoid being hit by their own fire.

Malviana turned in her saddle, scowling at the sight of the hated Rizelya standing on the highest wall. One of her hands rested on the flank of a creamy tan and brown Gryphon, and she stretched her other hand toward the group.

"She must be casting the shield," Malviana said. "Now's our chance. She can't defend against our attack while launching her own spell."

Malviana grinned, shooting a bolt of lightning into the shield. Rizelya flinched as if she'd been hit, but the shield held, even as Malviana and Borgedier continued to throw spells at it. Malviana's eyebrows raised when she sensed a powerful entity probing her. She strengthened her personal shield. If she didn't know any better, she'd swear it was someone with Black Talent. But the Malvers had eliminated anyone with that Talent.

Below, more fighters, including several centaurs, arrived. With their added numbers, they defeated the pack of skeaeters attacking the evacuees. Two humongous black Gryphons converged on a grifflyn from either side. Malviana gaped at how tiny it appeared compared to the massive creatures. Between them, they tore the grifflyn to pieces.

"Retreat!" she ordered.

The Malvers fled back to the safety of their camp. All the while, Malviana fumed. From her many forays into Rizelya's mind, Malviana knew the girl didn't possess any Black Talent, but that didn't account for what Malviana had just witnessed. Rizelya had cast the shield, and it had held against Malviana's greater magic.

Chapter 21

Wisah - 44 de Sandar, 1076

Wisah and Sheekeek sat in the hidden library, studying the ancient scrolls and books detailing the battles with the Malvers. She read every account of encounters with Malviana she could find, trying to learn how to fight her opponent. Wisah enjoyed the sound of pages being turned and the scent of old vellum and parchment. If only she were reading something besides war, she'd be content.

Sheekeek lifted his head, cocking it to the side and dropping his beak in a grin. *Moraak comes. Hurry! We still have time to reach the audience chamber before he arrives.*

Wisah hadn't heard anything, but the Gryphons could communicate much longer distances via mind-speech than the Posairs. She glanced down at her old tunic and trousers, stained with some substance and with small holes burned in them, and wrinkled her nose. They were completely unsuited to greet Prince Moraak, especially as the heir-apparent for the Supreme—even if no official announcement had been made yet. She dropped the scroll, raced up the stairs, through the corridors, and to her room, where she quickly changed into more appropriate attire.

She was braiding her sidelocks into the traditional priestess style when a young girl knocked on her door, bringing her the summons to attend the Supreme. Wisah finished her braid and affixed the white veil over her hair, now covered with black streaks. Her eyes had become so indigo as to appear black in most lighting. She wondered what Jaehaas would think of the changes in her. Hopefully, he wouldn't find her ugly.

Smoothing her skirts, she hurried to the Supreme's room, where she helped the old woman to her feet and escorted her to the audience chamber. As each day passed, she noticed it became more difficult for the Supreme to rise from her chair and to walk. A constant slight tremor shook her hands now. Wisah worried again she wouldn't finish her training before the Supreme died.

Even before they crossed the threshold into the audience chamber, the murmurs of quiet conversation reached them. Wisah gave the Supreme a quizzical look, wondering why she'd called the other priestesses to witness Prince Moraak's arrival. The Supreme only smiled and patted Wisah's hand.

When she stepped through the audience chamber's door, Wisah paused. Next to the crystal throne sat a replica, although smaller and made from rose quartz rather than clear quartz. They brought the rose throne out of storage only when the heir-apparent neared her ascension. Wisah's heart skipped a beat. She swallowed the fear, pulled her shoulders back, and lifted her chin. Mustering as much regal demeanor as possible, Wisah helped the Supreme to her throne, then glided to stand in front of the rose throne.

Prince Moraak and his four towering Thunder Wing bodyguards stood before the dais. Their eyes were bright with curiosity. Sheekeek's gaze meet her eyes, and he touched a talon to his chest as he bowed his head. He knew what was coming.

A murmur rose from the gathered priestesses, and as one, they dropped to their knees and bowed in obeisance. Wisah felt her face flush with heat. The whisper of cloth as the priestesses rose was the only sound in the room—and the thundering of Wisah's heart. The Supreme hadn't warned her about this ceremony. Now she was glad she'd changed her clothes.

"My people," the Supreme said, raising her voice. Her spell allowed her normally weak voice to resound in every corner of the enormous room. "Although it is a bit unorthodox, the Goddess has chosen a new Supreme to lead you when I cross the veil into the Mother's arms."

An older priestess stepped forward with an ornate jewelry box and held it so the Supreme could reach into it easily. The Supreme motioned for Wisah to kneel in front of her. She retrieved a ring set with a sapphire from the box. "This candidate has passed all the tests and levels of magic. I hereby declare Wisah an Adept."

Wisah held out her right hand, unsurprised at its quivering. The Supreme slid the ring onto her thumb. She added several more rings until only the fourth finger of Wisah's left hand remained unadorned. She'd receive the final ring upon her ascension as the Posair's spiritual leader. Last, the Supreme lifted a necklace identical to the one she wore from the box. A huge diamond sat in the center of the eight-pointed star.

"With this chain of office, I anoint Wisah as my heir. Let all know she is the next representative of the Goddess, chosen by Her will."

Wisah bowed her head. The chain slipped over her head and settled onto her neck. As she stood up, the pendant came in contact with her chest. Light blazed from the diamond and every candle in the room ignited. The sigils on Wisah's face and arms glowed a bright azure. Suddenly, her staff appeared in her hand, the crystal on it shining with white light, and her headband sat on her brow as if it were a crown.

The crowd of priestesses gasped, again dropping to their knees. The Gryphons also bowed, including Prince Moraak. Power thrummed through Wisah's body, and the presence of the Goddess whispered in her ear. Any lingering doubts about her calling fled.

When she lifted her head, the Supreme's eyes were wide with surprise and her hand covered her heart. "This didn't happen when I was named heir," she whispered. "The Goddess has great things in store for you, daughter of my heart."

A few milcrons later, the light faded from Wisah's tattoos and staff. The Supreme directed Wisah to her new throne. As she sat, she drew in a breath when the crystal underneath her buzzed with energy, and she heard a barely audible hum. Her mind opened, and she could perceive the thoughts and feelings of everyone in the room. Most were excited, a few held sympathy, while even fewer were envious. Didn't they know she hadn't asked for this position? Or that she'd trade it in a heartbeat to be with her love?

Moraak approached the dais and lifted his talon to his chest, tipping his head. *Your Grace, it is my great honor to bear witness to the naming of your heir, the Lady Superior. The Goddess has chosen well.*

"Did you succeed in your mission with your father?" the Supreme asked. "Has he sent more Gryphons to help us in the fight against the Malvers?"

He has, Your Grace. Four hundred Gryphons fly with me to join Histrun and the Posair army.

"So few. I had expected more." The Supreme's fingers tapped on the arm of her throne.

They are our best fighters. Moraak fluffed the feathers of his head. *They should be sufficient. Another flight of one hundred will follow and remain at Strunhelos to guard the pass should the Malvers attempt to cross it. Another two hundred protect our borders to drive any Malvers or their creatures from our lands if they reach them. Is that enough?*

The Supreme nodded. "It shall have to be. When do you propose to fly south?"

We hoped to prevail on your hospitality for a few days to rest from the journey from Alkaak before we fly the entire length of Lairheim to the Barrens.

"You have it." The Supreme waved her hand, and several priestesses rushed from the room to ready the Gryphon quarters.

A commotion arose outside the audience chamber doors, and a Gryphon and his Posair rider hurried inside. Dirt covered Derenposan's face, and Poraak's wings drooped with weariness. He straightened at Moraak's presence.

My prince, Poraak bowed. *Am I glad to see you!*

"The war has begun," Derenposan announced when they reached the dais. "The Malvers army attacked Haaslornde Keep. It has fallen."

Wisah gasped along with the rest of the gathered priestesses. No, it wasn't possible. The Malvers couldn't be that strong, could they? "How..." She swallowed, leaning forward in her seat. "How many dead?"

"Not many, Wisah—" His eyes widened as he took in her new emblem of office and the rose throne. "I mean, my Lady Superior. Histrun had sent most of the army north to Haasneven before the attack. Rizelya, Blazel, and the whole Black Weave team were brilliant in keeping the Malvers' evil magic from us."

Wisah slumped back in her seat. Her friends were alive.

The messenger continued. "The Malvers army followed us to Haasneven Keep, where they've laid siege on it." He turned to Moraak. "Prince Moraak, I'm glad you're here. We really need your help."

Their winged creatures outnumber ours twenty to one, Poraak added, then grinned. *Although we are better fighters.*

Moraak rubbed a talon across his beak. *It appears, Your Grace, we shall not need your hospitality after all.*

"So it does. Stay the night and rest in comfort. When you leave in the morning, the Lady Superior will join you."

Moraak uttered a startled squawk. *Surely the heir will remain here, where it is safe.*

The Supreme shook her head. "No, it is not her calling. Her work is to cleanse the land of the evil infecting it. Malviana."

At the mention of the Malvers' name, the crystal in Wisah's headband warmed, and the sigils on her hands glowed. Fear and excitement raced through Wisah in equal measures. She dreaded the coming fight with Malviana and using the unmaking spell, but at the same time she looked forward to being with her friends—and Jaehaas—again.

The Supreme stood, ending the audience. As Wisah assisted her from the chamber, two familiar Red Guards detached themselves from their ranks and followed them. She rolled her eyes at herself, finally understanding why the two had trained as her bodyguards during their practice sessions.

The Supreme stopped at her quarters. "Now you are officially the heir, you must be protected. Jaena—" she indicated the taller of the pair "—and Dejah are your new bodyguards. They will keep you safe and guard your back while you do what you must."

Jaena bowed to Wisah. "It is our honor to serve you, Lady Superior." She lifted the red veil covering her face. Lines formed around the older woman's citrine eyes, and strands of red hair curled around her neck. "Only the Supreme and the Lady Superior may gaze upon the faces of the Red Guard."

Dejah removed her veil, revealing a younger woman with soft-brown eyes and cherry-red hair. She smiled shyly at Wisah before letting her veil fall to once again cover her face.

Jaena also put her veil back on, adjusting it into place. "Sleep well, my lady. We shall guard your door." She and Dejah took up their positions.

Before Wisah could say anything, the Supreme waved her away. "Hush, my girl. We'll say our goodbyes in the morning." She turned and disappeared into her quarters, her own Red Guard standing on either side of her door.

Wisah slipped inside her room, gazing around it. She'd only had it for a short time, but it still felt like home. She gently placed the staff next to her bed and took off the headband, then started packing. As she folded a pair of trousers, her gaze fell on Chariel's small carved sabertiger. She picked it up, running her fingers over the carving, smiling as she thought of her friend. *Did she see my fate in one of her visions?* She tucked the figurine into her pack. Following her intuition, she also put the ancient spell book in her baggage.

Early the next morning, Wisah and the Supreme said their teary goodbyes in the privacy of the Supreme's quarters. Wisah slung her bags over her shoulder, settled the headband more securely over her forehead, and firmly grasped her staff. With her bodyguards a few steps behind her, she strode through the temple corridors, nodding at the priestesses as they dropped into curtsies as she passed. She wasn't sure she'd ever become used to it.

Outside, Sheekeek waited for her, along with two red-shouldered hawk-type Gryphons.

So we're off on another adventure, Sheekeek said as he winked at her. *Life around you is never boring, Lady Superior.*

"Please, don't call me that, Sheekeek. We're too good of friends. I'm not ready to lose my identity just yet."

As you will. Moraak is waiting for us to join him.

"Then let us go."

Wisah tied her packs to Sheekeek's back and watched as her Red Guard clambered onto the Gryphon's backs and fumbled with the harness's buckles. Wisah stepped over to Dejah and helped her, while Jaena copied her. She hopped onto Sheekeek and buckled her own harness.

As Sheekeek flew over the temple, Wisah wondered when she'd return, and if the Supreme would still be alive when she did. She looked away from it and toward the south where her heart lay. Soon, she'd see Jaehaas again. Would he still love her now that she was the Supreme's heir?

Malviana - 54 de Sandar, 1076

Malviana, Morvana, and Borgedier lounged in her tent after the day's battle. She'd been throwing her troops at the walls of Haasneven Keep, trying to pry them out for the past three chedans.

"The Posairs' defenses are surprisingly strong," Morvana commented. "We can't pierce their shielding to reach the keep's walls. A handful of the Maldiers have crossed the outer fences, protecting the fields and pastures, but only the outermost. Once they pass the second or third, that damned shield stops them."

Borgedier twirled his goblet of bloodwine. "Even though the number of Gryphons they have to field is laughable, they somehow manage to defeat our flocks. We should win with our greater force of banthues, grifflyns, and baethor. Even when we kill their rider, the Gryphons continue fighting with cunning and strategy." He grimaced and gulped at the wine. "They didn't behave like this, or show any intelligence when we fought them before."

"Nothing is like it was," Malviana complained. "While we moldered in our exile, the Posairs, and even the Gryphons, prospered and changed. I'm beginning to regret sending my sons in different directions." She drained her goblet and refilled it with fresh bloodwine. "I need to complement Magdelyn. This latest batch of bloodwine is particularly fine. "

Someone scratched on the tent flap. "My queen, I have a gift for you," Keandran said. "May we enter?"

Curious, Malviana waved her wand, opening the tent. She relished being able to do such simple magic again without strain.

A grin pulled at Keandran's lips, showing his fangs, as he sketched a bow to her. "We caught a band of Posairs spying on our army."

Malviana sat up straight, her eyes alight. "How many did you capture?"

"Ten."

"Ooh." Morvana licked her lips. "That many sacrificed to Mordaga will please him greatly. And provide us with a huge influx of power."

"It will indeed, my daughter," Malviana crooned. "Bring them to me!"

"They await your pleasure." Keandran made a sweeping bow and pushed aside the tent flap.

Six men and two women, clearly Posairs, cowered on their knees with their hands tied behind their backs. Two golden-haired, bronze-skinned men caught her attention. They were like nothing she'd seen before. Malviana strode to them, circling around them and stopping in front of them. She reached down and tilted one man's head back, examining him closer. His golden eyes held hatred, and he bared a set of small fangs at her.

"What are you?" she purred. Perhaps she'd save these two to pleasure her. Thinking about it, she ran her hands over her breasts and hips. Out of the corner of her eye, she saw his younger companion lick his lips. Oh, yes, he was definitely male.

"Vhelopsi," the older man spat, ignoring her flirting. He had a strange accent. The word held no meaning for her.

"Where are you from?"

"Vhel."

She plunked her hands on her hips and glowered at him, tired of his one-word answers.. "And where is that?"

He smirked as he shrugged and pointed up. He couldn't mean the stars, could he? Then she remembered the damned aliens who had attacked her island. They had come from the sky, but these two didn't look anything like them. They must be another species. She wondered how much power she'd receive from his death essence. The thought made her core tingle.

The two women she gave to Magdelyn to sacrifice for the others. After they left, Keandran and Borgedier tied the older Vhelopsi onto the sacrificial altar. Tears streamed from his wide eyes, and he gibbered in his own language. If it was a prayer to his gods, they held no power here. She plunged her hands into his chest, and his blood flowed over her hands. Only the smallest flash of power seeped into her from his death. No more than a normal animal. Her forehead creased in disappointment.

"How is this possible? He doesn't have any magic for me to absorb?"

Borgedier shrugged, not having any answer either.

Malviana glanced at the younger one, who knelt off to the side, praying. She'd save him and hope he at least provided her some pleasure before he died. He wasn't worthy of sacrificing to Mordaga. The Posairs, on the other hand, were supremely worthy.

When she sacrificed the fourth Posair, the power of her god filled her. As she writhed with ecstasy, Mordaga deemed to show her a vision.

Her hated enemy appeared before her, and the power within her overflowed, hiding her features from Malviana. She held the magical device that had killed Mordar. Tendrils of magic drifted from it, questing for a new victim—Malviana. She couldn't win against the combined power. Not as she was now.

Malviana pulled her hands from the victim's chest, stunned and shaking. Mordaga's message was clear: stay and die, or flee ahead of the terrible power coming for her. Even though her strength was steadily growing, she'd need to become even stronger before she faced the magnitude of power she sensed.

"Order the retreat!" she commanded, ignoring the stunned expressions of her courtiers. "We're leaving, tonight."

"But why?" Morvana had the temerity to ask.

Malviana backhanded her daughter. "Because Mordaga demands it. Go do my bidding!"

All desire to spend time with her new slave vanished as Malviana shuffled into her tent to change into riding clothes, her thoughts whirling from her vision.

Shandir was dead, wasn't she? How could she have survived the conflagration that destroyed Malvernlair Province? She wasn't immortal—at least Malviana didn't think she was—so how was she here, now, to torment her?

Rizelya - 55 de Sandar, 1076

Rizelya stood on the battlement walls, staring out over what had been the Malvers' army camp—the empty camp. During the night, they'd pulled up every tent and left. Although several packs of floxidor, skeaeters, and jallopsitor roamed the fields to discourage the Posairs from leaving.

"Where did they all go?" Keshanal asked. The old woman rarely climbed the stairs to the battlements. She lifted a shaky hand to brush back her thin, pale copper-red hair. "I don't like this at all."

Histrun pointed to the trail cut in the tall plains grass. "They went north. More worrisome is why. Why did they leave so abruptly and abandon the fight here?"

Before anyone could speculate, a golden sheen caught the light, and the sound of thunder rolled over the keep. An enormous gold Gryphon swooped down, with hundreds of Gryphons flying behind him. As Prince Moraak spiraled to land in the courtyard, Rizelya and Blazel followed the leaders, hurrying down the stairs to meet him. When Hairan didn't follow, Histrun turned around and motioned for him to join them.

Sheekeek landed beside Moraak. Rizelya stared at the woman on his back. Surely she couldn't be her niece and friend, Wisah? Black streaked the woman's creamy-white hair, and her eyes were an indigo, so dark they almost appeared black. She dismounted the Gryphon and laughed at something he said. Rizelya recognized that laugh. It was Wisah! She had changed in the intervening lunadars even more than Rizelya had.

Wisah unhooked a tall staff topped with a crystal from Sheekeek's harness. She scanned the crowd, searching for someone.

A few moments later, Jaehaas pushed through the crowd, then paused. A wondrous look of love crossed his face. "Wisah!" he cried. He trotted to her and picked her up, spinning her around. "I missed you so." He bent to kiss her, but she turned away, sadness filling her eyes.

The Supreme has an heir, Sheekeek said, his voice penetrating everyone's mind in the courtyard.

"My Lady Superior," Histrun murmured as he dropped to his knee.

Horror filled Jaehaas's eyes as he took in the badge of office hanging around Wisah's neck. With an air of resignation and loss, he awkwardly knelt.

Rizelya gaped at Wisah's diamond pendant. *How can she be the Supreme's heir?* As she bowed in respect and obeisance with the others, Rizelya glanced at Naila. Shock and wonder shone in Naila's face. Normally, no one knew the parents of a Supreme. As soon as a child with white eyes was born, they were whisked away to the Sanctuary to be raised and trained by the Supreme. Never before had a new Supreme been an adult when their powers manifested. Rizelya sneaked a peek at Wisah. Her eyes weren't white, but nearly black! And yet she wore the badge of office for the Lady Superior, and Sheekeek, who had been at the Sanctuary with Wisah, declared her the heir. Rizelya shook her head. These were indeed strange times.

Wisah intoned the traditional blessing of the Goddess. "You may rise." Her voice quavered.

Rizelya caught Wisah swiping her eyes, her gaze on Jaehaas. Tears streamed down Jaehaas's face as he awkwardly stood up. Wisah reached out a hand to him, but he turned on his hind hooves and trotted toward the gate, people scattering out of his way. His gait changed to a gallop as soon as he passed through the gates. Wisah looked stricken, her hand still extended. Rizelya's heart went out to the couple. A centaur being in love with a priestess had been challenging enough, but now Wisah was much more than a priestess. It would be impossible for their romantic relationship to continue.

Histrun stood, cleared his throat, and raised his voice to address the assembled crowd. "This is momentous and happy news. We've long awaited for the Supreme's heir. But it doesn't change the fact we're in the middle of a war, people. The Malvers army is marching north. We now must chase them rather than draw them to where we want them to go. They have a head start on us. Prepare to march within the octar. Dismissed!"

The crowd scurried to obey his command. As people jostled her as they left the plaza, Rizelya cursed being short. Elbows and shoulders slammed into her, while she struggled against the current to reach the keep-house porch. Blazel noticed and signaled to Aistrun. They moved to her side, blocking the worst of the inadvertent strikes. Finally, they made it to the porch.

Rizelya slowly climbed the steps, staring at her niece. The alterations in her hair and eyes weren't the only changes she'd undergone in the few lunadars since Rizelya had last seen her. Faint azure-blue tattoos covered every bit of Wisah's skin. Rizelya paused at the top stair, not quite certain how to treat Wisah in her new status. She snorted to herself. This was still her niece and still her friend. She crossed the last few paces separating them and threw her arms around Wisah.

"I'm so glad you're back!" Wisah relaxed, and Rizelya knew she'd made the right decision. She stepped back, examining Wisah, and decided her new appearance was stunningly beautiful. "Sweet Goddess, I've missed you. We've missed you. I'm glad I'm not the only one who attracts trouble."

Wisah laughed, then scowled at Rizelya. "My trouble started with that ancient book you gave me! This—" she waved a hand, indicating her body "—is a result of the damned book."

Rizelya squinted and realized the tattoos were actually sigils. "Do they cover your entire body?"

"Pretty much," Wisah said with a wry smile. Her face turned somber. "Have you seen Malviana?"

Rizelya nodded.

Histrun glanced around at the few stragglers hanging around the porch. "Let's take this inside, shall we?" He gestured at the doorway. When Hairan turned to go, he motioned to him. "You too. You're the leader of your people. I need your observations and input."

Hairan pulled his shoulders back and strode inside, following Blazel and Chariel. Moraak had already slipped in, using his people's magic to move through the walls since the door, even built for a centaur, was too small for him.

Wisah hadn't moved. Her gaze remained glued to the gate.

Aistrun paused. "I'll go find Jaehaas. He shouldn't be alone right now. And he doesn't know we're leaving soon. I don't want him to be left behind."

"Thank you, Aistrun." Wisah patted his arm. "Tell him... tell him I'll talk to him later in private. And tell him I'm sorry he had to find out this way."

Aistrun nodded, then jogged to the stables.

As Wisah turned to enter the keep-house, two red-veiled women stepped from the shadows to trail behind her. Rizelya's eyes widened. The Red Guards were another indication of Wisah's changed status.

When everyone settled in the entertainment room—the only room in the keep-house large enough for three Gryphons and several people—Histrun started the meeting.

"Welcome back, Moraak," Histrun said. "We've missed your council. It appears you were successful and brought more Gryphons with you."

I was. Moraak flicked his tail to curl it around his feet as he crouched. *Even more than I expected. Wisah isn't the only one with a change in status.*

Histrun raised an eyebrow. "How so, my friend?"

If we are successful in ridding the world of the Malvers, King Zorlaak will name me the Crown Prince and his heir.

"Congratulations!" Histrun said.

It is imperative that we win, Moraak continued. *For if we do not succeed, my brother, Daelaak, will become the heir. If he does, he'll end our beneficial partnership. He hates the Posairs for what he believes was our slavery during the Great War.*

But that is preposterous! Sheekeek cried. *Has he not read our histories or listened to our songs? We would not exist if not for the Posairs.*

Nevertheless, it is how he feels. Moraak's head feathers drooped. *No amount of discussions or arguments can change his mind.*

"Then we must win," Keshanal said with finality. "I value our friendship, and many of our peoples have formed close partnerships."

"Like me and Graak," Blazel spoke up, "or Rizelya and Glork."

"Or Sheekeek and myself," Wisah said, gazing at Sheekeek fondly. "But let's not forget the Malvers are evil incarnate and mean to destroy us."

"We haven't," Histrun assured her. His eyes and mouth hardened. "We've seen and experienced their evil firsthand."

Naila gazed adoringly at her daughter. *With your new powers, do you have a way to defeat them?*

Wisah solemnly nodded. "I possess the device that unmade Mordar. It will unmake Malviana too."

"Unmake?" Rizelya frowned. "That sounds bad, even worse than killing."

"It is. Her soul will be as if it never existed. It is a terrible spell, only to be used against the vilest evil."

"I'm glad it's you using it and not me!" Rizelya leaned back in her chair, crossing her arms over her chest.

"I'm not so sure," Chariel spoke up, "she'll be acting alone."

Rizelya turned to stare at Chariel. "Is that a prophecy?"

Chariel shook her head. "No, just a feeling."

Blazel rubbed the scar on his face. "For you, it amounts to the same thing."

"Other than the unmaking spell," Histrun said, "do you have anything else to help us?"

Oh, yes, Sheekeek breathed. *We found the ancients' cache of weapons.*

"The one under the Sanctuary library?" Blazel asked.

Sheekeek nodded. *Maendy and Maellyn are at Strunlair Keep with the other helstramiesters building you an armory. We even developed a way for the men to use them with their latent magical gifts.* He looked at Hairan and scratched his head. *I don't know if they'll work for your people, though, since you lack magic.*

Hairan smiled and patted the sword belted at his side. "It's okay. We have our own weapons. Our swords are sharp enough to decapitate our enemies."

"When will the magical devices be ready?" Histrun asked.

Wisah shrugged. "Soon, maybe? There are several types, and they're complicated to make."

Histrun gave a curt nod of understanding. "On to other business. Let's discuss our battle strategy, since Malviana's sudden departure has changed it."

A flock of my warriors can scout ahead, Moraak said, *to keep us apprised of their movements.*

"Just be careful that none of your people travel alone or they risk being captured," Histrun advised, his lips thinning in disgust. "Malviana has a way of twisting Gryphons into something else, like she does the Posairs."

No! Moraak reared onto his hindquarters. *It's impossible.*

Oh, it is! Graak shuddered from beak to tail. *Horrid abominations, too.*

"The Malvers' death magic not only sucks out and absorbs life energy," Wisah said, scrunching her nose, "but it can also transmogrify it. It's how she creates Maldiers."

"I'd say so." Rizelya made a face, thinking of some of the creatures she'd encountered. "Some of the twisted Posairs are truly grotesque."

Histrun cleared his throat. "In addition, we need to send an advance team ahead of the army. Malviana may have left more beasts behind than those milling around to slow us down, if not stop us in our tracks."

The Posair-Gryphon teams should be part of that force, Moraak added. *Especially since the Malvers have banthues.*

"It isn't just banthues anymore," Blazel said, leaning back in his chair and crossing his arms over his chest. "Wait until you see the new creatures they've created. One of them we're calling grifflyns. They are... what's the word you used, Wisah?"

"Transmogrify."

Blazel snapped his fingers. "Yes. Malviana transmogrified a Gryphon with the Scourge's lizards. Then there are the floxidor, a nasty canid creature, and the jallopsitor."

"And don't forget the skeaeter," Hairan added, grimacing.

Or the giant baethor, Graak said with a grin.

Moraak's head feathers lifted. *I have been gone too long. The Malvers did not have these creatures in the Great War.*

"No, they didn't," Wisah agreed. "Malviana's power is greater than I, or the Supreme, suspected if she has transmuted so many different creatures—and to build an army of them. How could she be so strong?"

Rizelya tapped her chin thoughtfully. "It's likely she's accessing the malignant magic pools. They'd give her the power she'd need." She grinned with malicious glee. "Although she won't be using them for much longer. We're draining them as fast as possible."

"You found a way to cleanse the malignant magic?" Wisah's eyebrows rose, and she gaped.

Rizelya nodded, a pleased smile on her lips.

The leaders hammered out the other details for the march north, and the army left the keep within Histrun's allotted octar.

Wisah disappeared after the meeting to seek Jaehaas and mend their relationship. But while Rizelya strapped her travel bag to Glork's harness, Wisah and Sheekeek joined their group. Wisah's eyes were red and swollen. She silently climbed onto Sheekeek's back and buckled herself in. When Rizelya tried to talk to her, Wisah shook her head.

As Glork gained altitude, Rizelya saw the contingent of Vhelopsi ride from the keep with a familiar centaur in their company. At least Jaehaas had friends around him. She hated seeing her friends hurting so much.

Wisah - 55 de Sandar, 1076

Wisah rode through the morning in a fog. She knew she'd doomed her relationship with Jaehaas as soon as she accepted her new office, but she'd hoped they'd have more time together before it ended. She recalled the look of horror on Jaehaas's face when he saw her. Wisah held out an arm, examining the faint tattoos on it. They, along with her black-streaked hair and dark eyes, made her a freak now. No wonder he'd run away from her.

She'd searched for him before the army left the keep, but she couldn't find him. Aistrun had approached her, shaking his head sadly, and told her Jaehaas wouldn't talk to her. He needed time to sort it out. Did it mean their relationship was over, but he was too cowardly to end it cleanly? Tears snaked down her cheeks, and the wind of Sheekeek's wings quickly dried them.

Wisah leaned over Sheekeek's shoulder, searching the army marching underneath them for the centaur she loved. Sheekeek sensed her need and adjusted his flight to crisscross over the army. When they flew over the left flank, she finally found Jaehaas trotting with the Vhelopsi contingent. *Why is riding with them and not our friends?* A shadow fell across her, and Glork's large form blocked the sun. Rizelya nodded to her. Wisah realized all their friends now rode Gryphons, which Jaehaas couldn't do. Of course, he'd have to find new people to travel with.

Come join me at the midday meal, Rizelya said, mind-speaking across the distance. *Our Gryphons need a break.*

We do? Glork asked. Rizelya thumped his shoulder. *Oh, we do.*

Sheekeek let out a burble of laughter, followed by a sigh of relief. *I really do need to rest. We didn't get much chance after our rushed flight from the Sanctuary.*

Glork turned away from the army, with Sheekeek following him. A lone tree reached for the sky, and they dropped down to land next to it. Blazel, Aistrun, and Chariel sat on a blanket tossed on the ground. Their Gryphons lazed in the grass nearby. Her friends greeted Wisah warmly as she and Rizelya settled beside them.

Aistrun passed her a basket filled with food. "Eat up. We'll probably be eating trail bars for the next few days as we rush to Haasneh Keep."

"Is that where we're going?" Wisah hadn't paid attention to the travel details during the meeting. The problem with Jaehaas had occupied her thoughts.

Blazel nodded. "It's the only keep in the direction the Malvers are marching. They can't hide their trail in the plains grass."

Wisah didn't want to think of the war, and what she'd have to do when they encountered Malviana. "So, tell me what you've been up to while I've been gone."

Aistrun laughed. "That's a lot. First, we had to defeat the Scourge." He proceeded to regale them with stories of the war, many of them featuring Jaehaas.

The picnic reminded Wisah of when they'd gone to the Seven Falls above the Sanctuary. It had been the first time she and Jaehaas had spent time alone and when she'd started falling in love with him. Tears prickled her eyes. Abruptly, she set aside her plate and walked away from the group.

Rizelya caught up to her and walked with her for several milcrons. "He'll come around. Give him time. It was a shock to learn you're the new Lady Superior."

"Do you think that's it? Or is it because I'm now ugly?"

"What? You're not ugly. You're stunningly beautiful. I like the changes. I think Jaehaas is dealing with being in love with the Goddess's representative. We've been taught the Supreme can't be in relationships."

"Well, if he'd just talk to me, I'd tell him I'm not a normal Supreme—"

Rizelya laughed. "No kidding."

"In more ways than my appearance. Our world is changing. Just look at who he's riding with—aliens! Integrating the Vhelopsi into our society will bring many changes. You destroying the malignant magic pools, and hence the Malvers' monsters, brings another change. My rule will have to deal with all those changes. Jaehaas becoming my consort would be simply one more change of many."

"Your consort?" Rizelya raised her eyebrows.

"The Goddess has a consort, so why not Her representative?" Wisah leaned in and whispered, "I read the First Supreme's journal. She had a consort. The concept of a celibate Supreme didn't come until much later. So I'm actually reinstating an original tradition."

"Jaehaas will be happy to hear that. Our people, on the other hand, may struggle with it. But, as you said, our world is going through many changes. If there was a time to make your revolutionary change, now is it." Rizelya glanced back at their group, and Wisah followed her gaze. Aistrun had his arm wrapped around Chariel's shoulders, and he bent down to kiss her. "There are other priestesses who will appreciate the change, too."

Blazel waved urgently at them. "It's time to go," he shouted.

A pack of floxidor are headed this way, Graak added.

While Aistrun and Chariel threw the blanket and lunch remains into the basket, Sheekeek and Glork ran-hopped toward their riders. Wisah was buckling the last buckle of her harness when a canid beast broke from the grass a few feet from them. Its long, straight horns stuck out from its head. Its blood-red eyes bored into them malevolently. Sheekeek squawked and threw himself into the air as the beast swung its tail at him. The sharp spikes whistled as they passed the spot Sheekeek had just vacated.

What are those things? Sheekeek pumped his wings vigorously to quickly gain altitude.

"Floxidor," Blazel said. "They're swamp creatures the Malvers have modified to be bigger and meaner."

Their small group flew back toward the army, and soon Wisah heard the sounds of fighting. The floxidor they'd seen hadn't been alone. A large pack harried a squad of fighters. The men used a combination of their shapeshifter forms and their pulsers against the creatures, while the women fired their helbraughts interchangeably with their pulsers.

A floxidor's tail smashed into the legs of a warrior, who went down in a swirl of blood. As he fell, the floxidor snapped its huge jaws over the man's throat. Wisah turned her head away from the spray of blood, choking on the bile rising in her throat. The struggle below was a vivid reminder they fought a war. And it was terrifyingly violent, bloody, and deadly.

She was here to save her people from an evil intent on their destruction, and to do so, she'd have to kill. She knew this, but while she'd been safe behind the Sanctuary's walls, it had seemed a simple thing. But here, now, with the suffering and dying around her, it wasn't so simple anymore. She wasn't sure she could kill anyone—anything. In her short sojourn at the Scourge war front, she'd only helped in the defense of their people. She hesitantly gripped her staff, unsure what sigil or spell to use. By the time she decided, the skirmish ended, and the two surviving floxidor slithered into the tall grass.

Wisah continued to struggle with justifying using her Goddess gifts to kill another being. A few octars later, a twisted creature appeared, and she used her Talent to examine its soul. She gasped, her grip tightening on Sheekeek's feathers.

Sheekeek squawked. *What is it, Wisah? What's wrong?* He turned his head around to gaze at her.

"Those creatures no longer have a soul! Malviana's evil has perverted it into something unrecognizable. Only a little bit of the original creature remains, and it's in pain." She closed her eyes and took a deep breath, coming to terms with what the Goddess was asking her to do. *I understand now, Goddess.* "This must be one reason I've received my new Talents, to right these terrible wrongs. The best thing I can do for the creatures Malviana has twisted is to put them out of their misery."

When they made camp, Wisah searched for Jaehaas. When she approached him, he shook his head and turned away from her with a flick of his tail. She returned to the tent she shared with Rizelya's Black Weave team, discouraged. Rizelya tried to engage her in conversation during dinner, but Wisah claimed fatigue and climbed into her bedroll before everyone else, where she cried herself to sleep. She wasn't sure what she'd do if Jaehaas never talked to her again.

Chapter 22

Blazel - 6 de Drudar, 1076

Fifteen days after leaving Haasneven Keep the Posairs were still fifty measures from reaching Haasneh Keep. The few days' travel between the keeps had turned into a grueling journey as they fought skirmish after skirmish. Blazel swore in frustration as another flight of banthues and baethors dove onto the advancing Posairs. No matter how many of the beasts he and the others killed, there always seemed to be more. Where was Malviana getting them all? Graak's sudden dive to escape a banthu's flames slammed Blazel into the harness hard enough he'd have a bruise in the morning.

Over the chedans of working constantly with his magic, Blazel's inner pool of power had grown. He now easily accessed his magic without needing to connect with the Black Weave. The most useful skill he'd developed outside the Weave was killing the Malvers and their beasts with his thoughts. He glanced over his shoulder at Chariel and Loshera, then twisted to check on his mother and Adara. The White Priestesses and the healers, Kaieli and Faliciden, appreciated not participating when he used his new Talent. His Talent wasn't the only one growing stronger. All the Black Weave members had developed new powers independent of the Weave.

Even Delestrun could do more with his Talent than simply shapeshift. A whirlwind formed above a cluster of baethor, flames licking the swirling air. It expanded until the funnel mouth extended over the baethor. The air funnel swooped down, gulping the creatures. As the wind whirled them around and tore them apart, the fire inside incinerated them. With a burst of light, the funnel consumed the ash and dissipated.

Ahead of Blazel flew a Malvers woman above Leistral and Morru. She pointed her wand at them.

Graak screeched. *We have to stop her! They don't know she's there.* He opened his magic to Blazel.

Blazel could use his mind alone; however, when Graak added his magic, it made the working easier. Plus, Graak enjoyed annihilating his enemies with their magic as much as Blazel.

I see them. Blazel wrapped his thoughts around the Malvers. He grinned when the woman's eyes bugged out as she gasped for breath. In his mind, Blazel added the burn of a janack's acidic saliva to his venom and injected the mixture into her neck. She screamed, clawing at her throat, and a moment later, tumbled to the ground, where Laynar's people swarmed over her.

Her banthu shrieked and dove at Morru. A pulser fired several rapid shots, the projectiles thudding into its hide. Sterkek attacked the banthu while Eidstrun continued shooting. Morru flipped on a wingtip, and Leistral shot a stream of fire from her helbraught. She paused when Sterkek gripped the banthu's neck in his huge talons and bit down. Blood gushed over his beak, and the banthu went limp. As Sterkek released the dead banthu, Leistral saluted her lover with her helbraught. She and Morru circled around to resume flying at Rizelya's side, protecting her.

Sterkek rubbed his beak on his breast fur, then spiraled to meet up with Graak. While Blazel and Graak fought with their minds, Eidstrun and Sterkek protected them from physical attacks. Blazel saluted Eidstrun, then pointed to another Malvers. Eidstrun nodded, and they flew toward her.

Blazel sent his thoughts at her, but his mind crashed into a shield. Stunned, he blinked and glimpsed the woman's black wand. Several gemstones glinted on it, and silver charms hung from its handle. She pointed it at him and Graak.

"Dive Graak! Dive! It's one of the older Malvers."

He'd found his new Talent didn't work on certain Malvers. He assumed they were the exiled Malvers rather than the newly transformed Posairs.

Graak squawked as he dove, Sterkek on his wingtip.

Blazel sensed the woman release a stream of baleful magic. If her blast hit them, they'd be dead.

Rizelya! Shield! he yelled.

Lightning crackled, and Graak darted behind a banthu while Sterkek swerved to the side. The banthu shrieked as the lightning struck its wingtip. Tiny flames marched from its wingtip, growing larger as they consumed the beast. The Malvers woman shouted curses, and magic surged from her wand.

Blazel gulped. His finger on the pulser's trigger tensed, and projectiles streamed from it. Sterkek rose from her other side, and Eidstrun also fired his pulser at her. They bounced uselessly off the Malvers' shield. Suddenly, Blazel sensed his team in his mind, and a shield formed in front of him and Graak. It extended to cover all the Gryphons in the air and the Posairs on the ground. Blazel added his strength to the net-shield. He blinked and rubbed his eyes. The shield glowed a red so dark as to be almost black.

"Are you seeing this, too, Graak?"

The net-shield? Yes.

What about you and Sterkek, Eidstrun? Blazel stared in wonder at seeing the shield with his physical eyes.

We are, Eidstrun said, awe filled his mind-voice.

"Mordaga, take you," the Malvers screamed. "How are you doing this? You can't be this strong!" She lifted her wand, and yellow light sprayed from it. A moment later, her banthu turned on its wingtip and retreated. The rest of the banthues and Malvers followed in their wake.

Blazel - 8 de Drudar, 1076

With the fighting for the day over, Blazel and Rizelya groomed their Gryphon friends, cleaning caked-on soot and ash from dead banthues from their fur. The others in their pack also cleaned their Gryphon partners. Graak and the other Gryphons purred or chirped in delight at the attention. The loudest purr rumbled from Sterkek's chest as he settled his head on Eidstrun's shoulder.

This may be the best part of being on the team, Blueek purred. Although as Blenora's partner, soot didn't cover his fur. He leaned deeper into the brush.

"Hey!" Blenora laughed as he nearly toppled her over. "If you're going to do that, then crouch down so you don't knock me over."

Blueek complied, but instead of crouching, he sprawled on his side.

Blazel widened his stance as Graak relaxed and his weight pushed against Blazel. He frowned at the furor overhead. A small flight of heavily laden Gryphons flew toward the war camp from the north, chased by a flock of banthues, baethors, and grifflyns. A dozen Thunder Wings leaped into the air to intercept the Malvers' creatures. The harried Gryphons zoomed toward the command tent.

"Who is it, Graak?" Blazel asked, squinting against the setting sun.

It's Jorreek. He has Maendy and Maellyn with him.

"They must have the magical weapons we've been waiting for. Come on, Rizelya, I want to see these."

"This should be interesting," Rizelya replied, giving Glork a last swipe with the brush.

"While I love my pulser—" Ambrelya patted the weapon cradled in her arms "—maybe there's another weapon more effective on the elder Malvers." She'd already groomed Maeaak, and stood guard while the others finished. One never knew when a floxidor or skeaeter would sneak into camp.

Baederposan rumbled his agreement. "The newly turned Malvers fall easily, but those exiled ones are damned hard to kill."

It bolstered Blazel's confidence to learn he wasn't the only who found it difficult to dispatch the exiled Malvers. He tucked Rizelya's hand in his as they crossed the compound.

"They've had longer for their dark magic to seep into their souls." Loshera shuddered. She patted Morlek, whose white chest fur gleamed. He carefully unfurled his wing and wrapped it around her shoulders, cooing comfort.

Before the end of the Great War, Sheekeek added, *the Malvers had become nearly immortal from their death magic.*

A haunted look clouded Wisah's eyes. "It's why Shandir resorted to the awful spell which created the crater. After unmaking Mordar, she couldn't stomach using the device again and believed the spell to rip their magic from them was a better option." She touched the headband she always wore.

"How do you know?" Rizelya's eyebrows crinkled.

Wisah grimaced, glancing down at her arms, which faintly glowed in the evening light. "I read it in her journal. It was included in the ancient tome you found."

"Oh!"

Blazel had heard about the miraculous discovery of the ancient temple and its immediate decay as soon as Rizelya retrieved the book. He hadn't realized the importance of the find until now. He scrutinized Wisah with new respect. Her unusual powers may be the key to winning this war against the Malvers. They arrived at the command tent at the same time as the Gryphons landed.

Wisah hurried forward, a huge smile on her face as she greeted the newcomers climbing off the Gryphons. "Maendy, Maellyn, Jorreek, it's so good to see you." She surveyed the large packs tied to the fifteen Gryphons' backs and whistled. "You've been busy."

Maendy brushed back her dark chocolate-brown hair, the corners of her red eyes crinkling as she hugged Wisah. "We have, Wisah." Her eyes widened as she took in Wisah's new badge of office. "I mean, Lady Supreme. Hopefully, we have enough to do some good. I saw what we're up against as we flew here. Sweet Goddess, some of those creatures are simply awful. And the Malvers—" she shuddered "—they're worse than I imagined."

"Maendy!" Histrun cried, beaming. "Your timing is impeccable, as always. We were just talking about needing the types of weapons the ancients used before. Even the newfangled pulsers we used on the Scourge aren't working on the exiled Malvers."

"These energy globes should work," Maendy said. "They're based on what our ancestors used during the last war with the Malvers. And our magic is stronger now." She eyed Blazel and Rizelya, her eyes narrowing.

Blazel fidgeted under her intense gaze.

She studied the other members of the Black Weave teams, her eyebrows disappearing into her hair at Saffren's royal purple hair. She gaped at the black strands woven through Chariel's hair. Maendy swallowed and shook her head. "Some of you even more. Blazel, how close are you and Rizelya to being fully Black?"

"What?" Blazel exclaimed. "Impossible!"

Maendy harrumphed and gestured to Wisah. "You're saying that after what happened to Wisah? Blazel, Rizelya, have you taken a good look at yourselves in a mirror lately? The last time I saw both of you, you had auburn hair. Not any longer. It's nearly completely black with only a few strands of red left in it, and your eye color is also so dark now to be considered black."

Rizelya blinked and stared at Blazel, her mouth dropping open. "You know, she's right. We're so used to seeing each other, I hadn't noticed how far the changes had gone."

"Really? You both didn't realize you were changing?" Wisah laughed. "But then I had to have it pointed out to me too. Oh, not the tattoos, but the Black Talent?" She picked up her sidelock and gave it a rueful frown. Black and dark gray now threaded her previously pure creamy-white hair. "I'm not quite sure what to do with it."

It's simple, Wisah, Sheekeek said, bumping her with his shoulder. *Your calling is to vanquish the evil queen Malviana.*

Wisah snorted. "And how am I supposed to do that? Every time she senses me, she hides behind a group of hostages. I can't use the unmaking spell on her when innocent lives are in the way."

"There will come a time when she can't hide," Histrun said, "and you'll send her back to the Void where she belongs. So, Maendy, show us what you brought."

Maendy walked to a box and opened the lid. Nestled inside were hundreds of globes in all the colors of the rainbow. They were small enough to easily fit in a person's palm. A blue globe, the surface swirling like a miniature thunderstorm, caught Blazel's eye. It reminded him of the one he'd unintentionally activated so long ago in the hidden room under the Sanctuary. He reached for it, and the lightning within the globe crackled.

"No!" Maendy cried, slamming the lid back down while Sheekeek flung out a wing and knocked Blazel away. "We don't need one of these to detonate while in the box with the others. It would be devastating. Blazel, you and Rizelya go stand over there." She pointed imperiously for them to move to a clear space.

Disappointment and anger washed over Blazel. He really wanted to try working the blue globe. But Maendy paused to study Wisah and the others in the Black Weave teams for a moment.

"You too, Wisah, and you lot," Maendy said, shooing them away.

With as much disappointment on their faces as Blazel felt, they shuffled to join him and Rizelya several feet away from the boxes.

"Warrior, all your Talents are so strong! I can still sense them. I'm afraid your very presence will activate these since I've calibrated them so those with a minimal amount of magic can activate them. Our magic impaired Vhelopsi friends may even be able to use them. It might be better if I showed you away from camp." She eyed the globes, then the crowded tents. Finally, she pointed to Aistrun, Leistral, and the other bodyguards. "You lot aren't as gifted, at least not yet. You can test them for us."

Leistrun's eyes lit up. "Those look like I could use them one handed. I can manage the pulser, but it's still awkward."

Maellyn nodded. "They should work for you. After a suggestion from Celedon, we made them small enough to fit an entire arsenal into a weapon's belt."

"Thank you, Warrior!" Leistrun pumped a fist into the air. Although he tried hiding it, the loss of his arm made him feel less of a Posair warrior. He worked hard to prove his value to the team, especially to Eiden.

Eidstrun and Nelstrun grabbed a leather handle on either side of the box and carried it as they trudged away from the camp. Moraak, walking beside Histrun and Naila, eyed the box with interest. The team's Gryphon partners joined them, none of them wanting to miss out on the demonstration.

"Psst, Aistrun," Blazel whispered and gestured for his friend to walk beside him. "Test one of those lighting globes for me. I want to see how they work. Maybe I can figure out how to replicate them with my Talent."

"I've got your back, buddy," Aistrun winked. "Just let me know which ones you want to study." If Rizelya and Blazel's growing power made him jealous, he never showed it. It hadn't ever seemed to matter to him either that Chariel's Talent far eclipsed his own. He'd had his chance to be part of the Black Weave and had chosen not to participate.

This is exciting! Graak gushed. *Do you think they'll work for Gryphons? While I have my own magic, this could be fun to use, too.*

They do! Sheekeek answered. *And it's exhilarating to focus your magic through an object.*

Graak tossed him a questioning gaze.

Sheekeek lifted a wing. *I helped develop them. Try the mustard-yellow globes.* He dropped his beak into a grin, then gazed around the open area. *On second thought, maybe not. The cyclone could be devastating here.*

When they stood a good quarter measure from camp, Maendy stopped. Aistrun winked at Blazel as he approached the open box.

"Can I try the blue one?"

Maendy handed a lightning globe to him. At his touch, lightning crackled across the globe and Aistrun grinned. She instructed him on how to use it. But before he raised his hand, she glanced over at the waiting Black Weave teams. "Saffren, Noriana, be ready with your water Talent. We don't want to set the plains ablaze."

Saffren and Noriana nodded and stepped forward. Blazel's eyebrows rose when Gehan and Eiden joined them. He didn't think they needed air to fan any flames. Then he noticed both the Yellows now had blue streaks in their hair.

Maendy put her chin on her fist, studying the box. "Hmm... none of these are safe. Wisah, you know what these are capable of. Can the Black Weave contain them?"

Wisah nodded. "From what I've seen them do, I'm sure they can."

Blazel and the rest entered into a light connection within the Weave, ready to stop whatever the globes spit out, but still able to watch the demonstrations. While Aistrun tested the lightning globe, Blazel studied it with his growing mental senses. After a few times, he thought he could replicate them.

Leistrun activated a yellow globe, and a mini tornado spun across the field.

"Ooh..." Rizelya breathed. "It's almost as good as what Delestrun does with his whirlwind. I want to do that!"

Blazel leaned close to her. "I completely understand," he whispered. "I like the lightning bolts. The Malvers use something similar, and I'd like to return the favor."

Graak approached the box and turned to look at Sheekeek. *The mustard-yellow one?*

Sheekeek bobbed his head. Maendy gaped and vehemently shook her head.

Rizelya, Sheekeek said, *a shield strong enough for a cyclone would be appropriate.*

Blazel gulped. They hadn't tried to stop any weather with their net-shield. But if it held against Malviana's magic, it should hold against anything. He reached out and laid a hand on Graak's shoulder. The others also initiated physical contact with their Gryphon partners.

Eiden, Rizelya said, *since we're dealing with something made from air, why don't you lead?*

Eiden nodded, and a moment later, Blazel gaped at the golden dome enclosing two measures of open plains.

"Holy mother!" Maellyn swore. "With them, do we need these?"

"We do," Histrun assured her. "You haven't experienced what the Malvers can throw at us yet."

Graak held out the globe, targeting a tree over a measure away. "Oyt," he said.

Air spun from the globe, forming a cyclone, growing larger as it barreled down the plains. It struck the tree with a thunderous clap and sucked it into the central funnel. The cyclone contracted, and the tree splintered.

"Stop it!" Maendy ordered. The cyclone had begun expanding again.

"No, let it go," Naila countermanded. "Need to see if shield will hold."

Blazel braced for the cyclone's impact. It hit and wind battered his senses. Eiden calmly wrapped the raging cyclone with their magic and whisked away the excess energy. Within moments, the cyclone dissipated. Blazel gaped in awe at what they'd accomplished with the Weave. He trusted his teammates to never use the power available to them inappropriately. If Malviana possessed even a portion of this power, he understood the temptation for her to become a megalomaniac.

"Impressive," Naila observed.

You're right, Sheekeek, Graak crowed. *It is exhilarating.*

Moraak's tail flicked and his eyes glowed. *At some point, I want to try these new weapons. But not tonight. Others need them more than I do.*

The teams held the shield while Ambrelya and the other bodyguards took turns testing the various globes. Blazel discovered he could easily maintain the shield and study how the globes worked. Once the bodyguards finished, they stepped aside to allow the small group of Vhelopsi to try their hand with the new weapons.

Hairan hesitantly approached the globes. From his time working with the Vhelopsi during the Scourge War, Blazel knew the Vhelopsi distrusted magic and preferred to rely on what they called science. Usually, only the foulest Malvers' spells worked on them.

Hairan gingerly held a blue lightning bolt in his hand, well away from his body. "What do I do with it?"

Maendy picked up a similar one and demonstrated as she explained. "Hold it toward what you want to incinerate and say, 'Oyt.' The word activates the spell."

Hairan raised a thin golden eyebrow before stretching his arm out and saying, "Oyt." Nothing happened.

"Say it with more feeling," Maendy suggested.

He tried several times with different tones, but still the globe lay inert in his hand. His uncle Agabus, then his brother Ninsun, tried, with the same result.

Maendy scowled at them. "It should have worked."

Hairan patted the sword at his side. "It's okay, ma'am. We have our own weapons, and they're sharp enough to kill the Malvers."

With the testing complete, the teams dropped the shield. Blazel waited for exhaustion to hit him from using so much magic. Instead, he felt rejuvenated—a welcome surprise.

Histrun surveyed the various globes. "How many of these did you bring?"

"Unfortunately, not enough for everyone in the war host to have one. We have two thousand. We're working on manufacturing more."

Histrun dropped his chin onto his fist as he conferred with Naila and Moraak via mind-speech. After a few milcrons, he nodded. "This is what we'll do. Since the Black Weave teams are on the front lines, their support team should have at least one each, if not a full set. We'll dole out the rest throughout the squad-packs and flight talons to spread the new weapons across the army."

The group hurried back to the command tent, where Aistrun, Leistral, and the others chose their favored globes.

Ambrelya hooted with delight when she selected a red globe for creating mini tornadoes. She eyed Delestrun and pointed between them. "Now, we can really have some fun, Delestrun! We can crush those damned banthues between our wind funnels."

The next day, when the Malvers' air forces struck at the Posairs, the globes proved to be effective, and the Posairs killed several elder Malvers.

Blazel celebrated with the others. For the first time, hope filled him that they could defeat their ancient enemies.

Malviana - 11 de Drudar, 1076

A thrum of magic broke Malviana's reverie. She glanced to her left, where it had come from, to see Borgedier pointing ahead of them. The one thing new Malvers and Maldiers grumbled about losing was their ability to mind-speak to each other. In situations like this, Malviana wished she and her people possessed the capability. The largest village Malviana had yet seen rose like an island from the golden grass. High stone walls surrounded it and the nearby fields and pastures. Herds of horses grazing in the plains made the scene idyllic.

The shadows of the approaching army fell on the horses roaming the plains. They whinnied in fright and fled deeper into the plains. She trusted Jorvelden to note the direction the herd took. The horses would provide subsentence for those in her army who still needed flesh to survive.

Malviana guided her banthu into a sweeping circle over the town, grinning at the shouts of terror her appearance elicited. *Fitting they should cringe at my presence.* She pulled back her shoulders and laughed in triumph.

Suddenly, arrows whizzed by her head, igniting as they passed. When one grazed her hand and stuck in the saddle, Malviana's pleasure quickly turned to anger. The arrows wouldn't kill her, but they were a pain to pull out. She formed the spell's pattern within her mind, while drawing it in the air with her wand and tapping into the death magic held within her jewelry's stones. The power built, and she released the spell, directing the magic through her wand. Below her, the archers dropped their bows as they burst into flames. However, it didn't stop the fire from jumping from the wood to their hands and traveling up their arms. They collapsed to the ground and rolled, but no matter what the archers did, they couldn't extinguish the fire.

Malviana smirked. *That will teach them to fire at me!* She chuckled when women with blue hair rushed to the burning fighters, drenching them with water. Her fire was impervious to water. Malviana scowled when a woman with canary-yellow hair ran to an archer and wrapped him in a blanket of air, snuffing out the fire. She hurried to do the same to the other archers. She didn't reach three in time, and Malviana siphoned off their death essence as they died.

Other Malvers riding banthues tossed spells at the people on the wall and in the courtyards. Amid the chaos of screaming and crying people, women with various shades of red hair and wearing red leather raced outside, each carrying a helbraught. They skidded to a stop, forming several groups spaced around the courtyards and plazas. They touched the ground with the now-glowing tips of their weapons, and a line of fire zipped along the earth, creating a circle. The fires flared, and domes of fire sprouted to surround the people.

Borgedier swore when his spell disintegrated against the fire dome. The fire-shields absorbed not only his, but every spell her people threw at them. And the shields became stronger.

"Damn them to Mordar's hells," Malviana swore. "Another siege!"

She'd hoped this keep was ill-prepared and would fall to her initial onslaught. She signaled to her people to leave off the attack, led them to the plains beyond the fenced pastures and fields, and landed. Her servants quickly unloaded and raised her pavilion. Gratefully, Malviana entered the cool, dark interior and sat on a chair, rubbing her achy eyes. As she rubbed her throbbing temples, Malviana wondered if the sunlight would ever stop giving her a headache. Her servant handed her a cup of bloodwine, which she sipped as she fumed.

Morvana swept into the tent, her black hair twisted into intricate braids. Tight-fitting black leather pants encased her legs, and she wore a black velvet vest, its laces loosened. She dropped to a chair, flung a leg over the arm, and took a cup from the servant. It shook in her hand, sloshing wine over the edge of it. "How in Mordaga's name did they kill Gordelven? I thought we were immortal."

"We're not immortal, not yet." Malviana glared at her daughter's leg until, with an exaggerated sigh, Morvana dropped it to the ground. "Once we sacrifice the Supreme, we will be. Until then, protect your head."

Morvana gulped and put one hand to her throat. She hadn't seen much of the Great War before their exile. She quaffed the contents of her cup and held it out for the servant to refill. "Why did we leave the other place? We're in another siege situation. And now they have these strange weapons."

"I told you, Mordaga ordered it. Besides, this one is less well-defended."

Morvana snorted. "Those fire-shields seemed to work just fine against our spells."

Malviana waved her hand dismissively. "We can penetrate them, eventually."

"But why did we leave so quickly?" Morvana pressed. "We were starting to gain the upper hand. We could have crushed their army right there, especially after sacrificing those captured Posairs."

"You know nothing!" Malviana slammed her cup down, red drops of bloodwine cascading over its sides to puddle on the tabletop. "Didn't you see how someone attacked and killed Gelposan without being touched? That, my dear daughter, was the power of Black Talent." She studied her daughter, debating if she should tell her the terrifying truth. Finally, she decided it wouldn't serve her if Morvana acted rashly because she didn't know the danger.

"During the sacrifice, Mordaga warned me we were in great danger. We needed to leave. There is one Posair who possesses the power to kill us all. We aren't ready to face that power yet. The same power killed your father."

Morvana's face grew pale.

"We'll continue to push north," Malviana said. "These little villages aren't our goal. The Sanctuary is. Once we're there, and we sacrifice the Supreme, Mordaga has promised we will have true immortality, unlimited power, and nothing can hurt or kill us."

Morvana grinned. "I like that. How long before we leave?"

"We shouldn't be here long, only until our ground troops catch up to us. I expect the Posair army is close behind them. We'll kill those we can here, harvest their death essence, grow stronger, and move on."

The next day, Malviana called a meeting with her courtiers in her tent.

"The new fire-shields the Posairs use are a problem," she said after her advisers had settled into camp chairs and had held goblets of bloodwine. It galled her that it had thwarted her magic. "There has to be a way to destroy them. Our magic is more potent than theirs. I can't believe the Posairs have grown strong enough to stop us. The fire-shields are normal elemental magic—unlike the other one." She stared into her cup. "If I didn't know better, I'd swear they had at least one Black Talent, possibly more."

"Impossible!" Borgedier trailed a finger over his chin. "Before we were exiled, we systematically eliminated any who showed signs of the Talent. Mordaga assured us the spells he gave us would ensure the Talent didn't return. It should be extinct."

Malviana leaned forward, her cup dangling from her fingertips. "And yet, I definitely sensed Black Talent being used to create the shield at Haasneven Keep."

"What about those globe weapons?" Magdelyn asked. "I remember only Black Talent could use those before. It amazed me how many the Posairs used in the last battle. There can't be so many Black Talents reborn, can there?"

Malviana shrugged and stifled a shiver, remembering Gordelven's slow fall from his banthu. "We can't be lax or lazy, thinking those we fight now are the same weaklings as their ancestors." She took a deep breath, letting it out slowly. "Real danger is on our heels. Shandir, or someone very like her, has the device that killed Mordar."

Magdelyn's cup clattered to the ground, the dark bloodwine pooling on the carpet. "No! It can't be. I helped you shatter the device."

"Nevertheless, Mordaga showed me a vision of it. Here. It's why I now always have a cadre of hostages in front of me."

"Then it's imperative we gather as much strength as possible," Magdelyn said, "and as fast as we can. We barely managed to destroy the device last time, and then we were much, much stronger than we are now."

"I agree," Malviana nodded. "Which is why we must penetrate these damned new fire-shields."

Borgedier raised a finger. "I have some ideas on how to do that."

"Good. Show me results. Dismissed."

Malviana watched her courtiers file from the tent. She tapped a long nail against her chin. The walled villages, or keeps, as the Posairs called them, were making it difficult to decimate the Posairs like they had in the last war. Surely not everyone lived behind walls, did they? She summoned Nelieh and asked her.

"Yes, my Lady," Nelieh said. "After the war, and with the advent of the Malvers' monsters, we found the only way to survive was to live in the keeps. The walls are made from sheadash stone, which repels the monsters. They nearly destroyed the survivors of the war."

Malviana smiled. Too bad she'd left the death device on the island. She needed it to control her pets. Although they should continue to rampage the countryside without her direction, seeking Posairs to eat, as she designed them to do.

"They're also why we developed the helbraughts," Nelieh added. "They help us focus our magic better."

Malviana's smiled faded. She dismissed Nelieh. Malviana hadn't considered her pets since returning to the mainland, especially after creating the other twisted beasts. Unlike the janacks and brechas, the new creatures weren't dependent on the magic pools for their continued existence. Thinking of the untapped energy of the pools and her pets, she picked up her small scrying mirror and focused her will.

It misted over. When it cleared, it revealed a roiling mass of tentacles and spikes, ready to emerge from the nest. She panned out, trying to sense the location of these pets. The landscape had changed over the years, but she soon recognized a landmark in Andranlair Province. She frowned, then refocused. The next landmark was even farther northwest, in Ledonlair Province. *Where are the pools in the plains? There should be some. I distinctly remember one glorious battle near here. And I recall seeing them when I arrived.*

She searched again, this time focusing on the magic pools and specifying the central plains. Half a dozen dots indicating a pool of magic north of her present position and close to Strunlair Province appeared on the surface of the mirror. *Good, we're heading in that direction.* Even as she watched, one of the spots disappeared, and she dropped the mirror into her lap.

"What in Mordaga's name is going on? How can they just disappear? Nothing can cleanse the perverted magic from the land." Not even the extinct Black Talents had possessed the power. Malviana's mouth went dry. Was there a new Talent? If it could cure the malignancy in the land, what could it do to her and her people?

Wisah - 12 de Drudar, 1076

Wisah's teeth chattered in the cold, upper-atmosphere air. "Can we go down now?" she asked. Although Sheekeek had extended his nimbus of flames around her, ice crystals formed on her goggles. Moraak and Histrun had ordered him to keep her away from the skirmishes as much as possible. His smaller size allowed him to fly higher than the larger banthues and baethor. But without fur or internal fires like the Gryphons, Wisah couldn't handle the high, cold atmosphere for long, even with his radiant heat.

Sheekeek bobbed his head in acknowledgment and dropped down. The height hadn't stopped her from using her new gifts to protect her people. In the past few days, she'd learned distance wasn't an obstacle for her sigil magic. All she needed was to see her opponent to strike them with her magic.

"How much further to Haasneh Keep?" Wisah asked, rubbing her hands together to warm them. They'd left Haasneven Keep two and a half chedans ago.

Histrun estimates another three days at this snail's pace, Sheekeek said after a few wingbeats.

Fire flashed ahead of them as a Gryphon flared. The pop and crackle of pulsers followed closely. Wisah gripped her staff, and a sigil on her side tingled as she readied a spell. A grifflyn dove at them from the obscuring clouds, spewing its noxious vapors. Sheekeek flared, neutralizing the vapor. Wisah released her spell, directing it at the grifflyn. It shrieked as it strained to flap its wings, but they wouldn't respond. They snapped closed, and the grifflyn dropped like a rock. Sheekeek plunged after it, his talons outstretched. He dug them into grifflyn's neck, just behind its head, and twisted. Wisah heard a loud crack, and the grifflyn's head hung limply. With a triumphant shriek, Sheekeek released the grifflyn.

Wisah activated another sigil. She directed the plummeting body to crash on ten skeaeters lurking in the tall grass, preparing to attack a group of fighters already engaged with a pack of jallopsitor. As Sheekeek overflew the fight, Wisah's heart lurched. Hairan fired his pulser at a beast barreling toward him. A projectile slammed into the beast's chest, but it kept running at him. He fired round after round into the creature. He swore as the load of cartridges emptied, and the beast still lumbered forward. Pulling his sword from its scabbard, he held it aloft. Wisah loosed another spell, and a red-hot beam shot from her staff, spearing the creature. It took two more running steps before it toppled over at Hairan's feet. He looked up and saluted her.

Jaehaas, fighting a tall horned man with his short helstrablade, caught Wisah's attention. The Maldier's whip flicked out. A scarlet line appeared on Jaehaas's hindquarters next to several others, and blood poured from the wounds. Jaehaas tried to rear, but his hind legs collapsed, and he tumbled backward to the ground. The horned man laughed, lifting his whip to strike again.

Before Wisah readied another spell, Hairan spurred his horse forward, his sword held level in front of him aiming at the horned man's back. His opponent twisted at the last moment, ducking his head and using his horns to turn aside Hairan's blade. Metal screeched against the hard bone. Sparks flew along the edge of the blade. Sheekeek flared, but they were too high for his flames to do any good. Wisah's stomach clenched. The fighters fought too close together for her to use one of her spells.

Struggling, Jaehaas rolled to his side and fired an arrow at the enemy. It pierced the horned man's shoulder. His orange eyes blazed as he howled. He flung out his hand and shouted. A wave of magic hit Hairan. Crying out with pain, he slapped his arms and legs and rolled on the ground as if trying to rid them of some nasty pest. Wisah tossed a protective spell over him, washing away the Maldier's mind magic. Bren ran to stand over Hairan and Jaehaas, swinging her helbraught at the horned man, who leaped to the side, the blade narrowly missing his side. He snarled and flung out his hand again.

"Oh, no you don't!" Wisah growled. She crafted her own spell, creating a protective shield between her people and the enemy.

The Maldier's eyes widened when nothing happened to his intended victims, and Bren used the distraction to lunge forward, thrusting her helbraught at him. He twisted away, slamming one clawed hand down on the blade, while the other grabbed the long handle. He pulled, jerking Bren off balance. She landed hard, face smashing on the ground in front of his feet. Grinning, he lifted a wide cloven hoof.

"No!" Hairan yelled, horrified. He fumbled to aim his pulser and fired. Blood blossomed on the Maldier's knee and he howled, grabbing it. Bren scrambled out of the way, searching for her helbraught. Sheekeek dove at the Maldier, but before he reached him, a banthu swooped in and plucked him up.

Another banthu dove toward Jaehaas. The centaurs seemed to be a valuable prize for the Malvers, and they tried to capture any injured ones. Luckily, so far they'd failed. Wisah wasn't going to allow Jaehaas to be the first one to suffer under Malviana's 'tender' administrations. Sheekeek changed targets, hitting the banthu and stopping it from grabbing Jaehaas from the battlefield. Wisah released another spell, and the banthu exploded.

All over the battlefield, banthues dropped from the sky and retrieved twisted Posairs from the fighting, flying away as soon as they clutched their prize. Within milcrons, only dead or dying Malvers were left on the field. Any jallopsitor still alive fled north after the retreating army.

Wisah turned in her harness to keep Jaehaas in sight. She kept expecting him to scramble to his feet, but he just lay on the ground, his hooves twitching. "He's in trouble! Where's Kaieli?"

I'll call for her, Sheekeek said. *She'll hear me over the din.* Even as he called to Kaieli, he angled his wings to land. At the same time, Hairan and Bren reached Jaehaas. Blood oozed from his hindquarters.

"What's wrong?" Hairan asked.

"I can't feel or move my legs." Jaehaas grimaced as he strained. "Nope, still can't."

Bren covered her mouth with her hand, her eyes wide. "I've never encountered such magic. But we're dealing with many unknowns with these Malvers." She looked at Wisah as she struggled to unbuckle her harness. "Is Kaieli on her way?"

Yes, she should arrive shortly, Sheekeek said.

Wisah finally undid the last uncooperative buckle and jumped from Sheekeek's back, running to Jaehaas. She slid to the ground, disregarding the muck, to cradle Jaehaas's face in her hands.

"My love," she cried. "Please don't die on me. Don't leave me."

"I not be dying," Jaehaas assured her, his voice a mere whisper. He tried to lift his hand, but it wouldn't move.

Kaieli! Where are you? Wisah cried out.

"I'm here," Kaieli said as Keeru landed next to Jaehaas, his talons digging furrows into the ground.

Wisah watched anxiously as Kaieli examined Jaehaas. She finally sat back on her heels.

"We've seen a few of these types of injuries," Kaieli said, "although none as bad as this. I think it's because you were whipped so many times, Jaehaas. The whips carry and focus magic, similar to our helbraughts."

She poured water from a canteen over the wounds and washed the blood off. Wisah coughed and turned her head away from the stink. Green-black pus oozed from the stripes.

"I'll need help to heal this," Kaieli said, sitting back on her heels, her mouth a grim line.

"Isn't there a safe-house near here?" Hairan asked. "Should we try to move him to it?"

Kaieli shook her head. "No. It will move the poisonous magic more rapidly through his system. Help is coming."

A few milcrons later, the sky overhead darkened as seven Gryphons winged toward them. Wisah sighed in relief when she saw Rizelya and Blazel and the rest of the sabertiger Black Weave team.

"Hurry," Kaieli urged them, "before the poison reaches his heart and lungs."

Rizelya and the others formed a circle around Jaehaas, with their Gryphons sitting or crouching behind them. Wisah's breathing eased when Aistrun, Broogk, Leistral, and Eidstrun, along with their Gryphon partners, Morru and Sterkek landed and formed a protective ring around them. Overhead, Leistrun flew on Brogkek and Nelstrun on Daerik, protecting them from the air.

Wisah maneuvered around, so she cradled Jaehaas's head in her lap. His eyes rolled to the back of his head, and his breath came in shallow gasps. She gazed up at Rizelya, tears streaming down her face. "Hurry, we're losing him."

She'd watched them work the Black Weave before, but hadn't experienced it. She caught the edge of their magic and gazed in wonder at the rainbow light flowing into the circle. The light intensified, but instead of turning into a white light, it darkened into deepest black as all the colors combined. The pure magic eased her heartache.

A few milcrons later, they dropped hands and stepped away. The wounds on Jaehaas's hindquarters were closed and scabbed over, as if it had been days since his injury instead of less than an octar. Jaehaas took a deep breath, his hooves kicking out. He opened his eyes.

"Wisah," he whispered. "I thought it be a dream."

"No, my love. I'm here." She smiled and dashed the tears from her face. "We seem to do this too often. You need to quit getting so injured."

"I can't help it if predators like my horse rump," Jaehaas grumbled.

"Shh... don't talk, my love," Wisah crooned.

"But I need to tell you. I acted foolishly. I be happy for you. The next Supreme, huh?"

She glared at Rizelya. "Yes, thanks to Rizelya finding that damned book. We can talk later, somewhere more comfortable than a battlefield." She held a hand under her nose. "Someplace less smelly."

Jaehaas tried to roll to his feet, but Kaieli stopped him. "No, not yet. I don't want you moving too much until I'm sure we purged all the poison from you."

"But how will I get to Haasneh? There be several more days march to the keep." Jaehaas flung his head back with a groan, closing his eyes. "No, just no. I be not riding in that damned sling again!"

Rizelya laughed. "Too late. The Thunder Wings are here."

On cue, two huge Thunder Wings landed a few feet away.

Kaieli put a comforting hand on Jaehaas's shoulder. "It's should only be for today. There's a safe-house close by where we're staying the night. The Thunder Wings will take you there."

Jaehaas complained loudly as they jockeyed him into the sling. Wisah and Sheekeek followed them to the safe-house, where she helped him into the house and made sure he was comfortable. She cuddled into his side. They were finally alone.

"I've missed you, Jaehaas," Wisah said. "Every day I thought of you and prayed to the Mother you were safe. I'm sorry I didn't tell you when I left. It all happened so fast."

Jaehaas brushed a thumb over her cheek. "I be understanding that. Rizelya and Glork told me what happened. When the Goddess called so clearly, you had no choice but to answer her. But how can we be together? Before you became the Lady Superior, we had a chance, a small one, but one nonetheless."

"When I become the Supreme, there will be many changes," Wisah said, turning slightly to kiss the palm of his hand. "The first one is to rescind the ridiculous celibacy rule. Did you know the First Supreme had a bond-mate?"

Jaehaas shook his head.

"Well, she did. And the Goddess has a consort. There's no reason why I can't have one. And I choose you!"

"I be glad it is me. As there is no other for me." Jaehaas bent his head and kissed her deeply.

Sometimes, like now, Wisah wished he could shift fully into his man form. Even though he couldn't, she still loved him. That night, Wisah slept the best she had in lunadars, snugged against Jaehaas's chest.

Chapter 23

Blazel - 15 de Drudar, 1076

The Posair war host continued to chase the Malvers army north through the plains toward Haasneh Keep. Moraak and Histrun sent ahead a contingent of fighters to supplement Haasneh's defense force, since most of their fighters had fought in the Scourge War. Finally, seven days after Maendy joined the war host, the towers of Haasneh Keep rose from the rolling plains.

Blazel's stomach dropped when the enormous Malvers army camped in front of the gates came into view. He hoped the noncombatant evacuees had escaped before the army had arrived. Blazel had met Jaehaas at Haasneh, and he had fond memories of the keep. It appeared lopsided now, with the tops of two of the corner towers blasted away, and a large chunk torn from a third. The wall still stood strong, and even as he watched, a new barrage of fire arrows streaked from the walls to bury into numerous beasts milling nearby.

Histrun called a halt. Moraak landed beside Histrun's large stallion, making the horse rear in agitation. As Histrun brought his horse under control, Graak and Glork landed several feet away.

"You'd think as often as he sees a Gryphon he wouldn't be so skittish around them," Histrun groused.

I try to tell him we don't eat friends, Moraak said, *but the animal doesn't trust me.*

"I wonder why."

Moraak's face took on an innocent look. *I have not eaten any horses that are friends.*

"That isn't saying you haven't eaten any horses," Blazel said with a laugh as he approached his leaders. "You underestimate plains-bred horses if you think they don't know the difference." He reached out and held Rizelya's hand. He loved flying with Graak, but it didn't give him any opportunity for physical contact during the day with Rizelya.

"From what I saw, sir," Rizelya said, turning the conversation to business, "the keep is holding on and the Malvers haven't breached it yet. What's your plan?"

Histrun gazed over the field, then climbed off his horse. "Naila, give the order to make camp here. Quietly. We've finally caught up to their army. Let's hope those in Haasneh hold their attention on them for a while."

Naila strode off, shouting orders via mind-speech. The only sounds were the creak of leather as people dismounted and tents and supplies being pulled off multas. Blazel winced as a pack with cooking pots in it crashed to the ground. His head swiveled to the Malvers' army, sure they had heard the noise, but the battle with the keep's defenders still raged.

Histrun turned to Blazel. "Your friend Jaehaas is from this keep, isn't he, Blazel?"

Blazel nodded. "He is."

Naila, Histrun called. When she looked over at him he continued, *Send the centaur, Jaehaas, to me.*

A few moments later, Jaehaas cantered up to their group. Blazel's eyebrows lifted. Only a few days ago, he'd been near death. Blazel enjoyed doing more than hurting with his Talent, and loved he'd participated in saving his friend from the Maldier's paralyzing poison with the Black Weave team. The only signs of Jaehaas's ordeal were the new scars on his hindquarters and a slight limp.

"How I be of help, sir?" Jaehaas asked, saluting Histrun.

"We need a better idea of the landscape around here," Histrun said. "You know this area and the secret entrances into the keep."

Jaehaas grinned. "Aye, I do. When I be younger, I loved to escape the confines of the keep to run with the wild horses." He studied the area in front of them. "If you send a division northwest, we can surround the Malvers. Our main force here, and one there, can squeeze the Malvers into the keep, where they won't have anywhere to run."

"But can a division get by without being seen?"

Using the Gryphon invisibility spell, they can, Moraak said.

"And there be a ravine that runs there." Jaehaas pointed at the spot. "It can hide many horses traveling around the army."

Histrun nodded sharply. "Good. Jaehaas, take the Vhelopsi division. I'm also sending Dolhaas's platoon with you. Go tonight under the cover of darkness. Who are the keep alphas?"

"Telekhaas and Belistril be the alphas when I left last year."

"Try to contact them and tell them help has arrived."

Jaehaas saluted, and reared, then turning on his hindquarters, he wheeled away. Blazel sadly watched him go. Ever since the disaster caused by the Scourge's bomb, and the return of the Malvers, he hadn't spent much time with his friend. He missed him. Someday, they'd be able to sit and play their instruments together.

Blazel paused in laying out his bedroll when the sentries cried an alarm. He glanced over at his mother and the rest of the fox team. They lay curled on their cots, exhausted from the day's fighting. Blazel doubted they'd need them, but they'd rouse if they did. He, Rizelya, and the others on the sabertiger Black Weave team ran from the tent.

At the perimeter, a pack of floxidor approached. Fireshields blazed up, and the floxidor yipped, their cry answered by the much deeper howls of men in their warrior forms. Blazel relaxed. The Black Weave teams weren't needed to fight off such a small pack.

Rizelya stood with one hand on her hip and the other shielding her eyes from the setting sun, and scowled. "This doesn't seem right. We should scan the area to ensure there aren't any other surprises hiding." Even as she talked, she initiated the weaving.

There! Chariel cried, indicating the northeast. *A squad of Maldiers is trying to use the floxidor attack as a diversion to sneak past our sentries.*

Blazel's mind followed Chariel's to the spot. Five men transmogrified into hideous beasts lurked at the perimeter, led by a man melded with a large feline. His eyes glowed dark red as daylight quickly gave way to darkness. Behind him paced a wolf-like beast. Blazel gaped in horror at the creature. It brought to life all his nightmares of becoming stuck between his natural form and his warrior form. Where a warrior was a beautiful, perfect meld of human and wolf, this man was a grotesque caricature. He appeared odd, running bent over, trying to hide his height and bulk. Like most of the Maldiers Blazel had encountered over the past chedans, cruelty and evil filled the wolf-man's aura. He glanced up, and Blazel caught a glimpse of pale watery-blue eyes.

Inside the Weave, Rizelya gasped. *I know him! That's Keandran. He's alive. If you could call that hideous form living.*

Before the approaching men took another step, Rizelya slammed the net-shield down in front of them. She anchored it in the ground and extended it to cover the entire war camp. The cat-man skidded to a halt, furiously rubbing his whiskers as they smoked. Keandran snarled at him. When he noticed his companion's singed whiskers and fur, he stood to his full height of over seven feet. Malice blazed from his eyes as he glared at the shield. He pulled a knife from the belt fastened around his waist, the only article of clothing he wore. His malformed lips moved as he lifted the knife.

"No, Keandran!" Rizelya shouted, out loud and in mind-speech.

But Keandran didn't hear her as he plunged the knife into the shield. Sparks flared, and smoke hissed from the blade. Fire blazed and traveled to Keandran's paw, but he still held onto the knife, pushing it into the shield, trying to break it. Blazel refused to let an aberration win and fed more of his strength into the shield at the insertion point. With a growl of his own, he pushed back. A bright light flashed, flinging Keandran into the air. He landed hard on his side, over twenty feet away.

Dazed, he staggered to his feet, and holding his injured paw to his chest, turned tail, and lurched back toward the Malvers army, his fellow Maldiers running after him.

By then, the perimeter guards had destroyed the floxidor pack. The Black Weave team checked the area again, but didn't find any potential threats. After three lunadars of working together to form and hold the net-shield, they'd become proficient enough they could maintain it without being fully immersed in the Weave.

Blazel came back into awareness, frowning at Rizelya's stunned expression.

"Who is Keandran?" he asked.

"Keandran?" Aistrun asked, puzzled. "Where did you see Keandran?"

"He was one of the transmogrified Posairs trying to sneak into camp," Saffren said.

Rizelya's forehead wrinkled. "That was him, then. When he didn't respond to my mind-speech, I wasn't sure."

"Why should he?" Blazel asked, confused.

"He was in our first squad-pack," Aistrun explained. "But we assumed, or in most cases, hoped, he was dead. He disappeared into the swamp on our way to Strunlair Keep."

"At least now I know what happened to him." Tears brimmed in Rizelya's eyes. "Although I can't help feeling I should have done more for him, and it's somehow my fault Malviana transformed him into that hideous creature."

Saffren put an arm around Rizelya's shoulders. "You did all you could for him. So did I. He heard Malviana's call because he was attuned to it. Remember what he did to his poor horses? Only someone depraved could cause so much pain to an animal for the sheer enjoyment of it."

"I should have killed him when I had the chance," Aistrun grumbled.

"Me, too," Eidstrun growled. "The damned caitiff caused nothing but trouble." He turned to Rizelya. "Can I kill him now? He's no longer pack, if he's a Maldiers."

Rizelya only shook her head, still in shock at seeing her former pack-mate.

Blazel nodded in her stead. "He's a priority target. I've seen him before, leading the twisted Posairs."

I'll help you, Aistrun, Broogk said. **Those twisted Posairs are just as much an anathema to you as the grifflyns are to us.**

You have my help, too, Eidstrun, Sterkek added. **Between us, we should easily kill the beast.**

Later, when the fox Black Weave team awoke to take over holding the net-shield, Blazel hugged his mother tightly. The image of Keandran still haunted him.

"What's this about?" Blenora searched his face.

"Thank you."

She raised an eyebrow. "For what, exactly?"

"I realized today how lucky I am." He told her about the encounter with Keandran. "Without your loving support, and Histrun's stern guidance and mentorship, I very well could have ended up like Keandran. You kept me on the Goddess's path."

"Oh, my dear boy, it was easy on my part. You could never become a Maldiers." Blenora placed a hand on his chest. "There is too much love and goodness inside of you. I've never worried you would become a rogue wolf. I'm happy you've found a pack." She gestured at the sabertiger Black Weave team streaming into the tent, and the fox team waiting for her.

Blazel bent and kissed her cheek. Even if she refused to take the credit, he knew she'd played a major role in the man he'd become. A smile played on his lips as he watched his mother join the fox Black Weave team. They—and she—was as much a part of his pack as those on the sabertiger team. Although he hated the Malvers, the war with them had brought him closer to his mother and he'd found his pack. He'd never be alone again.

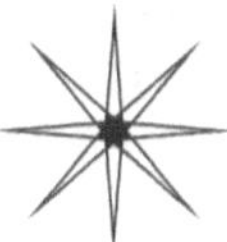

Malviana - 16 de Drudar, 1076

Malviana gaped at the sight of thirty thousand fighters, and five hundred Gryphons camped on the southern plain. She hadn't expected such a large force. When she'd first seen them, they'd been crammed into that little keep, making their numbers seem small. Her people were so few, especially since she'd split her army. Now she wished she hadn't.

But her forces were growing, even with the attrition of those few the strange Talent killed. Over a dozen Malvers and Maldiers had crept into her camp last night. New ones arrived nearly every day, coming from all parts of Lairheim. Her infection had spread nicely.

A strident howl pierced the twilight, and Malviana smiled. Malvidor's manipulation of the floxidor was magnificent. They multiplied rapidly and were effective in harrying the Posairs, as were all her children's twisted beasts. While her people may be few, her creatures outnumbered the Posairs. As long as she and her children had access to the magic pools, they could create as many beasts as they needed. However, they may not have that resource for longer. Malviana growled. The magic pools continued to disappear at an alarming rate.

Her head jerked around, seeking the thrum of energy skittering across her senses. She slowly turned until she faced the Posair army. The energy felt at once familiar and strange. Gripping her wand so tight the gemstones bit into her hand, she sought the source of the disturbance. It didn't take long to find it.

A young woman's aura shone like a beacon, glowing a dark indigo. Malviana scowled. *What is she? That isn't Black Talent. I've never encountered anything like it before.* She sucked in a breath at the power the woman barely constrained. It rivaled Malviana's. In a moment of unusual self-awareness, she admitted the woman's power eclipsed her own. After studying the woman's energy for several milcrons, Malviana finally decided her adversary wasn't Shandir, but someone new and unknown.

At the woman's side, another energy source pulsed, reaching across the space for Malviana. When it touched her, she screamed and toppled to the ground, curling into a ball. Pain—unlike anything she'd experienced, even while being tortured by Mordar—assailed her. Her heartbeat thudded in an ever-slowing rhythm. Fire made each breath an agony. The magic ripped pieces of her essential self from her, leaving festering, raw wounds, dripping acid and burning her alive.

She was dimly aware of when Morvana and Magdelyn raced to her side and threw their most powerful shields around her. Finally, the attack subsided, and Malviana lay panting and trembling, breathing in the dusty, dry earth.

"Mother, what happened?" Morvana asked, concern clear in her voice.

"It..." Malviana swallowed, her throat dry and her tongue swollen. The residual taste of coppery blood filled her mouth. Magdelyn handed her a canteen, and she gulped the contents, wrinkling her nose at drinking water instead of bloodwine. Magdelyn slipped behind her and helped her to sit up.

Malviana tried again. "It... it was the unmaking device."

Magdelyn gasped. "No! How did the woman find you?"

"She didn't. I found her... and the device. It sought me out on its own." Malviana pushed her hair from her face, surprised to find her hand still whole. "If the woman had been directing it, or if you hadn't shielded me from it, I'd be dead."

"Then we must leave tonight," Morvana said. "We need you to perform the final sacrifice to Mordaga." She held out a silver flask.

Malviana sniffed it, relieved at the scent of bloodwine. She took a large gulp, and a bit dribbled down her chin. She wiped her mouth with a shaky hand. "We can't leave until I regain my strength. Have Keandran bring me three Posairs to sacrifice. As soon as I'm recovered, we'll continue north and try to stay ahead of the Posairs and this woman who wields the device."

She tried to push to her feet. It galled her that she needed Magdelyn and Morvana to help lift her up and support her the few feet to her tent. She grimaced at the thought of someone in her army noticing her momentary weakness.

Within a couple of octars, Keandran strode into the tent with the three captives. This night, Malviana wouldn't be sharing their death essence with her courtiers—or even her daughter. It appalled her how much the device drained her after only a few moments. She couldn't imagine the depths of agony Mordar must have suffered before his end. And she had suffered much pain in her long life. She plunged her hands into the first man's beating heart. As she let the ecstasy wash over her, she prayed Mordaga would give her a way to stop the woman and capture or destroy the device. She'd just experienced how vulnerable she was to it—and to death.

In the gray light of predawn, Borgedier helped Malviana climb onto her banthu. She still suffered from her ordeal, even with the death essence flowing through her from her sacrifices last night. She left enough troops behind to keep the Posairs from following her and her courtiers too closely as they raced north. Her harrowing experience made it even more imperative for her to gain the last bit of immortality Mordaga promised.

Malviana shivered at how close the specter of death had hovered over her. She still felt its cold breath on her neck. She huddled deeper into her cloak. For once, she looked forward to the coming sunlight and heat.

Chapter 24

Rizelya - 43 de Drudar, 1076

Finally, after three chedans of intense fighting, the Posair army crossed the boundary between Haasneh and Haasper Territories. Only one more territory to cross, and they'd enter Rizelya's home territory. Under normal circumstances, it would only take two to three days to travel through Haasper Territory, then another five, and she'd be home. Rizelya glared in the direction of the Malvers army. Unless something happened, they'd reach it before her. She and Blazel walked to the command tent to report to Histrun and Moraak about the day's skirmishes. Rizelya wanted to ask Histrun to allow her and the Black Weave team to fly ahead. Strunland Keep was his home too—and Naila's. They'd want to protect it.

Ants crawled in her stomach as Blazel gave the commanders their report. Rizelya couldn't put forward her request until after the day's battle reports. Before she gathered her courage to ask, a messenger stumbled into the tent. Dust and grime covered the young man's face, and a cut on his cheek oozed blood. His clothing was little more than rags. Rizelya hurried to fill a cup with water and handed it to the young man, who gulped it down.

"Sir," the young man said, "I have news from Haaswyndir Keep."

"Go on, son," Histrun encouraged.

"Our Keep Alpha feared the Malvers would storm across our lands. After sending most of our fighters to the war front, we couldn't defend the keep, so we evacuated. The nearest Territory Keep to ours is Andranlyn, where we thought we'd find safety. The first two days went smoothly, and we crossed the Borleano River. We didn't even encounter any Malvers' monsters. However, things changed on the third day. We'd almost reached the safe-house twenty measures from Andranlyn Keep, when giant creatures appeared above us and nasty, canid-like beasts surrounded us.

"Our warriors and Reds fought, but our small force was sorely outnumbered. I'm not a warrior. I tend the sheep flocks, but I fought as best I could. Somehow, we reached the safe-house, closed the gates, and hid inside. But it didn't do any good." The young man stared into his cup for a few moments, tears streaming down his face.

Despair radiated from him, and Rizelya's heart lurched. She gritted her teeth, preparing for a gruesome tale.

The young man took another drink. "The winged beasts just flew over the wall. With a blast of magic, the door to the safe-house disintegrated. A creature who looked like a strange mix of a badger and a man led the charge inside. He attacked my friend, one of the few of us left who could maintain their warrior form, and the two fought. At first, my friend was winning, but then the badger-man threw a lightning bolt at him. He fell to the ground, writhing in excruciating pain.

"A man with gray skin and hair, holding an onyx wand encrusted with jewels, stepped through the door. He smirked when he took in my friend's agony. My... my lover blasted him with her fire magic, but it just washed over him, not even singeing his clothing. He waved his wand, and she started choking, and blood poured from her nose and ears. I tried to fight, but one of the Malvers pointed his wand at me, and suddenly, I couldn't move. I could barely breathe. I watched my beloved die, while the man—the others called him 'my lord Mordeven'—laughed. They subdued and tied up everyone who still lived. Mordeven told us we were now his slaves and servants. He and his people raped the women, and a number of the men. At midnight, he staked my friend out in the courtyard... and... and..." The young man's face drained of all color, and horror shone through his eyes. "Sir, he sacrificed him! He cut him open and—"

"How did you escape, son?" Histrun broke in. Rizelya was glad he did. She didn't want to hear any more gruesome details. She couldn't imagine watching a friend be killed so horribly. It sounded even worse than anything the Scourge had done, and she'd thought they had been evil incarnate. She'd been wrong.

The man gulped more water, although his hands still shook, and swayed on his feet. "They did something to our minds to make us docile and follow their orders, but for some reason, it didn't work on me. I pretended it did, though, and when we marched north, I managed to slip away. They had hundreds of Posairs with them, from several keeps, including Posanlair Clan Keep and Andranlyn Keep. It wouldn't have done us any good to reach it. It had already fallen."

Histrun put a hand to his face. They'd been so caught up in their own battles, they hadn't considered what else was happening in Lairheim. "When did this happen?"

"I... I don't know," the man stammered. "We left Haaswyndir Keep on 20 de Drudar. And it's taken me a long time to reach you."

"You're safe now, young man," Keshanal said. She motioned toward the tent door, where Bethlyn waited. "Bethlyn will see to your wounds."

The healer escorted the young man away.

"Damn! They split up their army," Histrun said. "But into how many forces?"

I will send reconnaissance teams to sweep the land east of here, Moraak said. *They will find them.*

"Send another team to the west, across the Storengher River," Histrun suggested. "We need to determine if they have a third force gathering people."

"But why would they, sir?" Blazel asked. "What's the purpose of capturing so many people?"

You heard him, Moraak grumbled, and rubbed his cheek with a talon. *Slaves and sacrifices.*

"It's more than that," Wisah added. She'd been sitting quietly off to the side. As the Lady Supreme, she was as much a leader of their people as Histrun and Keshanal. "The Malvers need to fuel their magic with death. Those people will eventually become sacrifices to their evil god, Mordaga. Some, if their hearts and minds hold evil, will turn into either Malvers or Maldiers."

"We must protect our people." Histrun stroked his beard. "But is it wise for us to split up our force as well and chase down these other Malvers?"

Blazel strode to the table with the map of Lairheim on it and studied it. "While this Malvers' faction has gone east and into Andranlair Province, they are still traveling north. Where are they going? What's so important to them that is in the north?"

Wisah stood up and paced the tent, the lantern light catching the crystal on the end of her staff. After a few moments, she stopped at Blazel's side and stared at the map. Her face paled as she placed her finger on it. "There. They are going to the Sanctuary. The records indicate it was Malviana's and Mordar's goal during the Great War. It seems her goal hasn't changed despite the intervening years."

"Then we can stop them!" Histrun said. "There's only one way into the White Mountains, and that's through Strunhelos Pass."

"But they have flying beasts," Rizelya interjected. "Can't they simply fly over the mountains?"

Moraak shook his head. *We had to fly through the pass on our way from the Deep Mountains. The mountains all around it are too high for even us to fly over.*

"It didn't seem like it when we traveled through," Rizelya said, frowning.

Wisah's fingers trailed on the map, pausing where the pass began. "You didn't notice because the tunnel takes us through the mountain. There's a magic barrier similar to the one that kept the Malvers on their island. Although it's weakening. I don't have the strength to restore it by myself. But—" she searched Rizelya and Blazel's faces "—from what I've seen you and your Black Weave do, I believe together we can rebuild it."

"Should we travel to Strunhelos ahead of the army?" Blazel asked, turning to lean against the table.

Histrun shook his head emphatically. "No. We need you with us."

"But you'd still have the fox Black Weave team."

"We need both teams here. Malviana leads this army, and she has too much magic for only one Black Weave team to counteract. However, now we know where they're headed, we can stop chasing them."

Histrun rubbed his jaw and stood up. Striding to the map, he gazed at it for a long moment. He placed a set of markers where the previously unknown Malvers force had attacked Andranlyn Keep. Another set marked the direction the main Malvers army marched. Which now he'd laid it out, Rizelya noticed the route was on a direct path to Strunhelos. After a moment, Histrun put a set on the west side of the Storengher River in Ronanlair Province. He motioned for the others to gather around the table.

"If we split our forces like this, we can cover all the Malvers army we're aware of, or suspect, exists. It weakens the main force, but our numbers are greater than theirs. They have stronger magic than we do, but the new weapons Maendy brought us are making a difference."

Let me send scout parties first, Moraak said, *then we will know what size the splinter forces need to be. It would be detrimental to send too small of a force or even too large and leave the main war host vulnerable.*

Histrun gave a curt nod. "That makes sense." He studied the map, stroking his beard. "Strunhelos is the strongest defensive fortress we have. It stopped the Malvers in the last war against them. I don't see why it won't now. This is where we'll push to make our stand. The pass will be at our backs. The valley is wide, giving us room to maneuver."

Moraak tapped on the pieces indicating the known Malvers army. *If we keep a smaller force following them, it will make them think we are still chasing them. Send a large portion of our war host directly to Strunhelos.*

"It might work."

"But at what cost?" Keshanal objected. She pointed to the numerous keeps in the Malvers' army's path, one of which was Rizelya's home keep, Strunland. "Do we sacrifice these keeps and let the Malvers raze them?"

Rizelya's heart dropped to the soles of her feet. How could Histrun even consider letting the Malvers demolish their home keep? She remembered the dreams she'd had of the Malvers' monsters attacking her home lunadars ago during the Scourge War. She still didn't know if it had happened or if it was a foreshadowing of what was to come.

"We can't let them fall, sir," Rizelya said. "Too many people remain in those keeps. It would give the Malvers too much power." She held her breath, waiting for his answer.

"We can't make any decisions or plans until we determine how large the Malvers' factions are. Moraak, send your scouts. We'll continue to chase the Malvers. We're headed to the same place. There aren't many routes the Malvers can take to reach Strunhelos from here."

Strunland Keep was right in the army's way, blocking its path to Strunhelos. Rizelya would soon see her home again, but what state would it be in when she finally did?

Rizelya - 49 de Drudar, 1076

The Posair war host stopped on a grassy knoll to make camp for the night. Over the past six days, they'd only traveled thirty hard-won measures northward. Even though the Posairs hadn't penetrated Haasper Territory much, neither had the Malvers. Rizelya glanced up from tying off the tent rope. Faekeek, the lead scout of the Gryphons sent east, fluttered to a lopsided landing near the command tent.

"The scouts are back," Rizelya said, finishing tying the knot. "I want to hear what they found."

Blazel tugged the opposite rope taunt and staked it into the ground. "I'll come with you."

"Yeah, leave us working," Aistrun growled, then ruined it with a grin. "Be sure to tell us the latest news. Hopefully, it's good news. We haven't had any in a long time."

"I doubt it is," Rizelya said, dusting her hands off on the seat of her pants. "Faekeek looked awful when he landed."

Rizelya and Blazel jogged the few feet to the command tent and slipped inside.

We found a large force marching here, Faekeek said, pointing a talon at a spot on the map near Andranlair Clan Keep.

Rizelya gasped as Histrun placed a token to mark the place. The Malvers force only had about 300 measures to traverse before crossing into Strunville Territory. If their destination was Strunhelos, they'd turn northwest before reaching Strunheim Territory. She could attest the route from Strunheim and Strunven was mountainous, treacherous, and dangerous. Rizelya shuddered, remembering the frightening scramble across a scree-filled path where she nearly lost Aistrun.

Histrun's mouth pulled into a grim line. "How many do they have?"

Roughly a third the size of the army we saw at the eastern fortress. A Malvers weapon had scorched the left side of Faekeek's cheek, as well as his left wingtips. Blood and pus oozed from the burns. Rizelya winced. They had to hurt him, but he still stood tall in front of his prince, making his report. *They have four hundred banthues, each carrying a Malvers, five hundred baethor, and fifty of the awful grifflyns. On the ground, two hundred Maldiers marched, and at least three hundred each of the various creatures at their command.*

"What of captives?" Keshanal asked, leaning forward on her camp stool. Strands of her pale pink hair escaped from her tight bun to frame her wrinkled face. "Did you see any? How many of our people have they captured?"

Faekeek started to scratch his cheek with a talon, stopping himself as he sucked in a pained breath. *We counted several hundred. We flew along their back trail.* He pointed out the route on the map as he talked. *Every keep south from where we found them through Posanlair Province to here has been razed.*

Rizelya gasped. He'd pointed as far south as Posandelvindir Keep, which was nearly to the Barrens.

"My home? Vhelkansti?" Hairan asked, his eyes wide with fear. He'd watched from the sidelines, not knowing the geography of Lairheim. "My wife... many of our women carry children."

It still stands, Faekeek said gently.

"Oh, thank you, Great Vheldura!" Hairan sank onto his knees with his hands clasped together.

Rizelya now understood how much of a difference the two Black Weave teams made in the fight against the Malvers. Numerous keeps in both Posanlair and Andranlair Provinces located along the route he'd indicated had fallen to the Malvers' magic. Those keeps should have been strong enough to defend against their foe.

Histrun drew a line on the map, indicating the expected route the eastern division would take to reach their final destination of Strunhelos. Keshanal leaned forward, watching him, and her face paled. The route took this secondary army right through her former territory of Strunell, and then close to the Strunlair Clan Keep.

"Do we chase them or put a force in front of them to try to stop them?" Keshanal asked.

Wrinkles creased Histrun's forehead as he studied the map. "It depends on what the scouts sent west of the Storengher River tell us. Have you had any word from them, Moraak?"

They return. Moraak's deep voice rumbled in Rizelya's head. *They should arrive within the octar. They do not have good news.*

While they waited for the scouts, they discussed their various options for splitting up the war host. When the scouts arrived, they too reported a third Malvers army marched through Ronanlair Province, also razing keeps, taking captives, and leaving a swath of destruction in their wake.

We found the army here, near Ronanlyn Keep, the lead scout, Polkeek said, tapping the map with his talon.

With this news, Histrun and Moraak decided they had to split the war host. They couldn't allow the two advancing armies to continue to take captives or destroy homes. Two hundred Gryphons carrying a Posair fighter, or in the case of the Thunder Wings, several Posair fighters, would fly ahead to Strunlair Province. Once there, they'd gather as many fighters as possible. Then they'd go to Strunell Keep, where they hoped to stop the eastern splinter force. The Gryphons would fly additional fighters from Andranlair to Strunhelos to bolster the garrison. They'd send another flight of Gryphons west to

Keistanlair and Ledonlair to fly fighters to join the Ronanlair fighters at the bridge over the Storengher River to Strunhelos. Their mission was to hold the Malvers' western force from crossing the river.

Rizelya, Blazel, and the two Black Weave teams would continue with the main war host as they chased Malviana and her army through Haaslair Province and into Strunland Territory. It took every bit of Rizelya's self-control—and quite a bit of Blazel's convincing—to remain with the troops rather than have Graak fly her to Strunland Keep. She desperately wanted to discover how her home fared.

Over the next few chedans, as they marched north, Rizelya worried about her friends left in the keep. Were they still alive?

Chapter 25

Wisah - 12 de Godar, 1076

As the heat of summer gave way to the beautiful, mild days of autumn, Wisah rode at Jaehaas's side whenever possible. Many in the war host questioned both her involvement with Jaehaas and her presence in the army, but she didn't care. She was determined to make him her consort, and she knew she was the only one who could kill Malviana.

A few times over the past chedans, as their armies clashed, Wisah and Malviana had flung spells at each other. Each time, Wisah sensed the unmaking device thrum to life. But she hesitated to fully activate it, fearing irrevocably harming the souls of the Posairs fighting between them. She didn't dare practice using the terrible spell. Simply reading what it could do had frightened her. And that had been in the hands of a normal Black Talent, not someone with her unknown powers. She would only use it when she and Malviana finally faced each other on the battlefield. The closer they marched to Strunhelos, the more anxious Wisah became, knowing the showdown between them also grew nearer.

Sudden movement caught Wisah's attention. She glimpsed the waving antennae of a dozen skeaeters. A grotesque combination of Posair and lizard rose from the tall grass directly in front of her, startling her horse, Telen, into whinnying and rearing. Wisah clutched the reins and squeezed her legs tight around Telen's sides to stay in the saddle. If she fell off, the skeaeters and Maldier would tear her to pieces, even with her new magic.

The crystal on her staff glowed with dazzling light, and the skeaeters keened a high-pitched click as they backed away. A sigil on her thigh flared to life, and the crystal in her headband warmed. She lowered her staff, pointing it at the nearest skeaeter. A beam of red light leaped from the crystal, cutting the skeaeter in half. Everywhere the beam touched, skin, bones, and muscle hissed, and blood quickly coagulated.

Telen twisted to the side, kicking a floxidor with his hind feet. Wisah gagged at the sickening sound of crushed bones. But she clamped her teeth shut against the bile rising in her throat. The destruction and death war brought made her sick, and she hated to kill. But this was the price she paid to ride with Jaehaas and the Vhelopsi rather than fly with Sheekeek. Wisah held the image of the temple mural, depicting the Goddess as a warrior, in her mind's eye. It reminded her there were times when death was necessary to preserve life.

The lizard-Maldier snapped its long jaws at Telen. Its black whip snaked toward her horse's neck. It would kill him if it touched him. Screaming defiance, Wisah pointed her staff at the Maldier. A sigil on her forearm flared, and a sonic wave traveled down her arm, to the staff, and out of the crystal. The sound wave crashed into the Maldier's chest, knocking him backward several feet to land in front of Hairan. He raised his sword, and Wisah turned her head away, unable to watch. When she looked back, Hairan had spun from the headless Maldier to face six floxidor racing toward them. She used the sonic wave again to knock a few down, giving him a chance to fight. An arrow thudded into the side of a floxidor as it leaped at Hairan. In quick succession, Jaehaas fired four more arrows, each taking down a floxidor. Hairan thrust his sword into the last one.

Wisah turned Telen in a tight circle, surveying the area, but the raid was over. A number of Posairs moaned, clutching at various wounds. The souls of three Posair dead rose from their former bodies and looked around, stunned. Wisah quickly opened the veil between the worlds. The warm light on the other side beckoned to the souls, and they sped through it. As soon as the last soul crossed, the veil snapped shut.

She turned her attention to the dead Maldier, waiting for his soul to leave the body. But nothing happened. Fighting her squeamishness, she nudged Telen closer to the Maldier. She activated her spiritual sight and probed the body. A small, foul thing skittered away. Wisah hurled a magical net around it, keeping it from escaping. She slowly stepped out of the saddle, making sure the thing stayed caught in her net. Squatting, Wisah examined it, then flung the back of her hand over her mouth, turning her head and gagging. The only thing remaining of Maldier's soul was the awful, black blob. She couldn't allow anything so loathsome through the veil and into the presence of the Goddess. *But what am I supposed to do with it?*

"What be you looking at?" Jaehaas asked, nearly stomping on the blob.

Wisah flung out a hand to stop him. "Don't come any closer. It's the Maldier's soul."

Jaehaas's forehead crinkled, but he stayed where he was. "I don't see anything except his body."

"Understandable. You don't have any White Talent."

The thing struggled against her net in an effort to reach Jaehaas's hooves. She suspected it would infect anyone who came into contact with it and contaminate their soul. She glanced around the battlefield and saw Bren burning the floxidor and skeaeter corpses.

"Bren! Come over here!" Wisah called. When Bren arrived, she pointed at the blob. "Burn that for me."

"Burn what?" Confusion wrinkled her brow. "I don't see anything except dirt."

"Oh, bother." Wisah pursed her lips, concentrating. She held her hand high above the soul-thing and activated the sigil for making the unseen visible. Both Bren and Jaehaas gasped when the net glowed dark blue, revealing the blob inside.

"That be hideous." Jaehaas made a disgusted face. "That be the Maldier's soul?"

Wisah nodded. "The transmogrification spell Malviana uses not only changes the shape of the person, but does this to their soul. I can't let this cross the veil. It's pure evil now. There is nothing good or right left in it."

"And you think my fire Talent will destroy it?" Bren sounded doubtful.

"I hope so."

Bren pointed her helbraught at the soul-blob. A blast of orange-red flames erupted, encapsulating the thing. She kept it going for a full milcron. When she released the fire, the soul-thing still wriggled inside Wisah's net.

"It didn't do anything to it," Bren sighed. "Doesn't it take the Crone's fire to purify a soul?"

Wisah absently nodded as she crouched again, frowning at the blob. How many Maldiers they believed dead had corrupted good people?

What Bren said finally hit her. "Crone's fires..." Wisah repeated softly, then lifted her hands and arms, studying her tattoos. One on the inside of her right arm, just above her elbow, caught her eye: the sigil for Crone's Fires. She abruptly stood and gestured to Bren and Jaehaas. "Step back. Farther. Farther. I don't know how big this will be, or if it will work."

She gazed at the sigil on her arm, mentally drawing it over the blob. The tattoo flared with indigo light at the same time the sigil burst into the air, glowing dark purple. It transformed into a pillar, surrounding the soul-thing. Wisah threw up an arm to shield her eyes from the brightness and activated another sigil to form a barrier between her and the Crone's fire. It continued to burn for five milcrons, then a quarter octar. Finally, half an octar later, the light dimmed and went out. Nothing remained, not even Wisah's magic net.

"It be gone!" Jaehaas said, patting Wisah on the back.

"It is," she agreed. "But it took a long time and Crone's fire. I didn't think I had the power to create that type of magic."

"We need to leave," Bren said. "It isn't safe to tarry much longer."

Wisah brushed off her hands and climbed onto Telen's saddle. As she rode next to Jaehaas, she pondered about the obscene magic it took to do such evil to the Maldier's soul. Over the past few chedans, she and others had noticed it didn't matter how many Maldiers and other creatures they killed, more always seemed to take their place. Wisah thought

Malviana was working her death magic to produce more—there certainly was enough death from all the fighting to fuel it. But now, Wisah wondered if the cause could be something much simpler.

"I think we keep fighting the same creatures over and over," she told Jaehaas. She explained her theory to him.

"If you be right, Histrun needs to hear this."

"But I don't know what to do about it. I can't be at every battle scene to burn the vile souls with Crone's fire."

"Be there someone else who could help you?"

Wisah started to shake her head. She'd never heard of anyone, not even the Supreme, who could do what she'd just done. Then she remembered the miraculous things the Black Weave teams were doing. Perhaps they could help. Rizelya and Blazel were becoming quite powerful in their own right, as were Chariel, Blenora, and the others on the teams. Based on their changing appearance, they were transforming into Black Talents from their constant use of the Black Weave magic.

As soon as the horse-master picketed Telen for her, Wisah hurried to the command tent and explained her discovery to Histrun, Moraak, and Keshanal.

"You're telling me we keep killing the same creatures over and over again?" Histrun asked, horror filling his voice.

Wisah nodded. "I think so. Their souls don't, can't, cross the veil, and if their body isn't too damaged, they reanimate it. I believe if it is, they invade a passing Posair with enough dissatisfaction or hate in them and take control of them."

Keshanal scrubbed her face in her hands, her eyes taking on a haunted look. "It may explain why good people are suddenly turning on their friends. We've had several incidences since leaving Haasneh Keep. It's like they become rabid animals."

"In a sense, they are." Wisah's jaw tensed at the news. Her dislike of Malviana grew the more she learned about the woman.

"Do the other creatures, the floxidor and such, infect our people too?" Keshanal asked.

"No." Wisah shook her head. "They are simple animals who've had their minds and bodies twisted. Their souls cross the veil."

Histrun rubbed his palms on his trouser leg. "So how do we kill them, permanently?"

"The same way we do the Malvers. Decapitate them or mutilate their body so much they can't be reanimated. Bren tried burning a soul-thing with her fire, but it didn't have any effect. Crone's fire worked by purifying the soul, which allowed it to cross the veil. I can create it." She glanced down at the sigil for it on her arm. "But my magic is different now. I don't know if anyone else can."

There are too many Maldiers' deaths in each skirmish or battle for you to be expected to destroy them alone, Moraak observed. He tilted his head to the side. *Perhaps our fire will burn these putrescent souls.*

Wisah shrugged. "If any could, it would be Sheekeek's or another mystic."

He is the only mystic who joined the army. Moraak's feathers drooped. *I tried to bring more, but he is the only one who dared brave the Malvers' evil. Unfortunately, I was not in a position to order any to come who did not volunteer.*

"It's possible the Black Weave teams can create Crone's fire. They do many things we previously thought impossible. I'll talk to them when we finish our meeting."

Histrun exchanged glances with his co-leaders, then gave a curt nod. "I think we're done here. We can't do much more except tell our people to brutalize the Maldiers' bodies." He shuddered. "I hate the thought of doing that. It makes us as bad as the Malvers."

Wisah leaned on her staff, and its crystal caught the lantern light, casting rainbows on the tent walls. "No, it doesn't. We don't feed on the blood or flesh of our enemies or serve a god of destruction and hate. Even after everything the Maldiers and Malvers have done, the Goddess and Her Consort will allow their souls to cross the veil once they are purified. They're given a chance to redeem themselves and to remember the divinity within them."

Your wisdom shines bright, my Lady Superior. Moraak dipped his head to her.

Wisah flushed and stood to leave. It disconcerted her when everyone else in the tent stood and made the gesture of obeisance reserved for the Supreme. She swallowed her embarrassment and blessed them. It would take a long time for her to become used to her new office.

She strode from the command tent in search of Rizelya and her team. At least Rizelya still treated her the same. She smiled as Jaehaas appeared out of the shadows to walk by her side. She linked her hand in his. A small tattoo on her left wrist glowed azure in the dark, and a moment later, her staff's crystal glowed softly, lighting their way. She wasn't like any other Supreme before her, not even the first one.

The strains of a Vhelopsi stringed instrument floated through the camp. Their world was changing—had changed. The new Supreme had to change with the world, and it started now, with her loving Jaehaas.

Wisah paused and stood on tiptoe to kiss Jaehaas's cheek. This was the first change of many in her rule as Supreme. Peace filled her, and she sensed the Goddess's presence.

Blazel - 12 de Godar, 1076

Blazel shivered at the cool breeze coming in from the open tent door. Dread skittered down his spine when he took in Wisah's face. Whatever happened during the day's battle didn't bode well.

"What's wrong?" Rizelya asked, hurrying to guide Wisah to a camp stool.

"I discovered something terrible about the Maldiers today."

As Wisah told them about the soul-thing, horror filled Blazel. All this time, they'd believed they'd killed the awful creatures, and instead, kept fighting the same ones.

"It's like what we discovered with the Malvers' monsters," Dehali observed, running a hand through her dark hair. Only a few strands of her original strawberry blond remained. "Until the first team cleared the malignant pool, we believed we killed the monsters when we fought them. Instead, they just slunk back to the malignant pools to regenerate."

"Would cleansing the pools work for the Maldiers?" Grazeen asked.

"No," Rizelya said. "The Bear Black Weave team traveled this route on their way to Strunlair Province. They'd have cleansed any pools in the area. I haven't sensed any."

"The Malvers' monsters are magical constructs." Ardela crossed her arms over her chest and stretched out her legs. Even she had changed since becoming part of the Fox Black Weave team. Her eyes had darkened to black, and her gray hair was a deep, warm charcoal, with silver strands running through it. "The Maldiers were once people, and therefore, have souls. From what I sense from Wisah's description, the magic Malviana uses to transmogrify them affects them at the soul level first. The outer transformation of twisted Posair and animal is a reflection of their soul, their inner essence."

"Bren's elemental fire Talent didn't do anything to it," Wisah said. She glanced at her right arm.

Blazel blinked when a sigil above her elbow glowed indigo. By now, he should be used to Wisah's unusual Talent, but once in a while, it still took him by surprise. He inwardly laughed. His new Talent, using his mind to kill, certainly wasn't usual.

"Is that the sigil for Crone's Fire?" he asked. Although the Posairs didn't usually use sigils, he'd read about them in the Sanctuary library. The sigils were remnants of their ancestor's early writing—and apparently magic.

Wisah nodded. "It's what finally destroyed the Maldier's soul. But I can't be everywhere and purge any rancorous souls left on the battlefield by myself. That's where you—" she pointed to the two Black Weave teams "—come in. I'm hoping with your growing power, you can create Crone's Fires within the weave, if not individually."

Blenora's face drained of color, highlighting her now dark gray eyes. Once, they'd been a soft, dove gray. "That type of soul magic is reserved for the Supreme. Only they can determine when someone has committed such evil their soul can't cross the veil. Even if we could create Crone's Fire, it is blasphemous for us to use it. We aren't the Goddess's avatar like the Supreme."

"I am the Lady Supreme." Wisah touched her pendant of office. The diamond flared, filling the dim tent with rainbow light. She stood, gripping her staff, which was suddenly in her hand, and not by the door where she'd left it. "It is by my decree you shall use this power to cleanse my land and my people of the curse Mordaga has brought to my world."

Blazel shivered as chills ran from the top of his head to his feet. Wisah spoke with the Goddess's voice. He dropped to his knees and made the gesture of obeisance. The rustling of fabric told him the others also knelt before their new spiritual leader and avatar of the Goddess.

The tent rustled, and the Gryphons on the Fox team appeared. Somehow, they all fit without knocking anything over or scrunching the people.

"Fox team," Wisah, as the Goddess, continued, "you are my chosen to heal my people of this curse. Come forward, and be blessed."

Blazel sank to his butt. Wonder filled him as he watched first his mother, then each member of the Fox Black Weave team, including the Gryphons, step forward. Wisah drew the Crone's Fire sigil over their heads. Dark purple light swirled around the Goddess's chosen. It plunged into them, and as one, they threw their heads back and cried out. When the light faded, the Posairs each sported a sigil tattoo on their right arm above the elbow, in the exact place where Wisah's tattoo was. Blueek, Blenora's partner, squawked and held out his right wing. In the juncture of his shoulder blazed an azure tattoo, burned into his fur.

"It is done," Wisah intoned.

Her eyes rolled to the back of her head, and Blazel scrambled to catch her before she slammed into the ground.

Raeleen, who was usually quiet and stayed in the background, held out her arm. "Wow! Just wow! So much power is pulsing through me." The sigil tattoo pulsed, and azure light danced over Raeleen's body. When it faded a moment later, the myriad scars covering her from working the sheadash stone had disappeared.

"I know what you mean," Gehan crowed with delight. She did a little jig. Her previously grass green eyes had darkened to a deep forest green. Now they also glowed with an inner purple light.

Blazel glanced around at the Goddess blessed. All their eyes contained the same purple glow, even the Gryphons. Briefly, he wondered if it was permanent, or only the residual effects of the Goddess's magic.

"I know exactly what we need," Gehan continued, "to do to cleanse the malignancy from the Maldier's souls. While we can generate Crone's Fires alone, our power is greater together."

Noriana nodded enthusiastically. "Together, we can clear an entire battlefield. But for small skirmishes, we can do it individually. The Goddess is wise."

Wisah moaned. Blazel helped her sit up, and she immediately put her head between her knees. After several milcrons, she lifted her head. "Channeling the Goddess has its price. A raging headache and nausea!" She gripped her stomach and moaned.

Kaieli rushed to her and placed her hands on either side of Wisah's head. Bronze light spilled from her palms, and in a moment, Wisah took a deep breath.

"Thanks. That helped." She gazed around at the Fox team, wonder in her eyes. "Even I didn't expect that to happen. I'm learning what it really means to be the living avatar of the Goddess. When she wills, she can step into my body and affect the physical world. Although she assures me it only happens when absolutely necessary."

Rizelya rubbed her arms. "I'm glad, niece, you're the next Supreme, and not me! I'm having enough troubles dealing with my newfound powers, let alone those of the Goddess."

The next day, after the battle ended, and the Malvers retreated, the Fox Black Weave team flew over the battlefield. They spread out in a complicated pattern. At Blenora's signal, they lifted their hands, drawing the Crone's Fire sigil in the air. The Gryphons drew it with their talons. The glowing sigils merged, and dark purple light fell like rain on the battlefield. Wherever it touched the body of any Maldier—or Malvers—it blazed into a pillar of purple light. Depending on the state of the soul, the pillar burned for a few milcrons to over an octar. Those whom the light bathed for a few milcrons crossed the veil, returning to the Goddess's arms. However, the Crone's

Fire completely annihilated the soul of those who took longer to burn. They'd crossed the bounds, making redemption impossible. Or, as Wisah told them later, the souls refused to be redeemed.

When Blazel reported to Histrun and Keshanal, Histrun slumped in his seat. "Does this mean we don't have to mutilate the Maldiers?"

Blazel nodded. "As long as the Crone's Fire touches the bodies, they won't affect our people. The Crone's Fire either purifies or destroys the Maldier, by the Goddess's will and their own actions."

"Thank Goddess!" Histrun prayed fervently. "The idea of brutalizing the bodies didn't sit well with me. It felt evil, even though Wisah assured me it wasn't."

"As Grazeen said, the Goddess is wise."

Malviana - 15 de Godar, 1076

The landscape changed from the vast plains into the rocky forests of Strunlair, and with it came the cooler nights of autumn. Malviana shivered in her tent. The brazier glowed with heat, and she wrapped a thick blanket around her, but she still felt chilled. The island of her exile had never been this cold.

Malviana leaned forward, studying the map Nelieh had brought her. They were two hundred measures from Strunland Keep, and from there, they had over three hundred measures to cross before reaching her first goal of Strunhelos Keep. If the last seven and a half chedans had taught her anything, those five hundred measures would be hard fought. At this rate, she wasn't sure if her force would arrive at Strunhelos at the designated time six chedans from now.

Keandran pushed open the tent flap, bringing with him a gust of frigid air.

"Shut the door quickly," Malviana ordered. "It's cold!"

Keandran retied the flaps, laughing. "This isn't cold yet. The breeze is refreshing."

"I don't have thick fur like you do." Malviana glared at him as she added more coal to the brazier.

"We're heading north, where winter comes early and stays late. What did you expect when you chose to cross the pass mid-autumn?"

"Not this." Malviana shivered as the wind found its way into the tent. "I'd forgotten what winter was like. The island only had one season—fog."

"We'll be lucky if we don't get any snow before then."

Memories of snow chilled her to the bone. She'd never liked winter and snow, originally hailing from the southern province where winter only brought rain. When she'd set her deadline for her sons to meet her at Strunhelos Keep, she hadn't thought about what the weather would be like in the northern climates.

Keandran poured himself a goblet of dark bloodwine and languidly strolled toward her. The chiseled muscles of his chest rippled as he moved, and his fur-covered phallus engorged as he gazed at her. He took a deep drink, then knelt in front of her. He slid his claws under the blanket, the sharp points sliding against her, shredding both cloth and skin. His wolf-teeth nipped the delicate skin of her neck. Warm blood oozed from the cuts, and she groaned with pleasure as he lapped it up with his rough tongue. She ran her own needle-sharp nails down his back, gouging long bloody furrows. He arched in pleasure. She'd been right. He enjoyed pain as much as she did. Octars later, they lounged, bloody and satiated, on the thick pallet of her bed.

"We're losing too many Maldiers," Keandran said. "We need more troops."

"Somehow that bitch White Priestess has learned how to stop them from reanimating their corpses or infecting someone new." Malviana's grip on her goblet tightened until the delicate glass shattered. Keandran grabbed a rag to wipe away the mess.

So far, she'd kept a group of hostages between her and the White Priestess Mordaga had warned her about. Over the last chedans, they'd tossed magic at each other, testing each other's strengths. But the damned unmaking device kept interfering and stealing Malviana's power. She didn't think the other woman knew, because she never pressed her advantage. After their fifth encounter, Malviana felt like she'd lost more strength from their confrontations than she regained from her sacrifices. Afterward, she avoided bandying any more spells with the priestess. The visions Mordaga continued to send her during the sacrifices showed her victorious over the White Priestess, but only if they fought at Strunhelos. Any time before then, Malviana would lose.

"Can't you make more of them?" Keandran brushed the glass from her belly.

She hissed as a shard sliced into her skin, and she flicked it away. "It takes time for the magic to work. I believe everyone infected has transformed by now, if they're going to. I only expect another fifty or so to join us in a few days."

"Fifty? Is that all?"

"How many rogues did you think there were?"

Keandran growled. "The bitch Supreme requires the Clan Alphas to put down any rogues as soon as they question her leadership. I only escaped because we were in the wilds when I heard your call. Rizelya—" he spat out her name as a curse "—was too soft to kill me. But her cohort, Aistrun, he could have. He tried once." Keandran's hand floated to his throat, and his watery-blue eyes took on a distant look. A moment later, he shook himself. "He can't now. I'm too strong. I'll kill him."

"You know this area. What predators can we pervert to our purposes? Morvana and I can produce as many of those as we need."

A grin pulled at Keandran's elongated jaws. "Paether and narhili beasts. Both are nasty and, if combined, would be formidable and hard to kill."

"Show me what they look like." They had shared enough blood over the past lunadars to allow her to easily peer into his mind. She encouraged him to believe she could only do it when he gave her permission. But in reality, she could pluck images from his mind any time she pleased—or see through his eyes.

He closed his eyes, concentrating, and a moment later, she saw a four-eyed, tusked creature. "Ah," she breathed. "I've used this beast before to attack Rizelya." She frowned at the memory. "But she destroyed the pack I sent."

"What about this one? It's a narhili."

The image he showed her was of a six-limbed, long, sleek-bodied creature. She scowled. It didn't appear like a deadly predator.

Before she could comment, he added, "Their bites are poisonous, and they can take down a billocks with little trouble. They're nocturnal, but you can change that easily enough. Combined with the paether fur, they could survive in the cold mountains. And best of all, Rizelya's terrified of them. A pack of them attacked her, and she nearly died from their poison."

"They will do nicely." Malviana stood and washed the blood from her body before wrapping a heavy, warm robe around herself. "Morvana! We have work to do. Keandran, three slaves should be enough."

He grinned and bowed to her. As he stepped from the tent, the gray light of predawn peeked through. Malviana grimaced. She and Keandran had played longer than she thought. She wouldn't have time to begin the magic and would have to wait until nightfall, when a Posair attack wouldn't disturb her. In addition, Mordaga required his sacrifices to be conducted at night. She viciously kicked the servant sleeping by the door.

"What's wrong, Mother?" Morvana asked as she slipped inside the tent, already dressed in black riding breeches and a black vest. The cold didn't seem to bother her as it did Malviana.

"I have a project for us, but I hadn't realized the night had fled." Malviana glowered at the growing daylight peeking through the gaps in the tent. "We'll have to work on it tonight after we make camp." She told Morvana what she planned.

Morvana flicked her riding crop against her hand. "As we ride, I'll have my people watch for these beasts and any others we could use. Too bad we can't control our janacks and brechas anymore. They'd be handy to harass the Posair war host and thin their numbers. They'd be too busy fighting them to fight us, too."

As Malviana dressed, she cursed again the necessity—or shortsightedness—of leaving the control device on the island. The first time, it had taken the combined strength of all the exiled Malvers to create it. As she strode from her tent, she stopped short at the sight of thousands of Malvers, Maldiers, and slaves rushing to break down camp. *Why can't I make another device? I'm much stronger now, and so are my people. We're no longer starving.* Her plans for the night changed.

Throughout the day, Malviana flew high over any clashes with the Posairs, unwilling to expend any of her strength or energy. She'd need it all to make a new device to control her pets. As she reviewed the process in her mind, she realized she would need a few undisturbed days to complete the project.

She called Borgedier to attend her. "I need a defensible spot where we can stay for several days. I'm recreating the control device for the janacks and brechas. Until I finish it, I can't be disturbed or move."

Borgedier thumped his chest in a salute. "As you will, my queen."

A few octars later, he directed the army to a small keep tucked into the trees with a stream running by it. Malviana smiled at the picturesque scene. It would be a pleasant place to construct her device, and best of all, the stout stone walls would keep out the frigid air.

Strunlandir Keep fell within an octar to their greater might. With deep satisfaction, Malviana took over the Temple, capturing the priestesses attending it. They'd make wonderful sacrifices to fuel her work. By midnight, she'd rededicated the temple to her god, Mordaga, sacrificing the head priestess on the altar dedicated to their foul goddess.

Chapter 26

Rizelya - 20 de Godar, 1076

The tall plains grass turned from gold to brown as autumn deepened. Rizelya breathed in the crisp air, throwing her arms wide and leaning back in the saddle to absorb the sunlight. She leaned forward to stroke Kymaya's neck. "We're almost home, girl," she murmured. "It's been a long time since we've been home."

Rizelya wanted to be on the ground when the war host crossed into her home territory and had insisted on riding her horse rather than flying on Glork. The Gryphon wheeled overhead, catching a thermal.

Kymaya snorted and bobbed her head. A grin lit Rizelya's face at the cairn marking the boundary between Haasper Territory and Strunland. Kymaya's next stride took them fully into Strunland Territory.

Home! I'm finally home!

Rizelya breathed in again and wrinkled her nose at the acrid smoke smell. The Malvers army had beaten them to the boundary. Tears welled up in her eyes.

"Are you okay?" Blazel asked, reaching over to pat her knee.

"Yes." She shook her head. "No. I can't help worrying about what the Malvers are doing to my home. We just crossed into Strunland Territory."

"Home!" Aistrun sighed next to her. "We're so close. Do you think we'll stop at Strunland Keep this time? On the way to the Barrens, Histrun bypassed it to shorten our travel time."

"How far is it to the keep from here?" Blazel asked.

Aistrun pursed his lips and tilted his head. "Normally, it's about a two-day ride from here, give-or-take, depending on how many Malvers' monsters we have to fight en route."

"But at this snail's pace, four or five days." Rizelya tipped her head back, finding the dark spot high overhead she thought was Glork. It would take them only a day to fly to Strunland Keep. "Maybe since we're so close, Histrun will allow us to go ahead. I want to be part of the team protecting the keep from Malviana and her minions."

"So do I," Leistral said, longing in her voice. "We've protected everyone else. I'd like to save our home."

Eidstrun, riding at her side, nodded in vigorous agreement. "I haven't slept in my own bed for over a year."

"The last time was 692 days ago," Aistrun said.

Rizelya turned in her saddle to gape at him.

He shrugged. "I've kept track. I like my bed." He winked at Chariel. "I think you'll like it, too. It's big and comfy, with just the right amount of spring."

Chariel rolled her eyes, blushing.

"While sleeping in my own bed would be lovely," Kaieli said, "I'm more worried about having a home to return to once we destroy Malviana." She looked away, dashing the tears from her eyes.

Rizelya's heart went out to her. Kaieli would never share her home with her beloved, Rolstrun. The constant fighting helped, but every so often, like now, Kaieli's grief at his loss overtook her.

"I'm sure Histrun and Naila want the same thing," Blazel said, tipping his chin toward the Supreme Alphas riding ahead of them. "This is their home, too."

"I know. But I should be there protecting my people."

"We evacuated all the noncombatants deeper into the mountains," Blazel reminded her. "They're safe."

Even though Rizelya knew that, it didn't stop her from worrying.

A small, brown owl-type Gryphon scout dropped down and flew over Histrun's head for several long moments before taking off again. Rizelya frowned, trying to recall which keep lay on its flight path. Strunland was in that direction. She kicked Kymaya into a trot and caught up with Histrun's party.

Histrun scowled at her when she rode up. "No. Not yet," he said as she opened her mouth.

"But—"

"I need you with the war host." Histrun's grip on the pommel tightened until his knuckles turned white. "It's my home, too. But we can't give it special treatment. We have to be fair. Additional fighters left this morning to supplement those at the keep."

"You didn't send a Black Weave team with them. How come? Are you going to send us?" Hope flared to warm her belly.

"Perhaps." Histrun stared in the direction the Gryphon had flown. "The scout reported a large contingent of Malvers captured the small keep of Strunlandir three days ago, and they haven't moved on. They are up to something. Tonight, when we stop, I need your team to determine what it is."

Rizelya scowled. "We can try. Malviana's magic is usually hidden from us. I can't promise we'll find anything out."

After dinner, Rizelya gathered the Black Weave teams and explained what Histrun wanted them to do.

"He does know we can't see what she does, doesn't he?" Saffren bit her bottom lip.

Rizelya rubbed her tired eyes. "He still wants us to try. They haven't done this before. We've only experienced the usual ambushes, not a full-out attack like you'd expect if they were digging in."

Blazel nodded. "True. Malviana is definitely up to something, and that is never good."

"She's probably trying to find a way to counteract our destroying her Maldiers," Chariel observed as she leaned back into Aistrun's embrace. She smiled at her fellow Gray priestess, Ardela. "Your team is making a difference."

"Even with everything else we've learned to do," Ardela said, "creating Crone's Fire still amazes me. I'd believed it was only a myth." She shook her head.

Grazeen shuddered. "I don't know how you can do it. Even creating the net-shield freaks me out. I'm simply a lowly Green. I shouldn't be able to do something so powerful."

Eiden laughed. "You're not a 'lowly' Green anymore, Grazeen. Your hair is so dark green now, it's almost black."

Grazeen ducked her head, running a hand through her hair, and said softly, "I used to make snelks to clean the middens and latrines. I'm nothing special."

Rizelya leaned over to pat Grazeen's knee. "But you are special. You wouldn't be part of this group—or going through the same changes we all are—if you weren't. Truthfully, all of this freaks me out, too."

Gehan pulled a lock of her own hair forward and examined it. The canary-yellow had darkened to a rich goldenrod streaked with onyx. "None of us are the people we were a year ago when Rizelya pulled us into her pack. The Goddess had her reasons for bringing Rizelya to Strunven Keep right when we were ready and itching to fight the Malvers' monsters. I never dreamed any of this would happen."

Rizelya bowed her head. She hadn't thought she'd been an instrument of the Goddess when Histrun had sent her on the quest to determine why the control-janack had appeared. Now that Gehan mentioned it, she saw how it all fit together. If she'd never gone to Strunven Keep and discovered women with other Talents, like Saffren, Grazeen, Gehan, and Raeleen, wanted to fight. They wouldn't have had developed the power to effectively fight the Malvers and their creatures. Her gaze landed on the Gryphons tucked around or behind their partners. It had taken melding all the Talents along with the Gryphon's magic to create the Black Weave.

The Posairs would have fallen to the Malvers in the first attack on Haaslornde. Their Black Weave magic saved them then. She believed it would save them now, and it would keep the Malvers from crossing Strunhelos Pass.

"Let's try," Rizelya said. "I suspect we'll need both teams to pierce Malviana's veil of secrecy." She held out her hands, feeling the need for physical connection for this work. Blazel clasped her right hand while Chariel held her left. She gasped at the amount of power coursing through them when Raeleen touched hands with Gehan, completing the circuit of energy. *With this much power, surely we can spy on Malviana!*

In three breaths, the Weave formed in the deepest, richest black she'd ever seen. It rivaled the night sky when all three moons were dark. Her consciousness guided the Weave toward Strunlandir Keep. Hundreds of sickening swirls of dark light popped into existence when they reached the valley where the keep nestled. Vile magic pulsed from its center. Both repulsed by it, and simultaneously drawn to it, the Weave consciousness honed in on the energy.

Chariel, Ardela, Blenora, and Loshera gasped at the number of souls crowded in the temple, trying to escape and cross the veil. Within the Weave's consciousness, Rizelya could also see the souls. Malevolent chains, oozing evil, wrapped around them, anchoring them to Malviana's magic. The same evil coated the temple, and Rizelya was glad Wisah wasn't part of the weave to see it.

Cautiously, the Weave consciousness approached the temple, but before they neared it, a flash of magic tossed them away. No matter how they tried, they couldn't pass through Malviana's shield. Or was it her god, Mordaga's shield?

As their merged consciousness flowed back to their individual bodies, Rizelya noticed a swamp near their camp. She frowned in confusion. The Lynx Black Weave team must have missed it on their way through the area. A whirlpool of rancorous magic swirled in the center—a Malvers' monster nest. The larvae within it were growing and maturing at an alarmingly fast rate. At the current pace, it would mature in less than an octar and unleash not a dozen, but hundreds of monsters.

The war host was in danger!

Rizelya's instinct to destroy the Malvers' monsters kicked in, and without thinking or consulting her companions, she unleashed the magic to drain the malignant pool. With their combined teams, their magic sucked the pool dry in one enormous slurp. The energy representing the Malvers' monsters shredded into thousands of pieces and disintegrated.

A blast of magic exploded, tossing her and the others back into their bodies. Before she passed out, Rizelya glimpsed Malviana, screaming in intense pain, and curled into a fetal position on the floor. Whatever had happened had also hurt her. Rizelya tried to wake up, knowing she had to tell Histrun. But pain wrapped around her, and her mind fled into unconsciousness.

Malviana - 20 de Godar, 1076

Malviana sat back on her heels, surveying the device on her worktable set up near the temple's altar. Bright moonlight from all three moons full, or nearly so, streamed through the crystal dome above the sanctuary and fell on the device. The matte black metal glinted and sucked in the moonlight. Malviana chuckled at the display of Mordaga's power over that of the Posair's goddess.

It had taken three days, the sacrifice of the pitifully few priestesses serving the temple as well as sacrificing fifty slaves to craft it. This device was smaller and more lightweight than the original one. It lacked the tubes extending from it to the black offering bowl. Although it still collected the death essence harvested by the janacks and brechas, it would only feed the user. She didn't need it to convert the essence into the black pearls her people had subsisted on during their exile.

As Malviana reached for it, revulsion slithered through her, making her want to vomit. The thousand years of exile and barely surviving marched through her mind. The device had been the only thing staving off starvation for those long years. Taking a deep breath and flexing her hands, she grabbed the device and slammed it onto her head.

The familiar pinpricks of evil shone in her mind, much fewer than she'd expected. She swore as she remembered the disappearance of the magic pools. Her pets required those pools to exist. She found a single nest close to the Posairs' camp, and she reveled in the beautiful magic. It reminded her of the spells she and Mordar cast so long ago, and the pleasure they'd shared watching the Posairs suffer.

With the fond memories filling her, she activated the spell to encourage the janacks and brechas to mature. But before they reached the stage where they could survive outside the nest, the magic in the pool began to fade. Just like a basin of water being drained, something siphoned off the magic. Her pets squealed in distress as they blinked out of existence. Malviana clutched her head, their agony reverberating a hundredfold, bouncing through the device and into her mind. After what seemed like days of anguish, she finally managed to pull the device off. She lay panting on the floor for a long time, willing the pain to recede.

Morvana found her curled in a ball, tears streaking her face.

"Mother! What happened?" Morvana used a damp cloth to wash Malviana's face. Tendrils of power seeped from the cloth into Malviana, reviving her and easing her pain.

She pointed weakly in the direction where she thought the device lay abandoned. "It worked. I connected with a nest of janacks and brechas—"

"That's wonderful! But why are you on the floor?"

As Malviana told her daughter what had happened, watching the horror cross Morvana's face was like reliving the event again. Malviana gulped back the pain. She'd suffered worse at Mordar's hands and had survived. It had made her strong and a Malvers. She could withstand this pain. It'd make her stronger, and she'd use it to exact her revenge on the ones who were destroying the beautiful magic left behind from Mordar's spells. Malviana added it to her growing list of offenses the Posairs must answer for. Vengeance would be hers, and they'd pay for their crimes.

And soon, she'd capture the Sanctuary. The Supreme would pay the ultimate price, and with her death, Malviana's beloved Mordar would live again.

Malviana - 21 de Godar, 1076

Even though every movement sent pain cascading through her body, Malviana ordered her troops to evacuate the keep. The Posairs had to know the encounter had weakened her and would be rushing to take advantage of it.

She surveyed the small temple she'd turned into her laboratory and shrine to Mordaga. Her dedication of the temple to Mordaga would infuriate the Posairs' Goddess and that bitch White Priestess. But it wasn't enough to exact her vengeance and make them pay for all they'd done to her. A cruel smile curved her lips, and she called for Keandran.

He trembled as he walked through the temple doors, his eyes darting to the darkened corners. Nothing had terrified him like this before.

"I hate this place." He curled his upper lip, revealing his fangs. "Rizelya forced me to allow a priestess to invade my mind and block your call. It was horrible." Keandran crossed his arms over his chest and pulled his shoulders back. "I am very lucky you are stronger and helped to break the barrier. I wouldn't be here otherwise."

"Would you like to vent your anger on this place?"

His eyes lit up, and he nodded. "I know several others who'd also enjoy the opportunity."

"Do your worst." She flicked a hand to the pile of bodies left over from her sacrifices. "Dispose of these, too. You may give them to your troops."

He licked his lips. "My queen is generous."

"When you finish, raze this place and follow the army. We march for Strunland Keep to join the rest of our forces."

"It shall be done, my queen." He bowed and whistled. Cloresh ran to him. She grinned, her long snake tongue flicking out with relish as he issued his orders. She practically skipped as she hurried outside.

Malviana strode from the temple as thirty Maldiers scurried inside. She cackled with delight as she imagined what they would do to the formally sacred place.

Malviana pushed her small contingent to speed toward Strunland Keep, wanting to reach it before her enemies. She'd sent Borgedier with the rest of her army to secure the keep for her. Keandran promised her the keep was Rizelya and the Supreme Alpha's home. Her people destroying the fortified village would devastate the leaders and demoralize their troops.

Throughout the day, she kept expecting to have to set her twisted creatures on the Posair army to impede their progress. But nothing marched on her back trail. Worried, she spurred her troops to move faster.

Rizelya - 21 de Godar, 1076

Shaking roused Rizelya, and she forced her eyes open. She immediately snapped them shut when the world spun around her, and a wave of nausea crashed over her.

"Rizelya," Aistrun's concerned voice pierced the fog in her mind as he shook her again. "Hey, Little Red, come on, wake up. Are you okay?"

Groaning, she rubbed her face. The vertigo eased, and she cautiously reopened her eyes. Aistrun bent over her, his forehead crinkled with worry. "What happened?"

He shrugged. "I don't know. All of you suddenly shrieked, then fainted."

"I didn't shriek," Blazel said flatly. He grimaced in pain. "Although I did black out."

Eidstrun, kneeling over Eiden, raised an eyebrow. "Yeah, you cried out. It sounded awful. I'm surprised the camp isn't in an uproar, it was so bad. What caused it?"

Rizelya lifted her shoulders and shook her head. Her companions were slowly coming around. Loshera lost her battle with the vertigo and bent over, heaving. Kaieli crawled to her side and administered some healing, even though pain lined her face.

"So much malevolent evil," Blenora groaned. Her face drained of color, and she leaned over Blueek's paw, vomiting. Faliciden valiantly battled her own vertigo to scuttle next to Blenora to help her.

"Mordaga... evil... temple... Oh, Sweet Goddess, no!" Ardela moaned as she rocked back and forth, hugging her knees.

Ambrelya had maneuvered to sit between Ryaak's paws and held Raeleen while she sobbed. Maeaak rested his chin on Ryaak's head, cooing gently, trying to ease his friend's distress.

Chariel leaned against Torlek's side. She appeared the most recovered of them all. Rizelya guessed Aistrun had woken her first.

Chariel rubbed her temples. "Not only did we brush against Mordaga's evil, we were caught in the backlash of two powerful magics colliding. Whatever Malviana was doing involved the malignant magic pool we drained."

"Malviana!" Rizelya flew to her feet, flinging out an arm to catch herself and closing her eyes as the vertigo returned. "I have to talk to Histrun. Malviana is hurt. The backlash hit her, too. Now is the time to attack while she's incapacitated."

Aistrun pushed her back down. "You sit. You're in no condition to go anywhere. I'll tell Histrun."

His gaze took on the distant look of someone communicating using mind-speech. Rizelya's head hurt too much to try to mind-speak or even listen in on a mental conversation.

"He'd already planned to attack at dawn," Aistrun informed them. "He's going to push it forward since there's only a couple of octars left before dawn."

Rizelya's eyes widened. "It's that late? It didn't feel like we'd been in the Weave for very long."

"You were gone over four octars. Eidstrun was worried and wanted to bring you out."

"As I should," Eidstrun said. He held Eiden's head in his lap and gently stroked his twin's hair. Eiden hadn't woken yet. "They were dealing with Malviana."

Aistrun waved a dismissive hand. "But you seemed fine. That is, until you all screamed and fainted." He smirked at Blazel. "It's taken us nearly two octars to revive you."

"That would explain the shakiness and vertigo," Kaieli spoke up. "Bethlyn is sending someone over with a healing brew to help us get back on our feet."

A few milcrons later, the tent flap opened and Leistral entered carrying a tray filled with steaming mugs, followed by Margandy and Faelyn. Leistral passed around the mugs, while Margandy and Faelyn hurried to those who were still struggling with the backlash. Margandy crouched next to Eiden, who continued to lay curled up on the floor. Bronze healing light seeped from Margandy's hands, bathing Eiden with it. Finally, Eiden struggled to sit up, her eyes blurry. Eidstrun held a mug out for her, and she blinked at Eidstrun's solicitude, which didn't happen often. Smiling, she took the mug from him and sipped on it.

Rizelya took hers and sniffed. It didn't smell too bad. She took a cautious sip, anyway. One never knew how a healing brew would taste. Tangy mint and sharp ginger played across her taste buds. She wrinkled her nose at the ginger. It wasn't her favorite flavor.

The brew soon settled her stomach. As the others perked up, they discussed what they'd experienced and speculated about what it could mean. What could Malviana be doing with the Malvers' monsters and the malignant magic pools? Hopefully, draining the pool had stopped it before she completed her magic.

Outside, the bustle of troops assembling and the thunderclap of hundreds of Gryphons taking off at the same time interrupted them. Rizelya snuggled into Blazel's side, his arm wrapped protectively around her. Even after finishing the brew, tiredness pulled at her. Being unconscious wasn't the same restorative as sleeping. Her head bobbed, jerking her awake.

"Aistrun, find out if we need to prepare to leave, will you?" Rizelya asked, still too tired to mind-speak with Histrun or Naila. If the backlash affected Malviana as badly as it had them, she wasn't going to rush to attack Strunland Keep anytime soon.

"Unless we're overrun, which Histrun highly doubts, you can catch some sleep. We might be here for a day or two."

Helping each other, Blazel and Rizelya stumbled to their tent. Rizelya collapsed on her cot, immediately falling asleep. Gratefully, she slept dreamlessly for several octars. Then she started dreaming.

Malvers' monsters ran amok, attacking Strunland Keep. Banthues and grifflyns breathed caustic fire onto its ramparts. Packs of floxidor, skeaeter, and jallopsitor roamed outside the gates, trampling the fields and killing any livestock left in the pastures. Just like at Haasneven, the Malvers changed the once small, gentle cardrolon lizards into huge monsters seven feet in length and six feet tall. This time, Keandran gleefully goaded them to attack Strunland's walls. At his demand, the lizards dropped their heads and rammed their bony plates into the walls. The stones shattered, and Maldiers flowed into the keep. People Rizelya knew and loved screamed in terror and pain as they died.

Her own screams woke her up. Blazel gathered her in his arms as she cried.

"What did you dream?" he asked, rubbing her back and soothing her.

"It must have been terrible," Aistrun grumbled from across the tent. "You woke us all up with your screaming."

Rizelya pushed her tangled hair from her face. "It was Strunland Keep. It's under attack." The terror and panic she'd seen her friends suffering in her dream assailed her again. She scrambled out of the cot, pulling on clothes.

"What are you doing?" Blazel asked, frowning.

"I'm going to go save my home!" She finished tying her boots and reached for her helbraught.

"But it was only a dream," Aistrun complained, even though he was putting on his boots. "Malviana is still in Strunlandir Keep, and Histrun is on his way there to attack her."

Rizelya tugged on her pulser. "It doesn't mean her army is with her. Keandran is at Strunland Keep, I'm sure of it."

"It might be more than a dream," Chariel said. She sat sideways on her cot, braiding her hair. "Rizelya's gifts are growing. It's possible her soul traveled there in her sleep, like we do during the Black Weave, or she's had a precognitive dream. She has seen into Malviana's mind before."

Saffren laced her vest. "I don't think it's coincidence Rizelya had the dream right after our encounter with Malviana. We need to go."

We are ready to fly, Glork said.

"The Fox team will stay here to protect the army," Blenora said. "You go. Save your people. We'll take care of things here."

A lump formed in Rizelya's throat. "Thanks, Blenora."

Everyone on the Sabertiger team was dressed and ready to accompany her. They were willing to fly into danger on just her word. They trusted her that much. She gave them a grateful smile, then ducked through the tent door flap.

Histrun and Moraak know where we're going, Graak told them as Rizelya and her team raced to the Gryphon camp. *Laynar's platoon is coming with us, as well as a flock of Thunder Wings.*

As Rizelya strapped into Glork's harness, gratitude filled her that Histrun believed in her. Less than a half octar from waking from her dream, a hundred Gryphons launched into the sky and winged toward Strunland Keep.

She was going home at last. But what would she find when she arrived?

Wisah - 21 de Godar, 1076

The Posair troops marched toward Strunlandir Keep, hoping to catch Malviana still weak from the magical backlash from her encounter with the Weave. Wisah glanced over her shoulder at her mother, Naila, riding behind her on Sheekeek's back. The Gryphons flew ahead of the main army, but without Blazel and Rizelya, the fighting force needed a battle commander. Wisah's eyebrows lifted in surprise at Naila's pale, drawn face, and the tight lines around her mouth. She'd always thought of her mother as a proud, strong warrior, unafraid of anything.

Wisah patted her mother's hands linked around her waist. "There's nothing to be frightened of, Mother. Flying is perfectly safe. Sheekeek won't let us fall."

"I know," Naila ground out. "Hate heights."

Wisah blinked at the admission. She'd wondered why Naila never rode a Gryphon. They had an octar or two of flight before they reached their destination. Conversation would help take Naila's mind from the heights, but Wisah wasn't sure what to say. When she'd turned five, Naila had sent her to the Sanctuary to begin her priestess training. She'd returned to Strunland for her apprenticeship at thirteen. But between her duties at the temple and Naila's as second in command to the Keep Alpha, they hadn't spent much time together.

"So," Naila said, then cleared her throat and continued in mind-speech, *do you think it wise to continue your relationship with the centaur?*

Wisah rolled her eyes. Of all the things they could talk about, of course, her mother would pick that one. "I love him."

That is obvious. But you're the Lady Superior. Someday, you'll be the Supreme. You know you'll have to end it when you ascend the crystal throne. It would be better for both of your hearts if you didn't prolong the inevitable.

"But it isn't inevitable. In case you haven't noticed, I'm not a normal priestess or a normal Supreme."

"I noticed." Pride filled Naila's voice. *I knew you were destined for greatness. The first time I nursed you, I sensed the presence of the Goddess. You opened your eyes—your white eyes—and gazed at me with such love and intelligence.*

"What?" Wisah exclaimed. "My... my... white eyes?"

Yes. Then you closed your eyes and slept. When you awoke, your eyes were pale blue. I thought I'd imagined them being white and never said anything to anyone. Truthfully, I forgot about it until you appeared as the Lady Superior and wearing your new tattoos. You see, you were always meant to be the Supreme.

I, too, sensed your greatness, Sheekeek said quietly. *The first time I met you, the Goddess whispered to me, 'This is the one. Serve her well.' It's why I volunteered to be your mount, as no other Silverbeak has ever done before. You will be a great

Supreme and unlike any before you. I'm honored to serve you—and be your friend.

And I'm honored to be the one who birthed you, Naila said.

A lump formed in Wisah's throat, and tears blurred her vision. "Thank you," she choked out through the emotions swelling through her.

She spent the rest of the flight contemplating this new information. Her life would be vastly different if she'd gone to the Sanctuary as a baby and lived her entire life as the Lady Superior and the next Supreme. She'd be a different person. Wisah wouldn't have had a friendship with Rizelya, or even known she was her aunt. She'd never have met or fallen in love with Jaehaas. The Supreme would never have allowed her to leave the Sanctuary on the quest to find the Gryphons and she'd wouldn't have met Sheekeek. Wisah gazed at her arm covered in sigil tattoos. Would she have received this gift of power had she grown up as a 'normal' Supreme? She doubted it. It amazed her how one small thing—her eye color turning pale blue rather than staying white—had changed her life. She hoped it meant she'd be a better Supreme because of her experiences.

"We're here," Naila said, breaking into Wisah's musings.

Black marred the white sheadash stone walls of Strunlandir Keep. A smoldering ruin marked where the stables had stood. The temple's crystal dome was smashed, and a horrendous stench wafted from it, making Wisah gag. Her stomach cramped, and bile filled her throat. She didn't want to know what the Malvers had done to defile a temple—one of her temples! Once Naila's people determined it was safe to enter the keep, Sheekeek landed in front of the temple. The noxious smell grew worse as Wisah climbed the stairs. She frowned at the doors blasted from their hinges.

The glow of Naila's helbraught startled Wisah. She hadn't expected her mother to accompany her. Wisah activated the spell to light the crystal on her staff, and Sheekeek increased his nimbus. Between the three of them, they cast enough light to see within the building. She carefully stepped over the piles of muck littering the floor as she approached the altar. A sob caught in her throat. Dark blood still dripped down its sides, and bloody white hair trailed from the body tied to its surface. She rushed forward, but the priestess had died octars ago.

Malviana had desecrated the Goddess's altar with her foul magic and sacrifices to Mordaga! Anger seethed in Wisah's heart, erupting in a blast of deep purple light. The Crone's Fire quickly immolated the priestess's body. The stone melted in the heat and intensity of her fury.

"Oh, Sweet Mother!" Naila gasped.

Wisah dragged her attention away from the altar.

Naila crouched over a pile of muck. *These are body parts,* Naila said in disgust. *Thrown away like trash. Someone has gnawed on most of them.*

That is not all. Fury and grief filled Sheekeek's voice. He pointed a talon at the walls. *Look.*

Wisah cried out in anguish. Blood, guts, and excrement defiled all the beautiful murals of the Goddess and Her Consort.

"She will pay for the defilement of my house!" Wisah yelled and the voice of the Goddess merged with her own. She turned unseeing eyes on Naila and Sheekeek. "Get out, now!" She heard their gasps and the clattering of boots and talons as they raced from the temple. Wisah—or the Goddess, she wasn't sure there was any difference at the moment—pounded the end of her staff three times on the floor. Pain flared as multiple sigils glowed and the Goddess's fire blazed in her staff's crystal.

With a boom, the light exploded.

When Wisah returned to her own senses, the temple was gone. Not even the foundations remained to mark where it had once stood. She trembled and wasn't sure whether to tightly grip her staff or throw it from her. *I have so much power at my disposal!*

She turned around. Naila stood shaking. The color had drained from her face, and her lips moved as she gibbered in terror. Sheekeek's feathers drooped, and he cowered on the ground. When they noticed her looking at them, they bowed low in obeisance. Wisah rushed to them. "Please, Mother, Sheekeek, don't be frightened. It's just me! I won't hurt you, I promise. The Goddess will never hurt any of her own."

Wisah helped Naila to regain her feet, then hugged her. She crouched to look Sheekeek in the face while she stroked his soft head feathers. "See, I'm just me now." He finally extended his beak to rub her cheek.

She stood up and anger flooded her at being forced to exhibit such power and scare her loved ones. Her tattoos glowed, and light sparked from her staff. "The next time," she vowed, "Malviana and I face each other across the battlefield, I won't hold back. I will eradicate the foul evil of Malviana and her god Mordaga from my world!"

Chapter 27

Blazel - 22 de Godar, 1076

Rizelya and Aistrun often talked about their home keep, Strunland Keep, but Blazel had never visited it. He considered settling down with Rizelya there. Going there with the specter of war hanging over them wasn't what he'd had in mind, though. For her sake, he hoped her dream hadn't been a true-seeing. They'd stopped for the night at a safe-house only a short flight from the keep. While the Gryphons could have flown the entire way in one day, they'd be too tired to fight if needed. Rizelya reluctantly agreed it would be better to arrive ready to fight rather than exhausted.

In the predawn light, their platoon left the safe-house. Flokeek, the owl-type scout who had replaced Baekeek, and his small flock of scouts flew ahead of them. A pang of guilt and regret filled Blazel at the thought of Baekeek. He hadn't seen the Gryphon alive since leaving him behind to surveil the Black Castle. The Malvers' grifflyns had the same coloring as the scout, and Blazel feared Malviana had transmogrified Baekeek into the abomination.

An octar later, the acrid tang of smoke tickled Blazel's nose. It didn't bode well for the keep. He glanced over at Rizelya. Her face was pale and lined with stress.

We're flying as fast as we can, Graak assured him. *We'll be there shortly.*

Not long after, Tuueek sounded an alarm. *Banthues, grifflyns, and baethors up ahead!* He and the other Thunder Wings put on a burst of speed and quickly outdistanced the rest.

Blazel slid his pulser forward and snapped a cartridge of projectiles into the chamber. Graak and the other Gryphons climbed higher so they could arrive at the battle scene above the Malvers' flying creatures.

They streaked through the clouds, Graak flaming as the first banthu came into sight. Blazel saved his projectiles, instead casting his mind out for the Malvers riding the banthu. He found the woman, and flung out his hand toward her, imagining her throat between his long warrior's claws. Her face constricted with pain as he pumped venom into her. She raked her throat, trying to dislodge his phantom hands, but couldn't touch them. He drew back his hand and swung it through the air, as if he slashed his helstrablade through her neck. Blood gushed as her head tumbled to the ground.

While he dealt with the Malvers, Graak attacked the banthu with both his claws and his mind. The banthu shrieked as a flaming hole formed in its chest. It twisted as it fell, belching a last gout of fire. Blazel threw a cold-air shield up in front of them. The banthu's fire bounced against it and flowed harmlessly around them.

As Graak spiraled up, the battle below them unfolded. Blazel swore as he took in the vast array of Malvers forces. It was worse than Rizelya's dream. Most of Malviana's troops had slipped ahead of her main force and had arrived at the keep several days ago.

A dark shape flew toward them. Blazel struggled to make out who—or what—it was through the thick smoke. He lifted his pulser, trying to sight the fast-moving object. Blazel sucked in a breath and dropped his weapon when Shokeek zoomed out of the haze and past them, winging back the way they had come.

He's going to tell Histrun and Moraak that the Malvers are already here, Graak said. *I expect most of the army will march here when they hear this news.*

"Thank the Warrior! The Malvers are flinging every foul creature they've created at the keep. It's as if they're practicing for the attack on Strunhelos. I don't think we have enough fighters to stop them."

A large banthu glided high over the battle. Gems glittered on the Malvers' wand. Over the lunadars of fighting, the Posairs had learned the Malvers who wielded bejeweled wands were the ones exiled and, therefore, old and powerful. They weren't as easily harmed as the newly turned Malvers and were even more difficult to kill.

However, Wisah's examination of the wand Rizelya recovered at Haasneven Keep revealed the stones on it stored the hateful death essence. Unlike the Posairs, who used their helbraughts to focus their magic, the Malvers' wands enhanced and powered their magic. Without their wands, the Malvers couldn't access the death essence and weren't any more powerful than a highly talented Posair. But targeting such a small object as the wands required extreme precision. Blazel preferred to attack the person rather than the tool. It gave him much more satisfaction to feel their death within his mental grasp.

"Let's fly closer to him." Blazel pointed up. "I think he's the leader here."

As do I, Graak agreed. *I've asked Glork to come with us. Those old Malvers are dangerous. Even with our growing skills, we can't take on one of them by ourselves.*

It would be better if the entire team joined us, Rizelya said as she and Glork flew toward them.

Blazel shook his head. *I don't plan on engaging with him. I just want to get a feel for what we're facing.*

In that case, we should go incognito, Glork said.

Blazel sensed Graak's invisibility spell wash over them. Although all Malvers had pale gray skin, black eyes, and charcoal-gray hair, they each had different facial features.

Malviana must want this keep badly to send one of her top commanders, Blazel said, recognizing the man.

Three short bursts of fire shot from his wand. Below them, the Malvers' flying creatures spun away from the keep. The Malvers waved his wand and uttered a string of nonsensical words. A gust of wind suddenly blew in the previously calm air, growing stronger as it fanned out. The wind funnel tossed the Gryphons, who hadn't moved out of its path, around like children's toys. They flapped their wings wildly to straighten themselves out. If the Posairs riding them hadn't been strapped into their harnesses, they'd have fallen off. In contrast, the Malvers employed a saddle and reins system similar to a horse. Any banthues with a Malvers on their backs didn't do any fancy flying or dives lest they lose their riders. The Posairs and Gryphons utilized this to their advantage, goading the banthues into following them in complicated maneuvers. The banthues were simply beasts the Malvers used for transportation, not a cooperative, thinking partner like the Gryphons were with the Posairs.

When all but two of the Gryphons flew out of the tornado's path, the Malvers commander swore. Although his archaic Posarian made him difficult to understand, Blazel caught the gist of it. The wind continued to batter the injured Gryphons, propelling them closer to the ground. Blazel's heart leaped to his throat as he recognized one pair as their friends, Dukaaik and Shaydan.

"No!" Rizelya cried.

She flung out her hand as Glork dove. Graak tucked his wings and followed them. Suddenly, Dukaaik and the other Gryphon stopped tumbling and hung in midair even though neither of them were using their wings. Finally, Graak caught up to Glork. Rizelya's hand trembled, and sweat covered her face. Blazel's eyes widened, surprised at her newfound telekinesis talent, and her strength to halt both Gryphon's fall. She lowered them into the courtyard, where women wearing healer green raced to help them.

The commander shouted in anger. The wind transformed into a tornado, barreling toward the keep.

If it hits, Rizelya said, *it will tear the keep apart. We have to do something.*

Blazel agreed with her. They didn't have time to join with their team to form the net-shield. After she used her new talent to save lives, Blazel considered his own burgeoning powers. All he'd done with them was kill. Could he use them for something else? He quickly communicated with Graak what he wanted to do. Graak agreed and joined his energy with Blazel's.

Blazel reached out with his mind. He'd found a physical motion helped him focus the magic, so he also stretched out his hand toward the whirling wind. First, he imagined tearing it to shreds with his warrior claws, but it only intensified the tornado. It touched down in an outer field, demolishing the stone fence and the few hapless skeaeters inside it. Next, he threw up a barrier, like a shield, to stop the wind funnel from moving from the field. It worked for a heartbeat or two, then the whirlwind broke through and into the next field, where a dozen Posairs fought with twisted Maldiers. Desperate to save their lives, Blazel flung out his hand again, this time imagining a blast of wind crashing into the tornado. He hoped to knock it off course and away from the people so engrossed in their life-or-death battle, they were unaware of the oncoming danger.

At first, nothing happened. He barely registered Rizelya yelling at the combatants, urging them to find safety. He couldn't take his concentration off the wind funnel to determine if they'd heard her or not. Graak poured more of his strength into the forming magic, and their wind grew more ferocious, beating at the tornado and slowly pushing it to the side. Blazel fed more magic into his wind and, to his horror, a second whirlwind formed. *What have I done?*

"Blazel! That isn't helping," Rizelya yelled at him, her words torn away by the howling wind. She switched to mind-speech. *What can I do to help?*

I don't know! Frustration made his eyes water.

With a growl, he envisioned slamming the two whirlwinds together and clapped his hands. The sound echoed as the two twisters met. Thunder and lightning rolled off them in wave after wave. Graak squawked in fear and dove toward a stand of trees. Gryphons attracted lightning. Electricity raised the hair on Blazel's arms, and he heard the sizzle of a lightning strike mere feet away. When he glanced over his shoulder, the two tornadoes had dissipated. Thunder boomed. Lightning cracked. The loud sounds reverberated through his skull.

Graak ducked under the spreading branches of an ancient oak. His shaking made Blazel's head wobble. Blazel started unbuckling his harness, and as soon as they were on the ground, he jumped from Graak's back and pushed his goggles onto the top of his head. The lightning continued to sizzle all around them. Glork tumbled into their refuge, his tail smoldering. Blazel jerked his bedroll off Graak. Unfurling it as he ran, he tossed it over Glork's haunches and tail, smothering the fire.

That worked to disintegrate the tornadoes, Graak grumbled, *but I could do without the lightning storm.*

"Sorry," Blazel apologized. "I didn't mean—"

A loud thunderclap stole his words. A heartbeat later, a torrent of raindrops pattered on the oak leaves above them. Blazel glanced up, and water splashed onto his face.

"I didn't mean to do that, either," he said, wiping away the water. He turned to Rizelya, who was examining Glork's injuries. "Did you see what happened to the Malvers commander?"

She nodded. "I did. Oh, stop complaining, Glork. Your fur is barely even scorched. You've suffered worse from battling banthues and grifflyns."

But it hurts! Kaieli! Kaieli! Come help me.

Rizelya glared at Glork, shaking her head and mouthing the word "baby" at him. *Kaieli, don't bother. He's fine. He just needs a healing salve, which I have. Are you and the others still fighting?* While she mind-spoke with Kaieli, Rizelya rummaged in her pack, and pulled out a small jar. "Ah, here it is." She liberally smeared the ointment on Glork's singed tail.

Thanks to the tornado and the resulting rain, we're done for the day. Kaieli's mind-voice sounded distracted. *The Malvers forces have also retreated, but there are many injured.*

We'll be there to help in a few milcrons.

Glork flicked his tail from her hands and gripped it carefully in his talons. *I'm not going anywhere while there's still lightning. It's too dangerous.*

Rizelya put her hands on her hips. "You mean you can fearlessly fight the Malvers and their creatures, but you're afraid of thunder and lightning?"

Yep. Glork turned in a circle next to the tree's base, preparing to lie down. *Lightning has hit me once already today.*

I'm not risking another strike. He settled down and tucked his injured tail around him. *It hurts.*

Blazel looked at Graak, who lay curled up under the tree. "What about you, my friend?"

I agree with Glork. This is a nice safe place to wait out the storm.

Blazel turned to Rizelya and gave her a lop-sided grin. "It looks like we're walking, in the rain, while our friends cower."

We're not cowering, Graak objected. *We're making a tactical retreat and staying out of unnecessary danger.*

Rizelya already had her waterproof poncho out of her pack. Blazel shrugged at his friend as he unhooked his pack and dug out his own poncho.

As he and Rizelya left the shelter of the tree, rain spattered his head. He'd rather stay safe, warm, and dry with Graak than tromp through the wet and mud, but he refused to let Rizelya traverse the battlefield alone. They couldn't be certain all the Malvers' creatures had fled.

"So, what happened to the Malvers commander?" Blazel asked after they'd walked for a while.

"When you smashed his tornado, a magical backlash hit him. He laid slumped over in his saddle, dead or unconscious. As hard as these bastards are to kill, I'd say he was unconscious."

They soon came upon an injured Posair. Blazel tore a strip from the man's undershirt to use as a bandage, then helped him to his feet. They trudged through the mud, finding more wounded. Twice, Rizelya's quick reactions saved them from an injured Maldier attacking them as they helped one of their people. Before they reached the keep, a flood of fighters converged on them and helped carry the injured inside. Blazel walked through the gates, wishing his first visit to Rizelya's home was under better circumstances.

After a few steps inside the keep, Rizelya stopped and flung out her arms, tipping her head up, disregarding the rain pelting her face. "I'm home!" she breathed.

Blazel's hand strayed to his jacket pocket, where he kept the bond-torque. A few chedans ago, he'd finally had a chance to ask Maendy to make it for Rizelya. In the chaos of the war with the Malvers, they hadn't yet had their bonding ceremony. If things calmed down enough while they were still in Strunland

Keep, he'd suggest they hold it here. Watching her as she took in the sights and smells of her home, he now understood how much the place meant to her. He'd never felt like that about any place before, not even the Sanctuary.

Rizelya held out her hand to him. "Come on, let me show you my room. I've let Aistrun know where to find us." She smiled happily up at him. "I can't believe it. I'll be able to sleep in my own bed tonight."

As they walked through the courtyard to Rizelya's pack-house, Blazel wondered if this could be his home too after the war. He hoped so.

Malviana - 23 de Godar, 1076

Finally, Malviana's banthu flew over a ridge. Before her, spread the largest village—really a city—she'd seen in these modern times. She scowled at her troops camping in the fields of Strunland Keep, and not inside it where they were supposed to be. She guided the beast to fly high over the keep. Malviana swore at the Posair army encamped inside the sturdy walls. How had they arrived before her?

A wave of magic quested for her just as a volley of arrows whistled through the air. She batted them aside with her magic and urged her banthu to speed to her people's camp. She landed next to Borgedier's tent and waited for him to come out and help her off her mount. Instead, Jorvelden offered his hand to her.

"Where is Borgedier?" she demanded.

"Inside, my queen, recuperating."

"Is he ill?" Her forehead crinkled in confusion. Mordaga's gift included never succumbing to illness.

"No, my lady. He's suffering from a magical backlash."

Trepidation made her steps falter. How could a spell gone awry also hit him? With his rank of Duke, there shouldn't be anyone here powerful enough to stop him. She entered the darkened tent. A single lantern set on low glowed near the doorway. Borgedier lay still as death on his cot. The slight movement of his chest reassured her he lived.

Malviana gaped at him, horror quivering in her soul.

The skin of his right cheek pulled his mouth into an unsightly grimace. His right hand was curled into a tight claw and trembled with every labored breath he took. This wasn't a simple backlash of power. Had Mordaga not granted him near immortality, he'd be dead. Even so, she wondered how he'd survived.

Blindly, she groped for a chair and collapsed onto it. She gently grasped his uninjured hand. "Borgedier," she breathed.

His eyelids fluttered and his left eye opened. He tried to smile at her, but it came out as a grimace. "My queen."

"What happened to you, and how?"

Through pain-filled breaths, Borgedier told her about his wind funnels being smashed to smithereens by a force he thought to never feel again—Black Talent.

Malviana slumped against the back of the chair. "But how? We eradicated all the Blacks. Mordaga assured us they would never be reborn."

"I know not, my lady. But the power that destroyed my spell was Black. One of the most powerful I've ever encountered. See what it did to my wand." He waved toward the chest by his cot.

His black marble wand lay in pieces. The six gemstones on it no longer gleamed with death essence, but instead were dull, lifeless, and had multiple cracks in them. They'd never hold and store magic again. It took an obscene amount of power to destroy a wand so thoroughly. As he turned his head away, she gagged. The shattered gemstone of his earring was embedded in his skin.

Her heart thudded painfully in her chest. Who could wield so much power? And how could they possibly gain it?

Stunned, she stumbled from Borgedier's tent in search of her own. Morvana met her outside.

"You look like you've seen a ghost, Mother."

"I think I did. The Posairs definitely have at least one Black Talent—and a powerful one." Instead of going directly to her pavilion, they wandered through their camp. As they walked, she filled her daughter in on what had happened to Borgedier.

Pausing on a slight incline overlooking the keep, Malviana contemplated what to do. The situation seemed dire, with her battle commander injured, perhaps even mortally wounded, and the Posair army firmly ensconced in the keep. To dig them out would take a major siege and possibly more troops than she had.

For the first time, fear wafted through her and she questioned if they would succeed. Her legs quivered from the short walk. Malviana shook her head. *It's only my exhaustion talking.* She still hadn't fully recovered from her own magical backlash. She considered advancing Jorvelden to the rank of Count to take Borgedier's place. Although Jorvelden didn't have the same gift for strategy as Borgedier. Then she glanced at her daughter. Why waste good sacrifices to elevate one of her people when Morvana was available? Over the lunadars, she's shown her capacity to lead.

"While Borgedier is incapacitated, I'm making you the new battle commander," Malviana said.

Morvana's eyes lit up, and she clutched her wand to her chest. "Do you mean it?"

Malviana nodded. "Work with Jorvelden. He's been Borgedier's second and knows Borgedier's plans."

"Do you want us to prepare for a siege?" Morvana's nose crinkled.

"Not yet. This isn't our goal." Malviana paused, pushing open her tent flap. "Keep them busy for today while I recover. At sundown, send ten slaves to me to sacrifice."

Morvana thumped a hand to her chest and strode off. Malviana gratefully entered the dim confines of her pavilion, unhooking her cloak and letting it fall to the ground. A servant would find it and take care of it. She shuffled to her padded platform and dropped onto it. The beautiful sounds of battle lulled her to sleep.

Blazel - 23 de Godar, 1076

Blazel stood on the keep's ramparts, glad to be out of the press of people. Thirty-thousand people and Gryphons crammed inside Strunland Keep's walls made it too claustrophobic for him. Since those first days traveling with Jaehaas, being uncomfortable to even stay in a safe-house with a small pack, he'd become used to being around people. But this many, in the small, enclosed space, made him twitch with anxiety.

"Ware!" he called out, seeing movement alongside the road leading to the keep. He scanned the skies, searching for the Malvers he'd faced a few days ago. But he hadn't directed any battles since then. Blazel hoped he'd killed the commander, but he doubted it.

A blue-black banthu rose from the Malvers' camp with a lean woman on its back. She wore black trousers and a vest laced tight over her bosom. A long, gray braid trailed behind her. Waves of evil and malice rippled from her. Blazel had faced her once before. With his increased abilities, he could now sense her energy signature mirrored Malviana's, but had its own distinct flavor.

Wisah climbed the stairs and joined him on top of the wall. She, too, stared at the woman, who directed her banthu high over the battlefield.

Not taking his eyes off the Malvers, Blazel asked, "Does Malviana have any siblings?"

"Why do you ask?"

At Wisah's cautious tone, he glanced at her, his eyebrows furrowed in confusion. He tossed his chin toward the woman. "She has a similar energy."

"No, it isn't her sister." Wisah took a deep breath and leaned her elbows on the edge of the balustrade. "Her sister died while trying to stop her."

Blazel frowned at the cryptic answer.

"Malviana has three children," Wisah continued. "That's probably her daughter, Morvana. Although the histories said they were adolescents when they were exiled with their mother."

Three short bursts of green light sprayed from Morvana's wand. Below them, half a dozen huge cardrolon horned lizards burst from the trees and raced toward the gates, their thick, bony heads lowered. Like at Haasneven, the Malvers had transformed the normally small, friendly lizards into gigantic beasts six feet high and seven feet long. They smashed through the first pasture's fence. Behind them ran several hundred Maldiers. All types of animals had been mashed together with Posairs in truly hideous ways. Fighters hiding in the walled fields engaged the Maldiers from the rear and sides.

"She seems to be the new battle commander," Blazel observed.

He hadn't tried using his magic from so far away before. After the last battle commander had fallen, the Malvers had stopped fighting and hadn't resumed until now. Blazel extended his hand, but his lightning bolt crackled over Morvana's head as it hit a powerful shield. He next formed a controlled whirlwind. The wind buffeted the banthu, but even when it tumbled upside down, the woman remained in her saddle and appeared to be laughing. Angered, he imagined choking her like the others, but he couldn't penetrate her psychic armor.

"Leave her for now," Wisah said. "Help me stop the lizards before they crash open the gates."

The wall under him shuddered from their onslaught. Rizelya, climbing a ladder rather than the stairs further away, lost her footing as the ladder swayed and flailed. Another lizard slammed into the gate, and Rizelya's hand slipped. Desperate, Blazel flung out his hand to grab her—even though he knew he was too far away. Instead of empty air, his hand caught flesh. Rizelya dangled in midair, an arm over her head. He quickly pulled her up, awed when she rose in response to his thoughts. As soon as she was safely on the rampart, he bent over, panting and exhilarated. He'd finally used his new Talent to save someone's life rather than take it.

Blazel turned his attention to the beasts. To his surprise, they had left the gate and ambled along the road leading away from the Malvers. Grazeen stood on the wall above the gate, gazing intently at the creatures. They stopped when they reached a grassy meadow far from the fighting and put down their heads to graze. His skills weren't the only ones growing by leaps and bounds.

When he searched the battlefield for Morvana, he could barely make out her banthu high above them. He doubted he could reach her at that distance. He shrugged, turning back to the fight at hand, sure he'd face her again.

After the battle, Wisah gathered the Supreme Alphas, Naila, Moraak, and the Black Weave teams together. Wisah trailed her fingers over the top of the silver chest she'd brought with her from the Sanctuary.

"Blazel reminded me today I've been remiss in sharing some vital information," Wisah said. She opened the box and pulled out a small portrait, handing it to Histrun, who gazed at it and then passed it to Keshanal, who gave it to Naila. "That is Mordeven. Malviana's eldest son."

This is the one leading the Malvers army in the east. Moraak tapped the image. *Though my scouts thought he was older than this.*

"These were painted before their exile," Wisah said, "when Malviana's children were adolescents. It makes sense they would age into maturity during their exile. This next portrait is of Morvana, her daughter, whom we encountered today." She handed Histrun the next painting as the others studied the pictures being passed around the room. "This one is Malvidor, her youngest."

He is the commander of the eastern faction, Moraak remarked when he saw the picture.

"We now know where Malviana's children are, and who leads her splinter armies." Keshanal grimaced at Malvidor's image. "He looks too young in this to be evil."

Wisah tapped the portraits she still held on the table. "Don't let their looks, or age, fool you. Malviana conceived her children in evil and breastfed them with blood. All they've ever known is serving the foul god, Mordaga." She shuffled through the remaining images and choose one. "This is Borgedier, rank of Duke, and Malviana's battle commander. At least he was. It appears Morvana has taken his place."

"He's who I clashed with the other day," Blazel said.

Rizelya ran a hand through her hair. "When I saw him after the magical backlash, he appeared severely injured, or, if we're lucky, dead."

"I doubt it," Wisah shook her head. "The Malvers, especially the top echelon and Malviana's family, are nearly immortal, but not fully. While they can be killed—" she grimaced as she touched her headband "—it takes immense power. A simple backlash of clashing magic would injure them, but not kill them."

"Decapitating them works," Blazel grinned. His recent confrontation with Morvana made him scowl. "If you can penetrate their shields, which are extremely strong."

Wisah handed out the last of the portraits. "These are her top echelon: Magdelyn, Valdorian, and Jorvelden. I'm sure we'll be engaging with these in the coming chedans. They all fought and survived the Great War. Do not underestimate their power. Histrun and Moraak, inform your troops to not try to fight them. Only those who are Black Talents, the Black Weave teams, will have the strength to survive a collision with them. "

"Thank you, Wisah," Histrun said, "for sharing these with us, and for the warning. It's good to know whom we're fighting."

Blazel gazed at the portraits spread out on the table, memorizing the faces. The Goddess must have gifted him with Black Talent to fight these Malvers and to save his people. He and those on the Black Weave teams were the only ones capable of ridding their world of this scourge of evil.

Malviana - 23 de Godar, 1076

Malviana awoke refreshed. While she'd slept, she'd absorbed a good amount of death essence from the day's battles. She stretched languorously and debated about calling Keandran or Korand to her. A scratch on the tent wall interrupted her, and Morvana stepped inside.

She raised an eyebrow. "You look better, Mother. Do you still want the slaves, or should I send Keandran to you?"

Malviana sat up, and the movement sent twinges through her body. "Slaves first. How did the day's battle go?"

Morvana screwed up her face. "Not well. We lost ten new Malvers. The power I sensed coming from inside the keep was tremendous. Three of them died without anyone touching them."

"That is definitely Black Talent," Malviana moaned, and rubbed her face. It didn't do any good to ask how or why. They now had to contend with it. While Morvana summoned the slaves, Malviana strode outside and stared at the keep. A familiar tendril of power wove toward her, and she immediately shielded. The bitch White Priestess and her hated device were here and seeking her. Malviana itched to put the bitch in her place, but now wasn't the time. She was still too weak, especially after the backlash. She returned to her tent and finished setting up her altar to Mordaga, grinning when Keandran dragged the first slave inside.

Blood spattered her face as she plunged her hands into the victim's chest. As the ecstasy of her god entered her, the vision assailed her again of fighting the woman who reminded her of Shandir while snow whirled around them. The high cliffs leading into the White Mountains rose in the background.

It could only be one place: Strunhelos.

The first rays of dawn lit the sky as she finished her sacrifices to Mordaga. Malviana's body hummed with power, but it wasn't enough to vanquish her enemy. She gave the order to march.

Let the Posairs stay huddled in their keep. She had a mountain to conquer.

Chapter 28

Blazel - 24 de Godar, 1076

Blazel climbed to the rampart, with Eidstrun following behind him. He didn't think he still needed a bodyguard while working the Black Weave magic, but Eidstrun and the others insisted on being at their side when they fought. Chariel had given up arguing with Aistrun chedans ago, accepting he'd guard her no matter what. Aistrun wasn't the only bodyguard who vowed to protect his love with his life if necessary. Nelstrun rarely left Saffren's presence anymore, especially since Maestrun's death. Even one-handed, Leistrun became a formidable fighter, protecting Eiden. After receiving the Crone's Fire gift, Raeleen had finally succumbed to Ambrelya's advances. She hadn't believed she deserved to be loved due to her multitude of scars. But Ambrelya didn't care. She had enough of her own from fighting the Malvers' monsters. The most surprising pairing was the much younger Baederposan and Noriana. The middle-aged Noriana blushed every time Baederposan brushed a kiss on her cheek or held her hand.

Blazel glanced over at Rizelya, striding to the next tower. Leistral trailed behind her, and Rizelya laughed at something Leistral said. While he also wanted to protect his beloved, she'd skin him alive if he tried. She was a capable fighter, and her burgeoning Black Talent eclipsed his.

"Warrior take you!" Gehan's strident voice rose from the courtyard. She faced down Korhaas with her hands on her hips and a scowl on her face. She stepped to the side.

Korhaas moved to block her path, crossing his arms over his chest. "You know you be safer with me."

Gehan rolled her eyes. "Fine. You can accompany me, but I don't need your protection."

"No, you be a fearsome warrior. But admit it, you like me." Korhaas winked at her, and without warning swept her into his arms and kissed her. Instead of pushing him away, Gehan wrapped her arms around his neck, pulling him closer.

Chuckling, Blazel resumed climbing to the rampart wall. "Damn them!" he swore when he gazed toward the Malvers army—or where they used to be.

Eidstrun jogged up the last step to lean on the wall and uttered a stream of profanities.

Blazel blinked at Eidstrun's creativity. When he finally ran out of breath, Blazel patted his arm. "Let's go inform Histrun that the Malvers have pulled their disappearing trick again and retreated from Strunland Keep."

Histrun and Moraak sent scouts after the Malvers army to determine their route, but didn't issue any orders to prepare to leave.

Later in the afternoon, they still hadn't ordered the march. Blazel paced the entertainment room where he and the others waited, too impatient to chase after them to sit. "They'll get too far ahead of us," he complained to Rizelya.

"Do you remember how we shaved off time to reach the Sanctuary?"

He glared at her as she calmly sipped her taevo. "I knew shortcuts you didn't."

"Yep. This is the same. This is Histrun's and Naila's home territory. They know it better than anyone else. There are several routes to Strunhelos from here. We need to discover which one Malviana is taking." She poured him a mug of taevo and held it out to him. "You might as well relax. For once, we aren't fighting any battles with the Malvers' creatures."

Sighing deeply, he took the cup from her and flopped onto the couch. The rest of their friends lounged in the entertainment room with them. His gaze fell on Wisah and Blenora, playing a game of keshe with Jaehaas, Chariel, Aistrun, Ardela, and Loshera.

Blazel jerked straight up and leaned forward with his elbows on his knees, staring at Rizelya.

"Uhm... Blazel, why are you looking at me like that?" Rizelya set aside her cup, her eyes round.

"I just realized we're in Strunland Keep."

"And..."

"My mother is here, and so is Wisah." He gestured to the keshe table, then around the room. "All our friends are with us. There isn't any fighting. It's the perfect time."

"For what?" Rizelya's hand fluttered over her heart.

"For our bonding ceremony." He knelt in front of her and held her hands. "We won't have another opportunity until after the war. I want to be your mate. Now." He pulled the bond-mate torque from his jacket. "Please, Rizelya, bond with me."

Tears streamed down her face, and she nodded her head. "But... I don't have a bond-mate torque for you."

Laughing, Maellyn glided across the room and stopped in front of Rizelya. "When Blazel asked me to make a bond-mate torque for you, I went ahead and made his, too." She shrugged. "You've been so busy."

"Thank you," Rizelya said, wiping away her tears. "Yes! Yes, let's do this."

"I hear we have a celebration to attend," Histrun said from the doorway. A grin lit his face. "I couldn't be happier!"

After a whirlwind of activity, Blazel found himself standing in front of the central altar inside the temple, with Rizelya at his side. On the altar lay the two bond-mate torques. Blenora, dressed in priestess white, stood across from him, beaming with delight. Next to her, Wisah stood with a white veil covering her black-streaked hair. The diamond in her pendant caught the light from the multitude of candles. Most of the time, Blazel forgot she was the new Lady Superior. But at this moment, the light inside her made her stand out from the other priestesses, even from Chariel and his mother. The Goddess peered out from her indigo eyes. Blazel bent his head, humbled to have the Goddess attend his bond-mate ceremony.

Rizelya's hand trembled in his, and he gently squeezed it as he gazed at her. Love shone in her eyes. He listened to the words spoken by his mother and Wisah in a daze. He couldn't believe the gorgeous woman at his side loved him and would soon be bonded mind, body, heart, and soul to him. His golden magic wound around her, as her silver magic wrapped him in love. They intertwined, a glorious melding of light, until there was no separation of them, no beginning or end.

"As a circle has no beginning or end," Wisah's voice echoed his thoughts, "the bond-mate torque reflects this truth. We join now the hearts and souls of these two people into one being." She placed the torque around his neck at the same time Blenora clasped Rizelya's on.

"I bind my heart to thee," he said, "as I am bound by thee."

"I bind my soul to thee," Rizelya said, "as my soul is bound by thine."

"We are one," they intoned together. He placed his right hand over her heart while she put her hand on his chest. He covered her right hand with his left. Their heartbeats synced into the same rhythm. "Our hearts beat as one. Our souls vibrate as one."

Blazel lost himself, gazing into Rizelya's eyes. He bent his head and kissed her. As their lips met, a shock wave bounced between their torques, growing in intensity. A maelstrom of light and magic spiraled around them. Ecstasy filled him. He drew her closer until their bodies touched and he felt her warmth through her gown.

"They are bound!" Wisah cried.

The crowd cheered, throwing kehani flower petals. Blazel laughed as the petals floated down, covering their hair and faces like fragrant white snow.

Blazel and Rizelya led the way from the temple to the dining hall, where the kitchen staff laid a sumptuous feast for the Keep. That night, they feasted, danced, and drank as if life were normal.

Blazel woke the next morning, groaning at his foggy head from too much drinking. When he and Rizelya were called to a meeting with the Supreme Alphas and Moraak, he regretted the return to battle. He would have liked more than one night of normalcy with his new bond-mate.

"The scouts have returned," Histrun said. "As suspected, the Malvers are heading to Strunhelos. The good news is they are taking a direct path and will bypass Strunlair Keep." Histrun pointed the route out on the map.

"It also means they're missing the other keeps in the Territories," Rizelya said. "If we take this one—" she traced the way with her fingertip "—we can arrive a day or two ahead of them, even though we're leaving here later."

"That is the plan," Histrun agreed. "I'm sending the two Black Weave teams directly to Strunhelos. Since we aren't chasing the Malvers, we don't need you with the army. Strunhelos needs you more. I'm afraid we're in for a long siege."

Moraak groaned. *Although I do not advocate a siege, I do not think we can avoid this one. We cannot let the Malvers through the pass.*

Blazel tapped the map. "Wisah mentioned there's a magical barrier which blocks the Malvers' access to the White Mountains."

Rizelya nodded. "She did. But she also said it needed strengthening. Sir, we need Wisah to go with us. We can work on the barrier while the army marches to Strunhelos."

"I concur. Leave within the octar." Histrun rubbed his temples. "I just pray this is the last war we have to fight against the Malvers."

Blazel couldn't agree more. They'd been fighting the Malvers in some form or another for over a thousand years. What would it be like not to?

Rizelya - 25 de Godar, 1076

As the Black Weave teams sped toward Strunhelos Keep, Rizelya touched the bond-mate torque hanging around her neck. Its unfamiliar weight made her conscious of it and the new connection she had with Blazel. She'd thought the ceremony wouldn't make a difference in her relationship, but she'd been wrong. Now all she had to do was take a deep breath and think about him, and she'd know what Blazel was feeling and thinking. She'd have to become accustomed to having him in her mind all the time and figure out how to find privacy when she needed it. Rizelya grinned at the buoyant joy filling him with excitement and wonder. Their lovemaking last night had been incredible, unlike anything they'd experienced before. Their magic fused them together, so what one partner felt the other did as well. She could become used to the indescribable ecstasy.

Rizelya glanced to her right, where Wisah rode Sheekeek. She regretted Wisah would never experience the same closeness with Jaehaas. But his choice to shift into a centaur had ended his ability to make love to a woman. It made Wisah's vow of celibacy easy to follow.

The flap of a red veil caught Rizelya's attention. The two Red Guards flying slightly behind Wisah were never far from her side, and most times, they were so unobtrusive as to be invisible. Rizelya gave Jaena a nod. She'd seen the guard fight to protect Wisah, although with her new sigil Talent, she didn't need their protection. But she couldn't be everywhere or see everything, and the Malvers targeted Wisah more than anyone else—even Rizelya.

The autumn sun warmed her back, and she laid her head on Glork's shoulder, closing her eyes. She trusted him to wake her if they ran into any trouble. She hadn't slept much. Blazel's smug satisfaction at keeping her up all night clearly came through their new bond. Grinning, she drifted to sleep.

The three days of flying to Strunhelos Keep were uneventful. The camaraderie and laughter the group shared in the evenings reminded Rizelya of their journey to the Deep Mountains to find the Gryphons, when life was simpler. She'd enjoyed the brief time of not fighting for her life or worrying if one of her beloved friends would be killed.

As they lounged on the safe-house floor in front of the fire, sipping taevo, she sighed in contentment and snuggled deeper into Blazel's shoulder.

"I sense your contentment," he murmured into her ear, "but not what's causing it."

"I'm enjoying the peace and good company. Do you think this is what life will be like when we end this war with the Malvers?"

"Possibly. But it might get boring. I think I'd need a bit of excitement now and again."

"Hey," Aistrun said, "life with Rizelya would never be boring. Remember, she's a trouble magnet."

Blazel mock growled. "Are you calling me trouble?"

"Absolutely." Aistrun laughed. "But we love you, anyway. We'll keep you."

"He's part of the pack now," Saffren said. "We have to keep him. Even if he is trouble." She winked at Blazel.

A mischievous twinkle lit Chariel's eyes. "Does that mean if I bond with Aistrun, I'll be pack, too?"

Aistrun gulped and looked like a terrified rabbit caught in a hunter's net. He opened his mouth, but nothing came out.

Blazel chuckled. It was the first time he'd seen Aistrun at a loss for words.

"Of course you would," Rizelya answered, a smile playing at the corners of her mouth. "But you're already part of the pack. You don't need to bond with someone so foolish to be family."

"So now I'm foolish?" Aistrun finally found his voice. He made a mocking gesture of being wounded.

"Yes, Wolf, you are. You haven't bonded with Chariel yet."

"But... but she's a White Priestess. They can't bond."

"Don't be so sure, Aistrun," Wisah spoke up. "Many things are changing in our world. That is likely to be one of them."

Aistrun's forehead furrowed. "How would you know?"

"Uhm... Lady Superior here." Wisah waved her hand where her pendant of office lay against her chest.

Aistrun turned a bright red. "Oh, I forgot. I still think of you as Wisah, an annoying pest—"

"Pest!" Wisah sat forward, her hands on her hips. "I wasn't a pest."

Aistrun doubled over with laughter. "Got you! You still fall for that."

A mischievous light gleamed in Blenora's eyes. "You know, Aistrun, there are two White Priestesses here willing to officiate. You wouldn't have to wait."

Aistrun gulped. "But we don't have bond-mate torques. Can't have a ceremony without those."

Maellyn laughed. Although she wasn't part of either Black Weave team, she and Jorreek flew with them to Strunhelos. Her mother, Maendy, had flown there earlier to assess the keep's fortifications. They'd work with Raeleen, a master stonemason before she'd joined the team, to add helstrim where it made sense. The Posairs developed the metal alloy after the Great War, and the building of Strunhelos Keep.

"Not a good evasion, Aistrun." Maellyn grinned. "I have all my tools with me and could whip up a pair of bonding-mate torques in a few octars."

"I'll hold him for you, Chariel," Eidstrun chuckled, "to make sure he doesn't run away."

Aistrun mocked-growled at him. Then a sly grin crossed his lips. "Leistral, do you need me to do the same for Eidstrun? He's big, but between me, Blazel, and Nelstrun, I'm sure we could manage it."

It was Eidstrun's turn to gulp in dismay, his mouth gaping like a fish out of water.

"Nah," Leistral drawled. "He's not that cowardly."

Eidstrun's eyes widened further, if possible.

Leistral laughed, patted his thigh, and winked at him. "We're not ready to become bond-mates. Life is too chaotic and unpredictable right now, and not everyone needs to cement their relationship by bonding." She shrugged. "It isn't necessary for us."

Chariel leaned against Aistrun and slipped her hand in his. "I don't need one either to know you love me. Besides, we can't become bond-mates until Wisah upends Posair society with the decree White Priestesses no longer have to be celibate."

"It's on my long list," Wisah sighed. "But hopefully, the current Supreme lives many more years before I must take her place."

"May the Supreme live long," Ardela intoned.

The other White priestesses repeated the blessing, along with the others.

The group sobered at this reminder Wisah would only become the new Supreme when the old one died. After fighting the Scourge War, and now this one with the Malvers, Rizelya was sick of friends and loved one's dying. The Supreme had treated Rizelya well during their few interactions, and she'd liked the old woman. The wars would change the Posairs' lives even more than they already had with the separation of clans no longer as well-defined. Thanks to Rizelya's role, the fighting-packs now included all the Talents. She brushed back a lock of dark hair, inwardly grimacing. Black Talent had returned to the world. Everyone on the two Black Weave teams now solidly wielded Black Talent. Rizelya hadn't met the other Black Weave teams after they'd been formed and sent across Lairheim to clear the malignant pools. But she suspected they too had changed due to the merging of Talents.

Many changes and challenges would confront their people when they finally defeated Malviana and the Malvers. Rizelya snuggled closer to Blazel, and his warmth enveloped her. She wouldn't face the future alone. She had a bond-mate to share it with.

Rizelya - 28 de Godar, 1076

When the Black Weave teams arrived at Strunhelos, Rizelya almost didn't recognize the keep. Workers had cleared the trees ten measures around the perimeter, leaving an immense area of open space the Malvers would have to cross to reach the gates. They'd filled in the moat and only one drawbridge crossed it. There hadn't been a moat around the keep the last time she'd visited it. Trebuchets marched along the battlements, and for the moment, their slings hung empty. The main gate now sported a portcullis.

A strange device mounted on a bracket sat on top of each bastion and barbican. Fighters could rotate it to face in any direction. Rizelya remembered seeing a similar bracket, without the device, in a ruined tower on their way to Strunheim Territory. Large baskets of arrows waited between each arrow slot. A Thunder Wing sat on each tower, facing outward, their wings folded close to their bodies, and their tails curled around their paws. They were so still, Rizelya wondered if they were statues, until one of them blinked, tilted his head back, and warbled a warning.

When Glork flew over the keep, Rizelya gaped at the multiple courtyards and baileys, several of which disappeared into the mountainside. When Histrun had mentioned housing the entire Posair army in Strunhelos, including the reserves streaming from the other Provinces, she'd wondered where they'd fit in the small keep. But the overhead perspective revealed the keep was much larger than it appeared at ground level or from the keep-house. In one bailey, she spied huge stacks of corded wood, bales of hay, and other fodder. Another courtyard held silos of grain. The garrison's people had had a busy summer preparing for a long, drawn-out siege.

Trukeek says we're to land in the main courtyard, Glork informed her as he tilted his wings and circled around. *There is enough space for us there.*

Rizelya gaped at the huge Thunder Wing, who was almost as large as Tuueek.

This keep looks much different from what it did when I first saw it last year, Glork observed as he landed. *It's ready for a siege. The Malvers will have a hard time reaching the pass.*

"We can't let them reach it," Wisah said, freeing her staff from its holder on Sheekeek's harness. "If Malviana sacrifices the Supreme, her god, Mordaga, will manifest on this world, and his cruelty knows no bounds."

Rizelya narrowed her eyes at Wisah. She hadn't known about that tidbit before. "What if she sacrifices you? You're the Supreme's heir."

"I don't know. It would be best if we didn't find out."

A tall, older woman with pale red hair and brown eyes strode across the courtyard toward them. A short, slight man with wavy brown hair and pale-yellow eyes accompanied her. Rizelya hadn't expected Keep Alphas Joydan and Bolstrun to greet them here.

A few feet away, Joydan stopped. "Lady Superior, welcome," she said, as she and Bolstrun dropped to their knees and made the gesture of obeisance.

Rizelya noticed her niece squirm a little before she intoned the Goddess blessing and bid the alphas to rise.

Joydan's eyebrows drew together as she studied Rizelya. "Rizelya? Blazel? Is that you?"

Rizelya nodded, shrugging at how much she'd changed. Her hair was black with gray and auburn streaks now, and her brown eyes had darkened to almost black. The gray streak in Blazel's hair had widened into a thick stripe, and it too, showed only tiny streaks of red amid the black.

"It's so good to see you again. But where are my people I lent you?"

Rizelya hadn't led the battalion that included the fighters from Strunhelos in many lunadars. Not since she'd formed the Black Weave teams. Later in the evening, she'd give Joydan an accounting of how her people had fared during the Scourge War.

"They're with the rest of the army," she said. "It's about a chedan behind us."

"The war is that close?" Bolstrun gulped and turned to face the south, as if he could see the marching army.

Joydan's eyes widened as she took in the thirty-odd people with Rizelya and Blazel, not counting the Gryphons. Other than their bodyguards, Rizelya's companions also had various shades of black hair and eyes. "You're not here just to inform us about the coming battle, are you?"

Wisah shook her head. "No, we're here to reinforce the magical barrier between the pass and the mountains."

"My ancestor's journals talk about the barrier," Joydan said. "It took Black Talent to create it and strengthen the walls. They lamented its loss." She paused vand studied the Black Weave teams. "It seems to have finally resurfaced."

"You have the details of the spell our ancestors used?" Wisah asked, excitement in her voice. She bounced on her toes. At Joydan's nod, she squealed, "Show me!"

As they trooped across the bailey to the main courtyard and keep-house, Rizelya whispered to Wisah, "I thought you knew how to strengthen the barrier?"

"I do, but not how to construct it. The Supreme believed we lost the spell after Shandir created the barrier around the island. The Supremes passed down how to maintain the barrier, but not how to make it." She gripped Rizelya's arms. "This is good news! Now we can set an additional barrier over the valley after the Malvers arrive. They won't escape us this time."

Rizelya's heart raced. *We can end this war!*

Wisah's countenance changed and her voice deepened. "This will be the last time the Malvers try to enslave my people."

Rizelya bowed her head, trembling at the Goddess's presence. A moment later, the presence departed.

"We can end this war, Rizelya!" Wisah exclaimed. "Just think. No more Malvers or their monsters to plague us. Our society can return to its greatness, and oh, Rizelya, you can't imagine how great we once were." Wisah practically skipped in her enthusiasm.

But Rizelya could imagine it. She'd spent most of her free time exploring the ruins of their ancestors and discovering the marvels left behind. Her parents had dreamed of this return to prosperity when they developed the Zehis method. It might have worked had they known about the connection between the malignant magic pools and the monsters.

While Joydan searched the archives for the ancient journals, Rizelya and the others settled into a large dorm room in the keep-house. Rizelya sprawled on the bed, luxuriating in its comfort and stability. "No more cots!"

Blazel knelt over her, grinning. "I couldn't agree more." On more than one occasion, their cot had folded in half on them as they'd made love.

The next morning, after breakfast, Rizelya shivered in the chilly air as the Black Weave teams walked across the courtyard to meet their Gryphon partners in the practice arena. She paused in the doorway, breathing in the warm air and the Gryphons' slight cinnamon scent. She'd spent most of the night worried about them being able to work the spell since it required Black Talent. Rizelya didn't think they were full Blacks, yet, since reminders of their former Talents remained. Although they'd all manifested new Talents over the lunadars.

As expected, none of them, including Wisah, could cast the spell when they tried it. But by late afternoon, first Wisah, then Rizelya and Chariel finally achieved a barrier across the practice arena door.

"This takes way too much energy," Chariel said, sinking to her knees. "If we're going to cast a barrier around the battlefield, which we'll need, we can't do it like this."

"We're stronger together," Kaieli reminded them. "It's only recently we haven't had to meld to do much of what we can in the Weave, or perform other magic we couldn't before."

"True," Rizelya said. "So why don't we try it as part of the Black Weave?"

Rizelya's team decided to go first, then Blenora and Faliciden's team would attempt the spell. As soon as they melded, Rizelya's greater consciousness perceived the similarities between the barrier spell and the net-shield. It only needed a few tweaks. Within moments, a barrier covered the practice arena. They anchored it to the walls, so it would hold even without their constant attention.

"It isn't much different from the net-shield," she said when she returned to her body. She explained the differences and the changes they made to Dehali and the Fox team.

"Oh, it seems so easy now," Gehan said. "We should be able to cast the spell."

The Fox team joined hands, and a barrier settled in front of the Sabertiger team's barrier. Rizelya raised her eyebrows. This adaptation would help them when they faced the Malvers and hemmed them into the Strunhelos valley.

With a bit more practice and coordination, they'd be ready when the Malvers arrived.

Rizelya - 30 de Godar, 1076

Rizelya and the others on the Black Weave teams gathered in the practice arena. Before they started on the mountain pass barrier, they created a net-shield around the keep, anchoring it to the walls. Whenever the army arrived, they could activate it and drop it in place at a moment's notice.

When they finished, they settled more comfortably, either against their Gryphon partners or on cushions, for the intense work ahead of them. For the first time, Wisah joined them in the Weave. She needed to guide them in the process of strengthening the barrier. Rizelya gasped, breathless, at the amount of power streaming from Wisah when she added it to the Weave. Her deep indigo light seamlessly wove through their strands of power, and Rizelya sensed the Goddess within the Weave more fully than ever before.

Oh, Sweet Mother! Wisah cried, within the Weave's consciousness. *It's so much worse than I thought.*

Instead of a strong barrier blocking access to the pass, only a thin sheet of magic remained. Over the years, and with the Malvers in exile, no one had maintained it.

We have to rebuild it, Wisah said, *not just strengthen it. Thank goodness we learned how to create a barrier. The Goddess is wise.*

As bad as this is, Blenora said, dismay filled her mind-voice, *we'll require both teams to reconstruct it.*

I believe this is a good thing, Chariel said. *With our combined power, especially with Wisah's added to ours, we can build it stronger than ever. Our ancestors didn't know how to meld their Talents like we can now do.* Her voice deepened into an otherworldly timbre. *Malviana must not reach the Sanctuary, or our world will be lost to Mordaga. And he can not have my world.*

With the Goddess's orders reverberating through their minds and hearts, the Black Weave teams began spinning and weaving the barrier magic. Once they stabilized the initial layer, they took turns in laying additional layers. Wisah used her power to weave and knit the layers, forming a densely packed barrier.

At the end of each day, Wisah cast an illusion of malice over Broogk, Sterkek, and the other Gryphon bodyguards, making their energy seem like the hated grifflyns. The team modified the barrier to block only those who were evil from passing through it. They wanted their Gryphon friends to be able to fly home after the war. The Gryphons cautiously flew to the barrier and attempted to fly through it.

Finally, on the fifth day, the barrier held and the "evil" Gryphons couldn't pass through it. Trukeek, as the largest Thunder Wing, agreed to test the barrier.

As the illusion settled over him, he shuddered. His black feathers made a hissing sound. *Ugh, I don't like this.* He took a few steps and stumbled. *I feel like I'm a hundred stone heavier than normal. It's a wonder the banthues and grifflyns can even fly, if they also carry this weight.*

"It's the evil," Wisah said. "Emotions have weight, and hate, anger, and malice are the most dense. Be assured it's only temporary. I haven't changed who you are." She stood on her tiptoes to caress his beak.

I still don't like it. After a few tries, Trukeek launched into the air.

As he dove for the barrier, Rizelya held her breath and crossed her fingers in a gesture of luck.

He hit the invisible barrier and bounced, tumbling end over end. Finally, he righted himself and tried again. After the sixth attempt, he dropped back to the courtyard where the Black Teams waited, panting heavily.

I can't penetrate it, he grumbled. The skin under his fur twitched like a thousand fleas attacked him. He whirled to Wisah. *Take this illusion off me! I can't stand it any longer.*

Wisah activated a sigil and indigo light surrounded Trukeek. When it faded, he sighed and slumped to the ground.

Rizelya pumped her fist in the air, whooping in delight. "It works!"

Blazel grabbed her and spun her in a circle. "We did it."

"We're not quite finished," Wisah said, gripping her staff tightly.

Blazel put Rizelya down. She frowned, trying to make sense of the look on Wisah's face. "What's that?"

"The last layer will ensure if any Malvers breeches the barrier, they won't live to reach the Sanctuary." Wisah gulped, then said in a rush, "We can't allow Malviana to sacrifice the Supreme to bring Mordaga into this world. I need everyone for this final step."

Within moments, the two Black Weave teams had slipped into their blended consciousness. Wisah joined them. The spell they cast was at once beautiful and terrifying.

Later, Rizelya flopped on her bed. "Who knew working magic would be so tiring?" Exhaustion made her voice thin and wispy.

Blazel flung an arm over his eyes, groaning. "I'm almost as drained as after the Scourge battle. At least we finished the mountain pass barrier."

"Hopefully, we have time to set one up around the battlefield before Malviana's army arrives. Goddess, grant it isn't for a few more days. I'm so tired, I couldn't even light a candle, let alone weave another barrier."

"Same," Blazel mumbled. His breathing deepened as he drifted to sleep.

Rizelya tossed and turned, trying to find a position where her body didn't ache so much. Finally, with her back curled next to Blazel's, her body and mind relaxed.

Chapter 29

Rizelya - 36 de Godar, 1076

Rizelya sat on the bench next to Leistral, sliding her breakfast porridge onto the table. The Black Weave teams hadn't needed their bodyguards while creating the barrier, and other than a few odd moments, she hadn't seen them.

"What have you been up to these past few days?" Rizelya poured a cup of taevo, and a rich, spicy scent wafted from her mug. She took a sip and sighed deeply as cinnamon and vanilla danced over her taste buds. Even after a good night's rest, she still needed the taevo's stimulant to function.

"Joydan put us all to work." Leistral spooned some porridge into her mouth.

"This keep may appear small," Eidstrun added, "but in reality, it's bigger than the Strunlair Clan Keep. Most of it is hidden in the mountains. We've stocked provisions in various places. In case the Malvers overrun one area, we still have food and supplies."

Aistrun pointed his spoon at Rizelya. "Hey, that isn't all we've done. We've added some nasty surprises to the outer perimeter. Bolstrun liked the idea of the emotion bombs."

"The alphas appreciated our input." Ambrelya drained her mug. "The sieges at Haasneven, Haasneh, and Strunland taught us much about how the Malvers fight. This battle will be different from our ancestor's fight with them. We've changed and so have the Malvers."

Trukeek's warble broke through the conversations in the dining hall. *Gryphons coming! To your stations.*

Rizelya's spoon clattered into her nearly empty bowl, and she gulped the last of her taevo. With Blazel at her side, and her people behind her, she ran to the main courtyard. Joydan and Bolstrun raced from the keep house.

Rizelya skidded to a halt, shocked. Histrun sat on the back of Moraak, fumbling with the harness buckles. Blazel hurried to assist him. Kaaik landed, and Rizelya had a second shock when Keshanal peeked from behind Derenposan. As far as she knew, neither Supreme Alpha had ever ridden a Gryphon before. Rizelya rushed to help the old woman off.

The rest of the army is behind us, Moraak said, resettling his wings. He glared with distaste at the harness on his back. *The Malvers are hot on our heels. We'll need your net-shield to protect our people if they are to beat the Malvers here.*

"The net-shield is ready for us to activate it," Rizelya said.

"Let's go up," Blazel said, pointing upward. "It will give us a better perspective if we need to adjust the net-shield, especially since the Malvers are pursuing our people."

Rizelya turned to Dehali. "Fox team, you're in charge of the shield above the keep. Allow the Gryphons in, but stop the Malvers' beasts from entering as best you can."

"Will do," Dehali saluted her. She and the others on the Fox team ran toward the walls. Kami, Ambrelya, and the rest of their bodyguards stationed themselves next to them.

In a flurry of feathers, Glork landed beside Rizelya, and she quickly climbed onto his back. Within moments, Rizelya and the Sabertiger team were aloft. The flight of Thunder Wings and Gryphons stationed at the garrison took to the air a few milcrons later, and not a moment too soon.

A flight of banthues and grifflyns zoomed toward the keep. Ambrelya hefted her pulser and fired at a banthu, flying close to the upper towers. Chaykraa, Kami's Gryphon partner, dove at a grifflyn, with Maeaak on his tail. They attacked, tearing huge chunks from the abomination.

The first horses raced into view, foam lathering their necks and shoulders, their riders bent low and standing in their stirrups, urging their horses to greater speed. A pack of strange-looking paethers, much larger than normal, ran under the horses' legs, snapping at them. One horse stumbled, throwing its rider over its head, her helbraught flying from her grasp as she landed with a hard thump. Three paether immediately pounced on the Posair, tearing her to pieces. Several more riders and horses went down under the onslaught.

Rizelya's team couldn't drop the net-shield around the perimeter until all the riders entered the keep. She reached for her pulser, and with an angry growl, realized she'd left it and her helbraught in her room. She hadn't expected to fight. Rizelya couldn't just sit and watch the Malvers' beasts ravish her people. But her new Talents didn't always require her to focus her magic through a tool. Blazel used his mind to hurl attacks at the Malvers. Why couldn't she?

Rizelya imagined small bolts of lightning, like a pulser's projectile, and tossed them at the paether. Her eyebrows rose in surprise when pinpricks of light exploded, killing several of them.

Ah, I see what you're doing, Blazel said. *Good idea! Graak, let's take down these pests.*

Gladly!

Blazel flung out his hand. A lightning bolt streaked from it, striking a paether before it attacked a rider. Graak flared, and a thin, focused beam of fire zipped toward another beast, engulfing it.

A few moments later, Saffren tossed ice spears into the paether, and Eiden hit them with hammers of hardened air. The ground opened and swallowed several skeaeter slithering on the side of the racing army as Grazeen added her magic.

In the meantime, Aistrun, Leistral, Eidstrun, and Nelstrun fired their pulsers. Leistrun held out a globe, and a controlled whirlwind scooped up several paether and flung them against the trees. Rizelya grimaced. They hadn't left their weapons behind. She blamed her lack of foresight on her exhaustion.

The next wave of riders crested the hill and sped across the cleared landscape. Floxidor snapped at the horse's heels. Gryphons dove, flaring at the banthues, their riders either shooting projectiles from their pulsers or hurling magic from their helbraughts at the floxidor. Chaos ruled as the Posairs raced toward the drawbridge before the Malvers army.

After what seemed like octars, the Vhelopsi contingent came into view. Rizelya spotted Jaehaas and let out a breath of relief, then frowned. He had someone riding on his back, which he never allowed. As they drew closer, she made out Bren clutching Jaehaas's waist, blood pouring from her side. Jaehaas thundered across the drawbridge, but before he could reach the keep, Bren slid from his back, tumbling into the deep waters below.

"Bren!" Rizelya screamed, searching with her Talent for the injured woman. She'd used her telekinesis to stop a Gryphon; she should be able to lift someone as small as Bren from the water. But she couldn't find her. A few milcrons later, Bren's body bobbed to the surface. Tears streaming down her face, Rizelya returned her focus on protecting the war host.

The last division bolted out of the trees, a swarm of Maldiers on their tail led by Keandran. The rearguard fell under the Maldiers' whips and claws. A flight of Gryphons flew to them, attacking from above and pushing the Maldiers back.

Keandran grabbed a Red from behind and locked his jaws around her neck. Blood spurted, covering his face. Grinning, he licked his lips, cleaning off the blood with obvious relish.

That damned caitiff! Eidstrun swore. *Sterkek, let's rid this world of his evil.*

Sterkek snapped his wings and dove.

Hey, not without me! Aistrun yelled. Broogk plunged toward the Maldier.

Keandran saw them Tond howled. He stood with his arms outstretched at his side, waiting. Sterkek pulled back his wings, leading with his bright orange talons. At the last moment, Keandran jerked his hand. His whip snaking out to wrap around Sterkek's talon. Magic skipped over the whip, and Sterkek shrieked in agony. Eidstrun fired a projectile. Keandran dodged it, but missed the one from Aistrun's pulser. Red bloomed on his shoulder, and he dropped his whip. Broogk swooped below the larger Sterkek, and Aistrun sliced the whip from his talon.

Keandran yipped. A flock of grifflyns broke from the main fight and zoomed toward Broogk and Sterkek.

Incoming! Blazel yelled. *Get out of there.*

Graak and Glork winged to join the fight, with Leistral on Morru following them. Nelstrun on Daerik and Leistrun on Brogkek remained with the Black Weave team, guarding them.

Graak tore into a grifflyn, while Glork attacked another one. Rizelya watched carefully, and when the grifflyn they fought opened its mouth to belch fire, she tossed a lightning bolt down its throat.

One ready to blow! she warned.

The Gryphons broke from their individual fights, putting on a burst of speed and rising above the grifflyns. Sterkek, flying slower than the rest, barely flew past the grifflyn when it blew. He tumbled from the shock wave, and Rizelya reached for him with her mind. She sensed Blazel doing the same, and together, they stopped the huge Gryphon's downward spiral.

Holding his arm, Keandran snapped his teeth at them, then shambled into the trees.

Rizelya and the others flew back toward the keep. Sterkek, keening softly, kept up with them, refusing to leave until the fighters were safely in the keep.

The drawbridge slowly raised, and the last rider urged his horse to jump the widening chasm. A feline-type Maldier leaped, his claws gouging the horse's flanks and making it stumble. The rider flew off, and twisted to land on the moat's bank. He shapeshifted to his warrior form. In a flash, the feline Maldier pounced on him. Pulser shots spattered around them as they fought. The warrior tore out the Maldier's throat. A large Gryphon dove and clutched him in his talons, carrying him over the wall as the drawbridge clanged shut.

Rizelya and her team activated the outer net-shield. She grimaced as warriors fought with paethers, floxidors, and even a few Maldiers who'd slipped into the keep with the war host. Outnumbered, they quickly fell to the Posair fighters. Graak and the rest of the Gryphon teams zoomed over the towers, landing in the outer courtyard. With the Posair army safely behind Strunhelos' walls, the Fox Black Weave team anchored the net-shield, and the two shields merged.

Rizelya gritted her teeth at the barrage of magic strikes slamming into the shield. After nearly an octar, the Malvers gave up. Finally, Rizelya slid off Glork's back, exhausted.

The long siege had begun.

Blazel - 39 de Godar, 1076

During the first few days of the siege, Malviana tested Strunhelos' defenses. Blazel and the Black Weave teams stayed busy ensuring the net-shield remained strong under the assaults. When the first flight of banthues and baethor attempted to cross the mountains, Blazel stood on the ramparts watching, the fingers of his left hand dug into his palms. Rizelya, standing by his side, gripped his other hand so hard it ached.

"I hope our barrier holds," she said, making the gesture to bring luck.

"It will," Blazel stated. "We're strong, and the Gryphons couldn't cross the barrier during our tests." He narrowed his eyes, studying the Malvers' creatures. "Those are all much smaller than Trukeek, and he couldn't penetrate it."

"The Malvers use different magic than we do, or the Gryphons. We don't know if the barrier will stop them." She fidgeted with the ends of her braid while rocking back and forth.

Blazel pulled his hand from hers, subtly shaking the feeling back into it before putting his arm around her, hugging her close. "It will work."

The barrier shimmered faintly in the morning light. Part of the last spell they cast made the shield visible, to warn any approaching it of the danger.

The first banthu reached the barrier and bounced like it had hit a wall. It shook its head as the Malvers riding it pointed his wand at the barrier. Sparks flew when his magic struck the barrier. Light sizzled across it several feet in either direction, then swiftly coalesced into a point with a boom.

Blazel threw up an arm to protect his eyes from the brilliant flash as a streak of magic zipped from the lights to pierce the Malvers. His anguished cry reverberated in the valley, and his body jerked, and for a moment, the light revealed the outline of his bones. He exploded, taking the banthu and those flying close by with him. The rest fled back to their camp.

"Our spell worked!" Rizelya exclaimed, clapping her hands, then whirled around to hug him.

Blazel awkwardly hugged her, still stunned at what their magic had done to the Malvers. "I didn't expect such a violent result. For some reason, I thought it would just repel them and not allow them to pass, like it did the Gryphons, not annihilate them."

Wisah turned away from the falling debris. "So did I." She covered her pale face with her hands and breathed deeply for a few moments. When she dropped her hands, she'd regained her composure. "When the banthu tried to fly through, the barrier simply repelled it. However, when the Malvers attacked, it responded in kind."

"The Malvers now know it's dangerous," Rizelya smirked. "We couldn't have asked for a better demonstration of the barrier's power. They may leave it alone after this."

"If they were reasonable," Blazel shrugged and pulled his eyes from the ash. "But I'm not sure Malviana is sane. They'll probably try again. Wisah, can you tell if the attack weakened the barrier?"

Wisah closed her eyes for several heartbeats. When she opened them, she shook her head and smiled. "No, the opposite, in fact. It's stronger than before. But I'll continue to monitor it."

Surprisingly, Malviana didn't attempt breeching the barrier. Instead, she attacked the keep, using the same tactics with her modified creatures as she had during the previous sieges.

Two chedans after Malviana's arrival, Blazel and Rizelya stood on the ramparts, repelling a swarm of angulete scurrying across the pasture fences to attack the keep's walls. He ripped the head off another flying snake with his mind. Beside him, Graak gleefully tossed fire bolts at the creatures. Eidstrun pumped projectiles from his pulser at them.

Don't fill them too full of holes, Graak complained. *While they aren't the best eating, they will give us fresh meat.*

"Fine," Eidstrun huffed. He fired again, aiming at an angulete leaping from the fence and spreading its wings, trying to reach the top of the wall near them. His projectile slammed into its head, instantly killing it. "Is that better?"

Graak bobbed his head, chuckling. *I knew you were a better shot.*

Leistral, on the other side of Rizelya, laughed. She leaned back to gaze at Eidstrun. "I bet I can kill more with a single shot than you, Eidstrun."

Eidstrun mock-growled at her. "You're on!" He targeted another angulete.

"I don't like this," Blazel said. "Do these attacks seem half-hearted to you?"

Rizelya flung an angulete off the top of the nearest fence with her new telekinesis magic. "What do you mean?"

"It's as if she's using them to keep her army busy. She's waiting for something."

Rizelya snapped the neck of another angulete. By now, the swarm had thinned. She leaned her forearms on the battlement wall, watching Eidstrun and Leistral systematically take out the remaining flying snakes. When the last one tumbled to the ground, Rizelya slapped her hand over her mouth and whirled to face Blazel.

"You're right. She is waiting. Her sons, leading those two factions of her armies, are headed here. We won't see any real battles until they arrive."

Blazel swore. "Do you think Histrun knows?"

"I'm sure he does. But when they get here—" she shrugged "—could be within a few days or chedans."

Graak joined them, resettling his wings. *The scouts can't fly from here to check. It's too dangerous. Moraak won't risk them being captured by the Malvers. We'll just have to wait.* He glanced over the wall and he sat up straighter. *Ah, the fields are clear. Time to grab dinner.*

He warbled, and within a few milcrons, the Gryphons on the Black Weave teams swooped on the angulete bodies. Graak hopped onto the top of the wall, then dropped off.

Blazel's stomach growled. He held out his hand to Rizelya. "It's our dinner time, too. Good timing, Eidstrun, finishing them off in time for dinner."

Chuckling, Eidstrun bowed.

"So who won?" Rizelya asked as they walked to the dining hall.

"I did!" Leistral crowed.

"Only by one," Eidstrun growled. He threw his arm over Leistral's shoulders and hugged her.

Blazel hated the idea of a waiting game, but until Malviana attacked full-out, he'd enjoy these moments of fun and friendship.

Blazel - 62 de Godar, 1076

A chedan after Blazel's realization, he sat in a conference with Histrun and Moraak. Maps of Ronanlair Province, to the west of them, and Strunlair Province lay scattered on the table. Markers indicated Histrun's best guess at the route Malviana's sons would take to reach Strunhelos.

Blazel leaned forward, idly pushing a map marker. "How much longer do you think we'll have to wait?"

Histrun pursed his lips in thought. "I doubt much longer. It's the last of Godar. We only have another lunadar before official winter starts. But here, this high in the mountains, it could snow in a few chedans. And fighting in the snow is nasty business. Footing is perilous, and everyone slips and slides."

We have an advantage. Moraak tapped a talon against his beak. *Our inner fires keep us warm. However, the banthues and baethor are lizard-based, making them cold-blooded. While the grifflyns are half Gryphon, the other half is sheezet, and we don't know how the invader's mounts fare in the cold.*

Blazel sat straighter, remembering a tidbit of history he'd read once. "I doubt Malviana considered the weather when she started marching north. She's originally from the southern subcontinent, where it only rains in the winter. And the island where they were exiled is also south. She doesn't know how to deal with cold weather and snow."

Histrun rubbed his chin thoughtfully. "So, how do we use our advantage the best possible way?"

A quick knock on the door interrupted them, and Polkeek rushed into the office.

The Malvers breached our defenses guarding the bridge across the Storengher River from Ronanlair, the scout told them, breathless from his flight. *The Keistanlair and Ronanlair war host is racing toward Strunhelos with the Malvers close behind them.*

Moraak warbled. Blazel covered his ears at the loud, high-pitched sound. Histrun winced and rubbed his ears.

The Thunder Wings will be in the air shortly to protect our people, Moraak informed them. *Another division only needs to pick up their riders.*

Blazel and Histrun dashed to the western ramparts, arriving at the battlement wall as the first beleaguered troops reached the no-man's-land. Over three hundred Malvers and Maldiers, plus a multitude of twisted creatures, blocked their access to the drawbridge. The leading Posairs would reach the blockade in milcrons.

"We have to do something to help them!" Rizelya cried, sliding to a stop next to Blazel and Histrun. A few moments later, the Black Weave teams joined them. Chariel's wet hair streamed down her back.

"What about our net-shield?" Loshera asked, tugging her jacket straight.

"It will work once they have a clear path," Blazel said. "We need to push the Malvers out of their way."

"How about shoving them aside with a wall of hardened air?" Eiden suggested. "Dehali and I can work together."

Dehali nodded. "I'll take the west side."

"A layer of earth would hide them," Grazeen said softly.

"Oh, I like that idea," Rizelya said, smiling at Grazeen. "My fire will encourage them to get out of the way."

"A coat of ice on the earthworks will keep them from breaking through." Saffren said.

"Especially if we add ice spears." Gehan crossed her arms over her chest. "That'll discourage them from digging."

"I'll throw in a few whirlwinds." Blazel rubbed his hands together. "I've become quite good at forming them."

"As have I." Delestrun lifted an eyebrow at Blazel. "Should we follow the ladies example and split the field?"

"Absolutely! I'll take the east side."

Delestrun raised a thumb in a gesture of agreement.

Raeleen frowned at the trampled ground. "Our fighters need solid footing. I can create a sheadash stone path for them, pulling it out after they pass."

"Their flying beasts will attack from above," Chariel noted, braiding her still damp hair. "The rest of us will cast a net-shield above them, then the Gryphons can concentrate on destroying our enemies."

We'll add our fire to yours, Rizelya, Glork added. He and Graak clung to the rampart wall's edge.

And support our partners where they need us, Graak said, shaking his head feathers, which had fanned out like a halo in his agitation.

Rizelya gave a curt nod. "Good plan. Those holding the net-shield, why don't you go to the courtyard, where you're safer? None of you are combatants."

Blenora glared at Rizelya a moment before sighing in resignation. "Let's go, ladies. She's right. We can defend our people and not place ourselves in danger."

"Unlike some of us who crave danger," Chariel added, wrinkling her nose at Rizelya and Blazel.

Blenora stomped down the stairs, with Kaieli, Loshera, Ardela, Faliciden, and Noriana following her. Their bodyguards close behind them.

"Stay safe, my friends." Chariel patted Blazel's arm. "Come on, Aistrun. Join me in our exile."

Aistrun rolled his eyes. "Why did I agree to this? I'm always out of the action."

"Complaints won't get you anywhere," Chariel mumbled, and tugged on Aistrun's arm.

Blazel breathed easier, knowing his mother and the other priestesses and healers were out of harm's way.

Rizelya clapped her hands. "Okay, everyone. Let's do this. Our people are depending on us." She leaned against the wall, gazing outward.

Leistral took a position at her side, her pulser raised. Eidstrun stood next to Blazel. Ambrelya guarded Raeleen, while Kami protected Dehali. Leistrun pulled a globe from his pouch, lightly tossing it, while he and Eiden found a spot a few feet down the rampart. Nelstrun stood between Grazeen and Saffren, where he could defend both women. Korhaas bent and brushed a kiss on Gehan's cheek, who blushed furiously.

Apprehension gnawed on Blazel's stomach. They'd never tried anything like this before. He swallowed, shoving any fear aside, then turned his attention to the approaching army. The first rider cleared the trees and entered the no-man's land. Blazel nodded to Delestrun and took a deep breath. "Now!"

Blazel flung out his hand, and a whirlwind formed below him. Delestrun added his power to it, and it blew down the center of the assembled Malvers troops, knocking them aside. The wind funnels separated, pushing the troops further away. Hardened air scooped the survivors up and hurled them to the side.

A stack of cobblestones appeared at the edge of the drawbridge, and like the children's block game, the stones tumbled down the path Blazel and Delestrun had cleared. It created a roadway four horses wide. When the Maldiers ran toward the drawbridge, an enormous earthen tunnel rose, encasing the stone path, and blocked them. Ice shimmered in the sunlight. A few Maldiers didn't stop in time, and sharp spikes of ice impaled them. Blazel's heart lightened when the first Posairs careened through the tunnel and across the drawbridge.

Banthues and grifflyns dove at the approaching fighters. Flames danced on the net-shield. Instead of adding her fire magic to the tunnel—or maybe in addition, Blazel wasn't sure—Rizelya had infused her magic into the net-shield. The Gryphons added their fire magic to Rizelya's, and the air above the net-shield ignited. Any creatures flying too close to the inferno immediately caught fire. Blazel and Delestrun guided their whirlwinds up and down the tunnel perimeter, flinging any

Maldiers trying to breech it away. Quite a few didn't rise from where their bodies crashed.

Wave after wave of fighters broke through the trees from the west, until finally, the last one rode through the gates. Exhausted, Blazel released his magic and slumped against the rampart wall. The tunnel collapsed, and the ice melted, creating a giant mud puddle the Malvers would have to slog through to reach the drawbridge. With a boom, the inferno above the net-shield extinguished, and with less fanfare, the net-shield dissolved.

Rizelya leaned against him, her head resting on his shoulder. "While exhausting, that was exhilarating!"

Histrun slapped Blazel on the back and patted Rizelya's shoulder. "Good work! Most of our people made it into the keep and you kept causalities to a minimum." He leaned his forearms on top of the wall, scrutinizing the newly arrived Malvers army. "Our wait is over. I'm sure that's Malviana's western splinter divisions." He peered toward the east. "I expect the other division to arrive soon. When they do, are you ready to raise a new barrier behind the Malvers army?"

"Yes, sir," Rizelya said. "Everything is in place. We just have to activate it."

After building the barrier over the mountain pass, the teams had laid the foundations for another barrier over the other end of the valley. It had taken less time and effort, since they'd remove this one once they'd destroyed the Malvers. Wisah, as the Lady Supreme, had decreed the mountain barrier to become permanent, with Chariel's vehement approval.

"We're waiting for your order to do so," Blazel added.

"The Malvers won't escape us this time," Histrun vowed. "Once all Malviana's people are here, we'll throw everything we have at them and end this war."

Blazel had wondered why they hadn't made any forays from the keep. Histrun had been waiting for the rest of the Malviana's army to show up.

Two days later, Blazel climbed the stairs to the rampart. He enjoyed watching the sunrise from the heights. He gazed out over the Malvers' encampment and blinked. The eastern border held new tents. Mordeven's troops had slipped in during the night.

Now the real battles could begin. He prayed the war would end soon. Too many lives had already been lost.

A horn blew, and the whistle of arrows followed, igniting in the air. The volley landed amid the newly erected tents, setting them ablaze. The first attack of the day had begun. Blazel took one last look at the rising sun. Would it bring destruction or victory?

Malviana - 64 de Godar, 1076

Malviana drank in the sight of her sons. Exhaustion lined their faces and dulled their eyes, but otherwise they appeared hale. Two days ago, Malvidor arrived with his division, and Mordeven's force had come in during the night.

The goblet shattered in her fist. She'd lost too many people and creatures to the Black magic, which allowed the Posairs to escape Malvidor's troops. How had they become so powerful? The ice-covered earthen tunnel was pure genius. When it collapsed, it trapped and killed fifty Maldiers, who'd infiltrated it, burying them under tons of dirt.

Early in the morning, before any sane person should be awake, the damned Posairs targeted the new arrivals with a volley of fire arrows. More than a hundred tents had gone up in flames. Mordeven barely escaped from his. The stink of smoke still clung to him.

"It's so good of you to join us," Morvana drawled as she gazed over the rim of her cup. She sat with her leather-clad leg thrown over the arm of the camp stool.

Mordeven glared at her, running a hand through his hair. "Don't start, Morvana. It's been a long night."

"We're early." Malvidor sat straighter. "Mother said to meet here the first of Rokdar. I rushed because I wanted to arrive here first."

"You're three and half chedans late," Morvana smirked. "What took you so long?"

Malvidor shifted in his chair. "We ran into trouble. Somehow, the magic pools started drying up, and I couldn't access them to create more creatures to replace those I lost. I can't believe how fierce their warrior forms are! Even the Maldiers have problems fighting them."

"They are," Mordeven said, pinching the bridge of his nose. "I experienced more difficulty battling against magic so strong I'd swear it was Black Talent if I wasn't sure it was extinct."

Malviana sat up and looked sharply at her eldest. "You did?"

He gave her a quizzical look and nodded.

"What about you, Malvidor?"

He tipped his head. "I did."

"Damn that bitch Goddess!" Malviana thumped her newly filled goblet on the table next to her. Glass and bloodwine flew everywhere. A servant scurried to clean up the mess, while another brought Malviana a fresh cup. She briefly considered using metal flagons, but she hated the metallic taste of them. "The only way Black Talent could resurface would be with her interference."

"If you've been here so long, why haven't you taken the keep?" Mordeven asked, changing the subject.

"The Posairs beat us to it." Morvana slumped back in her chair. "By the time we reached it, they'd fortified it. You'll learn how well-defended it is, damn them to Mordaga's seven hells."

"But what about just flying over the mountains?" Malvidor stretched his legs out in front of him and balanced his goblet on his stomach.

"There is now a magical barrier blocking access to the mountains." Malviana shivered at the memory of the banthu exploding. "It's even stronger than what kept us exiled on the island. The only way into the White Mountains, even via flight, is through the Strunhelos Pass. Unless..." She gazed at her children, squinting a bit to see their energy patterns. A pleased smile lifted her lips at how strong they were now. So were her councilors, except poor Borgedier. He still hadn't recovered from his magical backlash, and she doubted he would. She'd give him another chedan for old time's sake, then offer him as a sacrifice to Mordaga.

"Unless what?" Mordeven prodded.

"Unless we take it down. We're all at full strength now, something we haven't been since Shandir's spell. We should be strong enough. While we, and the higher nobility, work on it, we can throw the lower ranks and the Maldiers at the Posairs as a diversion. They're all expendable, anyway. Once we gain the last gift of immortality from Mordaga, it'll be easy enough to spawn more." She reconsidered her decision about Borgedier. She'd just found a use for him. Malviana needed his mind to formulate strategy and direct the others, not his magic.

"When will we hit it?" Mordeven interrupted her musing.

"Not today. First, we must stop that bitch White Priestess from stealing our Maldiers and Malvers." Mordaga had finally revealed to her in a vision what was happening. She still couldn't believe anyone was strong enough to create Crone's Fire. Malviana explained the problem to her children, and together, they devised a spell which activated anytime someone used Crone's Fire near the battlefield. Hopefully, it would catch Malviana's nemesis and destroy her.

With the additional slaves her sons had gathered, she possessed plenty of lives to sacrifice to fuel the spell. She laughed in delight at the thought of what would happen to the bitch White Priestess.

Chapter 30

Wisah - 1 de Rokdar, 1076

Alarm bells clanged, calling fighters to the walls and the Gryphon teams to the skies. Wisah peered from behind a tower window, and gasped at the number of Malvers, Maldiers, and creatures swarming the perimeter. She slammed the shutter shut and turned back to the room, where Rizelya and the Black Weave teams waited.

"There are so many out there," Wisah breathed.

"Malviana hasn't thrown such a large force at us before," Rizelya observed. "It has to be a distraction. I expect her to try to break the barrier."

"Then let's ensure she doesn't." Wisah settled on the floor on a pile of cushions. None of them knew how long it would take—or if Malviana would actually attack. But with the arrival of the rest of her army yesterday, she probably felt strong enough to attempt breaking the barrier. While it held against passive attempts, Wisah wasn't sure if it would hold up to a concerted attack.

No matter what, she couldn't allow Malviana access to the pass. She gritted her teeth and tightened her grip on her staff lying across her lap. Glancing around the room, she noted everyone here possessed power which far exceeded anything their ancestors had experienced. And they had defeated the Malvers once. The Posairs would do so again.

"I'm ready," Wisah said.

"So are we." Without holding hands, Kaieli initiated the Weave, including the Fox team in it. At her nod, Wisah carefully inserted her mind into the Weave, then directed their consciousness to the barrier.

Moments after they arrived, Malviana, her children, and several Malvers flew into view. The banthues' wings beat furiously as they hovered in front of the blockade. The Malvers pointed their wands, and malevolent magic pounded the barrier.

Shock waves rolled through Wisah with every hit as she worked to repair the damage before Malviana noticed it and had her people concentrate their strikes on it. She drew on the power offered to her within the Weave to close all the holes. But even that much power had its limits.

Blazel, she said, still awed at being able to mind-speak, *release your tornado spell. Drive them back. I can't continue patching the holes.*

A huge tornado popped into existence above Malviana and her people. A banthu screamed as the wind funnel caught it, and it spun out of control. The rider tried to jump off, but the wind held her in place. The whirlwind sucked in the banthu and Malvers, tearing them to shreds. Eyes wide, Malviana retreated as the tornado bore down on her. Her companions flew tight on her banthu's tail.

As soon as the last Malvers disappeared over the horizon, Wisah dropped out of the connection, breathing heavily. She looked at Rizelya, grateful to have had her and the others with her. "I could never have pushed back Malviana's attack or repaired the damage without your help."

"I don't think we helped that much," Rizelya said with a shrug. "Except Blazel. You did all the heavy spell work."

"Fueled by your power."

"Malviana won't stop with only one attempt," Chariel said, rubbing her arms.

"She won't." Wisah stroked the helstrim wire on her staff, absently watching the tiny sparks between her fingers and the metal. "Mordaga's promise drives her too much."

"Immortality?" Blenora's eyebrows rose. "That's what's pushing her to murder our Supreme?"

Wisah shook her head. "It's only one of his promises. The other, more important one to Malviana, is that he will resurrect her beloved, Mordar."

Blazel whistled and reached for Rizelya's hand. "If they were bond-mates, it would be a promise to drive Malviana to do anything he asked."

Ardela's eyes widened in fear. "Can he do that?"

"Not like Malviana believes. Mordar's body may resurrect, but Mordaga will inhabit it."

Rizelya swore. "What a sick bastard."

Wisah agreed wholeheartedly. The ancient tome included dire warnings about Mordaga and his evil.

After the battle, the Fox team and Wisah flew over the battlefield to cleanse the Maldier's souls with Crone's Fire. Dehali and Chekraa flew ahead of the rest, and indigo light flared around her as she activated the sigil. Accustomed to using her helbraught to direct her magic, Dehali pointed her weapon at a heap of Maldier's corpses. Indigo light, tinged with deep burgundy, flowed from the tip to surround the bodies in a pillar.

As soon as it touched them, sparks ignited and malevolent magic crackled. Putrid gray-green streaks slithered up Dehali's pillar of light. The corrupt energy leaped to Dehali's helbraught. She cried out, and Chekraa warbled in distress. Both spasmed and jerked, and if Dehali hadn't been strapped into Chekraa's harness, she'd have tumbled off. Wisah winced at a loud snap, and Chekraa screeched. His left wing hung at an odd angle.

Dear Goddess! Sheekeek cried. *He broke his wing and can't fly. Help!*

The Gryphons on the Fox weave team dove, trying to catch Chekraa, before he crashed. Two black shadows zipped past Sheekeek and the others. Wisah's heart thundered in her throat as the pair plunged ever closer to the ground. In a complicated and practiced move, the Thunder Wings flung a net under Chekraa, catching him inches above the ground.

Tears streamed down Kami's face. "Are... are they dead?" she stuttered.

No, just unconscious, Tuueek said. He gripped the net tighter in his talons as Chekraa and Dehali continued to jerk with convulsions. *They need a healer.*

"I'm right behind you," Faliciden said. Fear lined her face. "I've notified Kaieli. Take them to the infirmary." As she spoke, Faliciden spun soft, green light around the injured pair.

Kami looked uncertainly between her lover, Dehali, and the team, whom she vowed to protect.

"Go with them," Blenora told her. She waved at Ambrelya and the other bodyguards. "We have enough protection."

The Thunder Wings, Harweek, and Chaykraa sped back to the keep.

"What happened?" Gehan's helbraught trembled in her shaking hand.

"What else? Malignant magic attacked her," Noriana spat out.

Ardela glared at the untouched Maldier corpses. "Malviana's magic."

The hair on the back of Wisah's neck rose and her stomach roiled. Once before, Malviana had twisted a spell, turning it on its user. *Had she done the same thing to the Crone's Fire spell? But how could she? The Crone's Fire is a gift from the Goddess.*

"Sheekeek, land next to them, please. I want to examine the body and area."

What are you searching for? His mind-voice pitched only for her.

A twisted spell. It's the only way for Malviana to pervert the Goddess's gift.

He bobbed his head as he landed. *I'll help you.*

Maeaak hovered above them with Ambrelya training her pulser at the Maldier corpses. Korhaas, on the dark russet brown Horkeek, swept over the area, alert for danger. Baederposan on Kaereek, and Delestrun on Kaaik guarded the remaining Fox team members. Wisah breathed a bit easier with the precautions. They were unsure how long it took for the Maliders to reanimate.

Wisah paced around the pile of corpses, opening her senses.

Sheekeek padding at her side, inhaled deeply, then sneezed. *These corpses reek of recent malignant magic.*

Yes, I sense it, too. She muttered the spell to reveal the unseen. Streaks of Malviana's new magic twisted around her original transmogrification spell. Wisah studied the spell. She swore every profanity she knew when she understood the full implication of it.

Malviana placed a trap, specifically attuned to Crone's Fire, on her people—Maldiers or Malvers—anything with a perverted soul. When Crone's Fire touches them, it triggers her spell, and we've seen the results. It should have killed Dehali and Chekraa, but I think Malviana underestimates, or doesn't know, how powerful our new Blacks truly are.

They don't really know either, Sheekeek huffed. *We'll have to discover another way to cleanse these souls.*

I brought the ancient tome with me. I haven't read it completely. Perhaps it has something in it we can use or modify.

I've explored Strunhelos' library, and it has some surprisingly old scrolls buried in the back. I'll research them and hope we can find a spell we can use. Sheekeek crouched for Wisah to remount, and they flew back to their companions.

Blenora's eyes widened, and she covered her mouth with her hand as she took in Wisah's face. "You discovered something horrible, didn't you?"

"Malviana twisted the spell. You can no longer use the Crone's Fires without risking death."

Ardela gasped. "But Dehali and Chekraa aren't dead."

"Only because they are more powerful than Malviana believes. You all are. But it doesn't make you immune to her spell. I'll find something else we can do to stop the Maldiers."

As soon as they returned to Strunhelos, Wisah hurried to her room, while Sheekeek trotted to the library. She refrained from joining in the battles unless Malviana attacked the barrier. Finally, several days later, she found a reference about a sub-audible frequency only perverted souls could hear. Sheekeek appeared in her room, excited. He'd discovered a magical trap for perverted souls. Combining them, Wisah developed a spell to counteract Malviana's twisting.

The specific frequency of the spell drew the Maldier's and Malvers' souls to the trap like moths to a flame. Once trapped, they remained caged until Wisah or one of the Fox team could ignite the Crone's fire. The trap protected the team from the harmful effects of Malviana's twisted spell.

Wisah - 7 de Rokdar, 1076

Malviana's forces bombarded the keep with magic and physical attacks. They assaulted every side of the garrison, except the one abutting the mountain. Wisah grimaced. She hadn't thought she was claustrophobic, but the mass of fighters crowding the rampart made her heart race with anxiety. With their flying beasts, even the air above the keep teamed with fighters battling their enemy. Banthues, carrying a Malvers, swooped below the Gryphons to strike the net-shield. On the west side, a group of Maldiers attempted to cross the moat. The ground beneath them liquefied. Their screams and howls reverberated against the stone walls as the earth swallowed them.

Wisah blocked out the sounds. War wasn't pretty, nor was it easy on the heart. A few milcrons ago, she and Rizelya had stopped a vicious magic attack. Since then, their area was suspiciously quiet. She sensed a baleful presence nearby, so close it seemed to be at her feet.

She gripped her staff tighter and peeked over the edge of the wall. Frowning, she shook her head.

"What's wrong?" Rizelya asked, suddenly alert.

"I sense something, but nothing is there." Trusting her senses and intuition, Wisah activated the sigil to reveal the unseen and jumped back with a shriek.

Leistral swore as a swarm of cloaked anguletes, climbing the wall, appeared. She swung the butt of her pulser, knocking away the angulete posed to strike Wisah. Leistral fired her pulser, killing several. Rizelya shot the creatures with her pulser, while at the same time, used her magic to fling others from the wall. A snake slithered over the edge, and red light flared from Wisah's staff, nearly decapitating the creature. With another flash, Wisah finished the job.

A loud gong rang. One Wisah didn't recognize. "What..." Wisah glanced at Rizelya, but her question died on her lips. Rizelya didn't act like she'd heard anything. The gong went off again, this time louder and making Wisah's ears ring. Finally, Wisah understood the warning.

"Malviana is attacking the barrier," she told Rizelya. "We need to close any holes Malviana and her people make."

Rizelya shot an angulete, creeping over the wall. "Can you do it alone? We can't leave here. And the Fox team is struggling to hold the net-shield against the Malvers' magic attacks."

"I'll have to." Wisah's heart pounded. She ran down the stairs and into the temple. If she were to try this by herself, she needed to be some place quiet so she could concentrate. The temple's thick sheadash stone walls muffled the battle's cacophony and chaos. Wisah stopped at the altar to the Goddess as warrior. She said a quick prayer as she folded into a cross-legged position on a floor cushion with her staff in her lap. She closed her eyes and searched the psychic realm for the barrier. When she found it, she gasped at the small, jagged tear, steadily growing larger.

Oh, no you don't! The crystal in Wisah's headband warmed, and the sigil on her left wrist tingled. Using a psychic needle, she wove the hole back together like she was darning a sock. Another hole formed, and she darned it closed. After the tenth one, sweat dripped off the end of her nose. Power streamed from the altar and into Wisah. She wove the Warrior Goddess's energy into the barrier. In her psychic vision, the barrier pulsed, blasting Malviana and her cohorts from it.

Wisah waited for additional attacks, but when no more holes formed, she opened her eyes, yawned, and stretched. She raised her eyebrows, surprised. While she was tired, she wasn't exhausted. Wisah gathered her energy around her, stood up, and exited the temple. The setting sun gilded the clouds with golds, oranges, and purples. The chaos in the keep had changed from fighting to tending to the wounded and regrouping.

During the battle the next day, a banthu, carrying a Maldier in its talons, skimmed above the ground, rising to glide close to the outer wall. It flapped over the wall and over the heads of the defenders.

Swearing, Rizelya fired her pulser at the Maldier under the banthu. "They found a weak spot in our net-shield. We'll have to weave it tighter against the keep's walls."

Wisah kept her attention on the banthu as it dropped its burden behind a group of Vhelopsi running to the stairs. The Maldier raised his whip, aiming it at the trailing Vhelopsi. Wisah pointed her staff and unleashed a red light ray, slicing the Maldier in half.

"Whoa!" Leistral gaped. "Yesterday, you had trouble cutting an angulete."

Wisah stared at her staff, wondering where her increased strength had come from.

Over the chedans, Wisah noticed her magic grew stronger each time she defended the barrier and stopped Malviana's attempts to break it. She soon made the connection the large-scale attacks coincided with Malviana's assaults on the barrier. Wisah couldn't stop the distractions, but she could ensure Malviana didn't breach the barrier.

Chapter 31

Malviana - 40 de Rokar, 1076

Malviana, her children, and the upper-echelon Malvers worked tirelessly to break through the barrier blocking the way to her goal. Every time they succeeded in tearing a hole, it immediately closed. Malviana sensed the damned White Priestess mending the barrier, and each time she did, she seemed to grow stronger—as did the barrier—while Malviana grew weaker.

After nearly forty days of relentless effort and in the face of her flagging energy, doubt crept into Malviana's heart. That night, when she made her sacrifice, Mordaga whispered the promise of her beloved returning to her. She wept when he showed her Mordar, a smile lighting his cruel eyes as he reached a hand out toward her. With this vision firmly in mind, Malviana redoubled her efforts, refusing to allow anything to stand in her way of achieving her objective.

The next day, power surged through Malviana, and she tore the biggest hole yet in the barrier—large enough for a banthu to fly through. She counted to ten, and hope flared when it didn't shut. *This has to be the work of Mordaga!* The vision of Mordar seeped into her mind. She couldn't fail now when he was so close.

"Hurry," Malviana called to her children, "before it closes!"

She urged the banthu to greater speed. Ahead, the shimmering veil parted even further, revealing the mountains, snow covering their peaks. Victory was hers! Malviana imagined the foul Supreme's blood staining her hands while she tore the Supreme's heart from her. She could almost taste it sliding down her throat.

At her side, Valdorian whooped, striking her banthu with her whip. It shot forward. Not to be outdone, Malviana's banthu flapped harder. Neck and neck, they streaked toward the aperture. Valdorian's banthu crept ahead. The hairs on Malviana's arm raised, and she sensed the White Priestess' great power. She jerked on the reins.

"Valdorian! Turn back!"

But it was too late.

The orifice slammed shut, smashing Valdorian and her mount as if two enormous fists had squashed a bug. A light flashed, and nothing remained of the pair. Not even blood and guts.

Malviana slumped in her saddle. Horrified, she returned to camp. Another milcron and it would have been her squished to smithereens.

The only way to the White Mountains was through the pass. She couldn't break the barrier while the White Priestess lived. Malviana had tried to avoid a direct confrontation with her nemesis, but she finally admitted she must face the shadow of Shandir to reach her goal. Mordar hadn't survived the device the White Priestess carried. Malviana crushed the terror threatening to choke her. Mordaga would give her the strength to complete her mission.

As Malviana landed next to her tent, fat snowflakes drifted down. She turned to gaze at the keep as Mordaga's vision slithered through her mind.

It was time to end this.

Wisah - 40 de Rokdar, 1076

After five chedans, Wisah became finely attuned to the barrier and knew within moments when Malviana initiated her latest assault. Wisah rushed to the temple. While she could weave closed any holes Malviana created anywhere, she'd found it easier when in the comfort and serenity of the temple. The strength of the Warrior Goddess flowed through her, assisting her in keeping Malviana from her goal.

Wisah sank back on her heels, dropped her head to her chest, and breathed deeply. Malviana almost succeeded in breaching the barrier. Tears trickled down Wisah's face. Normally, her struggle with Malviana was strictly mental and magical. But this time, Malviana had ripped open an aperture big enough for a banthu to fly through. As Wisah finally pulled it closed, a Malvers had flown into it, and the shutting barrier killed her—no, annihilated the Malvers. Wisah still hated killing, and only did so when she had no other option to keep her people safe.

She stayed sitting in front of the altar, praying for the end of the war and for the end of all the killing and dying. Finally, she admitted she couldn't hide out in the peace of the temple any longer. Wisah stood and worked out the kinks from sitting so long. When she opened the doors and stepped outside, cold, wet snowflakes drifted down, coating her eyelashes. She flung her arms out wide, tilted her head back, and stuck out her tongue. She loved to catch the first snowflakes of winter on her tongue. It always seemed so fresh and clean. As the snow fell around her, a vision filled her mind.

The Posairs and Malvers fought a pitched battle on the snow-covered ground, many slipping and sliding in the mud. Malviana stood across from her at last. The vision faded before Wisah saw who won the face off.

She ducked her head and hurried to the keep-house. Wisah flung open the office door, startling Histrun, Keshanal, and Moraak.

"The battle to end this war is at hand," she said.

"When?" Histrun asked, surging to his feet.

Moraak fluttered his wings, hampered by the small space from fully extending them. *How to you know?*

"The Goddess just showed me. We only have a few days. The snow was only a few inches deep in my vision."

Keshanal beamed a wide smile and sat back in her chair, folding her hands into her lap. "The Goddess sent us this message so we'd have time to prepare. I have faith and confidence that we'll eliminate this threat to our people once and for all."

Wisah prayed it was so. She didn't tell the leaders the fight between her and Malviana would determine the outcome of the war. Wisah vowed she would be the one who walked away.

Malviana - 41 de Rokdar, 1076

The morning dawned bright and cold. All the previous day, the snow had continued to fall, and Malviana's army had huddled around their campfires. The anguletes, skeaeters, and cardrolon lizards had grown more sluggish the colder it became. When the temperatures dropped below freezing, they curled into balls, and no amount of prodding could make them move again. Malviana cursed losing a large portion of her fighting force. Luckily the paether-narhili hybrid thrived in the freezing weather, as did the grifflyns and floxidor. The slick, frozen ground made it difficult to walk—or to fight—but it didn't stop the fliers.

While she'd focused on the barrier, Borgedier and Jorvelden concentrated on the keep's fortifications. The protections laid on the stone walls blocked magical attacks, but with time and intense effort, they finally weakened a section on the southern wall. Borgedier's stone softening spell had worked on the sheadash fences at Haasneven Keep. Since he could no longer work magic, he taught the spell to Jorvelden.

"I'll wrench those damned Posairs from the safety of their walls," Mordeven vowed. He took their failure to breach the barrier as a personal affront and needed to salvage his pride. He sneered at Borgedier and Jorvelden. "Jorvelden's stone softening spell must be ready by now. He's been working on it for over a chedan."

Jorvelden stiffened. "While I might not be as powerful as Borgedier was, my spell is affecting the stone. You'll find out when we attack it."

Mordeven gulped the last of his bloodwine and tossed his goblet to the side as he stood. "Let's do this."

Jorvelden sucked in a breath and placed a hand over his chest. "Now?"

"No better time." Mordeven strode from Malviana's pavilion, shouting for his lieutenants to gather his forces.

Half an octar later, Malviana huddled in a thick cloak at her tent's entrance, watching a flock of banthues and grifflyns take off with Mordeven in the lead. She glowered at the barrier. She'd expected to at least penetrate it enough for her and her entourage to slip through. Malviana hated the bitter taste of defeat on her tongue. It reminded her of her loss at Shandir's hands. She shuddered at the power the White Priestess wielded. She had thought it impossible for anyone to be more powerful than Shandir, who had been the strongest Black Talent, besides herself, that had ever lived. Malviana wondered again if this new priestess was a reincarnation of her sister.

A cacophonous boom jerked her head around to the keep. Malviana pumped a fist in jubilation as the southern tower's top level crumbled. Mordeven had done it! He'd finally damaged the magically enhanced structure.

Two large Gryphons dove, attacking his banthu. Malviana scowled. Their riders possessed the unmistakable aura of Black Talents. She cast a spell to allow her to see clearly across great distances and swore. Malviana barely recognized Rizelya. She'd changed so much over the lunadars since Malviana had seen her last. *How has her powers grown?*

Although confident Mordeven could win a battle against a single Black Talent, she wasn't so sure about two. She pointed her wand at him and added another layer of protection to his shield. A moment later, a fiery, twisting cyclone of power slammed into Mordeven. The shock wave of the magic hitting her shield forced Malviana to take a step back. It battered both their shields. Gritting her teeth, Malviana poured more power into the shield. Mordeven slung spell after spell at the pair, but they just bounced off them like water droplets splashing on cobblestones. *They shouldn't be so strong!*

Furious, Malviana gathered her magic and channeled it through her wand, sending bolt after bolt of lightning at the Gryphons. She crowed in triumph when the dark brown Gryphon jerked as electricity tore through him. Malviana anxiously waited for him to explode. She'd learned in the last war Gryphons hated and feared lightning because it was so dangerous to them. It became the Malvers' weapon of choice against them. Malviana gaped when the Gryphon kept dodging Mordeven's spells. The man riding him had somehow neutralized the effects!

They'd drifted toward the mountains during their battle, and the barrier loomed behind Mordeven. He turned his head around and saw the danger. Malviana sensed his panic through her shield. They'd both witnessed what contact with the barrier could do. Together, they attacked the pair, giving Mordeven a chance to dive below them and race back to their camp. He landed his banthu next to her tent. When he climbed off it, his face was pale, and his hands shook.

"That was close," he breathed.

She followed his gaze back up to the pair, who had returned to the fight over the keep and engaged again. Suddenly, the Malvers facing the man clutched at his throat. A moment later, his head toppled from his shoulders and tumbled to the ground.

"Two Blacks!" Malviana exclaimed. "How is this possible?"

A grifflyn belched fire at a Gryphon with dark umber head feathers and rust on his shoulder wings and the woman with dark green hair riding him. Its higher position meant the pair didn't notice his attack. Malviana grinned as the fire streaked toward them. They'd never escape it in time. Green light flared around the Gryphon and woman before the fire touched them. She gaped as their shield absorbed it.

A smaller dark brown Gryphon with beige fur striped with brown on its chest and orange-red hindquarters and tail zipped to the larger Gryphon's side. Its rider, a woman with sapphire-blue hair streaked with black and purple, casually flung ice spears at the grifflyn. Malviana had never seen anyone with purple hair. Water and fire Talents didn't mix. The crystallized water sparkled in the sun before they pierced the grifflyn's side. As they did, orange light blossomed within the grifflyn. The woman yelled something, and every Gryphon in the area bolted. Blooms of fire ignited within the grifflyn, and a moment later, it exploded.

"Did you sense their power, Mother?" Awe filled Mordeven's voice—or maybe it was envy.

"Blacks," Malviana spat the word as a curse. "How many are there?"

Mordeven shrugged. "Obviously at least four." He waved a dismissive hand, then caressed his wand. "No matter. Our magic is greater than theirs. We'll be victorious."

Malviana didn't want to admit—even to herself—they worried her. The Malvers had eliminated Black Talent during the Great War because it rivaled their own power.

Malviana turned away from the battle and peered at the mountains and the snow that was visibly lower on them. She shivered as the frigid wind seeped through her cloak. She didn't want to spend the winter fighting a siege in tents. Her people would win, they had to. Mordaga had shown it to her.

She studied the crumbled tower. Only the top floor had fallen, but it was the first damage they'd made to the walls. The Gryphons were too good at stopping any air attacks and some sort of shield protected the keep from above. They'd have to force the Posairs out onto the battlefield somehow.

"Your attack proved the stone softening spell works," she said. "Work with Jorvelden to increase its potency. I expect you to create a gap in the walls by tomorrow."

"We'll create one by morning," Mordeven tapped his wand against his thigh as he considered the keep. "However, breaking through the wall won't be enough. We still have to contend with the moat and move our people across it. They'll destroy any bridge we construct, like they have our siege engines."

Malviana pursed her lips as she pondered the problem. A servant with an armload of wood slipped on a patch of ice. "We freeze it. The cold weather will help. And it's something they won't see, and if they do, they'll think it's natural."

Malviana fumed the next afternoon when she examined the moat. Even with the snowfall, only a few inches of ice formed along the moat's banks.

Mordeven slipped into her tent with his eyes downcast. "We need more time for the stone softening spell to work. The protective spells on the walls are blocking it from penetrating as much as we'd like."

"Have Morvana and Malvidor add their power and work on it around the clock." Malviana slammed her cup down, sloshing bloodwine on her hand. "I want in the keep and access to the pass before winter locks us out of the mountains."

Blazel - 43 de Rokdar, 1076

After the southern tower's top layer crumbled, Histrun realized what Malviana's people were doing. They'd experienced the Malvers use a stone softening spell before at Haasneven. This attack confirmed Wisah's warning the final battle was near. The Black Weave teams were the only ones strong enough to counter the spell.

Over the past three days, Blazel and the Sabertiger Black Weave team worked to stop their enemy's attempts to breach the southern tower. The first day, they'd easily blocked the spell. But on the second day, the Malvers poured additional power into the spells, and it had taken the full Sabertiger team to keep up with the damage. Raeleen, an expert stonemason, joined them, and she taught them spells to not only repair, but strengthen, the walls.

Blazel ran a hand over the southern tower's wall, and his magical senses detected a thin layer of stone and a hole behind it. The Malvers believed they'd tunneled through the stone. Blazel grinned. In a devious plot, Raeleen guided the team in allowing the Malvers to create a narrow tunnel in the tower while laying a spell to fill it in. Only a few Malvers would make it through the tunnel. The rest would be trapped within the stone forever.

Yesterday, Saffren detected the ploy to freeze the moat. She set a spell not only to unfreeze it but also to boil the water in the moat when the Malvers started crossing it.

Meanwhile, his mother's Black Weave team, the Fox team, erected a magical barrier around the outskirts of the battlefield, trapping the Malvers. Histrun didn't want them disappearing again. This battle would determine the fate of the Posairs. They'd either destroy the Malvers or fall, condemning their people to slavery. Blazel was vaguely aware of other measures Histrun and Moraak set in place as they readied for the confrontation with the Malvers.

An octar ago, the Malvers had stopped their attacks for the night, and Histrun called the battalion alphas into his office. He included Blazel and Rizelya as the leaders of the Black Weave teams.

Histrun paced the room with his hands resting on his lower back. "I expect the Malvers to attack in the morning. We have prepared as much as possible. Blazel, what is the status of their supposedly covert activities?"

"Only a thin layer of stone remains for them to break through. The spell to cave the tunnel behind them is in place. Saffren reported the moat near the tower is frozen enough for the Malvers to cross it."

Histrun gave Blazel and Rizelya an approving nod. "Thanks to our Black Talents, the Malvers assume they'll take us unaware. They won't be expecting to meet us on the battlefield. But that is where we'll be! At dawn, we'll march from the keep." He rubbed his hands together and sat down. "Now, let's discuss our battle plans."

Two octars later, Blazel gripped Rizelya's hand as they left the council meeting. As they walked to their room, he fingered his bond-mate torque with the other hand. Fear and apprehension sizzled through him, even worse than it had while waiting for the final battle to begin with the Scourge. Then they'd faced overwhelming numbers, but now they faced stronger magic. They'd lost thousands of people in the last battle of the Scourge War. How many would they lose this time? He didn't want to live if Rizelya wasn't in his life. After bonding with her, he understood Histrun's profound grief when his bond-mate and Rizelya's mother, Zehala, had died.

When they reached their room, he pushed the door closed, drew Rizelya to him, and kissed her deeply. Her hands pulled his shirt up and explored his back, and he shivered with desire. In a frenzy, they tore at each other's clothes. He picked her up and carried her to the narrow bed, where they made fierce love.

Chapter 32

Malviana - 44 de Rokdar, 1076

Malviana dressed in her battle gear. Last night, Mordeven had informed her they were ready to push through the wall, and the moat had frozen enough for her people to cross it. Snakes crawled in her stomach, and she doubled over. After several milcrons, she finally dispelled her apprehension and straightened. Taking a deep breath, Malviana stepped from her tent and into the dawn, blowing on her hands to warm them. Overhead, iron-gray clouds loomed, threatening another snowstorm. She shook with foreboding. The vision from Mordaga overlaid the scene before her. Today, she'd face her adversary.

Malviana gazed at her children, memorizing their faces. *Will they survive the coming battle?* Her army lined up, ready to race across the open land to swarm the keep. She climbed into the saddle of her banthu so they could all see her. Only her breathing disturbed the quiet.

She whirled toward the keep at the loud creaking sound.

The drawbridge banged opened, and the Posair forces streamed out. The breath of their horses fogged the air, and the morning light glinted off their weapons. Men in their warrior forms loped out. Gryphons landed to form a first line of defense. A huge golden one—the largest she'd ever seen—stood like a magnificent statue in the center. Around them flowed a phalanx of centaurs and archers.

Malviana turned her back on her enemies and faced her troops. She stood up in her stirrups and raised her wand in her fisted hand. "To Victory! To Mordaga!"

Her army took up the chant. She dropped her arm at the same time as she kicked the banthu to rise in flight. Her people rushed forward under her banthu's wings, screaming Mordaga's name. The Posairs thundered across the field. The two sides clashed with teeth, claws, weapons, and spells.

Malviana flew high overhead, searching for her enemy—the White Priestess. One of them would die this day, and Malviana vowed it wouldn't be her.

Blazel - 44 de Rokdar, 1076

As Blazel and Rizelya dressed in the dark dawn, they kept touching and kissing each other. Blazel couldn't keep from worrying that this would be the last time he saw her. Finally dressed, they stood in the center of the room and embraced.

"Be careful out there, my love," Blazel said. "It won't be like the skirmishes we've fought. Malviana and her children will be in the thick of it. They may be able to stop us from melding."

"From what I've seen, they don't work together well. But I promise to be careful if you do. I don't want to lose you either."

It's time, Moraak said in their heads.

There wouldn't be any horns or bells to gather their fighters. They didn't want to alert the Malvers before they were ready. In an eerie quiet, broken only by the creak of leather and the clink of metal, the Posairs saddled their horses and affixed harness to the Gryphons.

Wisah, dressed in white battle gear, appeared in the courtyard.

What are you doing? Histrun demanded in mind-speech. *It isn't safe for you to leave the keep.*

I'm going into the battle, Wisah responded calmly. She adjusted the headband she always wore now. An azure-blue sigil flared underneath it.

Histrun's face reddened. *You can't! You're the Lady Superior. We can't afford to risk losing you.*

If I don't go, you risk losing this war. I'm the only one who can vanquish Malviana. She patted the pouch at her waist.

The White Priestess unmakes the evil queen, Chariel said, a silver film covering her eyes. Even her mind-voice took on a spectral quality. *The world is reborn. If the White Priestess fails, the world falls to ruin.*

Histrun stared at Chariel for a long moment, then bowed his head. The Gray Oracle had spoken unequivocally. He stepped to the side and gestured for Wisah to go before him. She and those partnered with Gryphons slid into their harnesses and buckled in.

Dawn came with a slight brightening of the lead-gray clouds. Moraak gave the signal, and the gates slowly opened. The drawbridge lowered with a thunderous boom in the quiet.

Graak and the other Gryphons flew over the walls while the first of the troops marched out. As Graak landed next to Moraak, Blazel glanced to his right at Glork and Rizelya. She held her helbraught tightly, and her pulser peeked over her shoulder. He leaned forward to grin at Aistrun, who sat on her other side. Surprisingly, Chariel had demanded to be part of the fighting force rather than stay behind in the safety of the keep—and to protect it—with Kaieli and Loshera. The look in her eyes had stopped Blazel or Rizelya from questioning or protesting her decision. Blazel had been profusely relieved when his mother had opted to stay out of the active fighting. Ardela and Faliciden also joined the team who were staying in the keep. They'd anchor and hold the net-shield and ensure the barrier blocking the valley remained intact.

Behind Blazel, Eidstrun and Sterkek waited. The huge Gryphon's tail thumped, and it was only a slightly darker shade of white than the snow. Eidstrun held his pulsar in front of him, ready to protect Blazel. Next to him, Leistral gripped her helbraught. Like Rizelya, she'd strapped her pulsar to her back. Morru shook out his white and black striped fur, and resettled his light black head feathers. Leistrun held a yellow globe, and over the chedans, had become quite proficient with using the magic globes. Brogkek swished his red tail, forming eddies in the snow. Eiden looked over her shoulder and grinned at Leistrun, then patted the bluish-gray feathers on Korrik's neck.

Nelstrun sat between Saffren and Grazeen. He and his partner, Daerik, would watch over the two women. Ambrelya gazed adoringly at Raeleen. When she turned her attention to the waiting Malvers army, her mouth tightened, and she stroked her pulsar. Nothing would get past her to harm her lover. Chekraa rubbed his bright orange beak against Chaykraa's white cheek. The twins were as close as their partners, Dehali and Kami, were.

Dwarfed by Moraak's much larger stature, Sheekeek waited next to Moraak. Wisah reached out her hand to grip Jaehaas's. He leaned over and brushed a kiss on her cheek. He turned to face the Malvers assembling across the battlefield and nocked an arrow. Sheekeek stepped forward, and Wisah raised her staff. A beam of sunlight broke through the clouds and bathed her with its light. The crystal on her staff lit up like a beacon as the Malvers troops started chanting.

The Goddess's love emanating from Wisah filled Blazel with hope. His new Black Talent sensed it pulsing from her staff to touch every single person assembled on the field and to those manning the keep.

"For the Goddess!" he shouted. Everyone around him took up the cry. Across the field, Malviana dropped her arm. At the same time, Wisah thrust her staff above her head.

With a crack of his wings like the sound of thunder, Moraak leaped into the air. Sheekeek, Graak, and the rest of the Gryphons launched a moment later. With a screech of defiance, Graak quickly rose higher to meet the onrushing banthues, grifflyns, and baethors.

Even as he and Graak fought the first banthu, Blazel searched for Morvana. They had faced each other twice before. This time, he'd be the clear victor.

Rizelya - 44 de Rokdar, 1076

Rizelya waited beside Blazel for the order to engage. Behind them, Metherposan led the men who chose to fight in their warrior forms, using tooth and claw. Those who stayed in their natural form followed Aradehan and fought with pulsers and magic globes. Jaehaas now served as the alpha for the centaurs and archers, which included Hairan and the Vhelopsi. Laynar and Kothera directed the women fighting on the ground with their helbraughts, pulsers, and magic globes.

Rather than Histrun giving the order, Wisah stepped forward just as a sunbeam broke through the clouds. Radiance washed over her, and Rizelya squinted, trying to see her niece within the dazzling woman. After seeing—and feeling—the Goddess's presence in Wisah, Rizelya would never again question Wisah's new calling as the Lady Supreme. Then Wisah's staff glowed, and Moraak leaped into the sky. Rizelya slammed into the harness as Glork took off.

Within milcrons, she and Glork encountered a Malvers woman riding a banthu, and their battle began. Glork dove at the pair while Rizelya fired helstrim projectiles into the Malvers. While they wouldn't kill her, they would stifle her magic. Rizelya shoved the pulser behind her and unhooked her helbraught, feeding fire and ice into it. It glowed a bright purple, something Rizelya hadn't ever thought possible until she'd become a Black Talent. Glork pummeled the banthu with talons and claws, tearing great chucks of flesh from the beast. Hot blood splashed on Rizelya. Her red fighting leathers protected her from its heat.

The Malvers woman pointed her wand at Rizelya, moving it in a complicated pattern while shouting an incantation. Rust-colored light flared, looking and smelling like old, decayed blood. Rizelya called up a tightly controlled wind funnel and gathered the foul magic in it. A flash of emerald-green light neutralized it. The woman bared her teeth in fury and waved her wand again. Glork disengaged from the banthu and flew directly at the woman. She screamed, threw her hands over her head, and ducked down. He scraped her back with his hind claws as he passed over her. In a graceful move, he flipped over. The woman never saw Rizelya's blade as it slashed through her neck.

Several octars later, Rizelya and Glork soared high over the battle below, catching their breath after fending off five Malvers who had attacked them at the same time. Rizelya breathed on her hands. Her fingertips felt like icicles. As the day had worn on, the temperature had continued to drop. She hoped it would snow soon. Then it'd be warmer.

Here, Rizelya, Glork said, *I can help you.*

A moment later, heat rose from the harness under her, wrapping her in delightful warmth.

The bright lights from the light-type projectiles mixing with the various colored lights of the globes cast a strange beauty over the battlefield. Spells flew from both sides, clashing and colliding, sometimes in a sickening, writhing mess of magic. The melee made it difficult to pick out individual fights.

A gust of wind momentarily cleared the smoke and magic, and Rizelya glimpsed a familiar red-gold pelt. Her forehead puckered. "What is Aistrun doing down there?" Suddenly a malformed warrior form rushed Aistrun. "Keandran!" she said in disgust.

Look, Glork said, *Aistrun has already scored the caitiff.* He drifted closer to the fight.

A huge warrior with pale gold fur swiped at Keandran from the side. "Eidstrun is with him. It's time for those three to settle their differences."

Broogk and Sterkek are down there, too.

The two Gryphons fought a pack of Maldiers, keeping them from overpowering Aistrun and Eidstrun. While Sterkek wasn't quite as large as a Thunder Wing, his size made him a match for the brown bear-type Maldier attacking him. His bright yellow talons dug a huge furrow in the Maldier's chest. Blood dripped from an injury on Broogk's dark brown hindquarter.

He flared, and the wound sealed. With a hunting cry, Broogk leaped on the sabertiger-Posair Maldier. His weight took the Maldier down while his hind claws disemboweled it. Before he could move off his dead opponent, another Maldier, this one a wolverine mix, attacked him. Broogk tucked his wings tight to his body, protecting them as they rolled across the ground.

Keandran howled, and Rizelya's attention turned from the Gryphon's fight. She trusted they'd be victorious over their Maldier opponents.

Wide, bloody stripes marred Keandran's back. He bared his teeth, snapping them, and leaped at Aistrun, who almost casually moved out of the way. The Maldier whirled around, his tail thrashing, and dashed at his opponent. Aistrun whacked him with an open palm, the tips of his claws sliding against Keandran's jaw. Keandran shook his head, flinging blood, then charged again. Aistrun ducked under him, caught him, and threw him. The move reminded Rizelya of the fight between them so long ago when Aistrun had put Keandran in his place. Maybe she'd been wrong to stop Aistrun from killing Keandran then. They would have saved him from being twisted by Malviana into the evil creature he'd become. Aistrun was now taking the opportunity to correct that mistake.

Eidstrun slammed his clawed foot into Keandran's side, and as he flew, blood sprayed from the deep gouges. Keandran rolled several times. When he finally stopped, he pushed to his hands and knees, shaking his head. Aistrun gave him a chance to stand before backhanding Keandran. His head jerked back, and Eidstrun grabbed Keandran's horns, forcing his head even further. But before he could break Aistrun's neck, a black bear-type Maldier, almost as large as Eidstrun, bowled into him, knocking him away from Keandran.

The tip of a whip snapped beside Rizelya's ear, reminding her she couldn't sit and watch Aistrun's and Eidstrun's battle with Keandran.

Wisah - 44 de Rokdar, 1076

Wisah and Sheekeek flew high over the battle, higher even than the aerial fights between Gryphons and the Malvers' creatures. Her skin glowed azure with the numerous sigils she'd activated, using her magic to defend her people. Time after time, she'd saved a group of Posairs surrounded by the twisted beasts. She couldn't spare a moment for remorse as she tossed them aside like broken toys. If she did, they'd simply regroup and attack the Posairs. Her efforts helped her people overcome the animals.

But her and Sheekeek's main duty was to burn away the Maldiers' and Malvers' perverted souls, so they couldn't infect anyone else. Her sonic spell only held a limited number of trapped souls. There were so many Maldiers and Malvers on the battlefield that she needed to clear the traps often.

There! Sheekeek pointed out a pack of floxidor and Maldiers, his keener eyesight picking them out of the chaos.

The creatures circled twenty Vhelopsi and centaurs. Arrows flew, igniting as they hit their targets. The Vhelopsi shot projectiles into the floxidor surrounding them. Sheekeek dropped a bit lower, and Wisah sucked in a breath. *Jaehaas!*

A floxidor nipped Jaehaas's heels. He swung his bow like a cudgel, knocking the beast away. It snapped, catching the bow in its jaws, breaking it. Jaehaas didn't have a pulser; he hated anything to do with the Scourge. He grabbed an arrow from his quiver, and as the floxidor jumped at him, he thrust the tip into the floxidor's eye. Before he could pull the helstrablade strapped to his side, a great horned Maldier flicked his whip at Jaehaas. A multa's hindquarters formed the lower portion of the Maldier, and long, shaggy brown fur covered his upper body.

Jaehaas reared, his hooves striking at Korand and knocking the whip aside. When he came down, he clenched his helstrablade. He charged Korand, who laughed and bent his head. Using his huge antlers, he blocked Jaehaas's strikes. Wisah imagined hearing the clash of metal on bone. Even while he parried and thrust with his horns, Korand slowly swung his rope, gaining momentum. In a quick succession of moves, he twisted his head and Jaehaas's helstrablade flew out of his hands.

Korand threw the rope. It slid over Jaehaas's head, tightening around his neck. Jaehaas bucked and reared, but it only tightened the noose. He had both hands on it, straining to loosen it. Wherever the rope touched, pustules broke out on his skin, oozing bloody green pus. Korand wrenched the rope, pulling Jaehaas toward him. Jaehaas dug in his rear hooves and crouched down, but Korand dragged him relentlessly closer.

A red beam of light shot from Wisah's staff, striking Korand in the back and cutting him in half. As the two halves toppled away from each other, Jaehaas frantically removed the rope from around his neck, then bent over, taking deep gulps of air.

Thank you, my love, he gasped. *I was sure it was my time to meet the Goddess.*

You'll only see her through me for a long time to come. Tears fogged Wisah's goggles.

Watch out! Move, Jaehaas! Sheekeek cried.

Korand's corrupt soul flowed from his corpse. Wisah hurled the trap spell at it. The trap opened with a pop of light. Korand's soul struggled against her siren's song, wriggling toward Jaehaas.

"You can't have him!" Wisah yelled as she exponentially increased the volume and intensity of the spell. It tugged at Korand's soul, which thinned and snapped into the cage. Then twenty other Maldier souls were wrenched from their still living bodies and zoomed into the trap. Wisah gaped at the collapsing bodies, horrified. "Oh, Sweet Mother, what have I done?" Before she could end the spell, the souls from every Maldier, living or dead, in a two-hundred-foot radius were torn away and imprisoned in her trap.

I didn't think it was possible to separate a soul from a living being, Sheekeek said. His trembling matched her own.

Nor did I. Wisah gagged as the dark purple light of Crone's Fire ignited, burning the souls within her net. *Sheekeek, can you land? I'm going to be sick.*

I'll be joining you. Sheekeek swiftly dove and landed in an empty field.

As Wisah emptied her stomach, white flakes drifted through the sky.

Chapter 33

Rizelya - 44 de Rokdar, 1076

Even as Glork whirled to face their new opponent, the crack of a whip and a surging pulse of foul magic slammed into Rizelya's side.

"There you are, you bitch," a Malvers man sneered. Instead of riding a banthu, he rode a grifflyn. "I've been looking for you."

A circlet-type crown held back his longish black hair, showing off a hematite and black diamond earring dangling from his ear. Gemstones winked from the rings on his fingers. If not for the cruel set of his mouth and the malice in his eyes, she might have considered him handsome. She'd take Blazel's scarred face and kindness any day over this repugnant man.

"Mordeven, Malviana's eldest son," Rizelya sneered, recognizing him. "I thought Malviana would be the one to seek me out."

"She's busy with that bitch White Priestess, so it's between you and me." He smiled and licked his lips as he raked her with his eyes. "You've been troubling Mother for a long time. I had planned on killing you for her, but after seeing you, I've changed my mind. First, I'll beat you senseless, then take you for my pleasure. If you survive, which I hope you do, I'll sacrifice you to Mordaga. With your strength, he'd grant me vast power, maybe enough to challenge Mother."

Rizelya rolled her eyes. "Are you going to talk me to death, or are we going to fight?"

In answer, he pointed his black onyx wand toward her, fire crackling from it. Rizelya threw up an ice shield. Mordeven's strike sizzled against it, and she shifted the shield into a stream of water, quenching the fire. A dozen small, keen-edged daggers materialized, zinging at her like a swarm of angry hornets. She flung out her hand, catching them telekinetically, and tossed them back toward him. Rizelya cried out at the sharp sting in her arm. A dagger she'd missed quivered in her left biceps. As she negligently plucked it out, searing pain spread from her arm to her chest and her hand grew numb.

"Trust you to use poison," she sneered at him. She hurled the dagger at him.

Mordeven laughed as he knocked it from the air.

She continued to fight him, even as her movements became more sluggish.

Kaieli! Glork called, *Rizelya's been poisoned.* He attacked Mordeven's grifflyn with a fury that didn't give Mordeven a chance to fling any spells at Rizelya.

Kaieli and Loshera merged with her through their Weave connection. A small part of the others joined with them, but they couldn't merge fully. They were all engaged in their own desperate battles.

It's bad, Kaieli said. *You need to return to the keep now.*

I can't, Rizelya panted. *I'm fighting Mordeven.*

We'll purge what we can. But Rizelya, finish your fight quickly and get your ass back here. I can't lose you too.

Grief swamped Rizelya through their link.

I'll make sure she returns, Glork assured Kaieli. Fear slithered through his voice.

Bronze healing energy zapped the poison, and Rizelya's strength returned immediately.

This is only temporary, Kaieli reminded her. *Kill the bastard and come home.* Kaieli broke the connection.

Pretending the poison still affected her, Rizelya slumped in her harness, her arms hanging loosely over Glork's sides, hiding her helbraught with her body. After a flurry of attacks and counter-attacks, Glork drooped one of his wings, spiraling toward the ground.

Mordeven gave a gleeful laugh as his grifflyn dove after them. When the grifflyn flew alongside them, he pointed his wand at Glork. It glowed a vicious sepia color. Glork rolled closer to their enemy, and Rizelya rose off Glork's neck and swung her helbraught, pulling in some of Blazel's strength from their bond-mate connection.

Mordeven's mouth opened in a silent scream as his head toppled from his shoulders and tumbled to the ground. Glork ripped great chunks of flesh from the grifflyn. Rizelya took pity on the beast and shoved her helbraught into its heart.

That small bit of exertion exhausted her. "Take me to Kaieli, please, Glork."

I'm already on my way.

Rizelya hooked her helbraught to the harness, then laid her head on Glork's soft neck feathers. A numbing lethargy stole over her, and she no longer felt Glork underneath her. She closed her eyes against the blackness stealing away her vision. Her last thought was of Blazel.

Blazel - 44 de Rokdar, 1076

Blazel tried to track Rizelya's movements, but all the spells and magic flying in the air made it impossible to pick out a single person. Through their bond-mate connection, he sensed she was cold, but okay. Already this morning he'd fought and killed several Malvers with his Talents. He kept expecting Morvana, or another of Malviana's children, to find him. Until then, he'd continue to be a menace to any Malvers who flew close.

Three Malvers faced him on their banthues, smirks on their faces, thinking they outnumbered him. He feigned being afraid, forcing himself to shake and cower away from them. As usual, they miscalculated the effectiveness of having a Gryphon as an intelligent partner. Two of the Malvers drove their mounts to ram Graak from the side, while the third one attacked head on. Graak waited until the two banthues were on his wingtips and the Malvers pointed their wands at him. As soon as they loosed their spells, he snapped his wings back with a crack of thunder and dove under the banthues, cloaking himself in his invisibility spell.

The Malvers screamed as their spells slammed into each other. The man on their left grabbed his heart, while the woman on the right gagged and vomited black bile. Using his talent, Blazel squeezed his claws around the first Malvers' heart, injecting his venom into it. A lovely shade of purple covered the man's face as he gasped in pained breaths. At the same time, Blazel inserted snelks into the woman's stomach. She clutched her abdomen and doubled over, retching. The black bile turned bloody. She howled, staring at her stomach with a look of horror on her face. The growing snelks were visibly wriggling inside of her.

Now! he said to Graak.

Graak released his invisibility spell, sped into the opening between the two banthues, and flared. Blazel shot both hands out, armed with long helstrablades. Graak's momentum added strength to his strike, and both blades cleanly decapitated the Malvers. The third Malvers flung a hand up against Graak's fire. Graak flared again, aiming at the banthu's head. The banthu jerked back, its movement throwing the Malvers from the saddle. Blazel grinned; they still hadn't learned to strap in. The man screamed as he fell hundreds of feet, splattering on the ground. It killed the Malvers as effectively as beheading them did.

Blazel wiped the first accumulation of snowflakes from his goggles.

Suddenly, pain seared his back. Blazel glimpsed a familiar face as a grifflyn sped past them: Morvana.

How hurt are you? Graak asked. *I didn't see or sense them!*

"They must have used a cloaking spell. It isn't too bad. I can still fight." Blood oozed down his back, making his shirt sticky. While Morvana's mount wheeled to strike again, he concentrated on closing the wounds by borrowing a bit of Kaieli's healing Talent. The blood flow slowed to a trickle, but pain blazed with every movement. He really should return to the keep and have Kaieli treat his injuries, but he wouldn't run from this Malvers.

It was time to finish her.

He flung a red lightning bolt at her. Her lightning bolt met his in midair. They crackled and sizzled, his red blending with her blue into a purple stream. He added more power to his, and her portion grew smaller. She pushed, and her power ate at his. For several long milcrons, they played tug-of-war with each other. Graak wrapped his magic around Blazel's, and with a blinding flash, his bolt tore through hers and slammed into her. She toppled backwards with a cry, smoke billowing from her chest.

He gaped when she swiped away the smoke and sat back up, looking none the worse. She pointed her wand at him, and a wind funnel laced with scorching fire thundered toward him and Graak. He gathered the falling snow, compacting it into a wall. Her twister slammed into the snow, which collapsed around it, dousing the fire with water.

Graak zipped past it and dove at the grifflyn, flaring as he did. The two snapped at each other, their talons raking at each other's chests. Blazel and Morvana continued to throw spells at each other as their mounts fought. Graak's talons dug deep into the grifflyn's chest. It threw back its head and rammed it into Graak's forehead. Graak lost consciousness, and Blazel hung onto his harness as they plummeted. As they spun, he glimpsed Morvana's arms wrapped around her mount's neck, barely staying on. Graak hadn't let go of the grifflyn.

"Graak! Graak!" Blazel yelled frantically. "Wake up!" Graak's labored breathing beneath his thighs reassured him his friend was still alive.

The ground grew closer and closer. The grifflyn frantically struggled to free itself from Graak's grip while simultaneously beating its wings in a frenzy to stop their plunge. But Graak's weight pulled it down with them.

With a shake of his head, Graak regained consciousness, squawking when he saw how close they were to the ground. He beat his wings and released his hold on the grifflyn, sailing under it. Blazel's head brushed the red feathers of its belly stripe. Gritting his teeth against the pain, he raised his helstrablades, letting their tips slide along the grifflyn's underbelly. Hot blood dripped on him, and then Graak flew into open air. A moment later, he skidded into a landing in a snowy field.

Blazel hurried to unbuckle his harness. As soon as his feet touched the earth, he shifted into his warrior form. The grifflyn crash landed, and Blazel raced to it as Morvana dropped to the ground in a daze. He swiped his claws at her face, but she leaned back in time for them to swish at empty air. Her fist slammed into his belly, surprisingly strong. She danced away, and he lost the advantage of his larger size. He decided to stay in his warrior form. His back hurt less, and he could still access his Black Talent in it. He had a moment to glimpse Graak and the injured grifflyn fighting. The grifflyn's left wing dragged uselessly and was bent at an odd angle.

Morvana cracked a whip at him. Blazel twisted to the side and grabbed the whip, hissing and letting it go as it burned the pads of his claws. He reached toward her, imagining his claws around her neck, like he had with so many other Malvers, but he met resistance, and she pushed his attack aside. Her whip cracked again, snaking around his right wrist. Scorched fur filled his nostrils. Ignoring the pain, he wrapped his hand around the whip and jerked, pulling her off balance.

As she stumbled forward and into him, he plunged his left-hand claws into her side. Her eyes widened. He felt a stab and glanced down at the dagger in his abdomen. With a howl, he swiped the claws of his free hand across her neck. Blood spurted from the wound, and she grasped at her neck. He stepped away from her, dropping her to the ground. The pouring blood from her neck suddenly stopped, and she laughed at him.

"It will take more than that to kill me!" she taunted him as she struggled to rise.

He shifted and swung his helstrablade.

"Mordaga's power flows through me. I am immor—"

Her head wobbled, then bounced at his feet.

Groaning, he gripped the dagger still sticking from his abdomen. Blood poured from the wound. Sparkles of light danced in front of his eyes. His knees buckled, and he fell to the cold, frozen ground. The numbing in his limbs spread. Already he had difficulty breathing.

"Poison—" he mumbled. *Rizelya, forgive me.*

Malviana - 44 de Rokdar, 1076

Malviana floated over the battlefield all morning, searching for the hated White Priestess. She sensed her outside the keep walls, but she couldn't find her anywhere. Whatever strategy Borgedier had formulated dissolved in the melee below as individuals fought for survival.

As the day dragged into afternoon, Malvidor's energy pulled desperately at hers. He was in trouble. She followed the threads of magic that connected her to her children and found him on the ground facing a gray-haired woman. At first, Malviana thought it was another Malvers and couldn't fathom why they'd be brawling. Then the woman turned, and her face was a pale white, not gray. Black streaked her hair. *She's one of the new Black Talents! And a Gray, no less.* Malviana's brows drew together. *But why is she outside the Sanctuary and fighting?*

Malvidor and the Gray Talent continued to fight, flinging so much magic that their spent spells obscured them. Malviana didn't dare strike for fear she'd hit Malvidor. When the air cleared a bit, Malvidor's skin appeared more ashen and pale than normal. Blood dribbled from his nose and ears, while the Gray woman seemed unharmed.

Silvery light flashed from the woman's palms, slamming into Malvidor. He clutched his head and bent forward, weaving from side to side. He feebly brought up his wand, but before he cast a spell, another bolt of gray light zoomed toward him. *Why doesn't the silly boy shield himself?* Malviana inserted a shield in front of him and jerked back in shock as the spell smashed through her protections and ripped into her mind.

Panic and terror assaulted her. She once again saw the slow disintegration of Mordar, as the unmaking spell worked its magic on him. She frantically tried to stop it. But the more magic she used, the faster the spell unmade Mordar. *No, no, this is just a memory. Fight it.* Malviana struggled to wake from the nightmare. When she finally freed herself, she lay slumped over the neck of her banthu, quivering and sweat soaked.

Below her, the haze was even thicker with spent magic. The mind-spell had caught her for longer than she thought. A breeze blew the obscuring fog away, revealing the corpse of her beloved child. Malviana directed the banthu to land next to her son's body. She quickly jumped off the beast and knelt on the frozen ground, cradling his head in her lap. His unseeing eyes stared up at her accusingly. Why hadn't she kept him safe? A keening wail ripped from her throat, and tears, she'd believed long extinct, coursed down her face. The pain of his loss was nearly as bad as losing his father.

"This won't go unavenged!" she railed, shaking a fist at the sky. Coming back to her senses, she scanned the field for her son's murderer. At the far edge, the Gray woman climbed onto a tan-and-white Gryphon. Malviana realized they could have killed her while entrapped by the spell.

"Why didn't you kill me?" Malviana yelled.

"It is not your destiny to die by my hand," the woman answered. A vision of a white-and-black-haired woman glowing with strange symbols filled her mind. Radiance shone from her, and Malviana shuddered. It was the same woman she'd seen in her visions from Mordaga. When she looked back, the woman and Gryphon had departed.

She brushed Malvidor's hair away from his face, closed his eyes, and gently kissed his forehead. A searing pain tore through her as first Mordeven's, then Morvana's threads were sundered from her. "Agh..." she cried, "My children, my lovely, darling children—gone! Mordaga, how could you allow this to happen? I... we have served you faithfully."

Everything Malviana loved was gone: her mate, her children, and now her faith in her god. Doubt filled her mind. Would she win against the White Priestess as Mordaga had promised? Would she get the vengeance she deserved for her exile and her beloved?

She tilted her head back, screaming. Snowflakes fluttered into her mouth. Gagging, she spit them out and bent her head in surrender to her fate.

The power of Mordaga slowly seeped into her, and she realized her god hadn't forsaken her. She regained her feet and took a deep breath. "I will have my vengeance!" she vowed.

A few milcrons later, she heard the sounds of vomiting coming from the adjacent field. A tug of magic pulled her to the fence. She peered through a crack in the gate. At first, she only saw the small silver Gryphon she'd come to hate. But then she spotted her nemesis huddled on the ground nearby, puking her guts out.

Malviana grinned. She gazed over her shoulder at Malvidor's corpse, the snow slowly covering it. "I'll avenge you, my children."

She quietly opened the gate, gripped her wand, and readied a spell before stepping through.

Wisah - 44 de Rokdar, 1076

Wisah took a swig of water from her canteen and rinsed out the sour taste of vomit from her mouth. The crunch of snow alerted her, and she whirled around, wiping her chin clean. Malviana stepped through the field's gate.

A crown held Malviana's long charcoal-gray hair from her face, and jet earrings dangled from her ears. Seven gemstones winked from her necklace. Each one pulsating with malevolent death magic, as did the gemstones in the rings on her fingers and those on her obsidian wand. Sheekeek hissed at the Gryphon talon forming its handle and the Gryphon feathers hanging from it. As Malviana moved, her heavy black cloak opened to reveal a gray-and-white fur lining.

How dare she? Sheekeek spat. His head feathers ruffled, and his fur stood on end. *That's a Gryphon's pelt!* His tail lashed an angry staccato.

"Oh my. He's more beautiful up close," Malviana purred. "I'll have to be careful when I sacrifice him to be sure not to ruin it."

What? Sheekeek sputtered. *You'll not sacrifice me to your foul god!*

Hush, she can't hear you.

His tail thumped Wisah's legs, but thankfully he quieted. She was having enough trouble thinking from the growing buzz in her head coming from the unmaking device. The words of the spell whispered in her mind, even through the pouch's protective sigils and spells. Tendrils of power snaked up her arm, and the sigil on her forehead throbbed under her headband in rhythm to the beat of her thundering heart.

"You won't make any more sacrifices to your foul god, Mordaga," Wisah said. As she stood up, she kept her hands hidden while she carefully loosened the fastenings on the pouch holding the unmaking device. But she paused, unwilling to open it and dip her hands into it to retrieve the device unless forced to do so. Guilt still assailed her for using the Crone's Fire to pull the souls from those living Maldiers. The unmaking spell was much, much worse.

The two women slowly circled each other.

Malviana's eyes lit up when Wisah's pendant swung away from her chest and caught the wan light.

"The Supreme! Mordaga hasn't forsaken me. I thought I'd have to claw you from your crystal throne."

Wisah shook her head. "No, not the Supreme. At least not yet. I'm her heir."

"Oh, even better. Mordaga will surely grant me immortality and bring Mordar back to life."

Wisah frowned. "Mordar is gone, beyond even the reach of your god. He's lied to you."

"No! It is you who lies. He promised me. Sacrifice the Supreme, and Mordar lives again!"

"Not Mordar, but Mordaga." Suddenly, Wisah saw the god's purpose. He'd used Malviana's love for Mordar to manipulate her. She'd become his vessel—the only way he could walk on the Goddess's world. "The only immortality you'll receive is being his slave as he takes possession of your body."

Malviana's face drained of the little color it held. "Lies!" she yelled.

The sapphire in Malviana's necklace briefly glowed. Wisah wrapped a shield around herself. The blue blast of magic skimmed over her and slammed into Sheekeek. He keened in pain and his wing drooped, icicles hanging from his wingtips.

Sheekeek, get out of here! I can't protect you and myself at the same time. She thawed the ice and healed his injury.

But you need me.

No, I have the device, Goddess have mercy on me. Wisah swung her staff toward Malviana, and a red beam whooshed out. Malviana jumped out of the way, blocking it with a wave of her wand.

Please, Sheekeek, Wisah pleaded. *Go! I don't want you around when I use the device. I don't want to unmake you, too.*

Malviana pointed her wand at Sheekeek.

Sheekeek saw the danger and leaped into the sky. *I'll watch over you. Wisah, the Goddess loves you and chose you for this. You're strong enough. Rid the world of this evil blight.*

Wisah didn't have time to make sure Sheekeek left. Malviana had turned the spell from Sheekeek onto Wisah. The shock as it squarely hit her shield knocked her back several paces. Malviana followed it with spell after spell, not giving Wisah a chance to retaliate. She remembered the first time she'd put on the headband. Instead of creating a rose, she erected a stone wall in front of her. It gave her a bit of room to catch her breath while Malviana's magic pounded on it.

The stone splintered, and shards flew in all directions. Wisah readied her spell, and when Malviana charged through the ruined wall, Wisah hit her with a spray of lava. Steam rose as Malviana countered with a wall of ice, but not before lava hit the side of her face.

She screamed, but it didn't stop her from leaning around her quickly melting ice wall. A cyclone roared toward Wisah, throwing bits of broken stone at her and turning the snow into hard pellets of hail. A chip of stone raked across Wisah's temple. If not for the metal headband, she'd have lost her eye.

Wisah and Malviana continued to exchange spells. Wisah sent a wind tunnel at Malviana, only to have it ripped to shreds. Malviana countered with turning the ground under Wisah's feet into a marsh that tried to suck her under. Wisah froze the ground, then scrambled to heat up the area around her feet, where she'd inadvertently captured them in the ice. Her mistake gave her an idea, and she directed a ribbon of ice toward Malviana, wrapping her in its freezing embrace. Malviana struggled against the bonds. As she did, two of the jewels in her necklace cracked. She howled in fury, finally breaking free.

Malviana pointed her wand at a stand of trees, ripping them out by the roots, and hurled them at Wisah. Wisah gaped and formed a wall of fire. She hated to destroy the trees, but she doubted they could be saved. The firestorm engulfed the wood, raining burning limbs and ash on them. Wisah hastily wrapped a shield around herself while flinging the burning debris at Malviana. Several branches struck her before she could erect her own shield. She retaliated by hurling bolts of lightning at Wisah. She blocked the lightning strikes with her staff. They sizzled out as they touched the kehani wood. Malviana quickly switched to throwing dozens of daggers at Wisah, each one dripping with slimy poison. Using the electricity she'd gathered from the last attack, Wisah melted them in one sweep of her staff. Malviana cried out as another jewel on her wand and necklace winked out.

Wisah's breath came in deep gasps, and she hurt from multiple cuts and abrasions. Even with all the power she'd gained through the sigils, Wisah and Malviana's abilities were too well matched.

The device at her side called to her. Wisah shook her head. How could she do something so awful to another person? Even though Malviana was pure evil, she was still a person, still had a soul.

When Wisah brushed the snow from her eyes, her hand came away red. She looked across the field at Malviana, and suddenly, didn't see the woman she'd been fighting, but a strange, grotesque monster. It had ten tentacles waving from its chin, four eyes, and spines haloed its head instead of hair. It opened its mouth, and a round mass of churning teeth filled its maw. Five arms, each ending with long needle-sharp claws, waved various weapons at her. It stood on two thick legs, and a forked tail thumped behind it.

Mordaga!

Wisah fumbled at her side. She couldn't let the monstrosity enter her world. Her fingers wrapped around the cold metal of the unmaking device, and she pulled it free of its protective pouch. Chanting the spell, she placed both hands on either side of the pyramid. She aimed the clear quartz point at Malviana-Mordaga. The sigils of unmaking on her hands and forehead flared a brilliant indigo and zoomed into the device. Crone's Fire, the deepest purple Wisah had ever seen, pulsed from the pyramid, wrapping Malviana and her god in its light. They struggled, but the more magic they used, the stronger the unmaking spell became.

Wisah expected to feel pain, both physical and emotional, when she unleashed the spell, but instead, a sense of well-being filled her. She continued to pour her magic into the spell.

First, Malviana's feet began to disintegrate, then her legs crumbled. As the bits fell from her, the purple light consumed them. The god Mordaga roared and escaped from the bonds of Malviana's body. Blood drip from Wisah's ears, and still she held onto the device and chanted the spell.

At last, the unmaking device absorbed the final particle of Malviana. With a slight pop, the light fizzled out. Wisah collapsed on the snowy ground, vaguely aware darkness had fallen.

Awhile later, Sheekeek's cold beak stroked her cheek, then strong arms lifted her from the snow. She looked into Histrun's craggy face.

"Did we win?" she croaked.

"We did, lass. We did."

She allowed her exhaustion to pull her into oblivion.

Chapter 34

Blazel - 45 de Rokdar, 1076

Blazel slowly became aware of his surroundings. He reveled in not being cold anymore. He blinked his eyes open, surprised to still be alive. Kaieli and Faliciden bent over him. He turned his head toward the nearby quiet sobs. His mother held his hand, tears streaming down her face. The stone walls assured him he was back in the keep. Moans of pain filled the infirmary.

"Don't scare me like that, son," Blenora said, wiping at her eyes.

He tried to squeeze her hand, and even to him, it seemed weak. "Rizelya?"

"Glork at least had sense to bring her here immediately," Kaieli said.

"Graak was injured, too," Blazel said, defending his friend.

She pressed down on his stomach. "How does this feel?"

"Ow! It hurts."

"Good, the feeling is coming back. Now, wiggle your toes."

Kaieli flung aside his blankets and frowned at the meager twitch of his toes. She and Faliciden closed their eyes. Bronze light floated over him, centering first on his wound and then filtering throughout his body. The faint stinging from the grifflyn's gouges on his back eased, and the strange languor in his limbs lifted. He tried moving his toes again, and this time, they wiggled. He squeezed Blenora's hand with more strength.

Kaieli folded her arms over her chest. "We've cleared all the poison from you. The wounds from the grifflyn's talons and the stab wound will take another day to fully heal. I'll send Rizelya to you." She patted his shoulder and left to attend to other patients.

Blazel cocked his head toward the window, but only the normal sounds of the keep reached him. "Is it over? Did we win?"

Blenora nodded. "Once Malviana and her children were dead, their hold on the beasts evaporated. We have new predators to plague us, but they're simply animals, if a bit strange."

"They shouldn't be hard to deal with."

"It's the Maldiers who will give us grief," Rizelya said, coming to his cot. A sling supported her left arm, and her biceps had a bandage wrapped around it. Otherwise, she appeared to be hale. She slid into the chair as Blenora vacated it. "Many of them escaped. The cowards hid or pretended to be dead until we lifted the barrier blocking the battlefield, then they ran. We haven't captured them." Bitterness crossed her face.

"What's wrong? Did any of the Malvers escape?"

"That caitiff, Keandran, escaped! He disappeared before Aistrun or Eidstrun killed him. Aistrun has vowed he'll track down and kill the beast. Only two hundred Malvers survived, and none of them are the upper echelon."

"What is Histrun going to do with them?"

"Execute them," Blenora spat out, pacing the length of his cot. "I can't believe he's doing something so heartless. The Goddess always grants people the opportunity to change their ways and atone. Executing them doesn't give them a chance."

"But look at where exiling them got us." Blazel hissed as he tried to sit up. Blenora stopped her pacing to help him and put a supporting pillow behind his back, carefully avoiding his healing wounds. Blazel took in the full infirmary. "We had compassion for them after the Great War and gave them the chance to change, and they didn't. Our compassion bit us like a venomous snake. If we'd killed the Malvers then, we wouldn't have been fighting the Malvers' monsters for the past thousand years. And the thousands killed in this war would still be alive."

"I know." Blenora slumped to sit at the foot of his cot. "I'm having a hard time understanding how Wisah can condone their execution. It seems so against the Goddess's ways."

"She says it's necessary to prevent their god, Mordaga, from gaining a foothold in our world." Rizelya plucked at the sling. "She's terrified of him. Apparently, he's behind the Malvers' evil."

Blazel couldn't comprehend an evil god. But if the Goddess and Her Consort were the epitome of goodness, and the universe was balanced, it made sense that an equal force of evilness existed.

"I need to go," Rizelya said, standing up. "Wisah needs help with the Malvers' and Maldier's corpses. She and the Fox team cleanses their souls with Crone's Fire, while the rest of us burn the bodies. It's the only way to ensure their evil doesn't spread." She bent down and kissed him. "I'm really glad you're alive, love."

That evening, Blazel hobbled to the mass funeral services for their fallen people. Wisah stood in the foreground, her white robes dazzling. Her staff caught the light and sent rainbows over the faces of the attendees. Dark circles hollowed out her eyes, and her cheeks had a sunken appearance to them. Whatever magic she'd used to defeat Malviana had cost her dearly.

Chariel leaned against Aistrun. He did a double-take. In addition to the black strands in her hair, white now streaked the gray. Aistrun turned to greet Blazel and Rizelya, and Blazel drew in a breath. "That will be a nasty scar."

"It'll be almost as bad as yours." Aistrun ran a finger along the slash running from his left eyebrow to his jawbone. He squeezed Chariel's shoulders. "At least my lady love assures me I'm still dashing, and she loves me."

"I do." Chariel stood on tiptoes and kissed his uninjured cheek. "I think you're adorable, scars and all."

Jaehaas, standing next to the couple, sported healing sores around his neck. Bandages wrapped around both hands, leaving only his fingertips exposed.

Blazel clapped him on the back, hissing out a breath as the movement pulled on his own healing wounds. "Jaehaas, I'm glad you've joined us, but I thought you'd be with the Vhelopsi."

Jaehaas started to shake his head, then stopped, putting a hand up to his sore neck. "They be having their ceremony for the dead in the morning. Hairan lost his uncle, Agabus. They be heading back to Vhelkansti tomorrow afternoon. Hairan's anxious to return to his pregnant wife, and they'd like to leave before snow clogs up the roads. Where they be from doesn't have snow."

"Are you going to Posan... I mean, Vhelkansti with them?"

Jaehaas smiled and gazed at Wisah, who smiled back at him. "No, I be going to the Sanctuary with Wisah. She insists things under her rule will be different."

"Hey, I'm glad it will be," Aistrun said, kissing the top of Chariel's forehead. "Otherwise, Chariel would have to continue breaking the rules."

Wisah held up her arms, and the assembled people quieted. A gentle breeze carried her words to the back of the crowd. "Once again, we meet to send our beloved sisters and brothers to the Mother's Womb. Let this be the last time war with the Malvers causes us so much grief. Purge the greed and anger from your hearts and deny Mordaga anything to hold on to. We do not want to become like Malviana, Mordar, and their followers. We cannot allow his evil to walk upon our lands." She turned to face the multiple funeral pyres.

"Great Mother," Wisah intoned, lifting her hands toward the sky, palms upward, "accept these, your sons and daughters, into your loving embrace. Hold them close and give them comfort as they release the burdens and joys of this life. Gentle and Wise Matriarch, guide your children through the Summerlands, where they may remember and learn from the lessons gifted in this life. Gracious Crone, may your purifying fires be gentle as they burn away the dross accumulated in this life, so their next life begins in pure love and joy. Go with love and grace."

Wisah lowered her arms. A sigil glowed on her ankle as she pointed her staff at the pyres, and all fifty of them lit at once. If she heard the gasps in the crowd, she ignored them, her head held high as she watched the flames consume the last remnants of the fallen Posairs.

Two days later, Blazel tromped across the muddy ground to the edge of the battlefield. The late autumn sun had melted the early snow.

The two hundred Malvers, their hands bound and their heads shaved, stood in several long lines. Ten blocks of wood, divots carved into them, waited at the front of the assemblage. Beside them leaned thick, sharp blades. They appeared more like axes or the Vhelopsi swords than helbraughts. Blazel wondered when Maendy had had time to forge the executioner blades. Beheading was the only way to ensure the Malvers, even the newly transformed ones, died.

Blazel approached his assigned block, wearing a leather smock to cover his clothes. He didn't look forward to the day's work, even though he'd volunteered to be one of the many executioners. But he agreed with Histrun and Wisah about the necessity of it.

By the time he stepped away from the block, blood spattered his face from the ten Malvers, and the ground was soggy with it. Other Posairs carried the heads and bodies where Wisah and the Fox team waited to purge their souls. Once they did, Rizelya, Chariel, and the rest of the Sabertiger Black Weave team burned the corpses. He wrapped his arms around his sore abdomen, not sure if he'd torn the wound open with his exertions. If he had, he deserved it after what he'd just done.

He'd killed often enough during both the Scourge War and this last Malvers War. He should be used to death, but this was different. None of the men and women had held a weapon or threatened his life. He had to remind himself with each stroke of the blade that their very existence threatened his life, Rizelya's life, and the lives of everyone he loved. The Posairs couldn't risk allowing their evil to continue and fighting another thousand years of unrelenting war.

Rizelya's face tightened with revulsion as she burned another pile of bodies. He wanted their future to be one of peace, without the constant threat to their survival from the Malvers' monsters or creatures. He wanted to raise children with Rizelya, to play with them, and teach young boys how to shapeshift for the first time. To have that, he'd kill another hundred Malvers.

Rizelya - 47 de Rokdar, 1076

Rizelya burned the last Malvers' body. She should be jubilant her people's ancient enemies were gone and wouldn't ever bother them again, but instead, numbness filled her. She gazed down at her hands. Even though she hadn't done any of the actual executions, she still saw them covered in blood. Blazel approached her, his face, hair, and arms spattered red.

"It's over," he said, his voice hollow and his eyes haunted. He reached for her, noticed his bloodstained hands, and dropped them. "I need a bath to wash this off me."

"So do I."

They slogged through the mud with their friends back to their assigned pack-house. Rizelya sighed in relief when no one else occupied the bathing room.

"I'm not sure I'll ever feel clean." Chariel hugged herself and slid down the bench away from Aistrun. "All those souls gone."

"At least they had a chance for redemption." Wisah slumped on the bench and hadn't started undressing. Silent tears streamed down her face. "Unlike Malviana. My spell obliterated her soul, and it will never cross the veil, never be reincarnated. You can't imagine how evil it makes me feel."

"Evil?" Rizelya gawked at her. "How can you say that? You stopped a terrible evil, one which has plagued our land for over a thousand years. You freed us."

"I know, but I still feel sick and filthy for using the unmaking spell." Wisah patted her pouch as she carefully removed it.

"One the Goddess gave you," Chariel reminded her. "You saw what waited if you didn't cast the spell. Mordaga was pure evil."

"You saw him?"

Chariel nodded. "For many years now. My visions of him became worse when Malviana and the others escaped their exile."

"Why didn't you tell anyone?" Aistrun's boot plopped to the floor with a bang.

"I did. I told the only person who needed to know—the Supreme."

Wisah tugged off her tunic with her mouth hanging open. "She knew? She didn't tell me. Why?"

Chariel gazed at her hands, twisting together, then at Wisah. "Because you would have hesitated and second-guessed yourself, like you're doing now. When he appeared, you reacted and used the device. If you hadn't, we wouldn't be sitting here. Malviana and Mordaga would have won, and his evil would have enslaved our people. Forever, with no hope of escape." Chariel put her arm around Wisah. "You did the only thing you could do."

Rizelya moved to the other side of Wisah and hugged her. "Dearest niece, you're a hero. You saved us. You stopped Mordaga. And I'm extremely grateful you did."

Wisah turned into Rizelya's shoulder and sobbed. The numbness inside Rizelya's soul rupture as she bent her head over Wisah's and allowed the tears she'd dammed to finally flow. The others gathered around and held them, tears streaking their faces.

After a while, Rizelya sat up and brushed the moisture from her eyes. "Well, this cry-fest might be healing, but I still need a bath."

They finished undressing and padded to the scrubbing stools. Blazel took the sponge from her and soaped down her back. His trailing fingers made Rizelya shiver with desire, reminding her of the good things in life. She kissed him deeply, then washed the blood and dirt from his body. She helped him scrub the filth from his long, twisted hair. Over the lunadars, it had grown past his waist. "Are you ever going to cut this off?"

Blazel shrugged. "It's been this way so long, I don't even remember what it looks like without the locs." He patted the top of his head. "I'm afraid if I shave it, I'll lose my powers."

"The Scourge chopped the men's hair off as part of their induction to the slave camps," Kaieli said, sadness welling in her eyes. "Rolstrun complained about the loss of his hair, but he didn't lose his abilities. The nucla stole them."

Blazel raised an eyebrow. "Hm... I'll think about it. A new haircut to start a new life." He grabbed Rizelya by the waist and pulled her to him, kissing her deeply.

She leaned into it, enjoying his hard body until soap dribbled into her eyes from his hair. She pushed away from him and tugged on the chain, dumping water over them both to sluice off the soap, the pain, and the sorrow.

After dinner, the Black Weave teams gathered in the keep-house entertainment room. Rizelya and Blazel lounged on a couch, and she leaned back into his chest. Chariel and Aistrun snuggled in a big wing-back chair, while Saffren and Nelstrun cuddled in the one opposite the fire. Jaehaas had settled onto the rug in front of the fire, holding Wisah in an embrace. Noriana and Baederposan sat on a two-seater couch in the corner, and Noriana blushed every time he held her hand or brushed a kiss on her cheek.

Kaieli, Faliciden, Loshera, and Ardela sat at a table with an open book on it, quietly discussing some obscure healing modality and sipping taevo. Rizelya glanced around, and her eyebrows furrowed. Other than the Gryphons, who were too big to fit in the room—it hadn't been built with centaurs, or Gryphons in mind—Blenora was the only one missing.

A moment later, Histrun entered the room, escorting Blenora. Eidstrun, Leistral, Gehan, and Korhaas looked up from their game of keshe they were playing with Ambrelya, Raeleen, Dehali, and Kami.

Other than the fire, the only sound was Grazeen laying a card on the table. She had her back to the door and hadn't noticed the newcomers. She smirked at Delestrun. He dramatically put his hand on his chest. "No, you didn't just play that card. You sneak."

Chuckling, Histrun and Blenora found a seat on the couch opposite Rizelya and Blazel. As they sat, Histrun brushed a kiss on Blenora's forehead, and her cheeks flushed pink. But her embarrassment didn't stop her from snuggling into his side.

Blazel audibly gasped.

Chariel elbowed Aistrun in the ribs, stopping him from saying anything.

"When did that happen?" Blazel whispered to Rizelya. "I never saw it coming."

"You didn't?" Rizelya raised her eyebrow at him. "You weren't the only reason he traveled to the Sanctuary so often."

"Huh?" His forehead creased in confusion. "Oh!"

The keshe players returned to their game, while Grazeen and Delestrun continued playing cards. The others sat in companionable silence, listening to the crackle and pop of the fire.

Rizelya readjusted her position and studied Histrun. "So, sir, what are we going to do next? Are you planning on disbanding the fighting-packs?"

Histrun's brow furrowed. "Why would we do that? Plenty of Maldiers escaped." He glared at Aistrun.

"Hey, I didn't let Keandran escape," Aistrun howled with indignation. "The cowardly cur cheated. Just when I had him— his throat was between my claws—two floxidor attacked me. It's when I received this." He pointed to the new scar on his face. "When I finally fought them off, Keandran was missing. Eidstrun and I had severely wounded him, I thought."

"His blood was on my claws," Eidstrun growled, holding up his hand. "A damned bear-type Maldier jumped me. If Sterkek hadn't helped me, I'd be dead." He also bore a new scar across his left cheek, neck, and disappearing down his left shoulder.

"I tried to track him," Aistrun continued, "but his trail was mixed with too many other injured Maldiers, and I couldn't find his."

"You need my nose," Eidstrun said, tapping the side of his nose. He was an extremely good tracker. "I can pick up his trail. We won't let the cur escape us again."

Histrun gave a curt nod. "Good. Aistrun, you will be in charge of the force to track the Maldiers and put them down like the rogues they are. Eidstrun, you join him. In addition, too many twisted creatures survived. We'll need strong fighting packs to protect our people from them. There are some malignant magic pools to be drained, and until your Black Weave teams finish the task, we'll still have to contend with Malvers' monsters. Our way of life is changing—" Histrun raised Blenora's hand to his lips and kissed it "—but in many ways, it will stay the same. We'll have time to sort it all out."

Rizelya sat back and listened as her friends excitedly talked about how life could be different now that they weren't constantly fighting the Malvers' monsters for survival. Her fingers idly trailed along Blazel's strong arms wrapped around her. They were both fighters. It was all she knew. What would they find to do to contribute to the community if they weren't protecting it? She couldn't imagine herself tending livestock or working as a stable master. She'd never allowed herself to dream of a life where she wasn't part of a fighting-pack. And would there need to be packs in this new world order?

Blazel leaned forward and kissed her neck. "We'll figure it out, love. We have time. For now, we drain the malignant magic pools—"

"And help capture that damned Keandran." She tilted her head back to look at Blazel. "It's my fault he turned into a Maldier. I didn't allow Aistrun to kill him when we knew he was a rogue."

"Afterwards, we can decide what to do with our lives." He grinned at her. "Bonded to a trouble magnet, I'm not worried about living a boring life."

Rizelya laughed. Trouble did seem to find her.

Chapter 35

Wisah - 47 de Rokdar, 1076

Wisah let the talk of the future wash over her in calm waves. The love and caring her friends had shown her after the executions had begun the healing process of her heart. It would take time for the nightmare of Malviana slowly disintegrating to leave her.

She reached up and patted Jaehaas's hand on her shoulder. Wisah already knew one change she planned on making when she assumed the role of the Supreme. She glanced over at Chariel and Aistrun cuddling. Then her eyes flicked over to Histrun, holding Blenora's hand. She wasn't the only priestess who had found love. The tradition of the priestesses to be celibate didn't follow the precepts of the Goddess. It required the priestesses to leave behind an essential part of themselves: to love and to be loved. Even the Goddess wasn't alone. She had her Consort at her side.

Her thoughts flew to the Sanctuary and the Supreme. When Wisah had left, the Supreme had looked so old and frail. She'd come so close to crossing the veil when Malviana had attacked her and hadn't fully recovered. Wisah worried the old woman would pass before she'd learned all she had to know to become the new Supreme. She really ought to plan on returning to the Sanctuary soon. But she'd spent too much of this year away from Jaehaas. She sighed. *Decisions, decisions... What should I do?*

"What be you thinking, love?" Jaehaas whispered to her as he ran a soothing hand through her hair.

"How much I love it when you do that," she grinned at him. He raised an eyebrow at her. She sighed again. "Just debating with myself whether to stay here and be with you longer or go to the Sanctuary. The Supreme wasn't doing well."

"Go, Wisah, go be with the Supreme," he said. "I'll be here, waiting for you to call me to you. Perhaps I'll join Aistrun and Eidstrun in their hunt for Keandran and the other Maldiers."

Wisah kissed him. "Thank you. It makes my decision easier. I feel anxious and can't stop thinking about her."

"Don't fret, love. She be fine. I be exhausted. Let's go to bed."

She moved away so he could maneuver back onto his hooves. Their movement seemed to be the signal for everyone else. As she headed to the door, her friends dipped into a bow. Wisah flushed. They had been waiting for her. Instead of going to the temple and her lonely rooms there, she accompanied Jaehaas to his room. There would be plenty of nights to sleep alone when she returned to the Sanctuary.

Jaehaas settled down on his wide pallet and patted the empty space he'd left for her. Wisah quickly divested her outer layers of clothing, leaving on her under-shift. Shivering in the cool air, she scurried to the bed and Jaehaas's warmth. While his centaur form precluded them from having intercourse, it didn't stop them from making love. His very presence wrapped her in his love.

The next morning, Wisah and Jaehaas joined their friends in the dining hall for breakfast. The smell of smoked meat, toast, and eggs made Wisah's stomach grumble. She'd been too upset to eat much at dinner. Aistrun soon had their table roaring with laughter with his funny stories. Still chuckling, Wisah wiped the tears from her eyes. He wouldn't have any trouble finding a new line of work after he hunted down the rogues. She'd miss them all when she left.

"Rizelya, Blazel, everyone," Wisah said when the conversation paused, "I have something to tell you. I'm—"

The door banged open, and a Red Guard burst into the room. Her red veils clung wetly to her face, and she shivered. "Lady Superior!" she called. "Where's the Lady Superior?"

Wisah stood up, her heart racing, and she leaned on the table as a wave of dizziness crashed over her. "I'm here."

The Red Guard rushed to her and knelt before her. "My lady, the Supreme is dying. Jordelyna says for you to hurry."

Pandemonium erupted as the guard's message spread through the dining room. Wisah swayed. "No, she can't go yet. I have so much to learn. I'm not ready to be the Supreme."

Her bodyguard Jaena—usually so unobtrusive that Wisah forgot she was there—stepped from the shadows and bowed her head. "My Lady Superior, the Goddess will guide you. We trust you to lead us. I have watched you grow these past chedans, and I believe there has never been another Supreme as strong and compassionate as you are."

Wisah blinked back tears. She certainly didn't feel that way at the moment—or since killing Malviana. She turned to the table, where everyone stood with stunned expressions. "It isn't quite what I had in mind, but have to return to the Sanctuary."

"I'm coming with you," Rizelya said. "The Supreme helped me when I needed it. It's time I return the favor. Besides, this is a momentous occasion. My niece, the new Supreme!"

"You must hurry, Lady Superior," the Red Guard urged. "The Supreme was very ill when I left two days ago. Thank the Mother we now have Gryphons stationed at the Sanctuary or I don't think you'd make it back in time to see her before she passes."

"Get something to eat and some hot taevo," Wisah told the messenger. "We'll be ready to leave in an octar."

Wisah swept from the dining hall and hustled across the courtyard to the temple. Dry leaves skittered in the cold wind. In less than the designated octar, she'd packed her few things, and she and her bodyguards returned to the courtyard. Sheekeek waited for her, along with her guard's Gryphon partners. Moraak's golden bulk blocked much of the wind, which had grown worse while she'd been in the temple. She did a double-take at the harness affixed to his back and Histrun standing next to him.

We go to pay our respects to the old Supreme, Moraak said. *And to witness the coronation of the new one.*

Wisah's stomach fluttered. When Rizelya, Blazel, and Chariel hurried into the courtyard dressed in heavy, fur-lined leathers and cloaks, the tense fear inside her uncoiled. It completely released when Jaehaas clomped up to her, a padded blanket wrapped around his belly. Two Thunder Wings landed beside him, carrying a rope contraption.

"I be going with you," he said, plucking at the blanket. "You need me. I can't let my dislike of the damnable sling stop me from being there for you."

Tears welled up in her eyes, and she kissed him.

The others on the Black Weave teams ran into the courtyard as their Gryphon partners fluttered to land at their side. Wisah climbed into Sheekeek's harness and buckled herself in, then, glancing around at the small crowd accompanying her, she gave the command to leave.

Wisah - 50 de Rokdar, 1076

Sheekeek dropped down into the inner courtyard of the Sanctuary Temple as dawn brought light to the world. They'd flown directly from Strunhelos. The journey only taking two days riding the Gryphons. Worry had wormed in Wisah's stomach the entire journey. With numb fingers, Wisah unbuckled the harness and slipped from his back. At this altitude, winter had arrived several chedans ago and snow covered the Sanctuary grounds. Jaena and Dejah, her bodyguards, appeared at her side and escorted her inside the temple. Their strong hands on her elbows kept her from falling on the ice.

Once inside, Wisah forgot all decorum or her position as Lady Superior and raced through the corridors to the Supreme's rooms. Jordelyna met her at the doorway.

"How is she?" Wisah's voice trembled.

"Still alive." The healer placed a hand on Wisah's arm. "She's been waiting for you to arrive. It won't be long before she crosses the veil."

Wisah nodded, biting back a sob. Quietly, she opened the door and slipped into the Supreme's dim room. The antiseptic smell of medicinal herbs made her nose twitch and her eyes water. She knelt at the side of the bed and gently clasped the Supreme's tiny, frail hand in hers. The papery-dry skin was too cool. Numerous braziers circled the bed, a fire roared in the fireplace, and several thick quilts covered the old woman. Sweat trickled down Wisah's spine from the heat.

"Supreme, I'm here," Wisah said.

"Ah, my sweet child," the Supreme whispered. "I prayed the Goddess would wait to take me into Her arms until I could see you again."

"There are others here to pay their respects."

"They can wait. I have much to tell you before it's too late."

Wisah settled on the chair, leaning forward. "I'm ready, Supreme."

"No one is ready, child."

In a dry, raspy voice, the Supreme whispered to Wisah the secrets that had been passed from Supreme to Supreme. Many she made Wisah repeat until she was sure Wisah wouldn't forget them. After the first octar, Jordelyna came in and tried to usher Wisah away.

"No, I have to tell her this," the Supreme insisted, giving Jordelyna a stern look. "I'll sleep soon enough."

Jordelyna bowed her head but left a healing brew by Wisah's elbow, which she coaxed the Supreme to swallow in between messages. Finally, as the afternoon shadows lengthened, the Supreme leaned back onto her pillows.

"There is no more I can tell you," she said. "The rest you'll have to learn on your own—" she grinned at Wisah "—or change as you please."

Wisah blushed. "You know about Jaehaas?"

"Of course I do, child. It's one of the reasons your path to become the Supreme has been so different from anyone else's. Your world will be unlike what mine was. It needs fresh eyes and new ways." She patted Wisah's hand. "Now, let me rest. I'll see Moraak, Histrun, and the others when I wake."

The Supreme closed her eyes. The gentle rise of the quilts comforted Wisah. She slumped in her chair and rubbed her tired eyes. So many things to remember, so many secrets the Supreme kept. Wisah glanced around the room. In a few days' time, these quarters would be hers.

All through the evening, a steady stream of visitors filed into the Supreme's room, their eyes reddened from crying. Wisah sat vigil next to the Supreme's bed throughout the night. At times, making notes on the secrets revealed to her, and other times, simply holding the Supreme's hand.

"Ah, Wisah, my child," the Supreme said when she woke up in the morning. "Did you spend all night here?"

"I did. I didn't want you to be alone should you cross the veil during the night."

"There is one last thing I have to do before I go home." At Wisah's raised eyebrow, the Supreme continued. "I shall see you installed as the next Supreme. The Goddess assures me I have the strength for this. Call Jordelyna for me and let all those in the Sanctuary know. I can no longer mind-speak to so many people." She glanced at the timepiece on the fireplace mantel. "An octar. Tell them to meet in the audience chamber in an octar. You'll find a suitable gown in your room. Now go."

Wisah scurried out, doing the Supreme's bidding for the last time. When she entered her room, a dazzling white gown lay across her bed. Diamonds, rubies, emeralds, sapphires, golden topaz, even jet gemstones—the colors of the eight Talents—were sewn on it in intricate patterns. Upon closer examination, she discovered the patterns were sigils. A simple lace veil covered her hair.

The rustle of silk and satin and the swish of the full skirt hinted at the change Wisah's life would take when the ceremony she approached concluded. The tap of her staff reminded her how much it already had. Her stomach fluttered, and she wanted to wipe off her sweaty palms but didn't dare muss the delicate fabric of her dress.

Jaena opened the back door to the audience chamber and bowed. As Wisah stepped onto the dais, everyone in the audience chamber dropped into the gesture of obeisance. Moraak and the Gryphons dipped their heads in respect.

Gone was the rose throne. Only the huge crystal throne sat on the dais. Wisah's heart thundered in her ears. She searched the room for the Supreme. A moment later, Blazel lovingly carried the old woman into the chamber. She looked so tiny and frail in his strong arms. It seemed fitting to Wisah that he should be here, part of the ceremony. The Supreme had thrown custom to the wind when she'd allowed the young boy to remain in the Sanctuary. The Supreme nodded to her, the corners of her mouth slightly upturned.

"Blessings of the Goddess," the Supreme said. The crowd stood up and raised their heads.

Wisah's mother, Naila, stood in the front next to Rizelya and Histrun. Moraak stood out, his golden feathers and gold breast collar gleaming. Sheekeek preened at the right side of the dais. Chariel and Aistrun openly held hands. The members of the Sabertiger and Fox Black Weave team also made up the front ranks of the audience. The Gryphons either crouched next to their partners, like Graak and Glork did with Blazel and Rizelya, or they stood on the sidelines. So many people she loved. Her eyes found Jaehaas. He beamed and stood proudly on the left side of the dais, the traditional position of the Consort to the Goddess.

An older priestess stepped forward with a familiar box and held it open for the Supreme. A single ring nestled inside of it.

"The Goddess has chosen this priestess as Her vessel to represent Her. Let no one doubt the Goddess speaks through this vessel. Wisah, do you swear to serve the Goddess and Her people for the rest of your life? Do you swear to lead the Goddess's people on a path of goodness and right, always fighting evil whenever, however, it raises its head? Do you swear to be an example of the love, mercy, and compassion that is the Goddess?"

"I so swear," Wisah said and held out her left hand.

The Supreme slid the diamond ring onto the only finger devoid of a ring, the fourth finger of Wisah's left hand. "I hereby name you Supreme. From this day forth, you will walk with the Goddess beside you. Hail the Supreme!"

The sunlight caught the gemstones winking from her fingers, then a beam of pure white light shot from her staff, surrounding her in a luminous glow.

"Hail the Supreme!" Jaehaas shouted, and the room took up the chant.

Wisah bowed her head to hide her tears. After today, only close friends—and lovers—would remember her name. After the reception, she would log her name into the Book of Supremes, locking her prior identity away. When she emerged, everyone would only know her as 'the Supreme'.

A sunbeam cut through the curtains and played with the sigil tattoos on her arms. She'd expected them to disappear once the danger with the Malvers and Mordaga was gone, but she hadn't lost one, not even the unmaking sigils.

What could it mean for her people? What dangers lay before them that she'd need such power? She vowed to find the spell Shandir had used to place the ancient tome in a pocket between space and time and use it on the unmaking device. It was too dangerous to simply lock it in a vault.

The sigil for harmony flashed, and contentment replaced her fear.

She raised her head and met Jaehaas's gaze. She wouldn't face the unknown future alone.

Epilogue

The Supreme laid her head on Blazel's strong shoulder. She'd done it. The Goddess had kept Her promise to allow her to see her successor installed into office. Wisah looked gorgeous in the Supreme's traditional coronation gown. The white had offset the azure-blue of her tattoos to stunning effect. This priestess's rule would be different from any other's before her. The Supreme followed Wisah's glance to the young centaur and smiled at the love shining in both of their eyes. Tears prickled in her own. This Supreme wouldn't spend her life alone. She'd always thought the tradition of the Supreme never having a lover or mate was difficult to keep and unfair. She'd never had the courage to break it—or change it.

"Take me back to my room, Blazel," she said.

"Gladly, Your Grace."

She appreciated how carefully he stepped, so he didn't jostle her frail body. She reached up and patted his cheek. "You've done well, my boy. I'm so very proud of you. You've exceeded all my expectations in becoming the leader and man I knew you could become."

They entered her rooms, where she'd spent all her adult life. She envied Wisah the freedom she'd had to traipse all over Lairheim. The Supreme had never set foot outside of the Sanctuary's territory, even as a child. She'd been born here. She wondered what it was like to fly on a Gryphon and gaze down at the patchwork landscape. She'd never felt the crash of the ocean's waves on her toes, or heard the crunch of the Barren's sand-glass under her feet. What would it be like to have the wind rush past your face as you raced a horse across the tall, golden plains? She wished she'd experienced the camaraderie of sitting around a campfire and roasting fresh-caught fish and laughing at old memories. Perhaps she'd experience those things in her next life.

Blazel laid her on her bed and gently tucked the quilts around her. She waved Jordelyna away. There was no longer anything the healer could do for her.

A deep lassitude pulled at the Supreme, and she sensed the opening of the veil between the worlds. The Mother beckoned to her, calling her back home. But not yet. She still had one thing to do before she left this world.

"Blazel, my son, Lairheim isn't out of danger."

"What?" he gasped.

"Mordaga," she wheezed. Each breath becoming more difficult to take. She caught Blazel's hand, and her gaze bored into his eyes, willing him to listen, to know. "He isn't gone. You must eliminate the escaped Maldiers, or Mordaga will find one to follow his corrupt ways. He'll be after Wisah. Don't let him get her or all will be lost. Protect her, Blazel. Promise me."

"I promise."

The Supreme sank back into her pillows. She'd warned him of the dangers. There was nothing more for her to do.

She closed her eyes. The cord Wisah had painstakingly mended that held her soul to her body shredded. A bright light invited her to come closer. As she did, the Goddess appeared in all Her glory, waiting on the other side of the translucent divide between the spiritual world and the physical. The Supreme pushed it aside without a backward glance at her worn body.

The Goddess embraced her. "Welcome home, daughter. Welcome home, Shonaya."

What to Read Next

This book concludes the *Legends of Lairheim* saga. The next series I've written, ***The Sentinel Witches***, is an urban fantasy/ magical realism. Book 1, *Crossroads to Destiny,* is ready for your enjoyment.

You can purchase this, and all my books, directly from me at ***Shop.ToraMoon.com*** or at your favorite retailer.

Hecate calls...
A life changing choice...
A dangerous destiny...

Catlyn Hennessey struggles to survive as an energy healer and tarot reader. All her life, she's longed for the magic to make fire dance on her palm...until she comes face-to-face with it.

Now, her fate is entwined with a mysterious magical creature-- and the Goddess Hecate.

Catching the Iron Maiden Serial Killer consumes Detective Sean McLarkin. His suspect, the sone of the wealthiest man in California, always has an alibi.

Sean's path crosses with Catlyn's when the Iron Maiden Killer sets his sights on her.

Thrown into a world of witches, demons, and Gods, the unlikely pair must choose: join the ancient battle or return to their normal lives.

Turning away could spell doom for humanity.

Crossroads to Destiny is the first book in *The Sentinel Witches* series. If you love Dresden Files, Charmed, and Supernatural, you'll enjoy this edgy dark urban fantasy.

Discover the thrilling, magical world of the Sentinel Witches, today!

APPENDIX

THE CAST

(In Alphabetical Order)

THE POSAIRS

Aistrun - (Aye-strun) Co-squad-pack Alpha with Rizelya; Strunland Keep; Rizelya's squad-pack

Alestrun - (Ale-strun) Strunland guard-pack at crater

Ambrelya - (Am-brel-ya) Red; Haasneh Keep

Anyola - (An-yo-la) Red; Posanreande Keep

Aradehan - (Ara-de-han) Dehanrandean Keep

Ardela (Are-dell-la) Gray; Sanctuary; Black Weave Team

Baerenposan - (Bear-en-po-san) Posanreande Keep

Belistril - (Bell-ih-stil) Red and Brown; Haasneh Keep Alpha

Bethlyn - (Beth-lyn) Brown, healer; Strunhelos Keep

Blazel - (Blay-zel) Born and raised in the Sanctuary, no clan affiliation (main character)

Blenora - (Blen-or-ah) White Priestess; Sanctuary; Blazel's mother

Bolstrun - (Bol-strun) Strunhelos Keep Alpha

Borhaas - (Boar-haas) Little boy, Haasneven Keep

Bren - (Br-en) Red; Strunell Keep

Calistrun - (Cal-ih-strun) Strunland guard-pack at crater

Camerposan - (Cam-er-po-san) Posanvende Keep Alpha

Candriel - (Can-dree-el) Red; Strunhelos Keep

Celedon - (Cel-eh-don) Guard at the Sanctuary; Ledonlair Keep

Chariel - (Char-ee-el) Gray, also known as the Gray Oracle; The Sanctuary

Dalnevah - (Dahl-nee-vah) Red; Posanvende Keep Alpha

Dehali - (Dee-haa-lee) Red and Yellow; Strunland Keep; Rizelya's squad-pack

Dejah - (Dee-jah) Red Guard; Sanctuary, Wisah's bodyguard

Delestrun - (Del-eh-strun) Strunlair Keep

Derenposan - (Dare-en-po-san) Posanlair, assigned to Haaslornas garrison

Dolhaas - (Dol-haas) Haasneh Keep

Eiden - (Eye-den) Yellow, twin to Eidstrun; Strunland Keep

Eidstrun - (Eyed-strun) Strunland Keep; twin to Eiden; Rizelya's squad-pack

Elaehara - (Ee-lay-ha-rah) Blue; Ronanlair Keep

Faelyn - (Fae-lyn) Brown; a healer; Strunland guard-pack at crater

Faliciden - (Fa-leh-si-den) Green; healer; Posanlair Keep

Gedronan - (Gehd-ro-nan) Ronanlair Keep

Gehan - (Gay-han) Yellow and Green; Strunven Keep

Grazeen - (Gray-zeen) Green and Brown; Strunven Keep

Hadronan - (Had-ro-nan) Ronanlair Clan Alpha

Histrun - (His-strun) Supreme Alpha; Strunland Keep, Rizelya's father

Jaehaas - (Jay-haas) Centaur, Haasneh Keep

Jaelena - (Jay-lee-na) Yellow; Posanreande Keep

Jaena - (Jay-nah) Red Guard; Sanctuary, Wisah's bodyguard

Joydan - (Joy-dan) Red; Strunhelos Keep Alpha

Jordelyna - (Jor-del-nah) Brown; healer, Sanctuary

Julhaas - (Jool-haas) Little boy, Haasneven Keep

Kaieli - (Kai-ee-le) Brown and Blue; Strunland Keep; heart sister to Rizelya

Kami - (Cam-ee) Yellow; Strunell Keep

Kederposan - (Ke-dare-po-san) Posanreande Keep Alpha

Keshanal - (Khe-shan-al) Supreme Alpha; Red and Brown

Kolhaas - (Kol-haas) Haaslornas Keep Alpha

Kothera - (Ko-ther-ah) Red; Keep Alpha Posanreande Keep

Laynar - (Lay-nar) Red; Strunheim Keep, granddaughter of Layhalya

Leistral - (Lay-ee-straal) Red and Green; Strunland Keep; Rizelya's squad-pack

Leistrun - (Lay-is-strun) Strunland Keep; Rizelya's squad-pack

Lorenda - (Lor-en-da) Sanctuary

Loshera - (Lo-sher-ah) White Priestess; Posanreande Keep

Maellyn - (May-lyn) Brown with Red; Strunven Keep

Maendy - (May-end-ee) Brown and Red, with some Yellow, Helstramiester; Strunven Keep

Maheli - (Ma-he-lee) Red; Strunlair guard pack alpha at crater

Margandy - (Mar-gan-dee) Green; healer

Metherposan - (Me-ther-po-san) Posanreande Keep

Mujeen - (Moo-jean) Red; Ronanlair Clan Alpha

Naila - (Neigh-la) Red and Yellow; Strunland Keep Alpha; Rizelya's sister

Nelstrun - (Nel-strun) Strunven Keep

Noriana - (Nor-ee-an-ah) Blue; Posanreande Keep

Norvela - (Nor-vel-ah) Red; Dehanrandevir Garrison Alpha

Raeleen - (Ray-leen) Brown with Yellow; Strunven Keep

Rizelya - (Rha-zeel-yha) Red and Brown; Strunland Keep (main character)

Rolstrun - (Rolstrun) Strunlair Keep (deceased)

Saffren - (Saff-fren) Blue with some Green; Strunven Keep

Shandir - (Shan-deer) Legendary hero from the Great War, a White Priestess; the huge crater in the south is named after her, Shandir's Crater, also called Shandir's Misery.

Shanle - (Shan-lee) White Priestess; Sanctuary; Blazel's grandmother (deceased)

Shaydan - (Shay-dan) Red; Strunell Keep

Telekhaas - (Tel-ek-haas) Haasneh Keep Alpha

The Supreme - White; the Posairs' spiritual leader; The Sanctuary

Voledon - (Vo-le-don) Ledonlair Keep

Wisah - (Wee-sah) White and Grey with some Blue; The Sanctuary; Naila's daughter, Rizelya's niece

Wyshera - (Why-sher-ah) The First Supreme

Zehala - (Zay-hal-ah) Red; Naila and Rizelya's mother, (deceased)

THE GRYPHONS

Baekeek - (Bea-keek) Silent Prowlers

Blueek - (blue-eek) White Feathers

Boreek - (boor-eek) Brown Feathers

Brogkek - (braug-kek) Dark Talons

Broogk - (broo-gak) Thorn Claw

Chaykraa - (chay-kra-a) Thorn Claw

Chekraa - (chee-kra-a) Thorn Claw

Corraak - (cor-ra-ak) White Feathers

Daelaak - (day-laak) Gold Wings; the eldest son of king Zorlaak

Daerik - (day-rik) Dark Talons

Dukaaik - (du-Kaa-ik) Gray Feathers

Faekeek - (fae-keek) Silent Prowlers

Flokeek - (flo-keek) Silent Prowlers

Florrik - (floor-reek) Red Feathers

Geraaik - (ger-ai-k) Dark Talons

Glork - (glor-k) Brown Feathers

Graak - (grr-aak) Thorn Claw

Harweek - (har-wee-k) Brown Feathers

Horkeek - (hor-kee-k) Razor Beaks

Jorreek - (joor-reek) Red Feathers

Kaaik - (kaa-ik) Brown Feathers

Kaereek - (kay-ree-k) Gray Feathers

Keeru - (kee-ru) Red Feathers

Korrik - (kor-rik) Razor Beaks

Maeaak - (mae-aa-k) Brown Feathers

Moraak - (moor-aak) Gold Wings; prince

Morlek - (mor-leek) Razor Beaks

Morru - (mor-rue) Gray Feathers

Nealaak - (nae-la-ak) White Feathers

Oslerru - (os-ler-ru) White Feathers

Polkeek - (pol-keek) Silent Prowlers

Poraak - (poor-aa-k) Brown Feathers

Ryaak - (rye-aa-k) Razor Beaks

Sheekeek - (shee-keek) Silver Beak, a mystic

Sterkek - (star-ke-k) Razor Beaks

Torlek - (tor-lek) Razor Beaks

Trukeek - (True-keek) Thunder Wing

Tuueek - (Tuu-eek) Thunder Wing

Zorlaak - King of the Gryphons; Gold Wing

VHELOPSI REFUGEES

Hairan Aziru - (hi-ran ah-zee-rue) male; prince

Agabus Aziru - (ag-ah-bus ah-zee-rue) Hairan's uncle

Ninsun Aziru - Hairan's brother

Sangasu Musa - (san-ga-su moo-sue) male

Zebba Azirubi - (zeab-ba ah-zee-rue-bee) female; mate to Hairan

MALVERS

Exiled Malvers (by rank):

Malviana - (Mal-vee-ah-na) Queen of the Malvers

Mordar - (Mor-dar) - King of the Malvers (Deceased)

Malvidor - (Mal-vi-door) Malviana's youngest son; Prince

Mordeven - (Mor-dev-en) Malviana's oldest child; Prince

Morvana - (Mor-vah-na) Malviana's daughter; Princess

Borgedier - (Bor-gay-deer) Duke

Magdelyn - (Mag-del-lyn) Duchess

Valdorian - (Val-door-ee-an) Duchess

Jorvelden - (Jor-vel-den) Baron

Gordelven - (Gor-del-ven) Lord

New Malvers:

Gelposan - (Gayle-po-san) male

Nelieh - (Nay-lee-eh) female

Maldiers:

Keandran - (Kae-an-dran) male

Korand - (Core-and) male

Cloresh - (Clor-esh) female

The Horses

Brishna - (Brish-na) Rolstrun's mare

Caela - (Say-la) Leistral's mare

Chaezreen - (Chay-zreen) Chariel's mare

Gemmy - (Gem-mae) Rizelya's pack multa

Jezhan - (Jay-zhen) Aistrun's gelding

Julay - (Ju-lay) Dehali's mare

Kressy - (Kress-ee) Rizelya's multa

Kymaya - (Kai-may-ah) Rizelya's mare

Lighzel - (Lie-zel) Blazel's mare

Luchen - (Lou-chen) Eidstrun's gelding

Tejen - (Tee-jen) Wisah's stallion

BLACK WEAVE TEAMS

(Posair - Gryphon partner)

Sabertiger Team

Rizelya (Red) - Glork

Chariel (Gray) - Torlek

Kaieli (Brown) - Keeru

Loshera (White) - Morlek

Saffren (Blue) - Florrik

Grazeen (Green) - Boreek

Eiden (Yellow) - Korrik

Anchor: Blazel - Graak

Bodyguards:

Aistrun - Broogk

Leistral - Morru

Eidstrun - Sterkek

Leistrun - Brogkek

Maestrun - Oslerru

Nelstrun - Daerik

Fox Team

Blenora (White) - Blueek

Ardela (Gray) - Nealaak

Faliciden (Green) - Harweek

Noriana (Blue) - Corraak

Dehali (Red) - Chekraa

Gehan (Yellow) - Geraaik

Raeleen (Brown) - Ryaak

Delestrun(Anchor) - Kaaik

Bodyguards:

Kami - Chaykraa

Ambrelya - Maeaak

Baederposan - Kaereek

Korhaas - Horkeek

OTHER POSAIR - GRYPHON PARTNERSHIPS

Wisah - Sheekeek

Shaydan - Dukaaik

Derenposan - Poraak

Maellyn - Jorreek

THE WORLD

The main continent is called Lairheim. The Barrens is an area of desolation, with only petrified wood and sand-glass in it. It covers a hundred-mile radius from Shandir's Crater, which is in the center of the isthmus between the main continent and the sub-continent. After the Great War, travel south of the Barrens became taboo, and so no one knows what the area is like. The sub-continent is believed to be covered by one huge swamp and is located south of the Barrens.

No one sails the oceans anymore because of the sea monsters created during the Great War. There is limited travel along the coasts.

The Provinces

There are eight provinces, each divided into eight territories. Each clan takes the name of the Province.

Strunlair

Ledonlair

Andranlair

Posanlair

Haaslair

Dehanlair

Ronanlair

Keistanlair

Days and Time

Milcron - equivalent to a minute.

Octar - roughly equals an hour. There are 16 octars in a day.

Chedan - roughly a week, consisting of eight days.

Lunadar - a month consists of eight chedans, or 64 days.

A year is eight chedans, or 512 days.

Measure - term for distance, a little less than a mile (5,000 feet).

The Months

Ahdar - Month one; Spring

Neydar - Month two; Spring

Sandar - Month three; Summer

Drudar - Month four; Summer

Godar - Month five; Autumn

Rokdar - Month six; Autumn

Eyedar - Month seven; Winter

Hondar - Month eight; Winter

The Moons

Kelar - the largest moon takes 64 days for a full cycle, measurement of a month.

Zelar - the middle-sized moon takes 32 days for a full cycle.

Chelar - the smallest moon's cycle takes 8 days, measurement for chedan, or eight-days.

Magical Abilities of the Women

There are eight types of magic, called Talents, worked by the women. Men exchanged the ability to do magic (except very basic skills) for the gift of shapeshifting into their warrior form when the Malvers' monsters appeared after the Great War. Hair and eye color indicate of the type of magic the person uses. Hair color indicates the person's major Talent and the eye color their secondary Talent. The darker the hair or eye color, the more powerful in that Talent the person is. A woman with fire magic is called a Red, one with water is called a Blue, and so on. Hair color pales with age.

The Powers

Whites - have shades of white hair. Priestesses — mind and soul workers, spiritual leaders. (Unseen in men.)

Grays - have shades of gray hair. Priestesses — also mind and soul workers but they work more with the transitions of the soul. This is a rare Talent. (Unseen in men.)

Reds - have shades of red hair — the fire workers and warriors.

Yellows - have shades of blond hair — the air workers.

Blues - have shades of blue hair — the water workers.

Greens - have shades of green hair — earth workers, plants, and are healers.

Browns - shades of brown hair — earth workers, animals and minerals/metals, and are healers.

Blacks - shades of black hair (extinct) — can work all types of magic.

Gryphons

Gryphons live in flights of several generations. Most flocks can be mixed bird-type species; except the three flights a Gryphon must be born into.

The flights are:

Gold Wings (must be born into—the royal house)

Black Feathers

White Feathers

Gray Feathers

Brown Feathers

Red Feathers

Thorn Claws

Thunder Wings

Razor Beaks

Dark Talons

Silent Prowlers (must be born into—owl types)

Silver Beaks

Green Talons (must be born into—they have poison sacks on their talons)

Black Weave Teams

Seven Black Weave Teams have been formed to cleanse the malignant magic pools which form swamps around Lairheim.

Sabertiger (stays with war host)

Fox (stays with war host)

Lynx (sent to Strunlair Province)

Bear (sent to Haaslair Province)

Wolf (sent to Andranlair Province)

Badger (sent to Keistanlair Province)

Ducorn (sent to Ledonlair Province)

GLOSSARY

angulete - (an-goo-le-te) a flying serpent found in the swamps, a twisted, venomous beast

baethor - (bae-thor) a predator found in the Deep Mountains

banthu - (ban-thoo) reptilian flying mounts created by the Malvers

billocks - (bill-ox) a wild, large herd beast and resists domestication

brecha - (bray-cha) one of the symbiotic pair of monsters collectively called the Malvers' monsters

cardrolon horned lizard - (car-droll-on) usually only 12"-18" long, the Malvers used their magic to make them huge monsters

dracur - (dray-cur) a flying reptile found in the southern swamp

ducorn - (dew-corn) a type of antelope with two twisty horns

floxidor - (flox-eh-dor) canid-type swamp creature

grifflyn - (grif-lyn) a beast created by the Malvers; a twisting of a Gryphon with a Scourge's lizard-mount

helbraught - (hell-brac-kt) the magical halberd type blades the women use to fight the monsters; the wooden staff is the height of the woman with a 16"-24" inch blade made from helstrim attached to the end

helstrablade - (hell-stra-blade) knives made from helstrim but not keyed to any type of magic

helstramiester - (hell-sta-my-ster) masters of the helstrim alloy

helstrim - (hell-strim) a special alloy that accepts and holds magic used to make helstrablades and helbraught blades

jallopitar - (ja-lop-ih-tar) a reptilian swamp predator

jallopsitor - (ja-lop-si-tor) a beast created by the Malvers based on a jallopitar

janack - (jan-ack) one of the symbiotic pair of monsters collectively called the Malvers' monsters

jelehan - (jay-lay-han) a throwing game using sticks of varying lengths with colored bands

kehani - (kay-han-ee) the flowers of the kehani tree are sacred to The Goddess and are used by the priestesses in the temples as perfume and incense

keshe - (kay-she) a strategy board game. It can be played with as few as two players or up to ten players; the more players added, the more complicated the game becomes

mookti - (mook-tee) an early ripening spring berry that is sweet, dark purple, and grows in small clusters

multa - (mul-ta) a pack animal with cloven, platter-like feet able to carry heavy loads

narhili - (nar-hee-lee) also called narhili beasts, predators that live in the swamps during the day and hunt the surrounding area at night

oyt - a nonsensical term used to activate the fire arrows

paether - (pae-ther) a canid-like predator found in the northern part of Lairheim

sabertiger - a large white and black striped feline that lives in the Deep Mountains *sheadash* - (shea-dash) a type of white stone that repels and negates any malignant magic. The Malvers' monsters can't cross it and so it is used for buildings and roads

skeaeter - (skae-ter) a large insectoid carnivorous predator

sheezet - (shee-zhet) the Scourge's lizard mounts

snelks - (snell-ks) a grub which eats rotten matter

taevo - (tay-vo) a stimulating drink made from the leaves and berries of the taeve bush

Vhel - (veil) - the Vhelopsi home planet

Vhelkansti - (veil-can-stee) the Vhelopsi refugee settlement

Vhelopsi - (veil-lop-see) former slaves of the Scourge, now refugees on Lairheim

Stay In Touch!

This book concludes the Legends of Lairheim series. Let me know if you want more books in this universe. I have several in mind!

If you haven't already, sign up for Tora's newsletter to keep in touch with what's happening in the world of Tora. Receive exclusive extras, news, and discounts on my books, products, and art. I have lots of ideas and always have a project—or three—in progress.

ToraMoon.com/subscribe

Also By Tora Moon

Legends of Lairheim (Epic Science-Fantasy)

Ancient Enemies (Book 1)
Ancient Allies (Book 2)
The Scourge Incursion (Book 3)
Exile's Vengeance (Book 4)
Redemption - A Novel

The Sentinel Witches (Urban Fantasy)

Crossroads to Destiny (Book 1)
Descent Into Darkness (Book 2)
Well of Sorrows (Book 3)

Indie Author Guides

Business & Accounting for Authors
Business Plans for Authors

To get an up-to-date listing of all my books or to purchase visit
ToraMoon.com

THANK YOU!

I hope you're enjoying discovering the world of Legends of Lairheim world and Rizelya and her team's story.

If you have a moment, please help others enjoy these books too by leaving a review on my shop or the retail site where you purchased this book, review it on a blog, share it on your social media, or even just tell your friends about it.

Reviews help other readers choose what to read and authors depend on reviews to get the word out on good books. Honest reviews and genuine word-of-mouth recommendations make all the difference.

I'm not asking for one of those awful book reports we did at school. Leaving a review will only take a minute: it doesn't have to be long or involved, just a sentence or two that tells people what you liked about the book. This will help other readers know why they might like it, too, and help me write more of what you love. But please, no spoilers!

The truth is, VERY few readers leave reviews. Please help me by being the exception.

About the Author

Tora Moon writes Goddess fantasy and science fiction, skillfully melding different sub-genres to create unique, memorable stories. Her completed series, The Legends of Lairheim, combines elements of epic, paranormal, and science fiction into a breathtaking tale of magic, courage, and the enduring power of unity.

Her series, The Sentinel Witches, blends her love of urban/magical realism, mythology, and portal fantasy—and skates close to the edge of thriller and horror. Throughout all her works, you will find Tora's love of Goddess mythology as she weaves aspects of these into her stories.

As Tora-Iresh'nai Moon, she writes about Goddess Spirituality and shares her nearly fifty years of experience of connecting with the Goddess and the Feminine Divine.

Tora is also an artist who explores drawing and watercolor painting. Her current passion is creating and coloring mandalas inspired by the Goddess. Tora also expresses her creativity through various handcrafts.

You can find out more about Tora, her books, and her art at ToraMoon.com